Actress and theatre director Margaret Bard was born in New York, graduated from the University of Texas and Montreal's National Theatre School, as well as training as a director with Alan Ayckbourn in England. With her husband, she co-founded Calgary's Lunchbox Theatre, which is now in its sixteenth season. During the course of her acting career she has performed with major theatres across Canada, the US and Britain and her film credits include *The Good Mother* with Diane Keaton. *The Changing Room* is her second novel; her first, *The Women's Club*, is also available from Headline.

Also by Margaret Bard

The Women's Club

The Changing Room

Margaret Bard

KNIGHT

First published in 1993
by HEADLINE BOOK PUBLISHING

First published in paperback in 1993
by HEADLINE BOOK PUBLISHING

This edition published 1998 by Knight
an imprint of Brockhampton Press

10 9 8 7 6 5 4 3 2

ISBN 1 86019 6691

Typeset by
Letterpart Limited, Reigate, Surrey
Printed and bound in Great Britain by
Mackays of Chatham PLC, Chatham, Kent

Brockhampton Press
20 Bloomsbury Street
London WC1B 3QA

For Helen and for Bartley,
who have been instrumental
in my own makeover.

ACKNOWLEDGEMENTS

To the many people in the television industry, actors, writers, directors, producers, designers, technicians, and especially the press, thanks for sharing your professional information. Please forgive the places where I have altered fact to shape fiction.

Prologue

Julia Hudlow woke up in a flash, her heart pounding. Sweat was pouring off her, adrenalin racing through her. The dream had been frightening but exhilarating, and real, so vividly real. She closed her eyes for a moment and saw the myriad colors against her lids, the images of each scene still strong in her mind.

There was a woman seated at a dressing-table. Was the woman herself? She didn't know because at first she couldn't see the woman's face, only the curve of her naked back. Julia was used to being behind the camera, not the object of its all-seeing eye. The woman was nude except for a towel wrapped around her head like a turban. On the dressing-table in front of her lay a vast array of theatrical make-up, the brushes and pots of color carefully laid out in neat rows like surgical instruments. Circling the outer edge of the table were a number of different-colored wigs impaled on individual wig stands, like floating, disembodied heads.

The scene shifted and the face of the woman suddenly appeared, reflected in the mirror, but it was a face devoid of expression, the features nondescript, a blank canvas. In slow motion, she reached for a lip pencil and began to outline a mouth, a fine-pointed brush to elongate her eyes, shadow to highlight the cheekbones, slowly, stroke by stroke, bringing the face tantalizingly into focus, the features close to Julia's own, but larger and more sharply defined. She removed the towel, letting her pale, reddish-blonde hair fall to her shoulders, but she then covered her real hair with a long wig of a deeper, more vibrant red.

The faces of other women began to appear in the room, floating in and out of focus, surrealistic, like a Dali painting. The woman stood up and moved through them to a full-length mirror, where she found herself surrounded by a

1

blazing white light. The walls of the room were closing in behind her, around her, all avenues of exit cut off. There was nowhere for her to go but forward. For a moment, she stood there, frozen, unable to move, then she took a deep breath and stepped into the mirror.

Lying in bed, Julia went over the images, frame by frame, alternating different camera angles, until she came to the end of the series. Still the dream wouldn't let her go. She could feel the cold of the mirror pressed against her naked skin, the way the smooth, hard glass miraculously dissolved at her touch. She saw herself going through the mirror over and over again. Trembling, she sat up in bed and tried to will her breathing under control as she stared into the murky blackness around her. The bedroom was dark, shadowy, just as it had been in her dream, but the room in her dream was like her childhood room back home in Houston and the dressing-table much like one her parents had given her for her thirteenth birthday: a fancy, white and chrome affair with a mirror surrounded by lights, 'to illuminate your first step into womanhood,' her mother had said: a step that the shy, adolescent Julia had been all too reluctant to take.

She forced her eyes to focus on her surroundings. She wasn't in Houston. She was in Los Angeles: Brentwood, to be exact, in the townhouse she shared with her husband, Marty. The objects in the room swam hazily into view, the blurred outline of each shape made discernible to her eye only by the fact that it was familiar – the heavy antique Louis IV armoire Marty had scored at an auction, the Mexican silver and turquoise plate they had bought on their honeymoon in Mexico, the hand-painted rice-paper screen from Japan, the little Navaho blanket covering the television, and the oversized leather chair that had belonged to Marty's father. Their little townhouse, barely big enough for two to begin with, was jam-packed with artefacts from their travels and furniture they had accumulated over their thirteen-year relationship. If they ever stopped working long enough to look for a real house, at least they would have plenty of stuff to go in it.

Her gaze came to rest on the computer terminal sitting on a little desk in the corner of the bedroom next to the glass doors that led out on to a minuscule deck. Even though she

2

had a full desk-top computer and laser printer in their shared office space, Julia insisted on having a terminal in the bedroom: 'In case I wake up in the middle of the night with a brilliant idea,' she told Marty. 'Whatever happened to the old pad and pencil beside the bed?' Marty wanted to know. 'Besides, there's nothing that can't wait till morning.'

She looked down at her sleeping husband. He was curled up tight on his side, one arm clutching the pillow, the other outstretched, reaching for something that just eluded his grasp: her warm body, probably. He looked so peaceful, it was a shame to wake him, but . . . She reached over and jabbed him in the ribs. Marty was a tall man, twice her weight, and it took several jabs before he stirred.

'Marty, Marty, wake up,' she whispered urgently. 'I think I've got it.'

'Got what?' he mumbled, pulling the flower-sprigged duvet closer under his chin and rolling away from her, out of reach of her violent fingers.

'I dreamed my film. Or maybe I dreamed the opening credit sequence, I don't know, but the images were crystal clear at first, then dissolving one into the other.' Excitedly she began to tell him how each shot would unfold, ending with, 'It was me sitting at that dressing-table and yet, at the same time, it wasn't me. I was becoming someone else. And I was surrounded by other women, all of them different, but all in the process of being . . . not reborn exactly, but . . . made over. . .'

'Sounds interesting, Jules. Can I go back to sleep now?' he rubbed his eyes.

'I think I know what it means, too. It's my subconscious telling me "Julia, you want to make yourself over. You're thirty-five years old and you want a whole new life." Rebirth, renewal, are you with me?'

'Um hmm,' Marty said sleepily. 'Sounds kind of New Age.' He yawned.

'Reinventing the self, a great theme for the movie.' She jabbed him again to keep him awake.

'Ouch! Quit nudging me. Can we talk about this in the morning? I'm a lot older than you and I need my beauty sleep.'

'You don't have any idea what I'm talking about, do you?'

3

'Sure, I do. A cosmic beauty shop. Only I don't see it as a film. I see it as television.'

'You see everything as television. That's because you work in television.'

'We'll talk, Jules. I promise. In the morning.' Marty's head was just about to return to the pillow when he opened one eye and said very clearly, 'I think you might have an interesting concept there but, trust me, it's not a film. It's a sit-com.'

CBN   MEMO

FROM: Stanfield King, President, CBN Entertainment

TO: Tim Talbot, Head of Network Programming

cc: Charles Currie, Chairman of the Board
                     Patsy Rodman, VP Promotion
                     Lisa Pellegrino, VP Talent and Casting

Network television is under siege and facing severe economic crisis:

1. TV viewing is down generally
2. Ad revenues are declining
3. Affiliates are deserting like the proverbial rats from a sinking ship
4. Affluent and educated viewers are defecting to cable
5. We are competing with the older networks for the remaining audience

We are in danger of being 'zapped' out of existence.

As we prepare for yet another pilot season, our goal must be to move from last place to first place. In order to be number one, we must:

A. Develop programming specifically aimed at ethnic minorities and the 'under-educated'
B. Create bold new programming that will woo the defectors back to CBN

In other words, boys and girls, find me a hit that crosses as many demographic lines as possible!

Network television is no longer a business. It's a war. The bottom line here is survival.

Stanfield King

THE PITCH

Chapter One

Currie Plaza rose straight up, thirty-four floors into the hazy western LA sky, a breathtaking complex of Finnish red marble and smoky reflective glass, like a giant mirror ball or a Japanese sci-fi version of an American futuristic tower. Surrounded by tall pines and palm trees, with banks of landscaped foliage, ice-plant, snapdragons and blazing red poppies, it faced a sculpture of dancing fountains and was the newest showpiece of a section of prime real estate known as Century City.

Currie Plaza housed the offices of CBN, the Currie Broadcasting Network, along with the western headquarters of Currie Communications Corporation, as well as a prestigious law firm. CBN had been founded by the charismatic and iconoclastic millionaire, Charles Currie, owner of CurriCom, a vast media empire which incorporated book publishing, several newspapers, cellular phones, and now a television network. Still regarded as 'the new network', CBN was already giving the majors a run for their money. Reportedly Currie had a strong vision of where he wanted his new toy to go, but he was based in New York and entrusted the day-to-day running of the network to his senior management team; Stanfield King, president and head of CBN Entertainment, and Tim Talbot, director of Network Programming.

Century City, the sign read in gold letters, as Julia turned off on to the six-laned boulevard, Avenue of the Stars, heading for Currie Plaza. She and Marty were scheduled for a three o'clock meeting to pitch their sit-com idea, Makeover, to the top executives of CBN, along with Kathryn Grady, director of Development for Pacific Victory Studios. As a freelance producer, Marty already had a track record with Pacific Victory, so they had first pitched the idea for Makeover to Kathryn who said she was 'deeply in love with it', and she thought 'Pac-Vic would come in on a co-pro' if they could interest one of the networks. Kathryn targeted CBN and managed to score them a VIP meeting with both Stanfield King and Tim Talbot.

Julia's stomach was doing flip-flops. Everything was moving so quickly. Since getting the idea in the middle of the night, she and Marty had talked about nothing but Makeover for the past two weeks. She hoped he knew what he was doing because she sure as hell didn't. Marty kept assuring her that if by some miracle her idea got picked up as a pilot and went on to become a successful series, she might make as much as seventy thousand dollars per weekly episode, which could eventually lead to her being able to finance the small, quality film she was so desperate to make.

Currie Plaza had its own parking lot behind the building on Constellation Way. Living in LA had forced her to become an expert driver and she smoothly maneuvered her red Honda Accord into an extremely tight space. Taking a quick look in the rear-view, she was satisfied that she had achieved just the right combination of business and creative in her look for the pitch meeting. Her smoothly styled long page-boy neatly framed her small, oval face, and her tight-fitting Armani suit was cut to flatter her petite but well-shaped figure. The deep jade green suit and rust silk camisole set off her pale (especially for southern California) skin and reddish-blonde hair. The Armani was her one concession to the Hollywood rule, 'Dress for where you want to get to, not for where you are.' As she attempted to swing her legs smoothly out of the car in one fluid motion, her short skirt rode up, giving the parking attendant a bird's-eye view.

'Damn,' she said, slamming the car door behind her. 'I wish I was wearing silk underwear.'

'What?' Marty made a grab for his Condotti briefcase.

'I bet Kathryn Grady wears silk underwear. In really hot colors. What do you think?'

'What are you talking about?'

'Nothing.' Julia tugged at the short skirt to bring it closer to her knees. Typical Julia: perfectly together on the outside, falling apart on the inside. 'My stomach is hang-gliding and my tongue feels like it's wearing a sweater.'

'Relax,' Marty smiled at her from behind his hooded deep brown eyes: eyes you could get lost in, as her best friend,

Diane, had said. 'There's an old adage in television: "the buyer is only the seller sitting on the other side of the table." The trick is to dance in, turn them on, and dance out again.'

'I think I should have worn different shoes.' Julia was struggling to keep up with Marty. She had her heels on, but even at that, he was a full head taller than she and, at forty-eight, thirteen years older. Her small, slight stature made her look girlish, much younger than her thirty-five years; her soft features appeared not fully formed, as if she were frozen in transition between childhood and adulthood. Marty was tall and dark, with an air of authority, a sharp mind and a quick wit, somewhat moderated by a genuine desire never to hurt another human being. She loved him; God, how she loved him, but as he continued to stride along, she realized just how much of her life had been spent trying to catch up with him.

They walked up the palm-lined entrance to the broad steps that led to the big glass doors flanking the entrance to the dazzling building, its mirror glass façade almost blinding in the sun. The doors swung open, admitting them into the lobby of Currie Plaza. They gave their names at the desk, the security guard checked his list, signed them in, and handed them each a visitor's day pass.

As they stood waiting for the elevator that would take them to the top floor where Stanfield King's office was, Julia felt her stomach turn over again. 'Why did I let you talk me into this?' she said nervously. 'I'm a documentary film maker, not a television writer.'

'You said you wanted to make yourself over,' Marty reminded her gently. 'If you want credibility in the industry, you need to do something that's fiction. With your docs, no matter how many awards you win, there's always a question as to how much of their success is due to you and how much to the people and events you are documenting. It's the difference between reportage and art.'

'A sit-com is hardly art,' Julia snapped. 'I want to write feature films.'

'And you will. I have complete faith in you, but you can't make a low-bud feature with Makeover. It's too big a theme, too many stories to tell in a ninety-minute film. You need twenty-two half-hour episodes to really explore it. It's October already and we're almost past the pilot deadline, but according to the industry "buzz" none of the networks thinks it's got a winner yet. Makeover fits most of the criteria of Stan King's memo. Plus we've got a surprise ace in the hole with Diane Slater willing to play the lead.'

'I wish Di could have come with us.'

'We'll be OK on our own.' He gave her arm a reassuring squeeze as the elevator door opened and they stepped inside.

The elevator was completely glass, and Julia felt her stomach drop out and away from her along with the buildings of Beverly Hills as the elevator started shooting toward the top. The speed of her ascent underscored her nerves. She looked at Marty. How could he be so calm? They were about to brave a Hollywood lion's den and he appeared totally confident; but then he always did. That consummate confidence had really turned her on all those years ago at USC.

After her protected upbringing in Houston society, with its narrow set of values and private school rules of behavior, southern California was almost frightening in the freedom it offered. So many choices, but which one was the right one? By the early eighties, the sexual revolution was rapidly winding down, but you wouldn't know it in LA. Drugs were still sold openly on the streets. People were actually living on the streets, sleeping in cardboard boxes, and they looked at Julia with a mixture of fear, hostility and hopelessness. She felt confronted by danger at every turn, and so far the USC film school had failed to provide her with a safe haven. The other students were younger than she was but much more competitive, and seemed so sure of what they wanted to do. All Julia really knew was that she wanted to know more about the real world, to film real people in real-life situations, somehow to get under their skin.

Marty Turgov was known in the television industry as 'The Pitch King'. The son of a famous cinematographer who was always off on location, he grew up spending most of his time with his mother, who had a local TV show. In high school, instead of waiting for Mom to come home and fix dinner, he hung out at the TV station where she worked, doing odd jobs, learning basic camera technique and how to operate a boom. Perhaps as a rebellion against his absent father, Marty rejected film and fell in love with television.

When his mother insisted he leave the station to get a degree at UCLA, he didn't want to go but, as usual, Mom was right; his double major in communications and business opened the doors even wider. He learned his strength lay not in writing, but in bringing the right creative people together. He liked to call himself an 'ideas man' with the business acumen to carry out those ideas and keep them within budget. He had done virtually everything in the business, worked at the networks and with the networks as an independent producer, but what he was really good at was selling.

Marty came to USC to give a two-week workshop in 'The Art of the Deal'. In one of the seminars, each student had to pitch an idea to the King of Pitch. Julia was in awe of him, maybe even already in love with him, but she could tell right away that he wasn't impressed with her pitch.

'I want to document the homeless,' she told him, her voice trembling with nerves and sudden, liquefying, sexual attraction. This guy was so neat. First of all he was Jewish, which made him, given her own background, kind of exotic. He'd been born and raised right here in LA, which was almost unique for this town; and, in the cut-throat world of television, he was already a proven success. No way would he ever be interested in a naïve, insecure film student. Stay cool, Julia, she thought. She fought to control her emotions. 'What I mean is, how do they end up on the street, what life circumstances bring them so low, where are they headed . . .?' She was running out of breath when Marty stopped her.

'The homeless have been done to death. They're a documentary cliché unless you have an inside track to some new insight. You should write about what you know, and somehow I have the feeling that sleeping in your clothes on the beach for weeks at a time and hanging out at the food bank is not really where it's at for you. Where are you from?'

Julia turned red. Was it that easy to tell she was a product of privilege? 'Houston,' she said, her voice barely above a whisper.

'I thought I recognized the accent. What part?'

She might as well confess. 'River Oaks.'

Marty whistled. 'Pretty posh. So how are the folks doin' back in River Oaks? Rich as always?'

'No, since the oil business went bust, they're having real problems trying to make ends meet, but it's still just as important that they keep up appearances. God, it makes me sick,' she exploded, 'the hypocrisy of it all.'

Marty laughed. 'Then document that. Sounds like you know River Oaks inside out. When times are tough, poor people want to know that rich people aren't doing so well.'

By the time Julia went back to Houston to make the film, Marty was with her, as her mentor and as her lover. She didn't dare tell her parents the exact nature of her film, but even so, they refused to participate in the project. However, she was able to talk to a lot of their friends and, even more usefully, their domestics. 'River Oaks, From Boom to Bust', a study of the decline of old money struggling with the loss of new, turned out to be a powerful exposé of Houston society as it spiraled to the bottom. Marty was able to get the finished film to the right people, which resulted in Julia winning the prestigious Veritee Award, almost unheard-of for a student documentary.

The national award meant nothing to Claire and Leigh Hudlow. As far as her parents were concerned, she had used her position in the community to betray trade secrets.

'Talking to the help, Julia, how could you?' Her mother's eyes filled with tears. 'Our friends trusted you.' Julia had almost never seen her mother cry and it shocked her that she had caused this by making a little film that would only be shown at festivals and maybe on PBS. 'It's all right for you, you can hightail it back to California,' her dad said bitterly. 'We have to go on living in this town and you've made that well-nigh impossible for us.' Up until this point, she had been one of the Hudlows, their darling little girl, supported in every way, secure in their supposedly unconditional love, but now she felt almost, well, disowned. Of course her parents blamed Marty Turgov for everything: for steering her in the wrong direction, for being older than she was, for taking her virginity and, probably, as much as she hated to admit it, maybe even for being a Jew.

She married Marty in a civil ceremony. Claire and Leigh refused to come to the wedding. Marty's father was long dead, and his mother was in retirement in Hawaii. She and Marty were on their own. Julia had spoken only rarely to her parents in the past decade. At least she had Marty, along with her trusty Bolex camera and a career in documentary

14

film. So far, Marty had never steered her wrong.

The elevator was approaching the top floors. Julia could see all the way out to Catalina, the little island rising up like a jewel in the turquoise blue of the Pacific Ocean. 'I'll do the wind-up,' Marty said, 'but you do the pitch as we agreed. They already know me and view me as a "show runner". What they'll want to find out is if you can deliver. You've got to get Stan's attention with the opening pitch and then we'll both build on it from there. Could take two hours if he likes the idea, two minutes if he doesn't.'

'Stan's head of Entertainment,' Julia said. 'He'll know where we're coming from.'

'Don't count on it,' an edge crept into Marty's voice. 'The silver-haired daddy gurus are long gone; today's it's youth that's pulling the strings.' He was still a handsome man who looked better with each passing year, but lately he had become obsessed with age. 'Networks are run by the "whiz-biz kids"; lawyers and accountants. They don't deal in art; they call it "product". When we were both at ABC, Stan King was known as the Baby Boomer Boy Wonder. Here at CBN, his nickname is Standard King, not because he maintains a high standard, but because his taste is basic, mainstream. He knows what will play in Boisie, New York City, the deep south, Puerto Rico and Alaska; and what will play is what's safe. No-risk television.'

'What about the programming director, Tim Talbot?'

'Tim's more of a wild card. He's at the most, twenty-eight, twenty-nine? Came up the cable route. To Tim, TV is just one big video game. His official role is court jester to the King. Stan's supposed to be grooming Tim for his job as head of the network if he has to leave CBN.'

'You mean Stanfield King might lose his job?'

'Are you kidding?' Marty said, just as the elevator door slid open. 'These guys don't lose their jobs. The shit rises to the top and then it rotates.'

'Hudlow/Turgov Productions? Right this way.' An army of executive assistants surrounded them in the plush reception area of CBN. Each assistant was beautiful and, if Marty's industrial espionage was correct, at least marginally bright. New Hollywood: brains with boobs. Young women asking their plastic surgeons to make them look like Candice

Bergen, the thinking man's sex symbol, instead of Madonna. Julia and Marty were whisked into the conference room which was huge and contained a polished oak table long enough and solid enough to accommodate a full-scale production of *Swan Lake* on its gleaming surface. The walls were pastel and hung with muted art. Julia's heels sank into the thick pile of the dove-gray carpet. The assistants hovered, plying them with coffee, tea, and designer water.

'They offered us coffee, that's good,' Marty whispered as the bevy of assistants fluttered out.

'Why?' Julia tried to will the butterflies in her stomach to come to rest.

'It means they've scheduled enough time at least to drink a cup of coffee. And they've turned off the muzak. That means they're taking this meeting seriously.'

'Oh,' Julia nodded. 'Good.' The room was glass on two of its four sides, offering a spectacular view. Julia felt suspended in mid-air out over the Hollywood Hills. The effect was dizzying. How could anyone work in such a rarefied atmosphere? The door opened and the triumvirate filed in, presumably in the order of importance according to *Daily Variety*: Kathryn followed by Tim followed by the King himself.

Kathryn Grady, former 'D girl', now head of Development at Pacific Victory, with the unusual power (for a woman) to actually greenlight a project. Her voice was low, guarded, she chose her words carefully, but she had a wicked sense of humor and a keen eye for comedy. She was wearing a fedora and a man's charcoal-gray three-piece suit, the severity of the look broken only by her wild tangle of dark hair and sensuously full mouth.

Tim Talbot resembled a Jim Hensen muppet, genial at first glance, but with more than a touch of malevolence on further inspection. He had a round, cherubic face – collagen, it was whispered – and thinning blond hair which he kept covered with a baseball cap worn backwards. He was wearing a pink shirt with turquoise pants, suspenders, high top sneakers, electric blue socks and a Star Wars watch. It was hard to assess what he was thinking or if he was thinking at all.

Stanfield King's face was more angular, topped with a shock of strange hair, rumored to be dyed. Certainly it was an odd shade of tan. Julia found it hard not to stare. The man who had graced the cover of so many industry publications, Stan King, boy wonder, had grown paunchy, and his taste in clothes even more middle-America, although his carefully pressed Levis had certainly never been anywhere near the kind of animals for which they were originally intended. He looked California casual, as if out for a few rounds of golf, but as soon as he turned the full force of his gaze on her, she caught her breath. The man exuded power. Stanfield King was out to reclaim the crown that his last name once implied.

Marty extended his hand. 'Hi, Kathryn, great to see you again. Stan, Tim, this is my wife, Julia—'

But Stan cut him off with a cursory wave. 'Of course I know Julie. Post-Emmy party, 1991. Nicky Blair's. You ate all the chocolate-dipped strawberries, right?' He laughed a wheezing laugh that ended in a snort.

Julia gulped. 'Right.' She wondered if Stan had a giant rolodex with a little card marked: 'Julia Hudlow. Nicky Blair's. Strawbs.' Stan looked like a guy whose entire life was on rolodex.

'We're going to be pitching this idea to all the networks,' Marty continued, 'but we're coming to you first. We both felt, and Pac Vic agrees, that CBN should have first option.'

'Well, you picked the right time to pitch,' Stan focused on Julia, his face so close to hers that she could count three stray hairs on the bridge of his nose just below his Ralph Lauren glasses. He smiled at her indulgently. Julia figured he thought she was much younger. Sometimes that was a pain, sometimes it was a plus. In this instance it was probably a plus since Stanfield King was ready to give her a lot more leeway than he would if he knew she was thirty-five.

'Drama is dead,' Stan intoned. 'What I'm looking for is good, cheap comedy. Thirty-minute slot. Costs me half what a drama costs and I get more for it.' He spoke in short, rapid sentences, as if editing his own text under the principle that time is money. 'Kathy here is very passionate about your idea. She says I'm going to love it. So, dazzle me.' He stopped and looked intently at Julia. Marty indicated she should go ahead. Julia froze. Her stomach went into an intricate sailor's knot. Oh God, she couldn't breathe. Her mouth was full of cotton. She licked her lips, swallowed, plugged into the soft vowels of her native accent, and began to speak. 'Makeover is a southern sit-com that takes a satirical look at urban Texas from a female point of view.'

'Satire is what gets bumped in mid-season,' Tim interrupted.

Stan lifted a hand to stop him from going any further and Tim was immediately silenced. 'Three lines, Julie,' Stan smiled at her again. 'Give it to me in three lines.'

'OK.' Julia took a breath. 'Two sisters, working their way up, run a beauty shop called the Changing Room in a Houston shopping mall. They're trying to change their lives by changing others' looks.' She stopped for a minute, then realized she had one more of her three sentences to go. 'We follow the stories of the main characters and their retail neighbors as well as a number of guests who all, eventually, get made over.'

'Umm-mmm,' Stan nodded briskly. 'Why Houston?'

'Dallas is dead and buried,' said Tim flatly.

'Exactly.' They had given her the right cue. 'Makeover is the antidote to Dallas. Number one, it's a sit-com not a soap. Number two, we're dealing with a different kind of south. I'm originally from Houston and, believe me, it's a world unto itself. I'm not writing about the wheelers and dealers in the oil business, I'm interested in the regular folks, although your basic Texan is always a little irregular,' she was rolling with a theory she'd been formulating ever since she left Texas fifteen years ago. 'In Texas, everybody is a little crazy, the heat makes passions run higher, and the accent lends itself to situation comedy. You can say the most outrageous things and somehow a southern accent makes them funny.'

'Why a beauty shop?' Stan was firing questions at her.

Her stomach lurched again; her palms were sweaty. 'The Changing Room is more than just a beauty shop, it's a complete makeover centre. Women want to look different. There's a plastic surgery epidemic in this country, but surgery can have serious side-effects. Just look at breast implants. The wave of the future is the non-surgical makeover. Hair, make-up, nails, clothes, the works. Before and after. Change the outer image in order to find the inner self. Women go to the Changing Room to be "transformed", hoping their lives will be transformed in the process.'

18

Stan plucked a pencil out of the crystal jar on the table and rolled it around in his fingers. 'Why a shopping mall?'

Julia looked to Marty for back-up, but he was just sitting there quietly. You've got the ball, baby, keep on running. 'A shopping mall represents Main Street, USA. I'm not talking your little pissant Searstown strip mall and I don't mean the Galleria where you need a guide dog just to find your way out, just a middle-of-the-road place . . .' They laughed at her pun. 'The mall is what used to be "downtown"; it's replaced the village square where all the townspeople would gather. Now they hang out at the mall. Kids go straight from school to the mall. The stores are open on Sunday; people go to the mall instead of to church. That's the people who shop there. For those who work there, it's a second home, their own little neighborhood. *But*,' she leaned forward slightly, 'for our characters in Makeover, the mall is a trap. Here they are, making over other people, but what they want more than anything is to change their own lives. Like so many of us today, they're approaching the midpoint and they want something different, something more, a whole new life!' She stopped suddenly, breathless. 'Sorry, when I get excited, I get ahead of myself.'

'No, it's nice to see real, honest enthusiasm.' For the first time Stan relaxed his rapid-fire delivery. 'It's in kind of short supply around here.' He smiled at her again. 'I like the concept. Tell me more.'

Yes! Excellent! Ten minutes into the pitch and already he liked her concept. Only what next? She drew a blank.

'Outline the characters for us,' Kathryn prompted. 'There are some terrific casting possibilities here, Stan.'

Now she was on firmer ground. She'd created the people of Makeover, they were as real to her as her own family back in Houston, more real since she was now estranged from that family. 'Our heroine is Janine Barnett, manager of the Changing Room. She's mid-thirties, a widow: her husband, Carl, died in the Gulf War . . .'

'Good,' Stan murmured approval, 'the ramifications of that conflict haven't yet been fully explored.'

'It's Carl's insurance policy plus his military pension that gives Janine the money to start her own business. She's down-to-earth, funny, warm, but she doesn't know her inner strength yet. That will come out through the arc of our first season. I've written the role with Diane Slater in

19

mind. She can be very glamorous when she's made over, but she looks like the wrath of God first thing in the morning. That's true for most women and a lot of men, too.' Everyone laughed. 'Her younger sister, Nadine, is early thirties and neurotic about it. A former beauty queen. She gets hooked on the makeover process. Always dieting, changing the color of her hair, always looking for the right guy. Dates a continual parade of losers.'

'That could be a running gag on the show,' Tim said with the barest hint of enthusiasm.

'Absolutely!' Finally, a crack in Tim's china. 'Nadine's desperate to get married but as soon as a man gets to know her, he realizes what a flake she is and finds himself more attracted to Janine. So right away we've got conflict. Now our love interest—' A murmur of anticipation from around the table. 'Of course he doesn't start out as the love interest. In the beginning he's just the guy next door. Travis Kyle. Runs the Sports Chek, athletic equipment and fitness centre, where Changing Room clients can go for long-range changes. A former football player who got permanently benched by football knee, he's a good-looking, good ole boy, but with a Nineties' dose of sensitivity. Sexy, charming, great sense of humor. But,' she had them hanging on her next word, 'he's married.' A huge groan from around the table. 'No, wait. This marriage is sort of bizarre. His wife, Marcia, is in the Air Force and she's not around. In fact, she's often reported missing. Travis never knows for sure whether "Marcia" is alive or dead, which makes Travis's sex life pretty precarious if he's an honorable man.'

'We can get a lot of mileage out of the missing Marcia without ever having her appear as a character –' Tim seemed now to be on track – 'let an image of Marcia build up in the viewer's mind and maybe eventually . . .'

'You got it,' Julia exclaimed, 'the real Marcia turns up.'

Stan wanted to know: 'Do you see our Janine eventually getting together with Travis?'

Our Janine. Julia liked the sound of that. 'Of course, but not for a few seasons. I'll spin it out as long as I can.'

'The slow tease,' Tim chortled. 'Feel that steam rise.'

'Besides, our Janine's not ready yet. She's got problems at home. She's trying to raise her daughter, thirteen-year-old Carlene.'

Stan tapped his pencil rat-a-tat-tat on the polished oak

table top. 'What's the kid's character?' Grabbing a piece of yellow lined paper he began to make notes. Tim quickly followed suit. In the blink of an eye, they had shifted into mode Type A workaholic, a mode Julia secretly shared.

'Simple, sweet, genuine . . .' Julia began.

'Boring,' Tim yawned.

Julia couldn't figure him out. Was he on her side or not? 'Only in the beginning,' she defended her character, 'but over time Carlene starts to rebel. She misses her dad and her mom is over-protective. Janine's afraid she'll get in with the wrong crowd. Carlene's capable of being a smartass and that eventually develops into real rebellion as she becomes a teenager over the seasons.'

'That sounds better,' Stan said. Back-up chorus agreed.

'Our secondary characters are more off-the-wall,' Julia went on. 'We've got Samantha, resident cosmetician and part-time astrologer. Gives you your horoscope along with your facial. Concha, the Changing Room receptionist, is Hispanic, a real hot tamale of a girl, nineteen and street-wise.'

'How about a black character?' Tim suggested.

'Lyla could be black. She's the woman who runs Lyla Kaye's Lingerie, the boutique on the other side of the salon where the Changing Room clients can buy sexy lingerie for their glamor shots. The before-and-after photographs are taken by Troy Morrison in his photographic studio which is part of the Changing Room's full-package makeover. I'd like to see an actor with stand-up comedy skills as Troy. I'm toying with making the character Jewish; Jews occupy a unique position in southern society. Troy's sharp, funny, could be gay, but that's been done to death. At any rate, he shouldn't be competition for Travis, who has to remain our resident hunk.'

'There's plenty of room for guest stars to come on the show and actually be made over,' Marty spoke up for the first time. 'We build the stories around a physical change in look for each client.'

'Every week?' Stan said skeptically. 'Could get old fast.'

'Not every week. But lots of current issues lend themselves to the makeover idea. Julia's got some great plot angles.'

'One set?' Stan was scribbling furiously as was Tim.

'Basically one set, yeah. The Changing Room beauty

21

shop and make-up salon is where the main action takes place. Of course we can move out into other locations in the mall such as the lingerie boutique and the fitness centre, but the main interior is the shop itself.'

'I love it,' Stan said suddenly. 'I love Makeover.'

'You do?' Julia gasped. He'd already made up his mind!

'Yes! It's hot!' he pounded the table, all reserve gone.

'Me, too,' Tim pounded the table, too. Marty let out a yell and Kathryn's smile was nearly splitting her face. Julia levitated to the ceiling and spun around a few times.

'Only, CBN can't do it. It's not right for us.'

Julia came down to earth with a thud.

'No, not right for us,' Tim echoed his boss. Julia looked at Marty who turned white, then green. Her heart started to pound and she felt her face grow hot. Bastards! Keep us here on your turf for over an hour stringing us along and then cut the high wire just like that? Changing from we would and we could to we will and we can, then backing off in the point of a Neilsen number? Having fun, guys? She was shaking with anger and then suddenly, the anger stopped and something else clicked in. She really wanted to do Makeover now, she wanted it badly, and she was ready to fight. If they expected her to pick up her ideas and go home with her psyche between her legs, they had another think coming.

'Why can't you do it?' she said with deadly calm, glancing at Marty. Little beads of moisture appeared on his upper lip.

Stan removed his glasses and rubbed the bridge of his nose, 'Look, I've got to be honest with you. We're losing viewers. Once network television dominated the universe. Now we can't even run our own backyard. The Japs are standing by just waiting for us to commit hari-kari so they can take over. I get paid to know what works and what doesn't, but even I don't know any more.'

'Who does?' Julia knew in her gut she had to keep the conversation going until they could all agree on something, anything. 'When the best of television has been cancelled.'

'Exactly,' Stan slammed the table again, only this time in anger. 'China Beach, Thirty Something, Twin Peaks: they were great shows, the critics loved them, but not enough people watched them. Big casts. Sub-plots. Expensive. Confusing.'

'So what you're saying to me,' Julia said dryly, 'is that what you want is a high quality show that will win over the critics and still please the lowest common denominator; a show that has wonderful characters, but not too many of them; that costs you nothing but will make a fuckload of money.'

Stan burst out laughing, wheezing and snorting. 'You know the golden rule of television?' Julia shook her head. 'He who has the gold, rules.' His eyes narrowed. 'No, what I'm asking you is what makes your project different from what's already out there? How are you going to get them to watch us instead of the other guys? Why should we take a risk with you?'

Marty sat silent as stone. Julia attempted to reload her ammunition. 'Makeover is a working-class comedy . . .'

'We prefer the term blue-collar,' Tim sniped.

Julia, ignoring him: 'Our working-class hero is a heroine. Not a freak like Roseanne, but a real woman who just wants to be better. Designing Women, they all look like fashion plates; Murphy Brown, they're all brilliant. Makeover shows the average woman where she can get help.'

'Which is the bottom-line theme for the show,' Marty had found his voice again. Along with his color. The green was retreating from his face, leaving his natural, healthy tan.

Julia looked at him with relief. 'Exactly. It's never too late to be someone or something else. Jane Fonda is walking proof of that. The entire United States wants to be made over, but what's our new image going to be? We're no longer naïve, which was part of what made our values so idealistic in the sixties. Some of the best sit-coms have centered around the nuclear family but, hey, we're not living in the fifties any more. There are a lot of single parents out there. The racial make-up of this country has changed radically. A large part of the population is African-American and Hispanic and they want their television to show a world that has them in it. On Makeover we have an ethnic mix, living and working together. The Changing Room is their home and the people they work with are their family. You've got two levels of appeal here: real-life situations with good potential for laughs, and an underlying theme which reflects the complexity of the nineties. We're now living longer than ever before. We've had twenty years of one life, now we want a change. And nobody said we couldn't. We're the baby boomers. We get to have everything we want.' Stan was nodding in agreement as if every word was personally directed to him, Tim was leaning forward, and Kathryn and Marty were silently cheering her on. She had them, she knew she had them. 'I believe that Makeover will not only hook the network viewers, it will bring back the crowd who defected to pay TV . . . Makeover will help you rebuild that audience you've lost. So you see, Stan, it's not a risk at all. In fact, it could save your ass.' She came to a stop, out of breath, but exhilarated.

'OK, OK, good pitch.' Stan was nodding like one of those mechanical dogs in the back window of a car and Tim was smiling away. 'What about casting?'

'We need a strong ensemble who can create unique characters, people the viewers will want to invite into their homes every week and grow to love as familiar friends.'

Stan frowned. 'No. Ensemble takes too long. We can't wait ten or fifteen episodes to build an audience. When I was at ABC, they used to give a show a year, maybe two. Now . . .'

'Now you're lucky if you get a month,' Tim joked. 'Stan's right. We'll need a star in at least one of the two main roles, a name that will get people watching the first episode and keep them watching.'

'Julia conceived Makeover with Diane Slater as Janine,' Marty reminded them.

'Di's a very close friend of mine,' Julia reinforced the connection. 'I would have brought her to the meeting today, but she and her husband are away in Cabo San Lucas.'

'Diane Slater could pull the show by herself, but why would she commit to a series and tie herself up?'

'She swears to me she wants a nine-to-five "day job" that will keep her in LA. She's only been married a couple of months and she doesn't want to jeopardize her third marriage by going on location.'

'Excellent,' Stan was nodding again. 'So we can go with an unknown as Travis.' Now they were back to 'can'. 'Who's your "wish actor"? If you could have absolutely any actor you wanted, who would it be?'

'Well,' Julia let her mind fast-forward through the *Player's Guide*. 'Nick Nolte is too old, Patrick Swayze is too young, Tommy Lee Jones, maybe. . . . Brandon Tate! Someone like Brandon Tate would be perfect.'

'How about Brandon Tate himself?' Kathryn interjected.

'Oh, come on, Kathryn,' Tim said in a don't-waste-our-time voice. 'He'll never do episodic television. Brandon Tate's a bigger star than Diane Slater could ever dream of being.'

'A star that's more than a little tarnished,' Kathryn said. 'His last two films have only just squeaked by at the box office. Let me talk to him.'

'Isn't he too big for the small screen?' Julia wanted to keep the focus on the female character.

'Not at all,' Kathryn argued. 'Brandon's style is intimate. He's sexy, but mysterious; he presents a challenge. Every woman wants to believe she holds the key that could unlock Brandon Tate. It adds up to just the kind of sexual sizzle we need.'

'I didn't say I wanted Brandon Tate, I said I wanted a Brandon Tate type.' Julia was sending a distress signal to Marty who knew two stars could also blow the budget.

'If we can get Brandon, Julie, you'll take Brandon,' Stan said firmly. The network had final casting approval. 'But we'd consider giving you "star breakage" on that,' meaning the network might come up with the extra bucks. 'He'll have to be wooed in just the right way. Maybe we can tie him up with golden handcuffs, sweeten the offer by giving him a chance to direct an episode or two. Kathy, go for it.'

'I'll give it my best shot,' Kathryn promised. 'What woman wouldn't want to spend an afternoon seducing Brandon Tate?' They all laughed.

Julia looked at Marty who was surreptitiously circling his finger in the air, indicating that she should wrap it up. She gathered her nerve to ask, 'So if Kathryn is going to talk to Brandon Tate, does this mean CBN is interested in Make-over?'

Stan wheezed again. 'Julie, you're quite a little hustler. So, Marty, got a director in mind?'

As producer, it was up to Marty to hire the director and the crew. He nodded. 'Alex Jordan. Also a friend of Julia's.'

'Really?' Tim was impressed. 'He's wonderful with actors. Knows the camera, too. I think the network would approve him. One more thing, what do you see as the target demographics?'

Julia was ready. 'We're aiming Makeover at women between the ages of eighteen and forty-nine, but I'd like to think the characters cross all boundaries of age and sex.'

'You'd like to think that,' Tim said wryly, 'but it doesn't necessarily work that way.'

'What I mean is, we'll be dealing with socially relevant issues that should be of interest to everybody.'

'Wait a minute,' Stan looked alarmed. 'What I love about the show is that it's a return to traditional values. I thought that's what you said.'

Marty and Julia exchanged mutual panic. That wasn't what they had said but, inches away from a deal, neither of them wanted to correct him.

'Right,' Julia responded, 'but I want to try to give the audience something a little challenging . . .'

'Don't try too hard,' Stan chuckled. 'The best television is like Kleenex – disposable.'

'Excuse me, but I've got to run,' Kathryn stood up. 'I'm meeting my fiancé at Le Dôme.'

'You're getting married?' Marty voiced everyone's surprise. 'Congratulations. Is he in the biz?'

Kathryn blushed, an action foreign to her. 'No, he's got nothing to do with entertainment, thank God, except as a fan. He's an oil- and gas-stocks analyst. Jonathan Long. I met him on a scuba dive in Belize. We haven't known each other long; well, only two months actually.'

'A whirlwind romance,' gushed Tim.

'Sort of.' Kathryn turned a deeper pink. 'You'll all get to meet him, eventually, but I really do have to fly.' She gathered up her things in a flurry and raced out the door.

Julia snapped back to Stan. 'So what happens now?'

Stan laughed. 'What happens now is you write me a pilot script. Maybe also a storyline proposal.'

Julia opened her mouth, but Marty jumped in. 'Not on spec.'

Stan raised an eyebrow at Tim and then said smoothly, 'CBN will commission the pilot script for a negotiated fee. We'll draft a deal memo which will outline your responsibilities if the pilot gets picked up. Does Michael Taylor at CTA represent both you and Marty?' Julia nodded, her heart pounding with excitement. This was it, they were about to close. 'Have Mike call me and we'll hammer out a step deal.' Bingo! Stan rose. Everyone leapt to their feet. 'Great to see you again, Marty,' shaking his hand. 'You and I must win the prize for longevity in this business.' Julia was fraid to see how this remark would affect Marty – he was so ensitive about age these days – but Marty was beaming way. 'I'm looking forward to doing business with you, ulie,' Stan continued. A quick kiss on the cheek. 'Get that cript to me by Thanksgiving; I'll have a decision for you by Christmas.'

And suddenly Julia and Marty were out the door, into the elevator, and shooting down to the ground floor.

A deal, we got a deal,' Julia shouted. 'Was I good?'

'You were great,' Marty hugged her, 'Wonderful, amazng. Like a little tigress. I didn't know you had it in you.'

'Neither did I,' Julia laughed with delight. 'All these years of WASP repression and now I find out what I really ove is confrontation.'

'I hate it. Once I get angry, I'm lost.'

'You really scared me there for a minute, Marty.' She ooked at him with concern. 'When they first said no, you vent white as a ghost and didn't say anything. I've never een you like that. What happened?'

'I don't know,' Marty shivered. 'I just lost it in there. I ot so dizzy I thought I was going to pass out. But you kept our cool.'

'Oh, I was pissed off, too, but then I rechanneled it in the ight direction and it worked. We won,' she crowed, 'we von!'

'You won.' Marty picked her up and swung her around. I tell you, Jules, you are made for television.'

'Don't insult me,' Julia said, but she was beginning to hink he might be right.

TO: ALL TALENT REPRESENTATIVES
RE: SIT-COM PILOT EPISODE
'MAKEOVER'
SAG/AFTRA

Producers: Hudlow-Turgov/Pacific Victory
Writer: Julia Hudlow
Director: Alex Jordan
Shoots: 3/92 2 weeks with option
Location: Pacific Victory Studios
Burbank, Ca.

ALL WRITTEN SUBMISSIONS ASAP TO: Lisa Pellegrino
Director of Talent
CBN Building
Century City
1200 Ave. of the
Stars
L.A., Ca. 90314

CASTING:

JANINE BARNETT:
Leading role. Mid-30s. Warm, funny, tough businesswoman.
Owner of the Changing Room salon. Southern accent.
Looking to cast *name actress*.

TRAVIS KYLE:
Leading role. Early 40s. Runs Sport Chek and Fitness
Centre.
Sexy, charming jock but with sensitivity. CAST.

NADINE (LAMAR):
Principal. Early 30s. Sister to Janine. Beautician.
Former beauty queen. Ditzy, neurotic. Prototype: Faith
Ford.
Southern accent required.

CARLENE BARNETT:
Principal. 13. Daughter to Janine. Sweet, genuine but sassy.
Prototype: Sara Gilbert. Southern accent required.

SAMANATHA JAMES:
30–40. Support. Cosmetician. Wise-cracking, raunchy.
Prototype: Bette Midler, a warm Delta Burke.

CONCHA MARTINEZ:
19–24. Support. Receptionist. Spitfire type. Hispanic accent.
Prototype: A younger Maria Conchata Alonso.

LYLA KAYE:
30–40. Owns lingerie boutique next to the Changing Room. Support role. Working class. Friendly, chatty. Southern accent.
Could consider visible minority.

TROY MORRISON:
Support but may be upgraded to Principal. Late 20s, early 30s. Photographer. Slightly off-the-wall. Fast-talking.
Prototype: Young Billy Crystal.

CASTING

Chapter Two

'Would you like a magazine?' A handsome male flight attendant with an armful of magazines and a fixed smile attempted to navigate a path through the aisles of the business-class section of the Air Canada 727.

'No, thank you, I have some work to catch up on,' said the little red-headed girl sitting in the window seat, wearing a bowler hat and chewing nervously on her already stubby nails. She had a plain little face, but it was full of life. Her small, thin, freckled hands clutched a dog-eared script with chunks of dialogue heavily highlighted in yellow.

'I'll take *People*. Gotta catch up on who's zooming who,' Bonnie McKimmie reached out a heavily ringed hand and let it slide across the flight attendant's, giving him a little wink. So, the guy was probably gay – most of them were – but just in case she wanted to keep her options open, and he really was, like, gorgeous.

'Mum, there's not going to be any time for reading,' the little girl said in a surprisingly adult voice. 'It's not a long flight and you have to help me prepare for my audition.'

'I know, Melissa, but, like, there's a whole bunch of stuff on Beverly Hills 90210 in here,' her mother whined. 'It's the cover story. Don't you want me to check out the competition?' She rummaged in her purse for her cigarettes. God, she was dying for a smoke.

'No,' said Melissa, 'I think Northwood is way better. Beverly Hills 90210 is so plastic. Northwood has –' she searched for the word – 'integrity.'

'You better think that,' Bonnie laughed, easing the lines around her eyes and mouth for just a minute. She pulled out a pack of Export A and a throwaway lighter. 'Northwood's paying our rent out at Kitsilano and it's damn lucky for both of us that CBC has renewed the series for another season.'

'I'm not signing anything until I see what happens in LA,' stated Melissa. 'If I get this job . . .'

'Hey, do we have to talk shop now? While we're in the air? Before I've had a drink?' Bonnie placed a cigarette between two fingers and handed her lighter to the flight attendant. 'Could you light this for me, honey?' She smiled up at him seductively.

Melissa was so embarrassed she had to look away. Why did Bonnie feel she had to come on to every man they met? Why couldn't she act . . . well . . . more like a mother? She scrunched down in the oversized seat, trying to make herself even smaller, and whispered fiercely to her mother, 'Yes, we do have to talk about it now, which is why there's no time for you to be reading *People* magazine. This is an important career move for me and you promised you would help.'

'All right, all right, just let me have a smoke first.'

'Excuse me,' the flight attendant interrupted, 'there's no smoking on this flight.'

'What?' The lines on Bonnie's forehead tightened. 'I thought that was just domestic. Isn't this considered international?'

'Los Angeles is within North America, ma'am.'

'Can't you make an exception? My daughter's got an audition this afternoon for a new TV series and we're under a lot of pressure here.' She gave him another little wink. 'I won't tell if you won't.'

'Sorry, ma'am, it's against regulations.'

'Yeah, fine, they should have told me that when I booked. I would have flown American. Shit, then give me back my lighter.' She grabbed it out of his hand and tossed it into the abyss of her handbag. He was definitely a 'mo' for sure. Forget it. Lost cause. 'What's the movie?' she asked sullenly.

'There isn't one, ma'am.'

'There isn't one?' Bonnie's mouth dropped open in horror.

'The flight's not long enough.'

'Oh, great. Can we expect you to be bringing the beverage cart around any time in the near future?'

'Mum, it's OK, go ahead and take the *People* magazine.' Melissa's face was pink with embarrassment. 'And could you bring my mother a headset, too, please? She might like to listen to some music.'

'Certainly, miss.' The flight attendant ignored the mother and directed his attention to the daughter. 'You'll find New Kids on the Block on channel six.' He pressed the headset into Melissa's hand and moved swiftly down the aisle.

'Mum, will you get it together, please? You're making me nervous.'

'Oh, chill out, Missy.' Bonnie put on the headset and began to flip through the magazine. 'It's not every day I fly to Hollywood with my daughter to audition for the head of a big TV network. This is like a major event and it should be fun, OK?'

'OK, I'm sorry, OK.' Melissa touched her mother's shoulder tentatively. 'Love you.'

'Love you, too.' Bonnie flipped the audio dial on her armrest, looking for channel number six.

'I just want you to go over my lines with me so I don't blow it, you know?'

'Can we talk about this after the emergency procedures?' Bonnie's eyes were fixed on the screen for the welcome aboard video. 'If you don't mind, I'd like to learn how to save my own life if we happen to crash into the Pacific Ocean.'

'Mum, you've flown dozens of times. You're just using delaying tactics. We're going to be landing at noon. While we're waiting for the bags, I'll change into my black leggings and green sweater in the washroom. A studio car is picking us up at LAX and we go straight over to Pac Vic for the on-camera audition at one-thirty. I've got to be totally prepared.'

'You are always prepared, Melissa. It's like you were born thirty years old and totally prepared. Although,' she gave her a sidelong glance, 'maybe you should try to do something about your make-up and hair?'

'Like you haven't got enough make-up on for both of us, eh?'

'I'm not the one who's auditioning,' Bonnie snapped. 'You are.'

'What's wrong with my hair?' Melissa twisted a stray strand of her Botticelli strawberry curls, which she thought was her best feature. She was wrong. Her hair got attention first, but it was her eyes that held it. Deep-set, serious eyes, that came close to holding a Russian novel of character and emotion.

'Well, you said this "Makeover" is set in a shopping mall in a big American city. So you need mall hair. You're way too sweet and simple, too Canadian. I mean, we're not talking Anne of Green Gables here. You gotta look more like a mall rat.'

'You know this term? My mother knows this term, mall rat?'

'Sure. I'm like totally on track, baby, you know that. Oh shit, your hair's starting to fall. Let me tease your bangs straight up and spray them, OK?'

'OK,' Melissa conceded, 'but we can do that in the john, too. Come on, run my lines with me. Please.'

'How about something to drink?' the flight attendant was at their side again.

'I'll have a double rye and ginger.'

'Club soda,' Melissa said firmly, 'for both of us.'

'You'll want some peanuts with that.' The flight attendant deposited three packets of honey-roasted nuts on Melissa's tray and moved out of range.

'Don't eat those peanuts, Mum,' Melissa said as Bonnie instantly grabbed them off her daughter's tray and ripped open all three packets at once. 'Seven grams of fat and tons of sodium.'

'But I'm starving. Breakfast was hours ago.'

'Lunch will be along soon. Did you remember to order the vegetarian?'

'Yeah,' Bonnie sighed. 'Probably overcooked stringbeans and carrots. Gross. I'd give my left boob for a Big Mac.'

'Grow up, Mum. And I wish you wouldn't use that kind of language.'

'I'm only thirty-three. How grown-up do you expect me to be? I'm starting to get majorly ticked off here, Missy. Chill out, will you? It's a free trip to LA. Look on it as a vacation.' Seeing her daughter's anxious face, her tone softened. 'Honey, you're going to ace this role. You'll make us both rich, I know it.'

For the first time Melissa's determination seemed to falter. 'I just don't know if I'm right for Carlene. I mean, they want somebody who's thirteen. I won't be thirteen for five months.'

'You're very advanced for your age.'

'Yeah, right,' Melissa snorted. 'I haven't even pubed. I'm not exactly Shannen Doherty.' She reached for the *People* magazine with a glamour photograph of the star of Beverly Hills 90210. 'All the girls on that show have bazonga melons; I haven't even got raisins yet.' She looked down at her flat chest in disgust.

'So maybe they're not looking for boobs. They loved your tape, honey, and your résumé. I call that casting director, Lisa Pellegrino, and she goes, "Your daughter is very impressive, Mrs McKimmie." I go, "Yeah, you think so?" She goes, "Melissa's got triple the credits of most of the other kids we've been seeing." '

'Sure, it's Canada. We all work a lot.'

'I didn't when I was an actress,' Bonnie said sharply.

'OK, Mum, OK.' Melissa ducked her head. She still felt guilty that her own career had long-since surpassed her mother's.

'Well, this Lisa's right, how many other kids have a résumé like yours? Danger Bay when you were only seven,' she began to reel off the credits, 'two McGuyvers, a guest shot on 21 Jump Street, a continuing role on Northwood . . .'

'Two MOWs for Disney/Touchstone . . .'

'MOW? Baby, you're going Hollywood on me already and we're not even in LA.'

'That's what they call movies of the week,' Melissa said seriously.

'Hey, all right. If you want to make it big, you gotta talk the lingo.' Melissa's thumbnail, what was left of it, went back in her mouth. 'Are you worried about leaving Vancouver, is that it? Missing all your friends?'

'What friends?'

'All the kids you work with on Northwood.'

'They're professional colleagues, not friends.'

'Well, excuse me. Anyway, you still have me. We can hang out together in LA, have a great time.'

'Yeah, maybe, but sometimes I worry about being too, you know, different.'

'Face it,' her mother said, 'you've never been normal. You used to run up and down in the backyard, talking to yourself, making up stories with these really weird characters. Do you remember Donny Onny? Your imaginary playmate when you were five years old? You made him seem so real I swear I could almost see him myself. You've always been good at play-acting.'

'Yeah, but now I have to do it for a living.' Melissa's eyes filled with sudden tears. 'Mommy, I'm scared.' She reached out for her mother's hand but Bonnie pulled it away.

'Scared? I worked my tail off so that your talent could have what it needed. I gave up a bunch of stuff so that you could have dancing lessons and piano lessons and braces on your teeth, and my reward for that is "I'm scared"? It's not like I pushed you into any of this. You wanted it. You saw me modeling for catalogues, going out on auditions, and you said you wanted to do it, too. You said,' she repeated stubbornly. 'I gave up my career for you . . . no, wait a minute,' she put her hand over Melissa's mouth, 'I'm not saying I'm sorry, I don't have your talent, I never did. Now your career is my career, OK? You're going to make TBT, like I never did.'

'TBT?'

'The Big Time.'

'Now who's talking Hollywood?' Melissa managed a watery smile.

'If you get the job and we move to LA, I promise you one thing.'

'What?'

'I'll teach you how to drive.'

'I thought you had your license revoked.'

'I have not had my license revoked.' Bonnie was indignant. 'OK, so I got a few tickets, but they're not going to hunt me down across the border. Anyway, you can drive me around LA. I know you're too young for even your beginner's, but I'll take you out into the countryside.'

'If there is any countryside near LA. Isn't it all one great big freeway?'

'Right.' They both laughed. 'OK, then we'll find an empty parking lot. Living in LA, the sooner you learn to drive the better.'

'OK, great.' Melissa brightened. 'Mum, if I do get this, it'll mean a lot of money, eh?'

'More than we've ever dreamed of. We can have whatever we want. Now shut up and let me listen to at least one song.' Bonnie put her headset back on and reclined in her seat.

Melissa started to open her script, then she turned and pressed her face against the window, watching the fog clear and the fir-covered mountains below give way to a vast expanse of sunlit blue, the Pacific Ocean. I know what I'll use the money for, she thought. I'll use it to find my dad. Maybe he'll see me on TV. Maybe my dad is trying to find me.

Linda Earl stood in front of the tall, three-way mirror in her bedroom in Beverly Glen. She was completely naked with a pile of clothes at her feet. Behind her, the walk-in closet was almost empty. Virtually every piece of clothing she owned was on the floor and she still didn't know what she was going to wear to the audition which was only two hours, no – she glanced at the bedside clock – now an hour and a half away. The sight of three naked Lindas with three piles of clothing on the floor reflected in the three mirrors made her want to burst into tears.

For the last three hours she'd been putting on and taking off clothes. The Donna Karan catsuit with wraparound skirt? No, too New York. Makeover was set in Houston, Texas. The Adrienne Vittadini black-and-white houndstooth jacket with matching slacks? No, too executive. The character she was auditioning for worked in a beauty salon in a shopping mall. Besides, if she wore a suit she'd sweat buckets in this heat. Her long blonde hair was already sticking to the back of her neck, even with the air-conditioning up full. Jeans and a silk shirt? Too casual. Leather? Too butch. Also too hot. LA was experiencing record temperatures for February. Should she wear her hair up? Or down? Or partly cover it with a scarf? She picked up a lipstick from her dressing-table and applied it carefully with a brush, then deciding, no, too glamorous, not serious enough, she grabbed a tissue and began rubbing it off. Wait a minute, this was television; of course they'd want some glamour. She began putting on lipstick again. The tears were rolling down her face, smearing the mascara she'd applied so carefully and running on to her mouth causing the lipstick to bleed. She sank down on to the floor and began to cry on the oyster-colored shag carpet that looked so elegant but was such a pain to keep clean. Get a grip on yourself, Linda, she thought, wiping her eyes. Do they want what I look like? Or do they want me? She sat down on the big circular bed and began the litany: I am enough; I am enough; I am enough. But she felt the familiar gorge rising and she ran into the bathroom, quickly locking the door behind her and turning on the faucet full-force to let the water run loudly.

'Linda, Linda, are you in there?' There was a loud knocking on the bathroom door. She hastily splashed some cold water on her eyes, grabbed a hairbrush and began brushing her hair as she flipped the latch on the door.

'Darling, are you all right?' Her husband, Steve, stood in the doorway, wearing an expensive three-piece suit and a worried expression on his face. His sandy hair was neatly combed and the cool, crisp smell of his freshly applied aftershave brought her back to reality. He looked so handsome standing there, all scrubbed and shining, holding his leather briefcase like an assault weapon on the world. Seeing her naked, his eyebrows shot up. 'Didn't you say you had an audition this morning?'

'Yes, but I'm not sure if I want to go . . .' Linda's voice sounded frightened, muted, crazy, even to her own ear.

'Well, if you can get dressed in ten minutes, I'll drop you wherever you have to go. After the audition, you can stay in town, do some shopping, then come and meet me at the office and we'll have an early dinner together. Concepcion has everything under control in the nursery so you don't have to deal with the baby, but,' he glanced at his watch, 'you'll have to get dressed in a hurry.'

'I . . . I don't know what to wear.' God, she hated herself. What a pathetic mess she must appear to him.

Steve's eyes swept the bedroom, taking in the scene. 'What is the part? I know you told me it was a new series, but I forgot which role you said it was.'

'I'm not right for it anyway . . .' Linda followed him slowly into the bedroom.

'What's the part?' he repeated patiently.

'The character's name is Nadine,' she made a conscious effort to center her voice as she recited the description from the agency breakdown. 'Early thirties. Beautiful. Lives and works in Houston.'

'Well, the accent's no problem for you. Kentucky's not that different. This is LA. As far as they're concerned, the south is just the south.'

'She's a former beauty contest winner,' Linda went on.

'No, you're right,' Steve dead-panned. 'Nothing like you. If I remember correctly, weren't you Miss Bluegrass 1980?

And Miss Kentucky in 1981? Second runner-up for Miss America not all that long ago?'

'She's supposed to be sort of insecure,' Linda faltered, 'you know, ditzy . . . kind of flakey . . .'

'You don't think standing naked in the middle of the room crying over spilt clothes is just the tiniest bit flakey?' Steve tipped her face up to his and kissed her lightly on the mouth. 'Hmm? What do you think, hmm?' Linda started to giggle. 'OK, so let's take a look in this mirror.' He pulled her gently into the center of the room. 'What have we got here? Honey-blonde hair that's completely natural, yes?' He glanced down at her crotch and Linda giggled again. 'Yes! Now you don't see that every day in LA. Amethyst eyes that Liz Taylor would kill for.' Slipping into a bad southern accent, 'Magnolia petal skin. Perfect cheekbones. Highly kissable lips, I believe. Let's see,' he kissed her again. 'Right again. Definitely kissable. A perfect body, thanks to nature and a personal trainer. Legs that go on for days. In a town where beautiful women are a dime-a-dozen, you still stand out. Why? Because you are drop-dead gorgeous, my darling. I can't understand why you're so insecure.'

'Me neither,' Linda whispered.

'It's not as if you have to work. I make a hell of a lot of money to ensure that you don't have to and that I won't have to after the age of fifty when we will build our own boat and sail around the world. You've got a huge house and a beautiful baby. If this acting thing is so painful for you, why do you put yourself through it?'

'I don't know,' Linda said miserably. 'I just feel like I have to do it.'

'Well, do you have to do it today?' Steve took another look at his watch. 'Make up your mind. Are you going to go for it or not? Your choice.'

'I want to go,' Linda said quietly.

'Great. Then let me help you out here.' He rifled through the pile of clothes on the floor, found a white jersey jumpsuit and tossed it to her. 'Wear this. If they don't hire you in this, they're all brain dead.'

'Thanks, Steve,' she said gratefully. 'I really mean it. Thanks for getting me through this.'

'That's what I'm here for. Meet you out front in no later than five minutes, OK?'

'OK.'

'Linda, darling, please, just try to remember,' he paused in the doorway.

'Yes?'

'They may need you, but you don't need them.'

A small, select, highly talented group sat quietly in one of the 'waiting' rooms in the cavernous broadcast and production complex of the CBN network. The final callbacks for Makeover were being held in the screening room. Every person waiting was on the casting shortlist and the tension was high. There were two teenage girls accompanied by their mothers, two women who appeared to be Hispanic, three black women and one black man, and one short, wiry man with curly hair, merry eyes and a slightly sardonic smile. Sitting apart from all of the others was a tall, statuesque model-type with platinum-blonde hair and an impressive cleavage. For the most part they all kept their heads down, studying the xeroxed draft of the pilot of Makeover. Every once in a while, one would look up to mouth a few words, the face running through a myriad of changing expressions in an attempt to bring the words of the script silently to life.

Theresa Ruiz, volatile, compact, curvy, with upswept dark hair and snapping brown eyes, signaled to her friend across the way to come and join her in the hall for a smoke.

Shirley Bunting, a willowy black woman with almond-shaped eyes and a warm smile, leaned against the wall next to the elevator, her dancer's body curving into a graceful S.

'What are you here for?' Theresa lit a cigarette and inhaled it rapidly as if it might be taken away from her at any moment. 'Not the role of Concha, I hope?'

'No way,' Shirley drew on the cigarette slowly and deeply. 'I can pass for twenty-nine maybe, but Concha's supposed to be nineteen. I'm up for Lyla. I think you've got a real shot at Concha. Especially in that,' her eyes narrowed with friendly amusement, 'tasteful little outfit.'

'I hate it,' Theresa said fiercely, then laughed in spite of herself. 'I can play Medea or Blanche Dubois, but all they ever want to see is gold spandex and spike heels.'

'So, what do you think of the script?' Shirley blew the smoke out languidly.

'Good story, fun characters, but the dialogue for Concha is like from Charo.' She sent the smoke out in short, angry little rings. 'Total stereotype, you know?'

'It's a great part, though. My agent got hold of the "bible" for Makeover,' Shirley referred to the document that detailed each character's history and storyline for the first season. 'Lyla's kind of a nothing role, but you could make your mark with Concha.'

'Yeah?' Theresa looked surprised. 'All she does in the pilot is file her nails, talk on the phone, and jump every guy that walks into the place.'

'I'm just glad they're willing to consider me for Lyla. The part's not written black.'

'Well, she does run a trashy lingerie boutique in a shopping mall. That's not exactly breaking the mould.'

'Still, it's better than playing a hooker on Night Court or,' she looked meaningfully at Theresa, 'a crack addict who sells her own child on Law and Order.'

'Hey, that Law and Order gig has already brought in enough residuals to pay for the bonding of my upper teeth,' Theresa protested.

'My point exactly,' Shirley smiled. 'You got to take it one step at a time out here in the golden land of opportunity. Don't rock the boat too hard. At least we're working.'

'Do you know the employment statistics for black and Hispanic performers?' Theresa demanded.

'Lousy,' Shirley admitted. 'Unless Spike Lee loves you, you're in deep shit.'

'Spike's women are mostly stereotypes, too. What pisses me off even more is that it's the same in real life.' Theresa furiously ground her cigarette butt into the sand in the ashtray by the elevator. 'My VCR broke down last week and I had to rent one so that I could tape my cable MOW? The rental guy wanted my employer to guarantee the fee. I tell him, "I'm self-employed." "No offense," he says, "but I need another guarantee. A lot of wetbacks don't make their payments on time and skip town with my equipment." Asshole didn't even get the accent right. I'm Cuban, not Mexican!' Angrily she lit another cigarette.

Shirley nodded sympathetically. 'Listen, I walk into a boutique in the Beverly Center, the clerks follow me around wherever I go. They think because I'm black, I must be there to shoplift.' The two women laughed bitterly.

'You know,' Theresa said suddenly. 'If they were really smart in there, they'd let you read for Janine. You'd be

43

great in the lead. And I could play your younger sister, Nadine, what do you think?'

'Dream on, girl,' Shirley laughed even harder. 'Back home in South Carolina, my old mama used to say, "Nobody's gonna give you a break for free." '

'Well, your old mama was right. In this business – in this world – we make our own breaks. Listen, you want me to wait for you after my audition? We could go for a drink.'

'I'd love to,' Shirley said warmly, 'but I've got a date with my main man. He's promised we're going to do something special to take my mind off whether or not I get this job.'

'Sounds like he might be giving you a hug and a plug,' Theresa said, lowering her voice to convey every ounce of sexual innuendo.

'Let me tell you, the way he does it it's something special all right,' Shirley said, and the two women burst into wicked giggles.

The door opened and the CBN casting assistant stuck her head out into the hallway. 'Theresa? We're ready for you now.'

Theresa stubbed out her cigarette, smoothed the spandex over her hips and headed for the door.

'Hey, Theresa,' Shirley grabbed her arm and turned her back to face her, 'Good luck.'

'You can say that free and easy because you're not up for the same part,' Theresa teased her.

'No, I mean it,' Shirley said softly. Impulsively she kissed the other actress on the cheek. 'I hope you get this one, I really do.'

The phalanx of studio and network execs seated around the table laughed heartily and then broke into spontaneous applause. They put their heads together for a whispering session while Theresa picked at one of her press-on nails which was in danger of coming right off. She snuck a glance at the motley crew. So these were the top brass. Out of the sea of faces, she recognized just a couple. Stanfield King, *El Rey*, whose hair was even more beige than ever. Tim Talbot, his second-in-command toady, wearing Banana Republic shorts and a Hawaiian print shirt. The glamorous and mysterious Kathryn Grady, as famous for her GAP ads as for her actual work in the business. Lisa Pellegrino, CBN casting director, recently imported from New York, short and dark with a pretty, round face. Her assistant, Angela Santi, even shorter and darker and rounder. Writer/creator Julia Hudlow, executive producer Marty Turgov (they had just been profiled in *Entertainment Weekly*), and director Alex Jordan, tall, lean and lanky, in his early forties but still boyish looking, a sweater tied casually around his shoulders: these made up the creative team.

Behind them, seated around another table, were yet another group of CBN and Pac Vic underlings, none of whom had made a sound during the reading. They broke out of the football huddle and Kathryn Grady said, 'Thank you, Ms Ruiz. A terrific reading. Even better than your taped test. What are you, twenty-three, twenty-four?'

'Truth or résumé age?' Theresa shot back and everyone laughed.

'Never mind, we don't need you to reveal your age,' Alex said in a clipped English accent. 'You look plenty young enough. I guess you've heard we're kind of in limbo here . . .'

'Word on the street is you haven't a Janine yet.'

'That's right. Until we do, this pilot's on hold.'

Theresa took a deep breath. 'I may be way out of line here, but why don't you consider reading Shirley Bunting for Janine? She's out there right now.'

A murmur went through the room. 'That's not part of the breakdown for this character,' Kathryn said smoothly, 'but it's an interesting suggestion.'

'Don't worry, the casting of Janine doesn't really affect you, Theresa,' Alex reassured her. 'We don't have to match you up with anyone else on the show. Concha's an employee of the Changing Room, not a member of the Barnett family.'

'Now, don't take this as gospel,' Kathryn said, 'but at this point you're definitely our first choice. So you don't have to wait around by the phone. The minute we're ready to take this forward, we'll get in touch with your agent. Obviously if you get another offer, you should let us know right away.'

'We don't want to lose you,' Julia broke in.

Lisa stood up to escort her to the door. 'Thanks for coming in, Theresa.' There was a chorus of head-bobbing thank-yous from around the table.

Theresa held up her hand. 'Um, 'scuse me, but could I

45

have just a minute more? Auditions are always strange. You ask me a lot of questions. You don't always listen to the answers. That's OK, because I know you're just trying to relax me, but if I could have just a moment more of your time, I have a few questions of my own.' A series of quick looks were exchanged around the table, then another head-bobbing chorus of fine, sure, go ahead. Theresa moved to Julia. 'Where do you see the character of Concha going?'

'What do you mean?' Marty answered for his wife.

Theresa continued to look at Julia. 'You know, in terms of development? Will there be a growth over the first season?'

Marty looked uneasy. 'Concha's a delightful character, but as Alex just told you, not a member of the family. In a play, the characters do grow, they change and learn, usually ending in some sort of resolution. In a sit-com, there can be no resolution or it's game over. On Cheers, Sam must stay a womanizer. If the characters change and learn, you've got no storyline to continue.'

'I know how situation comedy works, Mr Turgov,' Theresa said very politely, 'and I understand the ratings battle, but personally I like the shows that are different, the ones that have high quality as well as high numbers. I think Makeover has a chance to be that kind of a show and I'd be honored to be involved with it. I just don't want to get trapped in a role I might feel uncomfortable playing.'

'Now, just a minute,' Stan spoke up sharply.

'It's OK, Stan,' Julia said. Then, turning to Theresa: 'Tell me exactly what you mean.'

Theresa swallowed hard. 'Well, your concept is great and I really like what I think you're trying to say about people wanting to transform themselves and everything, but right now Concha's written strictly for laughs.' To Marty: 'I'm not asking for the role to be increased, I just think she should be a real person. Not that you mean her to be a stereotype, I'm sure,' she quickly said to Julia, 'but you could go a lot further exploring the socio-economic demands that are put upon a young Hispanic girl in that position, and still keep her funny without being demeaning. Anyway, maybe I'm out of line here,' she trailed off, still looking at Julia.

'I'll think about it, Theresa, I really will,' Julia said slowly. 'Perhaps if you do end up playing Concha, you could have some input into how the role develops.'

'Jules,' Marty said warningly.

'Sure, right,' Theresa edged toward the door.

'Thanks for coming in. We'll be in touch,' Stan's tone was the ultimate dismissal as Lisa quickly led her to the door.

The door had barely closed behind them when Stan exploded. 'That was unbelievable. What does she think she is, a professional actress or a political agitator?'

'No wonder Castro expelled her family in 1980,' Kathryn said.

'She's still my first choice for Concha,' Julia said firmly.

'Let's table this discussion,' Marty said hastily. 'Ah, the lovely Lisa is back. Who's up next, Lisa?'

'Kelly Carmichael for Samantha. I happened to catch her doing an Equity waiver production of *Sister Mary Ignatius Explains It All to You* and she was off-the-wall funny. She doesn't have much background in the electronic media, but she's got a great raunchy quality and, well, you saw the tape on her. Super comic timing and a really distinctive voice.'

The door opened and a cloud of Ombre Rose wafted in, followed by a tall blonde wearing a Lana Turner style turban and oversized sunglasses, her spectacular bosom spilling out over the lace-edged neckline of her retro-forties suit. She had a gold crescent decal over her left breast and a silver star over her right.

'Wow,' she exclaimed, taking off her sunglasses and surveying the sea of faces in front of her, 'is this an audition or a security check for the CIA? Who wants to be the first to frisk me?' Her voice was a delicious combination of silk and gravel, the result no doubt of too many cigarettes and far too much scotch. When she laughed her throaty laugh, her features became almost cartoon-like, huge eyes becoming huger, wide mouth growing cavernous. Her hands were constantly on the move, circling in the air like large, graceful birds, and swooping down to make a point.

'This is Kelly Michelle Carmichael,' Lisa introduced her.

'Hi guys,' Kelly smiled and gave a little wave. 'I'm a twenty-three-degree Leo with Saturn at seventeen-degree Aries and boy am I nervous.' But her words belied her manner. She was full of wise-cracking bravado and brassy self-confidence. 'Does it take all these people to make up one mind? I mean, it is your decision, you're the head cheese here, right?' She winked at Stanfield King. 'Oops, I guess I should say head honcho. Head cheese is something else. Sean, that's my dad, he's dead now, used to force me to eat that stuff back home in Chicago. Hog butcher to the world and pig town to the rest of us. I'm a multicultural schizophrenic: part Irish, part French. Get me drunk and I'm Irish enough to be easy, French enough to be good, and Catholic enough to feel guilty an hour later.' Stan snorted. 'Eenywaay,' she dragged the sound out, 'head cheese is truly gross, looks like something you've already eaten, you know what I mean?' she laughed her infectious laugh. 'Stop me if I go too far. I'm afraid I like to teeter on the edge of bad taste. So, Stan,' she continued, 'we're right down to the nitty-gritty wire here with this casting, aren't we? Now you're a man of culture and breeding; naturally I'm your first choice. I'm on a spiritual path but I'm ready to make some bucks. I'd been gearing up for longevity, but I think I could handle instant success.' Everyone turned to look at Stan. Fortunately he was laughing. Julia was enthralled. Kelly was talking to them in the character of Samantha. Clever, very clever.

'We all enjoyed your tape, Miss Carmichael,' Stan said dryly, 'very original, but we wanted to have a chance to talk with you in person. Maybe even have you read again for us, if you don't mind.'

'Sure. I'll read, but you gotta know one thing right off,' Kelly's tone turned threatening. 'Now I don't want to put any heavy energy on you, but if Brandon Tate plays Travis—'

'Yes?' Kathryn looked worried.

'I'll work for free,' Kelly's sexy belly-laugh rippled over them all like a warm bath. 'That man can tease my hair any time.'

'Tease my hair,' Stan's laugh ended in a wheeze. 'I like that turn of phrase.' Marty looked at Julia. Julia wrote it down. Tease my hair? Don't tease my hair?

Lisa handed Kelly the sides from the script. 'You gonna eat?' Kelly focused her attention on Tim Talbot who was caught with half a banana in his mouth. 'Hey, I'm actin' here. What is this, the Dime Box Dinner Theatre?' Hastily Tim took the banana out of his mouth and stuck it in his pocket. 'Is that a banana in your pocket?' Kelly drawled, 'or are you just glad to see me?' Tim blushed the same pink as the hibiscus on his printed Hawaiian shirt. Stan laughed so hard he nearly fell off his chair.

'Kelly, perhaps you could tell us how you got started in the business,' Lisa interjected.

'I became an actress because it was a step up from being a stripper. Besides, my nails are too long to be a massage therapist.' Everyone laughed again.

'Most of your credits are in theatre,' Lisa went on. 'You were based in Chicago before coming to LA?'

'Yeah. No more freeze-your-buns winters. I did a stint in Cleveland –' she elongated the 'a' – 'and then I said to myself, "Go west, young woman." OK, not all that young,' she amended, 'but at least I'm here.'

'You've played some terrific leads,' Alex said, looking down at her résumé. 'Mama Rose in *Gypsy*, Lady Bracknell in *The Importance of Being Earnest*, and Brutus in *Julius Caesar*?' He frowned slightly, 'Where was that?'

'In England. It was a feminist interpretation of the play,' Kelly shrugged, 'what can I tell you? I played Bruta who suffered from serious PMS.' They all laughed.

'There's a pretty big gap in your résumé,' Alex continued to study the page in front of him. 'What were you doing between 1987 and 1991?'

Kelly's face clouded, instantly altering the cartoon features. The large eyes flickered, the wide mouth trembled, and she began to twist the gold band on her left hand. 'My husband was very ill,' she said quietly, all flippancy gone. 'Cancer. Terminal. I wanted to be there for him so I got out of the business for four years. He was the best thing that ever happened to me. Right up until the very end, he believed he'd make it, and I helped him to believe it. He fought like a lion, but it was a losing battle . . . Anyway, after that very real and challenging performance,' she blinked back tears, 'getting up onstage and pretending to be someone else suddenly seemed pretty meaningless. Then I realized that being someone else was a hell of a lot better than being myself right at that point, so I decided to try again. Only as far away from the east and all the memories as I could get. So,' the pain in her face eased perceptibly, 'I sold my soul, packed my bags and came to LA. So far I love it. Gorgeous weather, gorgeous people, gorgeous food. And absolutely no values. Acrylic nails are my life!' The resulting laughter was a release for everyone in the room.

Suddenly the door swung open and in walked Brandon Tate. His lizard-skin cowboy boots were custom-built and his black jeans looked as if they'd been spray-painted on. His physique verged on the mystical. He had a small scar near his left eye and his dark, curly hair was slightly streaked with gray, which only served to strengthen a face that had once been perhaps a little too pretty. The green of his silk shirt matched the green of those famous, dangerous eyes. His animal male aura illuminated the smoke-filled room. All conversation stopped.

'Hi,' he said, flashing that famous killer smile at Kelly. 'You must be Kelly Carmichael. I'm going to test with you this afternoon.' He took her trembling hand and looked up at her; like a lot of film stars, Brandon Tate was smaller in person than he was on the screen. Smaller but no less perfect. 'And you know what?' he said softly, looking deep into her eyes, sending shock waves throughout her entire central nervous system and every part of her body that had ever manufactured a hormone, 'I have to admit I'm kind of nervous. Can I kiss you for luck?' He kissed her lightly on the cheek.

Kelly turned bright red. She opened her mouth, but no words came out. Everything started to spin in concentric circles. Before anyone in the room knew exactly what had happened, Kelly Carmichael gave a little squeak and fainted dead away.

Chapter Three

'OK, people,' said Stanfield King, rubbing his hands together in that nervous way of his. It was the end of a long, grueling day and the minions had been sent away, leaving the major players in the game – Tim, Kathryn, Alex, Marty, Julia, Lisa, and of course the King himself – sitting around the conference table which, littered with coffee mugs, cigarette butts, empty bottles of Evian, banana skins, and the rubbery remains of takeout pizza, now looked like the aftermath of a rather nasty ground war. 'I've got a reservation for Morton's at –' he punched in a code on his watch – 'eight-thirty. Let's figure out where we are with this casting.'

All heads in the room turned to look expectantly at Stan. He turned his gaze on Julia. Immediately all the heads swiveled *Exorcist*-style to look expectantly at her. Right, Julia thought, he's pretending the buck stops with me when we all know very well the final decision rests with him. If we disagree on a piece of casting, my only trump card is to threaten to withdraw the project. Fat chance. She looked to Marty for instruction but his face remained blank.

She took a deep breath, 'Let me say, first of all, thank you, Lisa. You've done a terrific job, giving us so many excellent choices.'

Lisa glowed with the unexpected praise. 'Being a casting director is a little bit like being a caterer,' she said in her Queens accent. 'I try to find the best people possible for each and every role. Then I lay out this big spread, a banquet of talent. The best thing a director or producer can say to me is, "Gee, this all looks delicious, I don't know how I'm going to choose." '

'Well, now we're at the point where we do indeed have to choose,' Stan said. 'The old casting clock is ticking away here. We want to start shooting in March, not next Christmas.'

'OK, I think we're all in agreement about Brandon Tate as Travis,' Julia said immediately. 'Thanks, Kathryn, for facilitating that. I never thought you'd be able to talk him into it.'

'According to his agent, he's ready to sign,' said Kathryn, 'providing we find a Janine who's acceptable to him.'

'Absolutely,' said Julia. 'I can't believe Diane Slater went and got herself pregnant. Her test with Brandon proved the chemistry between them was absolutely perfect.'

'He's not called Brandon "I'm Yours" Tate for nothing,' Tim said snidely.

'Brandon "I'm Yours" Tate? I hadn't heard that,' said Kathryn.

'If we sign him, we'll have women aged sixteen to sixty-five fainting after every episode of Makeover,' Stan laughed. 'His affair with that pop singer has only managed to broaden his appeal.'

'I think that's over,' Kathryn said.

'I know it's over,' Stan replied testily, 'but it served its purpose, didn't it? Gave a boost to both their careers.'

Julia cleared her throat. 'So Brandon is our number one choice. Provided we can match him with Janine.' She sighed. 'We've got the same problem with the daughter.'

'I have the Breakdown Service working overtime on that one,' Lisa promised.

'Casting kids is so tough,' said Kathryn. 'Do we want someone who's bankable or do we want a fresh face?'

'Every kid we saw today was in the biz. Have you people considered a non-pro?' asked Stan.

'Look,' Lisa said a little waspishly, 'I've scoured the city, talking to kids. I've been to every junior high in the city, every dance school, hung out at playgrounds. I'm sure they think I'm some sort of pervert but, without a Janine, we can't cast Carlene.'

'What did you think of Melissa McKimmie, the Canadian girl?' Lisa wanted to know.

'Now there's a genuinely funny kid,' said Tim. 'The best we've seen so far. Smart without being obnoxious.'

'I like the reality of her face,' Julia agreed.

'After we sent her to the bathroom to comb her hair and wash off all that make-up,' Marty said wryly. 'All the girls

52

we saw at the cattle call were made up like little painted dolls. And the glamour head shots. Frighteningly close to soft porn.'

'The photographs are airbrushed,' Lisa informed them. 'You're also looking at hair extensions, highlights, and even nose jobs.'

'And probably not a one of them still a virgin,' Tim added.

'Come on, Tim,' Julia said. 'They were all under fifteen.'

'So? I'm pretty sure that, as far as most of them are concerned, innocence is a remembrance of things past.'

'What's Melissa McKimmie's green card status?' Kathryn asked.

'Her father's American.'

'Father? I got the feeling this was a single parent situation.'

'It is. Daddy's flown the coop but he stuck around long enough to bestow his citizenship on his daughter.'

'How about the accent?' Stan asked. 'Her southern wasn't bad but she's still got some of those Canadian vowel sounds creeping in there, and that "eh" is a dead giveaway.'

'Melissa's got a good ear,' Lisa assured him.

'Well, there's a bottom-line advantage to us if we go with Melissa,' Kathryn cut in. 'Up until now she's worked only in Canada. She'd do this for scale, plus ten per cent for the agent and a per diem.'

'I wouldn't count on it. Mrs McKimmie seems like one tough cookie,' warned Lisa.

'You're right about that,' Tim agreed. 'Love the kid, hate the mom.'

'This is all academic,' Julia said. 'She's going to have to look like Janine, and with Melissa's red hair, that won't be easy.' She took a swig of coffee from a mug emblazoned with the network's logo. It was cold and had the metallic, powdery taste of too much whitener. 'What about Paul Green as Troy?'

'Oh, yes, I think we're all agreed on Paul,' Stan said briskly. 'His comic star is definitely rising and we want to take advantage of that before another network ties him up.'

'I have an instinct about these things,' cautioned Tim, 'and I think Paul's about to hit big. I don't know how long we'd be able to keep him.'

'A couple of seasons, if we're lucky,' Lisa said. 'He's

known in New York but still pretty much of a secret here in LA. He may not translate right away; we'll have to see. Remember, it took a while for Billy Crystal to find his niche.'

'The features will come sniffing around, but let him cut his teeth on a series like Crystal did with Soap,' Stan said.

'If you know you want him, you better put a hold on him,' Lisa declared. 'He's not sticking around. He told me he's doing Leno tonight, then he's heading straight back to New York tomorrow. I think he's a bit unsure about moving his family to LA.'

'What, is he crazy? Doesn't he realize this is where it's at if he wants a film career?'

'I gather his wife prefers New York. They've got a lot of kids – three, I think – and he's only a little over thirty.'

'Catholic?' Stan asked.

'Hardly. Jewish. Used to be Greenblatt.'

'Well, I thought so,' Stan said. 'But it's hard to tell. Those New Yorkers, they all sound Jewish to me.'

'OK, moving right along,' Julia said. 'For Lyla Kaye: Shirley Bunting or Renee Thomas?'

'Shirley's solid and dependable,' Kathryn said. 'We know what we'll get with her.'

'She's a lot more than solid and dependable,' Alex spoke up. 'There are depths there that haven't come close to being tapped. I'm dying to direct her. Extraordinary actress with a very special kind of beauty.'

'Developing a taste for dark meat, Alex?' Stan chuckled.

'I don't appreciate that remark, Stan.'

'I vote for Shirley,' Julia said quickly.

'Make her an offer.' Stan began to lock up his briefcase. 'For Nadine: Pamela Coe or Linda Earl?'

'They're both risks,' said Kathryn. 'Pamela's a real helium head. Linda's not much better. Take off her shoes and she'd float away. I know that's what the part requires, but I was hoping we could cast against type.'

'I liked that white stretchy thing Linda was wearing,' Stan paused for a minute, 'whaddya call that, a body suit?'

'On her? Definitely,' Marty quipped.

'You should have checked your testosterone at the door, boys,' Kathryn drawled. 'Let's keep looking. If we don't find anyone else, we can always bring Linda and Pam back in for a directed read-off.'

Julia nodded. 'Samantha?' 'Kelly.' 'Kelly.' A chorus of Kellys filled the room. 'What about the fainting?' Julia asked. 'I mean, was that an act or what?'

'Could be just to get our attention, but Brandon is known to have that effect on women,' said Kathryn with a sly smile. 'Once she recovered, her reading was hilarious.'

'I love her quality,' said Alex.

'I love her voice,' said Tim.

'I love her body,' said Marty.

'Yes!' shouted Stan, raising his arm high in the air and pulling it down in a sharp, triumphant gesture.

Julia was appalled. All day long, the minute an actress left the room, the men were immediately dissecting her physical attributes or lack of. Even Marty wasn't above it. Was the concept of sexual harassment completely foreign to these men? Had they been living in a cave for the past six years? These were the men that made decisions that would affect the course of individual actors' lives, yet they appeared to take that responsibility very lightly. To Julia, the casting callbacks had been like one gigantic sandbox where network and studio execs came to play. Some threw sand at each other. Some ate the sand. Some peed in it. But all of them, even Marty, behaved like overgrown five year olds.

'Grow up, boys,' Kathryn snapped. Marty punched Stan on the arm. 'It's the end of a long day . . .' Stan punched Marty back. '. . . And we're all getting punchy.' Marty and Stan started to laugh. 'Look, we've got some tough decisions to make here.' The men continued to laugh helplessly, wheezing and snorting.

Julia stood up and put her coffee mug down with a bang. 'Theresa Ruiz,' she said. The room went silent.

Stan got up and began pacing about the room. 'Now, I know you're keen on her, Julie, but I think she spells trouble.'

'I agree,' said Kathryn. 'We do not need that kind of a shit disturber in the company.'

'It's a small role,' Julia pleaded. 'We could start her off as a daily player and see how she works out.'

'I'm with Stan and Kathryn on this one,' Marty avoided his wife's eyes. 'Theresa's a terrific actress, but I don't think she's worth the risk.'

'I do,' Julia said with unexpected passion. 'She was right in what she said and you all know it. If we're ever going to do more than pay lip-service to eliminating stereotyping, we have to start now.'

'It's too much of a risk,' Kathryn reiterated.

Julia felt the anger rise within her and come out at gale force before she could stop it. 'I'm getting a little tired of hearing that word. A show that's geared around a female character is a "risk". Setting it in Texas is a "risk". Working-class is a "risk". What is this business about anyway, if not taking risks? We all know that network television is one big fucking crapshoot. I mean, who are we trying to kid?' She stopped abruptly. They were all riveted on her, dumbfounded. 'Sorry, I'm tired, I'm not really sure what I'm saying . . .'

Tim Talbot smiled, a warm, genuine smile that transformed his entire face, from malevolence to benevolence, in the time it took to draw one breath. 'I hear what you're saying, Julia. Nobody's saying no to Theresa Ruiz right now. We don't have to settle Concha right now. The most important thing we have to deal with right now is . . .'

'I know, I know,' Julia said wearily, 'please, God, please, let us find Janine.'

Chapter Four

'From New York, it's Late Night with David Letterman. Tonight with Tom Brokaw, Andrea Martin, Grainger Paulson and Dave's special guest, J.C. Austin! Plus Paul Schafer and the world's most dangerous band.'

'Will you please turn that off?' Julia crawled into the king-size bed next to Marty who was precariously balancing a giant bag of nachos, a Corona Light, and a huge glass bowl on an oversized pillow in his lap. 'Jay Leno I can take, but I can't stand Letterman.'

'I'll keep it low.'

'Do you have to eat corn chips in bed?'

'Stoneground blue. The best. Here, you want some guac?' He held out a triangle covered with a thick green paste.

'No thanks. It looks like snot on a dog biscuit.'

'What a charming description of guacamole!'

'I can't get used to blue corn chips. They're just don't look right.'

'Fine,' Marty shrugged, chewing happily. 'You don't know what you're missing.'

'Will you be careful, please? You're getting avocado all over the duvet.' She tossed a box of Kleenex to him, aiming it directly at his head.

'Ow. Thanks a lot. What is the matter with you tonight?'

'Where have you been for the past two months, Guam? We don't have a Janine, that's what's the matter. And if we don't have a Janine, we don't have a show. Damnit, I could kill Diane for getting pregnant. I wrote it for her, she knew I was writing it for her, and then she opens her legs at the wrong time of the month and . . .'

'Calm down,' Marty patted her arm absently, his eyes fixed on the TV screen. 'This happens all the time. Kirstie Alley replaced Shelley Long and Cheers survived. Murphy

Brown was originally developed for JoBeth Williams, not Candice Bergen.'

'Yeah, but Roseanne was developed for Roseanne.'

'You don't want a Roseanne Barr. Janine is a real person, not a personality. I know Diane's your best friend and you envisioned her while you were creating Janine, but you're just going to have to let that image go.'

'Then I don't have any image at all. I left it loose because Diane's got a special quality that would have filled out the character. Now Janine needs a new angle to make her exciting. Oh, goddamnit all to hell!' Julia gave Marty a sharp whap on the arm.

'Ouch. Quit beating on me. You southern women are rough. Look, we'll find another actress who can be just as exciting.' Marty's eyes returned to the television screen.

'Thank you for that hollow reassurance.'

'Well what do you want me to say?'

'I don't want you to say anything. I want you to do something about it.'

'At 11.53 p.m.?'

'You don't understand,' Julia pounded the bed, sending powdery blue corn crumbs flying all over the room. 'I've seen every actress on the A list. We've worked our way through every actress on the B list. Now they're pushing me – excuse me, us; this is your project, too – they are pushing us to go with Stephanie Edwards. She's the flavor of the month right now. Stephanie's not even thirty. Janine is supposed to be a woman, not a girl. I've got Stan and Tim breathing down my neck, not to mention Kathryn and the studio execs, and I'm afraid we'll lose our creative control.'

'You wanted to get into this business,' Marty said mildly, picking up a stray crumb off the edge of the bed.

'Wrong. You wanted me to get into this business.'

Marty put his arms around her. 'We're not going to let them push us around. We'll find someone soon, I promise.'

'Welcome back to the program. My friend, Mr News, Tom Brokaw is here. We've got Andrea Martin, a very funny lady. And Grainger Paulson, an eighty-three-year-old man who has patented over one hundred and twenty inventions in his lifetime. And the reigning queen of country music, J.C. Austin, is making her very first appearance on our show.' Wild cheering and applause.

'Help,' Julia whimpered, pulling the duvet up over her head.

'Try and relax, Jules. Want to make love?'

'Make love? In front of David Letterman? How bourgeois.'

'I still don't know what you've got against Letterman.' Marty was using his fingers to scrape the last vestiges of avocado from the bowl.

'I can't stand his smarmy, supercilious, holier-than-thou schoolboy manner, he looks like Alfred E. Newman, his humor is sophomoric and it's a micro-thin cover which barely hides more than an edge of "I never get what I want and I'm going to make you pay for it" bitterness . . .'

'Take this pillow and stuff it into your mouth,' Marty said kindly. 'I want to watch the show.'

Julia grabbed for the remote control, but Marty snatched it out of her hand. 'You're not going to make me miss J.C. Austin. She's the sexiest female singer around.'

Julia stared at him in amazement. 'You think J.C. Austin is sexy?'

'Well, I'm a sucker for a redhead, I can't deny it. Look at you,' he reached out and tousled her straight reddish-blonde hair. 'You even look a little bit like her.' Seeing Julia's glare: 'Without the twenty pounds of make-up and with twenty pounds more class, of course.'

'Save it.' Julia buried her head in the pillow.

'I love that little dimple on the left side of her face when she smiles. Great body, too. Kind of like a cross between Dolly Parton and Bonnie Raitt. And those red curls, oy, save me, right down to her ass . . .'

'Undoubtedly not real,' Julia said acidly.

'Oh, they're real. I've seen pictures of her as a kid back in Texas. She comes from somewhere near Houston.'

'You know all this?' Julia sat up.

'Face it, kid, I'm not just attracted to brilliant young documentary film makers from USC. My tastes are eclectic, and J.C. Austin's no bimbo; she's been around the block. Her singing range is phenomenal. She's got those clear sweet soprano top notes that can sometimes make you cry and sometimes make you soar and then she's got a gutsy deep chest voice that's down and dirty.'

'Since when do you listen to country music?'

'Whenever I drive the freeway alone, to and from work. She sings these songs that are kind of like a Sam Shepard monologue.' Julia's mouth was hanging open. 'Sometimes,' Marty added sheepishly, 'I watch TNN when you're not home. When she sings one of her bluesy numbers, she makes me want to pull her down to the floor and just roll around . . .'

'That is so incredibly sexist. I can't believe . . .'

'It's always an event when our next guest releases a new album. Here she is with her new hit single, "What Do You Make Over Me?" Ladies and gentlemen, J.C. Austin!'

> What do you make over me?
> How can you make me feel free?
> Not just my hair or a new thing to wear
> I want to make over me.
>
> What can I make of my life?
> Am I more woman than wife?
> What can I make out of what's mine to take?
> How can I make over me?
>
> Now, all that I am with the people I love
> Is what they expect me to be
> But if I'm to fly with the wings of a dove
> Then their expectations
> Leave some limitations
> So new alterations
> Must happen to me
>
> Don't think that I want to hide
> The real person inside
> Bring out the truth
> That I've known since my youth
> What can you make over me?

Julia and Marty found themselves moving closer and closer together until they were holding each other tightly, listening in hushed silence. J.C. Austin lifted her arms high in the air, outstretched to embrace the world, her magical voice dropping down an octave and then, with lightning speed, swooping miraculously up to a high note, holding it for a long time until the steel guitar faded away and all that was left was the whisper of her passionate cry.

'We've got to get our hands on that song,' Julia said. 'Use it as our opening signature for the pilot. It would be perfect under the credits. Maybe try and get J.C. to sing it herself, you know like Ray Charles does for Designing Women?'

'Yes, yes. I'll get right on it. Wait, shh, I want to hear what she has to say.'

'Hey, J.C., take a seat. Great to have you with us.'

'Well, I'm real tickled to be here.'

'Love your boots.'

'Yeah, red's my favorite color when it comes to boots.'

'You want to mention the guests you brought with you tonight?'

'Sure do. That's Wayne Bosco on the amazing steel guitar and Johnny Winston on the sublime fiddle. I don't travel anywhere without these boys. They're like my brothers.' Applause and whistling. 'And Paul, you must be a country boy at heart. You did real good.' More applause.

'Now this is your fourteenth album. You've sold a lot of records. Do you write all your own material?'

'Yeah. A song has to come from me to be right for me.'

'Tom Brokaw was on right before you and he thinks you're really . . . "hot" was the word I think he used.'

'He's sweet. We had a real good time in the green room before he came on.' Whistles and cheers from the audience. 'Now, y'all, I didn't mean that the way it sounded. Tom's a gentleman. And I know his wife.'

'But, do you see yourself as a sex symbol?'

'Well, my husband, Mac, thinks I am. I do love to sing those cheatin' songs. Like Willie Nelson says, "All the best songs are about faith and unfaithfulness." '

'But this song is different.'

'Each of my songs is a personal statement about where I am at a certain point in my life. "Come On Home" was written in early 1991, just after I got back from entertaining the troops who were part of Operation Desert Storm. My bass player, Lyle Carter, was killed in a car crash in the fall of 1990, so "Highway of Life" was written for Lyle. If I want to remember what I was feeling for pretty near all of

1976, I just listen to "Low Down Blue Without You" and I know that's when Mac and I lost the baby.'

'Really?'

'You don't need to get uncomfortable, Dave. My life is public property. Mac and I have always wanted kids. I've been blessed in a lot of ways, but it just hasn't worked out yet. Anyway, we're having fun trying.'

'You married Mac at what, sixteen?'

'People get married young down south. The heat makes us mature faster.' Big laugh from the audience.

'Yeah, right . . . well, as I said, it's a terrific song.'

'It tells me where I am right now.'

'And where's that?'

'I'm not real sure. I'm looking for something, but I don't know what's coming next.'

'Hear that?' Julia sat up straighter. 'Even a successful star like J.C.'s feeling the same way—'

'Well, you've certainly done it all. You seem to glide easily between country and pop and rock.' He turned to his sidekick. 'Can I say that, Paul? Can you glide between country and rock?'

'I would say catapult, Dave.'

'Right,' turning back to J.C. 'You catapulted from country to rock.'

'I love doing rock, but my heart's still with country. Nowadays kids are listening to country. When I was growing up, country was called hillbilly and you weren't supposed to listen to it.'

'So country is America's shameful secret?'

'Hey, don't be snotty, Dave.' Laughter from the audience. 'Even George Bush listens to country.'

'Well, if it's good enough for George Bush and Tom Brokaw . . .'

'Country music is real. People need that right now. We're pretty sick of all the bull . . .' Audience roars approval. 'That's something George Bush or anybody else who wants to be our President is going to have to listen to.' More cheers. 'You know what they say, there's a little bit of country in all of us. Country is a state of mind.'

'They're eating her up.'

'She's saying exactly what that audience is thinking.'

'. . . Country music doesn't stand still. You can always

62

hear its blue grass roots, but it's constantly changing.'

'That's the theme of your song, changing.'

'We all rebuild ourselves physically every seven years, did you know that? The cells that make up our body, they die off and then renew themselves. I'm not the same person I was seven years ago and neither are you.'

'Listen, I'm not the same person I was seven minutes ago. Before you came on the show!'

'Every seven years I have to reinvent myself. I started out as a hairdresser, then I got into writing songs, then I began singing my own songs . . .'

'Hold it. You were a hairdresser? Where?'

'When I first went to Nashville, I got a job sweeping up hair in a beauty shop. One thing I'm real good at is hair. You want me to do something with yours? It could use some help. You've looked the same for the last seven years, Dave. You could do with a change . . .' More laughter.

'Whoa . . . wait a minute. Don't touch the hair . . . Maybe we should set up an appointment for after the show. OK, so what's next for J.C. Austin?'

'For right now, I'm heading back to Nashville. I've got lots of offers. I'm going to go sit on my front porch at my big old house on Hickory Lake and I'll just swing in the hammock until I figure out what's my next move. It'll come to me. It always does.'

'I believe you. Thanks, good to have you with us, J.C.'

'Good talking with you, and I mean it: you want to change your hair, just give me a call.'

'I might do that. Y'all come back now, you hear?' Thunderous applause, cheers, whistles, catcalls.

'I want her to play Janine.'

'Forget it, Julia. The woman's a country music superstar. She's making megabucks. That little house in Nashville she's heading back to where she's gonna sit on the front porch and swing is probably a mansion. No way she'd consider sit-com.'

'I can persuade her, I know I can. Just imagine her with Brandon Tate. Talk about chemistry.'

'We don't even know if she can act. As far as I know, she's never done any film or television.'

'She doesn't have to act. She is Janine. She's the essence of what the Changing Room is all about. Didn't you listen to

63

the words of the song? Didn't you hear the interview?'

'Jules, you're crazy. I love you, but you're crazy.'

'I don't care what you think. Hand me the phone. I want to give Stan King a call.'

'At home?

'Yes.'

'Now?'

'Yes. I want to see what he thinks of the idea.'

'He'll insist that she test. Provided the network will buy the idea at all.'

'I'll cross that bridge when I come to it. I want to get the pilot script to J.C.'s agent immediately.'

'I think you're going to meet with a lot of resistance from the network. From J.C. herself.'

'Give me that phone. I'm booking a flight to Nashville.'

Chapter Five

Julia was standing in line at the J.C. Austin Country Showcase, near to, but even more lavish than, the Barbara Mandrell Country Museum. Both housed exhibits of collectors' items, memorabilia, and treasured personal effects of their individual stars. Both were located on the famous Music Row, across from the Country Music Hall of Fame and close to a number of smaller giftshops such as George Strait's Texas Connections and the Ernest Tubbs' Record Shop. She didn't know whether J.C. had purposefully set out to outdo them all, but the line for her Country Showcase snaked half-way around the block.

Julia was sweating like a pig in the hot noonday sun. She glanced at her watch. She had flown in yesterday afternoon with less than twenty-four hours to get a crash course in country music before her arranged meeting with J.C. at two-thirty today. Country music had changed since she'd left Texas, when she'd turned her back on everything she'd perceived to be 'red-neck'. The country music she heard in Nashville had fresh contemporary themes, intricate harmonies and, with the influence of blues, and rock, even Zydeco, more complex arrangements. Last night she'd gone to the Grand Ole Opry to catch Garth Brooks and Reba McIntyre on the mainstage, and Clint Black in the Jackson Showboat Lounge. Opryland USA, a modern, state-of-the-art theater, had housed the Opry, the 'Mother Church of Country Music', since 1974, but she was sorry not to see a performance in the legendary Ryman Auditorium, a red-brick building with white trim and a battered wooden stage on which so many country greats had got their start.

This morning she'd toured the Country Music Hall of Fame where she'd seen Minnie Pearl's straw hat, a hit song written out on the back of a grocery list, and the original document granting Merle Haggard a full pardon for armed robbery, signed by Ronald Reagan himself. She'd visited Fort Nashborough and the Parthenon, an exact replica of the one in ancient Greece, a symbol of the city's image as the 'Athens of the South', and used with such chilling effectiveness in Robert Altman's film.

Nashville, or Music City USA, as the tour guides liked to call it, was an uneasy blend of old and new, richly rooted tradition and modern crass commercialism, historic landmarks and honky-tonks. There seemed to be a Baptist church and a Bible bookstore on every corner, usually with a liquor store in the same block. What singer had said, 'You can't be a country star without drinking hard and thanking God for your success'? The city was a study in contrasts.

Her agent had booked her into the Opryland Hotel, a luxury hotel with an indoor garden of ten thousand tropical plants crowned by a one-acre glass skylight. This morning she'd had breakfast at Shoney's, a southern chain restaurant which, although a step up from Po'Folks All You Can Eat Chicken, was still pretty depressing. She ate lumpy grits and runny scrambled eggs brought to her by a Faulkneresque waitress with a worn face and a name-tag that had Charlotte crossed out and Sharon written below. Sipping her lukewarm coffee, she watched a couple huddled together on one side of a booth, whispering intensely to each other. They both had shoulder-length blonde hair and matching red leather jackets. Their faces were worn. Charlotte/Sharon squealed and jumped, smacking the hand of an ancient cowboy sitting in the booth in front of Julia. His thinning hair was slicked back, he had a prominent Adam's apple and a worn face. Julia took out her compact and took a quick look. Maybe it was the lighting in Shoney's, but she got out of there as fast as she could.

Now, standing in line for J.C. Austin's Country Showcase, she was surrounded by plaid shirts and string ties, boots and jeans, denim skirts and long, Loretta Lynn locks. Old Nashville. There was also lots of pink suede, sequined high tops, feathers and beads, and wash-and-wear perms. New Nashville. Finally, the line started to move. The entrance to the museum was flanked by floor-to-ceiling glossy posters of J.C. lit by tracer lights. The tour guides were all wearing T-shirts with J.C.'s head-shot silkscreened on the front. As Julia made her way through the maze of glass cases, she saw numerous portraits of J.C.'s beloved grandfather, her first Bible, her wedding dress, and her famous Dobro blues guitar draped with an American flag. J.C. had been photographed in a Houston Oilers' football jersey, surrounded by the members of the team. She'd been photographed with Dolly Parton and Joan Rivers, Jimmy Carter and Jimmy Swaggart. There were press cuttings and rave reviews. Her eleven, cut-glass, People's Choice Awards were mounted in a special case along with her Grammys and her gold records.

'Welcome to my home, the Lone Star Estate. I named it as a tribute to my home state of Texas. Come on in, take your shoes off, and make yourselves comfortable while I show y'all around.' Julia whirled to see two panels open up revealing a giant television screen completely filled with J.C.'s smiling face. A crowd of tourists gathered to watch as the eight-foot-tall image of J.C. Austin guided them through room after sumptuous room of her Hickory Lake mansion, complete with indoor and outdoor pools (guitar-shaped), custom-designed marble bathroom with pink crystal chandelier, indoor solarium full of cactus, screening room with sensaround sound and a huge master bedroom decorated in peach with a massive oak four-poster bed. There was even a nursery ready and waiting for the child she had not yet had.

Now and again, J.C.'s husband, Mac, a dead ringer for Kenny Rogers, appeared in the video, shaving, barbecuing ribs over a mesquite grill on the back deck, or eating popcorn in front of the TV. The underlying message of most country music was that being poor was not only OK but even desirable. Yet the people who sang these songs had long ago transcended the poverty they claimed to celebrate. The folksy underscoring of the video and the casual tone of J.C.'s delivery attempted to make their life look simple and down-home, but the whole thing ultimately came off more like Lifestyles of the Nouveau Rich and Famous. Julia sighed. Marty was probably right. Even if J.C. Austin did agree to do Makeover, there was no way they could pay her price.

The video ended and Julia, followed by a clump of tourists, took another turn down one of the hallways in the complex. She stopped to catch her breath in front of a replica of J.C.'s huge four-poster bed. Two couples, who looked to be in their early thirties, stood close by, and Julia was just able to overhear their conversation.

'This is the bed that Mac built for her. By hand. In October of 1989,' said the plumpish, sweet-faced blonde wearing white jeans and red boots, just like J.C. had worn on Letterman. 'J.C. embroidered the peach coverlet and monogrammed the sheets. It's real important to her to have a home to come back to when she's been out on the road. They were married in June of 1973 and they've got one of the strongest marriages in the music business. No kids. J.C.'s had four miscarriages. Something wrong with her plumbing.'

She had a wispy little voice that was quite comic to listen to, but she seemed highly knowledgeable about the details of J.C. Austin's private life. Julia assumed she was a tour guide until the other woman, a sharp-eyed brunette with a strong jaw said, 'Debra Jo, you sound like Entertainment Tonight. How do you know all this?'

'I know everything there is to know about J.C. Austin; she's my idol. I can't believe we're actually here, all of us, in Nashville. That package out of Houston is great, isn't it? I mean, tickets for the closing performance of J.C.'s eastern tour at the Municipal Auditorium; seats at the taping of Nashville Now; a tour of the stars' homes this afternoon . . . it's really good value.'

'Yeah, you're right, honey. I have to admit even I think it's worth it,' said the good-looking blond guy next to her whose faded jeans fit his athletic build like a second skin.

'And tonight, I want us all to go to the Nashville Palace,' continued the blonde they called Debra Jo, consulting her brochure. 'That's where,' she read out loud, ' "the country music stars drop in".'

'Anything you want, honey,' said her husband. 'This is your special weekend. Now stand right over here. I want to get a picture of you in front of J.C. Austin's bed, so we can show the kids back home.'

Country music is not just entertainment, Julia thought, it's a religion. To these people, the singers aren't mere stars, they're deities. And if Elvis was the King, J.C. Austin was the Queen. Why would she even consider giving up all this for a weekly television show?

In her rented Opal Corsair, Julia drove down Music Square,

past the RCA Studio B, MCA Music, Sony/Columbia, and the new building which housed the American Society of Composers and Publishers, ASCAP. There were close to three hundred music publishing companies and over sixty recording studios. Huge billboards filled the landscape, advertising individual country artists' latest hit tunes. Travis Tritt: 'Power, Passion, Performance'. Dolly Parton: 'An Eagle When She Flies'. And J.C. Austin: 'What Do You Make Over Me?'

She passed a restaurant called Panama Red's Oyster Bar – We Shuck 'Em, You Suck 'Em – and a drive-in burger joint with a marquee that read, 'God loves you, Chad!' Why, she wondered, on this particular Saturday, does God particularly love Chad? Does he love him more than the rest of us? Is this like that magic marquee in *L.A. Story* that sent special messages to Steve Martin? Does Chad have an inside track to God or does God have a secret agenda where Chad is concerned?

Get a grip on yourself, Julia. Chad is probably some kid with leukemia and the local community is praying for his speedy recovery. Although maybe in this town it was more likely Chad had cut a demo and his friends were wishing him well. Growing up in Texas, living now in LA, she should be used to this kind of display, but Nashville was something else again.

She turned off Two Mile Pike at the exit marked Twitty City on to Gallatin Pike which, her map told her, led to the Johnny Cash Parkway. Suddenly she was in a scene of lush pastoral serenity. Rolling wooded hills, rustic houses with barns, wood-railed bridges over rippling streams, like every image she'd ever had of the backwoods of Tennessee. Turning on to Barbara Mandrell Boulevard she found J.C. Austin Avenue, a tree-lined lane leading up to the iron gate of the Lone Star Estate, a massive white edifice with Doric columns.

A couple of tour buses were parked in front with their loudspeakers blaring. 'This is J.C. Austin's famous three-million-dollar home, the Lone Star Estate. If we're really lucky, we may be able to catch J.C. herself at one of those windows. She just got back from her two-month tour of the eastern United States. Her new hit single, "What Do You Make Over Me?", has been number one in the charts for . . .'

Julia pushed her way through the gawking crowd, who were already starting to reach through the gate to pick the Texas bluebonnets growing in the garden, and rang the buzzer. There was enough security around the place to protect Fort Knox. She announced herself and the heavy gate swung open, causing shrieks from the tourists who rushed to try to follow her in, but the minute she was past the electronic eye the gate closed quickly. An armed security guard escorted her across the grounds to the front door but, as he reached for the bronze knocker, the door flew open and there stood J.C. Austin herself, wearing a peach-colored track-suit and a radiant smile.

'Hi,' she stuck out her hand in a very direct manner, 'I'll just bet you're Julia. Come right on in. I'm real glad you made it through the minefield.'

'It's a zoo out there,' Julia agreed, taking her hand. 'Is it like this every day?'

'Pretty much. Our house is one of the stops on the celebrity map you can buy all over Nashville. Sometimes I go out and sign a few autographs if I feel like it.'

'You don't mind?'

'Are you kidding? I love signing my own name. It took me a long time to learn to read and write, so now I practise whenever I can. Besides, I owe my career to those people out there. I don't mind anything so long as they don't take pieces of that gate home with them as a souvenir.'

'Well, the gate looks intact, but the flowers are going awfully quickly,' Julia said.

'Oh great,' J.C. sighed. 'Jackson, do you want to go out there and see to that?'

'Sure thing, ma'am.' The security guard tipped his cap and slipped away.

'You know,' J.C. let go of her hand and stepped back, 'you don't look anything like I thought you would. Somehow I pictured a TV writer would be a lot older and . . . bigger.'

'Same here,' Julia laughed. 'You look taller onscreen.'

'You know, I think you and me look a little bit alike.'

'That's just what my husband said. He's a big fan of yours. He claims your songs are poetic hymns to America.'

'Yeah? I think I like this husband of yours. When do I get to meet him?' J.C. chuckled. 'I was born real tiny. They didn't think I was going to survive. People are always

70

underestimating me.' She looked at Julia shrewdly.

'I doubt that,' Julia said hastily.

'I don't mind being short. I like being near the earth. Of course I admit I wear high heels and tease my hair way up to make me look taller. You know the sayin', "The higher the hair, the closer to God"?' she laughed. 'Now, you come on with me. I'll give you a tour of the house.'

Julia didn't have the heart to tell her that she'd just seen the video, and besides, she wanted a chance to get to know J.C. before they came to the business of this afternoon's meeting. She'd been afraid that being in the presence of the star would make her feel intimidated, but as J.C. led her from room to room, stopping to let her touch individual objects or sit on a piece of furniture, Julia's nervousness soon vanished. J.C. chatted away, pointing out photographs on the wall. 'That's me with George and Barbara Bush. When I was doing Austin City Limits, they used to come backstage. To this day, he still doesn't know if I voted for him.' Her grammar was slightly off and she had a marked Texas accent, dropping her g's and substituting her i's for e's. The very accent that Julia had worked so hard to eliminate, although she knew she had always sounded more educated than this woman. Now they had courses for southern businessmen to help them lose their accents so that they would be taken seriously in the corporate world. Julia had worked with a tape recorder to lose her accent. J.C. had obviously worked just as hard to retain hers. Or maybe she didn't have to work at it. She sounded completely genuine. Julia kept looking for the chinks in the good ole girl armour, the seams where she'd sewn the image together, but she couldn't find any. When J.C. smiled her famous smile revealing the dimple in her left cheek and accenting the crinkle lines around her worldly eyes, Julia wanted to reach out and hug her.

'How do you like the house?' J.C. was breathless from the whirlwind tour.

'It's just amazing. Huge.'

'Thirty thousand square feet. I wanted it to be in the same style as Loretta Lynn's place, you know, real southern plantation. And it's got some of the same features as President Andrew Jackson's mansion, the Hermitage. So what do you think of our little hick town?'

'It's . . . amazing,' was all Julia could manage. 'But,'

quickly, 'it's not a hick town.'

'Sure it is. We got our little hick town, we put up all these big houses with all the swimming pools and turned it into a slick town. It's a pretty exclusive club out here.'

'You mean restricted?'

'Lord, no,' J.C. whooped. 'Not if you're talking about race, color or creed. What you got to be to get in here is a country legend. I have to pinch myself every five minutes 'cause I can't believe I made it this far.'

'Well, you're a legend yourself.'

'It's real sweet of you to say so, but things are changing. The Lone Star Estate was just perfect when I had it built, but now, well, it is a bit much. Mac and I are rebuilding. Renovation's supposed to start in the spring.'

'What's the new house going to look like?'

'I don't know. Like I said on Letterman, I'm waiting to see what comes next.'

'Did you like the Makeover script?' Julia couldn't wait any longer.

'I truly did. It's like you opened my head and just climbed right inside. Everything I've been thinking and feeling . . . I mean the world is changing so fast, Lord only knows what's going to happen, but, hey, if we're going to get down to business, you have to meet Mac.'

J.C. went to the intercom mounted on the wall and pressed a button. Within minutes Mac appeared, looking ten pounds heavier than he had on the video, and sporting a full beard: an imposing figure of a man.

'Pleased to meet you,' Mac said. But his eyes belied his words. Julia had the feeling that at any moment, he might whip out a six-gun and tell her to say her piece and then get off his property. 'Is it Miss Hudlow? Or Mrs?'

'I am married. My husband's name is Turgov. I use my maiden name. Well, really it's my professional name. I started out in the business with Hudlow and that's how everybody in the business knows me so I've stuck with it – Hudlow, I mean,' she finished lamely.

'Uh huh,' Mac nodded noncommittally.

'Mac says I married him just to get his name,' J.C. interjected. 'Isn't that right, baby?' Mac nodded.

'Well, I don't blame you. Austin's a great professional name for a country singer,' Julia bubbled. J.C.'s southern charm was catching. Julia hadn't bubbled since 1975.

72

'You're from Texas, too, aren't you Ms Hudlow?' Mac lingered on the z sound for just a fraction longer than necessary.

'A long time ago. Now, of course, I'm based in LA.'

'Y'all want to sit out on the deck?' Mac said abruptly.

'Sure, sounds great.'

'I'll get Daphne to get us some beers. You girls go on out to the deck and I'll join you quick as I can.'

'OK, baby.' J.C. gave him a kiss and then, linking her arm through Julia's, led the way out to the deck which ran all along the back of the house. As Julia looked out over the lake, she gave an audible gasp. The video did not do justice to the view of the sweeping woodland hills and the landscaped terraces leading down to Hickory Lake.

'Pretty, isn't it?' murmured J.C. 'I walk out here; I shut those patio doors and I'm in another world.'

Mac came out on to the deck carrying a tray of frosted mugs and a bowl full of blue corn chips. 'Oh, you've got those blue corn chips here, too,' Julia said, taking a swig of the ice-cold beer.

'I've got 'em, but I can't say I like 'em,' Mac said, slicing a fresh lime into wedges. 'I thought you might want them.'

'No, actually, I agree with you. I like my corn chips to be yellow, white even, but not blue. Doesn't seem right.'

For the first time Mac looked at her and smiled. 'What do you think of the beer you're drinking?'

'It's delicious. What is it?'

'Dos Equis. Mexican beer. The best. Take a bite of lime, then a slug of beer. Beer drinking, Mexican style.'

Julia tried it. 'It's good. I like it.'

'Now you've got something to take back to LA with you.'

'I hope that's not all,' Julia said boldly.

Mac set down his beer mug and leveled his gaze at her as if lining up the bull's eye on a target. 'You might as well know I'm against J.C. even considering this.'

'Now, Mac,' J.C. interrupted with a laugh.

'No, she needs to know that right off,' Mac said flatly. 'You don't want to do some little rinky-dink TV show. Excuse me, Julia, but compared to where J.C. is at right now in her career, that's what Makeover is.'

'Brandon Tate's ready to sign,' Julia said smartly. 'If it's good enough for him . . .'

'He can make his own decisions. I'm not married to him.

I'm married to J.C., and as long as we're on the subject, I don't want my wife doing love scenes with Brandon Tate.'

Julia tried to ascertain whether or not he was joking. 'I don't think you have to worry about that at this point.'

'A sit-com's just not in the same league with what she's doing now.' Mac was trying to be polite.

'I can understand you would see it that way, but that's not necessarily true,' Julia said as calmly as she could. 'Sure, it's different from what J.C.'s been doing, but she wants a change. That's what she told millions of viewers on national television just a week ago.'

'I don't want her doing weekly TV,' Mac insisted again. 'A feature film, OK, even a variety special. Hell, she's done a bunch of those and the numbers shoot way up whenever she does.'

'I admit that's part of the appeal but, more importantly, I want someone who's right for the role I created. I believe there's no one more right for Janine than J.C.'

'Now hold on here just a minute,' J.C. drawled. To Julia: 'Pardon me for buttin' in, but it is the next six months of my life you're talking about. Y'all are acting like I'm not even here.' To Mac: 'Honey, we're talking millions and millions of people here. When I do a gig, even if it's a big hall, it's going to be fifteen to twenty thousand tops. Radio, I get a wider audience, but not many people listen to radio any more. My music videos get a lot of airplay, but that audience is random . . .' Julia was surprised to hear a word like 'random' come out of J.C.'s mouth. 'A sit-com is a guaranteed audience, maybe fifty million people watching me every week. There's the possibility of product tie-ins. Endorsements. Maybe even a line of haircare products. It could open up a wider market for our business. You can't just dismiss this out of hand.'

'What about your fans?' Mac countered. 'They want to hear you sing. What makes you think they'll follow you to the small screen?'

'My fans will follow me where I go. They've stuck with me this far.'

'You don't have enough experience in front of a camera.'

'I've done music videos.'

'That's two days shooting, three at most. This is like a real job. Nine-to-five every day for weeks at a time. That's hard on any actress, and you're not a real actress.'

'Neither was Roseanne Barr.' Julia had found her voice.

'Yeah, and it shows.'

'People love her, though, and they'll love J.C. even more.' Julia turned to J.C. 'You had David Letterman in the palm of your hand, and that's not easy. You got more laughs out of the audience than he did.'

'How are you going to read the script?' Mac demanded. 'Learn your lines?'

'I'll be OK.' J.C. avoided his eyes and Julia's.

'No, you won't. You'll get the letters all mixed up.'

'I don't want to talk about that now, Mac. Not in front of Julia.' It was the first time Julia had seen the star's easy confidence shaken.

'You read everything backwards,' he persisted. J.C. stared down at the floor and said nothing.

'Are you dyslexic?' Julia asked gently. J.C. nodded, her eyes still on the floor.

'I don't believe it,' Julia cried. 'Me, too.'

J.C. looked up in relief. 'You're kidding me?'

'It's kind of my deep, dark innermost secret.'

'Yeah, I know,' J.C. smiled ruefully. 'When I was a kid, they didn't know what to do with me. I knew I was smart, but everybody else thought I was stupid.'

'They put me in a remedial reading class,' Julia confided. 'I was mortified. I waited until everybody was out of the halls and then I would slip into class after it had started.'

'They were going to hold me back a grade, but I wasn't having any of that, so I quit school and went on to Nashville. I was just fifteen.'

'Fifteen.' Julia gave a little whistle.

'Yeah. A year later Mac and I were married.'

'How are you going to read your lines?' Mac repeated.

'A lot of actors have the same problem,' Julia said softly. 'We'll hire a dialogue coach to help you with your lines.'

'Look,' Mac's tone roughened, 'you don't seem to understand. We're talking business here. Loss of revenue. J.C.'s under contract to deliver one album every year. I've got gigs lined up right through 1994. Concert dates would have to be cancelled. You cancel too often and you get a reputation you don't want to have.'

'Not cancelled,' J.C. broke in. 'Rescheduled. For each hiatus. Isn't that how it works?' She looked at Julia. 'A couple weeks on, then a week off. Hiatus, right?'

'Right,' Julia whispered.

'You'd be exhausted. I don't like saying this in front of Julia, but you only do a sit-com on your way up or on your way down. Not at the peak of your career.'

'But I'm different. I don't do things the way everybody else does them. That's why I'm here and they're there.'

'Don't get smart with me, goddamnit. Are you listening to me? Have you heard a word I said?' Mac was shouting now. 'I'm telling you it's a losing proposition. I'm telling you it's bad business. I'm telling you it's too hard.'

'How hard can it be, Mac?' J.C.'s voice escalated to match his. 'Harder than what I'm already doing? I tour six, seven months out of the year. I get on the bus, I get off the bus, I sing my guts out, I sign autographs, I get back on the bus. Sometimes if I'm real lucky, I get to sleep on the bus. Half the time I don't know where I am. If it's Tuesday, it must be Denver. Or Shreveport. Or some damn two-bit town. I never get to see you because you don't want to travel with me any more, you just want to stay home and count the money I'm bringing in. No wonder we don't have any kids. We're never together long enough to make one!'

'Don't you discuss our private business in front of a stranger . . .'

'Excuse me, guys,' Julia broke in, 'we don't have to settle this right now. You still have to test for the role.'

'Test? She's not going to test.'

'The network won't make J.C. an offer unless she . . .'

'Not an offer?' Mac roared. 'What the hell are you doing here then, wasting our time?'

'Julia's right,' J.C. quickly changed gear. 'No point in getting all worked up over nothing. Baby, you have another beer.' Grabbing Julia and shoving her down the steps off the deck. 'I'm going to take Julia out and show her the recording studio, OK?'

'The studio's nothing special,' J.C. said, once they were safely inside. 'I just wanted to get you out of firing range. When Mac's like that, there's no reasoning with him.'

'Does Mac make all your decisions for you?' Julia asked.

J.C. picked up an old Martin guitar hanging on the wall of the studio and began to pick it softly. 'When I started out in country music, it was a man's game. They were the stars, they made the big bucks, they laid down the rules. Oh sure, there was Patsy, and then there was Loretta, but even they didn't have the clout of a Johnny Cash or a Hank Williams. Then Tammy and Dolly and Barbara came along and things started to open up. Now it's Reba and Tanya and me who are carrying it forward. We sell as big as the guys. Got our own rules. Of course, when we go into the studio, Mac steps in and takes the wheel so I can give myself over to what I do best, singing. Mac's the salesman, too. It was his idea that we build this complex right here on our own property. All my business comes out of here: recording, promotion, publishing, it all starts here. I tell Mac what I want and he makes sure I get it, right?' She looked intently at Julia.

'Right, but . . .'

J.C. laughed. 'You are a lot like me. You want to know where all this is headed. We'll get to what you want to talk about when I'm ready to talk about it, OK?'

Julia instantly changed the subject. 'What's it like, touring? They tell me your bus comes equipped with everything except an Olympic-size swimming pool.'

J.C. laughed again. 'No country singer would be caught dead in anything but a Silver Eagle. When I started out, Mac and I used to travel in a beat-up VW van. Now I tour with three buses, two semis and a road crew of thirty.'

'Do you have to tour?'

'In the old days if you wanted to make it as a singer you had to get out there on the road. I never played a Wal-mart like Marty Brown, but I played some real holes in my time. You got to take the music to the people wherever they are.'

'It sounds like a hard life.'

J.C. smiled. 'It's meant to be. That's what we sing about. You don't think much of country music, do you?' she looked intently at Julia.

'I'm beginning to appreciate it more,' Julia said honestly.

'Mac hired me some of the best musicians in town and most of them are still with me.'

'What's it like travelling with an all male band?' Julia wanted to know.

'Well, first off, you got to make a decision, are the guys going to be your lovers or your brothers? After I made the crossover into rock, I went pretty wild. I was upset about not being able to get pregnant and I didn't care what I did or what anybody thought about me. No hard drugs, but I did my share of Tequila Gold. Performing makes you high and sometimes the only thing that can bring you down is good sex. There's a lot of temptation out there, not just the roadies but other singers on tour as well. A country singer is always a gentleman during the day, but some of them turn into the devil after midnight.'

'Did you and Mac separate?'

'Yeah. He knew what was going on. Or maybe he didn't want to know. Anyway, he took me back. Lots of men wouldn't have. I'm very lucky.' J.C. stopped playing and hung the classic guitar back up on the wall. 'I truly love Makeover, Julia. Janine's a wonderful character.'

'Were you really a hairdresser?'

'What's so weird about that? We don't all spring full-blown from Butcher Holler or the Blue Ridge Smokey Mountains. Kris Kristofferson used to sweep the floor at Studio B. He was working as a janitor when he wrote "Help Me Make It through the Night", and you know Kris was a Rhodes Scholar. Randy Travis was washing dishes at the Nashville Palace when Libby discovered him. I waited tables there. Used to get up onstage and sing my heart out whenever they'd let me. I drop in every now and again. Sing with Steve Hill and Granny Johnson. Stay in touch with my roots. You know,' J.C. said suddenly, 'that's one thing that bothers me about Janine. If I can play her like myself maybe I'd be OK, but Mac's right, I'm a singer not an actress.'

'Television's easier than acting in a play. You just do little bits at a time. We can have an acting coach on the set if you think you need one, but I can shape the character around what you bring to it.' The two women looked at each other for a moment and then Julia said, 'I'm getting this crazy idea. I don't know what you think about this, but what if we make Janine a secret singer?'

'How do you mean?' J.C. was intrigued.

'Well, suppose she's got a great voice only she's shy about her singing, so she never sings if anyone can hear her . . .'

'But, in the shop, late at night,' J.C. said softly, her eyes glowing with excitement, 'when no one else is around, she sings like a bird. Just for herself.'

'You got it,' Julia said triumphantly.

J.C. reached out and put her arms around Julia. 'I want to do this. I really do.'

'You will have to test. I'm sorry about that. But both Pac Vic and CBN insist on it.'

'No skin off my back. I'll just do the best I can.'

'What about Mac? He seems totally opposed to the idea.'

'I've got my pilot's license, did you know that, Julia?'

J.C. looked her right in the eye. 'Did you see the airstrip out back? Mac's been real important to me, no doubt about that. But I want to fly my own plane now.'

'I have a feeling neither of us does anything half-way,' Julia said.

J.C. smiled her radiant smile. 'If I'm in, I'm in one hundred and fifty per cent.'

VARIETY

SLICK HICK QUICK PICK AT PAC VIC

By Larry Cohen

HOLLYWOOD. After months of searching and testing, Pacific Victory Studios has signed country music queen, J.C. Austin, as female lead in CBN's newest sit-com Makeover. Austin will star opposite Brandon Tate who signed in January. The show is Tate's début in series television and will also mark Austin's first venture into acting.

Pac Vic's Dev. Dir., Kathryn Grady, said she and Stanfield King, Pres. Ent. at the web, were at first wary of two genre novices in leads. But they were instantly won over by Austin's screen test with Tate. King said, 'The chemistry between these stars is truly amazing.'

Julia Hudlow, who created the show and is co-producing with her husband, Marty Turgov, said she had wanted J.C. Austin all along. 'She's exactly what I had in mind from the start.' Asked if the show, set in Houston, would include country music, Hudlow said, 'It's not a musical and J.C.'s character is not a singer. But J.C. brings unique talents to be explored in the scripting.' 'We might also introduce guest characters from the music profession,' adds Turgov.

Austin excused her inexperience at acting when she said, 'It's not completely new to me. The character is a hairdresser. I've been that.' Shooting begins in three weeks.

PRE-PRODUCTION

COUNTRY SINGER RISKS DIVORCE WITH SERIES

'J.C. Austin Makes Love to Brandon Tate'

Just as J.C. Austin is about to take on the biggest challenge of her career, starring in a brand new sit-com with a leading role tailor-made for her, her manager-husband, Mac, is suddenly talking divorce.

Makeover, a new half-hour comedy set in a beauty shop in a Houston shopping mall, is scheduled to begin shooting in a few weeks.

America's favorite country star has already signed her contract and claims she has been 'studying night and day' so she'll be ready to act with top comedian Paul Green and her even more famous co-star, Brandon Tate.

Now sources close to the country music super-couple say Mac is suddenly getting cold feet about his wife being on a set with hunky sex symbol Brandon. 'I don't trust the guy and I don't want him anywhere near my wife,' the irate Mac is quoted as saying. 'The man's a sex addict. He's got a reputation for going after every woman he sees and I don't want the woman I've been married to for twenty years to be the next target on his superstud hit list. Maybe only half of what they say about him is true, but where there's smoke there's fire, and I don't want our marriage to get burned. A husband would have to be crazy to let that loverboy get too close.'

J.C. insists that 'my marriage is sacred to me and I would never leave Mac for another man', but she wants to go ahead with her role as Janine, head hairdresser at the Changing Room salon in Makeover because, 'I want to prove I can do something else besides sing. I may make a real fool of myself trying to be on TV but I hope that my fans will just give me a chance. After all, that's what my song says, "You won't know, girl, unless you try to fly." Mac's my pillar of strength. I hope he can understand how important this is to me and stand by me in my new career the way he's done throughout my life.'

Does this mark the end for one of country music's longest-running duets? Is J.C. Austin looking to fly solo? A source close to the red-headed queen of heartbreak predicts that the twenty-year marriage 'won't make it through one more.'

J.C. Austin is on tour in western Canada and could not be reached for comment. Mac Austin declined to answer our repeated phone calls. The couple's publicist says their marriage is still 'solid as a rock.' A spokesperson for CBN says that there have been no changes to the shooting schedule and that J.C. Austin will be on the set as announced for the first day of Makeover.

Lance J. Sutton

Chapter Six

Waiting in line for the checkout at the Piggly Wiggly super mart, leaning on her cart piled high with groceries, Debra Jo Fawcett saw the front cover of the *Hollywood Insider* promising the real dirt on J.C. Austin's marriage. 'Look, J.C. Austin's on the cover,' she said to her best friend, Jackie, who was behind her, her own cart equally filled to the brim. Jackie's teeth were chattering from the cold. Outside it was hot and sticky, a particularly humid February even for Houston. The air felt oppressive like maybe a blue norther was on its way. Inside the Piggly Wiggly, it was like a mini-Alaska. Why did they always keep the air-conditioning up so high in these big supermarkets? The longer you stayed in here, the greater the risk of pneumonia, although probably it guaranteed you'd get the frozen yogurt home before it melted.

'Wasn't it great seeing J.C. live in Nashville?' Debra cried. They'd been back for a month and she still hadn't stopped talking about it. Picking up the tabloid, she began to thumb quickly through it. When she found the right article she scanned it, then stopped and squealed so loud she caught everybody's attention.

'There's going to be a new TV show. All about Houston and a big mall with this beauty shop they call the Changing Room. Brandon Tate is the star, and, can you believe it, J.C.'s going to be his co-star. That is, if Mac lets her. See?' She elbowed Jackie in the ribs. 'He says right here he doesn't want her doing the show because of Brandon Tate. He's afraid she'll fall in love with Brandon, divorce Mac, and run off with him.'

'I don't blame Mac for being scared,' drawled Jackie. She was a tall, raw-boned, rangy brunette with a dry sense of humor and a fairly laconic delivery. 'Give me two minutes with Brandon Tate and my marriage vows would be as cold as yesterday's grits.' She was working on her third marriage to a man much older with a couple of grown step-children who had moved in with them, against Jackie's better judgment. 'Pure d. hell' was the way she described it.

'Brandon Tate? I'd leave my husband in a flash,' said the woman behind Jackie, who was wearing cut-offs and a T-shirt that read 'Don't Talk To Me, I've Just Quit Smoking.'

'I'd leave my six kids,' the woman in front of Debra Jo turned around, pen poised over the check she was writing for the vast array of groceries the box boy was now bagging. It was a long weekend and the Piggly Wiggly was closed on Monday.

'Go on, read us what it says,' urged Jackie.

'Yeah, read it out loud,' said the checkout clerk.

Debra Jo realized she was surrounded by quite a little audience that was hanging on her every word. Eddie was always telling her to lower her voice. It wasn't that her voice was too loud, it was just 'distinctive', a funny combination of breath and squeak. She had always been the sort of person that anyone, even strangers, felt comfortable talking to, or joining in a conversation she might be having with someone else, the way she was with Jackie right now. She liked having a bigger audience than just Jackie because the one problem with Jackie was that she sometimes took it into her head to shoot down Debra Jo's natural enthusiasm. If there was one thing Debra Jo couldn't take in a person it was negativity. It was a wonder she and Jackie were still best friends.

Debra Jo cleared her throat. Other shoppers had crowded in around them. The clerk stopped ringing in the prices. The box boy moved in closer. For a moment, in the frigid air of the supermarket, time stood still. In a hushed, almost reverent voice, she began to read what was purported to be the God's honest truth about Mac and J.C. and Brandon: '". . . and J.C. Austin will be on the set as announced for the first day of Makeover."' Debra Jo finished reading with a flourish. 'Wouldn't it be awful,' she said dramatically, 'if she had to turn down this big opportunity because of Mac?'

'Debra Jo, it says everything's going ahead as planned, didn't you listen to what you just read?' Jackie asked. Everybody else had gone back to their own business, the little flurry of excitement over. 'Anyway, you can't believe anything you read in there. Those tabloids always make it sound worse than it really is, you know, like "teenage girl gives birth to baby calf all by herself" and then you find out that the kid lives on a farm and she had to help the family cow give birth because her father was out in the field or something.'

'It's not fair,' Debra Jo continued as if she hadn't heard a word. 'Mac can't make that kind of decision for her, even if he is her manager. It's her career and if she wants to be on TV she should just go ahead and do it. I'm going to write and tell her that.'

'Come on, Debra Jo, like she's even going to get the letter!'

'I wrote her once before when she lost the baby and she wrote me right back. A real sweet letter thanking me for my concern and asking me to pray for her.'

'That was probably a form letter. They have secretaries that answer all their mail for them. I bet she got dozens of letters over a personal tragedy like that.'

'It didn't look like a form letter.'

'No, well, computers can do amazing things these days.'

'It was her signature,' Debra Jo said stubbornly. 'She signed it herself.'

'That's part of the job of being a star,' Jackie said with exasperation. 'Sure she signed it, so what? That doesn't mean she's going to take your advice about a major career choice. Grow up, Debra Jo. She doesn't know you from Adam. You don't exist for her. You're a fan, that's all. She has thousands.'

'Well, I've always kind of thought,' Debra Jo said wistfully, 'that if we ever met, we'd really like each other and get to be friends. I think I understand some of what she's going through.'

'Oh, great,' Jackie snorted. 'Next thing you know, you'll be turning up at her place, knocking on the door, and asking to be her friend. Just like that crazy woman who wrote all those letters to Michael J. Fox. They finally put her in jail, you know.'

'I know,' Debra Jo smiled. 'I'm not really serious. Still, if she comes to Houston to make the TV series, who knows? Maybe somehow I could get to meet her.'

'They won't be coming to Houston to do Makeover,' Jackie said flatly.

'They won't? Why not? It's set in Houston, right here in Houston.'

'I know all about this and that's not how it works. I saw this really great interview with Larry Hagman after the final episode of Dallas where he talked about how they made the show. They weren't in Dallas. They do the shooting in LA.'

'Of course they were in Dallas,' Debra Jo said emphatically. 'They showed Southfork at the top of every episode. I've been there. I've seen the ranch house.'

'But they didn't do the show in it,' Jackie insisted. 'They sent a camera crew to Texas to shoot the exteriors, that's what they call it, the exteriors. Back in LA, they build the rooms that are supposed to be the inside of the ranch house and they shoot all the "interiors" in them. The actors never leave LA. Even if it's supposed to be New York City, they still do it in LA because that's where all the stars live.'

'Oh,' Debra Jo was crestfallen.

'Now if you could talk Eddie into taking you out to LA you could go see a taping of the show at the studio. People line up outside, you know, tourists, and they're given tickets to come in and be a studio audience. Like we did in Nashville with Nashville Now.'

'That was fun,' Debra Jo remembered. 'I'd like to have that kind of life. Be a star. Make a lot of money. Be famous. Go to work, kiss Brandon Tate, and then get paid for it. Ooowhee –' she gave a little whistle – 'that'd be the life.'

'It doesn't say she's going to be kissing Brandon Tate. I think her husband's overreacting. Look at all the problems those stars have, anyway. Drugs, alcohol, divorce. No privacy. People talking about your personal life all the time, just like we're doing now.' They both laughed. 'How would you like to have your face splashed all over this rag? I sure as hell wouldn't want my dirty laundry hung out on a line all across North America for everyone to see.'

'Like that fight I had with Eddie last night?' Debra Jo sighed, thinking about her husband who'd been so pissed off when she and Jackie got in late from a friend's stagette at Chippendale's.

'Can't you just see it now?' Jackie drew the headline in the air in front of her. ' "Houston Housewife Forces Hubby to Eat Catfood." '

'It wasn't my fault he thought it was chopped chicken liver,' Debra Jo protested, giggling.

88

'See what I mean? They can take anything and twist it and make you look bad. No, I wouldn't mind being rich, but I don't think I could take being famous.'

'Oh, I think I could handle both,' Debra Jo said, looking thoughtful. 'I'd live in a mansion like the one J.C. has in Nashville and I'd fly back and forth to LA. I wouldn't get snotty or stuck up either. I'd be nice to all my old friends. I'd try and stay friends with you.'

'Gee thanks,' Jackie said sarcastically.

'Otherwise,' Debra Jo said slyly, raising an eyebrow, 'I know you'd be right there, as "a source close to Debra Jo Fawcett", selling all the inside dirt on me and Eddie to the *Hollywood Insider*.'

'Forget the *Insider*,' Jackie said. 'I'd go after forty thousand bucks from A Current Affair!' And they laughed as they headed out to the parking lot to load their groceries into the car.

Chapter Seven

In the backseat of a Manhattan taxi cab, Paul Green checked his watch. Looking out the window, there was still some light in the sky but, according to the Rabbinical Council calendar, the official time for sundown on this early February date had been set for five thirty-seven. It was five thirty-eight. He tapped politely on the glass panel that separated him from the taxicab driver, a dark, heavy-set man with a stern face, wearing a flat cap and a black turtleneck sweater stretched tightly across his barrel chest. 'You can pull over to the curb and let me off right here.'

'No. Is thirteen, maybe fourteen blocks to number you gave me. West End Avenue, yes?' The cab driver had a thick, East European accent. The identification card read Karel. Hungarian? No. More likely Czech.

'It's OK. Here's fine. I'll walk the rest of the way.' Paul hastily began to gather up his stuff. The light was going down fast and the cab was still moving. Chaya would be upset if she looked out the window and saw him pull up in a cab.

'No. Not walk. Is too far. Loads bags to carry.' When he frowned, the lines of his broad face fell into a relief map of melancholy.

'It's all right. Really.' Paul did his best to sound friendly, but firm. Some of these New York cabbies were crazy. You never knew what to expect. All he wanted to do now was to get home as quickly as possible.

'You don't have money?' The creases in the driver's face deepened.

'I have money,' Paul assured him. 'Don't worry, you'll get your tip. I just have to walk from here.'

'As you say,' the cabbie gave a shrug that shook his massive shoulders and, with a blast of the horn and a screech of the tires, he maneuvered the vehicle through the line of heavy traffic and pulled up to the curb. He sat, sullen, impassive, as Paul clambered out with his two suitcases and one shoulder bag, narrowly missing a pile of dog poop on the sidewalk that someone had obviously forgotten to stoop and scoop. As Paul leaned back into the cab to pay his fare, the driver said, 'So, you a Jew?'

Paul felt his stomach churn. The last thing he wanted was a confrontation on the street. 'I'm Jewish, yes,' he said as calmly as he could manage.

A huge smile lit up the cabbie's face, his dark eyes crinkling into little slits almost disappearing completely in the folds of his cheeks. 'Good Shabbas,' he said. 'I wish I could take the time but I have to keep driving.' He gave Paul a friendly wave and pulled away from the curb to a cacophony of honking horns.

Adjusting the baseball cap that had become his trademark, Paul picked up his bags and trudged the remaining six blocks to his apartment on West End Avenue. The uniformed doorman opened the heavy glass doors to let him in and, without ringing the buzzer to let Chaya know he was home, he eschewed the elevator and climbed the eight flights of stairs to the top of the building, groaning under the weight of his heavy bags. He let himself into the apartment calling out, 'Hi honey, I'm home.' The apartment was spotless and filled with the wonderful smells of the dishes Chaya had prepared for the Shabbat dinner. She had lit the Sabbath candles just before sundown and delicate shadows surrounded all the objects that had become so familiar to him. The living-room glowed with an almost magical warmth, like a special secret retreat, a comforting haven from the swirling, hectic street life of the Upper West Side. Once he entered that room, it was as if the outside world ceased to exist.

Chaya sat quietly on the sofa, wearing an elegant but simple navy blue skirt and a modest long-sleeved blouse. A gold embroidered silk scarf had been knotted into a turban around her head, the long fringe falling gracefully over one shoulder. Even with all his favorite parts of her completely covered, she looked more beautiful than ever. It was kind of exciting that no one other than the children or himself was allowed to see her long black hair, and when she let it down at night, just for him, he had to admit it was pretty sexy. The turban defined her smooth, pale face; her skin was

91

opalescent in the soft candlelight. She had high cheekbones a model would envy and finely chiseled features.

Paul liked to say he was addicted to his wife, couldn't get enough of her. She reminded him of the Greek actress, Irene Pappas: beautiful, magnetic, and strong to the point of fierceness. It was hard to believe Chaya was once called Carol, a plump, pretty, seemingly malleable undergraduate at Brandeis who followed him around the law department like a puppy, her baby fat concealing a surprisingly strong-willed core. Then they moved from Boston to New York, Paul had left law for stand-up comedy (exchanging one set of jokes for another, he liked to say), Carol had left law for early motherhood, and their lives had irrevocably changed. Paul became a comic. Short, odd, funny. Carol became Chaya. Thin, gorgeous, and undeniably sexy. He gave her a discreet kiss on the cheek. No doubt about it, he was horny. Observing the laws of family purity only made him want her more. 'Hi, babe, where are the kids?'

'Next door. I told them to resist all invitations to have Shabbat dinner with the Gottliebs and to come home and have it with us. You look exhausted, honey.'

'Yeah, well, schlepping my bags up Eighth Avenue . . .' He sank down on to the sofa next to her.

'So?' She looked up at him inquiringly.

'Soooo . . .,' he drew it out as long as he could.

'Yes?'

'I've got it! Principal role, pilot episode. I phoned them from the airport just before I got on the plane and they told me they're sure they want me for the role of Troy. *Mucho dinero*, my little pepita. They've even put a hold on me so I can't take any other work for the next six weeks, so that means even more money. Hopefully I start shooting mid-March in LA.'

Chaya sighed. 'Then we've got a big decision ahead of us.'

'Look,' Paul started in, 'out of twenty pilots, maybe two get picked up. The odds on this are lousy, but if by some miracle it does go to series, we'll have to leave the Big Dirty and move to LA. Flying back and forth to do The Comedy Store or a guest shot on Arsenio Hall I can just about manage, but I can't commute to tinsel town to do a weekly sit-com. Besides, I'd want you and the kids in LA with me. It'd be exciting, a whole new life.'

'I don't want a new life,' Chaya said fixedly. 'I like our old one. I thought you did, too.'

'You haven't heard the kind of money they're talking. Not to mention options, commitments, perks, residuals. I went out there with stars in my eyes; they've been replaced with dollar signs.'

'We can't discuss this any further tonight,' she said resolutely, getting up from the sofa and moving away from him. Immediately he felt dismissed, abandoned, the way he always felt when she wasn't right next to him. 'Not on Shabbat. No money, no work, right? Besides, we went through this discussion before you got on the plane for the first audition.'

She was right. They had. Although discussion was hardly the correct term. Knockdown drag-out was more like it. Standing in the kitchen Chaya had so carefully kosherized, the talk started calmly enough and then quickly escalated.

'Look, Chaya, if we have to make some allowances to live in LA, then we have to make some allowances. It was your choice to live a more observant life. We both grew up in a secular world. It's not as though we were raised Orthodox.'

'That's what is meant by *baalei teshuva*,' Chaya said patiently. 'We have returned.'

'I mean, if you want to talk Judaic one-upmanship, my upbringing was more Jewish than yours. At least my mother kept a kosher home, although we cheated in restaurants all the time. You weren't even raised kosher. We had sweet-and-sour shrimp the first time you took me home for dinner.'

'Right, and that's why your parents are no longer together and my father's been married three times. I don't want that for our kids and, supposedly, neither do you. When you quit pre-law and went into stand-up comedy, I told you I'd help in every way possible, but if we were going to keep this marriage together, we'd have to have some kind of structure. You said you could understand my need for the security of ritual, my desire to have a family. Now that we have one, I like living a traditional Jewish life with real values, following the *Halakha*. Paul, you said you understood,' she stressed the word again, 'even though you knew it would mean sacrifices on both our parts.'

She was right. It had sounded OK at that time. In fact, terrified of being cast adrift in the dark and dangerous, available sex-, drugs- and booze-infested waters of the comedy club circuit, having a safe, warm place to come home to sounded more than OK. And, after all, she had given up her own chance at a law career to make that home for him, the least he could do was go along with what she wanted. But he'd had no idea then just how far Chaya intended to go. She had set about the task of changing the very essence of their lives, observing Shabbat, taking classes in Judaism at the Lincoln Square Synagogue, eating fish when they went out to restaurants. It wasn't that hard at first and it did seem to bring new meaning to their relationship. Then she decided to take the big step of truly keeping kosher. She had kosherized the kitchen, replacing some dishes, taking others to the *mikvah* for a ritual cleaning, taking the oven apart, shopping only at Miller's Cheese and Fischer's kosher butchers, drinking only kosher wine, and delving even more deeply into all aspects of Jewish law as it applied to modern Jewish life. It was a long and involving process, but Chaya said in some ways it made her life easier because certain decisions were made for them. However, lately it seemed to Paul that the further she went down this particular road, there was always a distance still to go.

'We're supposed to be in agreement on this,' Chaya persisted. 'I thought you didn't mind.'

'Hey, every once in a while I miss Zabar's, you know what I mean?' At the expression on her face, 'Sorry, kidding, just kidding. It's just that I'm only thirty years old, babe, I'm not sure I want every inch of the rest of my life mapped out in such structured detail.'

'We live in a world without much structure. You've chosen a profession that is completely crazy. You never know where you're going to be from one minute to the next.'

'What can I tell you, I'm a stand-up comic and a freelance actor.'

'A freelance career is one thing; I just don't want a freelance life. You're in a business where the entire focus is on the self,' her voice was rising with the passion of conviction. 'You have to be self-centered as an actor—'

'Hey, wait a minute here—' he was starting to feel under attack.

'Listen, I understand that,' she was like a very persuasive

prosecuting attorney lulling the defendant into momentarily thinking she was on his side. 'You're selling yourself; the product is you. That's why it's so painful when you don't get a job because you take it as a personal rejection of you. I watch you go through this and I agonize with you. I can see how hard it is on your self-esteem and how tempting it is to compensate with ego. If you could learn to define yourself as a Jew before you define yourself as an actor, it could make a big difference.'

'You mean like realizing that Paul Green is not the center of the universe. That there's somebody up there with top billing?'

'Exactly.' She almost turned to an imaginary jury as if to say, 'See what I mean?' 'It would help you to keep things in perspective. Live a more reasonable life.'

He could almost feel his one shot at stardom slipping away into the black hole of this 'reasonable life'. 'A long-running series could take us anywhere we want to go,' Paul's voice was rising now.

'Maybe it's a place where I don't want to go.'

'How can you say that? You haven't even experienced it.'

'I don't have to experience everything to know that some things are not right for me. For us.'

God, she was stubborn. 'Look, Chaya, I'm making a living in this city, but that's all. The clubs, Saturday Night Live; here in New York I've gone about as far as I can go. In fact, I'm virtually there, wherever "there" is in this city. In LA, the sky's the limit.'

'The limitations have to be inside you. You have to set your own limits.'

'This could be a big opportunity for me, excuse me, for us,' he was shouting now. 'I've got three kids to support. Doing a series is a hell of a lot more lucrative than playing beard stubble in an electric shaver commercial. I know you don't want to leave New York, but Los Angeles isn't exactly Sodom and Gomorrah.'

'You're right, I don't want to leave New York. I like our shul where the service is in Hebrew. The boys love Chofetz Chaim and Talia's really happy at the Manhattan Day School. This apartment building is close to one hundred per cent Orthodox. Who knows what we would find in LA?'

'Lots of Jews, believe me. According to all reports, we

run the place. Hollywood is Jews. Some of them are just bound to be observant.'

'Here we can live the life we've chosen to live, surrounded by people who think and feel the way we do. We have everything we need right in this neighborhood. I like being able to go out for a kosher pizza. What if we can't find all this in LA?'

'But we can. I've been doing some research. There's a neighborhood right off Melrose in West LA. When I was out doing the Tonight Show I checked it out—'

Chaya cut him off. 'You haven't even got the job and already you're planning where we're going to live without consulting me?'

'I am consulting you. That's what this is all about. Although let me remind you,' he was so angry and frustrated he couldn't resist slinging it at her, 'according to what you believe, the house and the children are supposed to be your domain. Work and study are mine, so the final decision is up to me.'

Now, five days later, they faced each other in much the same manner as Chaya repeated his words, 'Well, the final decision is yours.' They stood frozen for a moment, staring in angry silence, when the front door was flung open and the kids rushed in from next door, noisy, exuberant, full of excited chatter. They threw themselves on him. Talia was just eight, Nathan a year older at nine, and Aaron, at six, the baby.

All of them were sturdily handsome. Thankfully they'd inherited Chaya's strong good looks instead of Paul's own nebbish comic features. He'd grown up as the class clown; he had only to look into the mirror to understand why. Now his looks were considered hip as well as funny. Still, he was glad the kids took after Chaya. He was inordinately proud of his wife and three children. Chaya kept saying she wanted at least three more, wasn't the first law of the Bible to be fruitful and multiply? He'd already fulfilled his minimum obligation of one boy and one girl, but as Chaya reminded him, some Orthodox Jews felt an obligation to the *mitzvah* to have as many as possible, as long as they could be provided for. He just hoped she wasn't planning on the two of them replacing the entire six million all by themselves.

'Dad, Dad,' Nathan grabbed him around the neck as Aaron threw his arms around his father's knees holding him in a mini hammer lock. 'What's happening? Are we moving to LA?'

'Are we, Daddy?' Talia tugged at his sleeve.

'Don't pack your Nintendo yet, but if the next month goes really well,' Paul avoided his wife's gaze, 'the answer to that question is probably going to be yes.' He could sense she was furious with him, but would not press the issue and risk spoiling the Friday evening ritual.

He opened his arms and the family came together to sing *Shalom Aleichem*. The children bowed their heads and Paul put his hands on each of them to bless them. The candles blazed on the dinner table as Paul poured wine into the *kiddush* cup, filling it to the brim and passing it around so each member of the family could take a sip. Then they all headed out to the kitchen for the ritual of *netilat yadaim*, the washing of the hands, then back to the dinner table where Paul took off the *challah* cover and, lifting the loaves high in the air, blessed the bread. Almost roughly (the kids loved this part), he tore the bread into individual pieces, dipped them in salt and passed them around to each member of the family. Chaya and Talia brought in plate after plate of food, boiled beef, chicken, salad, cholent, Talia chattering all the way, Chaya remaining ominously silent. Usually the Shabbat dinner was a festive occasion, a welcome window of time in Paul's busy week, the one guaranteed opportunity for him to revel in having his wonderful family all around him, but tonight the tension covered the table like a heavily embroidered cloth, driving them further apart instead of bringing them closer together. Between courses, they all sang *smirot*, song poems that celebrated the human spirit and the glory of the Sabbath. Chaya joined in the singing but her face was impassive and her eyes were still blazing. Paul could stand it no longer. He reached across the table and took his wife's hand, saying, 'Don't worry, babe, we'll work it out, I promise.' But even as he said the words he wondered if he would be able to make them come true.

Chapter Eight

'Great chicken, Debra Jo,' said Eddie Fawcett, his mouth still more than a little full.

'Yeah, Mom, great chicken,' the two boys echoed their approval. Jim Bowie, the family's golden retriever named for one of the heroes of the Alamo, sat at attention between them, waiting vigilantly for any scraps that might come his way.

Debra Jo acknowledged their compliments gracefully but she knew they were well-deserved. Nobody in Sharpstown, probably nobody in all of metropolitan Houston could match her honey crisp-fried chicken, homemade mashed potatoes, and flaky buttermilk biscuits with cream gravy. Of course she knew, at least she'd recently learned, that cream gravy was just about the deadliest thing a man about to turn forty could eat. Flour, fat drippings, chicken skin, cholesterol-rich giblets, all sent the fat gram level way above the thirty per cent recommended on the healthy heart diet in *Star Weekly*. Cooking had been one of her greatest pleasures until the spectre of cholesterol entered their lives. Last Thanksgiving the magazine had a recipe for cholesterol-free turkey gravy using cornstarch and skimming all the fat off the top. Debra Jo tried it for Christmas Day along with a roasted free-range turkey and the family bitched so much that she actually had to get up from the table, in the middle of the holiday dinner, to go into the kitchen and whip up a batch of her famous cream gravy.

At least she was trying to keep her family healthy and, she had to admit, looking at them around the kitchen table, that each and every one of them looked glowing. Beau and Danny were cute enough to do commercials on TV, and Eddie, who she had always thought handsome enough to be a movie star, had just been given a clean bill of health by Dr Lester. Eddie had gone through some tough years there for a while; they all had. When they first got married, he'd had part-ownership in a drilling company, but then the oil business went bust and Eddie worked three different jobs to get the money to go into a new field, the installation of air-conditioning units. Now he was back on his feet again, making good money, enough to buy the new house in a nicer suburb of Houston. Debra Jo knew he missed being in oil, but he never complained, rarely lost his temper. That was Eddie, all right, the master of adjustment, taking it one day at a time, making the best of a bad situation until he could turn it into a good one. A truly sweet-natured man. As she looked at him now, with his straight, white-blond hair falling over his forehead, shielding those clear blue eyes, eyes that looked even bluer against his tanned face, she thought her heart would burst with pride and love. Then she remembered she had something important to ask him. 'Honey,' she said, folding her napkin and putting it over the remains of chicken on her plate, 'how would you feel about a trip to California?'

'California? We only just got back from Nashville.'

'There's this new TV show starring J.C. Austin. It's got a country-and-western theme and it's called Makeover.'

'Where'd you hear about this?' Eddie said suspiciously.

'Well, I read it in the *Insider*, but the *Star* and the *Globe* were talking about it, too.'

'You are addicted to those things. We've got so many of them all over the house I might as well start using them as toilet paper. Save us a bunch of money.'

Debra Jo chose to ignore this. 'Anyway, they'll be taping the first episode in a couple of weeks out in LA and they're looking for people to be in the studio audience. I was thinking maybe we could all drive out to California. Might be real fun.'

'Oh, wow, great, let's go,' Beau said in between cramming huge mounds of mashed potatoes into his mouth.

'Can we go, Dad, can we?' Danny was equally enthusiastic. 'I want to check out Disneyland.'

'Jackie says you can get special tickets to be in the TV audience,' Debra Jo continued, not wanting to look directly at Eddie. 'You know, like we did for Nashville Now?'

'All right!' Beau yelled.

'Don't be yelling at the table,' Eddie said mildly.

'Your father's right,' Debra Jo said. 'And please keep

your mouth closed when you've got mashed potatoes in there. It's really disgusting.'

'Dad chews with his mouth open.'

'He most certainly does not,' Debra Jo said. Immediately Eddie's mouth snapped shut over the chicken.

'So what do you say, Dad?'

'Yeah, what do you say?' Danny was singing back-up to his older brother's tune. Debra Jo wished she had not brought this subject up in front of the kids; she should have waited until they were alone in bed together.

Eddie put his fork down. 'We ain't going to no California.' Debra Jo knew he was starting, just starting, to get irritated with the direction in which this conversation was going. Usually his grammar was excellent. He was surprisingly well-educated for a man in his position. 'Now, I love you guys and I try to give you what you want. But we took you to Disneyworld a year ago and we took you to Universal Studios in Orlando last summer. Plus your mom and me just got back from Nashville. I can't take any more time off away from the business until next summer.'

'So next summer, can we—?' The chorus began again.

'And when I get my time off,' Eddie cut them off, 'I want to go to Laughlin, Nevada, and play the slot machines they got there. It's a brand new casino. Supposed to be great.'

'Well, what are we going to do?'

'There's a bunch of stuff for kids to do right there in the casino, in another part,' he said hastily, looking at Debra Jo. 'A movie theater, video games, great stuff. They serve free chicken wings at happy hour and you can get a full dinner for under five bucks. That's where I want to go next. I'm not interested in going to California and watching some TV show. What do you want to do that for, anyway?' This was directed at Debra Jo. 'You already watch more TV than any living human being I know, even the kids. I swear, sometimes I think you care more about the stars you see on TV than you do your own family.'

But he said it with affection. This was one of the best things about Eddie. He pretty well let her do whatever she wanted as long as everything was running smoothly at home, and keeping things running smoothly was a snap for Debra Jo. She was born to be a housewife and mother and proud of it. Not that she didn't believe in equal pay for women when they worked outside the home. Fair was fair.

100

She had even thought about starting up her own small business at some point. Like maybe a knitting crafts shop. But she was glad when the women's movement came right out and said that raising kids and working in the home was just as important.

One of the most interesting 'Can This Marriage Be Saved?' articles in the *Ladies' Home Journal* suggested that the wife draw up a list of everything she did around the house and then put an hourly wage on it. When it was all added up, she showed it to her husband and it turned out to be worth over twice as much as he was making as a bank manager in Allentown Pennsylvania. So their marriage was saved. Not that Debra Jo expected to be paid for it. Still, it was nice to know that some sort of monetary value could be fixed to what she did. Eddie was as generous with his money as he could afford to be.

However, his mind appeared to be made up as far as going to California was concerned. 'OK, kids,' Debra said, 'let's see how fast you can clear the table and get the dishes into the dishwasher. The faster you get it cleared, the sooner you'll both be out of here and over to the swimming pool, right? No bones in the garburator, OK? And wrap them up real good so the dog won't get them. Paper and plastic. I don't want to be dragging Bowie to the vet any more times this month, you hear?'

'Yes, ma'am,' Danny said smartly, in tune as always to the shift in her moods. Sometimes she thought she loved Danny more than anyone else in the world, even Eddie. Beau was a wonderful boy, but at fifteen he was growing up so big and so fast he didn't seem like a kid any more. He took more after Eddie, anyway. Danny was her boy, her baby, had been so right from the start and, at almost eleven, hovered in that category still. He'd had a heart murmur when he was born, they didn't know whether or not he would survive, and there was still an air of fragility surrounding him, no matter how hard he tried to conceal it with the macho cover of his father and brother. Beau had a natural hustler's ease and charm that allowed him to breeze through life, neatly avoiding all of its corners. Danny had an innate fearfulness of what might be lying in wait for him around each of those corners. Eventually, of course, she wanted him to be confident enough to take on whatever life dealt him, but for the moment, a little part of her was secretly pleased that he still came to her for reassurance.

'Hey, you want to watch a video?' Eddie said over the clatter of the kids in the kitchen as they scraped the dishes and ran them under the tap in the kitchen sink, while Bowie's nails scraped along the tiled kitchen floor.

'Sure, what did you bring home?' Debra Jo moved her chair closer to his and rested her head on his shoulder.

'*Terminator 2*.'

'Oh no, why? We've already seen it and I thought it was just dumb. All those melt-downs, who cares?'

'Just kidding,' Eddie kissed her ear. 'I got the new Mel Gibson movie, OK? So we'll send the kids out to the pool, make us some of that sour cream and onion microwave popcorn, pop a few beers, and then maybe I can talk you into laying down on the couch with me and watching *Love Bites* which is about . . . well, I think I'll just let it be a surprise.'

Debra Jo giggled. She knew Eddie was hoping that watching Mel Gibson would get her hot enough to sit through one of those stupid-ass X-rated videos. Jackie had already told her the entire plot of *Love Bites* (she and her husband had already rented it) and it sounded like the usual. The same sex parts over and over again, even if it didn't make sense in terms of progression of any act of love she'd ever been involved in. You'd see this blonde going down on a guy, both of them naked, and then the next thing you knew he was kissing her and taking her bra off, a bra she didn't have on just one second before. The sounds they put in after almost never matched the lips of the actors supposedly making them, nor did they match what was supposed to be going on at that particular moment. Like when you see the blonde going down on the guy, they've got her screaming 'Ah, ah', when it's so obvious she couldn't be making that noise because her mouth is full. Crazy. Besides, the women in these porn flicks all made her feel she had to hold her stomach in the whole time she was having sex. The men were usually fat and looked either like mental retards or convicts who'd just escaped from the Huntsville state pen.

Anyway, she didn't need Mel or an X-rated video to get her going. Eddie was good in bed. She liked just about everything he did and the order in which he did it seemed like a pretty good chord progression to her. Although she had to admit, tonight when the two of them finally made it into their big brass bed, she'd probably lie back, close her eyes, and pretend that the man making wild, passionate love to her was not Eddie Fawcett but Brandon Tate.

Chapter Nine

In his deep-forest-green, 1949 Cadillac convertible with a white rag top, Brandon Tate sped down Old Topanga Canyon Road heading into the San Fernando Valley. The classic car had once belonged to Al Jolson and it was in museum condition. At forty-five, Brandon Tate was somewhat of a classic himself. Like a good single malt whiskey, age seemed to only improve his smokey flavor, the lines around his eyes and mouth giving added strength and determination to his sensual features. He had a slight, barely discernible scar over his left eye, a constant reminder that nothing in life was to be taken for granted.

Brandon was on his way to Pacific Victory Studios in Burbank and the sky was remarkably clear for LA. With the top down, his head thrown back, the early morning breeze blowing his thick, dark hair, Brandon sang along to a CD of J.C. Austin's latest album, *Change of Heart*. J.C. could sing, no doubt about that, but could she act? They'd met just once, briefly, at J.C.'s screen test, in which she had been surprisingly funny. Funny, but all over the place. The next thing he knew, she was playing opposite him in Makeover. There was nothing worse than working with an inexperienced actress surrounded by a lot of hype, because so often they were afraid to admit what they didn't know. Today was the first read-through around the table. It would be a real test of whether or not J.C. Austin had what it took.

Brandon Tate was a household name, yet few people knew that as a young actor he'd played Shakespearean leads at the Bristol Old Vic, sung Gilbert and Sullivan in Australia, and was fluent in several languages. He preferred to talk about the fact that he was the son of a rodeo rider and that he himself had won the National Steer Roping Championship. The good ole boy persona had been his stock-in-trade, but secretly Brandon was a man of many parts.

He had an air about him of desires not fully satisfied, promise not quite fulfilled. His sexual track record was legendary, but what really made him tick, no one in his life so far had been able to pin down. That was the way he wanted it. The entertainment business was built on illusion and the name of the game was to keep them all guessing. Brandon Tate in series television? Why not? His new manager, Michael Taylor, could give him lots of reasons why not. Hollywood was so rigid, the lines so clearly drawn, as if every aspect of life could be reduced to an A and B list.

Young Michael Taylor had tried to persuade him not to do Makeover. Film was A list, TV was B list and sit-com was at the bottom of the B list. But the producers of Makeover had offered Brandon a chance to direct, and directing was at the top of the A list. Hell, everyone wanted to direct, even the talking freeway sign in Steve Martin's *LA Story*; hadn't Michael been around long enough to know that? It was all such a game, and the fact that he knew it was a game hadn't made it any less harder to play. Only now he had no patience for it. The air crash three years ago had made him reevaluate everything in his life.

He had been shooting an action comedy outside Monterrey, Mexico. Peter Chase, his manager and his closest friend, had come down for the last couple of days of the shoot. The wrap party was wild and the two of them were still feeling the effects of the night, no, morning before when they climbed aboard an AirMex 727, direct to LA. Almost immediately after take-off, they both shared a premonition that something was going to go wrong, but they laughed it off. Funny, that they had each thought the same thing right at the same time. Over northern Mexico the plane began to lose altitude, they could feel it drop out from under them. The captain came on the air and told them he was going to try to land in Tucson, but Brandon knew in his gut they would never make it that far, the aircraft was bouncing all over the sky. He found out later that the tail engine had blown out and they'd lost the hydraulics which powered some of the control surfaces, including the rudder and tail, but the captain gave them no details, only came on the air again and in a voice battling for calm told the passengers to brace for an emergency landing in Nogales, Arizona, not to panic but they were going down, down, down . . .

Miraculously, the pilot was able to land the plane, but he overshot the short runway and went into a field, where the plane started to break apart. Brandon must have blacked out and, when he came to, flame and smoke were all around him, parts of the fuselage torn off, flinging a whole section of seats out on to the tarmac, seats with people still strapped into them by their seatbelts; there was a gaping hole near him, he could feel the cold air rushing in over him, he reached out to pull himself through and something sharp and jagged zig-zagged into his eye, the pain was savage and he felt the blood gush down the side of his face, Jesus, he couldn't see out of his left eye . . . Then strong arms were reaching around him and dragging him out through the open hole. 'I've got you, old buddy,' Peter said, 'just hang on to me,' and he carried him for who knows how long and laid him down on the tarmac. Brandon clutched him, gratefully, like a baby, but then Peter pried his fingers loose and blurrily, through one eye, Brandon watched him head toward the smoking plane. He climbed back through the hole and handed out a child, a little boy of about two or three, who made no sound, his small face frozen, his eyes wide with fear, almost as if he were holding whatever breath was left in him. Peter handed the child out to safety, gave Brandon the high sign, and then disappeared from view. He drifted in and out of consciousness. The screech of firetruck sirens, the shouts of the paramedics running back and forth around him, the blinding white light as a section of the plane exploded, it all seemed like some horrific dream, an apocalyptic vision, but the child's face was emblazoned on his memory along with Peter's final salute.

The surgeons did an amazing job with his face. He still looked pretty much the same except for the scar over his left eye, but he retained only twenty per cent of his sight in that eye. Nobody could tell, at least not by looking at him, but he could tell. They didn't let him know Peter Chase had died until they believed he could handle it. Trouble was he still couldn't handle it, even after three years. Brandon now saw the world in a very different light. The crash had left him with a faint scar, blurred vision, and a feeling that if life could be snuffed out that quickly, what was it all worth anyway? Why was he still here and Peter gone? What did he have to show for his life except for his face on a few thousand feet of celluloid? Damn it, he missed Pete. He had been more than his manager, he was his best friend. He owed his career to Peter, fuck, he owed him his life. No way could a young asshole like Michael Taylor ever replace what he had shared with Pete. He was careful to pay the proper commission to Michael, but he didn't have to take his advice or his shit. He had made the decision to do Makeover on his own.

He came to with a start. Christ, it was dangerous letting himself drift back like that, especially on the freeway, and he'd almost missed the exit. He turned off the Ventura Freeway and drove into Burbank. He passed Warner Brothers with its big WB logo and huge poster billboards advertising Murphy Brown on CBS. Apart from Disney, which had a roof held up by the Seven Dwarfs, most of the studios looked like airplane hangars: low-slung, flat, unprepossessing buildings to house such magic. Taking a right turn on Olive Avenue, he drove past NBC and Warner/Elektra/Atlantic records until he came to the pastel stucco buildings of Pac Vic with a marquee reading, 'Keep It to Yourself' on NBC and 'Dads in Bondage' on CBS. With any luck, it would soon say 'Makeover' on CBN. He pulled up to the security gate and wiped his brow. It was always a good ten degrees hotter in the Valley than in Topanga Canyon where he lived. Inside the booth was a new security guard, a woman, a little tough-looking but very attractive, her full breasts straining against the crisp uniform shirt, the gun in her holster cradled cozily against her solid thigh. After a brief but delightfully sparring flirtation, he felt better. She asked him for his autograph. Once he had signed the only piece of paper she had in the booth, a well-thumbed copy of the *Hollywood Insider*, she attached a priority pass to his windshield and waved him through on to the studio lot.

He parked in the spot designated for him, outside soundstage six, checked in at the front desk, and was met by Cindi, one of the many production assistants on Makeover, a nervous, rabbity girl with a sibilant 's' and frizzy hair pulled back in a ponytail, who escorted him to his trailer. It was nice of Pac Vic to give him his own trailer just for the pilot. They didn't really have to do that, but obviously since they were doing it for J.C., they wanted to make sure their two principals started off on an equal footing. He took a quick look around. There was a large complimentary fruit

107

basket from the studio and from the network, a bottle of Maker's Mark bourbon with a personal note from Stanfield King, Head of CBN. Sitting on his dressing-table was a leather-bound version of the latest draft of the pilot script from Julia and Marty. The little fridge in the corner was stocked with a variety of mineral water, fruit juices, pop, cheese and crackers, and a couple of frozen Milky Way candy bars, the sweet that everyone knew was his favorite. A nice touch, although he knew no perks came his way without being attached to some hidden agenda.

For eight years straight he'd been in the box office top five; then action comedy pictures went out of vogue. He'd made a couple of bad career choices, and when the crash happened, he went into orbit. Did a lot of drugs, had a lot of women, although not to the extent that it was rumored. If he'd done everything people claimed he had done, he'd be dead by now. He had enough money to live more than comfortably for the rest of his life, but what was that rest of his life going to be?

There was a knock at his trailer door. It was Kathryn Grady wearing a severely tailored black-and-white suit and carrying a clipboard in her hand. She looked very sure of herself. Kathryn was expert at making decisions, in a town where that ability was often in short supply, where projects could go into 'development' for months, even years. Sometimes it seemed to Brandon that life itself was stuck in development.

'Good morning,' Kathryn said briskly. 'I thought I'd come over and sign you in myself. Our production manager, Doug Berkley, is going a bit insane because it's the first day.'

'Hello, darlin',' Brandon took the pen and signed his name with a flourish on the callsheet. 'You look as gorgeous as ever,' he gave her a kiss on the cheek. 'I always liked that suit on you. It's one of my favorites.' She did look stunning, taut and trim, her dark hair pulled back into an intricate knot at the nape of her neck, one loose curl caressing the side of her face. He had a sudden impulse to reach out and twist that wayward curl around his finger. He cleared his throat. 'Listen, Kathryn, thanks for pushing for me to direct. It's what I really want.'

'I know.'

'Thanks for arranging the trailer, too . . .'

'You deserve it,' Kathryn said warmly.

'I hope I'll be seeing a lot of you in it.' Brandon smiled a slow, dangerous smile.

'I doubt it,' she said, instantly all business. 'I have a big job to do on this one.'

'You know that suit sends out mixed signals,' he said quietly. 'It's an interesting paradox. All hard and aggressive on the outside, all soft and feminine on the inside. Like you.' He couldn't resist. He leaned forward and touched her cheek lightly with his hand.

'Forget it, Brandon. I'm engaged to be married.'

'What?' He stopped, surprised, but he didn't take his hand away.

'Yep. To a guy I met on holiday in Belize. Jonathan Long.'

'That was fast.'

'Well, if you're sure, you're sure.' She smiled a little tremulously.

'Do you love him?'

'He's a millionaire.'

'Well, then he can't be all bad. Congratulations.'

'He's based in New York because of his business,' Kathryn explained, 'so I don't know how much we'll actually be together. I guess I'm about to embark on what they call a "red-eye relationship", the bicoastal marriage.'

'Too much togetherness can ruin a relationship, or so I've been told,' Brandon maintained his light, teasing tone, but his eyes were boring into her. 'Go ahead, get married, have a great honeymoon in the Caribbean, then . . . what's his name?'

'Jonathan.'

'Jonathan can fly back to New York, you can wing your way back here to me, and we can take up where we left off.'

'I don't think so,' she said coolly.

'I don't want to lose you, Kathryn,' he said softly. 'I adore you.' He brushed the loose tendril of wild hair back from her face. Then, gently caressing her cheek, he moved down the side of her neck, touching her lightly, expertly, moving his hand inside the collar of her tailored blouse, massaging the back of her neck.

'Don't,' she said. But she didn't move away.

He lifted her heavy mass of dark hair off her neck, put his mouth on her neck, letting his breath warm her skin, his tongue sliding down to the hollow of her collarbone and then working its way slowly back up toward her ear. Reluctantly she turned her head toward him, finding his mouth and kissing him passionately. He slid his other hand up under her skirt.

'I love it when you wear silk stockings and a garter belt,' he whispered in her ear, and then he let his tongue follow his words.

'I said, "don't".' She pulled her face away from his, but she didn't remove his hand.

He looked at her quizzically, his head tilted to one side, a half smile playing around the corner of his lips. He kept his voice seductively casual. 'Why not?'

'I really want this marriage to work,' she said pleadingly, as his hand moved up the inside of her thigh, under the lacy garter belt, finding the smooth silk of her crotch.

'Do you love him?' he asked again, letting his fingers brush against the silk with ever-increasing pressure.

'I want to get married.' She felt his fingers pull back the silken shield and move inside.

'Why? In God's name why?' He looked at her with amusement, holding her at arm's length, his magic fingers doing all the work.

'Would you take your hand out of there, please? I don't want this.'

'Yes, you do. You're already wet.' He continued to move his fingers inside her, thrusting more deeply. 'I want to have a baby,' she said faintly.

'You've got plenty of time.' He could feel her warmth closing involuntarily around his fingers. The center of her. Liquid. Pulsing.

'No I don't,' she protested. 'And neither do you. When are you going to grow up, Brandon?' She tried to keep her voice level, but her breath was coming in quick little gasps.

'Never, my lovely. Marriage is the last step before the grave. Haven't you ever heard, "First you're born, then you die, and in between you get married"?'

'No,' Kathryn said. 'I thought it was, "First you're born, then you die, and in between you're an actor."'

His eyes flashed, deadly. He pinned her to the wall like a butterfly with his gaze, letting her flutter for a minute before he said, 'That was low.' His voice was barely a whisper. 'You're going to have to be punished for that. Is that what you want? Would you like to be punished?'

'Yes,' she nodded, barely able to get the words out.

'Tell me you want it.'

'Yes,' she gasped. She came toward him, but with one swift move, he backed her up against the trailer door, unbuttoning her suit jacket and letting it fall to the floor. Swiftly, he put his mouth to the top of her breast, and he heard her gasp again at the sensation as he licked along the edge of her lacy bra, outlining each breast with his tongue. He slid the straps of her bra down her arms, pulling her bra down under her breasts, freeing them from the wispy cups, but keeping her imprisoned in a lacy cage. He licked each nipple, sucking on it gently, then harder and harder, making her moan with pleasure. Almost roughly he hiked her skirt up to her hips, pulling her silk panties down to her knees, leaving the garter belt intact, the air cool on her bare skin. He knew what pleasure he was giving her. Already her hips were moving toward him in a simulation of sex. Her hands reached for the buckle on his belt and she quickly got it open, frantically grabbing his jeans, shoving them down, clutching at his ass, freeing his cock, pulling him straight toward her. But he held her away from him, whispering urgently, 'What does the lady want; tell me what you want?' and she moaned, 'I want you inside me, please, come inside.' She was shaking all over, sweat running down her face and on to her breasts.

He leaned down and licked it off.

'Please,' she begged. 'Fuck me, please.'

'Always give the lady what she asks for,' he said politely, and then entered her in one quick, hard thrust. She cried out but he silenced her with his mouth, his tongue meeting hers, sucking on it, drawing it out of her mouth and into his. His pelvis hard against hers, thrusting into her over and over again. He loved the way she kept clutching at his ass, grabbing at him, roughly, almost painfully, pulling him more deeply into her, harder and harder each time, calling out his name. Her long fingernails dug into his buttocks and, as she stiffened against him, he felt his own orgasm rising, scalding, within him. Stifling their cries, they came at each other one last time, arcing up, way up, and then collapsing, panting, over each other. They waited, breathing heavily, while time and space came back to normal.

'Goddamn it, but you're good at that,' Kathryn said, and

it sounded strangely like a complaint. Little rivulets of sweat were running down her cheeks.

Brandon kissed her face gently all over. 'I adore making love with you,' he whispered. 'You make me good. Don't marry this guy. Stay with me, please.'

'Then let me marry you.' Kathryn's mouth was swollen and bruised. Her eyes looked at him beseechingly.

He stopped and let her go. There was no answer for that. He picked her suit jacket up off the floor, smoothed out the wrinkles, and wordlessly handed it over to her. Silently she put it on and turned to go. Her hand was on the door. He reached out and touched her shoulder. 'Friends?' he said quietly.

She paused. 'Of course, friends,' she said. She leaned forward and kissed him lightly on the cheek. 'You're one for the books, Brandon,' she gave him a smile as she picked up her clipboard and left the trailer.

He closed the door behind her and leaned against it, still a little out of breath. He felt better, more alive. Well, he thought to himself, there's still one thing I can do. At least I can still get it up. The confined space and the danger of being discovered only made it more exciting. For Kathryn, too, he could tell. God, she could be wonderfully wild. He would miss her. If she truly intended to keep her promise to herself not to see him again. He opened the little fridge, took out a bottle of Evian and, putting it to his lips, drank greedily, letting drops of water slide down the front of his denim shirt, until the bottle was drained. There was another knock at the door. Was she back already? He opened the trailer door and found J.C. Austin standing there. 'Hello, darlin',' he said, 'welcome to the team. Come on inside.'

J.C. stepped into the trailer. 'Thanks. It's great to see you again, Brandon. I was going to call you from the road so we could get together and talk about today, but Mac had my tour booked solid and,' she stopped suddenly, staring at him. 'Are you all right?'

He quickly ran his fingers through his hair. 'Sure. Why?'

'You're looking kind of red in the face.'

'Oh, yeah, it's hot in here. I'll turn up the air-conditioning.' He turned away and fiddled with the dial, trying to keep the conversation going. 'So, it's a big day for you, isn't it, first read-through and all? How are you feeling?'

To his amazement she suddenly burst into tears. 'Oh man, I am really scared,' she cried. 'I'm like a damned hog on ice.' Only a woman with genuine country roots could get away with a line like that, Brandon thought. 'What am I doing here? I'm a singer not an actress. I should quit before I even begin, but I can't let Julia down, I know she really pushed for me to get this gig.' Brandon put his arm around her and she continued to sob on his shoulder, 'I just went in to say hello to everybody. The room is full of suits. All the big guys from the network, I guess. They're all just sitting there, waiting for me to open my mouth and screw up real good.'

'Hey, hey, hey,' Brandon handed her a Kleenex from his dressing-table. 'You're going to be great.'

'You think so?' She stopped crying.

'I know so.' He wiped a couple of tears away for her. 'You could mop up the floor with anyone in there, take it from me.'

'Really?' She looked up at him with watery blue eyes.

'There isn't a speck of talent in that room until you and I walk into it. That's what they're waiting for. Together, you and me, we're going to make this one hell of a hit.'

'Will you help me?' The blue eyes were suddenly fiercely determined.

'What?' He was completely thrown off-guard.

'If I get into trouble with this acting thing, will you bail me out?'

'Well, Alex Jordan is a top-notch TV director. You're in good hands with him.'

'I know, and I'm going to work real hard to please him. But you're an actor, you've been doing it all your life. If you see me messing up, just take me aside and let me know, OK?'

'Sure.' He didn't know what else to say. She seemed completely open in her request, her insecurity genuine.

'I can't believe this,' J.C. said, sitting up and moving away from him. 'I am never nervous, never. But I've kind of been under a lot of pressure lately . . .'

'From your husband?' Brandon tried to ask it delicately.

'You saw the *Insider* spread?' J.C. looked dismayed.

'Come on, nobody believes those rags. You must have been in them before.'

113

'Yeah, but it was always good stuff. This is really bad.'

'That's because you weren't as interesting to them when you were a country star as you are now that you're about to be a TV star.'

'Don't count those chickens too soon,' J.C. managed a little smile.

'They'll come after me too,' Brandon predicted, 'now that I'm doing TV. Tab readers don't go out to the movies. Most of them have little money and lots of kids so they stay home and watch TV. They want to know what goes on behind the scenes of their favorite shows and they want to believe that even though you're rich and famous, your problems are just as bad, even worse than theirs.'

'I know, but the attack was so personal. It's like the *Insider* is out to get me.' She shivered.

'At least it wasn't your sex life. My privacy's been smeared all over the tabs in graphic detail. And the *Insider*'s the worst. They pay for their information. A friend of mine told me that over half their editorial budget goes toward paying off their so-called anonymous sources, and most of it's phony anyway. You can sue, but it never does any good.' He gave her a comforting little pat on the shoulder. 'Don't let them get to you, J.C. Look on it as a sign of success. The time to worry is when they stop writing about you.'

'Oh, I don't. I'm a hard-headed iron ass, but Mac really hit the roof. He fired our security guard because he was positive Jackson had sold the information to the *Insider*. I can't believe Jackson would do that. It could have been anybody. I mean, we weren't exactly quiet about our disagreements. We like to fight hard and then make up real good. Everything's OK now, I swear.'

'Well, everybody's entitled to a little bit of first-day nerves.' He handed her another Kleenex.

'Not me. I didn't just fall off the turnip truck from Hemstead, you know, I been in this business a long time. I'm real sorry I snortled all over your shirt.'

'It's OK. Lucky it wasn't wardrobe.' They both laughed. J.C. blew her nose, wadded up the Kleenex into a little ball, then looked for somewhere to throw it. Gallantly he took it from her and tossed it into the concealed trashbin under his dressing-table.

'Thanks,' she said gratefully. 'Lord, I am starving. Mac

tried to get me to eat some breakfast, but I was afraid I would puke it up.'

Brandon opened the door to the fridge. 'Help yourself.'

J.C. stared wide-eyed at the contents. 'Wow, look at all that in there. I've got an ice chest, too, but I hadn't even bothered to look inside . . . Hey, Frozen Milky Way, my absolute favorite. Is it OK if I steal one of those?'

'Go for it, girl,' Brandon laughed as she tore off the wrapping and stuffed half a bar into her mouth.

She chewed noisily and happily for what seemed like a full minute. Then she stopped and looked up at him. 'You know, you're a lot different from what I expected. You're real sweet. One hunk of a good-looking man, too. No wonder you're such a stud horse with the ladies. You can be my brother any time.'

He hardly knew how to respond to that. 'Brother?'

'That's what I call my guys out on the road, my brothers.' She took his hand and gave it a sisterly squeeze. Her touch went through him mainline direct to his groin. What the hell? She was looking at him with open admiration, but there was nothing flirtatious in her level gaze. Friendly, but down-to-earth seemed to be her approach to everything, including him. He studied her for a moment. All that red hair was fabulous, but she wasn't exactly beautiful. At least nowhere near as beautiful as most of the thousands of women he'd had in his life. Certainly she was not young. A woman, not a girl. Her face had had a life. But he was suddenly finding her amazingly sexy. Much more so in person than in her famous videos. He felt an unexpected turning in his gut. Had he finally met his match? He realized he wanted her more than any woman he'd met in his life. And he knew, just as instinctively, by the straight-forward way she was looking at him, that there was no way on earth he was ever going to have her.

THE PILOT

Chapter Ten

Ten-thirty a.m. The cast and crew gathered on soundstage six for the opening read-through of the pilot episode of Makeover. A huge room several storeys high with insulated walls, concrete floors and wooden catwalks, soundstage six looked more like a warehouse than the birthplace of a new sit-com. Grabbing donuts and coffee from the catering station, the company took their places on metal folding chairs around the long makeshift table of trestles and boards. In the stands sat row upon row of network executives, blank-faced, waiting for the show to begin, looking, as Paul Green put it, like Saddam Hussein's Republican Guard. Only Brandon Tate and J.C. Austin were missing, each of them undoubtedly planning to make a star's entrance. The rest of the cast were taking bets on which of the two would risk being last.

Julia, Marty and Alex sat at the head of the table along with unit production manager Doug Berkley, known for running a tight technical ship, and Liam Carey, who at twenty-eight was already one of the top production designers in the business and responsible for conceiving the overall design concept for Makeover, the 'look of the show'. Liam Carey was far too handsome to be behind the camera. He had dark blond hair and intense blue eyes. He looked up and saw Julia studying him. He smiled shyly and she felt a quiver go through her. Keep your mind on the business at hand, Julia ordered herself. This is a big day for you. They were surrounded by a team of assistant directors, production assistants, script supervisors, lighting technicians, the list of personnel seemed endless. Not for the first time did Julia marvel at the army of talent it took to do one half-hour of television. With the new commercial ruling, that meant only twenty-two-and-a-half minutes of script. Given that producing this pilot was budgeted at close to a million dollars, each minute represented roughly forty-four thousand, four hundred and forty-four dollars.

As Julia surveyed the cavernous room, a thrill ran through her. All these dynamic, talented people were here in this place and time because a few months ago, she had woken up in the middle of the night with an idea. After weeks of endless meetings, writing and rewriting, battles lost and won, this was it, the big day, and it was happening because of her. Looking at the actors huddled together, clutching both their CBN coffee mugs and each other for security, Julia wished there could be a cartoon thought-bubble over the actors' heads to let her know what each person was thinking.

Paul Green's funny, rubber face was twisting itself into a mass of contortions, part-excitement, part-frustration that Chaya wasn't with him in LA. He had wanted her to fly out for the week, but they'd ended up in a big argument about the Friday night taping. 'I can book us a hotel close to the studio. You can walk to the taping. I'll be the one working. All you have to do is sit there and watch. You won't be breaking the rules of Shabbat.' 'But I would lose the quality of Shabbat, the whole purpose of it,' Chaya was adamant. 'This is really important to me,' Paul begged. 'I need you with me for support.' 'If you end up doing the series, I can come and watch another time,' Chaya said. Paul didn't have the heart to tell her that as far as he knew they always taped on Friday nights. Here he was in Hollywood with his big break about to happen and the person he loved most in the world wasn't there to share it with him.

Melissa McKimmie sat, trembling with anticipation, one hand turning the pages of her script in which she had already made numerous precise and careful notes, the other nervously tugging on a strand of long red hair. Getting out of her Northwood contract in Vancouver had not been easy, and the negotiations for Makeover had been lengthy; but now here she was, a working actress in LA. There were real oranges growing on trees, it hadn't rained even one minute since they got here, and Bonnie was hardly drinking anything more than a couple of beers and a scotch before bedtime. This morning when the limo turned into the Pacific Victory lot she'd seen Jason Priestley getting out of a red sports car. He must be making a movie here somewhere right in this very building. Hollywood was so much . . . she couldn't find the right word . . . so much 'more' than Vancouver. Everything seemed bigger, brighter, faster than she was used to. It was like her normal life had vanished and she had flown into Never Never Land. Normal life, who was she kidding? Living with Bonnie, her life had never been normal. She just hoped that with Makeover at last she'd be able to fit in.

Linda Earl was praying her perfectly styled honey-blonde hair and meticulously applied make-up hid the shadows under her eyes and the pallor of her skin. She had already thrown up this morning. Did it show? Could anyone tell? Stop it. Get a grip on the situation. A nervous stomach, that's all it was. Perfectly reasonable given the stress of the first day. What if she didn't get along with J.C. Austin? Were they believable as sisters? They didn't look anything alike. Linda was beautiful. Would that cause problems if she didn't handle it right? Hadn't she been fired once before when the star of a show decided she was too much competition? She could feel her stomach turn over. Was there time to get to the bathroom before the read-through started? Oh God, not today, please not today.

Theresa Ruiz checked her lipstick in the mirror. It was a bright tomato red, her one concession to her Concha character. On the first day of rehearsal, many actors liked to wear something that suggested the character. Theresa was wearing black jeans and a black turtleneck sweater. She wanted to keep the lines between Concha, the token hot tamale, and Theresa, the seriously committed actress, distinct for as long as possible. She was pleased to see that Julia had already changed a couple of the more stereotypical lines in the pilot script. Maybe Julia was more willing to listen than most of them. Her agent, all her friends, even her mother in Miami, had given her a lecture about not being difficult and screwing up a lucrative job that would bring in *mucho dinero* for the extended family. She knew that, young as she was in this business, she had already developed a reputation for being a professional firecracker, explosive, noisy, and not always equipped with a warning. Still, she wasn't about to compromise her principles, no matter how big the deal. Sneaking a glance at the packed bleachers, it appeared the deal was *muy gordo*. This read-through was like an audience with the Pope, well, lots of Popes and – her eyes flicked over the stands, landing on Kathryn Grady – one Popess. Only one woman of power among all those men. All the staff writers who would be working with Julia were male. This was a sit-com developed by a woman, about women, aimed at women. Hmm, she could feel those little explosions going off inside her already.

Shirley Bunting sat quietly, allowing a small, gentle smile to play over her graceful, dark face. She looked alert, ready to work, but she was actually counting the minutes until this day was over. She had a dinner date with her honey, Roy, and this dinner promised to be really special. By some miracle, Roy was able to get away from home for the whole night and he was flying her to Catalina in his private plane for a discreet little dinner for two on the beach. She didn't have a whole lot to do in this first episode anyway, so why sweat it? If Shirley was forced to examine her inner sense of self-worth, she would have to acknowledge that, as far as the pool of life was concerned, she had stopped swimming full force and was starting to tread water. But Shirley didn't hold much with self-examination. So, the role of Lyla was somewhat limited? It wasn't the first time she would have to make a silk purse out of yet another big fat hog's ear. If you wanted to talk swimming, Shirley Bunting believed that the most important thing was to stay afloat.

Kelly Carmichael recognized that her role of Samantha was underwritten, too, but she was damned glad to have it. The big, buxom blonde was wearing glitzy white sweats, the smile on her face as high voltage as the sequins marching unevenly across the hills and valleys of her prodigious chest in order to spell out 'I Love Makeover'. She'd had the sweatshirt made up specially, and already it was attracting attention. Kelly's thought bubble would have read: 'This could be the breakthrough you've been waiting for, big girl. There's not a lot of Samantha. Yet. But what there is, is, is perfect for me. She's funny, she's raunchy, and just a little larger than life. Thank you, Julia Hudlow. If I look right, I think I just might be able to pull this one off.'

To Julia, they all looked perfect, a smorgasbord of

delight, her newly created Makeover family. She crossed her fingers and prayed that Alex could make them into a true ensemble cast. At the sound of spontaneous applause, she looked up to see the entrance of J.C. and Brandon. They strolled in together, arm in arm, chatting easily, already exuding the illusive, highly prized commodity known as chemistry.

'Hi folks, sorry we're late, but the lady here had to raid my fridge. She can't act on an empty stomach.' Brandon slid in next to Kelly Carmichael who promptly leaned over and gave him a smacking big kiss right on the mouth, saying, 'It's OK, gorgeous, I'm cured.' Brandon pretended to collapse on the floor and everybody laughed. Kelly's fainting fit at her callback had become an industry joke as the word spread all over town.

Alex Jordan clapped his hands together and immediately the room came to attention. 'Hello everybody,' he said, opening his arms wide, 'I'd like to give you all one big communal hug and welcome you to our new family.' He did a quick round of introductions, whipping through the myriad of names with consummate ease, and then said, 'You are about to witness the birth of a new baby, Makeover. Julia Hudlow is the proud mommy, but all of us are parents and will take part in this creation. Makeover's kind of funny and she's kind of sensitive, she's tough and she's vulnerable. She's going to need some careful nurturing, along with a little pushing and shoving to make her grow up healthy and strong so that someday she can support all her parents.' Everybody laughed.

Alex looked intently at each member of the cast. He put on his glasses and picked up the latest draft of the pilot script. 'OK, people,' he said encouragingly, 'let's see what we've got here. Now you're all brilliant and absolutely perfect for your roles or you wouldn't be here at great expense to the network. Let's have a read.' Linda Earl's stomach jumped. Brandon reached out and gave J.C.'s hand a little squeeze. Paul cleared his throat, Theresa coughed, and Shirley swallowed. Melissa bounced in her seat (just a little) and Kelly felt her heart turn over. 'This is only a read-through, but I want you to trust your instincts and give it all you've got so that we –' he nodded toward the mass of executives – 'can see if our marvelous writers have done their work. We'll skip the opening montage sequence. I'll read in the directions. J.C., your first line is cut, so just come in with, "Hi guys. Boy, do I need a change." OK, everybody settle and focus. Here we go!' He began to read, 'Fade in. Interior. The Changing Room beauty salon. Monday morning. A busy morning in the salon. The main door opens and Janine bursts in. She is late, out of breath and apologetic.'

Alex looked at J.C. The air of anticipation, excitement and tension was so thick it demanded a chainsaw. The circle of writers leaned forward. The phalanx of network and studio executives sat back. The script supervisor, Laurie, had her finger poised on the stopwatch, ready to click in with J.C.'s first word. The other actors shifted uneasily in their seats. Alex nodded encouragingly toward J.C. She cleared her throat, took a deep breath, and began to read.

THE FIRST SEASON

Chapter Eleven

'Pigs at the trough,' Tim Talbot whispered snidely to Julia as they watched the members of TCA, the Television Critics of America, swarm the lobby of the Century Plaza Hotel. Every July, print journalists from all over the country descended on LA for a press junket with all four networks as the new pilots were screened and the fall seasons unveiled. NBC, ABC, and 'the Tiffany network', CBS, each had three days to make a presentation. Now it was CBN's turn to face the TCA firing squad, and Makeover was the first show up.

Since they'd shot the pilot, the response had been nothing but good. Makeover was a hit with the head office in New York. In May, at the Upfronts, where pilots are screened for advertisers around the country, the program had received a standing ovation from a tough audience of cynical professionals looking for the best bets on which to place their fall season money. The affiliates were equally enthusiastic in June. But the reaction of the press to the pilot was the most important of all. Today would be the real test.

Marty was backstage with the cast, waiting to lead them on to the platform immediately after Stanfield King's welcoming speech. He had suggested Julia hang out with Tim for a bit to get a feel for the event before joining them. Even after six months of working fairly closely with Tim, Julia still didn't feel comfortable with him. Her natural optimism seemed continually to clash with his youthful cynicism, but there was no denying he knew the business of television inside out. Today he was wearing a subdued – for him – mauve blazer, aubergine slacks, and turquoise tie. Tim explained to her that, depending on your point of view, the TCA press tour was either one big schmooze-fest or all out war. The job of the TV critics was to shoot holes in the network's creative policy by asking tough and often embarrassing questions. The network's job was to seduce the press with parties at the LA Athletic Club Sports Bar and tours of Larry Hagman's Malibu home and Hugh Hefner's Playboy Mansion, wining and dining them into a soporific stupor that might make it a little more difficult for them to go back to their home towns and savage the fall season in print. In the beginning the networks had foot the bill for the entire junket but now, in the hopes of maintaining a modicum of professional objectivity, the newspapers covered the airfare and hotel. The city of LA was a big draw and so was the Century Plaza Hotel.

The luxurious Century Plaza, with its helicopter landing pad, sushi bar, and clocks set at LA, London, and Toyko time. The hotel of choice for both former President Ronald Reagan and the Japanese, whenever they visited Los Angeles. The main lobby, a vision of cream and brass, heavy gilt chandeliers, huge pink marble columns, marble tiled floors, French provincial furniture, with touches of the Egyptian, including a bronze head of Nefertiti on display at the main entrance. Decorated to seem light and airy, but with an echo of old-world charm, unusual for California which continued to trash the past and court the future. The Century Plaza was the perfect setting to seduce the bloodhounds of the press.

Julia followed Tim along with the pack into the Century Tower, heading for the main ballroom where the opening press conference was about to begin. The CBN logo was plastered all over every available surface, and hanging from the ceiling were large, brightly-colored balloons, each bearing the name of a CBN show. There were special screening rooms where the critics could gather to view the pilots, or they could have them piped into their suites on closed circuit TV. There were rooms full of electric typewriters, computers, Xerox and fax machines, so that the critics could file their stories daily, and pick up written transcripts of the previous day's sessions. Everywhere there were banks of telephones at which, for this presentation, notebooks and ashtrays had been set, print journalists being among the last bastion of smokers. Monitors blared promos for the new shows, and red-ribbon banners stretched wide, proclaiming the slogan for the season: CBN the hot new network! Watch our temperature rise!

Just outside the entrance to the ballroom lay a sumptuous

breakfast buffet. 'Pigs at the trough,' Tim reminded Julia *sotto voce*, noting the swarm of critics falling over each other, loading their plates with giant muffins, assorted cheeses, and a vast array of tropical fruit. Julia watched in amazement as a man, whose press pass screamed New York, precariously balanced a cup of coffee and a thick, glossy CBN press kit along with what appeared to be a pyramid of croissants and Danish. 'New Yorkers are so provincial,' Tim said just under his breath. 'We call them the "mensa crush" because they view themselves as intellectually superior. They love to be snotty about LA but honestly their manners are from the barnyard. You'd think they'd never seen food before.' He poured himself a cup of black coffee and selected a spartan slice of fresh pineapple and moved into the ballroom. Julia, too nervous to eat, grabbed a glass of freshly squeezed orange juice and trotted after him.

At eight-thirty a.m. the ballroom was already packed with press at the individual round tables, all facing the platform stage with a speaker's podium and three screens. The female journalists were dressed to the nines in suits and high heels. Most of the men still embodied Central Casting's idea of a newspaper reporter: rumpled, pudgy, and balding. The only thing missing were the ink-stained fingers, as most of their work was now done on computer. Tim and Julia took seats at the back of the hall. As head of the Network, Stan was giving the opening presentation, followed by a session with the cast of Makeover. Tim wouldn't speak until tomorrow, so today his aim was to 'hang out and get a take on the buzz'. Julia sipped her juice and listened to the chatter around them.

A bleary-eyed critic from the *Chicago Leader-Post* slammed down the lid of his miniature laptop and thumbed through a stack of paper. 'Has anyone got a fucking schedule? Or a transcript from CBS? I need everything from Tuesday on.'

'Here you go,' the charming, bearded critic from the *Calgary Herald* slid a schedule in front of him. 'Weren't you here yesterday?'

'Nope. Mind you, I'm putting in for it as far as my paper's concerned. So, if you're questioned, you can say you didn't see me, but don't say I wasn't here, OK?'

Calgary Herald raised an eyebrow. 'Don't you think it's

exciting when they start rolling out the new series?'

'Are you kidding? I haven't even seen any of the pilots this time around. Look, if you've seen one you've seen 'em all.' Chicago Leader-Post took out a silver flask and poured a shot into his coffee cup. 'Half of them will be cancelled by December anyway.'

Calgary nodded sympathetically. 'Two weeks is a long haul. It's kind of crazy sitting here watching television about television, but I actually love it. The best reason to come to these things is to get a sense of how the networks themselves view what they're presenting.'

'Hell, the best reason to come to these things is a free trip to LA!' Chicago downed his coffee in one gulp. 'I'll be filing this story from the beach.'

Julia raised an eyebrow. 'Same old crowd,' Tim sighed. With so many of the network shows 'skewing' young in order to attract a new audience, the bulk of the critics remained, as far as he could see, close to a hundred and two years old and wielding ever-increasing power. 'Most of these guys were hired in the sixties when the television beat was low on the media totem pole. Now that TV has become the biggest influence on the American public today, it would take a bulldozer to get them to let go. A few seasons back, I was sitting in this very spot, watching the critics go after the pilot for Uncle Buck. They attacked the writers for allowing a seven-year-old girl to say, "You suck." When the show aired in the fall, the offending line was gone. Uncle Buck is gone now, too. Forget the viewing public. It's TCA that can make or break your show. And this year, they're rumored to be out for blood. They've been eviscerating even the experienced producers like Aaron Spelling.'

Read the subtext as, 'So you've got a snowball's chance in hell your first time out,' Julia thought as she shivered and glanced nervously around the room. The ballroom had been transformed into a Houston country-and-western bar with knotty pine panelling, neon beer signs, sexy lighting and a live country band. Each of the members of the press had been given a Stetson hat, courtesy of Patsy Rodman of the publicity department. CBN was pushing Makeover as its signature sit-com of the new season. The whole ambience was to create the image, not of a business but of one big party. Patsy wanted to wake up the critics who were burned out after viewing over a hundred shows in ten days and who always approached the CBN presentation with a 'we've seen it all, why should we like you?' attitude. Julia wondered if the decorations were a bit much for early morning. Too reminiscent of the high school senior prom, a night in a smelly old gym? No, it looked as though the critics were buying it. They were actually wearing the cowboy hats and talking about looking forward to this evening's BBQ on the Pac Vic lot where, it was rumored, J.C. Austin herself would teach them how to two-step.

Tim nudged Julia in the ribs and pointed to a woman sitting in the front row. 'That's Kay Gardella of the *New York Daily News* and, three tables over, that's Jay Bobbins who's with Tribune Media Services. Two of the most powerful critics in the country. We call them the Jay and Kay show. Jay holds the unofficial record for the most questions asked in one session: I think it was thirty. The networks are always careful to give Kay special treatment. But wait, look over there,' Tim pointed to a woman of about fifty wearing a bright floral print shorts suit, white stockings and high heels. 'In the ass-kissing department, nobody beats the critic from the *Houston Daily Star*. Mavis Beam, as in broad-in-the . . . Talk about your Texas battle-ax.'

'I remember her,' Julia shivered. 'I grew up with the *Houston Daily Star*. It's something of a red-necked paper.'

'Right,' Tim snorted. 'Their idea of artistic license is how high you allow your hair to go.' Mavis's hair was always skyscraper bouffant, but the original color was unknown, maybe even to Mavis. This year her hair was black with a dramatic white streak in the front. 'Mavis loves to go after the networks on the "family values" thing. She's addicted to star gossip and anything about Princess Di. Watch out. Mavis Beam is a force to be reckoned with.' Tim caught Mavis's eye and gave her what he hoped was a casual wave. The lights in the ballroom suddenly dipped. 'It's showtime, Julia. You'd better scoot backstage.' Tim urged her out of her chair and gave her a shove in the right direction. He watched her go, wondering if this tiny, red-headed woman really had what it took to write and produce a hit TV show. Well, only time would tell.

The band let loose with a drum roll, and the room went into darkness as up on the platform screens appeared a black and white video done in the style of the old Movietone News, announcing CBN's fall season. This segued into a pulsating color promo video, full of quick cuts and pounding music, more like MTV. There was another drum roll and the leader of the band called out, 'Here he is, the head honcho himself, the King of CBN, Stanfield King!' A follow spot picked up Stan as he loped on to the stage, wearing a slate-blue Hollywood power suit, narrow-collared white shirt and red striped tie, a pearl-gray Stetson balanced precariously on his head. 'Welcome friends and foes. I have new respect for you guys. You know I get paid big bucks to listen to pitches and watch TV, but you couldn't pay me enough to sit in a hotel room and do it for two and a half weeks straight. Talk about torture!' The critics laughed and Stan immediately jumped into a high-fevered pitch. 'Last year I stood here and told you the bad news, that network TV was in trouble because cable was siphoning off network programming. Some of that is still true. It's like a game of chicken between the networks and cable. But this year there's some good news, because CBN has finally joined the game. For the past season, we've been programming seven nights a week, just like the big boys. CBN is no longer the new kid on the block. We're a primetime player. We belong in the network line. And what we're aiming for is to be at the head of that line by the end of this season. We're not scared of cable. We're not scared of the other networks. We're going to concentrate on bringing you the hottest programming ever seen on national TV. And we're saying to the other guys, "If you can't stand our heat, get out of our kitchen!" ' The band played a fanfare while Tim and other members of the CBN staff cheered and whistled. Stan proceeded to tick off the successes of the past season, neatly avoiding the failures, then trumpeting his plans for the future.

Tim settled back in his chair and tried to assess the performance of his boss. The old guy was good when it came to showmanship and pizazz but now, as he began to talk about ratings and shares and demographics while a series of complicated charts and graphs were brought up on the screens, Tim could feel the attention of the critics beginning to flag. They didn't want a lesson in the business of television. They wanted to meet the stars. They wanted the dirt, the blood. Who was already causing trouble on the set? Who was sleeping with whom? Who was gay and who was ferociously straight? That was all that interested their readers and, if the truth be known, that was what interested these critics, too. Enough with the numbers already. You're putting them all to sleep.

The lights came up and Stan took questions from the floor. The critics were all over him. How could he possibly think he could go from number four to number one in a season? Where did he get off thinking he could show the fat cats how to do it? What about sex and violence? What about family values? Stan was squirming in the hot seat. Throat dry. Consonants popping in the microphone. Licking his lips and clearing his throat. Taking a sip of water before he answered a difficult question to allow himself some thinking time, knowing every missed cue would be reported the next day in the national press. Stan slipped and made a vaguely sexist remark. Whoops, way to go, Stan. The protofeminist knives would be out for that one. Face it, Stan was old news. Tim knew that. But how soon would Stan realize it? More to the point, how soon would Charles Currie realize it? Silently Tim raised an imaginary pistol and shot Stanfield King right between the eyes.

Patsy Rodman slid in next to Stan at the podium and whispered in his ear. 'Oh yes,' he nodded. 'We have a very special treat for you this morning. J.C. Austin is the star of our next presentation, Makeover. We were really lucky to score her for this series because, as you all know, J.C. is so hot right now, she's just about on fire. And here she is to sing for you the theme from Makeover, ladies and gentlemen, J.C. Austin!'

The lights went down and a spotlight picked up J.C. wearing a black body suit and sequined jacket, her red hair like a fiery halo blazing in the hot light. 'What Do You Make Over Me?' had grown from a torchy ballad to a driving, up-tempo number. The opening credit sequence to the Makeover pilot flashed by on all the screens as J.C. sang her guts out, strutting across the stage in her trademark red boots, flirting with the audience, playing with heart and groin, until they stood *en masse* and applauded for a full five minutes. Finally the lights came up and Julia led Marty and the rest of the cast up on to the stage. The only one missing was Linda Earl. Stomach flu, her manager had said. Something not quite right there. Flashbulbs were popping all around them as they sat down and their individual names appeared on the screens. The actors were visibly nervous.

The network had ordered thirteen episodes; they were to start shooting next week. Still, depending upon the reaction here today, there was always the chance that one of the actors could yet be replaced. It had been known to happen. Exposed on a brightly lit platform stage, they stared into the faceless dark, as questions were shouted at them. Julia looked small, pale, vulnerable. Tim prayed she would remember his advice. 'Never refuse to answer any question. If you do, the critics will hound you. Find something positive to say. It's going to feel like we've thrown you to the wolves. Think survival mode. If Makeover hits big, you'll be facing a lot of this.'

Lining each side of the ballroom were uniformed ushers who each held a microphone ready to leap in when a critic raised his hand, rush to his side, kneel down, and hold out the mic so a question could be asked. The questions were so fast and furious it was difficult to identify where they were coming from. Tim could almost visualize how the Makeover session would appear in tomorrow's transcript.

Q: For the producers, specifically Ms Hudlow-Turgov, from your bio material, I gather you consider yourself a feminist. How do you reconcile that with creating a show which features make-up and hair?

JULIA: Well, first of all, I'm a man-loving feminist . . .

MARTY: Does that make me a woman-loving chauvinist?

JULIA (laughing): No, no, that doesn't sound right. Let's forget the name calling. I write strong female characters. That's what I've created for Makeover. The outside trappings are there to make it fun. That's why it's called the entertainment business.

Q: Julia, honey. (A drawling Texas voice.)

JULIA: Where are you?

Q: Over here, to your left. Why set the show in Houston?

JULIA: Why not? Afraid I'll reveal all your secrets? Sorry, Mavis. You know I'm from Houston; I thought it would be fun to present a city that hasn't been done to death.

Q: So how come you've got accents that are all over the southern map?

JULIA: Mavis, as a southerner, doesn't it tick you off that when a show is set in the south, they give every single person in it a cornpone accent? Like as soon as you cross that Mason-Dixon line, it's a license to be Gomer Pyle. You and I know Houston's a cosmopolitan city and we want Makeover to reflect that. For instance, Paul Green is from New York and we're acknowledging that in the show.

Q: J.C., J.C., over here in left field. I loved you in the pilot, but you're primarily a singer. Are you just playing yourself?

BRANDON (leaping in): No, she's not. Take a look at today's *New York Times* crossword. 'Eight across, country singer turned actress.' The correct answer is J.C. Austin. When the *New York Times* says you're an actress, it's got to be true.

JULIA: Some of the best TV shows take a real personality and create around them. J.C. Austin is a personality so we will be writing specifically for her.

Q (pointedly): My question was for you, J.C.

J.C. (speaking up for the first time): Boy, I get the feelin' if I say the wrong thing, y'all'll skin me for rabbit stew. (Laughter.) Just look at you, starin' at me like 'show us what you got.' All I can tell you is I campaigned real hard to get on this show. I bribed Julia with a dozen jars of my homemade, hickory-smoked barbecue sauce. A woman in love knows no shame and I am in love with the character of Janine. I hope y'all are, too.

At the back of the ballroom, Tim could barely make out the figure of J.C.'s husband, Mac, skulking in the shadows ready to defend his wife from attack. This guy was going to be trouble. Second only to Melissa McKimmie's mom, Bonnie the Barracuda. Why couldn't all actors be single and orphaned? It would make Tim Talbot's job a hell of a lot easier.

Q: Brandon Tate, straight ahead, home plate . . .

BRANDON: Did I miss something? What's all this baseball terminology flying around here? (Laughter.)

Q: Why do you think your last film bombed?

BRANDON: Nice question. Are you into S and M?

135

Or do you represent the *Hollywood Insider*? (Laughter.) First of all, it got great reviews. You guys loved it. You're right, though, nobody came to see it. The public resists change. As an artist, you have to embrace change. Otherwise you die.

Tim had seen all this before, when he was working as a trainee with cable TV. Watching actors back pedal as they tried to whitewash defeat as 'artistic growth'. Seeing the producers sweat, trying to defend why they weren't on the fall schedule, but were being held in the wings as maybe a mid-season replacement. So much history on this tour, in this room, littered with the ghosts of failed pilots, the strong smell of broken dreams mixed with the faint scent of new hope. The hope that people might rearrange their lives to stay home and watch a TV show, their show. Yet with Makeover, the scent of hope was growing stronger by the minute. At least they were laughing at all the jokes. That was a good sign.

Q: Brandon, are you the sex symbol for the show?
BRANDON: What are you doing for dinner tonight? (Laughter.) Seriously, I didn't sign on to play a Bubba stereotype. I like women a lot, you all know that. But we won't be pushing anything macho with my relationships.
Q: In the pilot, you seem to already have your eye on Janine. In what direction is the relationship between these two characters going to go?
BRANDON: You mean, a horizontal direction? (Laughter.) Well, a man can dream, can't he? (Slow smile.)
JULIA (stepping in): We have no plans for romance. We want to develop a real friendship between a man and a woman. You don't often see that on television.
Q: Question for Paul Green. Are you going to keep doing stand-up? Usually when a comedian gets a series, that's it, they never perform live again.
PAUL: I'm staying on the circuit. I think one will feed the other. Course now I walk out on stage and the audience has heard I'm working with J.C. Austin so they expect to see her up there with me. The women expect Brandon Tate to be there, too. They're hoping

to get a look at Brandon's butt.

J.C.: Yeah, he does have a cute little butt, doesn't he? (Applause.) Kevin Costner, watch out. (Whistles and cheers.)

Q: Melissa McKimmie, do you like being on TV?

MELISSA (shyly): I love it. I really feel like J.C.'s daughter. We've got the same hair, eh? Oh crumbs, I can't believe I said 'eh'. Now you all know I'm Canadian.

Q: Question for Kelly Carmichael. I loved you in the pilot. As Samantha, you're kind of an off-the-wall babe. Is that acting or is that you?

KELLY: Is it real or is it Memorex? (Laughter.) An off-the-wall babe. Thanks, I think. Could you leave your phone number on the wall in the washroom for me? I'm not sure who the real me is. Every inch of this fabulous body is manufactured. I'm living proof of the success of Makeover.

PAUL (interrupting): You know Julia doesn't really have to write. We could just let Kelly talk.

The room was rocking with laughter. Tim was relieved. The questions were coming thick and fast and the cast, relaxed to the point of euphoria, was expertly fielding them all. Shirley Bunting was asked if, with the number of all-black shows, she felt like a token on Makeover. Shirley said that all-black shows presented an unreal picture. 'I have white friends, I have African-American friends. My life is not segregated.' Tim held his breath when Theresa Ruiz was asked if the character of Concha was there to attract the Hispanic audience, but Theresa smoothly endorsed the party line that the diversity on the show reflected the diversity of real life. They were doing so well that Tim was almost disappointed when he saw Patsy giving the signal to wind things up with a final question.

Q: Julia, the pilot made me laugh a lot but you really got me in the end when you had Janine sing that little bit of a song on her own. I literally found myself in tears, crying at a sit-com. Will there be more singing for J.C.?

Stan swept on to the stage and said smoothly, 'Tune in and

find out. That's the end of our formal session. You're welcome to stick around and do some "individuals" if you like. Just remember, Makeover is going to make Saturday nights on CBN the place to be.'

Tim helped Stan, Marty and Julia down off the platform and they stood together in a corner as the members of the press rushed the stage, heading straight for the stars. They crowded around J.C. and Brandon, snapping pictures, shoving tape recorders into their faces, trying to get an exclusive sound bite for the folks back home. Paul had launched into an impromptu stand-up routine that had everybody laughing. Tim gave Julia and Marty a conspiratorial high sign. 'Good work, kids. You've got the critics on your side. Now the real work can begin.' Julia nodded, relieved, proud of her Makeover family. But then another stone sank in her stomach. Would they make it through their first season? Would the show be a success? How many of the people in this room would still be here when the July press tour rolled around again?

Chapter Twelve

'We're a hit. Just look at these reviews.' Julia plopped a huge pile of newspapers down on top of Marty who lay in bed, still snuggling under the covers.

'Jules, we've been on the air for a month. You've got to stop this thing of staying up all night waiting for the reviews.'

'I haven't been up all night. I got up early and went out to get the papers. It's almost six o'clock and we have to be on the set by eight-thirty anyway.' Marty groaned. 'No, wait, listen to this.' Julia started to read the headlines of the reviews from the TV columns in the stack of newspapers. '"Putting A New Face On Comedy, Makeover A Change For The Better": *LA Times*. "Sparkling New Sit-Com Makes Over Tired Television": *USA Today*. "CBN Moving Up With Makeover Cit-com": *Daily Variety*. Even the *New York Times* calls us "the brightest spot in an otherwise spotty season." '

'Don't count your hits before they've hatched,' grumbled Marty. 'We've still got a long way to go yet.'

'But we've already come so far so quickly. Remember, Tim told us that for a new show you get most of your audience within the first three viewings? Makeover's aired four episodes and our ratings are continuing to climb.' As headliner of the CBN fall season, Makeover had premiered with great fanfare in late September, and was immediately greeted with rapturous reviews.

'Pretty amazing, considering we're in the death slot,' Marty continued to grumble.

'I know. I was sure Saturday would be suicidal.' Neither of them could figure out why Makeover had been scheduled for eight o'clock on Saturday night, the low-viewing night of the week. The wrong time-slot could kill a show, but Tim kept assuring them that people, especially female viewers, were more open to something new on the weekend, that Saturday had a different feel to it, less pressured, more relaxed. 'There is no easy time period out there,' he told them. 'Trust me. I know what I'm doing.' So far he seemed to be right. The ratings were climbing to the point which suggested that more than a few people stuck at home washing their hair had to be watching the show.

'This is so exciting.' Julia bounced up and down on the bed. 'I wake up in the morning and my creative juices are already flowing. I can't wait to get on the set and watch the actors become the characters I've created, hear them say the lines that I wrote. When the audience laughs at the Friday night taping, I'm laughing right along with them, and I have to remind myself that, hey, they're laughing because of me. God, it's heaven.'

'I think it's hell,' Marty groaned again. 'I'd forgotten how much pressure there is to doing a series. It's like going straight from the Korean Conflict to the Vietnam War to Operation Desert Storm. It never lets up. The actors work a couple of weeks and then they get a week off. You and I are already working seventy hours a week and we don't get any weeks off. No time to do laundry, shop for groceries or pet the cat. Since the show got on the air, we've hardly made love at all.'

'Aw, poor baby, are you feeling deprived?'

'Yeah,' Marty made a little whimpering sound. 'I kind of wish you'd share some of those creative juices with me.'

Julia glanced at the clock on the bedside table. Six thirty-five. Give it a good twenty minutes. Hop in the shower. Blow dry her hair. Jump in the car. Half an hour on the freeway. She and Marty could be in Burbank in plenty of time, no sweat. She lifted her arms in an extravagant gesture, peeling off her T-shirt in one swift move. Naked, she climbed on top of her husband and dangled a neatly curved breast tantalizingly close to his lips. 'Can you think of something interesting to do with this?' she said softly.

'Hmm . . .' Marty's mouth closed greedily around the already hardening nipple.

'Oh shit,' Julia suddenly yanked it away.

'What is it? What's the matter?' Marty sat up, alarmed.

'I forgot to read you one of those newspapers.'

'Later,' Marty reached to pull her down again.

'No, this is serious. I think we may have a real problem here. For some reason, the *Hollywood Insider* is out to get J.C. Austin.'

'J.C. AUSTIN CAN'T ACT.'
MAC SAYS, 'I TOLD YOU SO.'

J.C. AUSTIN, America's Queen of Country Music, has been forgetting her lines, bumping into the furniture, and falling apart on the set of her new CBN sit-com, Makeover.

A source close to the thirty-six-year-old singing star says the season has only just begun and already J.C. is showing signs of stress.

'J.C.'s a singer not an actress,' the insider says. 'She's finding it hard to be on the set every day with the long hours of rehearsal. She's not used to the pressure of TV.'

Touted by CBN as its signature show of the new fall season, Makeover co-stars Brandon Tate, big screen sex symbol, and popular stand-up comic, Paul Green, who are there to give J.C. Austin plenty of support.

According to the source, that's part of the problem.

'Everybody on the show has more acting experience, even TV newcomer, Kelly Carmichael, who plays make-up artist Samantha, and Theresa Ruiz, who has the smallest role on the show, Concha the receptionist. They're all so good they make J.C. look bad. Especially when it's supposed to be her show. To make things worse, J.C.'s pushing herself too hard to keep up with her supporting cast. She's even losing her voice.'

The popular singer has often been plagued in the past by 'Vegas throat' and apparently her laryngitis has returned to haunt her as she tries to cross over from a mega-successful singing career into the world of TV sit-com.

An eyewitness on the set said last week production ground to a halt when J.C. burst into tears and ran into her dressing-room trailer. 'She couldn't remember any of her lines. She's got little pieces of paper all over the set to remind her of what she's supposed to say, but nothing seems to help.' There may be a simple explanation for that. According to a source, 'Most everybody knows J.C. Austin grew up poor in the backwater piney woods of east Texas. She never finished high school. Her big secret, one only her closest friends know, is that J.C. Austin can't read.'

The source adds, 'Manager-husband Mac Austin was against his wife doing a series, but J.C. was determined to change her life. She has put her heart and soul into Makeover. If the show fails, it could be a major blow to both her career and her marriage.'

Susan Carroll

Chapter Thirteen

J.C. Austin felt like a gopher in the middle of the highway. Too frightened to go back and unable to make it to the other side. Frozen. Out there in plain view. Just waiting for a great big old eighteen-wheeler to come along and run her right over and turn her into a road rug.

Everybody on the show was being patient, but how long would that last? Alex Jordan, the director, spent hours with her, and Julia was behind her every step of the way, but it had to be a drag for the rest of their cast, hanging around on the set while Alex explained, once again, what she was supposed to do. They all must think she was really stupid, but shoot, they made acting look so easy. When it was her turn, she felt stiff and awkward. She never had that problem onstage, singing in front of thousands of people, but on this small, cramped set, with the crew, the designer, the team of writers, and often a bunch of network executives watching her every move, she just couldn't seem to put one foot right. It was, to borrow a phrase from her late grandpa, 'pure d. hell'.

And the pressure never let up. There was no chance to relax or let her guard down for even a moment. Every single minute of the day was important because every single minute was leading up to the taping in front of a live audience on Friday night. Usually she was great with an audience, but by the time Friday rolled around, she was so rattled by the whole week that she didn't know if she was coming or going.

How could she be forgetting lines? It was crazy. She never had any trouble remembering the lyrics to songs, even songs she hadn't sung for eighteen years, songs from her first album. Mind you, she'd written most of those words. These were somebody else's words and they felt strange and lumpy in her mouth, like a mixture of mashed potatoes and peas. Plus there were rewrites every day. After the read-through on Monday, she'd go straight home and Mac would drill her on her lines all night long. First thing on Tuesday, soon as she walked in the door, she'd be handed new script pages, based on the network response to the first read-through! Whatever got big laughs stayed in. No response, the line was out. It was like that all week long. No use blaming Stan and Tim. Julia was a perfectionist. Always 'improving' the script. Every day there were new pages, each set in a different color – blue, pink, yellow – so you wouldn't get them mixed up with the old pages. At the dinner break before the Friday night taping, sitting in the make-up chair, getting her make-up done, she'd try to stomach a little chicken soup while the hairdresser did her hair. She complained to Mac, 'I've eaten more hair over the last few months. I'm sittin' there and they hand me another set of new pages. Pink this time! Right before I have go out and face a real live audience.' Paul Green called the Friday script true Jackson Pollock, whatever that meant. To her it looked like one psychedelic rainbow. At night she dreamed of pages upon pages of script, all full of lines that made no sense to her, speeches leading nowhere, scenes she'd never heard of. 'The actor's nightmare,' Brandon reassured her. 'All actors have it. I'm onstage in some unknown play, I'm naked, and I don't know the lines. That means you're beginning to think like an actor.'

Sure. Right. That's when she started putting the really tricky dialogue on little yellow Post-it notes and sticking them all over the Changing Room set: on Kelly's make-up table, in the corner of one of the sinks, behind one of the hairdryers. As if she could even read them once the taping got going! Well, hell, at least it made her feel better knowing they were there where she could reach out and put her hand on them for comfort. She felt like she was buried in sand and there were plenty of shit-disturbers hanging out on the beach just ready to throw more shovels of dirt her way. Last week, it all got so bad she burst into tears right there on the soundstage and confessed to everybody she was dyslexic. The next thing she knew the *Hollywood Insider* was accusing her of being illiterate. It was so unfair. Talking to Mac didn't help. He'd just get upset for her and say they didn't appreciate their star, she was too good for them all, he'd have to come down to the set and punch a few folks out, wave his gun around, smarten them up a bit, which was the last thing she wanted. To his credit, and contrary to what the *Hollywood Insider* claimed, he never once said I told you so, even though she swore she could see the words hanging there, right on the tip of his tongue. What he did say, was to stop letting on how insecure she was. 'Everybody doesn't have to know your private business. Keep your distance from the rest of the cast. You're up to your ass in alligators, girl. If they smell blood, they'll be crawling all over you. They want to see you fail. Don't you dare give them the satisfaction.'

She knew he was right, but darn it, it was hard to hold her poker hand close to her chest and keep it all in, when her natural impulse was to let it all out, so here she was again, sitting in her dressing-room, crying like a baby, surrounded by Julia and Marty and Alex all trying to get her to go back on to the soundstage and finish the scene.

Julia put her arm around her. 'J.C., they're just words on paper. It's up to you to make them your own.'

'How?'

'Put yourself out there. Take a risk.'

'I don't even know how to start.'

'Look, love,' Alex said in his clipped British accent. 'It's basic acting 101. Put yourself in the situation. What if? That's all acting is. What if Mac died and you were on your own, a widow like Janine? You started out as a hairdresser. What if you'd never written that first song? What if you were still a hairdresser? And the Changing Room were a real salon?'

'I couldn't work in this salon.'

'Why not?' Marty asked suspiciously.

'It looks like a set. You wouldn't find a beauty parlor like this in a shopping mall, not in this part of Houston, it's too fancy. And the salon's not laid out right. Not for-real. Any beautician watching this show is gonna know it, too. In a good salon, the sinks would never be that close to the dryers. I'd need more counter space, real running water . . .' The words flew out of her. She could feel Julia's hand gripping her shoulder hard and Alex's mouth was hanging open. Was she going too far? Hell, she didn't care. If there was one thing she still knew about, it was hair. She finished up, breathless, 'If you're gonna do it, you better do it right.' The room was so quiet you could hear a bobby pin drop. Then Marty nodded sharply. 'I see. Right. Julia, Alex, let's go.' And the three of them marched out.

Shoot. She'd really done it now. Brandon stuck his head inside the trailer. 'What's up, Tiger Lily?'

'I just trashed the set. Really pissed Marty off. They'll probably fire me now. Oh, Brandon, I don't know diddly squat about this acting thing, I admit that, and now I've got the *Hollywood Insider* on my butt about how I can't even read and write!'

'Hey,' Brandon was beside her in a flash. 'Nobody's getting fired. Alex just called a break so we can all cool down.'

'That picture in the *Insider* makes me look like a midget halfwit. Where the hell did they get that?'

'Paparazzi. I call them the slimerazzi. They lie in wait to snap you when you're looking your worst. They've probably got choppers flying over your estate in Nashville.'

'Shoot. Now the cast is starting to hate me. I just wish a great big hand would come down out of the sky and forklift me right out of here.'

'You're being pretty rough on yourself. Remember, it's your first time out of the gate.'

'I have no idea whether I'm funny or not. It's all so hard,' J.C. wailed.

'Well, sure, haven't you heard? "Dying is easy, comedy is hard." '

J.C. managed a little laugh. 'I'm so confused. Julia and Alex keep telling me to take risks. Mac's warning me not to make a fool of myself. I don't know who's right.'

'Well,' he put his arms around her and held her close. 'You have to develop this "extra eye" as an actor, so that all the time you're out there taking those risks, this third eye knows everything you're doing. Julia's right, you have to let go, but at the same time, you have to remember all the technical details. You're ninety-seven per cent in the moment, but that other three per cent of you, your third eye, is making sure you hit your marks. It lets you go not too far, but far enough. Understand?'

'Yeah,' J.C. nodded slowly. 'In a weird way, I kind of do. But the *Insider*'s right, I can't read that great. Sometimes I see a word and I panic 'cause I don't recognize it. Ask me to spell it, I'm fine.'

'Julia writes from reality. If you come to something you

can't read, just close your eyes and imagine what Janine would say next. Nine times out of ten, I'll bet that's what Julia has written. If you panic, you won't remember your line, but if you stop and think, it'll come to you because with a good script one line follows the next, OK?'

'OK,' she said gratefully.

'Remember when we shot the pilot? And you asked for my help?'

'Boy, March, that seems like years ago. Or yesterday. I don't know which. Feels like we've been doing this for ever.'

'I know. Television compresses and elongates time. Anyway, I'd be happy to give you some coaching on the side.'

'Would you really?' J.C. looked up at him.

'Sure. I'll be your third eye. Until you find it yourself. And I know you will.' He gave her a little squeeze.

'From your mouth to God's ear, brother.' She sighed. 'You know, I think part of the problem is that I don't really feel like Janine yet. I still feel like me.'

'That's not so bad. J.C. Austin is a very special lady, don't you forget that. Makeover has got a strong cast, but you're the one the viewers are tuning in to watch.'

'And you.' She squeezed him back.

'Right. That's what being a star means. You watch someone year after year and what they are winds up being on the screen. It has to.'

J.C. looked at him with genuine admiration. 'You know, you're not just another pretty face. You're one smart guy.'

Brandon smiled, but his voice was stern, 'Mac's right about one thing, it is time for you to get tough. That doesn't mean hiding yourself away from the rest of us but, as Julia says, you got to put yourself out there. It is your delightful little ass that's on the line. Along with mine. The ratings aren't suffering because of your lack of experience, but you are. You're letting it get to you and if you don't pull yourself together, you may not make it through the season. You'll have no one to blame but yourself.'

'I love it when you talk tough to me,' J.C. said with a laugh. 'I don't know what it is about you, but every time you come around, I just feel real good. That's a rare trait in a man.'

'Well then, you'll have to let me come around more often.' His arms tightened around her.

148

'Whoa, Brandon, don't you go putting the moves on me now. Practise on somebody else. You and me, we're friends, that's all.' She pulled herself away. There was a pounding outside the room; it sounded like the walls were coming down around them. A deafening hammering, the sound of a chainsaw, it was coming from outside the room. They got up, ran out of the trailer, and toward the sound.

On the soundstage, as the rest of the cast stood and watched, pieces of the set were coming down around them. 'Holy shit,' J.C. grabbed on to Brandon. 'What did I tell you? It's game over.' Julia and Marty were coming toward them, with Liam Carey, the set designer, in tow. Her stomach flip-flopped. They were smiling.

'We decided you were right,' Julia said. 'I gave Tim a call and he's authorized the rebuilding of the set to your specifications. We want the Changing Room to look authentic. We want you to feel at home here.'

J.C. looked at the warm, sympathetic faces around her. The business side of her knew that right about now they would probably do anything to keep her on the show because if she went down the tubes, their jobs would go right along with her. But she had to admit, tearing down the set was a pretty extravagant gesture of faith in her. She couldn't let these people down. They were counting on her.

Over the next couple of months, under Brandon's coaching, J.C.'s confidence grew and, little by little, the work got easier. She began to open her heart to the company and they, in turn, gave her the support and protection she needed. Kelly Carmichael urged her to fight the *Hollywood Insider* by going public about her dyslexia. Julia joined with her and together they gave an exclusive story to one of the rival tabs, *Star Weekly*. This time the headline read, 'Dyslexic Does Not Mean Illiterate. Makeover Gals Succeed Despite Reading Problem.' Other industry stars, like Tom Cruise and Steve Bochco, announced they, too, were dyslexic. Letters poured in from all over the country as fans expressed their gratitude to J.C for bringing the problem out into the open.

Mac loved her, but he wasn't always right about everything. People didn't want to see her fail. They wanted her to succeed. And after all, it was her show. Maybe it was time she started acting like it.

Chapter Fourteen

In the beginning, Paul missed New York even more than Chaya did. 'As far as I'm concerned, I live in New York, I work in LA. I'll always be a New Yorker.' He felt he'd signed his life away and, for the next five years, he had. Of course he could be dropped from the series at any time, but he wasn't even allowed to read for other projects without getting permission from the producers. The first couple of weeks he had off, he flew the whole family back east for a hit of the 'Big Dirty'. 'My body is used to germs and dirt. I can't take all this clean.'

Even with the five-year commitment, he wasn't ready to hammer down stakes. They were renting. He had no respect for young actors who got a hit series, became the flavor of the month, and immediately bought into the Hollywood lifestyle: a lifestyle that was, he had to agree with Chaya, all about discarding the past. What was the point of buying the W.C. Fields estate if you then razed it to the ground and built something completely new? The conspicuous consumption of LA, the sheer waste all around him, disgusted him. In New York, sure there were rich and poor, but at least on the surface, the disparity wasn't so blatant. New York was full of hidden treasures. You could walk into an apartment building on fifty-sixth, one that looked like all the other buildings on the street – old, shabby, run-down – and discover an indoor garden with a skylight rising straight up through the center of it. The apartments inside were full of antiques and *objets d'art*, but you'd never know it from the outside. In LA, the display of wealth was even more important than the having of it. Everything had to be spectacular. Even the natural setting – the mountains, the ocean, the sunsets – was just that little bit overdone, like the early technicolor movies of the fifties. Dazzling tropical flowers, grass such a bright, unreal shade of green it almost hurt the eyes, and palm trees. Come on! Palm trees belonged only in a Club Med commercial. Civilized people did not live among palm trees.

Each neighborhood with its huge, sprawling, beautifully landscaped homes, seemed more magnificent than the next. Beverly Hills, Beverly Glen, Bel Air, Santa Monica by the sea, it was all Paradise. Paradise with a price. The vast expanse of manicured lawns with sprinklers gently misting over them, the banks of vibrant flowers, the gardenia bushes and magnolia trees bathed in a glow of the hazy southern California sun, it all looked so inviting. As if to say, 'Hi there, come on in.' Of course if you set even one toe on any of these properties, all sorts of World War II alarm bells and sirens would immediately go off. It took Paul a couple of weeks before he realized that Wes Tech was not running for public office. The Wes Tech signs stuck in virtually every yard indicated the top security system necessary to protect these mansions. The whole thing reminded Paul of the famous painting in the Winter Palace in Leningrad, the one depicting the peasant soldiers breaking into the palace of the Czars and seeing, for the first time, the splendour in which their rulers lived. No wonder there was a Russian Revolution. No wonder there were riots in LA.

As much as Paul disliked the town, he loved the work. He was addicted to showbiz, especially comedy. As a kid, he'd loved the comedy routines of Newhart, Cosby, Wayne and Schuster, and watched with envy the rise of the hip new comics like Belushi and Aykroyd, Martin Short and Jerry Seinfeld. Forget law school. This was what he wanted to do. 'I had to become a comic,' he joked. 'I'm not fit for anything else. I got fired from every day job I ever had. I'm a night person. I only come out after dark, like the werewolf.'

Now he had the ultimate day job, a TV sit-com. It meant that he had to get up at six in the morning for the long drive into Burbank, where the days might last until six p.m., except on Friday when the live taping could run until ten or eleven o'clock at night. But he didn't care. The minute he stepped on to soundstage six at Pacific Victory studios, he felt at home.

After years of doing stand-up, in semi-isolation, on the road, alone, going back to an empty hotel room, it felt good

151

to be part of a team. And what a team this was! He had a lot of respect for director Alex Jordan. Before moving into television, this guy had directed theatre, Broadway, with some of the greats. Hoffman, Duvall, de Niro, even Robin Williams, all doing Shakespeare and Beckett. Julia Hudlow was a talented writer and he was developing a good rapport with her husband Marty. Given the difference between west coast and east coast Jews, they actually had a lot in common. Politics that veered to the left. A wry, self-deprecating sense of humor. An ironic way of looking at the world. Marty and Julia were a terrific team, on the set every day, making sure things were running smoothly and that the cast was treated well. A great cast. J.C. Austin had gotten over her initial star trip, although her Husband Hulk was often there lurking in the background. Mac hadn't liked the scene where Troy flirted with Janine. Not to worry. Paul sensed that things were heating up in the Janine/Travis love stakes which meant that he'd have fewer scenes with J.C. and Brandon would have more.

Brandon Tate. A little tension there. Not sure why. Except that Brandon was part of that whole male macho competitive thing Paul had done his best to avoid for most of his life. He respected Brandon's tremendous talent, but they had different approaches to the work, that was all. Paul came out of the improvisational tradition, SCTV, Saturday Night Live. Julia wrote terrific dialogue but for Paul, that was just a jumping-off point. He could go off on a tangent and wing it. The cast and crew would be in stitches. Alex would urge Julia to keep it in and often she would agree, which seemed to piss off Brandon no end. Brandon called him 'New York', which, at least in the way he said it, implied some sort of eastern intellectual Method snobbism which was just not true. Of course Paul called Brandon 'the Cowboy', because of all the action buddy pictures he'd done in which climbing a mountain or leaping from a burning building took the place of real acting.

Probably Brandon was feeling a little threatened with all the fan mail Paul was getting. Paul Green, hip? Trendy? Sexy? Pretty funny for a guy who couldn't get a date in high school. No, Brandon Tate was just a teensy fly in the whole bowl of schmaltz. Paul was happy. He was finally beginning to taste his dreams. Along with a heady hit of financial freedom. He had the money now to fly members of his and

Chaya's family out to LA. Even their next-door neighbors in New York, Max and Ruth Gottlieb, had come out for a visit. Paul missed his friends and family back in New York but for him, LA was definitely where it was happening.

Precisely because they didn't have family here, Chaya was determined to immerse herself as deeply as possibly into the LA Jewish community. She was surprised to learn that LA has the second largest Jewish population of any city in the world and a climate which, according to the Third Jewish Catalog, was 'similar to that of Eretz Yisrael, enabling the Jewish Angeleno to begin to praise God for rain at the same time that the rainy season begins in Israel, just after Sukkot'.

There were a number of Jewish areas in the city they could choose to live, but Chaya was drawn to Detroit Street, an older neighborhood south of Melrose, that had a graceful old-world charm about it. Spanish-style architecture, stucco, wrought iron, red-tiled roofs, turrets, and wooden balconies, looking like Jewish centers in Sephardic Spain from centuries past, full of mystery and romanticism. There were a few of the ubiquitous palm trees, but many more eucalyptus and Mediterranean pine. Bearded men walked the street in dark suits, long coats and hats. Some of the little boys sported peyas, the side curls, and some of the women wore luxuriant, human hair wigs. They had their choice of synagogues, all within walking distance, and a number of reputable day schools for the children. It would be just as easy to live an observant life in LA as in New York, and the climate, the mountains, the sea, the desert, were reminiscent of the places where 'our ancestors first met their God'. 'I don't know if I'd want to live in this neighborhood for ever,' Paul voiced a tentative objection but, seeing the glow in Chaya's eyes, he agreed it was an interesting contrast to the plastic side of Hollywood.

Chaya felt more comfortable not working here, too. In LA even women outside the Jewish community were choosing to stay at home and either run their businesses out of their houses or focus on the job of parenting. Very quickly she became involved in the Jewish Community Foundation and Family Service. She needed to be around other obser- vant Jews to feel part of something, the way she could see Paul was becoming part of Makeover. Being married to an instant celebrity was not what she'd bargained for. As a stand-up comic back in New York, with the occasional guest appearance on Saturday Night Live, Paul was rarely recognized on the street. Overnight all that had changed. She tried not to let it bother her, but her own privacy was something she treasured. She didn't like drawing attention to herself. 'The light of the King's daughter shines within.'

Now they couldn't go anywhere without being mobbed. Strangers stopped him on the street to ask his advice about what film to buy, which lens to use on their cameras, as if he really were a photographer and not simply playing one. Chaya had heard this happened to actors who played doctors, but a sit-com photographer? Whose photography 'studio' looked patently fake? What did these people want? They wanted to touch him, shake his hand, even kiss him. He was married to her, but it was as if she didn't exist. Woman after woman sent him letters, describing in graphic terms exactly what she would like to do to him, often enclosing a bit of hair, hopefully from her head! Paul kept saying, 'Actors are nothing without their fans. They make you and they can unmake you. Be cool. They're paying their money.' He probably thought she was jealous, but it wasn't that. It was the daily invasion of their privacy that bothered her.

Last week, the car broke down and they had to take a bus to the Hebrew bookstore on Fairfax. They were sitting in the back of the bus, having a quiet but intense argument, one of those that started in a whisper and then quickly rose to full volume. Two silver-haired ladies sitting across from them just wouldn't stop staring. Finally Paul, forgetting who and where he was, screamed at them, 'What are you staring at?' They beamed back, 'We just want to tell you how much we love you on Makeover.' Paul was public property now and, basically, he loved it. Chaya hated the whole thing.

It was a relief to have the Jewish community welcome her with open arms. This grew more and more important, as the Friday night tapings often made it impossible for Paul to be with the family for Sabbath service and Shabbat dinner. She acknowledged that home and children were her domain, but she was beginning to feel like a single parent. How much were the children suffering from Paul's absence? The family's monetary needs were being met many times over, but what about their spiritual and emotional needs? She sensed the other women felt sorry for her. Having a TV star for a husband might make her more popular in some communities, but in this one it merely caused talk.

Her period had ended a week ago, so last night she had gone to the *mikvah*, the ritual cleansing bath. It was her quiet time alone where she didn't have to take responsibility for the kids or answer to anyone. There was just the *mikvah* attendant and herself as she stepped down the blue tile stairs and was immersed completely in the warm, filtered water. Water, the universal symbol of spirituality and purification. When she first began to investigate living an observant life, this was a tenet that had vaguely disturbed her. Orthodox men will not shake hands with a woman at any time because she might be having her period and therefore be unclean. But Rabbi Joseph, who was a bit like a stand-up comic himself, explained that human beings are neither animal nor angel but a combination of both. God fashioned man of the dust of the earth and then blew into his nostrils, a living soul. A perfect balance. Whereas *toomah* was a condition of imbalance, when the physical, earthly part overcomes the spiritual, godly part. It was important to regain that state of balance through immersion in the *mikvah*. 'The wellspring of marriage is *mikvah*.'

She and Paul liked the idea that their marriage must also be balanced. One of the best things about Judaism as a religion was that it actually sanctioned sexual gratification, recognizing the sexual urge as natural and important, and a happy sexual relationship as part of creating a bond and keeping the family together. For a little less than two weeks a month, Paul and Chaya practiced *niddah*, separation; living together but not touching. They slept in the same room, but not in the same bed, eating at the same table but not from the same plate, until the *mikvah* brought them together again. They had found the practice invigorating, because it built up sexual tension: every month had its honeymoon. Except that last night, Paul had got home so late from the studio he had been too tired to make love. A far cry from *shechina b'socham*, a love so unique and total, so powerful that it draws the Divine Presence.

Lying in bed, late Friday night, the children asleep, exhausted from another noisy, joyous Shabbat gathering with the neighbors, she felt saddened that, once again, Paul had missed a beautiful evening, full of ritual and meaning. She sighed and turned over. Did Paul have any idea how much he was missing?

He let himself in as quietly as possible so as not to waken her. It was late and all he wanted to do was to strip off his clothes and fall into bed. He crawled in next to Chaya. He was exhausted. The early call, the long hours, and some escalating tension with Brandon had left him weary and drained. Chaya's warm, sleeping body was like a welcome ballast in a turbulent, threatening sea. He cuddled up against her back, his eyes closing, and let her regular, even breathing wash over him like a gentle, comforting wave. Chaya rolled over and put her arms around him. 'Hello, love,' she whispered softly, 'how did it go?'

'I'll tell you about it in the morning,' Paul mumbled a promise. All he wanted to do now was to fall asleep and wake up with, hopefully, enough energy to get through the next day.

'I've missed you, sweetheart,' Chaya's breath was warm against his ear. 'I've been waiting all night for you to come home and kiss me.'

'Too tired. Early call,' Paul tried to disengage himself.

'I want you to make love to me. Please.' Her tongue traced the outline of his ear. 'I miss you so much.'

'Honey, I'm not up for this.'

'Then you shouldn't have tempted me by getting into bed completely naked.' She tongue-flicked inside his ear.

'It ain't gonna rise. No way.'

'Are you sure?' Her hand slid down his back to the top of his thigh.

'Not tonight, dear, I have a headache.' Paul tried to make light of it. He was on his side, turned away from her, his back to her.

'Let me see if my language of love can persuade you otherwise.' She opened the front of her silky robe, leaving it loose about her shoulders, and twined herself around him, pressing her breasts against him, rubbing her body up and down his back. He sighed. She was so hard to resist, the sweetness of her breath, the smell of her skin, the feeling of her bare flesh against his. Her hand slipped between his legs, her fingers searching until they found his cock, and closed lovingly around it. His body betrayed his mind as it grew into life. She guided him over to her and he had no choice but to follow the core of his desires. With her other hand, she reached up and took the pin out of her hair, the long luxuriant hair that no one else was allowed to see, and let it fall over her shoulders, all the way down her back. Rising over him, she let her thick, black hair trace a pattern along his body, the thick, curly black tendrils stroking the front of his neck, circling his erect nipples, making them reach up for more, harder, harder, down past the ribs, etched just below his smooth skin, the flat, taut belly and tantalizingly close, so close, but with a wide sweep, she bypassed his cock, standing at attention, and let the silken curtain fall over his thighs and between his legs and then, miraculously, up again as she swung her head slowly back and forth, gently brushing, so close, so close, he was aching to have her touch him, make contact . . . He gasped as she grabbed his throbbing cock and wrapped her hair around the base of it, tight, so tight he was afraid it would hurt but the throbbing only increased as she closed her hand around him and began to rub, up and down, the friction so pulsating, the throbbing so intense that he cried out, 'Please, please.' She unwound the hair and replaced it with her warm, wet mouth, teasing him at first, licking up one side and down the other, drumming against the head of him, thrumming, thrumming, like the steady beat of a butterfly wing and then suddenly pulling him deep into her throat, sucking hard, pulling on him as if she could suck him right into her, then letting him slip out, just for one agonizing moment before she captured him again with her greedy lips. Her hands cupped the weight of his balls, so heavy with promise for the future. She grabbed the cheeks of his ass and drew him deeper again into her mouth, feeling him pulse inside her and then suddenly tighten. He was pushing up, bucking wildly, when she took her mouth away and moved up over him, poised for just an instant as his hips strained up to reach her. Slowly, very slowly, she slid herself down on to him, and he groaned with pleasure. The room was dark under the private, protective cover of late night, except for a shaft of moonlight coming in through the venetian blinds. Her body gleamed in the moonlight, full and round, the silk robe sliding off her shoulders and on to his own skin. She leaned forward, her breasts on his chest, nipple against nipple, rubbing, harder and harder. He opened his mouth, hungry like a baby, and she gave him hers, lips, tongue, life. She could feel herself pulling him deeper and deeper into her. She grew enormous, powerful, life-giving, Mother Earth. 'I am to my beloved and he is to me,' she whispered as she rode him, guiding him exactly where he longed to go. He was hers now, they were one, melting together, fusing for ever, no one else in the world, only each other, love, love, for ever, now, and he cried out with her as there was a flash of blazing, blinding light and they both exploded in one, long, rare, final release. *Shechina b'socham.*

Half-way across town, in bed, Melissa McKimmie listened for the sound of the key in the lock at the front door. She felt like she was in one of those fifties movies that Bonnie sometimes rented on video, the ones where the parents anxiously waited up for their teenage daughter to come home. Only she was the mom and her mother was the town bad girl. Why, why was this happening now? She thought Bonnie had left all that behind in Vancouver. Things had been going so well for them in LA. Bonnie seemed to be thrilled to get out of boring old Canada.

Melissa loved doing Makeover. Everybody liked her. Everybody treated her with respect. Maybe not as an equal: after all, she was only thirteen, which could still be considered a child. But Mel had worked hard to ensure that everyone in the company viewed her as a real professional. Alex Jordan had told them all on the first day of the pilot shoot that doing a sit-com was like being part of a new family, and it was, kind of. Alex was the director and her boss, but he was so kind and gentle with her, protective even. He acted like her father. As if she really knew how a real father behaved. It was fun pretending that a big country star like J.C. Austin was her mother and that Linda Earl, who had to be the most beautiful woman Mel had ever seen, was her crazy aunt, Nadine. Soundstage six was bustling and busy and it filled her life, at least during the week. All those people, each with an important job to do, but all of them finding the time to be friendly and nice. Bonnie hated nice, but Melissa thought nice wasn't so bad. She liked being around a lot of people. Bonnie was always saying, 'It's just you and me, kid. You and me against the world.' But

Melissa didn't want to be against the world, she wanted to be part of it.

She was never happier than when she was on the set. The Changing Room salon, her pretend home, felt more like her real home than this empty apartment. OK, so it had a great view with a palm tree right outside her bedroom window, and a pool and a jacuzzi, but what good did they do her when she was all by herself at something o'clock in the morning? She heard a siren in the distance, then the whir of a helicopter overhead. Since the riots, the police were patrolling this area twenty-four-hours-a-day. She was used to the night sounds by now. Vancouver had been a lot safer.

There was a scuffling noise at the front door and she sat up, her heart pounding, then the scrape of a key in the lock, and the door creaked open as Bonnie tiptoed across the living-room floor. What a laugh. Did her mother really think she would be asleep? Melissa called out to her, 'I'm in here, Mom.'

Bonnie came in and plopped herself on the end of the bed. 'What are you doing still awake, baby? Don't you have an early call tomorrow?'

'No,' Melissa's voice cracked a little with relief that her mother was home. 'Tomorrow's Saturday, eh? I get to sleep in.'

'Oh, right,' Bonnie giggled, 'I forgot.' She lit a cigarette, the flash of the lighter flame igniting the darkness for a brief moment. Her face looked lined and puffy, her lipstick and her smile slipping off to one side.

'You missed the taping again,' Melissa said accusingly.

'Sorry, Mel, I just got caught up with . . . things,' Bonnie had the good grace to sound guilty, but then her tone brightened. 'Guess who I had a date with?'

'Who?'

'Christopher Max.'

'You're putting me on.' Christopher Max was the latest primetime teen heart-throb.

'Nope. We went to the Roxbory.' This was a trendy club that was the in place with the younger crowd. 'We hung out for a while in the VIP room.'

'What was it like?'

'Small, smoky, sort of like a black box, but cosy,' Bonnie laughed and blew a smoke ring. 'You'd hate it.' Her burning cigarette glowed in the dark.

Melissa suddenly had a weird, wild thought that she and her mother were the only two people left in the world, frozen in this moment in time for the rest of their lives. 'You smell funny,' she said.

'Yeah? Must be the smoking,' Bonnie stubbed out her cigarette on the brass footboard. 'I meant to make it to the taping, really I did. In fact, I was going to bring Chris with me; I thought it might be fun for you. But you know what it's like, one thing led to another, and all I can tell you is Christopher Max definitely lives up to his last name.'

Melissa got a sinking feeling in her stomach. 'You're high.'

'A little, yeah. So what?'

'Oh, Mom, you promised.'

'So what are you, the Virgin Melissa?'

'What were you doing with Chris Max? He's a teenager. I could go out with this guy.'

Bonnie snorted. 'Chris is not a teenager. He just plays a teenager. He's twenty-six years old. That's practically thirty. Only we're not s'posed to tell anyone, 'kay?' her speech was beginning to slur. ''Cause it might spoil his image on the show.'

'Believe me, Mother, he's not fooling anybody. Not many high school juniors have that heavy a five o'clock shadow.'

'Uh-oh. I can tell you're really mad at me when you call me Mother in that really snippy, tight-assed little way of yours.'

'I want to show you something I found today.' Melissa climbed out of bed, went out of the room for a minute, and came back with an oversized garment bag. 'This was on the top shelf of the linen closet hidden behind a stack of towels. Like you thought I wouldn't find it?'

'I don't know what you're talking about. I can't even see what you're holding,' Bonnie whined.

'Let me illuminate the situation for you.' Melissa's thirteen-year-old speech became more adult and formal the angrier she got. She snapped on her tiger-shaped bedside lamp. She unzipped the bag and took out a hot pink leather suit. 'How much did this little number cost? The price tag's been removed.'

'I'm not going to tell you,' Bonnie mumbled.

'There's a jacket, skirt, and pants here. Real leather. Must be over a thousand bucks.'

'None of your business.'

'It is my business. Whose money is it?'

'We can afford it.'

'Sure, thanks to me. You're spending money like it'll be around for ever. Who knows how long this series is going to last?'

'You're in a hit, Mel. Makeover is guaranteed to run lots more seasons. The bucks'll just keep rolling in.'

'You can't be sure of that. The gravy train could run out tomorrow. Besides, most of my money is supposed to go into the trust account and sit right there, earning interest until I'm eighteen. That's what the California Coogan Law is all about. It's supposed to protect minors like me. It's my money, not yours.'

'You ungrateful little bitch,' Bonnie's eyes were hard as little stones.

'Who said I wanted to use my money to buy you a leather suit? This is so unfair,' Melissa's chin was starting to tremble. 'I'm the one who's working while you're out partying.'

'Don't you talk to me like that, young lady. I'm your mother.'

'I wish you weren't,' Melissa shouted. 'Where's my Dad? I want my father.'

'Well, your father didn't want you,' Bonnie lashed out. 'You're lucky you've got me.' Seeing Melissa's face, 'Oh, God, baby, I'm sorry, I didn't mean that. Your father and I chose not to be with each other, but I chose to be with you. I wanted you. I love you.'

But it was too late. Melissa had run into the bathroom, locked the door, and was crying as if her heart would break.

Chapter Fifteen

'Boy, I'd love to date Carlene,' Beau Fawcett announced to his mother, Debra Jo. 'That Melissa McKimmie, she is cute.' The entire Fawcett family had just finished watching an episode of Makeover on the large-screen TV. The big TV was kept downstairs in the converted basement that Eddie liked to call the family room, although in Debra Jo's opinion it would need a lot more converting before it looked like anything other than an unfinished basement. Danny, the younger boy, sat on the floor, his arms wrapped around the dog, Jim Bowie. Danny had already had his bath and put on his pajamas. The Fawcett family were addicted to the show and each of them had a favorite character. Debra Jo loved J.C. Austin as Janine, Eddie thought Kelly's Samantha was a real hoot, and Danny thought Brandon Tate really was Travis and could do all the rodeo tricks that he had seen in Brandon's old movies on TV. Beau had been smitten with Melissa since the first episode.

'She's got a sassy tongue and that hot red hair; I'd really like to meet her.' He stretched his long legs out in front of him and admired his new Nike hightops. 'Of course, probably in real life, she's a stuck up, snotty little bitch. Most of those TV babes are.'

'Don't use that kind of language, son,' Eddie said, but he said it mildly. Debra Jo had outdone herself with a catfish and hushpuppy dinner; Eddie had allowed himself his nightly two beers, and he was feeling relaxed and mellow, happy to be surrounded by his wife and kids. People could say all they wanted about the danger of watching too much TV but, in a recession, at least it was something a family could afford to enjoy together.

'Your father's right, Beau,' Debra Jo agreed, 'but you know, I'm worried about little Melissa.' She picked up a section of the *Hollywood Insider*, the pages of which were strewn about on the family room floor. 'There's a picture of her mother here in the photo scandal section called "We Caught You" that shows her kissing the star of Sherman Oaks in the Year 2000. On the mouth! What kind of example is that for a little girl? The woman must be my age and he's barely older than you, Beau; young enough to be her son.'

'Yuck. Gross,' Beau took the picture from his mother, looked at it briefly, then wadded it up into a ball and tossed it into the waste-paper basket. 'No guy in my school would be caught dead going out with a woman like that.'

'Oh, I don't know,' Eddie contemplated having a third beer. 'You can learn a lot from an older woman.'

'Yeah? Like what?' Beau's eyes lit up with interest.

'Edward,' Debra Jo said sharply.

'We'll talk about it later son,' Eddie gave him a wink.

'Like what?' Danny wanted to know. 'I don't get it.'

'You won't talk about it at all,' Debra Jo said crisply. 'Not in my house. You're whistling out of your backside anyway, Eddie Fawcett. What do you think you know about older women? You married me right out of high school.'

Eddie snatched up another section of the tabloid. 'What do you read this garbage for anyway? You can't believe what's printed in these rags. Nothing but lies. And you never throw any of them out. I bet you're the only woman in America who has her own tabloid liberry.' He deliberately mispronounced it just to piss her off.

'You are so wrong. You can learn a lot from the *Insider*. Their reporters go undercover to find out the truth, how the stars and their families really live.'

'Sure, and half the time it's all a shuck. Didn't you tell me Roseanne and Tom Arnold sued one of the tabs for claiming they lived like pigs and destroyed a beautiful rental home? Didn't it turn out that it was the reporters themselves that snuck into the place and trashed it? I mean, these papers are dangerous. I don't know how you can read this garbage.'

'What are you getting so upset about, Eddie? I just happen to tell you that I don't think Bonnie's raising Melissa right and you get all bent out of shape.'

'Melissa? Bonnie?' Eddie's voice had lost its mildness. 'You don't even know these people and you act like they're

163

personal friends of yours. Calling them by their first names.'

'Mom? Dad? Are you fighting?' Danny's eyes were anxious, his face pale against the brightly colored Ninja Turtle pajamas.

Debra Jo and Eddie exchanged a guilty look. Danny had long outgrown his heart condition, but it had left him sensitive to emotional undercurrents. Why shouldn't he be worried, poor kid? Half his friends at school came from broken homes and were being raised by a single parent.

'No, honey,' Debra Jo said gently. 'Your dad and I don't fight. Sometimes we discuss in a loud voice.'

'Scaredy-cat. Wimp. Wuss.' Beau taunted.

'I am not,' Danny tried to defend himself, but his lower lip was already quivering. 'What's a wuss?'

'Never you mind. Beau, quit picking on your baby brother.' Debra Jo reached out and enveloped Danny in a hug. Beau wouldn't let her touch him these days, but Danny, if he was upset, still allowed himself to be kissed and cuddled. She loved holding him, breathing in the smell of his freshly shampooed hair and his clean, little-boy skin.

'Carlene wouldn't want to meet you,' Danny muttered in his brother's direction. 'Not in a million years. I'd rather meet Travis anyway. He's better than old Carlene any day.'

'What is with you guys?' Eddie exploded in exasperation. 'You're as nutty as your mom. You are not going to meet Travis. Or Carlene. They don't exist. They're made up characters on TV. The people who play them are actors. They're Brandon Tate and Melissa McKimmie. Probably totally different from what they play. And you're not going to meet Brandon or Melissa either. God, now I'm doing it! You've got about as much chance of seeing these people in the flesh as a snowball in summer.'

'Well, we could take that trip to LA and watch a studio taping,' Debra Jo reminded him. 'That would be a great Christmas present. Then we could meet them.'

'No, we could not. Don't bring that up again. It's way too expensive. You've been belly-aching to me all fall about how, now that Beau's in high school, it costs an arm and a leg to outfit him.'

'You're just going to have to stop growing so fast, big boy,' Debra Jo teased, reaching out to rumple Beau's hair before he had time to pull away. 'You must have grown an inch a month since you started LBJ High. Never mind what it costs to feed you, Mr Bottomless Pit.'

'Speaking of which,' Eddie stood up and walked over to the basement fridge, 'who wants ice-cream before we all hit the sack?' He opened the freezer compartment of the expensive new fridgedaire they'd probably be making payments on until the day they died.

Debra Jo sighed. It was a family bedtime ritual, but Eddie shouldn't be eating ice-cream at all. The fat content was way too high. She'd tried to get him to switch to frozen yogurt but he swore he could taste the acidopholous culture in it, and that made it a health food, not a treat for a man who worked hard all day. He wanted real, creamy ice-cream or none at all.

'I stopped at the Circle K and picked up a new kind. One of those gourmet brands. It's called Cherry Garcia. Real cherries and big fat chunks of chocolate.'

'Cherry Garcia?' Beau snorted. 'Weird name for ice-cream.'

'No, it's not. Named after Jerry Garcia.'

'Who's Jerry Garcia?'

'Boy, you don't know anything, do you? Jerry Garcia. Lead singer for the Grateful Dead. And don't ask me who they are or you'll make me feel really old.' Eddie pulled out a pint of ice-cream and got three spoons.

'Cherry Garcia, that's funny,' Danny giggled as he repeated the name over and over again, giddy with delight and relief that everything was now securely back to normal.

Debra Jo watched the three tow-headed men in her life, laughing and teasing each other, battling spoons to get at the sweet treat. Eddie was a wonderful father, so good with the kids. They were lucky. She wondered if Melissa McKimmie had a dad who remembered to bring home ice-cream for her.

Chapter Sixteen

'We're stealing Saturday night,' Tim Talbot triumphantly announced to Julia and Marty, pointing to the shaded box on the Neilsen rating chart in *Daily Variety*. As far as the network was concerned, the ratings remained the only measure of success or failure. A ratings point represented 931,000 TV households; shares were the percentage of sets in use. According to Tim, every primetime rating point meant one hundred million dollars in advertising revenue for the network. 'Makeover got a 12.4 rating and 25.9 share. That means we've squeaked into the weekly top ten for the very first time. The word has come down from on high—'

'Meaning Stan?' Julia interrupted.

'Higher than that. Mt Olympus itself. Charles Currie. He's thrilled with the show and he's ordered Stan to pick up the option for the rest of the twenty-two episodes.' Marty and Julia broke into a cheer.

On an early November day, they were gathered in his office in Currie Plaza for their weekly meeting. Tim's skyscraper view was almost but not quite as spectacular as Stan's. Today the Hollywood Hills were obscured by an off-the-chart smog index, and a slight drizzle fogged the wall of windows, but the spirits of all three of them were as bright as Tim's fluorescent lime-green Gap sweatshirt. Tomorrow was the US Presidential election; there was talk of a change; once again America was hoping to make itself over.

'So the first thing I have to discuss with you is whether Hudlow/Turgov will be able to deliver those extra episodes, on time, and maintaining the standard of production you've established. You're supposed to stop filming the end of February. I would guess you'd have to extend the filming schedule through mid-April. That puts the pressure on you, Julia, to write those new scripts; and Marty, you will have to get the Pac Vic production team working overtime. Think you can handle that?' They nodded vigorously. They had been hoping this would happen and were already prepared for it. 'Now, I want to talk to you about programming,' Tim said, picking up a pointer and extending it toward the board that covered an entire wall behind him. The board displayed, in multicolors, the schedules of all four networks. Julia had come to know that there was nothing the cocky, neurotic director of Programming liked more than moving the slots around on his giant game of monopoly, playing God with people's lives and livelihoods. He had grown up on television, it was his world, and now he was in charge of a universe. Stanfield King might be the standard-bearer of taste for CBN, but Tim controlled the menu, where and when the dishes were served. 'Makeover has beat the competition two weeks in a row now. We didn't just beat them, we brutalized them, right in the target audience, adults 18–24,' he indicated the demographic report. 'So now that we've won, we're moving the show to nine-thirty Tuesday night.'

Julia gasped. 'What?' A left hook, out of nowhere, knocking her flat.

'You're telling us we won and the prize is a move?' Marty was turning that awful green-white color again. This was so typical of the whole television business. That's a great leg you've got there. Thanks. Pardon me while I amputate it. 'Are you trying to kill us off?'

'No, now listen, kids, stay cool . . .' Tim held up his hand in amelioration. He had this annoying habit of addressing them as children even though they were old enough to be his parents. Well, Marty was. Almost.

'What happened?' Marty spoke through clenched teeth. 'Did Stan get into a tennis match with Big Bob Iger at ABC and decide this would be a neat thing to do?'

'Of course not. Saturday has always been the low-viewing "geriatric" night. We took on the challenge of getting young people to watch and Makeover shot up to number one. In just a few short months, you've developed a strong, loyal core audience that will follow you to another time period. Stan thinks you're ready to go out and anchor a week night.'

'But not Tuesday,' Julia begged. 'That's Roseanne's night.'

'Just the point,' Tim argued. 'Roseanne will be our lead-in. The idea being, "You're watching something you like, why not watch something similar?" In other words, when Roseanne is over, switch the channel to CBN! Another network providing the lead-in, it's a programming coup.' His eyes were glowing with the zeal of a fanatic.

'I don't know, I don't like jumping on the coat-tails . . .' Marty began doubtfully.

'The nine-thirty slot should please you, Julia,' Tim cut in. 'It'll give you a chance to push the envelope a bit.'

'Push the envelope?' She drew a blank. 'What the hell does that mean?'

Tim explained that it was a term developed by the air force to describe pushing the limits of aviation. 'Or, in industry terms, the politeness barrier. You've been aching to tackle some social issues with Makeover. A later time slot takes us out of family viewing.'

'True, but we've got kids watching now because of Melissa. They'll be in bed by nine-thirty.'

'So, the VCR's will get a good workout.'

'But . . .'

'Look, kids,' Tim cut her off. 'The decision isn't yours to make anyway. This move is in your best interests. Trust me.'

'Is that anything like, "Trust me, I won't come in your mouth?" ' Julia murmured under her breath, but Tim didn't hear. He raced on, high on caffeine and adrenalin. 'We've upped the advertising budget in order to promote the hell out of this move. Patsy's come up with a fab campaign of testimonial promos from real beauticians all over the country. Hook into the authenticity angle J.C.'s so hot on, you know? Real people telling the world why they love to watch Makeover.'

'Not a bad idea,' Marty said, attempting to recover the ball. 'Wish I'd thought of that when I was working on LA Law.'

'Are you kidding?' Julia joined in. 'Nobody would believe the testimonial of a lawyer.'

Tim graced the joke with the crumb of a chuckle before driving ahead. 'Patsy's also landed us the cover of TV Guide.'

'Well, it's about time.' Julia wondered why it had taken so long for them to sit up and pay attention.

'The cover AND a big feature article, which will tie in with the testimonials because we'll have some of the same hairdressers dishing with J.C. about the new spring hairstyles. Focus the viewers on the move and on J.C. as well,' Tim finished in a burst of triumph.

'I was right about J.C. wasn't I?' Julia felt the need now to score a few points.

'Yeah, she's getting better with every show. Singing works like gangbusters, too. The audience looks forward to that private little moment at the end of each show; it's a neat hook. Are you thinking of expanding it?'

'Wait till you see what I've got planned for later in the season. A tie-in with Elvis.'

'Elvis?' Tim raised an eyebrow.

'That's all I'm going to tell you. I'm glad J.C.'s finally settled in. She's bonded with Melissa now, too, so the mother-daughter relationship is working much more believably. I don't know about the sister bond . . .'

'No,' Tim said, 'Linda Earl isn't registering with the viewers yet, but give it time. The public is responding well to everybody else. Our black and Hispanic demographics are improving, thanks to Shirley and Theresa.'

Julia winced. Tim was only reinforcing Theresa's concerns that she was on the show to bring in minority viewers.

'Paul's been getting some amazing letters,' Marty laughed. 'He'd never kissed a leading lady before Makeover came along. We let him give Linda Earl one little peck and suddenly he's getting offers to play sexy roles, both onscreen and off.'

'I don't think Brandon Tate has anything to worry about yet,' Tim chuckled. 'When he and J.C. are in the same scene, you can't keep the chemistry apart.'

'Well, now, I understand Paul's appeal,' Julia volunteered. 'He's cute and cuddly, half innocent *bar mitzvah* boy, half Peck's Bad Boy. And Jewish men finally seem to be "in" these days. I can't understand why it took so long. They've always been my sex object of choice.' Marty leaned over and kissed her. 'To me, the real surprise of the cast is Kelly Carmichael. I never expected the character of Samantha to take off like this.' The fanmail was pouring in and Sam's catchphrase, 'Don't tease my hair!' meaning 'don't mess with me', was sweeping the country. Kelly had just signed with a new manager, Michael Taylor of CTA, who jumped on the bandwagon by ordering a line of T-shirts with the same slogan printed in sequins.

'No surprise to me,' Tim said smugly. 'She's got this unusual quality. I predicted the audience would go for her.'

'They love her hair,' said Marty.

'Her voice,' said Julia.

'Her tits.' Tim actually blushed. 'Ohmigod! I can't believe I said that. Stanfield King must have possession of my body. That's not me at all. Anyway, my point is, Julia, you may want to think about weighting one of the future episodes toward Kelly. She's quite a woman.'

Quite a woman, Brandon thought, as he leaned across the table and stared into the heavy-lidded eyes of Kelly Carmichael. They were sitting in a booth at Fracas, having an after-rehearsal drink, double Jack Daniels. It had taken Brandon longer than usual to decide which female member of the company to hit on. There was something so delicious about having a clandestine 'office affair', but if you didn't pick just the right partner, the whole thing could backfire and then you had to live with the mess and, worse, work with it. Tricky. Very tricky. J.C. was the one he wanted, but she was still keeping at arm's length, sexually. Friends, just friends. He had to admit he was enjoying their relationship, but it meant he would have to look elsewhere. Linda Earl was a knock-out, but she was married, too. Not that that had ever stopped him before. But there was something a little strange about her, what was the word, neuresthenic? He sensed she could be trouble. Theresa was too young. Shirley talked about a boyfriend, although no one in the company had met him yet. When she wasn't on set, she spent most of her time on the phone, presumably with her mystery man. Discreet to the utmost.

There was nothing discreet about Kelly, at least not on the surface. She sat across from him, wearing a skin-tight leopard jumpsuit unzipped half-way to her waist. Her make-up was heavy but expert, shadowed cheekbones, shadowed eyes, shadowed cleavage. Kelly brought new meaning to the words big hair. Flamboyant to the max, she was also warm and funny and surprisingly sensitive. He tuned back into the conversation to hear her say she spent most of her hiatus weeks, when the series wasn't shooting, at the Hospital of the Good Samaritan, working with terminally ill kids.

'Theresa and Shirley are starting to razz me about it,' Kelly confessed with a blush, 'they call them "Kelly's kids" because I talk about them as if they were my own. It's hard not to get too attached to them, especially when you know that eventually each and every one will be taken from you.'

'Cancer?' Brandon found himself drawn into her sympathy.

Kelly nodded. 'Some. I've also worked with kids with cystic fibrosis. Now I'm on a ward that's mostly infants and babies. They're all HIV positive. It's heartbreaking. Their fathers are dead, their mothers are dying, and yet they still greet each day full of life and hope. Pisses me off: this fucking government will spend billions on defense, but what they deign to throw at AIDS research is just a drop in the bucket,' her voice was rising in anger and her eyes were blazing.

'Hey,' Brandon reached out and put his hand over hers. 'I think what you're doing is wonderful, Kelly. I wish I had your righteous anger. It comes from a belief that things could be better, a hope I'm afraid I lost somewhere along the way.'

'I'm willing to wager you can pinpoint just exactly when,' Kelly held on to his hand and looked into his eyes as if she could see straight into his soul, and suddenly he found himself telling her about the air disaster and Peter's bravery and his subsequent death, something he hadn't let himself think about – much less talk about – for a long time. When he finally ran down she knew enough to let the silence hang there, for a time, before she reached out and delicately traced the faint, jagged scar by his eye. 'Hard to forget that when you have this reminder every time you look in the mirror,' she said gently.

He nodded mutely, and to his horror, his eyes began to fill with tears. Shit, what was the matter with him, crying in front of this woman he hardly knew?

'It's OK, really,' she read his mind. 'Believe me, I know how you feel. I lost the person I loved most in the world, too. Here, take one of these fancy little cocktail napkins and see if it'll fit your nose, a nose I've always admired, by the way, in the hopes that it might mirror the size and shape of other more interesting parts of your anatomy.' She shoved the napkin at him, 'Go on now, blow. And then let's have another drink. I'm just starting to get into this.'

'Me too.' Brandon signalled to the waiter for another round of bourbon.

'You know what you need?'

'What?' He watched in fascination as she tossed the whiskey, neat, straight down the back of her throat.

'You need to have a baby.'

Brandon choked on his drink. 'You mean together? With you?'

Kelly laughed so loudly that, even with the noise of the Fracas house band, people turned to look. 'No, honey, I think my babymaking days are over. David and I never had any kids. We thought about adopting but . . .' She went off in her mind for a minute, and then her gaze returned to him. 'No, I mean get yourself married and have a child. You should be working on your second or third marriage by now.'

'My second or third?'

'Listen, I read *Hollywood Wives*. I know love and lust are cyclical out here. No, seriously, don't you want kids?'

'Someday. Maybe. It's never been a driving force.' He couldn't look at her. 'Too selfish, I guess.'

'Can you be absolutely sure there aren't any little Tates running around out there somewhere?' she said mischievously.

'Not that I know of. God, no. I've had a couple of scares in my day. Mostly one-night stands. Women outside the business. The actresses I've been seriously involved with haven't been in a hurry to procreate either.'

'Too bad,' Kelly gave a mock sigh. 'There are a lot of gorgeous women in this town you could make a beautiful baby with.'

Brandon nodded. He was almost blushing. Sitting here in a packed bar, one of Hollywood's trendiest meat markets, full of hustlers and hustlees, music blaring all around them, they were talking about making babies. He felt a stirring in his groin. He took another look at Kelly. She really was a stunning piece of female work. What a beautiful body. Poured into that tight-fitting catsuit. It was hard to keep his eyes above her neck. Force yourself, Brandon, focus on her face. Strong bones, sharply accented with careful highlighting, she knew her way around a make-up brush, all right.

172

Suddenly the urge overcame him to see her without all that make-up. Barefaced, softer maybe, tousled even, after a marathon night of love-making. Platinum hair against his black sheets. Those softer than soft, finest percale, black cotton sheets. There wasn't a woman alive who didn't look good naked on black sheets. The smell of her all over his bed . . .

He leaned in closer. 'I love your perfume. It's wonderful. What is it?'

'Ombre Rose,' she said in that peach brandy husky honey voice that drove him crazy.

'It's almost – but not quite – over the top.'

'Baby, I was born over the top. No censoring device.'

He studied her intently, the heat radiating upwards from between his legs. Was he getting mixed signals here? She was a hard one to read. Should he go for it? Risk making a complete ass of himself? Nothing ventured, nothing gained. 'Would you hate me if I were to make a heavy pass right about now?'

For barely a second, Kelly looked startled. Then the mask of bravado returned as she purred, 'You just want the thrill of going to bed with a woman who's half a head taller than you are.'

'Oh no,' Brandon said smoothly. 'I've done that before.'

'I'll bet you have.' Watch it, Kelly girl, play for time.

'Your size is the first thing that attracted me to you.' That's right. Always compliment them on the one thing they're probably most self-conscious about.

'Could be interesting,' Kelly lowered her lids à la Dietrich. 'You'd have to go up on me.' No, wrong move, Kelly girl. Don't lead him on. This is not what you want. Talking dirty will only rev him up.

'Sounds intriguing.' Good move. Such graphic sexual allusion usually meant that what was on his mind right now was also on hers. Don't push it, let the string out just a little, see if she extends a paw to play with it . . .

'Brandon, you're a star,' Kelly broke the electrical cord. 'I'm – well, not much more than glorified atmosphere.'

'Not for long. "Yo, Kelly, don't tease my hair!" That made you famous overnight.'

'You know what I'm talking about here. Cards on the table. They've given me a golden opportunity. A second chance. I'm going to take it and run with it. Watch me fly.

And – now stop me if I'm going too far here – you've got a second chance too, Brandon. Stop thinking with your dick and let some of that blood flow back to your brain. Don't blow this one, baby.' She laughed as she said it, but her eyes showed genuine concern. Concern for him or concern about his reaction to what she had just said?

Brandon nodded thoughtfully. 'You're absolutely right. Very sensible. And since we both are smart enough to know exactly where we stand,' he took her hand, 'why not continue this conversation,' he ran his tongue between each of her fingers looking her directly in the eye, 'in a more comfortable setting. Your bed or mine?'

Kelly's palm quivered under his touch. 'I think I might be just a little too much woman for you.'

'How can you be so sure?' Brandon said softly. 'There's nothing I like more than a challenge.'

Kelly flushed and pulled her hand away. 'You'll have to trust me on this one, Brandon. Believe me, I'm sure.' Unexpectedly a tear rolled out of her eye and right down on to her magnificent bosom. 'God, how embarrassing. The first time in ages a man tells me he wants me and I start to cry.'

Brandon's tone changed instantly. 'Hey, there's already been enough crying tonight. I wasn't trying to pressure you, I swear. Just some good old flirtin' goin' on, that's all. I'll back off, I promise. See?' He stood up, out of his chair, and took a few steps backward. 'See? This is me backing off.' He gave a strange, almost courtly, little bow. 'Am I forgiven?'

'Of course. It's just . . . too soon after David's death.'

'Hey, I understand. No problem.'

'Friends?' Kelly looked up at him with moist eyes.

'Friends,' he said firmly. And immediately began to wonder. What was wrong with him? Lately every woman he met wanted to be his friend. Worse, why did he feel, deep down inside, just a little bit relieved?

Chapter Seventeen

The first time she'd seen him, lying in a hospital bed, his face turned to the wall, her heart went out to him. He was only a little boy, barely four years old, and he'd already given up. Who could blame him? His father had died of AIDS eight months ago, and his mother had recently died, too, in a room right down the hall from his. Carlos Miguel Carrera read the name on his chart. Both parents were IV drugs users. They had not been married anyway. His mother knew she was HIV positive when she became pregnant. She'd been counseled to have an abortion, but she refused. Kelly could understand that. The cards had been stacked against her right from the beginning. She wanted to leave some kind of legacy, even if only for a brief period of time. Besides, there was no guarantee her child would have AIDS. He might test positive at birth only because he still had his mother's antibodies in his blood. But Carlos was born and six months came and went. Still positive. Two years. Still positive. Now he was four and there was no hope, short of a miracle, that the findings were negative.

All the children on this floor of the Good Samaritan Hospital pulled at her heartstrings, but for some reason, Kelly felt particularly drawn to Carlos Miguel. She'd gone up to his bed and spoken to him, first in English, then in her high school Spanish, '*Hola*, Carlos. *Como esta?*' He didn't respond; she didn't give up. Every time she volunteered at the hospital, she made sure she went in to see Carlos and finally one day, '*Hola*, Carlito. *Como esta?*'

Maybe it was the diminutive of his name that made him turn his head to her and look up at her with those big, searching eyes. '*Jo soy enfermo*,' he said, then in English, 'my stomach hurts.'

'I know.' The nurses had explained to Kelly that he was having trouble with cramps and diarrhea. 'I'm really sorry

175

to hear that, *amigo*. Let's see if I can make it feel better, OK?' She reached out and cautiously placed her hand on his tummy and began to rub it, ever so gently, the way Kelly's mother used to when Kelly was sick with the flu. He didn't flinch or pull away; he seemed to accept her touch for what it was, a moment of comfort, a relief from the din of the hospital.

Kelly had learned that hospitals aren't quiet places where people tiptoe about and talk in hushed tones. In the face of death, they are often noisy and teeming with life. But that doesn't make them any less scary. The special children's ward at the Good Samaritan was not painted hospital green and the smell of disinfectant was less obvious than anywhere else in the hospital. It had been decorated in sunny primary colors. California colors. In the playroom at the end of the long hall, there were lots of toys and plants and pictures. Carlito's room was bright and cheery, but still it was a hospital, it wasn't a home. Although how would he know the difference?

He had come in with his mother to die and when she was gone, where else could he go? No friends or relatives appeared to be in evidence. Carlito was a 'boarder baby'. He was waiting to be placed in a foster home, but that hadn't happened yet. There was little chance of his being legally adopted. What would be the point? Although he was relatively healthy at the moment, he might be exposed to an opportunistic infection and die before the paper work went through.

The nurses treated him well. They were an enlightened group who didn't bury themselves in gowns and gloves just to take his temperature. They followed the same precautionary measures when handling bodily fluids as they did when dealing with hepatitis, which was far more infectious. Carlito was cute and should be so easy to love. He was half black, half Mexican, with velvety skin, huge brown eyes, and curly dark hair. The nurses gave him a cuddle whenever they could, but they were busy, and he was already old enough and smart enough to know that nobody loved him for very long. Ryan White had Elton John, Phil Donahue, Michael Jackson. Carlito was alone. Ryan White had a fiercely loving mother. Carlito's mother didn't even say goodbye when she left him for the last time.

He began to look forward to Kelly's visits. She baked him

cookies, she who rarely cooked, and brought them to him. She helped him redecorate the room that he shared with two other kids. She was teaching him to make the letters in his own name. He was only four, but he was bright, bright enough to know he'd been abandoned and he needed to find a protector. He picked her and, goddamn it, she would do her best. The first day he greeted her with '*Hola*, Sam' and favored her with a smile, it was like the sun breaking through the clouds. The kids on the floor knew her as 'Sam' because a lot of them watched her on Makeover, so Carlos called her Sam and she called him what he seemed to like best, Carlito. He giggled at her broken Spanish, but they were able to communicate in many ways. Last week he had drawn a series of pictures, they were almost a storyboard, of himself and Sam on a beach. As far as she knew, he had never been to the beach.

Kelly had done a lot of personal research and she thought she knew most of what there was to know about AIDS. Since volunteering at the hospital, she had learned that seventy-five per cent of children with AIDS belong to an ethnic minority. That the US used to have one of the lowest infant mortality rates in the world and now its rank was dropping with every year as AIDS became a leading cause of death in children. She tried to keep up with the latest developments, the newest discoveries. They were on the path of a vaccine. This drug worked better than that drug. No, better not to take any drugs. They were all toxic and only further weakened the immune system. A new strain seemed to be developing. There was indication that the presence of the virus was not enough to cause AIDS, a co-factor had to be involved. She knew so much, and so little of it was hopeful, but when she looked into Carlito's eyes what she saw there was a new-found, slowly growing hope.

After she had rubbed his tummy that day, she finally found the courage to pick him up in her arms. He didn't hug or cuddle her, he *suffered* her to hold him, as she told a friend afterwards. Kelly sat down in a chair by the bed. It was a straight-backed, metal hospital chair, not a rocking chair, but she rocked him, holding him as close as she dared. This must be what it was like to have a child. How much she had missed. She rocked him gently, back and forth, singing him the only song with a Spanish phrase in it that she knew, '*Via con Dios*, my darling, *via con Dios*, my love.' Kelly had a terrible voice, closer to whiskey baritone than sweet soprano, but Carlito didn't seem to mind. His arms crept around her neck and he buried his face in her ample bosom. She had an overwhelming urge to take him out of the hospital, right then and there, just walk right out the front door with him in her arms.

For Carlito, the future was not measured in years or even months, but in minutes and days. She desperately wished that each of those minutes could contain all the best parts of a happy childhood. She wanted to get him a dog, read him a story, take him trick-or-treating, help him decorate a Christmas tree, blow out the candles on at least one more birthday cake.

Kelly sat across from Monica Forbes, the Children's Aid representative who was interviewing her as a prospective foster parent. She tried to gauge how the interview was going so far. She'd dressed conservatively. No high heels, no cleavage. No raunchy remarks either. She was careful to give measured, thoughtful answers to all of Monica's questions. Monica had already told her she watched her on the show, so she knew what Kelly's 'normal' image was, but so what? She was an actress and other actresses had been allowed to take in foster kids. She had a good home to offer him with lots of love.

Monica Forbes finished making notes on Kelly's file, looked up and smiled. 'I think Carlos Miguel is lucky to have found you, Ms Carmichael. We haven't been able to place him before now. He's a bright boy and I believe he will benefit from some individual attention. The prognosis isn't great for any of these kids, but chances are he'll do better with you than if he stays at Good Samaritan. You'll just have to take it one day at a time.'

'Then you think my application might be approved?' Kelly was weak with relief.

'I have no reason to doubt it. Of course, this is just a preliminary interview.'

'Preliminary?'

'Of course. The department always does an extensive evaluation before potential foster parents are approved, especially in the case of a single parent like yourself.'

Her heart sank. 'What does that involve?'

'Well, a number of home visits, of course, to establish whether or not the home situation is conducive to having a child.'

'It should be fine. I've got lots of room.' She had a large apartment with an extra bedroom plus its own bathroom. The hospital staff had been trying to get Carlos into a special day-care program outside the hospital for HIV kids, but there was a day-care at the studio for the children of parents who worked for Pac Vic. She would explain the situation to them and, according to the rules of the State of California, they would have to accept him. Her role on Makeover was small, so that she didn't have to be on set every minute of every day. She'd be able to pop up to the day-care and see him often. 'There's a park nearby and we're not far from the beach. Carlito's just dying to go to . . .' She stopped, embarrassed.

'Don't worry. I say it all the time. Anyway, that all sounds ideal. Now, there's also the background and financial check. If you do decide to take in a child, you receive financial support from the government and payment for medical and child-care expenses. Of course, in your case, you seem to be financially comfortable, so obviously money is not the reason behind your application to be a foster parent. Believe me, we're used to people in the entertainment industry so that's not the hindrance it might be in another city. I've got your forms all ready to fill out. You can take them with you and if you have any questions just give me a call.' Monica smiled reassuringly. 'Don't worry. It looks like a mound of paper, I know. The background check is very thorough, but unless you've been arrested for drug dealing or prostitution, you shouldn't have any problems.'

'Thank you.' Numbly, Kelly stood up to go. 'I'll be in touch.'

After the interview, she walked down the broad steps and out into the blazing sunshine. For once there was no smog in the air. The sky was a deep, cerulean blue with not a cloud. The sun bathed the afternoon in a rich golden light. She stared down at the stack of papers in her hand, then crumpled them up and threw them away. It was no good. It was hopeless. Once they checked into her background, there was no way they would let her take Carlos Miguel as a foster child. She would have to find some other means of helping him. Maybe get him into a day-care at least.

She drew a shaky breath. If the powers that be wouldn't allow her to help only Carlito, she would have to do something to help all the HIV children. She would move to the front lines of a more organized battle, lobby Congress, raise funds. She knew how to hustle, how to get what she needed. Most of the time.

Chapter Eighteen

Monday, nine-thirty a.m. Marty and Julia, along with the Makeover production team, were gathered at a long metal table for the weekly production meeting, discussing the technical requirements for this week's show. The meeting was co-chaired by production manager, Doug Berkley, and the first AD, Tom Bentley. Doug, who was Marty's right-hand man, was responsible for keeping the set running smoothly, overseeing the camera crew, lighting, wardrobe and make-up. Tom, working closely with Alex Jordan, functioned as floor manager and handled the actors. Tom and Doug were a lot alike, neat, bespectacled and sandy-haired, with a passion for scheduling everything right down to the last second. The Anal Retentive Twins, Marty called them.

Marty insisted Alex sit in on production meetings and the crew had agreed. Alex was directing every episode, which was unusual for a situation comedy, but Marty wanted to maintain artistic continuity, at least for the first season. It was part of Brandon Tate's negotiated contract that if the series continued, he would have a crack at directing a couple of episodes, but for now Alex was at the helm of the Makeover ship and Julia trusted the director completely. 'Makes the actors feel more secure,' he said, 'if there's only one "Daddy".'

Julia read through this week's script entitled 'Elvis Is Sighted in the Mall' and everyone followed along, with Doug and Tom interrupting every now and again, to call attention to the technical details such as props, sound effects, costume pieces, noted on the scene-by-scene breakdown. The episode, which was scheduled to air in February during sweeps week, featured an Elvis impersonator who comes to the Changing Room to get advice on how to look even more like The King. The staff of the Changing Room know he's not the real Elvis but hysteria spreads throughout the mall as clerks and shoppers become convinced that Elvis is alive and well and living in Houston.

Julia explained the montage sequence (it was different each week), which opened every show with the credits and the Makeover musical theme. In a series of fast-paced clips, the audience would see Elvis having chicken-fried steak at the food court in the mall, buying a set of weights from Travis at the Sports Chek, autographing a photograph for Troy in his studio and, at the mall news-stand, picking up a copy of the *Hollywood Insider* with a headline reading 'Elvis Sighted in Houston Mall'. It sounded clever and fun and should make for a terrific opening to what Marty was already calling Julia's best shot at an Emmy nomination.

Julia was studying Liam Carey, the art director, who was responsible for the look of the show, as he presented his design. Before getting into television, Liam had been a visual artist and theatrical designer. His renderings were like paintings and his set models intricately detailed. As he described the escalator scene, where 'Elvis' is going up the escalator and a crowd of gaping, open-mouthed extras – mall 'atmosphere' – are going down, Liam cradled a miniature escalator he had fashioned out of rows of staples. It was a tiny, perfect centerpiece to what was a real work of art.

Initially, he had gone for a highly stylized approach to the set decoration, what he called 'Edward Scissorhands': pastel ice-cream colors, oddly-shaped fixtures, and bold furniture. The look was startling and original and earned him great reviews, but after J.C.'s tantrum about the set, Liam agreed to throw it all out and go for something much more realistic. He'd listened to J.C.'s ideas, saying, 'We can make the salon more a part of your personality,' and now her down to earth characterization of Janine infused every detail of the Changing Room. Viewer response had been overwhelmingly positive to Makeover's makeover.

For an artist, Liam Carey was remarkably free of ego, all his energy flowing directly into the creative process. Soft-spoken and gentle, he managed to convey a world of ideas in very few words. Julia watched his strong, expert hands moving the walls on the model in and out, with the skill of a prestidigitator, revealing hidden treasures, as he facilitated camera positions. Magic fingers. What did that say about a man? He had dark blond, longish hair curling slightly over his collar, a lightly tanned face the focus of which was a pair of riveting blue eyes, almost azure, with a penetrating gaze, and thick, dark eyelashes: God, you could harvest those eyelashes. He was an amazingly handsome young man, seemingly unaware of his good looks. Certainly he didn't dress in a way to knowingly set them off, although his strong, well-developed thigh muscles were outlined by the tight, faded blue-gray jeans he wore, along with a soft, blue denim shirt, the sleeves rolled up to reveal tanned, strongly muscled fore-arms, with a light dusting of dark blond hair. Macho sensitivity. She was a sucker for that. Those sculptor's hands, large, powerful, long tapered fingers moving gracefully through the air. What would those fingers be like moving over her body, unbuttoning the front of her blouse, sliding the silk off her shoulder? What would he be like in bed, this gentle, quiet young man? Would he make love slowly, with exquisite precision?

She looked up to see Liam staring at her intently with that all-seeing deep-blue gaze. Oops, watch it, Julia. How old was this guy, anyway, twenty-eight, thirty at the most? You're in danger of becoming a dirty old woman. Mind you, sex with Marty had taken a back seat for the last little while, with all the pressure and demands of running the show. She could be excused the odd salacious thought, couldn't she? Still, what if he could see into her X-rated mind? She shivered and the look between them was suddenly broken, as if severing an electrical connection.

Eleven-thirty a.m. The actors arrived, in high spirits, bubbling about what they'd all been doing during the previous week's hiatus. Melissa was always first on the set, J.C. and Brandon the last to arrive. They liked to go over the script together in Brandon's trailer, discussing character, working out bits of business, before joining the others around the table. Alex didn't mind. Despite Julia's faith in J.C., like the network execs, he'd been worried she wouldn't be able to cut it as an actress. Whatever Brandon was doing with J.C. it seemed to be working, and the results were worth ceding a little directorial authority.

'Hi, Julia,' Paul Green gave her a quick kiss on the cheek. 'And what did you do during the hiatus?'

'Worked on the next two scripts,' Julia said, 'as usual.' It never failed. After a week off, when the actors came back for the first reading of the table draft, invariably one of them asked her what she'd been doing on hiatus. As if time stopped for everyone just because it stopped for them. The actors got these mini-vacations while the writers and producers worked straight on through.

'Oy, I forgot,' Paul smacked his forehead. 'Well, you done good. This script's a winner.'

'OK, people, let's settle.' Alex made his usual welcoming speech and then announced the good news that CBN had ordered nine more episodes of the show, which would take them into the middle of April. A huge cheer went up around the table. 'I hope none of you have a conflict with that. Of course, it doesn't really matter if you do,' he joked, 'you've already sold your souls to the devil. Your contracts dictate your obligations to Makeover take precedence over anything else.' The cast nodded, smiling.

Julia looked at the happy, relaxed, faces around the table and remembered back to the pilot episode when a nervous, much less confident group of actors sat stiffly in those same chairs. They hadn't come together as a team then, but now they were 'our little family', as Alex liked to call them. Acting was all about presentation. Conceal, then reveal. What are you really thinking? she wondered as she looked at each of them. Let me climb inside your head.

Paul was facing a dilemma. He was just about to sign for his first major role in a feature film. *Shooting Blanks* was about a sperm bank and Paul played the friend of a childless couple who offers his sperm to his friends in order to save their marriage. He was really excited about the offer. In fact, he'd been planning to tell everybody of his coup during the lunchbreak today. He figured he was in for some razzing and a number of sperm jokes but he had his own in mind: 'A lot of sperm movies are shot, but only one makes it.' All right, it wasn't a class A project, but he didn't want to get stuck in television. To be immortalized on celluloid. That would last forever, long after a TV series was gone and forgotten. He crossed his fingers and prayed that the film company would be willing to delay the start date until after April.

Theresa saw that Paul was frowning. Did he have a conflict, too? She had already booked her ticket back to Miami. She'd agreed to spend the hiatus months working with *El Teatro En Mi Corazon*, a Spanish-speaking theater company, which was rapidly becoming an artistic and political force in Florida's Hispanic community. Fortunately it was a collective co-op so they couldn't start rehearsals without her. But her mother would be disappointed by the delay. She sighed and turned her attention back to the script where she had highlighted with yellow marker the few lines for Concha in the season opener. So what new twist on the chiquita cliché did they expect her to pull off this time? Kelly didn't have a big part either, but somehow she was able to make it work.

Kelly knew she was putting her own inimitable stamp on Samantha. She sensed Alex having to curb her natural exuberance so that 'Sam' wouldn't steal the show. Never mind, she knew how to bide her time, at least for this season. If only she could get Brandon Tate to leave her alone. He hadn't stopped bugging her to go out with him. Why couldn't he understand she just wasn't ready? She laughed silently to herself. Face it, Big Mama, it was Brandon Tate who wasn't ready for her. Probably the only way to get the star off her back was to let him think she was interested in somebody else. Shouldn't be too hard. One of the grips would undoubtedly be willing to go along with that. Kelly sighed. She was tempted by Brandon, but no. She'd landed in a tub of butter. No way she'd mess it up now.

Brandon gave Kelly a wink. God, she looked sexy in that tight black sweater. It was hard to keep his mind on the script. He was starting to get antsy. OK, so they didn't want him to direct until next year. Fine, as long as there was a next year. He could play Travis Kyle with one hand tied behind his back. He hadn't been offered a feature film in some time now. His career was in a holding pattern. His love life stalled. Right now, there was nothing he wanted more than to get out of Hollywood. Too many memories. Too much emotional smog and sexual pollution. He needed the clean, bracing air of his ranch in Montana. Ride the land, tend to his livestock, forget all about LA. Maybe this summer? But summer was still five long months away. It was only Monday and already he was wishing the week were over.

Shirley Bunting was already wishing this day were over. Mondays were rarely full days. Read through the script a couple of times. Eat a few donuts. A little discussion. Eat a few donuts. Then finish early so the writers could get right to the rewrites. Plenty of time for Shirley to get together for an evening session with her honey, Roy. They'd been taking big chances lately. A night together here. A weekend together there. Tentative plans for a whole week during the spring/summer hiatus. Shirley didn't mind the network's new plans to film right up until Easter. Roy was lost to her as of Good Friday right through the Easter weekend anyway. Maybe then he'd think about sending the wife and kids to his in-laws back in South Carolina. Or maybe they could stay in town and Shirley and Roy could go visit her mother. No, too dangerous. Besides Mama didn't approve of her relationship with Roy, never had, never would. It was as if she'd let her mother down twice. First, by becoming an actress instead of an elementary school teacher. Second, by getting involved (and staying involved) with a married man. Hell, it was too late now. Shirley was in over her head. All she could do was try to stay afloat and go wherever the current took her. She didn't have a rich husband to support her the way Linda Earl did.

Linda Earl's stomach was growling in a most embarrassing manner. Quiet. You can't possibly be hungry. You had breakfast. Of course then you . . . no, she didn't want to think about that. Locking herself in the bathroom and . . . But she had to do it. The camera added ten pounds and after all, she was supposed to provide the glamour on this show. Her husband, Steve, kept telling her she looked too thin, but what did he know? The tabloids were out there watching every move of her fork to her lips, for her tits to droop even a fraction or a new wrinkle to appear on her forehead. Right now her beauty was her trump card, her only ace in the hole. She couldn't seem to get a handle on her character, Nadine. For a while the heat had been off her and on J.C. Austin, but J.C. finally seemed to be getting the hang of it, and now Alex was turning his attention back to Linda. The order for the extra episodes was good news. They wouldn't dare drop her in the middle of the season, would they? She knew she wasn't popular enough yet with the viewers. She wasn't getting as much fanmail as J.C.. Of course, that was to be expected. J.C. Austin had a lot of cross-over fans from her country music career. But Kelly Carmichael was getting loads of fanmail. She'd started as a minor player and now, with every episode, they were giving her more lines. Kelly was the new enemy, Kelly was the one to watch. God, her stomach was really hurting. The bathroom. Could she make it? She felt like a kid, no older than Melissa as, raising her hand, she tremulously asked to be excused.

Melissa could hardly contain her joy at hearing the filming schedule would be extended into April. That meant a delay on going back to school. By the time she returned to school it would be Easter and then came May and then summer vacation. During the weeks of film, she had a tutor on the set for at least three hours a day. When there was a week of hiatus, she tried to catch up with her regular class work at a junior high school in the Hollywood Hills. She hated it there. The school was full of rich kids who thought they were so much more sophisticated than Canuck Melissa McKimmie. So she was on a TV show, so what? This was LA. All the girls talked about was boys and when they would be old enough to have sex. Mel couldn't even imagine it. She didn't know who she was supposed to be when she was at school. On Makeover she was Carlene Barnett, cute and funny, daughter to J.C. aka Janine Barnett. Always ready with a quip. America's smartass sweetheart. If the truth be known, she preferred being Carlene. It was a lot easier than being Melissa.

J.C. was recovering from another real nasty set-to with Mac. She counted on being able to talk straight with him. They'd always shared everything, that was one of the big strengths of their marriage. When she left the studio and went back to him at night, she couldn't wait to tell him all about her day, but no matter how hard she tried, she knew he felt left out of the fun. He didn't like spending so much time in LA and worried that he was losing control of business back home. Now he was back in Nashville and riding her about the album she was scheduled to record during the hiatus. At least now she'd been given a bit of a reprieve. J.C. had a lot of good ideas for her new record, but no overall theme had come to her yet. She guessed she was in transition. Probably Mac suspected that and was worried about what she might 'transish' to. In the beginning she'd loved it when he'd drop by the set and hang out with her on the breaks. Sometimes they'd sneak into her trailer for a quickie at lunchtime. But now Mac was complaining that the studio didn't treat her enough like a star. J.C. tried to explain that was part of Julia's ensemble concept, but Mac didn't buy it. He was protective of her, that was one of the things she loved about him, but right now she had to trust Julia. She had to believe Julia wouldn't take advantage of her or steer her wrong. The last thing she needed was for Mac to fly in and start making demands, in her name, and putting everybody's back up. No, the best thing to do was to try to keep Mac away from the set during the week. Let him come to the Friday taping and the party after. Still that meant she had to get through the whole long week of rehearsal all on her own. Lucky she had Brandon to pick up where Mac left off. She wondered if Alex was aware of just how much Brandon was helping her.

Alex clapped his hands to signal the start of the read-through, the production assistant, Cindi, stood by with the stopwatch, and the cast jumped into the story, instantly bringing to life the characters they now knew so well. Julia was amazed at how easily they shed the skins of Paul, Kelly, Shirley, Theresa and Melissa in order to become Troy, Samantha, Lyla, Concha, and Carlene once again. She had come to learn that an episode rarely sounded as good as the very first time the actors read it. Even with one of the writing staff reading in the minor roles, because Marty, his ever-watchful eye on the budget, refused to pay a day player for five days' work. Soon the room was rocking with laughter. Marty had assured her the Elvis episode was one of her best. The structure of the show displayed the ensemble cast to full advantage as well as showcasing the guest star, Todd Wright, who played the Elvis impersonator. Todd immediately hooked into the essence of what Julia had written. He made his Elvis wannabee pathetic and desperately hilarious. When the reading came to an end, the entire company burst into spontaneous applause, but Julia was not wearing her happy face.

The writing staff were taking bets on whether they would be stuck doing major rewrites and sure enough, 'Wonderful reading, gang, but we're just not there yet. It's not you, you're all very funny and very good; I need to do some tinkering with the script.'

'OK, everybody,' Alex stood up briskly, 'you know what that means. Actors, we'll work the few scenes we can. Writers, you can count on not leaving the building until

Julia is satisfied with the new draft. I have a feeling you may be pulling an all-nighter on this one.'

Monday, eleven p.m. The harsh fluorescent lights cast a greenish pall over the disaster area. Sitting at the head of the table in the writers' room, Julia presided over the cold remains of takeout Chinese as the staff writers tried to come up with a new hook for the Elvis episode. The table was piled high with stacks of paper, discarded pages of script, half-empty cardboard food containers, and the crumbs from half-eaten fortune cookies. A ripped packet of soy sauce had stained one corner of the table and grains of fried rice were everywhere.

They had been arguing back and forth for the past six hours. Pitching ideas none of them believed would make the show better, but justifying their position and their salaries. Every once in a while a staff writer manged to come up with a suggestion that resulted in Julia's changing a line, but it was slow going. They had spent the last hour and a half working on one joke. Comedy is not a funny business. It was Julia who set the tone for Makeover, Julia who embodied the voice of Janine as well as all the characters the viewers had grown to love. The staff writers had input, but they all knew the creator of the show was still young and enthusiastic enough to fight for her personal vision and resist any whiff of 'writing by committee'.

Her staff were, for the most part, male, middle-class and under thirty-five. Pac Vic had insisted Julia hire writers with a track record in television since she had none. Dave Fish was quick with the one-liners, Larry Bergman was strong on emotion and Ross Brown could usually be counted on to come up with an unexpected plot twist. They all had their favorite characters. Dave liked writing for Paul/Troy, Ross was having a ball with Kelly/Sam and surprisingly, thirty-two-year-old Larry was proficient at getting under the skin of thirteen-year-old Melissa/Carlene. As a female producer, Julia had, early on, established her male credentials by roughing up her language and telling a few dirty jokes to let the boys know, 'You don't have to treat me like Mrs Cleaver. You can be raunchy if it helps you create.' They were a great group of guys, but it did strike Julia as ironic that on a show created by a woman, where the main character was female, the writers, aside

189

from herself, were all men. A friend had told her, 'There's a perception in the industry that women can write women, blacks can write blacks, Hispanics can write Hispanics, but young white male writers can write anything.' The studio and network execs seemed to have a love-hate relationship with the writers. If the show worked, they praised the director; if it failed, they blamed the writer. She remembered a Canadian screenwriters' joke: 'Writers are like tampons: not well-regarded but absolutely indispensable.' Still she was being paid more money than she had made in all the rest of the years of her life, so why bitch?

Julia took a sip of tepid jasmine tea. 'I like the device of the Elvis impersonator but it isn't leading anywhere, there's not enough of a pay-off. I know we're all tired and desperate to get out of here, but we've got to lick this tonight, so let's do a little brainstorming. What is America's fascination with Elvis? What does the Elvis legend represent?'

'The death of the sixties.' With his bamboo chopsticks, Ross nervously poked a deep fried Bo Bo ball that was trapped in a sticky, translucent orange mass in the middle of the desk. Ross was a chain smoker and since the writers' room had been declared a non-smoking area, he was counting the minutes until he could gracefully slip out for a cigarette.

'No, idgit, that was the Beatles,' Dave picked at the mound of slimy, worm-like beansprouts which made up the bulk of the House of Chan's special subgum chow mein. 'Maybe Elvis needs to talk about drugs, you know, something along the lines of "Death, the ultimate popper." '

'Forget it,' Ross said. 'That line will never get past Standards and Practices.' He stood up. 'Time for a smoke break.'

'I've got to pee,' Dave got up too. There was a universal groan from everyone in the room. Dave always had to go the bathroom, every half-hour on the hour.

'Wait a fucking minute, you guys,' Larry was shoveling cold fried rice non-stop into his mouth, 'I think we have a chance to really say something here. Elvis symbolizes what's been lacking in America almost since he died, hope, innocence . . .'

'The loss of the American dream,' Ross agreed, still poking the Bo Bo ball.

'Guys, guys, you're suffering from too much MSG,' Dave

sat back down. He squirted plum sauce over a cold egg roll displaying a thick layer of congealed grease. 'Screw symbolism. It's the personal connection between Janine and Elvis, what Elvis represents to her, that's important.'

'Wait a minute, I've got it,' Julia shouted so loudly that Ross jumped and stabbed the Bo Bo ball, sending it flying out of the sweet and sour sauce, off the desk and on to the carpet. 'You're right about the personal connection between Janine and Elvis, Dave. What if we did a kind of *Ghost* twist at the end and have the "real" Elvis suddenly appear in the salon? Someone who looks and sounds even more like the real thing than Todd Wright. It's the spirit of Elvis and the only one who sees him is Janine. I don't know,' she started to trail off, 'maybe it's a wing nut idea . . .'

'No, it's not,' Larry jumped up from his chair. 'It's fucking terrific. Of course we'll have to find a second Elvis.'

'Lisa can handle that. Even if we don't get the new actor until Wednesday or Thursday, we can add the new ending then. So, what do you all think?' She looked around the room.

'I love it,' Alex enthused. 'It's weird . . .'

'Strange,' Dave added.

'Mystical,' Larry built the theme.

'Let's do it,' Julia said.

Tuesday, noon. 'Now look, New York, I've had just about enough of this shit from you,' Brandon shouted. They were in the middle of a blocking rehearsal on the set but work had ground to a halt as tension mounted between Paul and Brandon. Paul had gone off on another of his improvisational flights of fancy. The crew were in stitches. Alex was ready to kill both actors.

'Fasten your seat belts, it's going to be a bumpy ride,' Paul did an impeccable Bette Davis.

'Is that all you can do? Tell jokes, do impressions, one after the other, like some wind-up stand-up?'

The crew continued to giggle nervously. Tension was high.

'Watch it, Pilgrim,' Paul segued into John Wayne, then broke out of it to say, 'Stand-up is a lot more honest than doing a television series.' He turned to appeal to Alex, 'I want to go with the flow and the cowboy here keeps pushing the stop action.'

'I don't understand you,' Brandon said stubbornly. 'We've got a good writer here,' he indicated Julia who was standing at the edge of the set. 'Every word of this script has been carefully thought out, right down to the punctuation. What makes you think you can improve on that?'

'Julia's wonderful,' Paul agreed, 'but I like to use the text as a jumping-off point . . .'

'Excuse me, but are you a writer? No. You're getting paid to act, so why don't you shut up and do it?'

Alex could see that Julia, caught in the middle, was highly embarrassed. With a writer like Julia, every word was a gem, but on the other hand, sometimes Paul was able to put them in a flashier setting. But Alex could see that he had let this go too far. The first real confrontation on the Makeover set and it was in danger of getting out of hand.

'Look, New York,' Brandon ignored the warning signs and plowed ahead, 'if you'll just focus on your character, on what Troy is saying, instead of trying to second-guess what's funny . . .'

'Save the acting lessons for the star,' Paul snapped. 'What do you want me to do? Have us all stand around and wait while I find my inner child?'

J.C. Austin turned on her heel and walked off the set. Oh, shit, Alex thought, that's torn it. He's insulted J.C. Just what I need.

'You're the one who's Method,' Brandon retorted.

'Why do you keep saying that? What I do couldn't be further from the Method. I didn't go to the Bristol Old Vic and waste my time with acting training where you work in sense-memory-angst-and-preparation-hell. I'm improv. Improv is all about don't think, just do it. Run with it.'

'Why can't you "run with" what's on the page?'

'My feelers just automatically go up for funny. Sure, this scene is well-written but it ain't funny enough yet.'

'Then why don't you try basing your performance in reality?' Brandon said icily. 'First rule of comedy, "If it ain't real, it ain't funny." '

Paul exploded. 'Don't you try to tell me what's funny. I earn my living with funny. You don't know from funny, cowboy.'

'Stop calling me cowboy,' Brandon shouted.

Paul lowered his head like a bull, pawed the ground, and made mooing sounds. Brandon rushed toward him with fire in his eyes. Paul leapt up in the air, then fell on the floor in a melodramatic death scene. In a flash, Brandon was on top of him. The grips moved in to forcibly pry them apart. There was a hushed silence. The cast were dumbfounded. Alex saw that Melissa was crying quietly. Poor kid, she idolized both these men, and here they were revealing their feet of clay. Christ, actors were babies sometimes. He made a snap decision.

'OK, clear the set, please. Brandon, Paul, I'll see you both on neutral territory. In the production office. Five minutes. Be there or be square.' Alex marched off.

In the production office, Paul hung his head and dug his toe into the carpet. 'Sorry, Alex. What can I tell you? I've always been the class clown. Back in high school, the teacher made a deal with me. Be quiet during trigonometry and she'd let me have the last five minutes of class to do a routine. Turned out to be a great deal. I had a captive audience.' He laughed self-deprecatingly. Alex joined in.

Brandon didn't crack a smile. 'Do you have to be "on" all the time?'

'That's what I'm paid for,' Paul quipped.

'Your characters are still growing,' Alex attempted the voice of reason. 'Right now we have some, and I emphasize some freedom to play around a bit. We're on our way, I believe, to being a big hit, but we're not there yet. Once that happens, the characters do get locked in and the audience tends to want the same thing.'

'That's just my point,' Paul said eagerly, 'but for now, I've got to be loose and free. I don't want to get predictable.'

'Nobody's asking you to be predictable,' Brandon said icily, 'but professional would be a welcome change. I'd like to be able to count on you for my cues.'

'It's not my fault if you're developing Alzheimer's,' Paul came back too quickly.

'Why you little sonofabitch!'

'It was a joke, you jerk. If you'd get your mind off which bimbo you're putting the bricks to tonight, you might be able to remember your lines.'

'A little jealous there, son?'

'At least I'm married. To the same woman.'

'If your marriage is so fucking perfect, where's your wife? Obviously she doesn't give a shit about what you do, she never comes around. Or are you ashamed of her?'

'You asshole!'

'You arrogant bastard.'

They were at it again. Alex stepped between them. 'All right, that's enough. Brandon, you're letting this get to you. You should have enough class to be able to withstand a terrier nipping at your heels.'

'Thanks a lot,' Paul snapped.

'And you, Paul,' Alex held up his hand in warning. 'I have more faith in you than you have in yourself, but the improv is getting out of hand. You run the risk of not really acting but performing. I think you've got a shot at an Emmy nomination for Best Supporting Actor. If you work at it. It's up to you. Do you want my help or not?'

Silence.

'We're already up against it, schedule-wise this week, what with the rewrites. I don't have time for this shit. I'd like to point out that the Elvis episode is not about the two of you. I have more important fish to fry. So I'm warning you. Neither of you is leaving this set until you apologize to J.C. We will then go through the scene calmly and politely. If it takes all night!'

Wednesday, three p.m. The run-through for the network was going well. The writers were laughing at every line that was even remotely funny, but then they always did, in the hopes of avoiding a rewrite. Word must have got out that 'Elvis Is Sighted in the Mall' was a hot episode because one whole side of the stands was full of CBN executives, including Tim and Stan. Tim often came to the first run-through but Stan usually preferred to leave it till the Friday night taping. Julia kept glancing over at him. He didn't seem to be taking many notes and he was laughing a lot. Todd Wright, the Elvis impersonator, in his skin-tight white sequined jump suit with the wide silver belt, cut just the right figure of pathos and humor. He looked a lot like the real Elvis, until Elvis number two walked on to the set.

Lisa, the casting director, had scoured the town to find a second Elvis lookalike and the search was worth it. Julia wanted a thinner, more sensitive Elvis, Elvis in his early days, Elvis just out of the army. In his pink shirt, black jacket, black pants and black tie, Elvis number two was to die for. He had just the right crotch movement and, with his softly accented southern speech, had all the mannerisms down pat. They were coming up to the final epilogue of the show. Julia was especially proud of this moment.

INT. THE CHANGING ROOM – EARLY EVENING.
IT IS DARK AND SHADOWY.
JANINE IS ALONE IN THE SALON. SHE TURNS AROUND AND GASPS AS SHE SEES ELVIS PRESLEY LOUNGING IN THE DOORWAY. CAN IT BE? SHE LOOKS AT HIM CLOSELY. HE SMILES.
    ELVIS: Good evenin', ma'am.
    JANINE: Are you for real?
    ELVIS: Why don't you come on over here and find out.
SHE MOVES CLOSER TO HIM. HE TAKES HER IN HIS ARMS AND KISSES HER.
    JANINE (breathless, looking up to heaven): Oh please, Carl, forgive me.
    ELVIS: It's okay, Janine. Carl sent me to you. He remembers how much you always loved Elvis.
    JANINE: So, tell me, what do you think of your commemorative stamp?
    ELVIS: I would have voted for the old Elvis.
FADE OUT.
END OF SHOW

The run-through finished to cheers and applause. Network and studio execs flowed down out of the stands and on to the set. Spirits were high as the cast and crew accepted praise and congratulatory handshakes. Everybody knew this was going to be a landmark episode of Makeover.

'Another terrific script, Julia,' Tim actually gave her a hug. 'The whole Elvis theme, it's been done to death, but you've made it fresh, original, personal. You've got an Emmy nomination waiting for you on this one, right Stan?'

Stan nodded slowly. 'I liked it, Julie. Your second act sags a bit, you could tighten that.' That was the usual note from Stan. She wondered if he really knew what it meant. 'I liked it, but there's one thing that disappointed me.'

'What's that?' Julia felt her heart drop.

'I kept waiting for him to sing with J.C. What good is Elvis Presley if he doesn't sing?'

Thursday, four-thirty p.m. 'Shit, shit, shit,' stormed Julia, pacing back and forth in a vain attempt to let off steam. 'A little over forty-eight hours before we go to tape and he wants an Elvis who sings.'

'This Elvis doesn't sing?' Marty asked. They were crowded along with Alex, Doug and Tom, into the production office.

'No. Looks like an angel. Doesn't sing like one. I can't believe this.'

'Jules, the ending works fine as it is,' Marty said soothingly, then exploded himself with, 'What does Stan expect us to do? Lisa had enough trouble finding Elvis number two. She can't possibly locate a number three before Friday night. Stan wants them to sing a duet. God!' Marty was pacing too. Julia stopped so suddenly that he ran right into her.

'I've got an idea.' She turned to Doug. 'Could we, in fact, use the real Elvis?'

'What do you mean?'

'Could we do it technically somehow? You know, like that video with Natalie Cole where she sings with her dad?'

'Or like the 1991 Academy Awards where they took footage of Laurel and Hardy doing a dance, colorized it, and put Billy Crystal right in the middle of them,' Marty's voice rose with excitement.

'How do they do those Elton John, Paula Abdul coke commercials with Humphrey Bogart and Cary Grant? It's all done by computer isn't it?'

'Hold on a minute,' Doug said, 'I know one of the guys who worked on that process. His name is Mike Geneva and he's a technical genius. They had to find the right footage from an old film, isolate the dead performers out of the background and context in which they were originally filmed, colorize them, and drop them into the modern video picture. It's done by computer, but you're talking big bucks and a lot of hours.'

Marty began issuing orders. 'Find an expert, bring him in, pay him a fuckload of money in order to do it in forty-eight hours.'

'Do it,' Tim agreed. 'If you can make it work, it'll be worth every penny.'

'But what do we do about the taping?' Julia asked.

'It'll have to be done electronically. In the booth,' Doug said, 'but we can give the audience some idea of how it's going to work. We'll put J.C. smack dab on a mark. With an empty stool next to her. She starts to sing . . .'

' "Are You Lonesome Tonight?",' said Julia.

' "Are You Lonesome Tonight?", OK. On the floor the stool will stay empty because that part of the screen has to be empty in order for us to put in the image of Elvis. But we can do the mix in the control booth. All the audience has to do is look up at the monitor and they'll see the result: J.C. Austin singing a duet with Elvis Presley.'

'All right,' said Julia. 'Let's go for it.'

Thursday, one p.m. J.C. invited 'the girls' of the cast to her trailer for a special, private lunch. Their happy little family had had its first fight and after yesterday's emotional fireworks, they felt the need to band together. Despite Mac's advice to maintain her distance as the star, she had begun to let down her guard and get to know the other members of the cast. Linda Earl had taken her shopping on Rodeo Drive. That little escapade had ended up in the *Hollywood Insider* under the headline, 'Makeover Stars Drop $20,000 on Shopping Spree.' But Kelly's advice about going public with her dyslexia had paid off, winning her sympathy and respect from her fans. Theresa had shared her dream of one day being a writer, and even Melissa had confided her concerns about Bonnie's all-night partying. J.C. found herself in the surprising position of mother-confessor, a role she hadn't occupied since her early days of touring with the band.

Today, Melissa was spending her lunch hour studying with her tutor for an algebra exam, but the others piled into J.C.'s trailer while she played mother hen to their hen party. They'd already demolished a bottle of Pouilly Fuissé, something they rarely indulged in over a lunch hour, but what the hell? It was a rehearsal for camera positions this afternoon. Basically all they had to do was show up and stand in the right spot. They were gossiping, just a little, and giggling together, relieved that the tension of the past couple of days seemed to be dissipating.

'I was real tickled. They both came in here to apologize, their tails scraping the floor like a couple of hound dogs,' J.C. bit her full, lower lip to suppress another giggle.

'Well, so they should,' Shirley said indignantly. 'I don't know what got into Brandon out there. He was ready to rip

Paul up one side and down the other.'

'I thought we were about to see a real cock fight.' Theresa helped herself to the lush fruit basket that was placed fresh, every day, in J.C.'s trailer as part of her contract.

'A lot of big talent around this place,' J.C. said darkly. 'Big talent means big egos. Shouldn't do but it does. It's kind of strange for Brandon, though.'

'Well, lately, Brandon has been acting strange.' Kelly went on to tell them of how he'd made a pass at her.

'Hell, that's not strange for Brandon,' J.C. laughed. 'He can't help himself. He's just like my late granddaddy's old hound dog. Give him a sniff and he'll follow you around for ever. You can't fault him. He's had just about every piece of tail in town.'

'To hear him tell it,' Linda said.

'No, that's the point,' J.C. defended her friend. 'You never will hear him tell it. He's too discreet to talk about it. So everybody else does. He's got a big reputation to live up to.'

'That's not all that's big,' Theresa chuckled. 'From what I hear,' she quickly added.

'Yeah, the old guy's doing pretty good,' J.C. agreed, 'to end up on every woman's top ten list at his age.'

'Top ten?' Linda asked. 'What's that? Some *People* magazine sex poll?'

'No, no, the "end of the world top ten",' J.C. explained. 'Me and my girlfriends back home used to play that game all the time. You know, the top ten men you'd most like to be shipwrecked with on a desert island, after a nuculear,' she mispronounced the word, 'holocaust. It's up to you to sleep with each and every one of them. God has to absolve you of guilt because the future of the human race depends on it.'

'All right!' Kelly gave the high five sign. 'Mel Gibson.'

'Jimmy Smits,' Theresa jumped right in. 'Andy Garcia.'

'Mm, please,' Linda joined them. 'Daniel Day Lewis.'

'Clint Black,' J.C. sighed. 'Whenever I sing duet with him, I forget my lyrics. Those cute little squinty eyes.'

'Denzel Washington,' Kelly was getting right into it.

'Hands off,' Shirley chided, 'he belongs to us. Same thing goes for Wesley Snipes.'

'Not fair,' Kelly said. 'I want Denzel on my island. And Gerard Depardieu.'

'Who's he?' J.C. asked.

'*Green Card. Columbus.* He can discover my America any time.'

'OK. Al Pacino.'

'Still?'

'Still. He just gets better.'

'Yeah, but he's so short.'

'So's Baryshnikov and he's definitely island-worthy. So's Kenneth Branagh. Some of these short guys, they put out a lot more energy.'

'Robin Williams. For comic relief. You're stuck on an island, you need a few laughs. Besides he can impersonate hundreds of men.'

'Jeff Goldblum, Steve Martin, John Cleese. Any guy who has the guts to dance around with a pair of underpants on his head . . .'

'Tom Cruise?' Linda offered.

'No way would I sleep with a guy whose teeth are better than mine.'

'Tim Robbins,' Theresa added. 'Just give me one night!'

'No! He's got a face like a baby's bum.'

'Maybe, but what a body! And a brain! Antonio Banderas.'

'Anthony Hopkins, Liam Neeson, Jeremy Irons, Patrick Stewart,' said Shirley. 'I love those English accents.'

'Patrick Stewart? Who's he?'

'You know, *Star Trek: The New Generation.* He's bald but what a voice! I want to lie on a bed in silk sheets and let him read out loud to me. Victorian pornography.'

'Oh wow,' J.C. sighed, 'I never thought of doing anything like that. It sounds great.'

'Hey, hey, hey, *momentito, por favor,*' Theresa broke in. 'Are we thinking about perpetuating the species or just ten guys we want to have it off with? I mean I would want a selection of the gene pool in order to get the right balance. So far, we're only talking movie stars. We need some brains here. What about Carl Sagan? Stephen Hawking? Athletic ability? Dave Winfield, Wayne Gretsky, Daley Thompson. Music? Stevie Wonder, Harry Connick Jr, Brantford Marsalis, maybe a couple of rockers.'

'OK, I'm with you,' Shirley said. 'Politicians. Nelson Mandela. He's a little old so I'd have to get started right away. Same with Gorbachev.'

'Wait a minute,' J.C. said, 'Y'all are taking this way too serious. It's just supposed to be who you're attracted to.'

'No way,' said Theresa. 'On my island, you gotta be selective.'

'Oh all right then, Bill Clinton. That's the only politician I know.'

'The Pope,' Kelly said.

'The Pope? He's not allowed to reproduce.'

'Yeah, well on the island, he'd have to.'

'Let's get some writers in here,' Theresa said. 'Carlos Castenadas. Salman Rushdie? Too dangerous. Michael Ondatje? Julian Barnes? What's his name Amis? The son, not the father.'

'Stephen King,' said J.C. Then seeing their faces: 'Well, I like his writing. I haven't heard of half these other guys.'

'Graham Greene,' said Shirley.

'Not fair. He's dead. No dead people on the list.'

'I mean the actor, not the writer. You know, *Dances with Wolves*?' They were back to actors again and the names were coming thick and fast. Kevin Kline, Nick Nolte, Tom Skerrit, Robert Redford, Armande Assante, Harrison Ford . . .

'Steve Earl,' Linda shouted. The wine, on an empty stomach, had made her light-headed.

'Steve Earl?' Kelly asked. 'Who's he?'

'My husband.'

'No, no, no,' J.C. protested. 'No husbands allowed.'

'He's gorgeous,' Linda insisted.

'Gorgeous? What man is gorgeous?' Kelly sniffed. 'You have a picture of him? Let's see gorgeous.' The women crowded around as Linda dug into her purse and brought out a snapshot of Steve holding the baby. Everybody oohed and ahed.

'You ain't lying,' breathed J.C. 'He belongs on the cover of one of those romance novels. Your baby girl's beautiful, too. What's her name? How old is she?'

'Maggie,' Linda said proudly. 'She's eighteen months. I love her to pieces.'

'I don't blame you. I wish Mac and me had been able to have kids.' She went on to give the explanation she always gave. 'Bad plumbing. Fortunately, all the rest of the parts work pretty good. But that little baby's just precious. Mind you, just look at her mom. You are about the prettiest thing

I've ever seen,' she looked at Linda with admiration. 'I envy you those cheekbones.'

'You want 'em?' Linda's speech had begun to slur slightly. 'You can buy 'em.'

'What do you mean?' They all leaned in.

'My plastic surgeon's the best-kept secret in Beverly Hills. If you're interested, catch me after rehearsal. I'll give you his number. I guarantee you he's a magician.'

'Naw, I don't believe it,' J.C. dismissed her with a wave of her hand. 'You are naturally beautiful and you are married to one handsome hunk of man.'

'I'm married, but you know what?' Linda giggled. 'I couldn't have turned down Brandon Tate. You're single, Kelly. What made you say no?'

Kelly turned a bright tomato-red. 'I guess I just couldn't picture being number four-thousand-five-hundred-and-fifty-two,' she said. 'I mean, the man has sown his seed so far and wide he's not even sure how many illegitimate kids he has out there.'

'*Madre de Dios*,' Theresa gasped. 'Sometimes I think men are from Mars.'

'Amen to that, sister,' Shirley lifted her wine in a toast and they all clinked glasses as a knock came at the trailer door to call them back to the set.

Friday, two-thirty p.m. Dress rehearsal. On the floor of soundstage six, wearing a headset, the stage manager relayed Alex's instructions from the control booth to the crew who were down on the floor. In the control booth, Alex sat in front of a bank of monitors. His hair was standing straight up from the number of times he'd run his fingers through it in frustration. He had been there since early this morning going over script changes and rehearsing the camera positions with the actors' stand-ins.

'Is this the right light for this, Doug?' he asked. 'I mean it's supposed to be late afternoon. It looks like night. OK, this is good for the master. Now let me see camera two. When Todd Wright makes his first entrance, remember to stay a little tighter on him. Oh fuck! We've got boom shadow all over that back wall. Can you do something about that, Doug? On the double, please?'

Doug nodded curtly. He was run off his feet. His expert in computer generation, Mike Geneva, had been working non-stop on the Elvis-Janine duet. Julia had found the right Elvis footage, not the original black and white, but from an Elvis concert tour in 1968. Mike was working his tail off but he hadn't managed to get the insert ready for this afternoon's rehearsal. They all crossed their fingers and prayed that it would work tonight at the taping. In the wings, Todd Wright was practising his pelvic thrust movements. Kelly, Theresa and Paul were running through the lines for their scene, the price tags still attached to their costumes.

'Are we close?' Alex asked Doug. 'Bring the rest of the actors out and let's do it. Go, go, go.'

'OK, rack 'em up and let's go,' Doug announced. 'From the top, please.'

Alex kept his eyes fixed on the monitors, snapping his fingers in rhythm as each shot changed.

Even though it was just a dress rehearsal, there was a small invited audience made up a group of sick children from the Good Samaritan Hospital, kids who had tested HIV positive, 'Kelly's Kids'. Thin and fragile, eyes looking enormous in their unnaturally gaunt faces, arms like twigs, easily bent and broken, they seemed very much alive during the rehearsal. They laughed loudly at every scene in the show, cheered the Elvis impersonator and afterwards swarmed around the cast, begging for autographs. Every single cast member waved them goodbye as they boarded the buses to be taken back to the hospital. No time for individual actor notes, so Alex promised to meet them all in the green room before the taping for a quick pep talk.

Seven p.m. 'It's not easy to get two hundred people to laugh exactly when you want them to laugh,' Alex told his cast. Outside the green room, the stands were crowded with yet another live audience made up of tourists to LA along with friends and staff. They could already hear the small, four-piece band playing an upbeat version of J.C.'s Make-over theme which signaled the introduction of the stand-up comic who was there to warm up the audience, so they'd be primed to laugh during the taping. 'Remember, this is a team effort. The person who sets up the laugh is just as important as the person who gets the laugh. Support each other and let's try to avoid retakes. Think of tonight as a performance of a play. It's like a Broadway opening and closing all in one night.' He gave each and every one of them a hug and then went into the control booth where he would call the show with his first AD.

In the VIP booth sat Tim and a number of network executives including Stanfield King and his race-horse elegant wife, Demeter. Usually wives hated attending the tapings, but Demeter liked watching Brandon. Julia and Marty had elected to sit in the stands with the regular audience. The Makeover montage was flashed on to the monitors and the crowd went nuts and stayed that way for the entire taping. Audience reaction was recorded live and often sweetened later by adding a laugh track, but for 'Elvis Is Sighted in the Mall' no sweetening would be needed. The audience laughed hysterically at all the right spots and there was a hushed silence at the end as the dialogue turned serious. When Janine sat on her stool and sang 'Are You Lonesome Tonight?' Julia and Marty along with the audience looked up at the monitors and broke into applause at the clear image of J.C. and Elvis singing together in perfect harmony. Julia burst into tears.

Eleven p.m. The cast was flying, high on the overwhelming response from the audience. Champagne flowed freely as the entire company let down its collective hair. Cast and crew members from other CBN sit-coms dropped in to share in the celebration. Julia and Marty shared a congratulatory toast with Tim and Stan. Tim noted that Stan's wife, Demeter, had Brandon Tate backed into a corner. Tim sent him a signal but Brandon waved him off. Apparently he didn't want to be rescued. Well, who could blame him? Demeter was rapier-thin stunning with long blonde hair to her waist. Brandon had hoped to corner Kathryn Grady but she had her new husband, Jonathan Long, in tow. Mac had flown in from Nashville to be with J.C., Melissa was beaming because Bonnie had made it to the taping this time, and Linda Earl was proudly introducing everybody to her handsome stockbroker husband, Steve. Kelly was holding court surrounded by the younger members of the production team. 'Give me a techie any day,' she whispered huskily to Theresa. 'They always know what to do with their hands.' She leaned over and planted a smacking kiss on the lips of Doug Berkley and everybody applauded. The wrap party was in full swing.

★　★　★

Midnight. Most of the cast and crew had split. The food and booze were gone. Julia and Marty were huddled together finishing off the remains of the Moet et Chandon Stan had gifted them with for their extra hard work this week.

'An Emmy-worthy episode, I mean that, Julie,' he said. 'You better dust off a spot on your mantelpiece.' He clapped them both on the back and then drifted away to extricate his wife from the clutches of Brandon Tate.

'I'm really proud of you, Jules,' Marty said. They shared a quiet embrace as they surveyed the scene of their triumph. Looking up, they saw the lights go off in the control booth and a figure come out and slink toward them. It was Mike Geneva.

'Sorry, folks,' he said sheepishly. 'I just couldn't get the computer generation to work for the taping. But it's no great loss. We've got time to edit in the Elvis insert before the episode is aired two weeks from now. The effect will work, I promise you.'

'What are you talking about?' Julia and Marty looked at him in confusion.

'I tried to do the mix in the booth but something screwed up. I'm really sorry. Elvis just wasn't there.'

'What do you mean?' Julia's mouth went dry and her heart started to pound. 'I was down on the floor and I saw it. I looked up at the monitor and Elvis was there. It worked like a dream.'

'No, I'm not kidding. In the booth, Elvis wasn't there.'

'But he was on the monitor,' Marty said. 'The whole audience saw him. Why do you think they went nuts and applauded for five minutes straight?'

'You got me,' Mike shrugged. 'I don't think it bears investigation.' He zipped his leather jacket and sidled off into the night.

BRANDON TATE SLAPPED WITH PATERNITY SUIT

A sexy brunette waitress/model swears Brandon Tate got her pregnant in a sizzling one-night stand in Oklahoma City.

'When he walked into my restaurant, I couldn't believe my eyes,' says twenty-four-year-old Connie Machado. 'I bribed the manager to let me serve his section. It was instant attraction and we flirted like crazy all through dinner. He was on his own and seemed to need someone to talk to. When he asked me to go back to the hotel with him, it was like a dream come true.

'I'd heard all the stories about him, but I never thought I'd have a chance to find out for myself. Let me tell you, Brandon Tate is the sexiest man alive and that night he proved he deserves every inch of his famous reputation.'

The tall, busty brunette, who looks like a Playboy centerfold, had been studying to be a model with the John Casablancas Agency, but her surprise pregnancy has put her career on hold for the moment.

Although she never expected that one night of perfect passion would turn out like this, Connie has no regrets. 'I believe I'm carrying Brandon's love-child,' the twice-divorced mother of three declares proudly. 'I've got a little piece of this wonderful man inside me. I've already had a sonogram and I know it's a boy. He's due to be born on Christmas Day and if he arrives on time, I'm going to name him Angel.'

Connie has used up most of her savings preparing for the new baby, but she's got big plans for her future. 'Right now I'm living with my grandparents, but once little Angel is born, I intend to move the entire family out to LA and pursue my modeling career. I know I can count on Brandon for help. Yes, he's rich and famous, but I believe he's a decent man who will want to support his child. I don't expect him to marry me but I have to admit I'd love to pick up the pieces of our fantasy affair right where we left off.'

Brandon Tate, who plays Travis Kyle in the new hit series Makeover, could not be reached for comment.

His manager, Michael Taylor, would say only, 'There is no truth to this woman's claim and once the baby is born, a simple blood test will prove that once and for all. Unfortunately, for now, we'll just have to wait.'

But for the big screen star it's going to be a long, cold wait to find out whether that surprise present under the Christmas tree is meant for him.

Susan Carroll

Chapter Nineteen

On the Makeover set, nobody took the story of his love-child seriously, but nevertheless they teased Brandon without mercy. Kelly called him the Santa of Sex, Alex accused him of spreading his Christmas cheer a little too early, and Paul risked coming to blows again by accusing him of having the inside track on 'who's naughty and nice'. Brandon took it all good-naturedly, but J.C. could see he was really upset. On a break, she put her arm around him and led him off to her trailer.

'This is just so much bull-crap and everybody knows it,' she said, pouring him a shot of Tequila Gold from her private stock.

But he pushed the glass away. 'Don't give me any booze. The next thing you know, they'll be printing I'm drinking on the job. You know so much has been written about me, I've tried really hard not to give a shit and to let them know I don't give shit, but for some reason this really gets to me.'

'Is there any truth to this story?' She started to pour the liquor back into the bottle, thought better of it, and downed the shot herself. They were almost at the end of the rehearsal day.

'I doubt the baby's mine. I did sleep with her. I think. I don't remember much about the night. Or her.'

J.C. whistled. 'Boy, you have got to clean up your act.'

'That's exactly what I'm trying to do,' Brandon lashed out.

'I know, honey,' she said, soothingly. 'Don't beat up on yourself.'

'I'd like to go over to the office of the *Hollywood Insider* and punch out the managing editor. And that reporter.' He was fuming.

'They don't have an office here in LA,' J.C. said. 'At least that's what I've heard. It's somewhere in Florida. Who cares, Brandon? Nobody is going to believe the story anyway.'

'What does that matter? *Insider* readers don't want the truth, they want entertainment.'

'Well, remember what you're always telling me. People want to know about you. That's what made you a star. At least they're writing about you again. That means they're still interested.'

'I guess you're right,' Brandon nodded. 'Did you know that some stars actually inform on themselves?'

'You're kidding!'

'Nope. Rumor has it that Michael Jackson leaks information to the *National Enquirer* on himself. If they don't give him enough coverage he complains. Who knows if that rumor is true? But the whole thing is a lot more complicated than star equals victim, tabloid equals victimizer.'

'What are you going to do?'

'Nothing I can do except sit tight and wait for the results of the blood test and the paternity suit.'

'If the results are negative, can't you sue the *Insider*? I mean something's got to be done about these people.'

'That's tough. And expensive. Liz sued and won. Tom Selleck won. But it's rare. The tabloids have an army of lawyers who make sure the accusations are within the letter of the law. Look, this thing is very carefully worded. 'Fantasy affair.' 'I believe I'm carrying Brandon's love-child.' The quotes leave her open to suspicion. She was probably just a simple, hard-working single mother until the *Insider* tracked her down and put the bug in her ear about a paternity suit. She's being manipulated, too. The writers have done everything they can to make her look like a gold-digging little slut. They're very quick to tell us that she looks like a *Playboy* centerfold and that, at twenty-four, she's already got three kids and has been divorced twice. That way their ass is covered if the blood test proves I'm not the baby's father.'

'You could still sue. For libel.'

'No, that's the point. All newspapers, including the tabs, are protected by the First Amendment as long as the article was written without malicious intent.'

J.C. nodded thoughtfully. 'You know, I wonder if Julia's right?'

'About what?'

'She told me she knew she was taking a chance sending up the tabloids with the Elvis episode. They might try to get their own back. I just hope this doesn't mean a war between Makeover and the *Insider*.'

'I doubt it. They've got their own angle on every piece of crap, but so far we've come out of this pretty easily.'

'You think so?' J.C. raised an eyebrow. 'Obviously you didn't read the rest of the paper. There's a full-page spread on Linda Earl. This time, they got two of us in one issue.'

'BEAUTY QUEEN'S FACE EVERY INCH MAN-MADE', screamed the *Insider* headline. Linda Earl felt sick to her stomach. Really sick this time, not self-induced nausea. Where did they get this story? How did they find out? There were before and after photographs of her which practically filled the page. One of those luridly colored head-and-shoulder shots with little black arrows aimed at each feature of her face and the price it was estimated to have cost her to have it fixed.

Nose: rhinoplasty – $5,000. Cheekbones: implants – $3,500. Eyes: removal of bags – $4,600. Jaw: restructuring – $8,000. Teeth: bonding – $3,000. And on and on. The list seemed endless laid out and itemized like that and the pictures made her feel naked, stripped of all dignity. Fortunately she hadn't been called until late in the afternoon, so she hadn't had to face her co-workers yet.

'Linda Earl was born a nine,' Dr Robert Carriage was quoted as saying. 'I just made her ten.' Why would Dr Bob betray her confidence? This late in the game after keeping her secret for so many years? Especially since he was the one who had talked her into the surgery in the first place. Someone through the *Insider* must have paid him a lot of money to do this, but why?

Robert Carriage had been one of the beauty pageant judges early on in her career. What was it? Miss Louisville Legs? Miss Cajun Crawfish? Some dumb, small-time contest. Long before she was crowned Miss Kentucky and on her way to second runner-up for Miss America. Dr Bob stepped in and offered to 'shave a tiny bit off her nose, make it even more perfect'. Some people called Dr Bob a pageant-chaser, the way lawyers were sometimes referred to as ambulance-chasers, but Linda, at eighteen, refused to listen to them. She began a long, professional and personal relationship with Dr Bob, who put her in touch with a paid pageant-trainer. The trainer taught her basic posture and poise, coached her on her talent, grilled her on the right answers to possible interview questions, selected the right clothes for her and, most important of all, helped her lose seven pounds of baby fat.

For four years of her life, it seemed to Linda she spent every waking hour either working out in the gym or stretched out like the cheese of a grilled sandwich in the tanning machine while listening to Dr Bob's motivational cassette tapes. Every couple of months, she went into the clinic for a little bit more improvement. A naïve eighteen, even Linda drew the line at liposuction – after all, women had died from it – but she went along with everything else. She couldn't remember eating a thing during that four-year period. Of course she must have, but she had certainly starved herself, knocking back laxatives and popping uppers in order to drop a few more pounds quickly. In fact, it was from one of the other pageant girls that she'd learned to stick her finger down her throat. What a magical way to get rid of unwanted calories! More than anything, she wanted to win, and her parents wanted that for her, too. By the time she made it to Atlantic City, her body was lighter by twelve pounds and her parents' wallets by close to sixty thousand dollars.

Still, it was worth it. She hadn't been crowned Miss America and she was just as glad. She would have had to travel as a goodwill ambassador and lose a year out of her life. Instead, a talent scout offered her a recording contract. She couldn't really sing but the record deal led to a lucrative stint on a New York soap and then a jump to a night-time romance series in LA. And now Makeover. But for how long?

There was a knock at her dressing-room door. First AD Tom Bentley stuck his head round the door. Linda flashed him a dazzling smile, revealing her perfectly even white teeth. He might as well see what she'd paid for. 'Hi,' she said brightly. 'Ready for me on set?'

'Actually, no,' Tom's gaze shifted uneasily. 'Tim Talbot's here. He wants to see you and Brandon in the production office ASAP.'

Oh, please. No. Not yet. Silently, Linda gathered up her script and her bag. She followed Tim out the door, convinced the axe was about to fall.

Stan and Tim faced Brandon and Linda in the production office, the late afternoon light streaming in through the window. 'I'm sending you two to Houston,' Tim said looking at a fax he was holding in his hand. 'We're doing a joint promotion thing here, kids. There's a Mrs Houston Mom contest being held downtown at the Hyatt. It's a contest for married women between the ages of twenty and forty-five. The top prize is a complete "Mommy Makeover" for the winner, plus a small role on an episode of Makeover. Don't know how we'll handle some housewife who's never acted before, but we'll cross that tightrope when we come to it. In the meantime, the Houston Chamber of Commerce has faxed me a message asking that Linda Earl and Brandon Tate be part of the panel of judges. OK with you, kids?' For the first time he looked up and saw them staring at him. 'What's the matter? We're not talking some tacky beauty contest here. Can't get away with that in the nineties. There's no swimsuit competition. Physical beauty is not an important criteria. These women have all contributed something to the home and community. They're supposed to be judged on their achievements. And how badly they need to be made over. Eat some good Mexican food, take in an Oilers game at the Astrodome, you'll have a ball. What do you say?' Neither Linda nor Brandon could speak.

Tim and Stan looked at each other and burst out laughing. 'What is it with you two? Is it the *Hollywood Insider* garbage? Did you think you were going to be called on the carpet and given a slap on the wrist for being bad kids? Come on. This is great for the show. They're really starting to pay attention to us. You can't buy this kind of publicity.'

Tim was nodding in agreement. 'You have a reputation to live up to, Brandon. The female viewers expect you to do something like this and they'll all get a vicarious charge out of it. Linda, cosmetic surgery is hardly a dirty secret these days. Listen, if I could pay to look as good as you I'd do it. Why do you think the sponsors of the Mrs Houston Pageant sent me this urgent fax? Why do they want you? Because right now you're in the public eye. So go home and pack your bags, kids. You're getting a free trip to Houston.'

Chapter Twenty

'What am I doing here? This is crazy.' The thought was so strong in Debra Jo's mind that she looked around the crowded room to make sure she had not spoken out loud. The Hyatt Regency Houston had given over several suites of rooms on one of their top floors to accommodate the contestants getting ready for the Ms Houston Pageant. Downstairs the banquet room was already filling up with guests when Eddie let her and Jackie off at the main entrance. He said he was going to hang out in the Backroom sports bar and take advantage of the all-you-can-eat Mexican buffet until the contest started. Beau and Danny could occupy themselves in the video game room.

Standing in her bra and halfslip, jumbo hot rollers in her hair, Debra Jo felt vulnerable and exposed in the midst of the whirlwind of activity around her. The prizes for the contest were fabulous. A top-to-toe 'Mommy Makeover' that promised to show the three finalists how to play up their best features with easy-to-manage hairstyles and make-up. For first runner-up, a complete spring wardrobe for the mom and her kids to be photographed by the fashion photographer from *Houston* magazine. But the grand prize, the one Debra Jo would almost be willing to give up her firstborn for, was the chance to appear on an episode of Makeover with three, count them, three guaranteed lines of dialogue. Imagine actually being in a scene with Linda Earl or Kelly Carmichael. Having the chance to be near that hunky Brandon Tate and the hilarious Paul Green. Wouldn't her neighbors in Sharpstown just die? What if she got to meet J.C. Austin? They'd have lots to talk about, that's for sure, because Debra Jo had followed J.C.'s career from the very first record she cut in Nashville. She knew everything about her country singing idol that it was

212

possible for a mere fan to know. Wouldn't J.C. Austin be surprised?

Wait a minute. Hold the line here, girl. What chance did she have of winning this contest? Beauty pageants had always been big business in Texas, with a support industry of trainers, corporate sponsors, and advertising that made the Olympics look picayunish by comparison. Growing up, Debra Jo watched the finals for the Miss Texas Pageant with envy. Never in a million years would she be tall enough, thin enough, or just plain – might as well face it – pretty enough. She hadn't even made cheerleader in high school. President of the Junior Homemakers of America was more her speed. Still, all the publicity the Chamber of Commerce had put out about this contest stressed the concept that they were not looking for just another pretty face. Leadership skills and the ability to communicate were at the top of the list. As far as Debra Jo was concerned, any thirty-four-year-old woman who could communicate with a teenage boy and get him to do what she wanted him to displayed exceptional leadership skills. And she had to admit she'd always been popular in her own way. Everybody liked her. Even now, her best friend, Jackie, swore Debra Jo Fawcett was the only woman she knew who didn't have a single enemy.

Jackie burst into the hotel room, breathless.

'Did you find them?' Debra Jo demanded.

'I found 'em. And it wasn't easy, honey pie.' Jackie reached into the pocket of her sweater coat and triumphantly brought out a little cardboard egg containing a pair of Leggs super sheer pantyhose. 'They had plenty of regular but I had to look high and low for shadow toe light beige.'

'I'll love you for ever, I promise.' Debra Jo plopped down on the nearest pink plush chair and began to roll the stockings on to her legs. 'These are the only kind that can hold in my thighs. It's like wearing a girdle on your legs. Who knows how long I'm going to be standing around tonight? I should have had my veins stripped after Danny was born.'

'Guess who I saw sitting and having a drink in the Park Lounge in the lobby?'

'Who?' Debra Jo was trying not to huff and puff in front of the other contestants. Darn, these stockings were snug.

'Mayor Bob Lanier and his lovely wife, Elyse.' Among

213

Houstonians this was how the mayor and his wife were often referred to.

'Wow. Wouldn't you just love to sneak a teensy peek inside that mansion they've got on River Oaks Boulevard?'

'Yes indeedy. Oh, and coming up in the elevator, I saw . . .' Jackie held the pause for dramatic effect, '. . . Jimmie Joe Johnson.'

'No!'

'Yes!'

'Isn't this event kind of small potatoes for Jimmie Joe?' Debra Jo said apprehensively. Fat, balding Jimmie Joe Johnson was legendary throughout Texas as a sponsor and private coach for the Miss Texas Pageant. Over the years, an unusually high percentage of Miss Texas graduates had placed in the top ten at Atlantic City along with several Miss America winners.

'Believe me, if Jimmie Joe's hanging around the Ms Houston Pageant, it's a big, big deal.'

'You're right.' Debra Jo was starting to get nervous again. She stepped into her yellow satin shoes and let Jackie zip up the matching yellow chiffon dress while she took the hot rollers out of her hair. 'I don't know why you didn't enter, too, Jackie.'

Jackie blew a raspberry. 'Somehow I don't think a thrice married woman who is secretly planning the murder of her current step-children is a prime candidate for Ms Houston Makeover Mom. Listen, you did just fine with your pre-interview interview. You're perfect for this, honey pie. Everybody knows you live for Ed and the kids.'

'That's true enough,' Debra Jo fluffed out her hair and pushed her way through the group to a full-length mirror. 'How do I look?'

'Great,' Jackie drawled in that laconic way of hers.

'No, I do not,' Debra Jo wailed. 'I look like a demented baby chicken. I don't think blondes are supposed to wear yellow anyway. I wish I'd had my colors done when you did. I tell you, if anyone needs a complete overhaul it's me.'

'You look fine,' Jackie smoothed down the layers of the chiffon skirt. 'You don't want to look too perfect. There's got to be some room for improvement. That's the whole point of Makeover Moms. Now shut your face and move your buns.'

★　★　★

The banquet room was already packed. Debra Jo gasped at the magnificent chandelier which cast a rosy, seductive glow over the contestants. A chamber orchestra played softly at one end of the hall and the judges' platform was ringed with interconnecting arches of real silk flowers. Everything was so beautiful it made Debra Jo want to cry. She spotted Eddie and the boys in the crowd, blew them a kiss, and made her way on to the platform where the rest of the evening passed like a dream.

Once again, Brandon Tate read aloud the pageant guidelines: that the contest was to honor the total woman, 'one who gives equally to family, friends, and the state of Texas'. Along with Debra Jo, the finalists included a twenty-nine-year-old Hispanic social worker who ran a drop-in centre for runaway teens, a forty-year-old black mother of three who was the top woman in real estate in Harris County, and a single mother of five who worked three jobs in order to put her children through private school. Debra Jo didn't see how she could possibly compete in this group of high-powered over-achievers.

The ultimate decision was to be based on a description of each finalist and a public interview in front of the crowded banquet room. When drop-dead-gorgeous Linda Earl, who played Nadine, one of her favorite characters on Makeover, asked her the final question, Debra Jo was quivering with nerves and excitement.

'How do you value your worth as a wife and mother?' Linda asked, smiling at her encouragingly.

In a flash, Debra Jo remembered the *Ladies' Home Journal* article about putting an hourly fee on the work she did around the house for the family. 'I don't work outside the home like these other ladies,' she said in a whispery little voice. 'But I estimate that at ten dollars an hour, working at the very least seventeen hours a day, seven days a week, I'm worth exactly sixty-one thousand, eight hundred and eighty dollars a year. That's twice what my husband, Eddie, makes, so I figure he's getting a bargain.' She hoped Eddie wouldn't mind her saying that, but everybody in the hall – roared with laughter. They thought she was funny and cute. It felt wonderful to have that laughter coming back at her, rolling over her like one great big wave of love. With her natural spontaneity and her weird little voice, she was always making people laugh, although she never understood

215

quite why. She must have said some more funny things because the crowd kept laughing, wave upon wave, and suddenly it was all over and dream stud Brandon Tate was putting a crown on her head and the room went nuts and oh my lordy, she had won!

Linda Earl watched her joy with a mixture of nostalgia and cynicism. Debra Jo reminded her a lot of herself back in Sweetgrass, Kentucky, before a life and career in LA was anything more than a fantasy. When Linda had asked her about her children, Debra Jo had immediately pulled out a plastic folding photo-holder that she just happened to be carrying in her tacky little yellow evening bag. Linda flashed back to that day in J.C.'s trailer when she'd brought out her mini album of Steve and the baby. This little housewife was sweet and shy and so open. What if Linda had stayed in Sweetgrass and allowed her hips to spread with a couple more babies? What if Steve supported the family by installing air-conditioning units instead of wheeling and dealing in high finance? What if all she had to worry about was keeping a house clean and figuring out a hundred different ways to use Hamburger Helper? No, there really wasn't that much difference between Linda Earl and the cute, pudgy blonde in front of her except for a few pounds, a little luck, and a lot of money.

Wearing a crown, holding a giant bouquet of roses, with the chamber orchestra playing 'The Yellow Rose of Texas', Debra Jo was smiling so broadly her cheeks were in danger of splitting. Linda saw tears of happiness rolling, unheeded, down her face. She wanted to whisper to her, 'This isn't as much fun as you think it is. Go home. Be safe, be loved, be happy. That's worth more than all of this.' But what did it matter? For Debra Jo Fawcett, this was just one special night out of her life. For Linda Earl, it was the rest of her life.

Linda and Brandon leaned over the balcony which looked down on a fifty-foot drop to the main lobby. They were both giggling uncontrollably. It was four o'clock in the morning and, after a night on the town culminating in a visit to a local country-karaoke bar where they ate sushi and sang off key to a back-up rhythm ace, neither was feeling any pain. The Hyatt Regency Houston was famous for its huge swimming pool in the center of the lobby. Surrounding the pool were tiers of balconies going up to the very top floor with rooms overlooking the pool. This open plan had resulted in a rash of suicides where guests walked out the door, climbed over the balcony, and threw themselves fifteen-odd flights down to the pool. Brandon had just finished telling her a popular Houston joke with the punchline: 'Check into the Hyatt and drop down to the lobby.'

Linda laughed long and hard, then draped herself seductively against the door to her hotel room. 'Given your reputation, I suppose it would be rude of me not to ask you in?' She kept her tone light so that the invitation could be genuine or could be a joke depending on how Brandon chose to take it.

Brandon seemed to sober up instantly. 'Darlin', thanks but no thanks. Right now my plate is full. Just remember what brought us both down here. Those lovely little spreads in the *Hollywood Insider*. There's probably an undercover reporter under your covers right now with a tape recorder hidden under the pillow just waiting for us to jump into bed together. That's all we need. I've got to wait until this paternity thing is settled, one way or the other, before I can be bad again. So,' he leaned in and kissed her lightly on the mouth, 'give me a rain check, please?'

'Sure thing, darlin',' Linda matched him. 'Give me a call tomorrow, not too early, if you want to take in some of the city sights.' She flashed him a whiter than white smile and slipped into her room.

Inside, leaning against the door she was red with shame. How could she even think of doing this to Steve? She'd never been unfaithful to him. What was she trying to prove? Whatever it was, she'd been turned down: gracefully of course, but still, a rejection was a rejection. And from Brandon Tate of all men. Why? What was wrong with her? Everybody could see that he was head-over-heels in love with J.C. Austin, even if she was too stupid to notice, but that hadn't stopped him from going after anything with a slit between the legs. Why would Brandon 'I'm Yours' Tate make a pass at Kelly Carmichael who had to be close to forty, for God's sakes, and say no to Linda Earl? Obviously she was not sexy enough. She walked over to the mirror and stripped off her black velvet bustier. She'd never had any work done below the neck. The thought of cutting into her breasts had always frightened her. But now, as she studied herself naked to the waist, it seemed to her that they were drooping, just a little. So what if Dr Bob had betrayed her in the press? He had always been loyal to her on the operating table. Maybe it was time. And as for Brandon, her pain was turning to anger, he would be sorry he had done this. Damn him! Somehow, at some point, she would make him pay.

Chapter Twenty-one

Bonnie and Melissa were driving along the freeway in their brand new Miata. A pink Miata with a vanity license plate. The law of Hollywood: you are what you drive. The freeways of LA kept the neighborhoods separate and the people from connecting. Lonely occupants, locked in their automobiles, speeding along the freeway, their vehicles intricately weaving in and out, narrowly missing each other, noted the color, make and cost of a car, but rarely acknowledged the presence of a human being inside the package. In a faceless city which celebrates only famous faces, the vanity license plate provided a personal stamp of identity, defined the driver as unique and special, someone with a business, a relationship, an attitude, something that elevated them above the throng. The vanity license plate said, 'I have a life.'

The vanity license plate on the pink Miata read BON MEL, which meant that technically the sports car belonged to both of them, although Melissa couldn't legally drive it for another year. Bonnie had always called her daughter Mel, but since they'd moved to LA, Melissa had taken to calling her mother Bon. Like they were best friends, just hanging out together, instead of mother and daughter. Bonnie loved it. Why not? She was still young, wasn't she? Melissa could sense her childhood slipping further and further away.

'See that guy over there?' Bonnie indicated a man in a Lotus Europa two lanes over. 'Check it out.' The windows were rolled, the driver had both hands on the wheel and was talking away animatedly.

'Who's he talking to?' Melissa stared, fascinated.

'Well, that's the question, isn't it? He could have a cellular phone with a speaker so no hands. Or he could be crazy and talking to himself. In LA,' Bonnie looked over at

Melissa and they said in unison, 'you just never know!' They both laughed. Melissa was chewing bubblegum. Bonnie was chain-smoking. 'How was school?'

'It's crap.' Melissa grumbled. 'None of the kids have any real values. Most of them get allowances bigger than my college fund, you know? All the boys can talk about is the maintenance on their Mercedes, pumping up their muscles and surfing on the beach. The girls are a bunch of rich bitches. Heavily into shopping. Designer labels only, puleeze!'

'Sounds OK to me.'

'Yeah right. Plastic surgery's a fave topic, too. Half the girls in my class have already had a nose job.'

'Is this your method of telling me you're ready to have your nose done?'

'No way.' Melissa blew a bubble.

'It'd be fun. We could do it together. During your hiatus. Lie in bed, eat Häagen-Dazs, watch the soaps, and recuperate.'

'Mother-daughter nose jobs? That is so sick!'

'Will you please stop popping that gum? You're too old to be chewing bubblegum anyway.'

'Yeah, well you're too alive to be smoking. It's going to kill you someday.'

'Thanks Miss Moraler than Thou.'

'You can't say that. It would have to be Miss More Moral than Thou.'

'Is that one of the really important things they're teaching you in school?' Bonnie blithely tossed her cigarette out the window on to the highway.

'No. They don't take learning seriously. I mean, look, it's only three-thirty and we're already out for the rest of the afternoon so everyone can go to the beach and "catch some rays". They don't take anything seriously out here. Everything's got to be "cool" and "fun". I hate fun,' she said darkly.

'Would I ever like to change places with you!' Bonnie aimed a quick squirt of breath freshener vaguely in the direction of her mouth.

'I hate everything except work. I don't want it to be over. I can't stand it when we have those weeks off. What am I going to do with three whole months on hiatus?'

'Have a vacation. Like a normal person. You better start

thinking about what you want to do or the time will be gone before you know it.'

'I'm going to miss everybody so much. Especially Alex.' Melissa sighed.

'I think somebody has a crush on her director,' Bonnie teased.

'I do not,' Melissa said defensively. 'I just think he's a neat, classy guy, that's all. Is Alex anything like my real dad? I just have this feeling he is.'

'Get real. Nothing like him. Alex is rich, your father was always flat broke. Alex is smart; Gord was, now that I think about it, pretty stupid. Bear of little brain, if you remember your *Winnie the Pooh*. Great bod, though. My guess would be he could beat ole Alex in the bed department.'

'Mom!' Mel squirmed uncomfortably on the leather seat.

'I know, I know, you hate it when I talk about sex. If you want to stay a prude for the rest of your life, fine, but you're going to miss a lot.'

'Bon, don't get mad, but . . .'

'What?'

'I'm scared to ask you.'

'What? Goddamn it, what?' Bonnie swerved dangerously over into the next lane, narrowly missing another car.

'I want to use the hiatus to try and look for Dad.'

'OK.'

'Just like that?' Melissa was incredulous. 'OK?'

'Yeah. I can't work here in the States because I'm Canadian. Technically I'm still married to your father, who is still, as far as I know, American. If we could find him, maybe I could get my green card. Or at the very least, I could divorce the asshole.'

'Tell me what you remember about him.'

'Right now?' Bonnie was never willing to talk about that part of their lives. Not even when she was piss-drunk.

'Please,' Melissa begged. 'I need this from you.'

'OK,' she said surprisingly. 'I guess it really is time. But let's go to Point Mugu. We'll walk along the beach and I'll try and tell you what few things I remember about Gord McKimmie.' Bonnie reached over and turned up the cassette player to let Nirvana blast out. For the rest of the way they drove in what passed for, as far as Bonnie was concerned, silence.

At Point Mugu they parked the car, put on their identical

pairs of Ray Ban sunglasses, grabbed a couple of sweatshirts in case it got cold and hit the beach. Way out here, there was nobody around. Mel could see why her mother wanted to come here. On a deserted beach, time stopped. Real life ceased to exist. They could walk for miles and anything that passed between them would be heard only by a few moth-eaten seagulls pecking away at a dead fish washed up on the beach.

'What was Dad—dy like?' Melissa stumbled over the second syllable.

'You've seen pictures. That's where you get your red hair. Gord's was lighter than yours. Kind of strawberry blond.'

'No, I mean what was he really like? What made you fall in love with him?'

'Well,' Bonnie started to walk faster. 'He smelled fabulous. Kind of musky and spicy. At first I thought it was patchouli oil. Everybody wore it in those days. But it turned out that he wouldn't be caught dead wearing a scent. It was just his natural smell. That's what made me go to bed with him on our first date. Oops, shouldn't have told you that.'

'It's OK.' Melissa was struggling to keep up with her. 'Is that why you married him? Because of his smell.'

'Of course not, dweeb. I'm not brain-dead. We loved each other. No, wait, that's not exactly true. I promised myself I wouldn't lie to you about this.' She stopped for a minute and looked out to sea. 'Your dad was a draft-dodger living in Vancouver when I first met him. Oh, hell, let's be totally honest. He was a deserter. There were a lot of them in Canada even as late as the early eighties. They just couldn't or wouldn't go back. I was getting the odd job now and again acting, and I thought it would be really neat to marry Gord and get my green card and move to the US. Gord wanted to marry me so he could get resident immigrant status in Canada. He said he never wanted to go back to America, but of course I always knew that he would and I would go with him.'

'That's it?' Melissa looked dismayed. 'You didn't love each other or anything?'

'Sure. Well, a little bit. And, after you came along, it was really important to be married. But I insisted that you be identified as an American. The minute you were born I marched your dad down to the US consulate and had you registered as a dual citizen, Canadian and American. Amnesty was declared and . . .'

'What's that?'

'It meant that the draft-dodgers were forgiven and could go home, back to the US, if they wanted to. Your dad didn't want to, but this was a good chance for both of us, so I pushed him to accept it. He told me he was going back to California to see his folks . . .'

'California?' Melissa gasped. 'He could be near here right now.'

'Yeah, well, maybe. I don't know if he was really from California, or whether he just said he was because it sounded glamorous. I'm telling you he went across that border and he just disappeared. I drove him down to the Peace Arch in Blaine, Washington. He kissed me goodbye, promised once he connected with his folks, he'd send for you and me.'

'And that was it? He just forgot us?'

'I don't know, Mel. For the first couple of years, I'd get a postcard from him from different cities all over the US. Never a California postmark. And never any money. He obviously didn't give a shit whether you had clothes or food or an education. I mean, sure things were a lot more casual back then, but you would think he would have sent something?' Melissa started to cry. 'Oh, shit, baby, I'm sorry. He probably really did care about you as much as he knew how to. He wasn't exactly the most together person, you know what I mean? His brain was fried from all the drugs. It was one of the things we did together – only I grew out of it and he never did.'

Melissa wanted to scream out, No, you haven't completely grown out of it, you're still a drunk and a pothead, because she knew her mother still smoked grass and who knows what else she snorted. But she was so devastated by the story that her legs went right out from under her and she sank down on to the sand and began to sob, her entire body reverberating with grief. She cried, 'Daddy, Daddy,' over and over again, as if that would somehow make him materialize right there in front of them on the beach. How could he just leave like that, without looking back, without once trying to find her? She was a part of him, living and growing every day. Didn't he want to know how she'd turned out? Wherever he was now, did he ever wonder if she still had the red hair she was born with? His red hair? Wasn't he at all curious about how she looked, what she thought and felt? Or had she been such an awful baby, he just couldn't stand to be around her any more? Of course that was it. Not only had her father not loved her, maybe he had actually hated her. After all, she had some of Bonnie's genes, too, and being around Bonnie for any extended period of time was enough to make anyone want to get the hell out of there. She was her mother's daughter, and she and her mother were responsible for driving her father away and leaving them all alone. Guilt overwhelmed her, driving a stake through her heart. It hurt so bad Melissa folded her arms around her stomach and rocked back and forth to try and make the pain stop, her thin little body reeling with anguish. Finally, Bonnie put her arms around her and held her until she'd cried it all out.

'I don't care, I still want to go ahead and try,' Melissa wiped her nose on the sleeve of her sweatshirt. 'But how are we going to find him, Bon?'

'Well, don't ask me,' Bonnie said crossly. 'You're the one that makes all the plans around here. We'll do it somehow though, I promise.'

'Slut's honor?' Melissa sniffed.

'Slut's honor. Now come on, it's over a mile back to where we parked . . . Let's haul ass.'

They turned around and started walking in the direction of the car. It was getting cooler. A light wind blew across the beach, stirring up the sand. At the very same time, mother and daughter removed their Ray Bans and pulled up the hoods of their identical Gap sweatshirts. They looked at each other and started to giggle. Mel felt her heart twist with love for her mother. Maybe Bon wasn't perfect, but at least she was there. After all, she had kept her daughter and raised her all on her own without any help. Didn't that mean something?

'Hey, Bon?'

'Hey, Mel?'

'Race you to the car.' And the two of them tore off across the sand.

Chapter Twenty-two

'The network has approved your season finale,' Stanfield King told Julia and Marty. 'It's a helluva script, Julia.'

'Brilliant concept,' agreed Tim. 'You've handled the whole Debra Jo thing really well.'

Julia breathed a sigh of relief. The season finale had been hanging over her for weeks. It had to wrap up several storylines, leave the viewers hanging and eager to tune in next season, plus incorporate the winner of the Ms Houston Mom contest, Mrs Debra Jo Fawcett, in her promised guest appearance. All of America was looking forward to seeing a real live fan, a normal person just like themselves, appear on Makeover. Who knew if this woman could remember lines, much less attempt to play a character? Julia had come up with what she thought was a brilliant idea. Why not recreate the Ms Houston pageant, call it Ms Texas Belle, and give Debra Jo her makeover right on the show? That way she could play herself, art could imitate life, and everybody would be happy. They had managed to get a videotape of Debra Jo onstage in Houston giving the winning answer to her question which gave her some idea of what the house-wife was like. She had already loosely drafted a scene of Debra Jo walking into the Changing Room salon and saying something along the lines of what she had said onstage at the Houston Hyatt. Once Debra Jo flew into LA to shoot her scene and they had a chance to meet, Julia could adjust the dialogue as necessary.

'It's funny and, I have to say, intelligent.' Stan was rarely this extravagant in his praise. Julia gave Marty a smile of triumph. Marty had worried that Stan would find the episode too 'issue-oriented'. They both knew how that label struck fear into the heart of Stanfield King, but this time he seemed to be buying into the underlying theme of the show.

As a judge for a local beauty contest, sponsored by a line

of hair-care products used at the Changing Room, Janine comes face to face with the issues of sexism and the beauty trap. Through the eyes of her daughter, Carlene, Janine is forced to question the value of outer beauty for women in today's world.

> CARLENE: I don't get this. What's so great about wearin' a bathin' suit and a crown and paradin' around in front of a bunch of guys? What does a Ms Texas Belle do?
>
> JANINE: Win a prize for lookin' pretty and actin' stupid, I guess. Maybe it's time to change the rules.
>
> TRAVIS: What's the point of a beauty contest if Ms Texas Belle has a high IQ and hairy legs? Call me an oinker, but when you and I talk about a woman with somethin' upstairs, I guarantee you we mean different things.

Janine goes back to the sponsors of Ms Texas Belle and tells them she won't be a part of a contest that's just for the prettiest popsie. Nor does she want the prize to go to the best wife and mother. She wants to open up the Ms Texas Belle to any and every woman who chooses to enter. Janine's new found 'feminism' causes problems for the staff at the Changing Room and threatens the future of the business. Great cliff-hanger for the viewers. Would they be tuning in next season to see Janine running a shelter for battered women, as Carlene was pushing her to do?

Pretty basic stuff but still Julia hoped it would make the Beverly Hills 90210/Melrose Place addicts sit up and take notice. If there was anything Julia wanted to do, it was to buck the current network trend of courting the youth market with sun, sand, and interchangeable blondes. Julia had also scored a coup by getting the governor of Texas, Ann Richards, to fly to LA and be on the show as a guest along with Debra Jo. 'Ms Texas Belle' should be one hell of a hot season finale.

'In fact, we love the initial script so much,' Stan went on to say, 'that we've come up with a number of exciting ideas to make it even better.' Julia's heart sank. Here it comes, the double whammy punch. 'Tim, tell her.'

'I want you to expand it so we can get an hour-long show out of it,' Tim said. 'If this works, we'll run it as a special hour-long episode and program it directly opposite Rose-anne starting at nine instead of nine-thirty.'

'Wow,' Julia said. It was a bold move, but if it worked, what a coup! Provided they could keep the programming ploy a secret from their rival networks until the show aired.

'Wait, there's more. We want to do some on-location shooting in Houston. You've used Houston as a backdrop. Now it's time to see some of the real thing. There's a term called "fly-over" country for the land between New York and LA, meaning nobody knows what's really going on anywhere else in the country. I want to send some of our execs to Texas to visit our affiliates out there and get a sense of who we're programming for. Houston's the third largest viewing center in the US. We need to know what that market is really like.'

'This doesn't involve me going to Houston, does it?' Julia was getting a sick feeling in the pit of her stomach.

'Of course,' Tim said enthusiastically. 'We're going to tie it all in with a big promotion. Shoot the pageant scene at the Houston Hyatt where it actually happened . . . We can use a local Houston crew, send the minimum of cast members, J.C., Melissa, maybe Linda Earl and Brandon again. The Hyatt has already agreed to this, in fact, they're going to put everybody up. Delta Airlines will fly everyone out. It's a terrific publicity gimmick and we'll save bucks on the deal.'

'But I don't want to go to Houston. I don't need to go to Houston to write this.'

'Tell her about the *People* tie-in,' Stan urged.

'The publicity department's already working overtime on the idea. *People* magazine wants to do a joint cover story. You and J.C.'

'Me? On the cover of *People*?' Adrenalin short-circuited throughout Julia's body.

'Yep. "Two Hometown Girls Go Home". One to the city, one to the country. You're both from the Houston area, you've both made good. *People* wants to do a spread with photographs of you and J.C. at all your old haunts. Where you went to high school, where you used to hang out, J.C. doing a gig at one of the places where she first started singing, throwing the opening pitch at an Astros' baseball game . . .'

'I don't think so,' Julia tried to stop him.

'A couple of shots with you and your folks. They still live

in the same house you grew up in, don't they? Hometown Girl Makes Good. Let Houston welcome you home.' Tim was beaming as he finished his spiel.

'I don't want to do this,' Julia said falteringly. 'I don't want to go back to Houston.'

'Look, I know what you're worried about,' Stan broke in. 'You don't want a camera crew invading your folks' privacy. I understand how you feel. *People* doesn't have to come into the home. They're willing to do a group shot out in front of the mansion on – what is it – River Oaks Drive?'

How did they know that? How was Julia going to get out of this? She hadn't been in Houston since the screening of *Boom to Bust* over ten years ago, the controversial award-winning documentary that led to the split with her parents. A couple of polite, dutiful, filial phone calls over the years, an exchange of Christmas cards, were all that was left of her relationship with Claire and Leigh Hudlow.

'I don't want to go to Houston.' Since leaving Texas, she had not looked back. That was how she and they had wanted it.

'I'll be there with you,' Marty said. He sensed what she was feeling. It was partly due to Julia marrying him, a Jew, that the rift in the family had become a canyon.

'I won't go back to Houston.' Now she would be forced to confront everything she'd left behind.

'It's the cover of *People* fucking magazine,' Tim lost his cool and shouted at her. 'Of course you'll go.'

'I don't want to do this,' J.C. complained to Mac. She had a week off from the show and was back in Nashville relaxing on the front porch when Tim's call came about location shooting in Houston. 'It's fine with me to entertain *People* magazine right here at Lone Star Estate. This is my home.'

'You better think about this long and hard,' Mac warned her. 'You haven't had a full *People* cover before. You've had lots of those little inserts with your picture at the top, but you've never been the main story.'

'I don't want to go anywhere near Houston. You know how I feel about that place. I managed to stay away even when I was touring and I don't aim to change that now.'

'I'd be right there with you, baby, protecting you from anybody who tries to do you dirt.'

'What are we going to tell people? That the piney woods of Hidden Valley, my so-called rural roots, never even existed? My country background's a shuck? We made the whole thing up?'

'No, we can't ever admit that.'

'Well, where are they gonna photograph me? In front of the Red Oak Trailer Village on Telephone Road? Or Jerry's Round-up: Beer, Set-Ups, Dominos and Pool. Liquor stores and pawn shops, that's my real roots. Not hills and pine trees, log cabins and runnin' brooks. It's Telephone Road and that's the truth.'

'Hush, don't you say that.' Mac's voice was comforting but stern. 'There's lots of ways around this. We can tell them Hidden Valley no longer exists. It's been swallowed up by the city; there's a freeway running right through it. They'll have to photograph you somewhere else – down at the Saddle Tavern where you used to sing. Take 'em to Gilley's so they can two-step. We'll think of something.'

'I'm not goin' to Houston.'

'It's *People* fuckin' magazine,' Mac shouted. 'Of course you're gonna go.'

Houston. The first word ever spoken from the moon. Half cow-town, half cultured cosmopolitan metropolis. Built on six thousand acres of swampland on the gulf coast of Texas. A modern mixture of chrome and contemporary art deco skyscrapers, rising out of the thick, black, wet gumbo clay. The seventy-five storey Texas Commerce Tower, the Pennzoil Building, the Transco Tower, and the Republic Bank Building thrusting up into the blazing blue sky. America's third largest port. The Buffalo Bayou of 1836, the Houston Ship Channel of today.

Houston. Manic-depressive city. From boom to bust, Houston has seen it all. A love-hate relationship with oil. The high-rolling, free-wheeling, big-spending days of the boom in the seventies before it all went dry hole in 1983. As oil prices fell along with the dollar and the pesos, the office towers continued to go up, with no thought of tomorrow. When the reality of bust finally sunk in, the value of real estate plummeted along with the Texas braggadocio and optimism. It's tough for a town of oil junkies to kick the habit and find another big-business fix, but a Texan never gives up easily. Houston was hell-bent on recovery, attempting to diversify the economy, ready to be born again.

'Huge, hot, and tacky' was how the *San Francisco Chronicle* described Houston at the 1992 Republican convention. 'Big, Brassy and Bodacious' was CNN's assessment. Downtown was pretty well dead. Although the odd crane graced the skyline, many of the office buildings were empty. The downtown business core looked like a George Lukas Star Wars ghost town. Houston had become a city of suburban centers, planned communities, little pods of activity complete on their own and separate from each other. Venturing into the heart of the city was hardly necessary. Race and class were polarized, living in separate neighborhoods and rarely mixing.

'You were right, Jules,' Marty said as they toured the area in a rented Camry, 'this place is god-awful. It's full of people wearing prole hats.'

'What's a prole hat?'

'You know, those baseball caps, the plastic ones that say John Deere on the front and are adjustable in the back? The ones that sit up high on their heads and make them all look like congenital idiots.'

'Don't be such an intellectual snob. That's exactly how the average Texan expects a Jew to behave.' Julia had a city map spread out on her lap and was desperately trying to locate Sharpstown, the area of Houston where Mrs Debra Jo Fawcett lived. 'It looks like it's somewhere off Bellaire Boulevard.' They were on their way to meet Debra Jo and discuss her guest spot on the show.

'I'm not being snobby. I'm shit-scared. These good ole boys all look like they're carrying guns. That's one of my worst persecution nightmares. Right out of *Deliverance*.'

'Marty, you are such a wuss. They are not all carrying guns.'

But Debra Jo Fawcett, declared winner Mrs Houston Mom and about to be guest on Makeover, welcomed them into her home and proceeded to confirm Marty's worst nightmare. 'What's gone wrong with Houston?' Debra Jo mulled over Julia's opening question for a millisecond before answering, 'Too many drugs and too many guns.'

It had taken them an hour and a half to drive through a number of equally depressing little neighborhoods, full of Pepto Bismol pink Taco Cabanas, Family Fun centres, and kids selling the *Houston Daily Star* on street corners, before finally pulling up in the driveway of the low-slung, ranch-style Fawcett family home. It was actually quite pretty the way the backyard backed on to an old creek – 'crick', Debra Jo called it – with leafy green trees and a basketball hoop attached to the garage. A two-car garage that could accommodate the family station wagon and Eddie's pick-up truck. Inside the house was warm and friendly, comfortably decorated to make a visitor feel right at home. After plying them with iced tea and fresh Rice Krispy squares, Debra Jo cuddled next to husband Eddie on the chintz sofa like something right out of *Good Housekeeping*. The boys, Beau and Danny, had briefly introduced themselves before rushing off to a nearby mall for two-for-one Tuesdays at the movies. It was obvious to Julia that Debra Jo was as excited as all getout to be entertaining a real life TV writer in her very own home. She had already confessed that the whole family was addicted to Makeover, never missed an episode, and could remember whole plot lines, individual costumes, and the different opening montages for almost every show. Eddie appeared less thrilled to be there. He held his wife's hand tightly, thinking long and hard about each question, as though polite conversation was a trick quiz.

'To be safe here, you have to have a gun,' the plump little blonde was chattering on. 'I heard that at that party for Clint Black and Lisa Hartman, eight out of ten people were "carrying heat". How else can you protect yourself?'

'It's the immigrants,' Eddie spoke up. 'Asians, Central Americans, Mexicans, they all pick Houston and move right in. We got seventeen registered gangs, all separate according to race. They don't question, they just kick down the door and take what they want. If you're attacked, don't look at their faces, and don't go with them,' he directed this at Marty, 'or you'll never come back alive. Better to let them shoot you right there where somebody might hear the shot and be a chance of rescuing you than to go quietly along at gunpoint to some deserted road where they'd just shoot you and leave you to die.'

Marty swallowed nervously. 'I'll remember that.'

'Eddie, you can't blame people from other countries for wanting to come here. Texas is one of the best places in the whole world to live, so naturally people are going to flock to it, and naturally they're going to have problems fitting in.'

231

'I don't think you can call Houston a best place any more,' Eddie grumbled. 'Galveston Bay isn't fit to swim in, and we're second in the nation in air pollution.'

'OK, I hear you, but that's why our city officials have a big campaign to clean up the air and water,' Debra Jo's cheeks were pink with the exertion of proudly defending her birthplace. 'Every city has its problems, honey pie. Houston'll be back in the ballgame before you know it, wait and see. But Eddie's right, there's some not so good stuff going on here right now.'

'Crack cocaine, rape, car muggings, welfare babies, AIDS,' Eddie seemed almost to relish listing them all.

As Julia listened to their strong Texas twang, she was reminded of what made her want to get out of Texas in the first place. The unconscious racism, homophobia and right-wing fundamentalism that no honeyed Texas twang could sugar-coat. At least it was all out front. In LA, the same attitudes existed but were never acknowledged in polite society. At least Houston recognized its problems and was trying to do something about them. The collar around the red-neck was beginning to chafe a bit, beneath the surface there actually were the rumblings of change, while LA preferred to draw a veil of smog over its racial tension and violent crime. Plenty of lip service was paid to it, but not much had been done about it.

'The economy is fixin' to turn around,' Debra Jo declared vehemently, although not as strongly as she would have liked to. It wouldn't do to have her and Eddie fighting in front of the Makeover writers, not after she had just won an award for best wife and mother. Still, she couldn't sit by and let Eddie trash their home town. 'You can tell by the Galleria. Y'all just have to get out and see it. I swear, you won't recognize the place, it's been completely redone.' Ah yes, the famous Galleria. Grande dame of all shopping malls. Flashy showpiece of the boom years. Julia remembered it well. It was so big that, at ten, Julia got lost in its intricate maze of boutiques and had to have mall management call over the PA system to find her mother, which mortified both of them. With its skating rink, video arcade, and pushcart peddlars rubbing shoulders with Gucci, Neiman Marcus and Tiffany's, the Galleria remained a local barometer of the economy. When the Galleria was looking shabby, the Houstonians' spirits were down. Every time the

Galleria got a facelift, the economy had to be improving. 'I think things are looking up,' Debra Jo assured them all.

Surprisingly. Julia found herself moved by her stubborn optimism. There was a lively charm about her and, despite her fuzzy little voice, she saw some things quite clearly. Debra Jo Fawcett was honest and genuine, exactly what Julia had written the winner of the Ms Texas Belle contest to be. If Debra Jo could just be herself in front of a camera, her appearance on Makeover should win the hearts of all the viewers. The thrill of watching someone like themselves on national television: how could it miss? The episode was destined to rack up the rating points and let them end the season on a high.

Frequently throughout their meeting, the doorbell had rung numerous times as people from the neighborhood 'just happened to be passing by and thought they'd drop in'. It was obvious that, to the inhabitants of this suburban community, Debra Jo was already a star before she'd even said one word on TV. A string of neighbors trooped in and out to get a good look at Marty and Julia – 'writers from Hollywood', as Debra Jo introduced them. The last guest was Debra Jo's best friend, Jackie, a tall, rangy brunette with a lazy, corn syrup drawl. Watching Eddie smiling indulgently in the background as Debra Jo bubbled on to Jackie about how excited she was to be on the show and how much she was looking forward to meeting her idol, J.C. Austin, Julia suddenly flashed back to her trip to Nashville and her visit to the J.C. Austin Country Showcase. Seeing Debra Jo next to Jackie, she was almost positive that this was the woman she had mistaken for a tour guide, the one who had seemed to know everything there was to know about J.C. Austin.

'Excuse me,' she interrupted their chatter, 'but have the two of you ever been to Nashville?'

'Well, sure, honey,' Jackie slid all over those vowels, 'just last January. Me and my fiancé who's now my husband, and Debra Jo and Eddie went on a package tour. It was a special weekend for Debra Jo because she's such a big J.C. Austin fan. Why?'

'Nothing, no reason, really.' Amazing. Talk about synchronicity. She remembered at the time thinking the little blonde in the red boots was quite a character. Certainly the more time she spent with Debra Jo, the more that was being

233

reinforced. She could be really funny. Funny and somehow endearing. There was something about her that pulled you right into her. Maybe she should consider writing Debra Jo a few more lines? Suddenly she could hardly wait to get out of there and back to the Hyatt to her word processor. She intended to make Debra Jo Fawcett Cinderella for one brief, shining week. Certainly anyone who was willing to pledge her heart and soul to a place like Houston, Texas, deserved at least a fleeting taste of happiness.

Debra Jo was having a ball. Each of the seven days the Makeover company was in Houston had been more exciting than the last, a whirlwind of activity for all of the actors on location. J.C. and Julia had been photographed all over the place for *People* magazine, and a lot of the time Debra Jo had been right there along with them. Sharing a Mexican dinner with Marty and Julia at Ninfa's, dancing the Texas two-step at Mickey Gilleys, visiting Rocket Park and the Lyndon B. Johnson Space Center with Danny and Beau and little Melissa McKimmie who played Carlene, and going to the Livestock Show with Brandon Tate, whose father had been a genuine rodeo champion. Debra Jo could still only manage to say two words to Brandon without stammering and blushing, but Julia liked that so much she wrote it into the script. On the set, everybody was real nice to her and treated her just like a professional actress. Mavis Beam of the *Houston Daily Star* did a big spread on her TV debut. Even the kids were impressed and Eddie was getting razzed at work about being married to a movie star.

Who would have ever thought that she and Eddie would be double dating with Mac and J.C. at the opening game of the baseball season for the Houston Astros? Eddie had to pinch himself to make sure that the whole thing was real as they sat in the special press box and listened to J.C. sing the National Anthem with a live country back-up band. Debra Jo's head was in a whirl, working during the day and partying at night, getting her picture in the paper, enjoying her fifteen minutes of fame. It was like a dream come true and she wished it would last for ever.

'I can't stand this place any longer,' Bonnie McKimmie was throwing clothes into an open suitcase on the bed in their suite at the Hyatt Regency. 'Nothing but cowboys and heat and humidity.' She had been in Houston on location with Melissa for exactly forty-eight hours. 'I'm going to back to LA.' Seeing her daughter's stricken face: 'Oh, come on, grow up. You'll be fine on your own. You've got plenty of mothers to look after you here. That Debra Jo woman is just dying to get you over to her house for a backyard barbeque. Yuck. I'm outta here! Now call me every night after the shoot to let me know how you are doing. I'll be at LAX to pick you up, promise.' She slammed the suitcase shut and was out the door before Melissa had time to say goodbye.

Melissa wandered listlessly into the bathroom, pulled down her jeans and sat on the john. She could see herself reflected in the mirror immediately opposite on the bathroom door. What a stupid place to put a mirror! Who wants to look at themselves taking a dump? Her bare legs seemed unnaturally white and freckled in the strong light. She snuck a look at the crotch of her underpants. Yep, it was still there. A dark, reddish-brown stain. Could this be it? She'd been waiting for this for months. Ever since her breasts started to grow, just a little bit. She'd check her underwear every couple of days but, until now, nothing. A sudden, sharp cramp seized her gut. She was starting to feel sick to her stomach, too. Great. Undoubtedly Bonnie had taken all the tampax with her back to LA. She didn't know how to put it in anyway. Wouldn't it hurt? She thought about going down to the smoke shop on the mezzanine. They'd have the necessary supplies, wouldn't they? No, wait, then everybody would know that Melissa McKimmie, America's Smartass Sweetheart, was having her period. Late bulletin to the *Hollywood Insider*, eh?

She stuck some toilet paper in the crotch of her pants and made her way to the phone. The toilet paper made a rustling noise. First she dialed J.C., who was a couple of doors away. No answer. Next she dialed Julia and Marty, who were on the floor below. No answer. They all must be out somewhere together. Great, just great. Another cramp gripped her gut. She got out her contact sheet with the names and addresses of the Houston cast and crew, found what she was looking for and dialed the number. 'Hi, Debra Jo? It's me, Melissa. I'm really sorry to bother you at home like this, but my mom's kind of left me on my own. My stomach hurts, and I'm not feeling too good.'

★ ★ ★

Melissa was in heaven. She never wanted this to end. She was actually sitting at a real dining-table eating a family dinner with a real family. Just like on TV. Debra Jo's kids, Danny and Beau, kept sneaking looks at her all through the meal, especially Danny, but she didn't mind. Since Make-over she was used to people staring at her, stopping her in the street, screaming at her from a passing car. Danny and Beau were just curious. Well, maybe Beau was something a little more than curious. No problem, she could handle it.

'That was super-good, honey,' Eddie wiped his mouth with a napkin and pushed his plate away with a satisfied sigh. 'Great baby back ribs, just like always.'

'You don't notice any difference?' Debra Jo said almost flirtatiously.

'Like what?' Instantly Eddie was suspicious. He didn't like anybody messing with his food. Ribs were ribs and as far as he was concerned there was only one way to fix them.

'J.C. Austin's secret sauce. She broke down and gave me the recipe this morning, wasn't that sweet?'

'Um-mm,' Eddie knew it was best to stay noncommittal when J.C. was under discussion. According to Debra Jo, the country star could do no wrong. 'Did she give you a secret recipe for dessert, too?'

'No, but I made a deep-dish pecan pie. Want a piece?'

'Tempt me, woman, tempt me,' Eddie rolled his eyes and groaned and the boys laughed, sneaking another look at Mel across the table.

Jim Bowie's head was resting on her knee, his big, brown watery eyes begging for a gnawed-on rib bone, but Debra Jo had instructed Mel in no uncertain terms not to give in to his silent plea. 'We don't want to be putting that dog in the station-wagon and trying to find a vet open past eight o'clock at night the way we did last time.'

Melissa had spent the last three days with Debra Jo's family. She went to bed when they went to bed, in a beautiful guest room with a canopied bed and macramé hangings on the wall. She got up and had breakfast with them, breakfast cooked by Debra Jo. When was the last time Bonnie had done that? Then she and Debra Jo piled into the station-wagon to head for the set downtown at the Hyatt while Eddie took the boys in the truck and dropped them off at school on his way to work. It was all so normal, so simple really. Nothing extraordinarily exciting about regular family life. Unless you'd never had it before.

When Mel first arrived, Debra Jo had hustled her past the other family members, straight into the bathroom. She had given her two tylenol, helped her get out of her clothes, and taken a look. 'Yeah, you're perkin' right along there,' she said in a matter-of-fact voice. 'That's good. Your body's workin' just the same as any other girl's. I'll get you a maxi pad. Later, when your flow's not quite so heavy we can try a tampon if you want. It took me a fair bit of practice but, once you get the hang of it, believe me, you'll never go back.' She giggled conspiratorially. Bonnie would have made a huge deal out of the whole thing. Maybe even blabbed it to everybody on the set. Who could predict these days? She was so nuts. But Debra Jo treated it like a special secret between two women, herself and Melissa.

The boys stood up and took their plates out to the kitchen to put them in the dishwasher. Melissa followed suit. Danny went off to his room, but Beau just stood there, white blond hair hanging sexily over one eye, his thumbs in the loops of his jeans, shifting from one foot to another.

'Um, I guess you have to be on set early. For the shoot, I mean,' he spoke the words as if they were a foreign language, and to him they probably were. To Melissa it was all she'd ever known.

'Yeah, I guess.'

'Um, it's not too late yet. You want to drive over to the mall? Hang out? Grab a Häagen-Dazs or something?'

Melissa's heart was pounding. No, she didn't know how to handle this. She wasn't ready. This great looking high-school guy had a crush on her. What was she supposed to do now? She'd have to meet his friends. No, no. 'I can't, Beau. I have to talk to your father this evening.' God, why did she have to say it like that? What a dweeb. She sounded like an adult.

'Oh, OK.' Disappointed but too polite to show it, he slouched off.

Mel was torn. He was cute, a lot cuter than that Christopher Max Bonnie was still sleeping with, but what she had said to Beau was true. She had to talk to Eddie before he settled down in front of the TV with his nightly beer allotment. Debra Jo had told her Eddie was a Vietnam vet. Maybe, just maybe, he could help her find her dad.

★　★　★

237

Julia had been surprised that her mother was willing to see her, but apparently the prospect of appearing in *People* magazine was too tantalizing for even a Hudlow to miss.

'Do you want me to go with you?' Marty asked anxiously. He had a million things to do with budget and set for these location scenes, but he didn't want her to face her parents without back-up.

'No, thanks. I've decided to take J.C. to River Oaks.'

'J.C.?' Marty looked incredulous. 'Is that wise?'

'Damn straight,' Julia was slowly reverting to good ole girl the longer they stayed in Texas. 'Bringing a country singer into the mansion is destined to piss Leigh and Claire right off.'

Chapter Twenty-three

The gates at Locke and River Oaks mark the entrance to the most exclusive and fashionable neighborhood of Houston, where high society meets high rollers, old money rubs shoulders with self-made millionaires, oil barons entertain genuine titled barons and other European royalty. A broad street with a tree-lined divider, River Oaks Boulevard leads directly to the Hogg Bird sanctuary, the golf course and the country club, a club so private it needs no sign to identify it. River Oaks, Republican bastion, home of hunt parties and hoedowns, champagne breakfasts and beef barbecues, and the Team 100, some of the richest men in all of America. White colonial mansions with columns or red brick with wrought-iron gates, homes that rival the southern plantations of J.C. Austin and her friends back in Nashville.

Julia dressed carefully for this meeting with her parents. Claire had always preferred her in a skirt, so she decided to wear her latest Armani, a black and white silk suit. She hadn't felt comfortable telling J.C. what to wear and, anyway, wasn't the whole point of this little visit with her folks to shock them? But J.C., sensing the importance of the occasion, had on a softly tailored jade green sheath with a matching jacket. Julia would never have imagined J.C. to own such a classic outfit.

The Hudlow family home was set back from the road with a circular gravel driveway and high privacy walls surrounding the front and back yards. Ancient oaks and elms, trees dripping with Spanish moss, rose twenty to thirty feet in the air. The front lawn looked slightly less manicured than Julia remembered it. Could it be that the recession had invaded River Oaks? A uniformed black maid let them into the front vestibule. Instantly Julia felt embarrassed. What would Shirley Bunting think about this? In Houston, most of the black maids had been replaced with

Spanish-speaking help, but not at the Hudlows. Her father trusted no one whose first language was not English. Loretta had been with the family since Julia was in grade school. Looking at Loretta's still smooth, unlined face, Julia realized, with a shock, that there was maybe only about six years difference in age between them. She had always regarded Loretta as much older.

Loretta gave her a hug and said, 'Welcome home, Ms Julia. We're mighty proud of you.' Well, this was a surprise. Did Loretta include all members of the Hudlow family in this pride? She shook J.C.'s hand shyly, telling her, 'This sure is a pleasure. My husband and I, we must own every album you ever made.' Turning back to Julia, 'Ms Hudlow's waiting to see y'all in the sun room. I'll just let her know you're here.'

'Where's Dad?' Julia suddenly felt uneasy.

Loretta looked at her strangely. 'Hasn't your mother told you?'

'No. I haven't heard anything since Christmas.'

'Oh.' Loretta was obviously embarrassed. 'Well, I'm sorry to say your dad ain't been feelin' so good. We're doin' the best we can in a difficult situation, but it's hard.' She stopped, as if she'd already revealed too much. 'I'll let your mother fill you in.' She led the way and Julia and J.C. followed.

Almost everything inside the house had changed. She wondered if her bedroom upstairs had been redone, too. Was her old dressing-table with the mirror and lights still there? The white eyelet-covered bed? Certainly there was practically no stick of furniture or piece of decoration left on the main floor that she remembered or recognized. Claire should have been an interior decorator. With impeccable taste she managed to keep up with the Houston trends, from antiques and Oriental rugs through Danish modern to Santa Fe Chic. The thought of her mother living amidst all these wild, exuberant colors, silver and turquoise, woven blankets hung on the wall, was incongruous. Claire had always been more of a pastel person, controlled, tightly gracious.

Claire sat in a chair in front of the fireplace in the sunroom, where she had been photographed a number of times for *Town and Country* and *Architectural Digest*. Even though it was spring and already hot, with the sun streaming in through the long, paned windows, she had a small fire going. The sunroom looked out on a vast backyard, swimming pool, tennis courts, and huge flower beds, where so many garden parties had been held among the blossoms. Known for having a green thumb (and a high-priced landscape architect) Claire was proud of her garden. 'Lousy with people, great with plants,' is how Marty once described her mother.

Her hair was just slightly bouffant and a perfect ash-blonde. The color had not changed one iota since she and Mr Marcus settled on the formula twenty years ago. Was she perhaps a little thinner? Hard to say. Claire Hudlow monitored her weight as closely as financial experts monitor the price of gold. Her attempt at a smile was tight and frozen. Julia wondered if her mother had had any face work done: her skin was taut and still relatively unlined.

'Welcome home, dear,' she said, in that refined, educated Houstonian accent she'd worked so hard to instil in her daughter. Julia leaned forward to kiss her mother's cheek, but surprisingly Claire rose and clutched her in an awkward hug. It had been years since her mother hugged her and never in front of a guest. No PDAs had been a family rule ever since Julia could remember. The tight smile pushed at the corners of her mouth, but there was hint of some other emotion in her eyes. Fear? Disgust that she had brought J.C. Austin into the house? Her parents had always disdained what they called 'hillbilly' music. Claire and Leigh considered themselves patrons of the arts, contributing generously to the Alley Theatre, the Houston Ballet and the Grand Opera in an attempt to distance themselves from anything that smacked of Texas working class. That was one of the few attitudes Julia had shared with her parents. Now, after getting to know J.C., Julia was beginning to find poetry and pathos in much of country music.

But no, her mother grasped J.C.'s hand almost warmly, saying 'It's a delight to have you in our home. Leigh and I really enjoy you in Makeover.' This was news to Julia. Her parents watching her show? They'd never said one word about it to her. While her mother chatted away with J.C., Julia found herself tugging at the short skirt of her suit. Thirty-five years old and still worrying about whether or not her mother would approve of what she was wearing.

Claire turned her focus on her daughter, 'I told the folks

from *People* magazine they could take pictures of anything here on the main floor like this room, the living-room, even the kitchen, but anything upstairs is out of bounds. Your father's not well.'

'That's what Retta said.' Julia's heart twisted again. There was something her mother was not telling her. 'What's wrong with him?'

'Well, he had a little funny spell back in the fall. For a couple of days there, his speech was slurred and he had trouble remembering things, but we went to Dr Walker to get him checked out and they didn't find anything. By the end of the week he seemed to be his old self again. Now Trace Walker thinks he must have had a mini-stroke, because Thanksgiving Day he had another one, a big one this time, which landed him in the hospital. He'll be fine, I know he will,' her mother's bright tone never wavered, 'it's just taking him a while to recover.'

Julia wanted to reach out and shake her, hard. Six months, six months ago this happened, and nobody had told her about it? Why? But she knew she had forfeited all her rights a long time ago. 'I want to see him.'

'Well, of course you should see him. That's what you're here for. You go right on up. He's in the guest bedroom right at the end of the hall.' Her mother made it sound as if her father was on display, like one of her prize-winning flower arrangements at the Bluebonnet Festival.

'I'll go with you,' J.C. offered.

'Oh, no,' Claire said quickly. 'I don't think that's a good idea.'

Something in her mother's tone was really frightening now. Julia suddenly didn't want to go upstairs and into that room without J.C. right beside her. 'It's fine for J.C. to come with me, Mother. I'd like her to meet Dad.'

'Up to you, dear. When you girls have had your little chat, come on back down and we'll discuss the schedule with *People* magazine. I'm really looking forward to that.'

What Julia saw when she entered the bedroom almost made her heart stop. Her father, her big, tall handsome father, who seemed to fill an entire room with his presence, had now shrunk to something that could easily be contained in one single bed. His silver hair was much thinner, with a yellowish tinge, and he had a beard. A beard! She couldn't remember him as anything but clean-shaven, with a short, almost military haircut. She stood there for a moment, hovering in the doorway, while J.C. went over to his bedside. Julia didn't want to go any closer and have to see what she didn't want to see. He already looked dead.

J.C. leaned over the bed. 'Are you awake, Mr Hudlow?' His eyes were closed and his breathing was labored, a whistling, raspy sound. J.C. leaned in closer and spoke softly right next to his ear. 'Hello, Leigh.' The use of his first name seemed to get through to him and he opened his eyes. 'Julia Catherine, is that you?' His words were slurred and he squinted to get a better look at her. 'What have you done to your hair?' A hand reached up, faltering, toward J.C.'s red curls. 'No, it's not your daughter, but she's right here. Julia's here.' J.C. beckoned for Julia to come closer.

Julia sat awkwardly on the edge of the bed and looked down at her father. His eyes, those clear blue eyes, were now milky and vague as he searched her face. For a moment, she was afraid he wouldn't recognize her, but then his hand moved to touch her cheek. 'You look beautiful, darling. It's good you're here.' He spoke slowly, trying to form his thoughts into words. Already Julia could feel the tears in her eyes spilling on to her cheeks, but he didn't seem to notice. 'They almost lost me . . . but I'm still here.'

'I'm glad to see that.' Feelings she thought were gone for ever, memories came flooding back to her. Digging for clams on the beach in Galveston, her father following her across the wet sand, his big footsteps eradicating her small ones, patiently holding the red plastic bucket out for her to drop the shells into. The time he had taken her, without her mother, on a dinner 'date' to the Oilman's Club, and when the maitre d' had refused to seat them because women weren't allowed in, he had railed at everyone in the dining-room, saying that was the last they'd ever see of him or his money, and had then driven her to the Holiday House for burgers and fries. How could she have stayed away from home so long? Let her parents grow old without her? He was trying to lift his head off the pillow. She slipped her hand under his neck to give him support. His voice was barely a whisper.

'Julia Catherine?'

'Yes, Dad?'

'Are you still married to that Jew?'

Julia stiffened but did not pull away. He's sick, he

doesn't know what he's saying, he's not himself. Or maybe, if she's really honest, he's more himself than he's ever been. 'Yes, Daddy, I'd afraid I am.'

'Well, that's a hell of a surprise. I never thought it would last. You've got the jump on your mother there.'

'How's that, Dad?'

'I guarantee you she's never seen a circumcised dick.'

Julia was mortified. J.C. burst out laughing. 'The old guy's not dead yet. Still some fight in him, although it may not be politically correct, according to you, Julia.'

Her father pulled her face down close to his. 'Don't tell your mother, but I still love you anyway.' His eyes fluttered and closed, and his shallow, slower breathing told them he had instantly fallen asleep.

'Why didn't you tell me?' Julia demanded of her mother.

'I didn't want to worry you, dear,' her mother said guiltily. 'Dad expressly didn't want you to know.' She was close to cowering in front of them, as if the roles were suddenly reversed and Julia was the mother, Claire the recalcitrant daughter.

'Daddy is long past knowing what he wants. Have you been trying to take care of him all by yourself?'

'Retta's here. She helps. He didn't want the neighbors to see a nurse coming in and out of here.'

'Goddamn it, Mother . . .'

Swiftly J.C. stepped in between them, took Claire's hand and held it tightly. 'Listen to me, Ms Hudlow. You have to get your husband some help. You can't handle this all by yourself, do you hear what I'm telling you?'

Her mother started to cry. 'I promised Leigh I'd never put him in a home.'

'And that's real good of you,' J.C.'s voice was calm and reassuring. 'My granddaddy died in a home and I wouldn't wish that way to go on anyone. You're doing the right thing.'

'The right thing,' Claire repeated dully.

'Yes ma'am. But you need some help here. You got to get yourself a full-time nurse. Otherwise you won't be able to sleep and there's a good chance you'll make yourself sick. You can't let that happen because Mr Hudlow is depending on you, right?'

'A live-in nurse is too expensive.' Her mother seemed

even more immobile than her father trapped upstairs in that bed. Frozen. Unable to face the reality of the situation.

'You can afford it, Mother.' Julia was angry, furious, that Claire would let things deteriorate to this extent. Her parents have been married for thirty-seven years. Did they know each other at all?

'I'd have to sell the house.'

'Then sell it. Move to a high rise.'

'You don't understand. Even if we did put it on the market, we wouldn't get near what it's worth. Mayor Bob Lanier hasn't been able to sell his million-dollar residence. What makes you think we'd have better luck?'

'So, you take a bit of a loss.'

'Selling the house wouldn't save your father, it would kill him. It's all we have left.'

Julia understood this. The house in River Oaks represented their life, who they were, who they wanted to be. They had bought it for cash when they were into rice. When the rice business failed they sold the land, but retained the mineral rights which gave them enough money to get into the oil business. Now that the oil had failed, this generation of the Hudlows had nothing else to get into.

'If we sell the house, we'll wind up no better than the folks on Telephone Road. Starting with nothing and ending with nothing.'

'Well, if you can't afford round-the-clock nursing, then I can.'

'I don't want your money, Julia,' her mother's eyes flashed with anger.

Again J.C. stepped in. 'It's not the money, Ms Hudlow. You have to let Julia help out. She's your blood daughter. She'll never be able to forgive herself if you don't let her back into your life.'

'Please, Mother. Let me help. I really need to. Don't you think I've been made to feel guilty enough?'

'All right,' Claire said surprisingly. 'We'll look into hiring a private nurse.'

'Good.' Julia's relief was overwhelming. 'I'll start making inquiries this afternoon. Maybe we can find someone by the day after tomorrow.'

'Oh, no,' her mother looked alarmed. '*People* magazine is coming the day after tomorrow.'

'Forget it, Mom. They can photograph the outside. I'm

not letting them into the house.'

As they drove down to the Houston Hyatt, Julia was burning with shame. 'J.C., I had no idea about any of this. I thought it was going to be a simple afternoon tea. Thanks for helping out with Mother.'

'Sure thing.'

'God, I feel I have to apologize to you.'

'For what? Everybody's family's got problems. I know you're worried about your daddy. What you have to realize is that your mama is worried, too, but she's just as stubborn as you are. You're more alike than you know.'

'He's always been the dominant one in the family. Is it that she can't love him if he's not strong?'

'No. You got to understand. Acknowledging his weakness means facing her own. She's in shock; she's not herself.'

'Believe me, that's herself. She's much more interested in keeping up with the Joneses, excuse me, the Laniers, than keeping my father alive.'

'Honey, I know you're wrong about that. You get a full-time nurse in there to help out and you'll see a big difference in your mama. You want some help interviewing people?'

'No thanks. You'd better spend some time with Mac.'

'He's left. He had to fly back to Nashville. One of our recording artists is having some booking problems. Mac had to be on the spot to figure it out. So I'm here for you if you need me.'

Her concern made Julia feel even more guilty. 'God, I hate River Oaks. It's conservative and racist, totally out of touch with the rest of the world. That's why I've never wanted to admit that I come from here.'

'You don't have to apologize to me.'

'Yes I do,' Julia said grimly. 'You don't understand. I used you. I took you there to embarrass my mother, to flaunt my new life in her face.'

'I figured it was something like that. It's OK, I don't mind.'

'I've always been ashamed of my parents.'

'That's just a lot of wasted energy,' J.C. said emphatically. 'Take it from me, you are not your parents, you're your own person.' She studied Julia for a moment as if she were trying to make up her mind about something. Then:

'Now it's my turn. We've got a full day on the set tomorrow, but next day, I'm not called till after lunch. Can you meet me early on that morning?'

'As early as you want.' Right now Julia would agree to anything to assuage the guilt she was feeling: about her parents, about her friendship with J.C., everything.

'I want to show you something. I'm going to take you to where I grew up.'

'I thought you told *People* magazine that Hidden Valley doesn't exist any more.'

'That's right,' J.C.'s eyes were clouded but her mouth was firm with determination. 'I'm going to trust you with the truth, Julia. I want to show you my real roots. Day after tomorrow I'm going to take you on a trip down Telephone Road.'

Chapter Twenty-four

It was still warm, but the sky had clouded over and it was starting to drizzle as they set out in the morning. J.C. had dressed down, in a pair of old jeans and a nondescript shirt, her bright red hair concealed by a scarf and her eyes shaded by sunglasses. Clearly she did not want to be recognized by anyone on Telephone Road.

As they turned off Harris Boulevard, Julia asked, 'Why is it called Telephone Road?'

'Used to be the main trunk-line of telephone cable that originally came into Houston along this road. You have to remember that where we are now used to be right on the edge of what was then Houston city limits. Pretty charming and quaint, isn't it?' She gestured out the window at a collection of low-slung buildings with peeling paint, faded signs with missing letters, graffiti scrawled on the walls. Telephone Road was like any industrial strip in the boondocks. Tire shops, discount grocery stores, autoparts, a Salvation Army thrift shop, the Acme Truck Line, a Church of the Seventh Day Adventists and numerous pawnshops. Hymie's Hamburgers. The sign was still there, but the place had long gone out of business. The Josephine Motel was officially closed, too, but squatters and derelicts had moved in, slouched on the front steps, sipping furtively out of brown paper bags. There were barbecue joints and fast food places. None of the big chains like McDonald's, but sad little fried fish huts and rib shacks, smoke curling out of broken chimneys up into the dull sky.

Julia had never seen anything so depressing. She thought of her mother's crack about Telephone Road yesterday and her embarrassment deepened. 'I don't quite understand all this, J.C.,' she said cautiously, 'I thought you came from Hidden Valley and were . . .'

'Raised by my grandfather in the piney woods,' J.C.

finished bitterly. 'Yeah, well, that's always been the official party line. What I'm showing you today is just between you and me, OK? To be a country singer, you got to be country. You can't grow up on Telephone Road. It's always been white trash. Oh, sweet Jesus,' she brought the car to a halt. 'Look at that,' she pointed out the window to a small, pink stucco building with a sign that read 'Hair By Elva'. I can't believe it's still here. I ain't been back here in twenty years. That's where I used to sweep up hair after school. My first job. Not legal, of course. I was only fourteen. Elva was real good about paying me under the table. She knew how much we needed the money.'

'Do you want to stop and go in?' Julia asked.

'No,' J.C. paused, then: 'No. Elva's dead by now for sure, anyway. She had one foot in the grave when I was working for her. Lord, nothing around here has changed. There's the Red Oak Trailer Village. We lived there for a while. Course now the trailers have all been fixed down. More like houses. Ours was mobile. That was Daddy's favorite word. Mobile.'

'You lived in a trailer?'

'Yeah, some of the time. We had a real house once. For seven months. Hell, I'll show you. Might as well go all the way.' J.C. swerved quickly off Telephone Road on to a quieter, more residential side road. She pulled up in front of a small, yellow, wood-frame house with a porch. On the porch was a sagging sofa and an old refrigerator. A tire swing hung from a tree in the overgrown front yard. Parked in the driveway was a tractor rig. 'Well, what do you know? Looks like truckers still live here.'

'Where's the rest of his truck?'

J.C. laughed. 'Honey, you don't know anything, do you? A trucker owns the tractor part, the controls and the motor, and the power wheels. There's a universal hook-up on the back to which the trailer parts will attach. Means you can drive for any company.'

'Did your dad drive trucks?'

'You bet. He was on the road a lot. Came home less and less.'

'Are you still in touch with him?'

'Nope. He was killed in a pile-up near the Mexico border. Fell asleep at the wheel. He was responsible for a lot of deaths. Lucky he didn't live. He was a sweet man and he could never have forgiven himself. Played a mean guitar. We used to sing together. After he died, my mama didn't want any music in the house. If I started to sing, she'd tell me to hush up and not disturb her peace and quiet. Not disturb her drinking was more like it.' A scowling face peered around the curtain on the window of the house. 'Oops, somebody's home. We better get a move-on or they'll be out here to shoot us for trespassing.' Seeing Julia's face: 'Not really. But I've had enough, haven't you?'

Julia nodded. How could she have ever complained about growing up in River Oaks when this is what J.C. had to remember as childhood. She'd known little about Telephone Road except that, as J.C. said, it was white trash, one step above shanty town because it was white not black.

'One more place we got to visit. I'd never forgive myself if I didn't go check in on Luther.'

'Luther?'

'He runs a liquor store. If we're real lucky, he might give us some lunch.'

In the gray, murky light, the bleakness of Telephone Road was broken only by brightly lit marquees and flashing neon signs for various bars and liquor stores. Jerry's Round-Up: Beer and Set-ups, Dominos and Pool, the Lucky Time Club and Happy Lounge, and Sheryl's, which claimed to serve 'Houston's Finest Mixed Drinks'. They parked in front of a gray slate building with a red and white sign that said only 'Maddie's'. As they walked into the dimly lit liquor store, J.C. took off her glasses and removed the scarf, letting her long red curls fall on to her shoulders.

'Maddie?' a voice called out to them. 'Bless me, Jesus. I swear, I'm seeing a ghost.' A tall, heavy black man was making his way toward them. 'Hey there, Julie Carol. Long time no see.' He enveloped her in a massive bear hug. 'This sure is a surprise. Baby doll, you look good.' Tears streamed down his broad face. He was crying and laughing, holding on to her tightly as if he never wanted to let her go, his deep, booming voice reverberating in the small room. He could be anywhere from fifty to seventy-five. He had a large head with a leonine mane of tightly curled gray hair. He was wearing a checked shirt and neatly pressed tan corduroy pants.

J.C. hugged him back and said, 'Hey, Luther, this is my good friend, Julia. She produces my show.'

Julia held out her hand, but immediately Luther was hugging her, too. 'Pleased to meet you, ma'am. It's a grand show. Never miss it.' He smelled wonderful, warm and smoky.

He grabbed J.C. by her shoulders and said, 'You done real good, Julie Carol. All grown up. Damn, I just can't get over how much you look like Maddie.' Now J.C. burst into tears and the two of them hugged again.

Julia felt her own eyes growing wet. Julie Carol. So that's what J.C. stood for. She looked around the room. Hanging on the walls were signed eight-by-ten photographs, some in black and white, some in garish color, all in cheap gilt frames. They looked like Hollywood glamor shots from the fifties and were all of the same woman. Masses of auburn hair hanging over one eye, a slash of bright red lipstick in a pale face. In some, the woman was wearing a tight, fluffy angora sweater; in others, an equally tight black turtleneck, accentuating her pointed breasts. Julia recognized the dimple in the left cheek. 'Wow! Is that your mom?'

'Yeah,' J.C. snorted almost derisively. 'That's Maddie. There was a special on photographs at Woolsworth,' (like a number of people in the south, she mispronounced the name of the five and dime store). 'Maddie could never resist getting her picture taken.'

Julia would have liked to know more, but Luther said, 'I was just fixin' to sit down to lunch. Y'all want somethin' to eat?'

'Ribs?'

'Yeah.'

'Cornbread?'

'Sure enough.'

'I thought you'd never ask.' J.C. turned to Julia. 'Luther's the best cook in Harris County. He missed his calling. He should have been a chef at K Paul's in New Orleans.'

'You got that right.' Luther flipped the sign on the front door from Open to Closed and led them to the back of the store where he had built-on living quarters. The tiny kitchen was immaculate. They sat at a table covered with a red and white checked oilcloth, while Luther piled their plates with barbecue baby back ribs, smoky tasting beans, collards and freshly baked cornbread.

'So now I have to confess,' J.C. wiped her greasy fingers on a piece of paper towel, 'my secret rib sauce comes from Luther. It ain't mine at all. I wooed you under false pretenses, Julia.' She told Luther how she sent jars of her barbecue sauce to Julia to bribe her into casting her in Makeover.

Luther laughed, a warm, gut-shaking laugh. 'I tell you, you take after your mama, no two ways about it.'

'You do look like her,' Julia offered. 'She's gorgeous. Pretty sexy for a mom. Well, you've seen what my mother looks like.'

'Oh yeah, Maddie was hot all right. In and out of my life, too. Just like Daddy. She'd go off for weeks at a time. We never knew where she was. Luther did a pretty good job of raising me,' she reached over and gave his large, square hand an affectionate squeeze.

'Wasn't easy neither. You ran off just about as often as Maddie did. Then one day you just up and left for good. I couldn't even find you,' Luther's face was suddenly stricken as if reliving the panic.

'Don't you have anything stronger than this?' J.C. took a slug of iced tea. 'Oh, no, I forgot. You sell booze, but you never touch the stuff yourself.'

'That's right,' Luther said strongly.

'Look, I still feel guilty about all that. But I couldn't stand it any more. I didn't want you or Maddie to come after me. I made Granddaddy promise not to call you till I was already settled in school.' J.C. told Julia how she left Telephone Road at fifteen and ran away to her grandfather who lived in East Texas near the Louisiana state line. It was real bayou country, green and wet marshlands, quiet and safe, right on the banks of the Trinity River. 'You talk about country, this place was it. Granddaddy was Mama's daddy, but he didn't really approve of his daughter. He was real religious and he didn't hold with drinking and screwing around. He got me singing gospel. I must have won every gospel-singing contest in the state. I never sang children's songs. I latched on to cheatin' songs before I knew what cheatin' ever meant. Granddaddy didn't approve of that. He loved music as long as it was for the glory of the Lord. That wasn't enough for me. He didn't want me to go to Nashville – said it was full of sin and I'd really have to mind the good book – but he didn't try and stop me going. When he put me on the Greyhound bus for Nashville, that's when he gave me his most prized possession, his Dobro blues guitar.'

'That's the one in the museum in Nashville!' Julia remembered seeing it in a glass case.

'The very same. I near about hocked it a million times when I got to Nashville, but fortunately something always saved it. Granddaddy was right about Nashville. I was so disappointed. It was just another big city. Nothing country about it except the music. It was all just business. I expected to be discovered, you know, just stand there in Music Square, open my mouth and sing, and somebody would come rushing up to offer me a record contract right away.'

'Is that what happened?'

'Well, not really, but pretty near. Mac latched on to me quick. He said I had a woman's voice in a girl's body. He had big plans for me right from the beginning. I married him just before my seventeenth birthday. Granddaddy came out for the wedding to give me away.'

'What about your mother?' Julia asked as gently as possible.

'Oh, she was already dead. Got stoned on vodka, fell asleep with a cigarette in her hand, burned the trailer to the ground. I came back for the funeral, but I knew there wasn't nothing for me here on Telephone Road. 'Course Maddie didn't have anything like a will, but that meant the liquor store went to me. So I signed it straight over to Luther. He deserved it. He'd been running the place for her for years, hadn't you, Luther?'

'Yes, ma'am.' Luther nodded reluctantly.

'Oh, I know you hate it when I trash Maddie 'cause you thought she was great. She gave you a job when you needed it, but you know she never really loved me.'

'No, I don't know that,' Luther said firmly. 'The problem with your mama was she never got what she wanted and sometimes she took that out on you. That don't mean she didn't love you.'

'You're probably right,' J.C. sighed. 'She'd have loved having what I've got now. Plenty of people taking my picture. Granddaddy lived long enough to see me win my first Female Vocalist of the Year award. Damn, he was proud, although he hated the song I won it for. "Other Women's Beds". Now that's something Mama would have really understood.' She laughed wryly. 'No, I don't miss

253

Maddie at all. I sure miss Granddaddy, though. He was a true believer and he made me one, too, even though I don't get to church as much as I'd like to.'

Luther smiled at her. 'Julie Carol, you're in church every time you open your mouth to sing.'

'God, J.C., what must you think of me?' Julia asked when they were in the car and driving back down Telephone Road. 'Bitching about growing up in River Oaks when you had all that to deal with?'

'Julia, I didn't show you this to rub your nose in it. I needed to come to terms with it myself. I couldn't have faced it without you. I counted on you for support just like you counted on me the day before yesterday.'

'What must you think of me?' Julia said again.

'I think of you as a woman. To me, you're a real lady. And you're my friend. Stop beating yourself up over it. My problems are in the past. Yours are in the present. How's your daddy doing? Is the nurse working out OK?'

'Yes, so far. I was over there this morning just before you picked me up, and she seems to be handling things well. She's Vietnamese. Dad must hate that. He loves to complain about how the influx of immigrants has ruined Houston's economy.' Julia closed her eyes for a minute and saw Boni's small, deft hands changing the soiled bed linens under her father, rubbing cream on his back, soothing the loose, papery skin that hung like Spanish moss from his gaunt limbs. 'Mother's dealing with it better than I thought she would. I really appreciate you helping me arrange it all.'

'No problem.' J.C. reddened slightly. 'I bet you don't have a clue how important you are to me. You've given me a whole new life with the chance to do this show. I mean it when I say I feel we're friends, Julia Catherine. By the way, I like that name.'

'I like Julie Carol, too.'

'Forget it. I'm J.C. now and that's it.' Quickly she changed the subject. 'I'm glad they're picking us up for next season. What are you going to do during the hiatus?'

'Write scripts, what else?' Julia said. 'You get time off. Marty and I will be busier than ever.'

'Shoot, I don't get time off. I've got to record a new album and I haven't even finished writing the songs. I'm kind of stuck. I want to say something different this time

254

around, reach a new audience, really affect people's lives. Mac wants me to do the same old thing, but Makeover has made me push myself and I need to show that on the album. I've done my bluegrass roots album, I've done my rowdy, hardcore honky-tonk, I've done my hurtin' songs. Now what? I feel the need for some kind of catharsis, is that the right word?'

Julia nodded. An idea was forming in her mind. 'Look, I don't know anything about country music except what I've learned from you, but if you want to be really bold, do an urban album. Write about what you just showed me.'

'Growing up in a trailer park?' J.C. laughed ironically. 'I don't think so.'

'Why not? Make it real, grittier than anything you've done before.'

'And destroy all the mystique I've built up about myself?'

'You don't have to say these are your roots. Just acknowledge that there's country in the city.'

'It's too risky,' J.C. said, her eyes clouded with fear. 'I couldn't.'

'Telephone Road, just the name is so evocative,' Julia was suddenly seized with excitement. 'It sounds like a metaphor: poetic, haunting, do you understand what I mean?'

'I guess,' J.C. looked doubtful.

'Forget it. I don't know what I'm talking about.'

'It's OK. You got me thinking. I'll keep it in mind, I promise.'

Chapter Twenty-five

The popping of champagne corks signaled the end of production of the first season of Makeover. The final hour-long episode, entitled 'Ms Texas Belle, Skin Deep', was in the can, although it wouldn't be edited and broadcast for several weeks. Tim Talbot was playing his cards close to his chest, but Julia knew he had high hopes of pulling off the programming ploy of the decade. Plan A of his scheme had already worked. On Tuesday nights, Roseanne fans watched the ABC show at nine and then switched to CBN for Makeover at nine-thirty. The show was consistently in the top ten week after week. Now he was plotting an even bolder move. He intended to schedule the season finale, 'Skin Deep' for nine o'clock, in the hopes that viewers would skip the rival show completely in order to catch the full special of Makeover. If it worked, next season the show would stay in the nine o'clock time slot and go head-to-head with ABC's most popular sit-com. The entire company had been sworn to secrecy not to reveal that the final episode was an hour instead of a half-hour.

The end of production felt like the last day of school, as if they were kids going off to camp or summer jobs or whatever to pass the three- or four-month hiatus period before returning to 'real life', the start-up date for shooting the next season.

Brandon was smiling. Out of the blue, his agent had called with a film offer. *Vengeance*. A western. His first feature film since the plane crash that killed Peter. He was so used to seeing his face on the small screen he could hardly remember what he looked like on the big screen. Would they be able to conceal his scar? Did it matter? *Vengeance* was not your typical rawhide and bullets, good guys, bad guys story, but a complex, serious examination of violence in the old west. The part was that of an American Cavalry officer, a blue-coat from Fort Whoop-up in Montana, who comes up to Canada to help Northwest Mounted Police, the red-coats, wage war on the American whiskey traders. The traders ran rotgut liquor across the border to the native peoples, selling them a home brew that, if it didn't kill them, often drove them crazy. The story was told from the native point of view. Except for his role, most of the major characters would be played by North American Indians. There was a revenge plot with an interesting twist which involved his character 'becoming' a native, going through a rite of passage to win their trust and gain their assistance in order to exact his revenge.

Intriguing story. A sparsely-written screenplay, the dialogue was almost poetic. Of course he would prefer to be directing the picture instead of starring in it. But Richard Flint claimed to be one quarter Choctaw and he had a good feel for this kind of sweeping saga. The western was a tricky genre to be selling at today's box office. Still, a strong script coupled with famed director of photography, Eric Vasily, *Vengeance* had the potential to attract critical attention, maybe even become a classic.

The prairie sequences would be shot at Morley Flats, Alberta, but the quest for vengeance would lead his character up into the Rocky Mountains of Banff. Brandon could hardly contain his joy. A chance to get out of the LA smog and into the fresh air of the Canadian Rockies!

Smug bastard! Linda Earl sent Brandon a silent message. How dare he sit there with that superior smile on his face? Did he enjoy making a fool out of her? Oh, outwardly he was friendly enough, but she knew how he really felt. Every time she thought about putting the make on him in Houston, she relived the shame of his rejection. Maybe he really had forgotten about it? She couldn't. Her stomach had been one great big knot for the rest of the season.

Being away from the set for a few months should ease the tension, but it meant she would be eating more at home. Here at the studio she could control her caloric intake the way she wanted to and nobody paid any attention. Meals with Steve were always a problem. He fussed if she didn't eat enough and accused her of trying to starve him and the baby. Nervously, she ran her hand under her chin. A bit of loose flesh there. Summer was a good time for a quick tuck.

Leave her looking smooth and refreshed for the new fall season. It was important to look her best and television was such a demanding medium.

Television paid the rent. True art lay in the theater. In between scenes of Makeover, Theresa had stayed in her dressing room, working on a play, and now it was actually going to be produced by *El Theatro En Mi Corazon* back in Miami. *El Cigaro de Mi Padre* was a bilingual comedy, half in English, half in Spanish. Set in a cigar factory in old Havana, the play chronicled the lives of four women. In three days she would be winging her way to Miami for rehearsals. Hearing the words she had written spoken aloud for the first time on a real stage. Mamacita was planning an opening night party at a restaurant in Little Havana. The Versailles. A cool combination of tacky and chic, full of cut glass mirrors and chandeliers. A favorite spot with Cuban exiles, who often met there to plot, over numerous pitchers of beer, their eventual return to their country and over-throw of Castro's communist government. She could almost taste the garlic roasted chicken, the *moros y christianos* (black beans and rice), and the fried plantain. *Hola*, little Havana! *Hasta la vista*, LA.

New York, New York! The producers of what Paul and Chaya were calling the 'sperm bank movie' were so eager to have him involved in the project, they delayed the start date until he finished on Makeover. Next week he and the whole family would fly back to New York (Chaya could hardly wait) where he would begin work on *Shooting Blanks*. He smiled ruefully at the title. Obviously it didn't apply to him. Chaya was pregnant again. Their fourth child. *Vay'z mir*, he was barely thirty-two. So many people around all the time, so many kids underfoot. He loved his family but sometimes what he wanted, more than anything, was a vacation not with them but from them.

A paid vacation. With Elizabeth Taylor. Kelly could hardly believe it. Liz, her longtime personal idol. Beauty, talent, and a 'fuck you, I'll do what I want' attitude. Liz wasn't afraid of anybody. It was Liz who had publicly slammed George Bush by telling the world he wasn't doing anything about AIDS, that he was so ignorant of the disease, he probably didn't even know how to spell it.

Liz had called Kelly, to tell her she knew of Kelly's involvement with pediatric AIDS and she wanted to help make 'Kelly's Kids' official. Liz was asking her to join, along with a group of Hollywood stars, in setting up a special camp for HIV positive children. Spend the summer in Mendocino helping the kids to forget, at least for a time in their brief lives, that they were sick, and throw themselves into having some real fun. She would be working closely with Liz to increase AIDS awareness and to raise money for Hollywood Helps, a non-profit foundation providing care for those with AIDS.

But how could she leave Carlito behind? He wasn't well enough to go with her. The AZT did not appear to be working. He was losing weight and his stomach cramps were worse than ever. The nurses told Kelly that since she had entered his life, he rarely cried and was much more cheerful. He was still boarding in the hospital. So far, nobody else had come forward to adopt him. She spent every moment away from the set with Carlito. He was depending on her. If she went off to Mendocino, would he still be here when she got back?

It was ending too soon. How could she leave her friends on the set for three whole months? What would Melissa do without Alex? The way his face lit up when she ran on to the set, that special note he got in his voice when he told her, 'You don't have to act funny, just be yourself, Mel. You are delightful enough.' Always willing to take the time to talk to her if she had a problem or to give her a hug if she needed it. Boy, she was going to miss those hugs. There hadn't been that many hugs in her life. In a couple of years, there would probably be lots more, but at the moment she was suffering hug deprivation.

Bon wanted to go back to Vancouver for the summer, but what was the point of that? Northwood, the Canadian show, which had once been the center of Mel's whole life, seemed like small potatoes compared to what she was doing down here. The kids would probably accuse of her being stuckup and full of herself now. What was she going to do with herself day and after day? When she didn't have to report for work on the set? She was supposed to be starting her first year of high school in the fall. Why not get a class out of the way? Biology, maybe. Lab work, dissecting, stuff she couldn't easily do with a tutor on the set. Beverly Hills High, ugh, she hated the very thought of it, but at least summer school would give her some place to be every day. She felt lonely already. What was so great about getting away from everybody?

'We've got to have some time on our own,' Marty was pushing Julia to find a couple of weeks for them to get away together, but how could they manage it? Now that Make-over had been picked up for a second season, Julia had twenty-two scripts to write and pre-production on the technical side had already begun. Marty kept complaining he was exhausted from the grind of the series and bored with the whole show, but Julia could hardly wait to get started on the writing. She'd held back a lot in the first season but now that it was a hit, she was eager to stretch the boundaries of the sit-com and explore more current social and political issues on the show. 'Ms Texas Belle, Skin Deep' had pilloried sexism and body image to great comic effect. She was aching to do more of that. Not that she viewed Makeover as her own personal soapbox, of course, but still, she sensed their loyal viewers were ready for her to 'push the envelope' just a bit.

As she drained the last of her champagne, she saw J.C. in a heated conversation with her husband, Mac, in the corner. J.C. pulled his bearded face down close to hers in an attempt to give him a kiss, but he shrugged her off and walked away.

Julia went over to her friend and saw that her eyes were brimming with tears. 'Is everything OK between you and Mac?'

'Oh yeah, sure,' J.C. flashed her a watery smile. 'He's just ticked off about the new album. I'm going into studio next week back in Nashville to start recording. Ever since we got back from Houston I been working like a woman possessed getting the new songs written. I took your advice, Julia, and Mac don't approve of me listening to anyone but him. He doesn't want me to go public about my past, but you know what? I just don't give a shit. I've already written the title song. You dying to know what it is?'

'Yes,' Julia gave her friend a hug.

'"Telephone Road."'

TELEPHONE ROAD

On the southeast side of Houston
Is a place called Telephone Road
Where I grew up from a little girl
While my daddy drove a heavy load
Where I learned to read the Bible
And know where the line is toed
But, then Daddy ran off and Mama ran a liquor store
On Telephone Road.

I was fifteen goin' on twenty
When I told my mama dear
This ain't the land o' plenty
And I just gotta get outta here
Mama said, 'Girl, you can leave us
But you'll reap just what you've sowed
And you'll never erase the trace on your face
Of the place called Telephone Road.'

But my granddaddy lived
In a neat little shack
On the banks of the Trinity
He taught me some gospel singin'
But it still weren't enough for me
So he gave me his Dobro blues guitar
And I learned to jump and shout
Then I packed my bags for Nashville
'Cause my music was my ticket out.

Now I play my country music
Like a farmers' market town
Like the piney woods, or the bayou floods
Or the mountains all around
But my truth is southeast Houston
And I guess it's always showed
It's the beater cars, and the pawned guitars
And the bars of Telephone Road.

You can take the girl out of Houston
But she can't shake Telephone Road.

Chapter Twenty-six

'I don't know about this,' Marty grumbled, 'Stan's liable to blow me out of the water. I haven't played tennis in years. I hope it's like riding a bicycle.'

'Relax,' Julia urged him. 'We'll scarf a few margaritas, you can bat the ball around, we'll sign the contracts for our new deal with CBN and beat a hasty exit. Get home in time for Nova.'

'Easy for you to say. All you have to do is sit in the shade and watch. It must be a hundred degrees today.'

'There are advantages to not knowing the game,' Julia admitted.

They were on their way to Stanfield King's house for an afternoon of tennis, tequila and deal clinching. Because Makeover had proved to be such a success, they were in a position to renegotiate a better deal for another season. CBN had offered them a lucrative pay-or-play clause which meant the network would personally pay them to develop future projects, even another comedy series, specifically for CBN, relegating Pacific Victory to a lesser position and guaranteeing more money would go directly to Hudlow/Turgov, a lot more money. The negotiations had been hard-fought and now Stan wanted officially to celebrate the deal they had hammered out so carefully.

Stan was famous for his 'margarita matches' and for his home, which was unique in both style of architecture and natural setting. He and his wife, Demeter, lived in Pacific Palisades, in a mansion reportedly worth over three mil with a collection of contemporary art estimated at a couple of million more. The entire area was peopled with money. As Marty maneuvered the winding mountain roads, each home appeared to be more magnificent than the last.

'Wow, look at that one,' Julia pointed to a

Mediterranean-style villa surrounded by landscaped olive trees and orange groves.

'Maybe Makeover will become such a mega-hit we can buy a place like that some day.'

'I'd settle for a bigger house in Brentwood,' Marty groused. 'We could afford to move, you know. We're not exactly poverty-stricken even now.'

'Who has time to look? It's not the money, it's finding enough hours in the day to trot around after some leathery blonde real-estate agent with a rolodex the size of Russia. We're fine where we are for now. Oh, wow, look at that view,' Julia pointed out a white, Andalucian-looking edifice with a long terrace facing out to the Pacific Ocean, sunlight glinting off the water. 'I've never really been in Pacific Palisades before. Too rich for my blood.'

'Probably Stan and Demeter keep in shape with a personal tennis pro,' Marty continued anxiously. 'I mean, I know my way around a tennis court, but it's hardly my sport of choice.'

'What is your sport of choice? Sex? Food? Talk? Those are the only things I've seen you work up a sweat over.'

'Very funny. It's one hundred and ten in the shade today.'

'You'll be just fine,' Julia soothed. 'Didn't you tell me that getting an invite to an industry executive's home and being introduced to his family is a privilege extended to only a select few? We should feel honored.'

'Yeah right. I'll be glad when this afternoon is over.'

'Quit kvetching. It's only a friendly little game. Oh my God,' Julia gasped as they pulled up to the gates of the Kingfield Estate. Set into the mountains, looking out to the sea, the house was large, rectangular and mostly glass.

'This place is called variously the Ice Cube, the Glass House, or the Crystal Palace.'

'Whew. It makes J.C.'s Lone Star Estate look like a shanty-town shack.'

Marty pushed a button to announce their arrival and the tall gates swung open to let them drive in. As they got out of the car, Julia went around back to get her Bolex camera out of the trunk.

'What are you doing with that?' Marty asked. 'You're not going to schlep your old Bolex to the party.'

Julia reddened. 'I thought it might be fun to shoot some footage of the game.'

'Oh, great, I'm going to look like a schmuck. I told you I haven't played in years.'

'I've got some film in the camera I want to burn off. It's no big deal.'

'Well, be discreet about it, OK? You've been in TVO for a year now, forget about documentary film.'

Demeter King herself met them at the door. Julia knew Stan and his wife had kids, but there was no other 'family' in evidence. Demeter had blonde hair to her waist and a lean, hard body kept in fighting trim, rumor had it, by a diet of speed and rigorous sex. Marty said whenever she smiled at him, he wanted to run for cover. She smiled at them now and led them down steep stone steps, past an Olympic-sized swimming pool with an intriguing looking beach house to the pristine tennis court with its earth-red surface and shimmering white net. The court was enclosed on three sides by a high, chain-link fence, but the drop off over the mountains gave one the unnerving sensation of playing tennis in mid-air. Recalling the dazzling view in Stan's CBN office, Julia wondered, what is it with this guy and heights?

The sun was blazing hot. Tim was already stretched out in a lawn chair, his white tennis shirt open to the waist in order to, as he put it, 'bag some rays'. Stan was at the bar mixing up a batch of margaritas. He strode over to meet them, bearing each a frosty, salt-rimmed glass the size of a fishbowl balanced precariously on its glass stem.

'Oy, if I drink that,' Marty said into Julia's ear, 'I'll have to take a nap in the middle of the game.'

'Or drop dead of sunstroke out on the court.'

The drinks were downed in a flash and Stan was urging them to jump into the fray. Marty was relieved to find that he was playing with Stan against the team of Tim and Demeter.

'I prefer doubles,' Stan told them, leading them to the court. But once the game was in play, he and Demeter played as if they had no partners at all. Demeter led off with a vicious serve that sent the ball whizzing like a Scud missile to the other side of the net. Julia whipped out her Bolex and began shooting the highlights of the game.

Whatever was going on was not a game but deadly

serious, not just sport, but blood sport, the net a dividing line for two enemy territories. Stan and Demeter were playing by some secret code, rules that only the two of them understood. A private ritual between them that had been played out many times before. Marty was holding his own, but taking it easy. The last thing he wanted to do was to put his back out. Tim played with caution, too. He was fifteen years younger than his boss and the last thing he wanted to do was beat him on his own tennis court. In the boardroom maybe, but not on the court. Stan and Demeter were out for blood. It was riveting to watch. Tim and Marty hardly ever got their racquets on the ball.

Slam. The tennis ball seemed to appear out of nowhere as the couple, both in tennis whites, glistening with sweat, smashed the ball back and forth with the powerful force of a jet breaking the sound barrier. When it ricocheted off the chain-link fence, the noise was deafening. Julia thought of tennis as a quiet, graceful, loping game, gently lobbing the ball back and forth. Maybe that was table tennis. What she was seeing unfold in front of her third eye was a grudge match. She was fascinated not so much by the game itself but by the driving emotions behind it. Stan had seemed so easy-going at their initial pitch. At subsequent meetings, he was calm to the point of comatose. Nothing got under his skin. Except, it seemed, his wife.

It was unbearably hot. Julia was slick with sweat. She could feel it running down the back of her shorts. Poor Marty. Running his ass off out there, trying to find the ball. Mercifully the match ended. She had no idea who won until she saw Stan hold up Marty's hand in a team victory gesture.

Stan and Demeter went off up into the house, taking the stone steps two at a time. Julia brought Marty some ice water and a towel. He was dripping with sweat and gasping for breath, but he took the opportunity of Stan's absence to ask if the changes he'd requested in the contracts had been approved. Tim told him the clauses he'd requested had been added right on the front page. Julia knew that if she wanted to stay in television, she would have to learn the business side of the business, but at the moment she could barely keep up with the output of scripts necessary to keep the series going, and was grateful to Marty for handling the the tough and intricate negotiations.

As Stan returned with the contracts, Julia picked up her Bolex again and resumed shooting. Here we go. Coming up on the big moment. He put the contracts down on the patio table and she zoomed in for a close-up. Good one. Stan's cellular rang. He excused himself to his guests and wandered off to the other side of the tennis court, taking the contracts with him. Julia panned after him until Tim wooed her away with another mega margarita.

The telephone conversation seemed to take for ever. Hurry up, Julia willed, get your ass back here. We're just getting to the good part. Finally Stan was off. Tim yelled out, 'Do you want another 'rita?' Julia zoomed in on Stan who waved and gave a high sign indicating he'd be right back. He held up two fingers signaling he wanted a double. Damn. Now he was dialing another number. More talk on the phone. Come on, Stan. We haven't got all day. It's hot. We're all bombed. Let's sign this sucker and clinch the deal.

Finally Stan returned, precious documents in his hand. He signed for the CBN network. Marty signed for Hudlow/ Turgov. Tim signed as witness. Then they toasted each other. Julia kept the camera running the whole time. She thought her heart would burst with excitement. They had done it. They had their deal!

On the way home, Marty groused, 'I hate all that "schmoozing" shit.'

'You were fine.' Nothing could bring her down now. Ideas and concepts for new shows were dancing in her head. She could hardly wait to begin.

'So whaddya think of Hollywood's happiest couple?'

'What an experience,' Julia exclaimed. 'That tennis match was like something out of *Raging Bull*. I'm glad they're them and we're us. Oh, Marty,' she squeezed his arm, 'we're going to do more projects. I can't believe it's happening.'

'Look at it this way, if the whole thing falls apart, you've probably got enough footage there to do a La La Land documentary exposé on the Stanfield Kings.'

'Call it "Inside Hollywood"?'

' "Lifestyles of the Bitch and Heinous".'

HIATUS

Chapter Twenty-seven

'The advertisers are in a bidding war for Makeover,' Stan looked like a cat who had swallowed a gold canary. He had just come back from the 'upfronts' in New York, where the advertisers gathered to buy for the season ahead. 'We're going to be charging three hundred thousand dollars for a half-minute of commercial time on Makeover this season.'

Marty did a quick calculation in his head. 'Wow! That's ten thousand dollars a second!' Along with Kathryn Grady, Marty and Julia were gathered in Stan's office to discuss plans for the second season. The cast was on hiatus for the summer, but for Hudlow/Turgov Productions, the real work was about to begin.

'More money in the till for CBN,' Stan shouted. He no longer bothered to disguise his true agenda, which was to make as much money for the network as possible. 'In exchange for these mega bucks, we have to guarantee to deliver to the advertisers the ideal demographic audience.'

'We should have no trouble making good on that promise,' Tim said proudly. 'We've won that coveted eighteen to forty-nine age group so vital to advertisers, but we've gone beyond it. The show's skewing younger than we thought it would. My nieces and nephews are watching because of Melissa. The baby boomers are watching because country music has become hip and they love J.C. My gay friends watch the show for Kelly. She's so bitchy and funny.'

'Demeter watches because of Brandon,' Stan said. 'She thinks he's really hot.'

'Even my eighty-seven-year-old grandmother watches it,' added Kathryn. 'She loves the makeovers.'

'All of this increases our audience,' Marty agreed. 'I think the other networks are crazy to ignore the older viewer. These people have very strong buying power. The whole country's growing older.'

'Our black and Hispanic demographics have increased, albeit marginally, thanks to Theresa and Shirley,' Tim went on. 'There's room for improvement there, but still the show is crossing age, gender and race barriers. Everybody in the country is watching it.'

'Do you realize how rare this is? It calls for a real celebration.' Stan opened his private bar and brought out a chilled bottle of Crystal champagne. He handed it to Tim who popped the cork and poured it into the delicate, tulip-shaped glasses. 'It took Cheers three years to find its audience, Mash a year and a half, Miami Vice the same. The success of Makeover has raised ratings for all our shows on Tuesday nights. Thanks to you, Tuesday now belongs to CBN.'

Kathryn raised her glass. 'Here's to a long and happy partnership. We're on our way to one hundred episodes where we get to make the really big bucks. Just remember The Cosby Show was sold for four million dollars per episode in syndication. This is only going to get better. Congratulations to you both.'

Julia sat back and quietly sipped her champagne, letting the talk swirl around her. She could hardly believe it was little more than a year ago that she and Marty had been in this very office, feverishly pitching the idea for Makeover, desperately hoping Stan would accept it. She remembered her sweaty palms, dry mouth, and churning stomach. She'd known she was talking too much and pushing too hard, but she couldn't seem to stop, so eager was she for a chance to prove herself. Now there was no need for her to say anything. Let them come to her.

'You're an extraordinary writer, Julia,' Stan continued to heap on the praise. 'You've given us some wonderful scripts this past season. I'll be very surprised if you don't receive an Emmy nomination or two. You seem to have unlimited energy, and you've done an excellent job of handling the star talent and staying within budget. You've certainly earned your new title of Executive Producer.' He paused then, almost as an afterthought, nodded in Marty's direction and said, 'I'm sure Marty's been a useful resource for you. Both of you work well under pressure and, believe me, we all know the time and financial constraints of producing a hit series week after week.'

Julia snuck a look at Marty. She was getting all the

accolades these days. She knew he was really proud of her, but she sensed it was beginning to wear on him. Lately, he'd been complaining about being too tired to go on with the show. She was really beginning to worry about him and wonder whether he was up to another season. She'd promised him a vacation. If they could just get a couple of weeks together, on their own, somewhere far away from LA, she knew he would regain his usual good spirits. His enthusiasm was one of the things she loved most about Marty, and it frightened her to see him even a little depressed, especially when she herself had never been happier. She felt guilty at being so happy. She was making good money, maintaining a measure of creative control over her work in a very tough business, and gaining confidence in herself for maybe the first time. She felt she was finally coming into her own.

'The success of the show flows directly from you, Julia. And of course you too, Marty,' Stan refilled their glasses. 'CBN wants to do whatever we can to keep you happy, create the right atmosphere, so that you will learn to trust us and want to stay with us for all your future projects. Having said that, I hope you'll be open to a new suggestion . . .'

Right, here it comes, thought Julia. Stan was a master of the cuff/caress approach. Warm them up and then move in for the kill.

'Our research department has been busy,' Stan handed them each a stack of reports. 'Now you remember that I believe strong ensemble characterization is the key to a hit show.'

No, that was not what Julia remembered. She distinctly recalled Stan saying that ensemble took too long to build and that individual star power was what counted.

'CBS has done a very interesting study called "The Changing Characters of Primetime", which has to do with the characters viewers recognize and love the most. A survey was done by telephone, asking people to name their favorite television characters, the ones they identify with, admire or relate to. Murphy Brown, Roseanne and Sam Malone are the top, but our Makeover characters are hot on their heels. J.C. as Janine, Brandon as Travis, Paul as Troy, all have a high recognition factor. And, amazingly for such a small role, Kelly Carmichael as Samantha is right up there, too. What a surprise.'

'Not to me,' Tim said, 'I predicted Kelly's popularity right from the beginning. I hope we're going to see more of her next season.'

'Yes, we are,' Julia said enthusiastically. 'In fact, with the scripts I'm prepping, I've already begun to expand her character. Kelly is so easy to write for. She's quick, she's funny, she's got tons of sex appeal, and now that I'm getting to know her as a person, I'm discovering there's quite a unique woman under all that hair and make-up.'

'Maybe,' Stan said, 'but given the results of our market research, you've got a problem with your female characters.'

'What's that?' Julia said quietly. Watch Stan slip the knife in.

'The problem seems to be that all your female characters are considered to be somewhat unusual, extraordinary.'

'That's a plus, right?' She intended to make this difficult for him. Stan was not a writer nor a producer; in his soul he was a bean counter. There was nothing creative about him. Where did he get off telling her how to write?

'Not necessarily. There's no female character the average woman can relate to. Now it should be Janine. Warm and funny, tough yet vulnerable, she's the queen bee. Makeover revolves around her, right?'

'Right. And the viewers love her.' Julia was having trouble following just where Stan was headed with this line of reasoning.

'Yes, they do, and now that she's singing on the show, they love her even more. But she isn't really your average working mother. She sings like an angel and she can't hide the fact that she's a star. Linda Earl occupies the role of resident flake, but the viewers researched think she's too neurotic. They can't really relate to her problems. Kelly's popular because she's so outrageous. She says the things we'd all love to say but never dare to. All three of these characters are funny, but they're not average women.'

'What about Shirley? She's completely down-to-earth.'

'She's black. That doesn't count.' Stan quickly covered his ass. 'What I mean is, blacks represent only sixteen per cent of the population. Shirley is not your average . . .'

'Woman,' Julia finished it for him. 'Who wants to see the average on television anyway? I thought the whole point of fiction was to take us out of ourselves.'

'Not according to our viewer research. They would like to see a female character that is closer to themselves.'

'Wait a minute,' Julia suddenly got the point. 'You're asking me to add a new character to Makeover?'

'Yes.'

'Because of some telephone poll the research department did?' Julia was ready to explode. He was asking her to write on demand, as if Makeover was some fast-food joint looking to change its menu. Drop the fish sandwich, add a chicken burger, who cares, it's all the same. She looked around the room to try and gauge Tim and Kathryn's reaction, but they were both sitting there in stunned silence.

Marty quickly stepped in. 'Stan, any change in cast would be dangerous, especially this early in the process. To bring a new character on in the second season could upset the whole balance of the show.'

'Maybe that's just what it needs,' Stan said eagerly. 'Stir things up a bit. Keep the cast on their toes. After all, we don't want any of them to think they're indispensable and give us contract renewal negotiation headaches.'

Julia opened her mouth, but Marty signaled her to stay quiet. 'Look, Stan, I don't think the budget will stretch to this. We're already planning to make over the set for the new season. Creating another character means adding another actor and that would increase the budget at a time when Brandon, J.C. and Paul are all demanding a raise.'

'Oh, that's no problem,' chirped Stan. 'We can increase your license fee. We've got that big jump in advertising revenue and I have even more good news for you; we schmoozed it up at MIP, the television festival, and we scored a sale to the UK. Channel Four. We test-marketed a couple of episodes, and the Brits love it because it's working class. Roseanne's already popular; no reason to think Makeover won't do the same. I realize this all comes as a bit of a shock to you, Julia.'

'I have already started working on the twenty-two scripts for this season,' Julia demurred. 'Marty and I haven't had one day off in over a year. We were hoping to grab some time together. Creating a new character would mean going all the way back to square one.'

'Ah, but that's the wonderful surprise about my suggestion. You won't actually have to create a new character.'

'What do you mean?'

'I want you to consider bringing Debra Jo Fawcett on to the show as a regular.'

'What?' Julia gasped. 'The Houston housewife?'

'Exactly. She's real housewife and that's her appeal. You told me yourself you loved working with her.'

'Stan, listen to me. Debra Jo is a lovely woman,' Julia fought to be diplomatic, 'but she's no actress.'

'Don't be so sure. You said she has a special quality and I agree with you. One thing I pride myself on is having a nose for talent, and I just know Debra Jo Fawcett has talent.'

Julia wanted to scream that, so far, Tim had it all over Stan in that department. Tim had predicted Kelly's instant fame and had backed Julia on the hiring of J.C. Stan, on the other hand, had pushed for Linda Earl who, according to the hallowed viewer research, was coming across as a nut-case. Tim had been concerned about Linda's emotional stability right from the beginning. 'Let me get this straight here, Stan,' she said in a murderously calm voice. 'You want me to write a continuing role for someone who isn't a professional actress, who has no training whatsoever in how to play a character?'

'She'll play herself. That's what she did on the "Ms Texas Belle, Skin Deep" and our ratings went right through the roof. The female viewers can relate to her. My wife absolutely loved her.'

'Demeter is hardly your average housewife,' Julia snapped. Demeter King, regent of the Hollywood cocktail set, art collector and behind-the-scenes power broker. Rumored to have an insatiable appetite for kinky sex. A rumor that everyone in Hollywood was party to, except, it seemed, her own husband. This was the woman Stan thought of as just an average stay-at-home mom? She turned to Tim, 'What do you think of this idea?'

'This is the first I've heard of it, actually,' Tim stammered, obviously caught with his bicycle shorts down. 'It's a fascinating idea you've come up with, Stan, but if you don't mind my saying so, Julia's thinking on this is probably right. Bringing a non-pro on to a weekly series could be awfully tricky. Her whole life would be turned upside down. I can't imagine Debra Jo and her family would want to move lock, stock and barrel to Los Angeles.'

'Well, we'll just have to wait and see what they say,' Stan said smugly. 'I've already sent the Fawcetts a telegram.'

'What the hell is going on here?' Julia completely lost control and began to shriek at him. 'How could you make them an offer without consulting with us? Or Pac Vic?'

'I've already consulted with Charles Currie,' Stan said coldly. 'He thinks it's an excellent idea. He believes Debra Jo Fawcett has star quality. So do I. It's a top executive network decision. We want her written into the show.'

Jackie squealed like a stuck pig when Debra Jo called her on the phone and told her CBN wanted her to come out to Hollywood to be on Makeover for a whole eight months.

'I can't believe it,' Jackie said. 'This kind of thing just never happens, not in real life.'

'I know,' Debra Jo exclaimed. 'How do you think I feel? I keep pinching myself to make sure I'm not dreaming.'

'Who are you supposed to be on the show?'

'Me. Isn't that a hoot?' she giggled. 'Well, not exactly me. They think I should play a housewife who's worried that her husband's gotten bored with her so she's always going to the Changing Room to get a new look. They're going to call the character Debra Jo, my real name, isn't that exciting?'

'Yeah, I guess.'

Debra Jo sensed her friend might be jealous. 'It's just a little bitty part, but I'd be on almost every week. I think it'd be fun. When we did that special episode in Houston, everybody was so nice to me, it didn't even seem like work. I mean, it's not like J.C. Austin and I are best friends or anything, but we sure had a ball together. Can you imagine being close to her every day?'

'I'd prefer to imagine being close to Brandon Tate even one day,' Jackie sighed huskily.

'Oh, please. I was nervous just being within ten feet of the man. He is so sexy. I liked the little girl, Melissa McKimmie, a whole lot, too. She spent most of her time off at our house, remember? Now, there's a kid who really needs her mother. I don't know what that woman can be thinking of, leaving her on her own like that all the time.'

'So what about your kids? Do the boys want to go with you?'

'Sure thing. Wouldn't you rather live in Beverly Hills than Houston?'

'I don't rightly know,' Jackie said thoughtfully. She went

silent for a moment and Debra Jo could hear her breathing over the phone. Then, 'We all thought you were fabulous on the show, but we assumed it was a one-shot deal.'

'That's what I thought, too,' Debra Jo said breathlessly, 'but I guess a lot of people wrote in to the network saying they wanted to see more of me. The publicity department even forwarded some of the fanmail on to me.'

'Fanmail? Debra Jo Fawcett, you mean you got letters from total strangers?'

'Oh yeah.'

'And you didn't show them to me, your best friend?' Jackie's usually deep, laid-back voice rose half an octave in indignation.

'Well, most of them were really sweet. One or two of them were kind of weird. Like this guy who wrote from Chipley, Florida, listing all the ways he'd personally like to make me over, starting with shaving my pubic hair? Boy I didn't dare show that one to anybody, least of all, Eddie.'

Jackie laughed. 'So what does Eddie think of all this? Is he going to let you go?'

That, of course, was the one question Debra Jo didn't have a good answer for yet. Ever since the telegram had come from Stanfield King, the big head honcho at the network, followed by a long letter on embossed CBN letterhead outlining in detail the offer to become a regular on the series, she and Eddie had been arguing about what to do. She kept telling him that this was the chance of a lifetime, her dream come true. He kept on warning her, in that maddeningly reasonable way he had, that sometimes dreams can turn into nightmares. She was getting more than a little anxious. The producers wanted to know by the beginning of next week if she would be ready to report for work at the end of July.

'I don't have a good feeling about this,' Eddie said quietly. It was late at night and they were arguing in bed, whispering so as not to alarm the boys. 'They want you to use your real name on the show. Why? Everybody will know that it's you. Mrs Debra Jo Fawcett. You'll be living in a fishbowl where the whole world sees your private business. I'm afraid you're going to get your head turned and your heart broke. You think you know what show business is all about because you read those crazy tabloid newspapers, but that's all made-up stuff. It's not near as

276

glamorous as they make it out to be.'

'I know that, Eddie,' Debra Jo whispered fiercely. 'You don't have to treat me like I'm totally stupid. I do know the difference between reality and fantasy.'

'Yeah, well, that's the trouble. I'm not sure you do.'

'Don't you realize what an opportunity like this could mean for our future?' She couldn't see his face in the dark, but she suspected he was wearing his 'I hate to think about this shit' look. Eddie liked it best when he was allowed to take things one day at a time, when he wasn't forced to examine the past or to consider what lay ahead.

'In the grand scheme of things, it won't mean nothin', and you can count on that.'

'Damnit, you can't stand that I've got the chance to do something that's just for me.'

'Don't go throwin' that women's lib shit all over me. Of course I want it for you if that's what will make you happy. LA scares me, that's all. Nobody in their right mind would want to live out there. They got earthquakes, they got riots, they got drugs, the rate of violent crime is unfuckingbeliev-able.'

'We got all that right here in Houston. No earthquakes, but plenty of tornadoes and floods. Drive-by shootings, drugs sold on the street corners in plain daylight. I read in the paper yesterday that the rate of juvenile homicide has nearly doubled in one year. No place is truly safe any more, Ed.'

'I won't have you takin' my kids into a war zone.'

'I would never put my boys in danger and you know it.' Her voice was trembling with anger. She was right on the edge of bursting into tears. 'I'm a good mother and don't you dare tell me I'm not. In the end, you have to trust your kids and hope and pray you've raised them right.'

'Of course you're a good mother, Debra Jo. It's just I hate the thought of you bein' all on your own out there.'

'Then come with me.' Even in the dark, she could feel her cheeks flaming red. She had never stood up to Eddie like this before. She'd never had to.

'I've got a business to run,' he said loudly. 'I can't just pick up and move to California for a year.'

'You could get somebody else to run it for you. Jackie's husband keeps pestering you to take him on as a partner. Give him a chance. Sugar pie, please, it'd be so much fun,' she was begging now. 'They've offered me enough for us all to go. Airfare for the whole family. Plus a rented house.'

'No, goddamnit. Quit pickin'. My life is right here. We had our family conference and Beau already told you he don't want to leave his high-school friends.'

'Danny's dying to go.'

'It ain't good for kids to be movin' schools all the time.'

'One year isn't exactly all the time.' She could tell he was getting really mad, too. His grammar was starting to slip, which was always a sure sign. For a moment her heart went out to him, he was so afraid of anything new, but then she hardened herself. This was her big chance and she'd be a fool not to take it. 'I'm sorry, Eddie, but I have to give this a try, at least see how it works out.'

Eddie got out of bed abruptly and snapped on the overhead light. He went over to the dresser and took out the package of Marlboros he kept hidden in the bottom drawer. He put a cigarette in his mouth and lit it.

'Now don't start smoking again just because you're mad with me,' Debra Jo said softly. She had only just got him to quit smoking six months ago.

'I ain't,' he took a long drag and defiantly blew the smoke in the air. 'If I do, it's none of your business anyway.'

'I guess you know the Marlboro Man died.'

'Look, Debra Jo, if I'm going to be a single parent stuck here raisin' a teenage boy all on my own, I'm goin' to need somethin' to get me through it.'

Debra Jo knew right then and there he'd made the decision to let her go.

Chapter Twenty-eight

'Desperado Productions, Banff location office.' The young, female voice on the other end of the line sounded half-way between British and American, the elusive Canadian accent.

'I'm trying to get a hold of Brandon Tate,' J.C. said.

'You and just about every other woman in North America.' The young woman allowed herself a small giggle before someone else grabbed the phone and J.C. heard, 'Sorry about that. May I help you?' J.C. repeated her request and a much crisper, more authoritative voice told her, 'You'll have to contact Mr Tate through his personal manager at CTA.' Of course he would be hard to reach. J.C. insisted on the same protective shield between herself and the public. But she wasn't about to give up. Besides, she could hear a man's deep voice and muffled female laughter in the background. No doubt Brandon was around there somewhere.

'Look, y'all, I swear this is urgent business. It's J.C. Austin calling and I'm down here in Calgary.'

'Wow, really?' the voice went up an octave with a shriek that blasted her ear. 'Just a minute, I'll fetch him.'

There was a pause and then: 'Brandon Tate here.'

'Hey, Brandon. How's the film shoot going? Sounds like you're having yourself a ball up there.'

'Hey, J.C. This is a surprise.' He sounded sheepish, almost guilty. What for? She didn't own him. 'We were just fooling around, waiting for the call to set.'

'Haven't you learned to keep your paws off all those little starlettes?' she said teasingly.

'What can I do, darlin'? You're not around. I miss my favorite redhead. I can't function unless I'm giving acting lessons. That's the only way I can relate to women these days.'

'Brandon, you tickle me, you really do.'

'Any time, darlin'. Just give me the chance. Where are you calling from?'

'Don't drop the phone. Calgary.'

'You're kidding me?'

'No. I'm the headliner at the Calgary Stampede this year. That's why I'm calling. They've asked me to lead the parade and I thought maybe you'd like to haul your handsome ass down here and give 'em two stars for the price of one.'

'Where's Mac?'

'Still in Nashville. Directing the sound mix on the *Telephone Road* album. It's turned out to be trickier than we thought. Otherwise he'd be up here with me.'

'Honey, I am on my way. I can't believe that old bird dog let you out of his sight for one minute.'

'He didn't know I'd be on the phone to you as soon as I got here,' J.C. giggled. It was fun when Brandon flirted with her. Harmless teasing, but it made her feel appreciated in a female way. Locked in a recording studio for the past month working on the album with Mac, she had begun to feel that all that mattered to him was her larynx. 'How's the film going?'

'Great, I think. At least the scenery's playing its part. It's magnificent. Big sky, tall mountains, wildlife roaming all over the place. The director, Richard Flint, is one of those Method directors. Everything has to be as genuine old west as possible. No automobiles or trucks allowed. He's insisting we all ride horseback to and from the set. Aside from me and my co-star, the rest of the actors are mostly native Indian and they're all terrific. I think they're going to give real strength to the picture. I have a good feeling about this one. J.C., I love it up here. They've actually got air you can breathe.'

She laughed. 'OK, OK, you've convinced me. But do you think you could drag yourself away for twenty-four hours to come down to Calgary? The parade's on Friday morning and then I sing at the Grandstand Show Friday night.'

'My day off, as it happens.'

'All you have to be able to do is sit a horse.'

'Exactly what I'm doing here. A beautiful mount she is, too. Pure Arabian. Black and tan. Sensitive to my feelings, responsive to my every move, what more could I ask?'

'She sounds pretty sexy.'

'Not as sexy as you. But she definitely has more to offer than my co-star, Steven Fleetwood.'

'Well, now I don't know about that,' J.C. drawled. 'Steve's got a pretty cute little butt.' She was enjoying this. It felt good to practice her flirting.

'Hey, wait just a minute here. My feelings are hurt. I thought you gave your highest cute-rating to my butt.'

'I do, I do,' she laughingly reassured him. 'So just bring those sweet cakes on down to Calgary. I'm staying at the Palliser. In the Royal Suite, I'll have you know. Real fancy. All oak panelling. It's even got an electric suit-press and shoe-polisher. Queen Elizabeth and Prince Philip once stayed here. There's a big old carved wooden mantelpiece and a four-poster bed bigger than the one I have back home.'

'Sounds tempting. If I come down there do I get to see your bed?'

'You keep those kind of thoughts for your horse.' At last she had made him laugh. 'The Stampede Parade will last a couple of hours. Then the mayor wants to present us both with traditional white cowboy hats. There's a ceremony in the afternoon in Olympic Plaza, then the singing gig at night.'

'Should be a lot of fun.' He sounded as if he meant it.

'Wait till you see me with brown eyes. You won't be able to keep your hands off me.'

'What happened to your green eyes?'

'I've got contact lenses for the shoot. I have to pass as part native. I'm wearing them as much as I can to try and get used to them.'

'I can hardly wait. See you Tuesday, bright and early. Bye, bye, brown eyes.'

Thousands of Calgarians lined the streets to see J.C. Austin and Brandon Tate ride horseback in the Stampede Parade. J.C.'s Grandstand concert was a triumph, an electrifying performance. She wore the traditional white hat but eschewed simple Stampede denim wear for glitter and spandex, which was what her fans had come to expect of her as glamorous country. The tight-fitting white pants and low-cut sequin top made her look sexy as hell, and when she sang one of her raunchiest tunes, 'Basic Needs', every man in the audience wanted to leap up and offer to fulfil every one of them. The crowd refused to let her go. They were stamping their feet on the floor and calling out her name, 'J.C., J.C., J.C.!' They brought her back for encore after encore, and when she finally ended the night by giving them a preview of *Telephone Road*, they went nuts, on their feet, cheering and stomping. She could see Brandon in the celebrity box, waving and blowing kisses to her, tossing his white cowboy hat in the air.

It was a clear summer night as they headed back to the Palliser. Calgary was far enough north that, although it was already close to eleven o'clock, there was still light in the sky. They had decided to walk, and a clump of fans followed them, hooting and whistling, until they ducked into the King Eddie, a funky bluesy place where some of the best underground bands in the country came to play. They drank Tequila Gold and ate pickled eggs while listening to a down and dirty group called Triple Threat, the 'sensitive acoustic blues pigs'.

'So when do I get to see this famous bed Betty Windsor slept in?' Brandon leaned across the table and said directly in her ear, raising his voice above the wail and whine of Tim Williams.

'Are you kidding me?' J.C. raised an eyebrow. 'You think I'm going to let a man with your dangerous reputation into my private boudoir?'

Brandon laughed. 'Believe me, darlin', your virtue is safe tonight. José Cuervo has taken possession of my body as well as my soul. Even if you took off your clothes and danced naked down Ninth Avenue, I don't think I'd be able to do you justice.'

'OK, come on back then.'

Brandon let out a whistle when he saw the room. The Royal Suite lived up to its palatial name. They took turns helping each other off with their cowboy boots, tossed the white hats on to two of the posts at the end of the enormous four-poster, and piled on to the bed, giggling like high-school kids on a clandestine sleep-over.

'My mouth feels like a boll of cotton. Man, it's so dry in Alberta.' J.C. opened the miniature bar fridge and poured herself a glass of mineral water.

'Here, you can give me some of that.' Brandon held out his glass and she filled it with the cold, bubbly water. 'You were terrific tonight, by the way.'

'It felt so good, right, to be singing again, and that audience was hot. I love that. It really gets me going.'

'You got them going, too. Your voice, I don't know what it is, a certain quality, the way you phrase things, it connects with something deep inside. It's like a total surrender to the emotion of the thing. You go away, somewhere else, and everybody listening to you goes there, too. Even me. I've never told you this, but I can't talk for five or ten minutes after I've heard you sing. I just want to hold the sound of your voice inside my head for as long as I can.'

J.C. looked at him in surprise. 'I didn't think you paid much attention to my singing.'

'I forget it's you. No, that doesn't sound right. What I mean is, you're so different when you sing. It never fails to astonish me. I like to think I know you pretty well by now, we're comfortable together, good friends, I hope, but when you open your mouth to sing, I don't feel I know you at all. All I can do is marvel at the amazing sound that comes out of that little body of yours.'

'That's the sweetest, most personal thing you've ever said to me.'

'Well, I mean it.' Brandon reached across her to get the bottle of mineral water and J.C. held out her glass so he could refill it, too.

'So tell me,' she said, leaning back against one of the oversized brocade pillows. 'We been friends for over a year now and I been studying you up close, but I still can't figure you out. What's your secret?'

'What do you mean?'

'Why are you so successful with women? OK, so you're handsome, although without those famous green eyes,' she peered at his brown contact lenses, 'I have to say you're just another cowboy.' He hit her on the head with a pillow. 'Kidding, just kidding. You're mighty studly whatever color your eyes, but it's got to be more than that. What do you think makes the women fall, like a stack of dominoes, right into you waitin', willin' arms?'

'Well, now, to be honest,' Brandon stretched out his taut, denim-covered body the length of the bed. 'Some of it remains a mystery, even to me. I couldn't even talk to a woman until I was twenty. Of course, once I got the hang of it, I was hooked. I guess they recognize that I really and truly love women. You're by far the superior sex, in virtually every way.'

'That's a line if ever I heard one.'

'No, I mean it. I would rather be with a woman than a man any day. I find you all endlessly fascinating.'

'All of us? You must have a type.' J.C. wrapped the satin comforter around her and snuggled down, ready to hear more. 'What do you like in a woman?'

'Hey, if you restrict yourself to a type, you limit the possibilities. Every woman is interesting and worth loving once you really get to know her. It's a matter of taking the time to look. I'm looking into her eyes, I'm looking at her life. Most of us, we're afraid to look too closely at one another, afraid of what we might see.'

'Something we won't like?'

'No, something we might like too much.'

'Are you talking about sex?' She felt comfortable and relaxed, a little high, but pleasantly so.

'Of course. Between a man and a woman, it's always there. We may seem friendly on the surface, but an unspoken connection, that male/female thing, is always humming along underneath.'

'I don't believe that.'

'You can't get away from it. It's how we are made, it's why we were made. But that's the difference. I admit it, other people don't. I think about sex every fifteen seconds.'

'Every fifteen seconds?' She smacked her head in mock surprise.

'We all have the impulse for sex, but we rarely act on it. I always act on it, given the chance. I've been lucky, I've had a lot of chances.'

'Have you taken a lot of chances? The free ride is over. It's pretty toxic out there.'

'I always wear my raincoat,' Brandon smiled. 'That's why I was sure that waitress, Connie, was lying about my being the father of her child. And I've been tested for AIDS so many times my doctor thinks I'm paranoid, but with my history, you can't be too careful.'

'So you admit you're proud of adding all those notches to your belt as you go through woman after woman.'

'No, you've got me all wrong,' he protested. 'I like to take things slow. I'm a sensualist, not a sexualist.'

'Still, you like the chase, you love the conquest.'

'Never. Conquest is based on oppression. Men who think that way are not really looking at women. No wonder they can't communicate.'

'Come on, Brandon, you're not known for being faithful.'

'But the strange thing is I am.'

'What?'

'Faithful. Me and Liz Taylor, we practise serial monogamy. When I'm involved in a relationship, no other woman in the world exists for me. I've got great powers of concentration.'

'What about when you're not involved?'

'Then, I have to say, I like to eat around.'

'Oh, Brandon, you make me laugh, you really do.'

'A good sense of humor is part of the art of seduction. I've had many panties down around the ankles because I know how to be funny.'

'Oh, you are so bad,' she gave his leg a poke with her bare foot. This was fun. Hearing a man talk about women and sex. Enlightening, too. When she was on the road with the band, the guys in the group used to boast about the women they slept with. The basic attitude always seemed to be that they were sluts, vessels to be used and abused. J.C. wanted to be one of the guys, so that's how she treated the men who came after her, when she went through what Mac called, 'her wild spell'. They were there to be enjoyed for a night, or maybe two, then left behind when she moved on with the band. Being able to take her pleasure when and where she wanted it had given her a sense of power and control in a life full of uncertainty. Still, that was no excuse. She felt ashamed now she'd ever done it. She'd been completely faithful to Mac for the last six years. 'You're not taking this seriously at all.'

'Oh yes, I take it very seriously. I believe it's women who hold the key to love.' He sat up and in a low, melodic voice, began to recite:

> 'From women's eyes this doctrine I derive:
> They sparkle still the right Promethean fire;
> They are the books, the arts, the academes,
> That show, contain, and nourish all the world.'

'Now there's one helluva good line,' J.C. sighed. 'That's beautiful.'

'Shakespeare's *Love's Labour's Lost*,' he said softly.

'You know Shakespeare so well you can just say his words right out loud like that?'

'I played Biron when I was at the Old Vic.'

'I didn't know you could act Shakespeare,' J.C. looked at him in genuine surprise.

'Well, darlin', I can't let you know everything about me all at once. Then there would be no mystery.'

'That's real important to you, isn't it?' she said, looking at him shrewdly. 'Not giving too much away.'

'I like to be a challenge. Everyone wants the unattainable.'

'Yeah, like Marilyn Monroe. All the men I know, including Mac, think they were the one that could have saved her.'

'It's a little the same with me. Not that I need to be saved, but every woman thinks she's the one I'll stay with.'

'So is that the game? If you stay, you lose, if you go, you win?'

Brandon stopped suddenly. 'This is weird. I've never had such a conversation with a woman before. Why am I telling you all this?'

'Probably because I asked. It's interesting. Believe me, I could never talk like this with Mac. I'm real jealous. I wouldn't want to hear him go on about other women. And he sure wouldn't listen to me talking about other men.'

'What would he do if he knew you were in bed with me right now?'

'Oh, probably shoot you,' J.C. said casually.

'Shit.' Brandon sat up.

'It's OK. He won't find out. Anyway, we're not doing nothing. Course he'd never believe that.'

'Neither would the *Hollywood Insider*!' They both laughed and then shuddered at the imaginary headlines. 'Holy shit!'

J.C. wiggled under the comforter. 'OK, back to the topic. What happens when you leave?'

'We stay friends.'

'I doubt that.' She reached over and tousled his hair.

'I try and make them feel wonderful about themselves. Usually they move on to bigger and better men.'

'How long do you usually stay?'

'Two years is my limit. That seems to be it for true desire.

After that, the feeling is still there but it becomes something else.'

'Yeah, I know what you mean,' J.C. sighed. 'Love starts out as an undiscovered country, then moves into familiar territory, and eventually becomes armed truce. Maybe you're smart to get off the train at the familiarity stop.'

'Now it's your turn, Ms Austin,' Brandon said. 'You're regarded as pretty hot stuff yourself. I wager I could walk from here to China on the carcasses of men who would die for you. What do you look for in a man?'

J.C. smiled. 'I thought you'd never ask. One who can sit a horse, play a tune, and kiss real slow.'

'That sounds like something out of your press kit. Come on, level with me.'

'OK, stamina. Intellectual or physical brawn. Preferably both. And I think I just added something to the list: one who can speak Shakespeare and make it sound like he means it. No, seriously, I want a man who is truthful, who doesn't bullshit me to get me into bed.'

Outside the balcony window, it had gone from light to gray to dark and then to light again as the first streaks of the morning sun appeared through the sheer lace curtains.

'You got to go,' J.C. pushed him toward the door. 'If you're going to make the hour-and-a-half drive up to Banff in time for your call, you have to leave now.'

'You're right.' Brandon looked at the digital clock on the table by the bed. 'We've been talking all night.'

'Just one more question before you go.'

'What is this? Are you doing some sort of psychological study here? Women Who Love Brandon Tate Too Much?'

'No, this one's really important. Sex is one thing you've mastered, but are you good at love?'

'What?'

'Have you ever really been in love?'

'Of course. Yes. I don't know.' Brandon suddenly looked uneasy. They were both completely sober by now. 'Sure I have. I love love.'

J.C. burst out laughing. 'Brandon, you are full of shit, you know that? But you know what? That's OK.'

Brandon gave her a goodbye peck on the cheek. 'Well you know what John Barrymore said—'

'What did he say?'

'Women sleep with assholes and marry gentlemen.'

It was mid-afternoon. Brandon picked up the phone and quickly dialed the number of the Palliser. He hoped he would catch her before she got on the plane.

'Hello?' She sounded breathy and more than a little hung over.

'Hey, it's me.'

'Hey. I had a ball last night.'

'Me too.'

'So, you made it back all right?'

'Fine. I don't remember much about the drive though. How are you feeling?'

'Like a herd of buffalo are camped inside my head. That's the trouble with Tequila Gold. You don't even realize you're wazooed until it's too late to redeem yourself. I'm trying to pack here but just the sound of my clothes hitting the suitcase gives me a headache.'

Brandon laughed. He could picture her tossing clothes willy-nilly into her bag, undoubtedly having to sit on it in order to get it zipped up. Her dressing-room was always a mess, unlike his, which she said looked like a gynecologist's office with everything neatly laid out on a towel. 'Listen, something's come up. We just lost an actress for *Vengeance*. It's a really small role, there's hardly any women in this picture, but we're set to shoot tomorrow. If we wait to bring someone in from LA it'll put us behind schedule. Would you be interested in doing it as a cameo? I talked to the director and he'd love to have you.'

'Oh, Brandon, I don't know. I'm supposed to be at the airport in an hour.' She sounded tempted. 'When would you want me?'

'First thing tomorrow morning. I'm telling you, this happened very suddenly. We're really in a bind here.'

'What's the part?'

'A farmer's wife. But she's got two good emotional scenes. Her daughter is raped and killed. They think it's by Indians but it turns out the whiskey traders did it and blamed it on the natives. That's why I have to seek vengeance. It could really show you off to great advantage. She's there in the early part of the picture to get the news of her daughter's death. That's a real gut-wrenching tear-jerker. Then there's another short scene at the end when I come back to tell her that the revenge has been carried out.

It's just the kind of part to get you some serious attention if you can pull it off.'

'I'm not a serious actress, Brandon. I can handle Janine, barely, but if there's crying and stuff, I don't know.' He could imagine her chewing on the inside of her cheek and narrowing those crinkling blue eyes the way she did whenever she was forced to make a difficult decision.

'I'll help you through it, I promise. You need the experience on the big screen. Even Mac agrees with that.'

'I doubt it. He's expecting me home tonight.'

'It's only a couple of days' shoot. You'd be staying in Banff and then going to and from Morley Flats to shoot your prologue and the epilogue. I really want you to do this, J.C. Please. For me.'

'Why Mr Tate, I don't believe I've ever heard you beg.'

'As your personal acting coach, I see you as absolutely perfect for this role. Besides, you've got one talent that's vital to the production.'

'What's that?'

'You already know how to ride a horse.'

J.C. made it through both scenes with flying colors. Brandon coached her every step of the way and, when she finished her big breakdown, the director and crew applauded. Brandon had another ten days to go on the shoot, but he promised J.C. her own private little wrap party. They started with mulled wine, followed by dinner and a bottle of Bordeaux at the Banff Springs Hotel, where he watched her polish off a plate of blood-rare prime rib, mashed potatoes and vegetables.

'I don't hold with California cooking,' J.C. said. 'I can't get into sushi and I'm not ready to give up red meat. This is perfect. What's this popover kind of thing called?'

'Yorkshire pudding.'

'It's tasty.' She slathered it with gravy.

'Save room for dessert. You should sample the trifle.'

'What is that? I've read about it in books.'

'Heavy cream, sponge cake, sherry and raspberry jam.'

'Bring it on,' she pounded the table with her spoon. 'Tonight I'm ready for new experiences.'

He ordered them another bottle of wine. 'You look terrific on a horse. I guess it comes naturally to you.'

'Not really. I didn't learn to ride until we bought the

spread in Hickory Lake and Mac started breeding horses.'

'Really?' Brandon was surprised. 'I would have thought with your country background you would have been riding since you were three.'

J.C. smiled wryly. 'My background isn't what you think it is.'

'That sounds mysterious.'

'You'll find out soon enough. Once my new album, *Telephone Road*, is released, everybody will know I'm nothing but trailer trash.' For a moment she looked like she were about to cry, then her mouth tightened with determination. 'What the hell. I don't care.'

He was curious but he didn't press her. 'Are you pleased with the album?'

'Mac's got some reservations, but I can't be letting him pull the strings all the time. I got to do what's right for me and I think *Telephone Road* is more "me" than anything else I've done. Releasing a new album is always a crapshoot. Must be kind of like giving birth to a baby.' Her face saddened.

He didn't say anything. He knew her well enough by now to realize how much not having children had hurt her.

'You know it's bound to have at least some of the right genes but you're never positive exactly how it's going to turn out. I really believe the songs on this album celebrate the wisdom of growing up and looking back. I never believed I would stay alive long enough to get this far, and that's one of the things I'm trying to say with my lyrics this time around.'

'You were running pretty wild there for a while, weren't you? I remember reading about it in *Rolling Stone*. A lot of booze, a little blow, maybe even some raunch on the side?'

'Yeah, I was kind of rowdy. I wanted to be like the big boys of country music, the legends: hard drinkin' and hard lovin'. I aimed to experience it all and then write about it. I learned, first-hand, that that's not always the best approach. Anyway, *Telephone Road* will have a different sound, that's for sure.'

'But still country, right?'

'What the hell's that supposed to mean?' J.C. displayed a flash of her famous temper. 'Ultimately it's all country, because it's me singing it and country is what I am. Besides, I don't want to be labeled any more. For a long time I was just the singer. Mac chose the songs, the back-up musicians, the arrangements. He's got an ear for hits and he was responsible for getting me the right exposure, making sure I hit the charts on a regular basis. You could say he was riding in the front of the Silver Eagle bus while I was in the back. Hell, he was the driver and I was just a passenger along for the ride.'

'I thought you wrote all your own material.'

'I do now. It was kind of my own personal "outlaw movement",' she chuckled, referring to the revolution led by Waylon Jennings against the Nashville establishment, when recording artists began to take control of their own careers. 'Still, I trust Mac's opinion on just about everything. He's real good at seeing through all the bullshit. I take everything too personal. If the critics say I'm bad, I just fall apart. If they tell me I'm wonderful then I'm likely to go out there and push it and be too wonderful, if you know what I mean. Mac keeps my feet on the ground. He could be dead right about *Telephone Road*, we'll just have to wait and see.'

'He wasn't right about your acting.' Brandon was usually careful not to criticize Mac or their relationship. 'You were wonderful today.'

'Do you think so?' J.C. instantly looked anxious. 'It was hard for me to tell if it was working or not. I was crying so hard I didn't know what was happening. Pretty powerful emotions to get into and then try to get out of. You don't think my part's going to end up on the cutting-room floor?'

'Not a chance. You had the whole crew bawling along with you. You were terrific.'

'I hope you're right. I'd like this to be a new start for me.' She still seemed nervous. Her eyes were narrowed with anxiety and she hadn't laughed much at his jokes.

Suddenly he wanted to soothe her fears and take away all her insecurities. He paid the check and took her for a therapeutic full body massage and a dip in the Sulphur Mountain hot springs. The sulphur springs were right out in the open with a spectacular view of the snow-capped mountains. The steam rose from the water, a soporific warmth gently lapping at their bodies, while their faces felt the sting of the cool night air. He was glad to see the worry leave J.C.'s eyes and her tensions finally melt away. She lifted her arms up, stretching them above her head, her breasts rising out of the top of her simple black bathing suit. He was very aware that this was the first time he had seen her in any stage of undress. She had a small waist, round hips, full, gently sloping breasts. It was a woman's body, not a girl's, and yet it seemed more desirable to him than any of the more perfect bodies he had possessed in the past. They soaked as long as they could stand it, watching the sun go down leaving a few pale orange streaks against the dark sky. Then they dressed and took the long way back to the individual chalets the Desperado Production Company had booked for them.

Neither of them felt like talking. J.C. reached out to take his hand and they walked along together, without saying a word, feeling the powerful force of the natural beauty of the Rockies all around them: the jagged peaks thrusting up into the night sky, patches of snow still glistening on the tops, even in July. Further down the side of the mountains, rivulets of water rushed down, becoming instant falls. The air was crisp and scented with pine. Pine needles crunched under their feet. It was dusk now, Brandon's favorite time, a mystical period between day and night. Suddenly a deer appeared on the path before them, its antlers quivering. Then, out of the depths of the forest, came two Rocky Mountain Big Horn sheep. They all stopped, startled by each other and by the humans in front of them, then lightly, gracefully, bounded away.

'Wow,' J.C. said in a hushed voice. 'You would never see that in LA.'

'Maybe where I live,' Brandon said quietly. 'Topanga Canyon has wildlife. That's why I like it out there. It puts things in perspective.'

By the time they reached the door of J.C.'s chalet, the moon had risen, big, round and full, so bright it lit up the surrounding trees with an almost unearthly glow. She was telling him about the design for the *Telephone Road* album cover, how different it was from the usual soft focus, color-washed, backlit stuff. 'In fact, the whole thing is in black-and-white. Very stark, very real.'

'Black-and-white? What about your red hair?' J.C.'s flaming hair blazed in the moonlight like a fuzzy, surrealistic halo.

'That's the point. When people think of me, they think of my hair.'

Or your mouth, Brandon thought. That sweetly curved small upper lip and the sexy, slightly protruding lower lip, jutting out defiantly, daring itself to be kissed. God, what he wouldn't give to slide his tongue all around the edge of her mouth and then slip it inside, just once . . .

'I want people to see the real me this time. So I'm naked from the waist up. Just a pair of black jeans and nothin' else.'

Brandon snapped back to attention. 'Just how much of the real you do we get to see?'

'Actually not that much,' she grinned infectiously. 'My hair does cover the rude bits.'

He remembered her full, curved breasts. 'Lucky for you you've got a lot of hair.'

J.C. laughed. 'It just about does the job. On the other side of the cover you get to see my bare back. Anyway, it's a real eye-catching photograph.'

'I'll bet it is.' She was acting so natural about all of this, but Brandon was suddenly sweating, his voice thick with desire. He could barely resist the urge to reach out and unbutton the top, pearl-edged button on her western-style shirt. The soft chamois next to her smooth skin, the intricate stitching cupping each gently curved breast. It made his heart ache. He cleared his throat. 'J.C., I behaved myself in your bedroom the other night.'

'You sure did. Bet no one would believe it either.'

'I promised you I would, but I don't know how much longer I can go on being good. We're good friends now and I like being close to you, but this closeness, it's . . . God, I know this sounds crazy, but I think I'm in love with you.' He was amazed to hear himself saying the words and the minute they were out of his mouth he was afraid she wouldn't believe him.

She didn't laugh, but her lips curved into an amused smile. 'Mr B., you are a pure master at layin' on the bull. Down in Calgary, you spent a whole night telling me all your secrets about how you go around seducing women, and here you have the gall to try and lay the same old line on me. Give it up, baby. I know it's late, you've had too much wine and you're feeling horny. I got to admit I'm a little horny too. I've been away from Mac too long.'

Of course she didn't believe him. He'd spilled his guts to her and now she was throwing it right back in his face.

Well, not exactly throwing it, but at the very least, holding up a mirror so he could see what a fool he'd been. 'No, no, I really mean it, J.C. I'm in love with you.'

'It's the booze talking, brother.' She gave him a sisterly pat on the arm.

'No, it's not. I love you. I've loved you from the very first moment I saw you.'

'What a bold-faced lie. You first saw me at my screen test for Makeover. You were too polite to say anything, but it was crystal clear you thought I was a two-bit singer who was going to ruin your chance at a comeback.'

'You got all that at our first meeting? Oh God,' he said miserably. 'I'm stupid, stupid, stupid.' He hit his forehead with the back of his fist.

'No, you're not.' Her eyes were warm and wise. 'You let your guard down with me because we're meant to be friends not lovers. Don't fret yourself. I'm not about to go running to the *Hollywood Insider* and tell them all your sexy little secrets.'

'Please. Let me love you.' He had never had to beg before.

'How can you think you're in love with me? We've never even kissed.'

The usual Brandon would have responded with a flirtatious joke: something like, 'that's easily remedied' or, better yet, would just have taken her in his arms and kissed her. But somehow he couldn't move. He stood there, frozen to the spot. He could only repeat, 'I'm in love with you.'

For a moment, her eyes narrowed and she looked almost frightened, then she doubled up with laughter. 'You're a persistent bugger, ain't you? Is this how you do it? You just keep pushing until you wear a lady down?'

'I want you.'

J.C. nodded judiciously. 'Sure you do. I'm warm, female and I'm here. That's enough for you."

'I'm sorry.' He quickly moved away from her.

'Are you sulking?' she said teasingly. 'You trying to make me believe you've never been turned down before?'

'As a matter of fact, I haven't.' He was frantically trying to regain his equilibrium.

'I believe you,' she said solemnly. 'And your stud card can keep its perfect score because you know, deep in your heart of hearts, that wasn't a genuine offer.'

He couldn't pursue it any further. He was suddenly deeply embarrassed and desperately afraid of losing her. 'J.C., please don't stop being close to me. I need you.'

'Don't worry. You've still got me.' The warmth was back in her eyes. 'Give me your hand.' He held it out to her and she kissed his palm and folded his fingers over the kiss. 'Now you take that little kiss and hold on to it, Brandon, OK? You'll find it means a lot more than a big old kiss on the lips. I'm flying out of here real early in the morning so I got to get some sleep now. I'll see you back in LA.' She unlocked the door to the chalet and quickly slipped inside.

He stood there in the moonlight, his fist tightly closed, hanging on to her kiss. He couldn't understand why he was so upset. He was drunk and he'd made a pass at her. She'd forgiven him. Supposedly nothing had really changed, but he felt such a longing. The pain of loss was almost overwhelming, which didn't make sense at all. How could he lose something he had never had?

Chapter Twenty-nine

Marty lay on the living-room sofa watching Julia get ready to leave the townhouse. She could feel his eyes on her, following her around the room, as she picked up her daytimer, stuffed her draft of the script and a sheaf of notes into her briefcase, and grabbed her purse. It was if he were actually leeching the energy from her.

'So, what's on your agenda for this morning?' she asked brightly, hating herself for sounding like her mother.

'Nothing much,' he said, staring at the shoe that balanced on the end of his foot, half on, half off. It was obvious he was not intending to come with her. 'How about you?'

'I've booked a story conference with the writing staff at eleven; but first I've got a meeting with a representative from that lingerie company. Next of Skin. Believe it or not, they want me to model their underwear for a series of print ads.'

'You're kidding?' For the first time all morning, he seemed interested.

'If I say yes, I'll be down to my knickers, posing in various states of undress for some pretty high-class maga-zines in North America and in Europe. *Elle, Mirabelle, Vanity Fair*.'

'You mean *Vanity Feh*?' He reminded her of their private Yiddish joke about the glitzy publication.

'I've come a long way, baby,' she was glad to coax a smile out of him.

'Are you really going to do it?'

'It's great publicity for Makeover. Good link with Lyla's Lingerie on the show. Why, don't you think I have the body for it?'

'You have a delicious, delectable body. Not that I get to see much of it these days.'

Let it go, Julia, let it go. He was always complaining that

he never saw her when certainly he knew exactly where to find her. What did he think she was doing with her time? Out on the town, hitting the clubs, doing the scene? For the past year she was always either at the studio, on the set, or in the editing suite.

'Why do they want you to wear their undies? You're not a model.'

'That's the whole point of these ads. They're using real people instead of bimbettes. The thrust of the campaign is that women in positions of power can still be feminine and seductive, that underneath the herringbone beats a heart of silk and lace. You must have seen the ads. They've got a research scientist, a judge, a concert violinist, even an astronaut.'

'In her underwear? This does not bode well for the future of the space program.'

'Well, we're not talking Frederick's of Hollywood G-strings here. Next of Skin is all very tasteful. Pure silk, just the kind I like. That's the best part of the deal. Along with the fee, they supply me with a whole new wardrobe of lingerie.'

'For you, I know, a dream come true.' He seemed to be perking up. 'For me, I want us to get out of this house. It's closing in on us. We promised ourselves that once the season was over we'd concentrate on finding a larger place. I feel like that commercial where the couple is buried under a mound of paper. I've already called the real-estate agent and she's got a bunch of places lined up for us to see . . .'

'What, today? Are you out of your mind?' Julia exploded. 'I'm covering your ass right now because you don't feel up to working and you want me to take time off to look at pretty houses?'

'OK, OK, sorry I mentioned it. You don't have to bite my head off.' He sank back down on the sofa.

Instantly she was flooded with guilt. 'No, I'm sorry. I shouldn't have snapped at you. I'm on edge, I guess. I'm not looking forward to this story conference. We're going to talk about expanding Kelly's role and, your favorite subject and mine, how we're going to deal with Debra Jo Fawcett.'

'Has the happy hausfrau arrived yet?'

'She'll be in town tomorrow. She and her son are booked into the Burbank Plaza until their condo is ready. Hubby is staying in Houston so the older boy can finish high school.

That should be just great for family values. Oh well, it's not my problem. My job is to make her look good on the show.'

'Or so bad Stan will come to his senses.'

'Fat chance. He's got a bug in his headset on this one. At least Debra Jo seems smart enough to do whatever we tell her to.'

'She's a nice woman.' He was responding to Julia, but not really engaging. What was wrong with him?

'I'm meeting Tim for lunch at the Sakura Club. Then I have to drive all the way out to the studio to discuss the changes to the set with Liam. Will you join us?'

'Is that the Euro-Japanese place?' Julia nodded. 'No thanks, I'm pretty well sushied out. I miss the good old days when it wasn't considered a war crime to eat red meat, and seafood meant lobster.'

'I could use you to play good cop, bad cop with Tim. You're much better at intimidation than I am. And you really should take a look at how the set's coming along. You're the one in charge of the money.'

'Can't you handle it? You know what the budget is.'

'I think so, but Tim's going to wonder. This will be the third lunch meeting you've missed.' Don't push it, Julia. Even though he hasn't been out of the house the entire weekend. Let the guy relax if he wants to.

'I just don't have the energy to face Tim today.'

Lately he didn't have the energy for much of anything except lying around, watching TV or sleeping, while she seemed to be busier than ever. Hudlow/Turgov was deep in pre-production, developing storylines, finalizing the first scripts of the new season, not to mention creating a brand-new character for Debra Jo. Working sixteen hours a day for six and sometimes seven days a week, by all rights, Julia should be exhausted. Instead she felt positively rejuvenated, full of life and raring to go, if a little short-tempered. Of course it was natural for Marty to be experiencing a bit of burn-out, he'd been through all this before; but for her it was still new and exciting.

'I just find Tim so overwhelming these days. It's all one big video game. What excites him is who he gets to shoot down next. To Tim, everything is "fun",' Marty grumbled. '"We're launching a new series. Oh, that'll be fun." "We're the number two network, that's fun." "We're in the Neilsen dumpster." "Well, it was fun while it lasted, now let's blast toward another planet." I don't relish being called "kid" by someone wet behind the ears who's been promoted at the network three times in the past two years. And those clothes he wears. Exposing parts of his body no real man was ever meant to reveal. Colors I don't want to see except as a warning signal on a bicycle at night. That stupid baseball cap that he wears backwards. As if we're all supposed to be players on his home team.'

'Now let's examine this social-sartorial phenomenon,' Julia desperately wanted to make him laugh, 'the ever-present baseball cap, what does that tell you about a man?'

'That he's a case of arrested development?'

'No, that he's bald. Wearing a baseball cap indoors or on "Arsenio Hall" screams, "I'm losing my hair. If I hold this hat tight on my head, the few strands left will be unable to escape." Easy for you to laugh. You've still got a beautiful head of hair. Tim's not even thirty.'

'And he wants to be taken for twenty-three. Pretty soon, you won't be able to run a network if you're over twelve years old. Tim will probably be replaced by Macaulay Culkin.'

'Oh, honey, you can't take these people seriously. We have to laugh at them. It's the only way to keep their power in perspective. I suspect Stan's losing his marbles but I've grown to like Tim. He's been supportive of us.'

'I know,' Marty admitted grudgingly. 'Maybe Tim's got the right idea. Maybe I care too much, more than it's ever been worth. But he makes me feel old.'

There it was again. That word. Recently Marty had taken some of the earlier credits off his résumé because he thought they dated him. 'I can't understand it,' she had argued, 'you won awards for some of those shows. Why would you want to deny your own success?'

'Because,' Marty told her angrily, 'they're part of my history and in this town, anything before 1980 is ancient history. We're living in a time when a screenwriter who's only twenty-eight drops his age to twenty-two. His agent markets him as a wunderkind fresh out of film school and his screenplay is auctioned for three times its real value because he's "young" and "hot". You can't blame them. The studio heads and network execs are all babies. They want to work with talent their own age.' A couple of times she'd caught him plucking gray hairs and staring into the mirror, lifting the loose skin under his chin and sliding it from one side to the other. Who said men weren't vain? Although he'd probably hate the word, he'd grown into a distinguished, handsome man, who looked better than he had when she'd first met him, but she sensed that mirror was revealing something more to him than physical appearance.

She tried again. 'Why don't you meet Tim and me at Sakura? It's right here in Brentwood, just a couple of blocks over.'

'Not today.'

'This is too big a job for one person. I need you. We're a team, remember, partners, produce as a pair? Now that I've been upgraded from creator to creator/producer. Hey, I wonder if that's how God bills herself? Mere creator will no longer suffice.'

Marty refused to laugh. He looked at her accusingly. 'With you as my partner, I expected there to be less pressure. Instead there's more. I thought by bringing you into the business, we'd be able to spend more time together.'

'Instead, you created a monster?'

'I'm lonely, Julia. We're supposed to be married. I shouldn't have to feel so alone.'

She felt her guilt barometer shoot straight to the top, threatening her emotional Richter scale. Marty's mother had recently died and it had shaken him badly. She put her hand on his shoulder, but he shrugged it off.

'I'm almost fifty years old.'

'Well, you don't look it.'

'I know and I appreciate your saying that to me, but it doesn't change the fact that it's true. Fifty. Half my life is already over.'

'That's not so bad when you consider the alternative.'

'What do you mean?'

'That you never reach fifty.' It was a very Marty thing for Julia to say, and normally it would have made him laugh, but not today. He was hardly at his most attractive, sprawled on the sofa in his T-shirt and undershorts, with a two-day growth of beard, a cup of soup balanced on his chest, and various sections of the newspaper strewn all over the living-room floor. The TV was on, but the sound was turned down, so the images flickered brightly across the screen, the actors, none of whom she recognized, opening and closing their mouths as if in a dumbshow, their hands gesturing in silence like some obscure mime. She wanted to grab him and shake some life into him. Get up, get moving, do something. Stop lying there feeling sorry for yourself. You could be fighting for your life in Bosnia Herzegovina. You could be watching your child waste away in Somalia. It's not like either one of us has cancer. What is your problem? The old guilt blanket enfolded her again. How could she be so insensitive? He had a headache. He was tired. Hadn't he told her that he hadn't slept very well last night? That he'd been up at four a.m. unable to go back to sleep and ended up doing the *New York Times* crossword puzzle until finally he dozed off on the couch. Not that that explanation was particularly reassuring. Crosswords, for God's sake, the activity of the old and infirm. She'd called her mother last week and Claire had said Leigh was on the road to recovery because he was finally 'starting to take an interest in his crosswords again'. Julia couldn't see the point. You spend hours filling in the blanks and when you've finally found all the right words, you throw the whole damn thing away. God! She never thought she'd be married to a man who did crosswords.

When he was in one of these moods, she was probably better off taking the meetings without him. He was right, she could handle today on her own. In fact, it would good for her. Still. She tried one more time. 'Well, if you feel like dropping out to the studio this afternoon, the set should be almost built.'

He waved her off. 'You'll be fine. You're young, you're fresh, full of ideas. You're getting lots of attention and you deserve it. Enjoy it while you can. I'm happy for you.'

'Boy, if Alex were here right now, he wouldn't let that little speech pass as a performance. Your line readings lack a certain sincerity.'

At last he smiled. 'You're right. OK, erase tape. Let me try that again. I'm proud of you, Julia. And I love you.'

She leaned down to give him a quick kiss. 'I love you, too, Marty.' She hoped her own delivery still had the ring of truth.

She was over two hours late arriving at the studio. Lunch with Tim had gone on far too long. People kept stopping at their table to tell Julia how much they loved the series and to wish her good luck with the Emmy nominations just a few weeks away. By the time she left Sakura, it was getting on to late afternoon and the freeways were jammed, but she'd promised Liam she'd look over the set and, if she didn't do it, who would? Certainly not Marty.

Pac Vic studios, usually a hive of activity during the day, were already quiet. She parked casually, taking up two parking spots, signed in with security, and then went looking for Liam. She hoped he hadn't already left, but she knew he usually worked late hours. She pushed through the heavy steel door that led to soundstage six and found him, standing in the middle of the newly constructed set for the Changing Room, meticulously applying the last touches of highlight and shadow to give the color depth for the camera. She gasped.

'Oh, Liam, it's wonderful. Completely transformed.' It was all art deco, in soft shades of peach and green. Over the top of the Changing Room salon was a faux skylight through which the bright TV lights could create the effect of sunlight. There was a fig tree and potted palm trees. 'I don't know how you do it. I mean, you showed us the rendering for the new design, but this is so much more. The skylight is a lovely touch.'

He smiled shyly. 'I wanted that to be a surprise. I think the deco works, don't you? When we were on location in Houston, I noticed the abundance of art deco. It looks so un-Texan to me, but it seems that architectural style is really popular right now with south-westerners. I think it makes the salon a little more upmarket, which reflects your storyline. The Changing Room has become more successful, Janine's business has finally taken off and she's attracting a better class of clientele, which will eventually lead her to question her own principles, right?'

Julia gulped. 'Right.' It was the longest speech she had ever heard out of Liam. Obviously he'd been spending a lot of time thinking about this. And listening to her. She was impressed with his attention to detail, the way he could sense the shift in her thinking and incorporate it into the design for the show. She loved the fact that he'd become so involved with the characters she'd created.

'I wanted the overall color to be deeper, too. Since we're moving from videotape to film this season, visually everything's going to appear richer, more three-dimensional than the look we had with tape. I've already talked to the lighting crew about how it will affect them, because film makes a difference as to how the show is lit.' Julia and Marty had pushed for film this season for just those reasons; it made for a classier looking product. 'You want to have a look at the set for the Food Court? We've expanded Travis's Sports Chek and fitness centre, too.'

'Sure.' She followed him as he took her through all the new locations that had been built by the carps, as he called the union carpenters. Last season they had concentrated most of the scenes in the makeover area with its adjoining lingerie boutique and photography studio. This year they planned to use more 'swing sets', 'open up' the show, take some of the scenes out of the basic salon location and play them in other parts of 'the mall'.

'Let's go back to the Changing Room,' Julia urged. 'It's so glorious, I want to see it again.' The fluted walls and broad curved steps made everything seem larger, more open. 'It's not a set, it's a living, breathing environment. You could almost live here.'

'At the very least, spend a couple of nights.' Liam was turning red with her praise.

She suddenly felt tired, as if her legs were about to collapse under her. 'Could we just sit here a minute in a couple of the salon chairs? As if we were waiting for a makeover? Do you have time to talk?' she asked him.

'Sure. Would you like a glass of wine?'

It probably wasn't such a great idea: it'd been a long day and she still had the drive home, but one glass couldn't hurt. She was in desperate need of relaxation. She nodded and he went back into the production office and returned a moment later with a chilled bottle of a rather pricey Chablis.

'You just happen to have this lying around?'

'No,' he reddened. 'J.C. stopped by this afternoon to see the set. Fortunately she gave it her stamp of approval. Peach is her favorite color and, lucky for me, the sinks are all in the right places.' They both laughed. 'You were smart to have faith in her, Julia. She's really come through for you as an actress. She told me she just finished shooting a film up in Banff.'

'I know. Brandon called to tell us her dailies look great. Well, J.C.'s the epitome of what the show is all about:

change. I'm as excited as she is by all her new directions; it can only help the show.'

Liam smiled and looked into her eyes. Julia stopped talking. It felt strange just to sit there quietly, in this lovely setting, sipping wine and not saying a thing, as though they were operating in language other than her own. She couldn't figure him out. Was he simply shy? Or did he not feel the urge to speak unless he had something vital to say? She wasn't used to that. The men in her life were all marathon talkers, giving everything they said a weight of epic proportions. For Marty, the smallest problem loomed as a crisis. 'This is the worst year of my life,' he would say. He'd been saying that for the last ten years, which didn't say much for her effect on his life, since she had been a major part of it for all of those ten years. She was reaching the point where she wanted to scream out to him, 'Make up your mind. Which year is really the worst, this year, last year, or the one before that? Or is it all just an accumulation of shit?'

Liam's eyes remained fixed on her, and Julia found herself opening up to him about her desire to take the show in a different direction this season, make it more topical, reach a more sophisticated audience, people who normally didn't watch television. She confessed how she herself had sneered at television before she started working in the medium, and how she was just beginning to understand the importance of pop culture, the sweeping influence it had over the imagination of a nation, the impact even a show like this could have on the hearts and minds of people. As she expounded on her favorite subject, she knew she was not following logic, but jumping from point to point, letting her fancy take flight.

Liam listened. He was very good at listening. Marty was good at talking. Liam seemed genuinely interested in what she had to say, while Marty was always waiting for her to finish so that he could tell her what he thought. Liam sat there quietly, his azure-blue eyes fixed on her, nodding every once in a while rather than telling her she was wrong or, even more frustratingly, that she was absolutely right only she'd better hurry and do something with those ideas before somebody else picked up on them. It felt good to be able simply to toss thoughts out and let them lie there, floating in the air, not feeling she had to immediately focus them and apply them to a definite project.

But she hadn't given him a chance to get a word in. She stopped, out of breath, and said apologetically, 'Now it's your turn. What made you want to be a designer anyway? Were you one of those kids who was drawing while still in the crib? Do you come from an artistic family?'

'No,' he ducked his head in embarrassment, 'farmers. Iowa. I had no idea what I wanted to be. Didn't know what an artist was. I'd never seen a play, been to a gallery. So much was missing when I was growing up.'

'So it was not what you were drawn to but what you were repelled by.'

'That's it.' He was pleased at her understanding. 'I didn't want to be like my father or my brothers.'

'How do you mean?'

'Well, I'm not interested in land, I'm interested in buildings, architecture. Color, shape. I liked clothes.'

'That must have made you popular on the farm.'

'Yeah, right. Some relative from the city sent me a marionette when I was about nine. I ended up designing backdrops for puppet shows in the barn. In high school I "designed" the class play. I didn't know what a flat was. I painted a piece of plywood and put doors in it.'

'Did you go to university?'

'First member of my family to graduate. By then I was painting, doing my own stuff. But the hard thing about painting is that you're so isolated, you're always alone when you do it. In theater, there's other people around. I'm not a very good team player but I like being part of the team.'

'What got you into TV?'

'Miami Vice. High concept style. Defined color palette. Of course, I didn't realize how unusual Miami Vice was. It's hard to make magic with television the way I used to in the theater.'

'Magic?'

'Look, I'll show you what I mean. Let's play with a little light here.' He moved the dimmer console closer to them. 'You like the sunlight effect?'

'I love it.'

'Now I'll give you moonlight. This switch is difficult to accomplish with film and TV lighting, which is where my background in theater comes in handy. Another surprise, especially for you.' He pressed a button, and immediately

305

the set was plunged into radiantly soft moonlight, a little hazy, the feel of a balmy Texas night.

'Oh wow,' Julia couldn't help gasping. Suddenly she was sixteen and back in Houston sitting on a blanket on a hillside watching a performance of Shakespeare under the stars. 'It's like another world right here inside the salon. Everything looks so soft and beautiful. Liam, this is incredibly romantic.'

'That's the idea.' The sharp planes of Liam's face were bathed in a warm, rosy glow.

It was a very seductive setting he had created. She wondered if he knew how stunning he looked. She wondered if the effect was equally flattering for her. 'The moonlight is very effective,' she said, 'but I'm not sure I see the purpose. When would we ever have a scene in the shop at night?'

'Well,' he stumbled a little, 'I'm wondering when J.C. and Brandon, I mean, Janine and Travis, are finally going to get it on. I don't know if I can last another season.'

Julia giggled. 'You and everybody else in America. I haven't decided. Something's definitely in the wind, but whatever it is, it may hang out there for a long time before it's acknowledged.'

'Just like real life,' Liam said. He was staring at her so intently she had to look away.

She cleared her throat. 'So J.C.'s back in LA?'

'Yes. The new album she's just released is getting a lot of airplay, isn't it? I saw her on Oprah last week talking about the courage it took to come clean about her roots with *Telephone Road*. I guess she was afraid the public would stop liking her if she told the truth, but all it's done is boost record sales. Did you know about any of this?'

'Sort of.' Julia would never betray J.C.'s confidence, but suddenly she longed just to keep on sitting here with Liam and tell him all about the trip she'd taken with J.C. down Telephone Road, how she'd helped her have the courage to break out with her new album.

'I actually went out and bought the CD. Each song is different, but every one of them is good. I've been playing it over and over again.'

'You sound like Marty,' Julia laughed. 'He's a big J.C. fan.'

'That doesn't surprise me,' Liam said shyly, 'she looks a lot like you.'

'A little, maybe, but he's really hot for her. Not that he would ever do anything about it, of course. I know he loves me, but I have to face the fact that he would probably give his entire collection of Emmys for just one night with J.C. Austin. I imagine you feel the same.'

'Not exactly.' Now it was Liam's turn to look away. 'She's wonderful to design for. No bullshit factor, she's straight ahead, knows what she wants and how to get it. It's weird, but I think maybe the things I like about her keep me from finding her sexually desirable?' The statement turned into question. He was struggling to keep up with the turn their conversation had now taken. 'Aesthetically I respond to her coloring, as I do yours. I love red hair and pale skin, and I like petite women. But J.C.'s a little too simple to interest me. That sounds sexist. I didn't mean it that way.'

'Don't sweat it, Liam. Believe me, there's no politically correct answer here. It was just a casual question.'

'I'm not very good at explaining how I feel.' He seemed to want her to understand. 'For me, sex is most exciting when there's some reserve, mystery, something that I can discover. Are you following this at all?' He smiled at her hesitantly.

God, he was young. She couldn't remember the last time she had sought anyone else's approval. 'I think so, but J.C. is actually quite complex. That's why we're friends.'

'She wrote that song for you, didn't she?' He took a gulp of wine. 'I'll probably make an ass of myself doing this, but I'm going to do it anyway.' He drained his glass and then sang, very softly, in a clear, sweet voice, the first lines of the song to her, ' "She's a woman, she's a lady, she's my friend." ' He stopped, looking embarrassed. ' "Julia's Song." I figure she means you?'

'I'm the one. She gave me a wonderful present when she told me she wrote that song for me.'

'It's my favorite cut on the album. She knows you well.'

'Liam, it's so sweet of you to say that.' Julia smiled at him warmly. Why not flirt a little? It couldn't hurt, could it?

'I mean it. I love working with you. You let me run with an idea. That's rare in this business. But if you find the right creative relationship, it's worth more than anything.

It's almost like having an affair. The chemistry has to be right, you know what I mean?'

Julia was now very aware that they were completely alone together in the deserted studio, close to each other, so close they were almost touching, sitting on an empty set, which was supposed to be in Houston. It should have all been amusing, but instead it felt almost suggestive. She was feeling uncomfortably warm, as if the faux Texas night air was enveloping them both in a hot, humid caress. It took a surprising number of lights to create this moonlight effect, and they gave off a lot of heat. She unbuttoned the top of her blouse and fanned herself lightly with the back of her hand. 'It's hot,' she said. 'The lights.'

Liam sat there quietly, just looking at her. Why was it she couldn't stop thinking about his body, what lay under the clothes? Tonight he was wearing a simple white cotton sweatshirt and blue jeans, nothing particularly revealing or even artful, so why was she suddenly so aware of his strong thighs, the powerful arms exposed by the sleeves of his shirt pushed casually up to his elbows, the long, sensitive fingers toying idly with the buttons on the dimmer control. She moved away slightly and crossed her legs. The expression on Liam's face was virtually unreadable in the shadows. Only his laser eyes blazed bright. Could he possibly know that she was sitting here fantasizing about him? Of course not. He was, in a manner of speaking, an employee of Hudlow/Turgov, which made her his boss. He would never suspect her of coming on to him. Could it be that he was coming on to her? Ridiculous. He was seven years younger than she, for God's sake.

Liam looked concerned. 'OK, I've given you a nice glass of wine, I've dazzled you with my light show, and you still seem pretty tense. What's wrong, Julia?'

For a moment, she had an overwhelming urge to blurt it all out, to tell him how worried she was about Marty, that she couldn't handle this by herself, making decisions for Hudlow/Turgov all on her own, but instead she said, 'I'm sorry. It's been a rough day and I woke up this morning with a sore neck. Sleeping the wrong way, I guess.'

He reached out and touched the side of her neck. She almost jumped, it felt so hot. 'I can fix that,' Liam said at once. 'I give great massage. I know acupressure. Give me your hand.'

Reluctantly she held it out. This couldn't possibly be a good idea. He took her small hand in his large one, and with a strong, downward move, began pressing firmly on the soft, fleshy part of her thumb. It sent a shock wave, not to her brain, but straight to her nipples. Down girls, she ordered them silently, you don't know where this is headed. 'There's a system of nerve endings,' he explained, 'and they're all linked to each other in ways you can't possibly imagine.' Try me. She needed to get up and out of here right now. Gently, he began squeezing each of her fingers, pulling on them as if removing them from her hand, closing them into a fist, and then releasing them. His hand moved up to her forearm, kneading gently, methodically, just the right amount of pressure. The shock waves had established an electrical pattern, running between crotch and breast. He stood up and moved behind her. She thought she would faint. His hands were on her neck, under her hair, his thumbs pressing down the base of her spine. 'See, already it's a bit looser.' No kidding. 'Now let the energy go, think about the tension leaving your body.' She closed her eyes and leaned her head back against him as he let his fingers do the walking, down, down. Her silk blouse had somehow slipped off her shoulders. His hands were sliding down over her bare skin, heading straight for her breasts. The pulsing between her legs intensified, as if an invisible hand were peeling back the folds of her cunt, petal by petal.

Slowly, he lifted her out of the chair and turned her to face him. They locked eyes. Only a minute, but it seemed like an eternity. She could feel his closeness, so close she could smell the sweetness of his breath. And then, almost abruptly, he pulled away from her, 'I've got to get going. The freeways are going to be nuts.'

'Where do you live?' Inside she was shaking.

'La Canada. In the hills.'

'Long drive.'

'Yeah. Better get going.'

'See you.'

'See you.'

THE SECOND
SEASON

Chapter Thirty

Usually the start-up of the second season of a successful sit-com is a breeze compared with the uncertainty of the first. If the show's a hit, and the actors have become, if not megastars, at least household names, the tension of having to prove oneself should be eased. No doubt about it, *Makeover* was now an unqualified hit. They were being hailed as the saviours of the network, responsible for bringing CBN from last place into second place, and moving closer to number one all the time. So why, as the cast gathered for the Monday first reading of the season opener, was there such a feeling of unease around the big table? Sure, they'd been away from each other for four months and, except for the odd personal appearance to plug the show, their paths had not crossed, so it was a bit like starting over again, the first day of school. It was the end of July and the season opener would not air until the end of September, but next week the Emmy nominations would be announced, and they all knew that immediately the balance of the famous ensemble would change. The 'For Your Consideration' ads were already appearing in *Variety* and *Hollywood Reporter*. Of course the studio was shelling out a lot of money to push J.C. and Brandon, but everybody knew those ads rarely had an impact on the voters. There had been so much hype surrounding the show's first season, they were bound to receive some nominations, but who among the cast would be the chosen ones to get the industry nod?

Last season they had become part of a tight little group, unified in their struggle to make sure the show and their jobs survived. They were used to seeing each other's faces around the table, but now there was a new face at that table, Debra Jo Fawcett, a housewife, who had never acted before. A new sibling had joined their close-knit family and the rivalry was about to begin.

When viewers last left Makeover, they were wondering if Janine's new-found awareness of 'the beauty trap' would threaten the future of the Changing Room salon. This season, they would see Janine finally accept the death of her husband and start looking for love. Travis would now realize he was attracted to Janine but he was supposedly still married to his wife, Marcia, out there somewhere. Samantha would buy into the business and become a more active partner. Melissa, the good daughter, would begin to get into trouble. In the carefully balanced mix of comedy and real life, all of these were interesting storylines that, if they did not keep the viewers hanging on the edge of their seats, were at least guaranteed to keep them hooked on the characters. The viewers had started a write-in campaign for Julia to bring Janine and Travis together. Brandon was pushing, too, for the sparks to fan into a fire. J.C. was happy to wait; Mac still wasn't keen on the idea of a romance between the two stars. Julia wanted to spin out the chemistry for as long as possible. That kept the viewers tuning in to see just when the pot would boil over. But the most explosive development was the addition of Debra Jo to that boiling plot pot.

The *TV Guide* log line for the first episode simply read: 'Janine does a deal with Debra Jo, winner of the Ms Texas Belle contest, to be the Changing Room's celebrity rep for suburbia.' That didn't begin to explain the complexity of the season opener. The idea was that Debra Jo's contest prize of a makeover at the Changing Room had led to a boost in business among suburban housewives. Janine then gets the bright idea of hiring Debra Jo to bring the makeover concept to the people. She and Debra Jo go into homemakers' homes and do a beauty demo for the women in the neighborhood: a makeover 'tupperware party'. Soon Houston housewives are lining up in the mall for a Debra Jo makeover.

Stan thought Julia's concept for integrating Debra Jo was a brilliant example of art imitating life. A new form for television, situation comedy meets reality programming. Debra Jo's position on the show was the same as her position in real life. Mrs America, this is about you!

Julia was not so sure. Just when she thought she was getting somewhere, there was Stan putting her back in her place. In the beginning it was Stan who had seemed to be in full support of her, while Tim was the one she thought she had to woo. Now Tim was finally on side, while Stan was sticking his fingers in her every pie, meddling a hell of lot more than she liked. Add a character here, expand a character there, where was all this leading? Linda Earl would have to be blind not to see that Debra Jo was encroaching on her territory. Giving Kelly more to do had to mean giving J.C. less. She had only twenty-two minutes per episode, and juggling the dialogue among the principals was already a nightmare. The worst of it was that she couldn't be open with any of the cast, especially J.C., who had now become a good friend. J.C. trusted her to do what was right for her star. How long would it take before she began to feel betrayed? More and more Julia's job seemed to be about lying, or at least concealing the truth.

For the first time, Julia felt she was out there on her own. Marty was at home with the flu today, and she really missed his presence. The company depended on her to make it work, more than the director, more than the producer. She was Big Mama and it was up to her to help her little family grow and thrive. The responsibility weighed heavily on her. As a documentary film maker, she had been a one-woman band, responsible only to herself. If she let these people down, if the show were somehow to fail, she would put hundreds of people out of work. Great, it was the beginning of the second season and already she was envisioning her own demise. Get a grip, Julia. She shook her head vigorously to clear it of unwanted thoughts, but they came stampeding back again. The tabloids had been relatively quiet about Makeover during the early summer. So why did she have such a strong sense of the shit before the storm? She glanced over at Debra Jo, who was listening round-eyed to Alex's welcoming speech. Her hair had been darkened slightly at the network's request. Stan had also decreed she go on a diet. So far Debra Jo seemed only too happy to oblige. Did this sweet-faced young woman have any idea what she was getting into?

Debra Jo was in hog heaven. Here she was actually sitting at the same table as J.C. Austin and Brandon Tate, a script for her favorite show with her name on it right in front of her. Her very first scene was with Brandon. Oh Lord, how would she ever get through it? Would she be able to remember her lines? He was so gorgeous, sex just oozed out of his every pore. It was going to be awfully hard to concentrate on the job at hand. She was trying her best not to look at him, but she could feel his eyes on her, a friendly, curious, burning, penetrating – don't use that word – gaze. He was drawing her to him right across the big table, forcing her to meet his eyes. She looked up at him, and he gave her a conspiratorial little wink, as if to say, are you ready to play?

It had all happened so fast she could hardly believe she was here. Once the decision had been made and the contract signed, the weeks had gone by in a blur of packing and cooking and cleaning, and making arrangements to insure Beau and Eddie's comfort while she was away. The *Houston Chronicle* put her on the cover of their weekend magazine, the neighborhood threw a going-away party, she and Eddie made love for the last time and before she knew it, she was on a jumbo jet with Danny, winging her way to California. At the very last moment, she started having second thoughts. Well, that was all Jackie's fault. Her best friend got drunk at the send-off party and began bugging her about everything under the sun like what made her think she'd be able to keep up with the real stars on the show? Wasn't she worried about leaving part of her family behind? Wouldn't she be lonely so far away from home? And, most annoying of all, how could she possibly expect Eddie to do without sex for such a long time? Thanks, Jackie. Just what I need to hear right about now. What are friends for? Next day at the airport, saying goodbye, she sobbed uncontrollably all over Eddie, shaking so bad Danny had to drag her on to the plane. The minute she was on board, she threw up in the washroom.

But now that she was here, it was all so exciting. She hadn't had this much fun since her high-school graduation which ended up lasting for eight weeks. Her stint on Makeover was guaranteed for eight months. She'd already been fitted for her wardrobe for the first four episodes. With all this free food, she was going to have to be really careful or she'd balloon right up. Every time she turned around, someone was offering her donuts or a bagel with cream cheese or a croissant filled with crab salad and she hadn't been charged for any of it.

She wasn't used to having other people fulfil her needs.

When she got up the courage to tell them she wasn't used to living in an apartment, they'd found a house for her and Danny in Sherman Oaks, just twenty minutes away, by freeway, from the studio. The house had three bathrooms and a big backyard with three orange trees, a lemon tree, a peach tree, and wild plum trees. She had never seen fruit growing before. There was a huge kitchen, just the kind she liked and a swimming pool out back, which totally thrilled Danny. Already he was running up the phone bill calling all his friends back in Houston.

Of course the shooting schedule looked pretty rough. Each show was done in five days and it would be four weeks before she got any time off. She realized she had a lot to learn, but there were plenty of people standing by to teach her what she needed to know. And why not? She was savvy enough to realize that the success of the show depended on their getting her through it. Come to think of it, the people sitting around this table were probably worried that she was going to mess up. Troy, Samantha, Lyla (it was hard to call them by their real names because she already knew them as the characters they played on the show) all seemed a little nervous. Funnily enough, Debra Jo wasn't. Maybe she just didn't know what there was to be nervous about. This acting thing didn't look that hard. Everybody kept telling her all she had to do was be herself. It could be a chance at a new life, but if it didn't work out, she could always go back to her old life in Houston. No big deal. She'd do this as long as it was fun and when it stopped being fun, that was it. In the meantime, she'd be socking money away for Danny and Beau's college education. They could go to school out of state now if they wanted to. Just one year of Makeover would insure the future of the entire Fawcett family.

She looked around the table at the rest of the cast. The women were all rail-thin, skinny little wrists with bones sticking out. They looked completely normal on TV, which probably meant she'd photograph like one of the three little pigs. Aside from being thin, the stars weren't nearly as glamorous as she'd expected. J.C. had hardly any make-up on, her long red hair was pulled back in a ponytail. The women dressed like the counselors at Danny's summer camp. Everybody was wearing sneakers, jeans and sweaters (it was surprisingly chilly on the soundstage), and here she was in a skirt and pumps.

Even in jeans, Linda Earl sat there looking like the beauty queen she had once been, that magnolia petal skin, perfectly white teeth and her honey blonde hair tumbling on to her slim shoulders. She was so gorgeous, Debra Jo couldn't help staring and when she caught Linda's eye, she gave her an admiring smile.

Linda Earl gritted her teeth and smiled at Debra Jo. Another blonde on the show? What was the point? Unless it was to ease her out. 'She's not even beautiful,' she had cried to her husband, Steve. 'At the very most, cute. And kind of dumpy.' But Steve was not his usual sympathetic self these days. Her plan to have a little tuck under the chin had escalated into something more. In June, she had told Steve she needed to be on her own, and she was going away to a spa for a three-week vacation, leaving him at home with the baby. Instead, she flew to the Caribbean to a plastic surgery resort center where she had the works: facelift, liposuction, and breast augmentation. The night she returned to LA it was Steve's birthday and as a special treat, she plied him with his favorite single malt scotch, turned on the stereo, and did a striptease to show off her newly voluptuous, sculptured body. 'This is my birthday present to you,' she purred, lying back across their big brass bed. Instead of being pleased, Steve burst into tears. 'What happened to your beautiful breasts?' he sobbed. 'You lie down and your tits stand straight up. It's unnatural, in fact, it's revolting. Jesus, Linda, what the hell is going on with you? You're my wife and I love you. But, godamnit, I'm worried about you.' Linda couldn't blame him. She was worried about herself, too.

Debra Jo could see that Linda's smile was strained. Maybe she was going to be snotty to her because she wasn't a real actress or maybe she was just shy. Not like Kelly Carmichael who had immediately taken her under her wing, showing her where to sign in, and where the main fridge, stocked with juice and Evian, was located. Kelly Carmichael's jeans were white and studded with little silver studs. A tiny silver rhinestone was embedded in the nailpolish on each of her long nails. Her platinum hair was obviously bleached. Touch-ups for those roots would have to be every two weeks at the very least. The white-on-white

318

look Samantha was famous for had to be expensive to maintain. Kelly must be making a bundle.

A year ago Kelly had been living on unemployment insurance and Kraft dinners. Now they were giving her a raise and expanding her role. She had prayed for a break like this, a second chance at happiness, and here it was. Most of her previous work had been in small theaters where you never got over your fear of where the next job was coming from. To have a gig like this, where she got to go to work every day and do what she loved doing meant that by her own terms, she was rich (well, relatively) and famous. The famous part was happening more and more and it was not her favorite side of this deal. Flamboyant as she was in appearance, Kelly thought of herself as a very private person. She couldn't believe the effect she was having on people. All over North America, men and women were wearing sequined T-shirts and saying 'Don't tease my hair.' With the money and fame came power and with power came a certain responsibility. As far as Kelly was concerned, the only value to all the hoopla surrounding her, was to focus attention on her major cause, pediatric AIDS. Kelly's Kids was bringing in money from all over the US as she worked to raise awareness of the disease. She was glad to be back at work again but the best news was that Carlito was feeling better. In a miraculous turnaround, the AZT appeared to be finally working. This afternoon, the minute rehearsal was over, she was picking him up at the hospital and taking him to his beloved beach. She'd buy him a fish sandwich and one of those giant cones of curly fries. The water was too polluted for anyone to swim in, let alone Carlito, but they could walk on the sand and gather shells. She couldn't wait to see the expression on his face when she showed him the famous antique merry-go-round at Santa Monica Pier. She wanted to sit him up on a brightly painted wooden horse and let him ride around and around as if he never had to get off.

Debra Jo thought Paul Green was pretty cute as Troy. Not that he'd beat out Brandon Tate in the hunk department, but he had funny, twinkling eyes and a naughty smile. She liked the fact that he was a family man. She'd read all about the pressure of Hollywood, the strain a hot career can put on a relationship, and here was Paul Green, successful at both.

Paul's career was hot, his home life was not. It had been wonderful being back in New York for the filming of *Shooting Blanks*. Chaya was so happy she didn't want to come home to LA and in fact she hadn't, yet. She was big as a house waiting for the birth of their next child and she wanted to be close to her mother. OK, well and good, but here he was on his own and she was dictating policy to him from half-way across America. *Good Housekeeping* magazine had approached them about doing a spread on the Detroit Street home and their 'unusual lifestyle'. Paul thought it was a terrific idea but when he called Chaya to tell her the wonderful news, she was less than thrilled. 'I don't open my doors to the secular world. They won't understand and it's none of their business anyway. I won't allow my privacy to be invaded or have our children subjected to ridicule.' A moot point since the kids were still with her in New York. 'This is *Good Housekeeping*, not the *Hollywood Insider*,' Paul tried to convince her, but when Chaya said no, that was the end of it. The publicist he'd hired to help him take full advantage of his new career visibility was not pleased. Paul was paying her a couple of thou a month to give him advice and then his wife wouldn't allow him to take it! Sure, he understood Chaya's desire to keep their private life separate from their public profile, but he was beginning to feel more than a tug between the personal and professional.

Concha was not one of Debra Jo's favorite characters and she was reserving judgment on the actress who played her, too. Theresa Ruiz wore no make-up and dressed only in black, which seemed weird for LA. She and Shirley Bunting mostly stuck together. She'd been polite enough to Debra Jo, but there was something behind her eyes, like she didn't really want to be there and thought acting was beneath her, though Debra Jo knew most every woman in America would give their eye teeth to be an actress in Hollywood for even one day.

Returning to Miami for the summer, Theresa had discovered the face of the city continued to change just in the short time she'd been away in California. Thousands of Cuban refugees had fought their way through the dangerous shark-infested Straits of Florida to look for a new life in

America. Miami had become a center of Spanish speaking business. It was possible to live and work in that city without ever hearing a word of English. Here in LA, the Hispanic community had swelled to 1.4 million, forty per cent of the city's total population, but were their faces on television? No way, Jose! At least the other networks were actively going after minority viewers while CBN only paid lip service to a vague concept of ethnic representation. They decide to bring a new character on to Makeover and who is it? Another blonde. Her own role on the show remained generic Latina. It was starting to bug her that they never identified what country Concha was from. In every episode she seemed to have a line that began with 'In my country, we . . .' but which country? As though it didn't matter whether she was Mexican or Cuban or Salvoran. All they wanted from her was the house-brand, mildly spicy salsa without any real heat or flavor to it. With this *gringa* Debra Jo joining the show, there were bound to be even fewer tortillas to go around. She took some comfort in the fact that her play, *El Cigaro de Mi Padre* had been a huge hit in Miami. Maybe it was time to start pitching herself as a writer. It was crazy to think she could make a difference as an actress.

Debra Jo beamed fondly at Melissa. Aside from J.C., Mel was her favorite. She hoped they'd be able to spend more time together. It had been clear to her in Houston that Melissa needed some real mothering and that mother of hers didn't seem the least bit interested in doing it. How could she ignore her own daughter that way? Melissa was such a sweet kid. Although she hardly had any time to be a kid at all. What chance did she have at any kind of a normal life?

Melissa had become a star almost overnight. She'd gone from having no friends to being mobbed by strangers who thought she was their best friend. She couldn't go anywhere now without being hit on for an autograph. People came right up to her and started talking like she was some long lost member of the family. Maybe to them she was. After all, she came into their living-rooms once a week. But did that give them the right to act like they owned her? Yesterday, on the freeway, driving in to the Farmer's Market, a car had honked at them so long and loud that Bon assumed something was wrong with the Miata. When she rolled down the window, the driver of the other car leaned out and shouted across at Melissa, 'Hi Carlene, we love you. Stay as cute as you are. Please don't ever grow up.' So how was she supposed to stop nature? She was developing by leaps and bounds, or mounds, if you wanted to get specific. It felt weird 'pubing' in front of millions of people week after week. Complete strangers knew that her breasts had grown. Shouldn't that be her private business? Bon was just as nuts as ever. Teen idol Christopher Max was supposed to be engaged to one of the bimbettes on his show, but he was still sneaking around with Bonnie. Boy, was that ever weird. Her mom screwing a guy she should be dating herself.

At least Debra Jo knew what being a real mother was all about. It was so neat to have her new friend from Houston out here in LA on the show. J.C., her pretend mom, was always really nice to her on set, but when the rehearsal day was over, she went home to her husband. Melissa went home to Bon. Bon never wanted to do anything except get high and hit the clubs which, technically speaking, Mel was too young to be allowed into, although they often made an exception because they recognized her from the show. Now that Debra Jo had come to town, she wanted Melissa to go sightseeing with her and Danny. Melissa wished that Debra Jo had brought her older hunky son, Beau, instead of eleven-year-old Danny, but still, it was better than nothing. They'd been to the beach, Knotts Berry Farm, the Griffith Park Planetarium (Debra Jo told them it was very educational and besides it was the setting for the big knife scene with James Dean in *Rebel Without a Cause*) and of course, Disneyland. Debra Jo couldn't believe that Melissa had been in LA for a whole year and had never been to Disneyland. Mel was too embarrassed to tell her that Disneyland was a day place and Bonnie was a night person. Debra Jo was really good at giving hugs, too. Now she had another reason to look forward to going to work every day, Debra Jo. And Alex.

Alex Jordan signed out with security and headed for the parking lot. The first day had been bound to be a bit tricky, but hopefully they were over the hump now. Debra Jo, although not a trained actress, did have a unique quality, a natural ditzy delivery that was actually quite funny. She looked perfect for the part of a suburban housewife, probably because she was a suburban housewife, but in TV, image was almost – if not quite – everything. It would take work, he thought, but with very specific direction and Julia's clever writing, they might get quite a good performance out of her. At least she seemed willing to learn. He would have to keep an eye on Linda Earl until the network finalized the decision about her; obviously they were waiting to see how Debra Jo worked out. Melissa had certainly changed over the summer. She was growing into a young woman. He was very fond of her. She was such a talented kid with, he truly believed, a very big future. He would hate it if she went off the rails. It was bloody difficult trying to keep all the various factions happy and productive. Sometimes he thought they were paying him the big bucks to act as psychiatrist rather than director. He sighed. Time to go home, pour himself a drink, and relax in the hot tub while he fine-tuned his camera blocking for tomorrow's rehearsal on the floor. He stepped outside and immediately saw a Toyota with its hood up and what appeared to be the long legs of Shirley Bunting, the upper part of her figure concealed by the hood as she bent over the inner workings of the engine. 'Car trouble?' he called out, heading over to give her a hand.

'Battery's dead,' Shirley told him, squinting up at him from a twisted pretzel position intended to keep the grease of the car away from her gleaming white outfit. 'I've called AAA and they're on their way, but I have a dinner date in Santa Monica and now I can't possibly get there on time.'

'Do you have triple A plus?' Shirley nodded. 'Then leave a note on the windshield with your card number. When the truck gets here, they'll punch your number up on the computer and, if everything checks out, they'll not only get the car started, they'll deliver it to your front door. I can give you a ride to Santa Monica. I live in Marina del Rey and it's on the way.' Alex unlocked the door to his Land Rover; Shirley hiked up her tight skirt and climbed in. He unfolded his long, lanky frame into the leather seat next to hers. As they sped along the San Diego freeway, they exchanged few words. It had been a long day, and somehow the breeze whipping through their hair was both calming and exhilarating. Alex turned on to the Santa Monica freeway. 'Should I take the exit for Lincoln Boulevard or are you off the Pacific Coast Highway?'

'PCH,' Shirley replied. That was all she said for a number of miles. The beach was almost deserted, the sun was just beginning to set, as they neared Santa Monica.

'Which restaurant?' Alex asked.

Shirley hesitated. 'Actually, my dinner's at home.'

'OK, what's your address?'

Again Shirley seemed to hesitate. She looked at her watch. 'You know, I'm a bit early and the dinner's being catered. It was sweet of you to drive me. Can I buy you a drink? There's a new place just opened up on the pier.'

'Sure.' Alex parked the car in the lot at beach level and they climbed the steps to the pier.

As they passed by the building that contained the wooden carousel, the strains of a ragtime number drew them to take a peek in. 'This is the famous carousel that was in *The Sting*, right?' Alex asked.

'Yep, the very same,' Shirley smiled. 'I've always loved it. I come down here sometimes even when it's not moving and just stare at it. It's been around for at least forty years. Hey, wait a minute, isn't that Kelly over there?' She pointed toward a tall blonde who stood holding the hand of a very small, very dark boy. 'That must be one of Kelly's Kids.' He did look thin and fragile, but his smile lit up the whole room, his little face blazing with excitement at the whirling horses circling before him.

'Do you think we should go say hello?' Alex asked. 'I have a feeling she's trying to be in disguise.' Kelly was wearing dark glasses, most of her platinum hair was tucked under a big, floppy hat, and baggy sweats hid her voluptuous curves. Just at that moment the merry-go-round came to a stop. Kelly gave the boy a gentle kiss and carefully lifted him up on to one of the huge, wooden horses. Slowly, gracefully, it began to move, up and down and around, the boy clinging to the brass pole, his eyes wide with wonder, looking up into the brilliantly colored canopy overhead, gazing so intently at the painted silver stars that he didn't even see Kelly waving at him every time he came around. Alex and Shirley sensed they were witnessing a very private moment, so they turned and went back out on to the pier toward the restaurant.

'Isn't this gorgeous?' Shirley asked when they were seated on a deck that looked right out over the water. 'You can't beat that ocean. Especially at sunset.' She ordered oysters on the half-shell and a shot of vodka.

Alex raised an eyebrow. 'Ah, a woman who enjoys oysters.'

'Don't read too much into it, honey,' Shirley laughed. 'My mother ran a boarding house on the Isle of Palms back in South Carolina. I grew up on the coast so I learned to love my seafood. Now Mama's retired to Charleston.'

'Which has pleasures of its own to offer.'

'You are right about that. I miss it,' Shirley gave a wistful smile. 'LA's no substitute for Charleston.'

'You look, I don't know, different tonight,' Alex realized, his eyes taking in her white, form-fitting Chanel suit, matching heels, and the single strand of pearls knotted loosely about her neck.

'You've hardly ever seen me off the set,' Shirley laughed. 'Do you expect me to be wearing maribou and see-through chiffon from Lyla Kaye's Lingerie?'

'No, no,' he said hastily. God, she was a beautiful woman. The heavy eyebrows, almond-shaped eyes, full, sensuous lips, dark, velvety skin.

'I'm very much aware of who I am, once I put that costume on. I know that when I walk on the set I'm Lyla Kaye and not Shirley Bunting.'

'And what's the difference between Lyla and Shirley?' She paused. 'Balance,' she said.

'Oh.' He didn't quite know how to respond to that. 'Are those pearls real? Not that it's any of my business.'

'They're real. A gift from a friend. Believe me, I couldn't afford these, not even with the jump my bank account's taken thanks to Makeover.' Silence fell.

'I'm more contained, I guess.' Shirley said suddenly. 'I think that's the difference between Lyla and me. I'm more guarded.' She checked her watch again.

'Did you always intend to be an actress?' Alex didn't want her to leave. He felt he couldn't bear it if she got up and left him sitting there all alone in this beautiful place with the sun streaking the sky orange and pink and purple.

'Oh no, I started out as a model. That didn't make Mama too happy, let me tell you. Nothing but face and body.'

'Which in your case happens to be everything.'

'No, no, you're not getting it.' She swallowed the oyster whole and took a sip of vodka. 'If you get lines on your face, it affects your job. You get a scar, it threatens your livelihood. Acting's not much better. It's so easy to feel you're the victim of other people's decision-making. That sense of knowing yourself, being yourself, seems to take a long time to build.'

'It's the most important thing you can have,' Alex said seriously. 'And the most vulnerable. You must guard it.'

'You think so?' Shirley looked startled.

'I do.' How did they get here? One minute they were not saying a word to each other, the next minute they were in the middle of a philosophical conversation. Shirley must have felt the same way because she changed the subject.

'It's crazy to be talking about this stuff. Just look at the light on the water. Show me how brave you are, Alex. Prove your manhood. Try one of these oysters.' He couldn't resist an offer like that. He brought the oyster shell up to his mouth and slid it gracefully down the back of his throat.

'Way to go, Mr Director,' Shirley applauded. 'You are a very good director, you know. That's rare in television.'

'Well, what is it they say?' Alex boldly popped another oyster. He could finish off the entire dozen if only she would keep looking at him like that. 'Theater is the actor's medium, film is the director's, and television the producer's. It's hard sometimes not to feel like a hired hand.'

'At least you're sticking around for the whole season.'

'No point in being a guest on my own show. That's how I felt when I was one of a team of directors on other series.'

'So what would you really like to be doing in, say, five years?'

'Oh, film. Like everybody else in LA. Sometimes I feel I'm compromising myself with television . . .' He stopped and made a face. 'God, that sounded pretentious. Erase that, please. I actually like the challenge of directing TV. Having to stay ahead of the audience, making it just challenging enough to keep their attention but not so difficult for them that they'll hit the remote and change the channel. They hold the power, in a little black box, in their hand. You've lost them, you're gone. I have great respect for Julia's talents as a writer. I've known her since USC. She has a very strong vision and all I'm here for is to help support that.'

'Don't underestimate yourself, Alex,' Shirley took the last oyster, then stood up abruptly. 'I'm late. I have to go.'

'Do you really have to? I'm convinced all your talk about a dinner party is just a sham. Won't you stay and have dinner with me?'

'I'd love to, but I can't. Tonight is a long-standing engagement.' She was polite but firm. Alex offered to drive her home, but she said it was close enough to walk. It was obvious she didn't want him to know where she was going. He was tempted to follow her, but, of course, he didn't.

Shirley took off her heels to walk across the beach and over the bridge on to Ocean Drive. As she rounded the corner and could see the softly lit entrance to the Palm Court, she brushed the sand off her feet and slipped her shoes back on. Her heels made a light tapping sound on the terrazzo floor of the elegant lobby. There were palms everywhere, on the front grounds, closing off the land at the back on the hill that overlooked the ocean, potted palms in the lobby of the posh apartment hotel. She stopped at the front desk to pick up her mail and check her messages. Roy usually left a cryptic note, cryptic to anyone but her, letting her know that he would be waiting for her upstairs in the suite.

'He said to tell you he couldn't make it tonight,' the desk clerk said with an apologetic smile. He looked a hundred and two years old and had probably been there since the thirties when the Palm Court was built. The bellboys seemed to come and go around the place, but the desk clerk went on for ever. 'He had some flowers delivered to you. A great big fancy arrangement. Too big for you to carry yourself.'

'Thank you,' Shirley managed stiffly.

'I'm sorry.' The sympathy in his eyes made Shirley want to reach across the desk and strangle him. No, it was Roy she wanted to murder. How could he do this to her? And it was happening more lately. Now that he was running for office, his visits were few and far apart. What did he think she was, some obedient geisha sitting around waiting for him to turn up so she could massage his back for him? Damn, she was sick of this shit! She made a snap decision. She reached down, took off her shoes, and ran back across the expansive lobby and out the front door. Maybe, just maybe, Alex would still be there.

Alex sat watching the last vestiges of the sun sink slowly

over the sea. He had been too perplexed to move from his seat on the deck, so he had decided to go ahead and have dinner at the same place. He couldn't stop thinking about Shirley, how beautiful, how intriguing she was. She was right when she said she was nothing at all like the character she played on the show. But what if he were able to bring some of that mystery out of her onscreen? Get Julia to write it into the part. No, forget it, it was totally wrong for Lyla. That amazing stillness Shirley had, the ability to sit there and convey worlds with her eyes. God, how he would love to direct her in a film some day. He looked up from his plate of Dungeness crab to see her standing in the doorway, breathless, holding her shoes.

'You were right,' she said, 'my dinner party was a sham.'

'Pity for you, lucky for me.' He could hardly contain his joy. 'I'm afraid I went ahead and ordered.'

'No problem,' she smiled at him. 'I'll catch up with you.'

They had a wonderful dinner together, laughing and drinking wine. Shirley told him more about her family back in South Carolina. Alex regaled her with tales of his father, Andy Jordan, an actor-singer who had been on the music-hall stage. He loved seeing her reserve and composure break down. He loved making her laugh. When she stood up to go at the end of the evening, he knew he had to make a move. 'I've so enjoyed spending time with you, Shirley. Could we, perhaps, do this again sometime?'

Her whole demeanor changed. 'If you mean what I think you mean, sorry, no.'

He was completely taken aback. It was like night and day. 'Why ever not?'

'You're white.'

He could tell she hadn't meant to say that. 'So?'

'I'm sorry, that was rude. You're my director.'

'Now that's rather a better answer. You know, color is not really a matter of skin, it's an attitude.' Seeing her face: 'That was a simplistic thing to say. What do I know about it?' He tried to lighten the mood by giving a melodramatic sigh. 'You're right. We wouldn't want to sully a perfect professional relationship.'

'It's not just that, I'm not . . .' She stopped, confused. 'I'm not completely free.'

'I understand.' Although he didn't. 'I suppose you don't want me to take you home either.'

'No, really. I live just around the corner.'

'I don't feel comfortable about this. You're sure you'll be safe, love?' She nodded. 'All right.' He sensed there was no point in arguing. 'See you tomorrow, then.'

'See you tomorrow.' Impulsively she leaned forward and kissed him on the cheek. 'You're a nice man, Alex Jordan.'

'That's what they all say.'

Chapter Thirty-one

The champagne was flowing again on the set of Makeover. Charles Currie had sent them cases of Moet et Chandon, along with several pounds of beluga caviar, for a bang-up post rehearsal bash right in the middle of the week. Why? Early this morning, the Academy of Television Arts and Sciences had announced the nominees for the Primetime Emmy awards, and there was plenty for cast and crew to cheer about.

CBN had scored forty-three nominations, not a lot in comparison with the other, more established networks, but a big jump from last year's sixteen. Finally they were playing in the big leagues. And eleven of those nominations belonged to Makeover, unheard-of for a show that had been on the air for only one season. They had done well in the highly visible 'glamour' categories, with Brandon being nominated for Outstanding Actor in a Comedy Series, Paul for Supporting Actor, Kelly for Supporting Actress and, in a surprise move, Theresa for Supporting Actress as well. Julia was up as Outstanding Writer of a Comedy Series for both 'Elvis Is Sighted in the Mall' (as Stan had predicted) and the season finale about the Ms Texas Belle contest, 'Skin Deep'. She had two chances to bring home the most prestigious award the television industry had to offer. Alex was up for Best Director and Liam Carey was up for Production Design. The rest of the nominations were in the less exciting technical categories, but still they all focused attention on the series. Shows like Hill Street Blues and Cagney and Lacey were legends for having been saved from cancellation by the Emmys. Not that Makeover needed saving, but taking home a number of the coveted statuettes known in the industry as TV's Golden Girls, would get them off to a good start with the new fall season, and make an already hot show fairly sizzle in the ratings.

Stan, Tim, the entire company and their friends all gathered to celebrate. Julia and Marty and Liam were standing together in the corner. 'Way to go, Jules!' Marty toasted her. 'You too, Liam.' Liam acknowledged him, but his eyes remained fixed on Julia, his expression unreadable. What was it that he always seemed to be trying to tell her? Standing between Marty and Liam, Julia was suddenly very uncomfortable. She found herself babbling, 'I can't believe all this. A year ago I was dreaming about changing my life and, thanks to you, it's actually happened.'

Liam's smile vanished. 'I believe we all have more than one life we could lead. The choice is up to you. You decide.' His piercing blue eyes were sending her another one of his cryptic messages.

Julia felt her face grow warm. 'Maybe, I don't know. This has happened pretty fast. I guess I'm just surprised.'

Paul wasn't at all surprised by his nomination. *Shooting Blanks* had just been released and was doing boffo box-office biz. Now that a spark had ignited his film career, he wished he hadn't committed himself to five years of Make-over. If he won an Emmy, he would be in a position to have his agent renegotiate his contract to give him more freedom for other projects. Kelly was absolutely thrilled. There was nothing she would be rather be doing than this show for the rest of her life. She was trying desperately to hold on to her usual cool, cracking jokes and flirting with the crew, but underneath the bravado, her heart was leaping with joy.

For Theresa, the nomination was just the leverage she needed to push her case. Finally, some good had come out of this unpredictable and frustrating business. This morning she'd been interviewed via satellite by Bryant Gumbel as well as being pursued by all the print media. Her mother, back in Miami, loved it when she could read about her daughter in the newspapers. The members of the Academy, her peers, who voted to select the nominees, were paying attention to her, even if the writers and producers weren't. She raised her glass triumphantly in the air and declared, 'Here's one for the bastards!' The little group standing next to her assumed she somehow meant everyone who had voted for her, until she confessed, loudly and tearfully, that she was illegitimate and had no idea who her father was. 'Even my mother's not sure. Havana offered freedom in some areas if not others. Undoubtedly he was some charismatic communist,' she said, draining the glass and reaching for another mound of the prized black pearl eggs, 'with high principles and low morals, leaving my mother to fend for herself and me. My mother and I nearly died getting to this country,' she said dramatically, feeling the eyes of the room riveted upon her. 'Sunstroke, dehydration, blisters on our hands, close to starvation, but we made it. Hooray for America!' She was talking too much, crying and laughing, but so what? She was bombed and she didn't care who knew it. This was the biggest night of her life and, *Madre de Dios*, she was going to enjoy it.

Debra Jo listened to her tirade, mentally filing away all the details to write to Jackie later. This was everything she'd expected show business to be: champagne, caviar, back-stage melodrama, tearful revelations, the most famous stars in America cutting loose and letting their hair down. She sipped her champagne and listened, wide-eyed, to everything going on around her.

Linda Earl had had plenty to drink, too. 'This town loves to suck celebrity ass,' she muttered to Shirley, 'that's why Brandon got an Emmy nom. But, Theresa hardly says one word on the show and she rates a nomination? Give me a break.'

'She's a good actress,' Shirley said firmly. 'She deserves to be nominated.'

Linda drained her glass and reached out to grab another from a passing drinks tray. 'Oh come on, Shirl, everybody knows the Emmys are rigged. They just want to be seen nominating someone with an accent. The whole thing's political.'

'Shut your face, Linda. Theresa's my friend. I don't have to listen to this shit.' Shirley turned on her heel and walked away.

In the corner, J.C. was losing the battle to hold back her tears. 'Baby, I don't blame you,' Mac looked utterly miserable. 'It's your show, you are Makeover; I know this is a real slap in the face to you, but you can't let them see you cry. You're a star.'

'Why would they do this to me?' J.C. asked. 'It's like saying everybody else belongs here and I don't. Even Kelly Carmichael got nominated, and her part's not much more than a cameo. Don't get me wrong, I don't grudge her the honor and all, but hey, these people are supposed to be my friends, my peers. I've worked my ass off and they still won't take me seriously.'

'Oh, they take you seriously all right,' Brandon, who had been deep in flirtation with Stan King's wife, overheard the last part of their conversation. He pried himself away from Demeter and moved into their little circle. 'They see you as a threat, J.C. They're protective of their turf and you come along and invade it and show them in one short season that you're better at this game than they are.'

Mac nodded. 'Well, for once, you and I are in agreement about something,' he said grudgingly.

'Baby, could you go get me a refill?' J.C. handed him her empty glass. 'Forget the champagne. I need something stiffer to get me through this.'

Mac shot Brandon a look. He didn't want to leave the two of them together, but he said, 'Sure thing. Be right back.'

Brandon watched him go with an amused smile, then he turned back to J.C. 'Darlin', you not being nominated isn't an oversight, it's an obvious slight.'

'But why?' J.C. wailed. 'I come to TV from country music, OK, but you come from movies and they let you have a nomination. Not that you don't deserve it.' The tears were welling up in her eyes. 'Oh, shit, I'm sorry, that sounds so little and mean, I despise myself. But why you and not me?'

'Well, in my case it's different,' Brandon gave an ironic chuckle. 'This town is so screwed up it's hard for me to explain it to you. I've been up for the Oscar a couple of times, so for me an Emmy nomination is actually a demotion. What they're telling me is, "We've got you now and you're no better than any of us." '

'Really?' J.C. was amazed. 'Boy, that's cockamamy. I don't know whether to be sad or mad.'

'Put it behind you,' Brandon said. 'You're the reason people watch the program and no gold-plated statuette is going to change that.'

Alex had been watching Shirley work the room, hoping to get a private word with her, but she seemed to see the party as business rather than a chance to relax. She shared a drink with J.C. and Mac and the group of friends that had flown out from Nashville, stopped to congratulate Theresa, and laughed at a joke Kelly told to the crew, but she spent only the minimum amount of time with each group before excusing herself to move on. For a moment, he thought he'd lost her when, from clear across the room, he saw her slip out the side door. He followed her into the moonlit night, but something about her hesitant steps toward the edge of the lot made him pull back into the shadows. She was looking around furtively, checking her watch, and then glancing over her shoulder. Why? It was late and there weren't many people around: the security guard was stationed outside, a couple of crew members shared a joint in the parking lot. The night was hot, even for LA, and Alex watched as Shirley took off her tailored blazer revealing a low-cut bustier. Several minutes went by before a sleek, black Cadillac pulled up in front of the studio. Like a scene from *The Godfather*, the back door swung open slowly, silently, and Shirley got in. Alex squinted to try to see who was in the back seat with her, but it was dark and the windows were all tinted glass. As the car sped off into the night, Alex caught a glimpse of the vanity license plate on the back of the Cadillac. It read 'REV ROY'.

Flashbulbs popped as Julia and Marty made their way up the steps to the Pasadena Civic Auditorium for the Emmy Award ceremony. Even though the paparazzi didn't recognize the couple, they weren't taking any chances. The photographers were vying to get the right shot of the best- and the worst-dressed for the tabloids. In her black beaded bustier dress and high heels, Julia wasn't likely to end up in the 'Would You Be Caught Dead in This Outfit?' category. She looked as glamorous as any of the television stars who followed her.

As the stars and their publicists paraded in front of the fans, reporters and photographers yelled out their affiliates – 'LA Times', 'Associated Press' – and shouted questions. 'What are you wearing?' 'Who designed your dress?' 'Armani, Armani, and Armani,' came back in a chorus. The fans, kept safely behind a velvet rope watched over by police, cheered and applauded for their favorite actors. Julia had learned that if the stars didn't acknowledge them and wave to their fans, the cheers would turn to invective as the fans showered them with abuse. 'Who do you think you are?' 'We made you!' The line between idolatry and condemnation was as flimsy as the one that separated the fans from their object of desire.

Inside, the auditorium was packed. Professional seat-takers, extras, were hired, so that every seat would be full for the ceremony which was broadcast on national television from the West Coast. If the stars got up to go to the bathroom or hit the lobby for a drink at the bar, someone would immediately fill their seat and hold it for them until they came back. The Emmys were like the Oscars, maybe not quite so glamorous, but becoming more important with every year, as staying at home and watching television surpassed going out to the movies as entertainment of choice for most Americans. Surrounded by all the lights and glitter, Julia squeezed Marty's arm in excitement. She'd attended the Emmys before with Marty, but this time was different because she herself was nominated. Even though she knew she wouldn't win. A first-time writer, with a background in film documentary, up against heavyweights like Cheers' Jim Burrows and Designing Women's Bloodworth-Thomason? She didn't stand a chance.

Two hours later, Julia was standing on the stage of the Pasadena Civic Auditorium, clutching her Emmy Award for Outstanding Writing on a Comedy Series, Episode 'Elvis Is Sighted in the Mall'. The walk down the broad steps and up to the podium had been one of the longest of her life. What if she tripped and fell? What if she forgot her acceptance speech? which she'd been practicing in front of the mirror even though she was absolutely positive she wouldn't win. She was so short that she could barely reach the microphone at the podium. This year's Miss Universe adjusted it for her. Miss World handed her the prized gold statuette.

Julia took a deep breath and said, 'Thank you all so much. Just a year and a half ago, I was half-way up a mountain in India, making a documentary, virtually all on my own, just me and my Bolex camera. Now my life has been completely made over by Makeover. I want to thank my husband for pushing me in this new direction. I want to thank everyone on the show, behind the show, responsible for the show, especially J.C. Austin, my dear friend, without whom there wouldn't be a Makeover. I know at least some of you agree with me on that.' Outside the Pasadena Civic Auditorium, demonstrators were already protesting the lack of nomination for J.C. 'I'm giving you all fair warning. There's going to be some big changes on the show this season, so watch for the "before and after".' The crowd roared with laughter. 'All I can tell you is, "you ain't seen nuthin' yet." ' Holding tight to her trophy, Julia managed to make her way off the stage and back to her seat.

The Governor's Ball. The Awards Ceremony was over. The broadcast had run close to four hours, the longest in industry history, and was only slightly less vulgar than those of the past few years. There had been the loquacious recipient who was personally responsible for adding seven minutes to the broadcast by thanking everyone from God to the nursery school teacher who started her career by casting her as a carrot in Mr MacGregor's carrot patch. There was the blonde starlet whose heels were too high and dress too long, who fell splay-legged on the stage, her humiliation broadcast before millions of viewers. And there was the embarrassing off-color comedy routine from the stoned stand-up comedian. Why did this always happen? The Emmys were broadcast live, so no matter how strictly rehearsed, some presenters always ended up making public fools of themselves. They tried to be hip, they wanted to seem young, so it was always a crapshoot as to how far they would go.

After the long ceremony, everybody was starved. There were never enough places to sit at the Governor's Ball, so the winners stood around, juggling a plate of food in one hand and an Emmy in the other. Marty leaned down and gave Julia a huge kiss. 'Welcome to the wonderful world of the Emmys. Not bad for your first time out.' They both knew that tonight was a big step for Makeover. Paul had won for Outstanding Supporting Actor in a Comedy Series, Theresa had won as well, and Liam had snagged the Art Direction, and there were two other technical awards for the show. 'Yeah, but I'm disappointed we didn't win the big one, Outstanding Comedy Series.'

'You can't expect to the first year on air. We have to prove we can do more than just stay in the ballgame. We'll set our sights on next year.' He smiled indulgently and then said, 'Listen, Jules, I'm exhausted. Have you got your heart set on going to the Pac Vic party at Spago's?' The studio had rented the back room at the restaurant for a private celebration.

'Well, sure, kind of. Besides, we've only got the one car here.'

'Hi guys,' Liam appeared next to them. 'Congratulations.'

'You, too,' Marty put his arm around him. 'I'm really proud of you both. You two have a set of bookends there.' He smiled benevolently down on them. 'Liam, have you got your car here?'

Liam blushed. 'I hate to admit it, but I actually rented a limo. It should be picking me up out front.'

'Great. Julia wants to hit the Spago party and I've just about had it for one night. The ceremony went way overtime.' He stopped and waited for Liam to pick up his cue.

'I'd be glad to take her to the party and then bring her home.' His eyes bore into her once again.

Don't do this, Julia pleaded silently, although she didn't know with which man. Say no. This is dangerous, can't you sense it?

But no. 'Hey, terrific, thanks,' Marty leaned over and gave her a kiss on the cheek. 'I'm going to split, then. Have fun, Jules. This is your night. Enjoy.' And then he was gone.

Julia and Liam were left standing, staring at each other. The noise of the party swirled around them. Julia dropped her gaze. Liam looked over the room. 'So what do you think?' he asked. 'You had enough of this yet? Ready to go?'

Her sweaty palm gripped the little statuette and her heart was pounding so loud she was sure he could hear it. 'Sure,' she tried to shrug, 'any time you say.'

They never made it to Spago. Liam let her into his apartment and headed straight for the kitchen. He opened the fridge, reached for a bottle of wine, changed his mind and closed the door. He turned around and their eyes locked. Julia couldn't bring herself to look away this time. Neither could he. They stood, frozen, looking at each other, for what seemed like an eternity.

Julia's heart was racing. She didn't know what to do. Liam didn't move. He wanted her, she was sure of that now, and oh, God, she wanted him. She realized that if anything was going to happen, she would have to make the first move. She had never done that before. She wasn't sure she even knew how. Tremulously, she reached out to touch him, letting her hand gently brush his cheek. It was like releasing a volcano. He grabbed her and instantly they were clutching at each other, mouth against mouth, breast and crotch and thigh slamming up against each other, breathing heavily. Their hands moving all over, seek and find, search and destroy. His mouth was on hers, tongue mixed with tongue, as he backed her up against the kitchen table. His hands, those hands she'd been fantasizing about for months, pulling down the top of her dress, freeing her naked breasts in the air. She shut her eyes and felt his hands, those strong, beautiful hands, closing over her breasts, pressing them together, squeezing them gently, then harder, rubbing the nipples till they were hard as diamonds. His breathing was ragged. She gasped as he brought his mouth down to her nipples, sucking each one, hard, pulling on her fiercely, as if he could take all of her body straight into his. His hand crept up under her taffeta skirt, fingers searching blindly as he brushed against the crotch of her panties, sliding under the lace, losing themselves in her slippery, silken wetness.

She couldn't bear it. Her hands tore at his belt buckle, fighting to unclasp it, yes, there, open, tugging at the zipper of his tight black pants, please, come, free, yes, her hand sliding down the front of his pants, searching, where is it, please, yes, grabbing on to his cock, finding it hard, so hard. He was kissing her all over, her neck, her breasts, back to her mouth, the only sounds in the room, the ragged sound of their breathing. They'd said not one word since entering his apartment.

He lifted her up in his arms, she had no idea where his bedroom was or if they could even make it that far, but he pushed her back on the table, back on to the antique lace tablecloth that covered the long hard wood table. He was standing over her, holding his cock in his hand, stroking it as if it were something to be proud of, not furtively touched and then crudely shoved into her. The sight of him, the finely muscled chest, the powerful arms, curling dark blond hair, bright blue eyes, was so erotic that for a moment she closed her eyes, blinded by the danger of his beauty. Then, slowly, wantonly, she lifted up the taffeta skirt of her black cocktail dress, inch by inch, revealing the black silk stockings, wispy garter belt, and fragile silk panties. He groaned and brought his mouth straight to her crotch, his breathing hot against the silk. She was melting, melting, the fragile silk of the panties dissolving under the heat of his kiss. She reached out for him blindly, wordlessly begging him to come into her, everything seemed to melt away and he was inside her, plunging deep inside her, her hands gripping the sides of the table for ballast, her head thrashing back and forth; her skirt was up around her hips, her legs were wrapped around his. The friction of her silken stockings against the hair on his bare legs was heavenly. She had never worn stockings before. She had never felt so wild, so abandoned. Her body was shaking with the force of his, the colors were unfolding within her, red and orange and purple and then a series of silver, white-hot explosions. It went on and on, she was pulsating, contracting, little spasms of exquisite pleasure until she screamed from the joy of it. He was still plunging, faster and faster, with more and more urgency. His face changed, he threw his head back, and he gave a long, low growl of release.

They lay there, sprawled on the table, feeling each other's rapid heartbeats slow, the room stopped spinning, everything swam into focus and they came back to earth.

'God, Julia, I am so sorry,' Liam looked totally remorseful. 'I've never done anything like that before, but I saw that underwear and I just went crazy.'

'Believe me, I've never owned anything like this before. It's all from doing that lingerie ad for Next of Skin.'

'I love that ad. I have to admit I've got about a dozen copies of it hidden in my sock drawer.'

'You beast,' she smacked him hard on his bare ass. 'I think we ruined your tablecloth. I'll pay to have it drycleaned.'

'No way. We're already even. I'm afraid these will never be worn again.' He dangled what was left of her black lace panties over her. Then he brought them up to his face. 'Hmm, delicious,' he said, tasting them.

'Don't. Liam, that is disgusting.'

'No, it's not. It's you. You taste wonderful. You want to see?' He sucked them hard into his mouth, growling like a dog with a bone, and then bent to kiss her.

'You know . . . this was not how I expected it to be.'

'You mean you envisioned this moment before it happened?'

'Yes,' she felt the heat rise in her face.

'Oh, God, Julia, so did I, over and over again. I used you to go to sleep at night and then it didn't work any more because I couldn't sleep for thinking of you. I just never believed it would happen.'

'No the reality of it is a surprise. But you're not how I thought you would be.'

'What do you mean?' He was crestfallen. 'Didn't it work for you?'

'Oh, yes. Believe me, I'm not complaining. But somehow I always imagined you soft, gentle and,' she giggled, 'slow.'

'I am, I swear it, I can be.' He moved over her again and gave her a long, slow kiss that started the colors growing inside her again. 'If you'll give me another chance, I'll show you.'

Blame it on the bellboy!

LYLA CAUGHT IN LOVE NEST
WITH REVEREND ROY

*Revealed! Reverend Roy Williams' Secret Eight-Year Affair
with Makeover Star, Shirley Bunting!!*

Reverend Roy Williams, long-time leader in the black
community and candidate for Mayor of Los Angeles, has
been involved in a sizzling love affair with actress Shirley
Bunting who plays Lyla Kaye, the flirtatious manager of a
peekaboo lingerie shop on the new sit-com, Makeover.

Their cover was blown by an anonymous tip to the
Hollywood Insider. The *Insider* has discovered the couple's
secret love nest is a suite in none other than Santa
Monica's ritzy apartment hotel, the Palm Court. Reporters
caught Reverend Roy, as he is affectionately called, red-
handed (and stark-naked!) in bed with sexy Shirley.

Until this year, Shirley Bunting was a struggling actress,
earning bit parts here, a guest role there. Now the African-
American beauty has hit it big with Makeover.

Minister of the famous Dawn of the Day AME church
located in the heart of Watts, Roy Williams is known as a
powerful political leader who is able to both move a
congregation to tears and spur them to action, pushing his
parishioners to get personally involved in the social issues
of their own community. Reverend Roy was instrumental in
easing racial violence both in the 1964 riots in Watts and
the more recent protests over the Rodney King verdict.

According to sources, this is no one-night stand or casual
fling. The affair has been going on for eight years but hotel
management have discreetly turned a blind eye. Recently
hired bellboy, Harold Booker, observed the high profile
couple's comings and goings. 'I never actually saw them
together, but right from the beginning I was suspicious. She
was getting a lot of gifts and flowers from somebody. Late
one night, after I finished my shift, I stuck around and saw
Reverend Roy go up in the service elevator to Shirley's
floor. He went into her penthouse apartment and didn't
come out for thirty-six hours. I can't believe it would take
that long to give someone religious counseling.'

A spokesperson for the Williams campaign has gone on

record as saying that, 'Reverend Roy Williams is an extraordinary man who has waged a war against drugs, gangs, and drive-by shootings. His church has brought a ray of hope to young people trapped by urban blight and his political activism has provided a focus for the disenfranchised. I don't believe responsible voters, black or white, who want to see real change come about, will be influenced by these allegations about Reverend Williams' private life.'

At a hastily called press conference, Roy Williams today admitted he knows Shirley Bunting as a volunteer worker with his political organization. 'I respect and admire her but we are just friends who share a political ideology and hope for the future.'

Mary Anne Williams, his wife of twenty-five years, says she accepts her husband's explanation without question and will continue to stand behind him every step of the way.

Shirley Bunting could not be reached for comment.

Chapter Thirty-two

Shirley could avoid the Makeover set no longer. She only had a couple of lines in this week's episode. The article came out on Monday and she hadn't been called until Wednesday. She'd had forty-eight hours to sort out her life. It hadn't been easy. Half the time she was filled with rage, an emotion foreign to her until now, a murderous anger directed at nobody and everybody. If anyone came near her she wanted to bite and scratch and claw them, make them hurt, bad. Her fury frightened her as though some alien force had taken over her being. The rest of the time she just lay in bed and cried.

The only call she took was from Roy. After agonizing over the situation, they had reached a mutual and painful decision to sever their relationship immediately and completely. She had lost him, the person she loved most in the world, and there was no one she could cry about it to. None of her friends knew the extent of her involvement with Roy. They wouldn't have thought it politically correct or personally wise.

If only she could fly home to Mama, climb into her lap, bury her head against her bosom and cry her heart out the way she had as a little girl. But she wasn't a little girl any longer and she knew her mother, while opening her arms to comfort her, would be secretly relieved that the affair was over, even if it meant bringing it out into the open. She didn't care about Roy's wonderful work or his political future. Her daughter's future happiness was all that concerned her.

Shirley's picture was splashed all over the front of the tabloids. Photos taken inside her apartment with a hidden camera, showing where and how she lived, the table she ate off, the bed she – they – slept in. It was such an invasion of privacy. There was nothing she wanted to do more than just

343

run away. Instead she had to report for work at soundstage six.

Shirley's eyes were so red and swollen there was little the make-up artist could do. The set was unnaturally quiet. She could tell the cast had no idea what to say. Brandon's paternity suit had been regarded as somewhat of a joke and Linda Earl's plastic surgery was easily dismissible, but this was bound to change people's lives. They didn't know whether to offer sympathy or ignore the whole thing. She could feel their eyes on her but the minute she connected with them, they shifted away. She refused to feel shame. A wasted emotion that wouldn't do either Roy or herself any good. Anyway, she was not sorry she'd been involved with Roy. She was only sorry it was now over.

Alex broke the tension by acknowledging the situation immediately with, 'Well, Shirley, the *Insider* obviously thinks you've been a naughty girl. We still love you and certainly there are far more major crises in the rest of the world. So give us a hug and let's get to work.' He reached out and embraced her and the rest of the cast followed suit. Then they all went about the business of the day's rehearsal and Shirley, surprisingly, found she was able to lose herself in the work.

At the end of the day, Alex came over to her and put his arm around her. 'If you want to be on your own, that's understandable, but if you feel like some company, why not have dinner with me?'

'Not in a restaurant,' Shirley said quickly. 'The press are hounding me. I had trouble getting to work today.'

'OK, then. My place. I'll cook for you. I can't guarantee gourmet but at least it's quiet and private.'

'Thanks,' she nodded gratefully.

'Grab your things and let's go out the back. Might be easier that way.'

But outside there was a crush of reporters, photographers, and a TV news crew, all lying in wait for a photo-op or sound bite to make the six o'clock news. As soon as they saw Alex and Shirley come out of the studio, they rushed forward to surround them. 'Stick with me, kid,' Alex took her firmly by the arm and steered her through the crowd. There were questions being shouted at them from all sides, but Alex offered only a terse, 'No comment,' and hustled her toward the parking lot, shoving her unceremoniously

344

into his car and slamming down the locks on the doors. Huddled in the front seat, with reporters clawing at the windows and aiming cameras at her from every direction, for the first time, Shirley felt truly frightened. This was not something that was going to blow over in a day or a week; this was going to take a long time to go away. Alex slammed the car in gear, gunned the motor and sped off, leaving the media vultures in a cloud of dust.

'I imagine you could use a drink,' Alex said as he let her into the living-room of his condo, 'what would you like?'

'Vodka. If you have it. Straight. On the rocks.'

'That bad, huh?' He headed for the bar.

'That bad.' Shirley stood frozen in the doorway for a moment. She remembered very little of the hair-raising ride from Burbank through Van Nuys over the Sepulveda Pass toward Marina del Rey. It seemed one moment she was getting into the car, the next moment they were at his place.

'Why don't you take off your coat and stay awhile?' Alex motioned for her to come on in. He put on Wynton Marsalis and the smooth, cool jazz invaded the room.

She shut the door behind her and looked around the apartment. It was very simple. Large, open rooms, high ceilings, lots of windows, but very little furniture. Off-white walls broken only by huge, colorful photographs mounted on matte board. She looked at the pictures more closely and recognized them as photos of some rather exotic places: Singapore, Tangier, Budapest. They looked professional, like something out of the *National Geographic*.

'Did you take these?' she called out over the music.

'Yes. It's my hobby.'

'You must travel a lot.'

'I consider myself a citizen of the world. LA is the worst place on earth for an artist to live. No sense of history, no semblance of spirituality, total lack of values. It's where I work, but it will never be home. Here,' he handed her what looked like a tumbler full of vodka, 'get that down you. It'll make you feel better. Why don't you bring your drink and come and sit on a stool in the kitchen while I fix dinner.'

'All right.' Her body wasn't performing well. She was finding it difficult to move, as if under water.

'I hope you don't require meat. I'm vegetarian.'

'Sure, fine, anything.' Shirley followed him in a fog, then

345

stopped, embarrassed, 'And I made you swallow all those oysters the other night.'

'It's OK. I eat seafood. Just no red meat. I thought I'd make something simple. Pasta with vegetable sauce. Maybe a green salad?'

'That's fine. Whatever you're having is fine.' They lapsed into silence. She couldn't think of anything to say. She didn't really feel like talking; she just didn't want to be alone. She sat on the stool, nursed her drink, and watched him prepare the food. He moved easily around her in the kitchen, opening cupboards, chopping vegetables, lighting the gas stove. He worked deftly, carefully, making decisions quickly about which spice to add, which dish to use. Maybe she should offer to help, but at the moment, she felt heavy, as if she would never be able to get up from this stool. She had no idea how much time had passed when she looked up to see two places set at the round table, complete with red-cloth napkins, wine glasses, fresh flowers and lit candles.

'Hey, that looks . . . nice.' It was an effort to summon up anything more than the basics of polite conversation. She tried again. 'You cook the way you direct.'

'How's that?' He held the chair for her.

'Fast and precise. You're very sure of yourself.'

'In some areas.' He poured a little wine into her glass and it took every ounce of strength she had not to down it in one gulp. Although, hell, why not? Maybe if she got very, very drunk, it would deaden the pain. But she couldn't do that here, not in front of Alex, her director, no matter how kind he had been. She forced herself to sip slowly. Dinner passed without conversation. He must sense that jazz and wine was about all she could handle at the moment. She didn't think she'd be able to eat much, but she found it went down easily. The food was simple but superb. A fine, thin capelletti pasta with egg-plant, olives and roasted peppers. Fresh sourdough bread. A mixed salad with a lot of greens she didn't recognize. The wine was especially good. He poured her another glass. An hour passed. Or maybe more. She had no idea. The alcohol and the food numbed her but it was a comforting, warm numbness that went a long way toward melting the block of ice she'd been carrying in the pit of her stomach for three days.

'OK,' Alex got up from the table and turned off the

346

stereo. 'Do you want to talk about any of this?'

'Why?' she said vaguely.

'Because I think you need to. Tell me what you feel.'

All right. If this was to be the payment for dinner and wine and a tiny margin of safety, OK, she would try. She took a shaky breath. 'I guess I feel betrayed.'

'I don't blame you.'

'How could they know all this? It's like they were right there in bed with Roy and me.'

'Maybe they were. These papers have spies everywhere. Your hairdresser, your bank teller, the person sitting next to you on the plane the last time you flew home to Charleston, who knows? But given Roy's profile, wasn't this bound to happen eventually?'

'I hate it that we've been used like this.'

Alex looked confused. 'You mean you've been used? By Roy Williams?'

'No, goddamn it, no,' she exploded. 'You don't understand anything. The white press loves this kind of dumb shit. A scandal that pits black against black, there's nothing they like better. This thing is deep. I've got the *LA Times*, the *New York Times*, the tabloids, *A Current Affair*, all after my ass to sell my story. But my story is not the story here.' Her language was loosening, she tried to hold on. 'None of this garbage means anything to anyone. Damn, Alex, don't you see? In comparison to what Roy has managed to accomplish for people, our relationship is not important. I'm talking crack babies, getting people off the streets and out to vote, rebuilding after the riots. There are so many real life crises out there, what does it matter who's sleeping with who? His wife knew about us, for God's sake; if she didn't care, why should anybody else?'

'What about his children?'

Shirley didn't say anything. Then: 'What I mean is, our relationship was not something either of us went into with our eyes closed. He always said if he had met me twenty years ago things would have been different. But his life was already established: the wife, the kids, their shared goals. I couldn't interfere with that and I didn't want to. I've always preferred my privacy and now that's all blown to hell. Roy had a real chance of winning this race, first black mayor of LA, think what changes he could make? But they'll go after him now for something that doesn't amount to a hill of beans, not in the big picture. I feel sick. This could split the black community, which is just what they want.'

'They? They who?'

'The forces against him. All right, you want me to say it, white people. Get us fighting with each other and we won't go after them, leave them alone to hold all the power, run the country and keep on running us into the ground.' She couldn't believe she was shooting off her mouth like this, saying these 'activist' things. She had never even thought them before tonight. 'Damn, Alex, I'm sorry, you just wouldn't understand. You're not even American.'

'You think we don't have racial tension in Europe?' Alex gave a dry little laugh. 'God, you Americans are so insular, so self-obsessed. What about what's going on in Germany right now? Yugoslavia? France? There are plenty of people all over the world who believe blacks are subhuman and Jews are part of an international conspiracy. You think LA is the only place that has race riots? Britain has them, too, you know. Remember Brixton? It's not about race anyway. It's about feeling threatened. It's about power.'

'Shit, Alex, don't you see?' Shirley started to cry; hard, big, wracking sobs that shook her whole body. 'I haven't just lost Roy. I've lost my entire sense of direction. Everything took a backseat to being with him. That's what defined me, that's what shaped my daily life. Maybe that was wrong, I don't know . . .'

'Is it definitely over?'

'If he has any chance at all of continuing his political career, it has to be over. I understand that, I accept it, but what am I going to do? For a long time I felt like I was floating, not touching bottom, but not really in danger of drowning either, know what I mean?' Alex nodded. He was listening hard. 'Now I just want to run away. I feel like I'm about to fly off into a million pieces. What's going to stop that from happening? What's going to hold me together?'

'Work.'

'Work? Don't give me that shit. I've been working.'

'No, you haven't, not really. I've watched you. You're just going through the motions.'

'What do you mean?' Shirley stopped crying. 'Is this just your opinion?'

'You haven't yet put your stamp on Lyla, made her your own. I agree there's not enough there in the writing, but right now she is just a token, no matter how much we all try to deny that. Lyla's not integral to Makeover.'

'Are you saying I'm in danger of being written out?'

'No, I'm just . . .'

'Thank you,' she squeezed back tentatively, 'I mean that. Thank you. I want to keep my job. I guess I didn't realize just how much until now.'

'Good. Now what about the apartment at the Palms? Is it Roy's?'

'You mean, was he keeping me?' She was screaming at him again. Crying and screaming, crying and screaming, that's all she seemed to be able to do these days. 'None of your fucking business.'

'No, that's not what I meant,' he said gently. 'I just wonder if you really want to go back there.'

'Oh, sorry. You're right. I don't. I can't. I have to get out by the end of the month. Only I have no idea how or when I'll be able to look for a new place. Our shooting schedule is tight for the next couple of weeks.'

'There's an empty condo one floor below mine . . .'

'I'm not ready to buy anything yet.'

'No, no, of course not. But I could ask the manager if he'll rent it to you for a few months. They do that sometimes while they're looking for a buyer. It's not bad. Same layout as this. Give you a chance to regroup. Figure out what you want next.'

'Please. Thank you.' She didn't know what else to say. Why was he doing all this for her? Why was he being so nice?

'You can stay here tonight if you want.'

Oh, so that was it. She felt the fury rising again. 'Is that what this is all about? Are you after my ass, is that it?'

'Hey, wait a minute. I've got two extra bedrooms. You may use one of them. For tonight only. No strings attached.'

'I'm sorry, Alex, please, sorry.' Now she was embarrassed. He was doing his best to help her out and she just kept biting at him.

'I had no idea you were this volatile.'

'Me neither.' Shirley managed a small smile.

'I'm really quite repressed. You don't have to worry about me making a move on you. I'm interested in you, I can't deny it, but I promise never to mention it again.

Unless you mention it first. I'd be honored to have you as a neighbor, that's all; OK?'

'OK.'

'Come out on to the balcony. I think we both need to cool off a bit.' He slid open the door to the deck and they went outside. She could hear the gentle murmur of the ocean and there was a balmy breeze off the water. The view was not as magnificent as the one from her top-floor suite at the Palm Court but it was nice. Soothing. Peaceful. 'Look out there,' Alex pointed to some dim, faintly glowing lights far off in the distance. 'Beyond those lights is who knows what? Entire countries, whole groups of people, working, fighting, loving, just simply trying to survive. Right now everything seems focused on you, like one of those tiny little lights, just barely there. You said it yourself. There are far bigger tragedies in the world, OK?'

Chapter Thirty-three

'I'm not in favor of this episode, Julie,' Stan said sternly, holding the current script out in front of him as if it were a dead fish that was beginning to smell.

Julia and Marty and Tim were in Stan's office. Whenever they were in conflict with Stan and he had a particularly difficult pill for them to swallow, he always called them into his office so they could meet on his turf. Julia looked at the room in amazement. In just one week, everything in the office – furniture, pictures, posters, awards – had all been completely rearranged.

Stan caught her staring. '*Feng shui*,' he said.

'Pardon?'

'*Feng shui*. I've been studying Oriental mysticism and I've redone my office according to the principles of *feng shui*. That's the ancient art of enhancing fortune and luck through aligning a building and its interior with the environment. See, I've moved my desk so that my back is now against the wall. That way I can see everything. Nobody can attack me from behind.'

Julia and Marty looked at Tim to see if this was all a joke or if Stan was in danger of losing his marbles. Tim merely smiled and shrugged. 'How interesting,' Julia said politely. 'Now, what don't you like about the episode, Stan?' Be diplomatic, be reasonable, her inner general ordered her troop of emotions who were instantly ready to do battle.

'The theme, the characters, the storyline, just about everything.'

'I see,' she said noncommittally. He was such an idiot but an idiot who held the power. 'Actually, Stan, I was following one of your suggestions. You suggested I write an episode featuring Samantha and this is what I came up with. Kelly loves it. You heard the first reading, didn't you think it was funny?'

The new episode, entitled 'There Is Nothing Like a Dame' dealt with a Halloween fundraising event in Houston's gay community, a drag ball which raised money for AIDS research. The logline read: 'Samantha's powers are put to the test when she is called upon to make over twenty-five men for the Halloween Drag Queen Ball.'

'It's hilarious, but I think it's in poor taste.'

'I see,' she said again, trying to hold on to tact. 'I believe it got by Standards and Practices, didn't it, Tim?' Julia was referring to the network censors who had to approve everything that went on the air. Tim nodded. 'There's no profanity, no skin, very little sexual innuendo. If they don't have a problem with it, why do you?'

'It sends the wrong kind of message out into the community.'

'Oh come on, Stan, it's not as if we're telling everyone to get out there and cross-dress. Homosexuality is a part of real life. What's wrong with presenting it in a humorous but positive way?'

'Middle America is extremely homophobic,' Stan cautioned.

'Not half as much as Hollywood,' Tim interjected. 'Supposedly thirty per cent of the industry is gay and most of them are still in the closet. Rock Hudson and Magic Johnson haven't changed that much.' Julia and Marty had often speculated about Tim's sexual proclivities. He was seen in the company of women, but rarely the same woman twice. He never talked about his private life and deflected anything more than superficial questions. A man of mystery was Tim.

'I don't think the viewers are ready for this,' Stan insisted.

'I think they are,' Tim said. 'Our research tells us Kelly has a big gay following.'

'You mean she's a fag hag?' Stan looked alarmed.

Tim winced. 'No, that's not what I mean. Like Bette Midler and Delta Burke, she's got that larger-than-life appeal. I think Julia's come up with a good tie-in here, a drag ball to raise funds for AIDS and Kelly's own work in that area with Kelly's Kids. Everybody knows about Kelly's activism. Even the President of the US knows. She's just been appointed to his Action Committee On AIDS. That's a great publicity tie-in for the show.'

'I like to make it as personal as possible,' Julia admitted. 'If something interesting is happening in an actor's life, I'm going to use it. This is an opportunity for the average viewer to learn something. Why should I write for the lowest common denominator?'

'Your job is not to give lessons,' Stan said nastily, 'your job is to entertain. Mine is to make sure it sells. We've got to get those ratings, deliver those viewers to the advertisers.'

'I guarantee you this episode will get you the numbers,' Julia said. 'It's bold, it's daring, but there's nothing offensive about it.'

'You want to push the envelope a little, OK, but I don't approve of shock for shock value. You writers think you want to be on the cutting edge,' Stan sneered, 'whatever that means. What it means to me is there's a great danger of falling off.'

'It's a different world out there, Stan, don't you agree? Nobody lives in the Little House on the Prairie any more.' She was so tired of trying to toe the line. Yes, she said, when she really meant no. I understand, she said, when in fact she didn't. You're wrong, she wanted to yell at him, you're wrong, you dickhead. But of course she didn't. And what was going on with Marty? Why wasn't he backing her up on this?

'You liberal baby boomers think you can change the world by rejecting traditional values. You think they're boring. What you don't realize is that values become traditional because the majority of people, not a few eastern intellectual snobs or westcoast forest faggots, but the majority of the people really believe in them.'

Tim winced. 'All Julia's trying to do,' he ventured hesitantly, 'is to anticipate a change in the nation's taste for comedy. After all, CBN is supposed to be the alternative network. Julia has her finger on the pulse and I think we ought to allow her some leeway and support her on this . . .'

But Stan overrode him. 'Makeover is not your personal soapbox. It is not a political show. That's not what the network bought in the first place and it's not what we want.'

'What the fuck are you going on about, Stan?' Julia totally ignored her own inner direction to be tactful. 'There's nothing political about this episode; it's a reflection of real life. There are things going on around us that we simply can't ignore. A recession, racism, sexual harassment, and yes, AIDS. Am I supposed to pretend these issues don't exist? Janine and Carlene are a modern family unit living in contemporary times. Do they never read the paper? Don't they watch the news? Everybody I know is in the process of re-examining their lives. Why doesn't that apply to Janine and Carlene?'

'Re-examining their navels is more like it,' Stan grumbled.

'What are you telling me here? Am I supposed just to go on writing joke after joke in order to fill a meaningless twenty-two minutes?'

'No, of course not,' Stan said calmly. 'Just don't start taking yourself too seriously, Julie. People will take a little controversy with their laughs, a little bit of poking fun at politicians, but do you really think any of this shapes people's opinions or really changes their minds?'

'Of course I do,' Julia said hotly.

'Take it from me, Julie. You can't change the world through a sit-com.'

'What a pompous toad he is,' Julia griped to Marty as they were on their way home in the car. 'I used to be afraid of him, but now he just pisses me off. Why does he resist anything new I try to do with the show? Haven't you always told me that the only thing that really succeeds in television is breakthrough, not copy? Stanfield King may have a lot of experience in television, but he has practically none with real life. And for someone who's supposed to be an expert in comedy, the man has no sense of humor. Now, Tim, I think, is beginning to come on to my side, which is all to the good. "He who sets the entertainment schedule for network TV sets the agenda for the nation." We have the power to shape opinions and move people to action. That involves responsibility. I resent being told I'm taking myself too seriously. Well,' she looked at Marty accusingly, 'how do you think the meeting went? Am I overreacting?'

'Julia, do we have to review every single moment of our lives? Can't you just let the performance stand? You got what you wanted, you won. The episode will air exactly as you've written it. So enough with the diatribe.'

'I don't get it. You were the one who politicized me in the first place. You made me open my eyes and see the injustices in the world. Now you want me to shut them and not do anything about it?'

'Of course not,' Marty said tiredly, 'but much as I hate to agree with Stanfield King, I think you may be exaggerating the importance of our influence. Now would it be too much to ask for you to keep your mouth shut until we get home?'

Julia leaned her head back on the seat, closed her eyes and allowed herself to think about Liam. Whenever things got too stressful these days, she hooked into her own private sexual reverie. It was her escape route; her 'secret garden'. Thinking about Liam when she was with Marty almost made her more guilty than when she was actually making love with Liam. It seemed more of a betrayal somehow, perhaps because Marty had had full ownership of her thoughts for so long.

The affair with Liam had changed all that. Not that it was a real affair. Just a dalliance. He was younger, which should render the relationship harmless. There was little danger of getting too close. She'd slept with only three men in her life. Two of them before Marty. None since. Unlike many of her female friends, who talked about their numerous affairs, Julia had felt superior, proud of the fact that she was naturally monogamous. Now that she had slept with Liam, strangely she felt proud of that, too. She did it, she went home, nobody knew about it, everything was fine.

With Marty it had become a continual power struggle. With Liam she had the upper hand. Little things. For instance, for ten years Marty had insisted on sleeping on the left side of the bed. He even made love to her from the left side. He wouldn't consider changing sides, not even as an experiment, not even for one night. Naturally Julia had developed a craving to be on the left side. Liam didn't care which side of the bed he was on. It was proving to be deliciously exciting. Probably Liam had his own little idiosyncrasies which, if they were together for some time, she would eventually discover. What she found charming and titillating now would eventually drive her nuts. But she wasn't in this for a long time, just a good time.

Liam was her reward for standing firm on her principles. He was her treat for suffering all the shit. She'd been living and breathing Makeover for almost two years now. She deserved a little recreation, didn't she? It wasn't that sex with Liam was better than it was with Marty. It was just different. He was different. Such a contrast to the man she had known for most of her sexual life. It was like exploring foreign terrain, a surprise mountain here, a hidden valley there, an unexpected cove, a forest of delight. Her own body felt new and exciting, too. Having someone view her breasts, her thighs, the curve of a hip, without familiarity. Touching her in new ways as if for the first time. She responded differently when she was in bed with him. She felt wilder, more passionate. She wasn't in love with Liam, but she sensed he might be falling in love with her. For all his handsome, sensual good looks, he was not a man to be toyed with. He was too sensitive, too sincere. He wouldn't know how to use a woman, so was it wrong for her to use him? She would have to be very careful. Let it go on just a little while longer, then break it off. For now, she would think about the way he kissed the back of her knee, how his tongue moved along the back of her thigh, licking the curve of her . . .

'I'm sorry I snapped at you,' Marty interrupted her fantasy. 'What are you thinking about?'

'Liam Carey,' the words were out of her mouth before she realized.

'You know I envy that guy,' Marty said.

'Why?' Julia's heart skipped a couple of beats.

'Everything comes so easily to him.'

'What makes you say that?'

'He's a natural. Talent, skill, vision, it all just seems to flow out of him without his even trying. I have to work so fucking hard just to hold on to what I've got.'

IS THERESA RUIZ CASTRO'S LOVE CHILD?

Emmy Winner Rumored To Be Illegitimate

Theresa Ruiz, Makeover's jalepeno hot receptionist, Concha, has dropped a bombshell by admitting she is illegitimate.

'I don't know who my real father is,' she says, 'but he could be still alive and living in Cuba.'

Now the truth may be about to come out. Sources close to the fiery actress's mother, Margarita Olivera Ruiz, who now lives in Miami, say the Cuban émigrée was once a high government official, working for the CDR, the Committee for the Defense of the Revolution. She was special assistant to the speaker of the Supreme CDR, attended cabinet meetings, and accompanied Castro frequently on school visits. How close was she to the dynamic dictator?

'Castro was very handsome and charming in those days,' says an unidentified source, another expatriate Cuban living in Miami, nearby to Margarita and her husband, Jorge. 'He was tall and powerful, with an eye for the ladies. Women were always throwing themselves at his feet and he took advantage of many of them.'

Faithless Fidel never married, but is rumored to have a number of children by different women. Could Theresa be his long-lost daughter?

When questioned, Margarita called the cigar-smoker potentate by his first name. 'I did work for Fidel and the CDR, but got out when the government became corrupt. I was lucky to be able to leave before everything fell apart.'

Our reporter asked if Margarita had denounced Castro. 'No, I still love Fidel,' she told us. 'When I knew him he was a man of ideals but he is only one man. Everybody knows he is going to die soon. There is a struggle for power raging all around him. It was very dangerous for me. I had to get out and I'm glad I did.'

When asked if Castro could be the father of her child, Margarita became angry and slammed down the phone.

But our source says she was forced to leave Cuba because she married Theresa's stepfather, Jorge Ruiz. 'Castro was wildly jealous and had them all deported. Just ask anybody at the Versailles in Little Havana.'

Theresa Ruiz says she was raised by her mom and

stepfather. 'Jorge Ruiz gave me a loving home and treated me as one of his own. I consider him to be my true dad. I'll thank you to leave my mother alone. At great personal risk, she left her old life behind. Please allow her, and me, to enjoy our new one.'

Theresa denied any link with Fidel Castro. Nevertheless, as our photos below show, torrid Terri bears a striking resemblance to the revolutionary leader. Theresa has a reputation in Hollywood for political activism. Like father, like daughter?

Lance J. Sutton

Chapter Thirty-four

'I wanted you all together in the same place when we discussed this,' Tim said to the cast, 'because I know you're upset, kids. Theresa, you requested this company meeting. I've asked Stan to join us.' Stan nodded and bared his teeth in a smile. He was growing his hair long, in search of a ponytail, and he looked uncomfortable, as if he would prefer to be guzzling Evian on Ocean Avenue, facing the accusatory stares of the homeless in the park across the street, rather than a group of confrontational actors. 'Stan's been in the business a long time and knows that when you're dealing with this kind of tabloid trash, the best thing to do is ignore it.'

'Look, they can say whatever they want about me,' Theresa gripped the *Hollywood Insider* in one hand and a cigarette in the other, 'but when they start dragging my mother's name through the mud, I get so angry I can't see straight.' She threw her head back and exhaled a gunshot of smoke into the air. Smoking was not allowed in the green room, but no one dared tell her to butt out. All day she'd been storming around the set, muttering under her breath, glaring at everybody like a thick, dark thunder cloud rarely seen in southern California. 'It's lies, all lies. They took everything she said and completely twisted it. Margarita didn't mean that she was in love with Fidel, she hardly knew the man; she meant she loved what he stood for, in the beginning, before everything changed. And this bullshit about calling him by his first name. In Cuba, everybody does that, even today. Whether you're a top government official or just the guy on the street, you say "Fidel". It's part of his Papa image; it doesn't imply a close personal relationship. Lies, blatant lies! Just look at these pictures,' she pointed to a blurry photograph of a young Castro in his trademark green fatigues next to one of herself in an army uniform. 'This is a still from a guest shot I did on China Beach. This is supposed to prove we look alike?'

'Be grateful they didn't give you a beard or superimpose your head on his body,' Paul joked.

'That's not funny,' Theresa snapped. 'I'm not in this business for the fame. I'm in it for what I can say through my work. This type of slime goes against everything I'm fighting for. Theresa's Cuban, oh, she must be a whore, a radical. When will Americans realize Cuba is not just about a revolution? They keep saying "source",' she hit the tabloid with her fist, 'what source do they mean? And who is Susan Carroll? Or Lance J. Sutton? Sometimes they use a byline, sometimes they don't. All the tabloids cover us, but the *Insider* articles have all been personal and very specific. Someone has to be leaking information to the *Insider* and it could be one of us.' Puffing furiously, she glared around the room. 'In this country, only my mother and stepfather know I'm illegitimate. I never told anybody else until the night I got drunk and told you.' She zeroed in on Linda Earl. 'The night of the Emmy nominations.'

'Are you accusing me?' Linda went ashen.

'I'm not saying that. But how do I know it wasn't you? It's no secret you're pissed off I got nominated and you didn't. You've hardly said two words to me since I won the award.'

'Terri, I would never do something like that,' Linda began in a shaky voice. She looked as if she were ready to cry.

'What are you blaming Linda for?' Paul demanded. 'Where's your mother in all of this? Why doesn't she just come right out and say who your real father is?'

'Because she doesn't know,' Theresa retorted. 'At the time, she had a lot of lovers. Oh, don't look so shocked. This country is so puritanical. She was an artist. She ran in literary circles. She was sleeping with more than one man but, according to her, none of them was Fidel Castro. Just because you have the perfect little nuclear family unit, Paul, doesn't mean everybody else in the world lives that way. Funny, the *Insider* hasn't gone after you yet.'

'Now hold on here, kids,' Tim gave Stan a nervous glance. Obviously neither of them expected to have a mutiny on their hands. 'There's nothing to be gained from accusing each other. I didn't allow this meeting to take place

360

so that you could start pointing the finger, Theresa. There were lots of people on the set that night and you weren't exactly quiet about your little announcement.'

'If I thought that anyone in this room was responsible for giving information to the *Hollywood Insider*, I couldn't go on working with you, not for another minute,' Shirley said strongly. The room went deadly quiet. By now most of the cast were fully aware of how much Shirley had been hurt by the exposé of Roy Williams. Alex, who was closer to Shirley than anyone else, had let Julia know, without revealing all the details, that Shirley was barely managing to hold herself together these days. 'These stories are so ugly and so mean. They're destroying the lives of really good people and they don't even care. Nothing is sacred to them.'

'What do you think?' Julia appealed directly to Stan. So far, he had sat there, stone-faced, not saying a word. Surely he must be concerned himself by the constant *Insider* attacks on the cast of Makeover? If he were as confident as he appeared, he wouldn't have taken the time to come to the studio to talk to the cast. He rarely mixed with the actors, except for the occasional get-together after the Friday night taping. According to Stan, getting too close to the talent opened the door to contract demands. 'Why are they singling us out? It's been that way right from the beginning. Other shows were more important, but it's like we're on some kind of hit list. The *Insider*'s cranking out stories as fast as we're cranking out episodes.'

'Yeah, Julia's right,' J.C. broke in. 'I thought at first it was me they were after, because most of the articles were about me, but now they've hit on practically everybody.'

'Not me, so far,' Paul offered. 'As Theresa so graciously pointed out.'

'That's because, as Theresa says, you're too boring to make good copy,' Brandon sniped.

'If sleeping with one woman, and spending as much time at home with my family as I possibly can makes me boring,' Paul said, 'then I guess, as far as Hollywood is concerned, I'm a freak.'

Julia looked at Marty. Why didn't he say something? The fear and anger at the *Insider* attacks was already causing division among their ranks.

'What about me?' Kelly asked. 'Nothing on me so far either.'

'No one could call you boring, darlin'. They're probably lying in wait, saving their big guns for you.'

'Don't say that,' Kelly shivered. 'Sometimes I get the feeling that somebody's going through the things in my dressing-room. It's creepy.'

'Now there's no need to be paranoid, folks,' Stan finally spoke up. 'Believe me, there's no rhyme or reason to the tabloids. It's a business, that's all. Circulation, that's what it's all about for them. The only magazines with a circulation equal to the *Hollywood Insider* are *TV Guide* and *Family Circle*. We're popular, we make good copy.'

'But where are they getting the information, if it's not one of us? Who are these so-called sources?' Theresa violently ground out her cigarette and instantly lit another.

'Who knows? They quote supposed sources to cover their asses in case of libel. The retainer fees for their lawyers come out of their publicity budgets. They have a legal staff who make sure that what they've got will spark a reaction, generate publicity, sell more papers, but within the realm of truth so they can't be sued for libel.'

'These guys are devious,' Brandon agreed. 'They steal your mail or they fill out a change of address card so your mail is rerouted to an address where their reporters can get their hands on it. They go through your garbage, they go after your hospital records, they bribe your supposed friends. Believe me, they'll stop at nothing.'

'How do you know all this?' Theresa asked suspiciously.

'Don't look at me, chiquita. I ain't been slipping them hot tips. They've already come after me. My paternity suit made front page news. The blood test that proved I couldn't possibly be that baby's father rated just a couple of lines at the back of the paper. That's the way they operate. When you've been in the business as long as I have, you just hope and pray that people realize if all the sleaze they print about you were true, you wouldn't still be around.'

Shyly Debra Jo raised her hand and said, 'Y'all are making me feel ashamed. I buy those papers in the super-market every week. Eddie says I'm hooked on them. I read about all of you. When I came on the set the first day, I believed everything they told me was true. For me and my friends, reading that big stars like you have problems just like us made me feel better somehow.'

'Ah, yes, the tabloids, the great equalizer,' Alex said

sarcastically. 'You may be rich and famous but you too can get cancer, lose your husband to a younger woman, be caught shoplifting, have a kid arrested for selling coke. We all smell the same when we're covered in shit.'

'I guess I thought you were too big to care what was said about you.' Debra Jo was red with embarrassment. Alex still intimidated her. She was doing her best to please the director but sometimes he made her feel stupid, like one of those episodes of Masterpiece Theater where everybody talked with British accents and the story, when there was one, was almost impossible for a normal person to follow.

'Don't feel bad, Debra Jo,' Brandon said kindly. 'We're no different from you. I bet there's not a person in this room who can truthfully say he's never snuck a peek at the *Insider* while standing in line at the supermarket. That goes for just about everybody in the industry. We're all ready to dig in the dirt provided none of it clings to us, right?'

Debra Jo nodded gratefully. 'I guess. I just feel dumb. I didn't realize it could hurt you.'

'Well, it does,' Melissa's eyes filled with tears. She'd sat quietly all by herself through the meeting until now. 'It's OK what they say about me, but when they make my mom look stupid, it hurts a lot. I go to school and everybody's staring at me, like my mom's the slut of all time. It's so embarrassing. I wish they'd just leave us alone. They act like they know us but they don't know anything about us.'

'Oh, Missy, don't cry.' Debra Jo's face was stricken with guilt as she reached out and put her arms around her.

Julia felt sorry for the newest cast member. Probably she took this gig thinking it was going to be a lark. Now she was beginning to get a taste of the realities of the business.

'The *Insider* really scares me,' Melissa said. 'It's like they hate everything about Makeover. What if it really starts to hurt the show?'

'No,' Tim said decisively, 'it may be hurting some of you personally and I know that's hard to take, but it's not hurting the show. Stan's right, it's all part of the business. Bad publicity is better than no publicity. It drives up the ratings. The more they read, the more they watch; the more they think they know about you, the more they want to find out. Shirley, your TV Q has shot way up since the *Insider* spread. Sad but true, that's just par for the course.'

Shirley smiled wryly. 'My mama always used to say, "Be careful what you wish for, you just might get it." If I'd known it was going to be like this, I would have opted for rich and bypassed famous.'

'Hey, *compadres*, we can't just lie down and play dead,' Theresa persisted. 'We've got to go after these guys, get them before they get us.'

'You try that and you'll only make it worse,' advised Stan. 'Don't give them more to feed off. That only increases their circulation. Don't give them the satisfaction.'

The actors looked at each other uneasily. Julia looked at Marty. Obviously this answer was not enough. The atmosphere of mistrust and division had infiltrated their tight little group. If it were allowed to make further inroads, it would threaten the ensemble they had so carefully built. Each of the cards was important to the deck. Even the addition of a wild card, Debra Jo, seemed to be OK, but they would have to keep a close eye on morale or the whole house could come tumbling down. The cast depended on Marty and Julia to find the right key to make them whole again. She didn't know what to say. Come on, come on, she pleaded silently with Marty. Don't sit there like a Sphinx. Help me out here.

'You're in a hit show,' Marty spoke quietly and slowly. 'You're working when a lot of other people in this town can't get arrested. We're all having a good time on the set. Of course, the *Hollywood Insider* doesn't bother to print anything about that. We simply have to be on guard. We don't even know who their reporters are. They may try to get to you by any number of ways. Debra Jo, you should be especially careful. You're a newcomer to Hollywood and the tabs figure you don't know the rules. Don't talk to strangers on the street. Be careful what you say about the show. Warn your son, too. They may try to phone your home, pretend to be a colleague of yours, and pry some onset gossip out of Danny. That goes for all of you. Don't give out any information unless it's cleared through the network and studio public relations department.'

'Security's already tight here at the studio, but we'll beef it up,' Stan promised. 'Make sure all interviews are scheduled and that anyone with a press pass is legitimate press and not this scum sheet.'

Marty was gaining strength. 'We need to close ranks and

circle our wagons. From now on, don't talk to anybody except family or friends.'

'Who knows who your friends are these days?' Paul said with a sidelong glance at Brandon. 'Whom do you trust?'

'If we stop trusting each other,' Marty said with conviction, 'believe me, we'll have nothing left.'

'God, that was a tense meeting,' Julia commented as they were in the car whizzing down the freeway. 'I'm glad I'm just the writer and the tabloids don't think me glamorous enough to attack.'

'Don't be so sure. I'm thinking of spilling the beans on your Next Of Skin deal.' His tone was teasing but there was an edge to it.

'What, you mean like, "Makeover Creator Took Bribe of Underwear!"? I feel for Theresa and Shirley though. I just hope we can keep our happy little family from splitting into warring factions. Certainly Stan and Tim weren't all that reassuring with their focus on the bottom line. Listen, that was a nifty metaphor you came up with in there: "Circling the wagons." They all seemed to respond to that.'

'I must admit I did feel a little like Pa Cartright.'

'Not the most relaxing way to gear up for our first meeting with the elusive Charles Currie. Are you nervous?'

'No. Godamnit, can't you see I'm signaling to get over in the next lane,' he swore at a driver. 'Are you going to let me in or not?'

'What do you think he wants?' She looked at the pink slip she was clutching in her hand. 'C. Currie flying in from NYC. Dinner at Morton's, 8 p.m. Discuss future projects.'

'He wants to discuss future projects. Obviously.'

'Marty!' She whacked him on the knee.

'Jesus, Julia, I'm trying to drive in very heavy traffic. I really wish we had a sign in this car like they have on city buses, "Don't talk to driver while vehicle is in motion." '

'When was the last time you were on an LA city bus – 1973?' She tried to keep her tone light and joke him out of his bad mood. He said he wasn't nervous but he was hunched over the wheel and he looked a little green around the gills. 'Are you all right? You didn't say much in the meeting until the very end.'

He shrugged. 'You were handling it all right on your own.'

'No I wasn't. I was waiting for you to jump in and save me.'

'Right now I'm busy trying to save myself.'

'What's that supposed to mean?'

'Nothing. Believe me, you're doing fine. I'm really proud of you.'

'Will you stop saying that?' It came out more sharply than she meant it to. 'That's just an excuse to get me to do your job for you.'

'It's really your job now.'

'No, it isn't. We're in this together. I hate it when you drop off the edge of the earth like that, leaving me to pick up your shoes on the beach, as it were.'

'I just feel overwhelmed with dread, this strange sense of impending doom.'

'Great, that's great. I always advise meeting a VIP wearing doom and dread. Personally, I intend to change.'

'Leave me alone. I'm tired. Didn't sleep last night.'

'Look, let's get through dinner, do your usual snake-charming bit, then we'll go home and go straight to bed, I promise you. This is an important meeting, Marty. Charles Currie, the owner of the network. It could change our life.'

'I thought we did that last year. With you, everything's about to change our life. You're so busy reaching you can't even enjoy the changes that have already happened.' He turned off the freeway, suddenly, sharply, on to an exit ramp.

'What are you doing? This is the wrong exit.'

'Not for me. I'm going to see if I can find a convenience store, grab a cup of coffee.'

'Now? Before dinner?'

'Julia, I'm exhausted. I won't make it through this dinner if I don't have something to wake up my brain. Everything's fogged over.'

'No wonder you can't sleep.'

'Shut up. Just shut up for once, will you?' With a sharp right turn and a squeal of the brakes, he pulled into a Seven–Eleven. 'Stay in the car. I'll be right back.'

Julia sat in stunned silence, her body still reverberating from the force with which he had slammed the car door. What was wrong with him? One minute he seemed perfectly calm, the next he exploded with rage. Through the wind-shield she could see him already arguing with the clerk at the front counter, his mouth tightening with fury, his arms starting to wave in the air. Probably complaining about the coffee, the price, the temperature, the styrofoam cup, who knew? She put her head in her hands. Why was he always doing that? Taking out his frustration on some hopeless bozo who was clinging to the only job he could get without a high-school diploma. With Marty, if a sign was misspelled, immediately it had to be fixed, even if it was misspelled on purpose. Dew Drop In or All Nite Grocery always elicited a lecture from Marty on the preservation of the English language. A missing price on artichokes at the corner grocery store brought a tirade about keeping the customer informed. She could just hear him now. 'You advertise hot coffee, to go, quik. This coffee is cold. If you have to take the time to make it, it won't be quick. You don't have any takeout lids that fit these particular cups. If you can't deliver the goods, then remove the sign. And learn to spell. What is it with you people that you can't do the simplest job?' On and on and on.

She looked up. Oh God. Marty was collapsed over the counter. Oh my God. He was down on the ground. She threw open the car door and ran into the convenience store. Marty was lying on the floor with the Korean grocer bent over him, applying a wet paper towel to his head. 'What happened to him?' she cried.

'Sick, no breathe, not my fault.' The thin, anxious clerk, still gripping the cup of coffee, leaned in and haltingly attempted to explain, his smooth face knit with worry and resentment, undoubtedly already anticipating a lawsuit.

She crouched down beside her gasping husband. 'Marty, what's wrong?'

'Ground . . . dropped out from under me. Weak in the knees. Started to feel dizzy. Heart pounding. Leaned over to catch my breath, like you're supposed to when you feel faint? Next thing I know I'm on the floor.' He was clutching his chest, trying desperately to get the words out between gasps.

She tore open his shirt. She could feel his heart racing. She put her hand on his forehead. It was dripping with sweat. 'Dial 911,' she said to the clerk.

'No,' Marty's hand shot up to grab his sleeve. 'I'll be fine. I'm seeing my doctor in three days. Just let me lie here for a minute and catch my breath. Give me a sip of that coffee.'

The clerk brought the cup down to his lips, but Julia knocked it out of his hand. 'No coffee. Get him a glass of water. Cold water. Quickly!' The clerk scuttled away. 'You've had too much coffee already. Look at you, your whole body is shaking. Have you eaten anything at all today?'

'Yeah. Seafood crêpe. Lunch. But my stomach's churning. I think I'm going to throw up.'

'Maybe it's food poisoning.' She grabbed the paper towel and tried to blot his face. Sweat was pouring off him.

'I don't know. My skin feels like it's on fire. Needles sticking into me. My chest; Christ, Julia, it really hurts. Pain, white-hot, burning sensation. Spasms up my arm. I can't breathe. I think I'm having a heart attack.' He was clutching at the front of her blouse, frantically pulling her down to him. The clerk came running back with the water.

'Which arm?' she was screaming at him. The pale, worried face of the clerk swam in and out of focus. 'The left side, Marty? Damnit, which side?'

'Everywhere. Julia, help me, please. I think I'm dying.'

Chapter Thirty-five

The hair-raising ride to the hospital was a blur. The paramedics arrived at the convenience store, the stretcher was out and Marty was on it and being lifted into the ambulance before Julia had time to think. Even as she climbed in after him, an oxygen mask was being placed over his face and the doors slammed shut behind her.

She held his hand tightly as he stared up at her, too frightened to speak, his eyes flickering over her face as if studying it for the last time. She was searching his face, too, for some clue as to what was going on inside him. He had changed before her eyes, his color waxen, his sensual features drawn and constricted, the lips tight. It was like looking at a line drawing instead of an oil painting. He was still sweating profusely and there was a bitter, acrid smell to the sweat, something she had never smelled on him before. This was her fault. She had ignored all the signs. He had told her often enough he was at the breaking point and she hadn't believed him. Kept on pushing him for more meetings, more decisions, oh God, I'm sorry, I'll do anything, only please let him live.

The ambulance rattled through the streets, siren blaring, red light spinning, until it screeched to a halt at the emergency entrance. The emergency room was packed, but the medics lifted him on to a gurney and wheeled him through the mass of humanity waiting with sprained ankles, broken noses, cuts and minor burns, straight into a smaller room, where the wheels of the gurney were locked in place and curtains immediately drawn all around the bed. It was all happening so fast. That's why it's called an emergency, Julia told herself; it's urgent and must be dealt with quickly. But her level of fear was escalating as things were taken out of her hands.

A female doctor and several nurses clustered around

Marty, taking his blood pressure, hooking him up to futuristic-looking machines, then unlocking the wheels and sending him out the door and down the hall for an electrocardiogram. Julia stumbled after him, but a nurse stopped her to take her aside and ask her a barrage of questions. How it had happened? Where had it happened? Was her husband on any drugs? Did he have a history of illness? Julia was numb as she tried to give the nurse the right answers, but finally she cried out, 'Why are you keeping me here? I want to be with my husband, he's having a heart attack.'

'We don't think so, Mrs Turgov,' the nurse said calmly. 'We think it's an anxiety attack.'

'What do you mean?'

'It feels like a heart attack, many of the symptoms are the same as those of a coronary, but it's triggered by the mind and not the body.'

'Wait a minute. You're telling me it's all in his mind?' She felt like screaming at the stupidity of the woman. What were they trained for if they couldn't recognize a heart attack happening right in front of their very eyes. 'I don't believe you. You didn't see it happen. He was gasping for breath, he changed color, he had nausea. He's in terrible pain.'

'Yes, he's in pain. But he's not in danger, at least not life-threatening physical danger.'

What was the matter with this idiotic woman? She didn't even seem sympathetic. 'I don't believe you,' Julia repeated.

Neither did Marty, but after the electrocardiogram along with a battery of other tests, the hospital staff gave him a cheese sandwich and a glass of apple juice and sent him home. Marty was furious. 'Some health-care system we have in this country,' he railed. 'Enough tests to blow my Blue Cross for the rest of my life and they tell me it's nothing but stress. I've been mainlining stress, I thrive on it. The pain was real, the symptoms were there, it has to be something serious.'

'Wait and see what Dr Ross says,' she tried to assuage his fear and hers. 'You've got your annual check-up the day after tomorrow. I'm going with you. I want to tell Ross everything that happened.'

But Ross subjected Marty to the same intensive battery of

tests and gave him the same clean bill of health. He could lose a little weight, maybe watch his cholesterol a bit, but basically, for a man approaching fifty, he was in excellent shape. Then two weeks later, it happened again. The shortness of breath, the heart palpitations, the sweating, a fluttering in the throat and an inability to swallow.

'Jesus, Jules, it's come back,' Marty cried, as she watched him turn ashen and his features transform once again, Jekyll and Hyde, before her eyes. 'I'm going crazy. Do something, please!' She called Dr Ross who immediately made an appointment for him with a therapist. Maybe he was right, maybe they were all right, maybe it was panic.

Marty was ebullient as he left the therapist's office. 'Lorna's wonderful,' he exclaimed. 'Tall, blonde, beautiful, warm, nurturing. I already feel much more secure. She's so gentle and calm. With one of those soft, musical voices.'

'Well, that certainly makes me feel secure,' Julia said. 'She's everything I'm not.'

'She's also a lesbian.'

'Ah.' She wondered if her guilt and relief showed. Her parents dismissed the entire psychiatric profession. The Hudlows wouldn't dream of discussing their emotional problems with anyone, certainly not someone paid to listen. Claire believed if a problem really existed – and in her opinion very few of them did – they must be dealt with, on your own, and in secret. Probably her father placed going to a therapist in the same category as eating at a New York deli: Jew food, heavy, over-priced, and not good for the digestion. Julia had lots of friends in therapy, but she had to admit even the idea of it made her nervous. Part of her worried that any right-thinking, conventional therapist would blame her for Marty's problems. After all she had been neglecting him, pushing him too hard, a regular modern day Lady Macbeth.

'Does she know what's wrong?'

'Yep,' he said triumphantly. 'Diagnosis is anxiety disorder. I gotta admit, I'm a little disappointed. I thought I had something exotic, something special, you know? Now I find out fifteen per cent of the population suffers from this. It's second only to the common cold. Pretty simple.'

'Hey, listen,' Julia was trying to remain upbeat. In Hollywood, anxiety disorder surpassed the common cold. She'd read about it and it didn't sound that easy. 'What's wrong with a little anxiety. Keeps you on your toes and you've got to be on your toes if you're going to survive.'

'No, no, you don't understand,' he began to explain the difference between anxiety and anxiety disorder. 'Before every Friday night taping, you feel a little anxious, right? But once you're out there, on the floor, with the cameras rolling, you forget about it. If anything, a little extra added tension makes you do a better job, it means you care. But if you get so anxious, so dizzy, then you can't make it through the taping, you can't do the job, that's anxiety disorder.'

'So it's kind of a heightened sense of fear?'

He nodded with the zeal of the already converted. 'Fear without any real danger. Let's say I'm the Korean running that convenience store. Someone comes in with a stocking over his face, points a gun at me, and demands my money. The adrenalin starts shooting through me. Fight or flight. Nature's way of telling me I'm in danger. Normal panic. But let's say I'm just a customer who goes into said convenience store to buy a cup of coffee and suddenly adrenalin is coursing through me. My body is telling me I'm in danger when there's no danger evident. That's a panic attack. Simple really.'

Only it wasn't. Over the next month, for both of them, it was like a descent into the Snake Pit. Marty was put on a beta blocker. It blocked the panic attacks but it made him paranoid. He became obsessed with his body, what he was putting into it, what was coming out of it. Dr Ross had told him to cut down on fat to lower his cholesterol, but didn't fat affect the nerves and the brain? Was he somehow depriving his nerves and short circuiting his brain? Meat, meat was poisoning him because it was red. He must eat only white foods. Vegetables, his system was missing vegetables. He would rush out in the middle of the night to the twenty-four-hour Ralph's to get a pound of broccoli, cook it and eat it all at once. The drugs made his mouth dry. Julia offered him a stick of gum, but he refused.

'Gum is really bad for me right now.'

'Why?'

'Chewing makes my mouth tense. Could give me lock-jaw.'

The doctor switched him to an anti-depressant. He no longer felt anxious. He no longer felt much of anything. Except sad and tired. Julia wished he would get angry again, rant and rave at bad service, lecture someone on the misuse of a word, even scream at her. Instead he was frighteningly quiet. Polite, if a little spacey. This was no Marty she knew. It was like living with the male equivalent of one of the Stepford Wives.

He wasn't eating his usual bedtime snack of corn chips and guacamole. He wasn't eating much at all now. Julia wondered if she was going to have to start liquefying his food, a possibility that one of the books she'd read suggested as a last resort. If he was calm during the day, he was tormented at night. She woke to hear him screaming and thrashing about. 'What is it? What's wrong?' she cried, reaching out for him, but he pushed her away.

'Flashes of light, bright light. The room is moving, the walls are closing in on me, crushing me. I can't stop the zapping in my head.' He was frantic.

She didn't know what to do. He was so afraid he made her afraid. Turn on the radio. Music, something soothing.

Whip through the stations. FM. Classical. Pachelbel's *Canon*. All the rage a few years ago, it had become a cliché, but Marty said it reminded him of water. She opened the patio doors on to the deck. A light breeze blew in. Gently, she urged Marty out of bed. Come. Sit with me on the floor. They sank down together, her arms went around him. The music washed over them. He was clinging to her. She stroked his brow. 'I'm here, I love you,' she whispered to him, her hand moving back and forth over his skin, 'it's going to be all right.'

The next morning he felt better, but she insisted he call his therapist, Lorna. 'There's something very wrong here; this drug can't be helping you.'

'Lorna didn't prescribe this,' he told her. 'She's a therapist not a psychiatrist. This is Dr Ross.'

'Then get him on the phone.'

She went into the other room and surreptitiously picked up the extension phone. She listened to his halting, listless responses to Dr Ross's routine questions. No, he hadn't slept well, he'd had a bad dream, he was having a few flashes. In a calm, measured voice, Dr Ross suggested increasing his dosage and, to her amazement, Marty agreed that sounded like a good idea. She broke in on their conversation. 'What the fuck is going on here? This is a man who never smoked grass, who rarely drinks, is afraid of taking an aspirin, and you're giving him mind-altering drugs?'

'Well, I have the pharmaceutical encyclopedia here in front of me,' Dr Ross said reassuringly, 'and this is the drug suggested. Marty is not a small man and he may require more in order for his symptoms to be alleviated.'

'You're reading this out of a book?' Julia said in utter disbelief. 'Are you telling me you don't really know anything about this Aldous Huxley nightmare we're living in?'

'It's a system of trial and error,' the doctor said matter-of-factly. 'You just have to keep rotating the drugs until you find the right one.'

'I want him off this one,' Julia said with as much strength as she could muster.

'I think that would be a mistake. You haven't really given it time to work.'

'Now,' Julia shouted into the receiver. 'Right now.'

'It can't just be stopped. There's a possibility of a seizure if he isn't weaned off it slowly and carefully.'

Julia felt her blood turn cold. Seizure, my God. 'All right, then perhaps the book you have there in front of you can tell me how to get him off this fucking thing safely, the sooner the better.'

Julia couldn't talk to Marty any more. She wanted to tell him about the ever-increasing conflict between herself and Stan. She had won her point with the Kelly episode. 'There Is Nothing Like a Dame' drew over forty million viewers who responded favorably to raunchy Kelly making over men into women for the Houston Halloween drag ball. Makeover was being touted by critics as an All in the Family for the nineties, ready to take on any red hot issue and make it palatable to the American public. Now Stan was demanding equal time for Debra Jo. Julia was already tailoring her dialogue ultra-carefully, and Alex was just barely getting her through the few lines that she had each week. An episode built around Debra Jo would be much more difficult to pull off than the one featuring Kelly. Never mind Linda Earl's reaction to Debra Jo's expanding role. Julia felt like she was maneuvering a swinging rope bridge of diplomacy and tact with Linda right now while the network execs were pushing them to dump her from the series altogether. It was almost funny. She desperately needed to discuss this with Marty, but she couldn't. He'd lost his sense of humor along with his perspective.

Sometimes she looked at him and it was like seeing a stranger: his face, his body, his entire being seemed altered. *Night of the Living Dead. Invasion of the Body Snatchers.* Which B movie was it where aliens landed on earth and inhabited the bodies of human beings? Human husks, people pods? Cheap in terms of the special effects budget, but much creepier than any monster that Industrial Light and Magic had come up with. The people in the town looked and sounded the same but there was something weird about them. You never knew who you could trust; might be a human being, might be a pod. Marty was like that now.

Psychic pain, wasn't that the term for it? As though the very essence of him, his inner spirit, was somehow broken, torn apart. She alternated between wanting to hold him tight and cry with him, and wanting to grab him and shake him and tell him to snap out of it. But of course if he could snap out of it, he would.

The worst part of it was, she couldn't tell anybody about it. Her best friend, Diane Slater, was now living in Europe with her third husband and first baby. She never got to see Diane any more: the relationship had cooled when J.C. ended up playing Janine although she'd originally created the role for Diane. Even though Diane was pregnant at the time so it could hardly be called Julia's fault, she still felt guilty. It made her sad to think that what she thought was her closest friendship couldn't survive the television business.

Marty was insisting she keep quiet about his condition saying that if the network were to find out, they might decide he was unable to fulfil his producing duties and start looking to replace him. 'They can smell the dust on me,' he kept saying. She was having to do the work of two without letting anyone become aware of it. Any discussion of future projects had to be put on hold. Charles Currie had flown back to New York without meeting either one of them. Co-producing and writing the series was a huge responsibility; having to constantly cover for Marty was wearing her down.

Liam sensed there was something going on, but she couldn't talk to him about it. Waking up in the morning, lying next to Marty, when she knew she would be seeing Liam, she felt only dread and revulsion for what she was doing. How did I get here? This isn't me. Looking down at her sleeping husband, battling with his own inner devils, she thought: nobody deserves what I'm doing to this man. But the minute Liam opened the door to her, the moment he reached out to touch her, she was gone. What she'd thought was a gossamer web of desire between them was now so strong it seemed impossible that she could escape.

'You don't look too happy, girl,' J.C. stopped her coming out of the studio commissary. 'You're walking around with the weight of the world on those puny little shoulders.'

'That's what it feels like,' Julia admitted with a sigh.

'You want to come into my trailer for a little while and shoot the shit? Mac's away so I'm in no hurry to get home.'

Julia looked at her watch. They'd stopped early today, so Marty wouldn't be expecting her for a couple of hours.

'OK.' She loved J.C.'s trailer. It had all the star trappings, but J.C. had added her own personal touches: posters from her road shows; a hooked rug from her place in Nashville, the Lone Star Estate; a Texas flag. An actor's dressing-room is a home away from home and often reflects her personality. J.C.'s was messy and comfortable and lived-in, along with a hint of raunch.

She closed the door to the trailer and turned to give Julia a long, hard hug.

'What was that for?' Julia asked.

'You look like you need it.'

'I do.'

J.C. opened the door to her minibar and said, 'I'd give you a drink, but it's an early call tomorrow, so I shouldn't have one myself, and if you have one, I'll want one, so I'm giving you a mineral water, OK?'

'OK.' Julia had gotten used to her friend's thought processes.

J.C. poured them each a tall glass of Pellegrino and sat down. 'Boy, if my roadies could see me now. They think all this designer water is for pussies. Why drink water when there's real booze around? But I've learned I got to be careful. The "been there, seen it all, done it all" look is great for a singer, but it doesn't read so well on camera, so now I save my tequila drinking for Saturday nights. I shouldn't deprive you, though, but I'm mean and selfish that way.'

'It's all right. I don't want to drink either. Booze just makes me more depressed these days.' Julia sipped her water and stared off into space.

'Everything OK with you and Marty? He don't seem to be around much lately.'

'No, no, he's fine. Touch of the flu. I've been running back and forth with ginger ale and chipped ice. He's such a hypochrondriac anyway. I think he sees being sick as a sin and therefore some sort of guilty pleasure.' The minute she'd said it she wondered if it were true. Did she really think Marty's illness was a bid for attention? Or some kind of divine punishment for her affair with Liam?

'Tell me about it,' J.C. laughed. 'Mac's a big old bear when he gets even a cold. If his head hurts, he's convinced he has a brain tumor and is about to go crazy.'

'He must be thrilled with the success of *Telephone Road*.' Julia was eager to change the subject. 'It's been number one for months. Up for a Grammy. You two must be raking in the shekels.'

J.C. shrugged. 'I guess. He was so against me doing it, he's too bull-stubborn to say he likes it. Sometimes I think he'd rather be right than rich.' She studied Julia's face for a minute. 'There's something you're not telling me. Sure you don't want to talk about it?'

Since being on location in Houston, their relationship had deepened. Julia had started out protecting J.C., taking her under her wing, teaching her the ins and outs of the business as she had learned them herself from Marty. But J.C. knew more about real life. Julia wouldn't betray Marty's desire for secrecy, but there was one thing she needed to talk about.

'Out of the blue, Marty's fixating on the fact that we don't have any children. He lies there on the sofa, watching TV, flipping channels, and every time he sees a baby he bursts into tears. We decided when we got married this was what we wanted, and all of a sudden he's changing his mind on me. Now it's like I've cheated him of life experience, it's all my fault.'

'I know what you're talking,' J.C. said, and her voice had a note in it that Julia had never heard before. Bitterness. 'Mac still blames me and my plumbing. I guess men, as they

377

get older, start feeling broody just the way women do when they're young.'

'I guess. I've never felt it.'

'What?'

'Broody. Maternal. I never played with dolls. Just wasn't interested. I love my work too much. When I'm working, I forget who and where I am. Marty calls me, I don't even recognize his voice. If I had a kid, I'd probably forget to feed it.'

'Don't be silly,' J.C. laughed. 'I think you'd be a fine mom. You mother everybody on the show. You make all of us believe we can do our best and we end up being even better.'

'Thank God,' Julia said melodramatically. 'I am normal, after all. I do have maternal impulses, but they're all going into my work, nurturing the writers and the actors.' She laughed. 'Maybe you're right, but I doubt it.'

'You could have a child if you wanted, couldn't you?'

'Sure, at least I think so, but with Marty ill . . . I mean, it's only flu, but still, our lives are so complicated right now, it's hardly the best time to be thinking about getting pregnant.'

'Have you ever been pregnant?'

'Maybe, I'm not sure. I thought I might be just before Marty and I got married. I even thought about having an abortion, but then, I got my period, although it was so late it might have been an early miscarriage. Certainly we've never really tried.'

'I don't believe in abortion,' J.C. said.

'Not ever?' Julia put her glass down. 'Funny, we haven't talked about this before. I mean, I understand, you're in the country music business and it wouldn't be too smart for you to come out publicly as pro-choice, but surely that's not how you really feel?'

J.C. looked her straight in the eye. 'If you ever found out for sure you had no hope of having a kid, you'd change your tune pretty damn quick. A woman's body is not her own if she has no choice in the matter.'

Chapter Thirty-six

She had to do it. She just had to make it through her first featured role on the show without flubbing any of her lines. Of course now she knew learning her lines was the easiest part of the whole thing. Even hitting the taped marks on the floor wasn't that tricky once you got the hang of it (J.C. had given her some pointers). Remembering to do everything exactly the same way each time a scene was shot, that was the real tough patooty. Pick up the brush on this line, dip it in the blush, hold, stroke it on her cheek, then on another line, toss it in the air. Lucky she was playing herself. If she had to remember to be someone else plus all of the above, she would never make it through.

Hearing the band play the Makeover theme, live. The warm-up comedian's jokes tonight were centered around Debra Jo. The bleachers were packed. People had lined up for blocks to get inside and be part of the studio audience. She wished that Eddie and Beau could be here, but they weren't coming out until Christmas. Oh well, they would see 'her episode' – that's how she was already thinking of it – when it aired a few weeks from now. At least Danny was in the stands, along with a couple of his pals from school. He loved having a mom who was a TV star. He liked the money, too. When Debra Jo held that first check in her hand, she nearly died, thinking they must have added some extra zeros by mistake.

She was determined to stick to her plan to live simply in LA and save the money for the kids' college fund. But that was hard. Danny saw LA as one big Toys R Us. He wanted every electronic gizmo going and it was hard for her to say no when the other kids had them, too. The clothes kids wore out here made the Houston Galleria look like J.C. Pennys. Two-hundred-dollar sneakers. Designer sweats. Leather jackets and matching pants. Leather, for kids!

Debra Jo firmly believed that you shouldn't be allowed to wear leather until you were old enough to drink and vote.

'Quiet on the set.' Her stomach lurched.

'Sound.' She was nervous.

'Sound rolling.' Why had she thought this would be easy?

'Speed.' She had the first line.

'Action.' Okay, D.J., this is it!

Then the sound of laughter coming from the live audience. Washing over her like the warm waves of the Gulf of Mexico. People had always thought she was funny, even though she could never understand why. Now it was OK, she was supposed to be funny.

The filming went by as if in a dream. They shot a couple of scenes twice so that they could edit the best takes. Debra Jo kept her cool. She said her last line, the audience was applauding her, Alex gave her a thumbs up, and her part was over. She stood by, watching J.C do the signature final moments of the show, singing alone in the shop, until the phrase, 'it's a wrap', signaling the end of the show. Everyone was cheering, her fellow cast members were hugging and congratulating her. The big boss, Stanfield King, shook her hand and introduced her to his gorgeous wife. J.C. kissed her on both cheeks and told her, 'You did real good. A lot better than me the first time out, I can tell you. You didn't seem nervous at all.' Only Linda Earl was less than enthusiastic, but she acted stuck-up to everybody these days, spending a lot of time alone in her dressing-room and refusing to eat with the others in the commissary.

'I'm totally impressed with you,' Danny was beaming from ear to ear, his pals in tow. 'Mom, you were awesome.' The boys were excited to have a chance to meet Brandon Tate. Brandon had promised Debra Jo that if the filming went well, he would take her out for a real Hollywood-style night on the town. She'd got over her shyness with him and he had taken her under his wing, as if he really cared whether she succeeded or failed at this, the most important change in her life. She'd brought a fancy dress, just in case, and now she would get a chance to wear it. Danny was spending the night with his friend, Tucker, so she could stay out late. Debra Jo wasn't positive that she liked Tucker. For a twelve-year-old, he had a sly, mean little mouth and off-kilter eyes, but he came from a well-to-do family. She'd met Tucker's dad, they lived in Bel Air, so

Danny should be safe. Besides, he was almost a teenager. She had to learn to trust him away from her, at least for one night.

'Give me some sugar, son,' she planted a kiss on his face before he wiggled out of her embrace, embarrassed to have his mother manhandling him in front of his buddies. Too bad. She wanted to be sure she left her mark on him.

There was the usual wrap party for family and friends in the green room, but Brandon quickly spirited her away. 'LA's not a late-night town like New York. If we want to have dinner, we need to leave now.' They hopped into his vintage Cadillac convertible and sped, top down, to a popular industry dining spot on La Brea. If it were a Monday night, Brandon had told her, he would be taking her to Mortons, on the Sunset Strip, but instead they were going to La Brea. Debra Jo knew that half the women in American would give anything to change places with her right now on her Hot Date with the Hollywood's King of Love. Goodness, she was actually starting to think in tabloid headlines.

There was a crowd of people waiting out front of the restaurant. Debra Jo wanted to let them know they didn't have a hope in hell of getting in. Already, she knew La Brea was one of those places where it took six weeks to get a reservation. Unless you were Brandon Tate. The restaurant was full, but as they went through the front door, every head in the place turned to look. All too late, Debra Jo realized that her black, low-cut cocktail dress, was totally out of place. No matter how expensive the food, the dress code was California casual. Oh, no. Two photographers were moving in to take their picture. Brandon whipped off his suede blazer and slipped it on her. 'I love the dress, it's wonderful on you, but this makes for a hot combination. Lingerie and leather, sort of Malibu Madonna.'

Studying the menu, the combinations of food were equally exotic. Debra Jo would never have thought of putting these tastes together in a million years. Grilled salmon with chocolate and fresh strawberries, scallops with apple crème fraiche. Lobster-stuffed ravioli and black pepper pappardelle with shreds of stewed rabbit. Fresh artichoke with warmed goat's cheese in leek and fennel broth. Didn't they have any nachos? She decided to let Brandon do the ordering for both of them. Brandon chose the wine and then suggested they each have a Kir Royale as an aperitif.

'This is good,' Debra Jo said, downing it instantly. It was obviously booze and she was nervous.

'Champagne and cassis. I thought you'd like it.'

'Tastes like grape juice and club soda, but with a kick.'

Brandon laughed. 'That's what I like about you, Debra Jo. That's what makes you different. You're real.'

'Thank you.' What did he mean? What were human beings if not real?

'Is everything all right?'

'Perfect.' Normally she had the appetite of a truck driver but she was too excited to eat. The procession of famous names and faces by their table, idols from the past and present, kept her from paying attention to the food. Studio heads, agents, movie stars, they all stopped to pay homage to Brandon Tate and to be introduced to Debra Jo Fawcett. Like one cover of *People* magazine after another. All the stars seemed to be much smaller in the flesh than they appeared up on the big screen, and at the same time, larger than life, somehow. Her best friend, Jackie, was fond of saying, 'Underneath the façade, movie stars are people just like you and me, only with advantages.' But it was hard to find even a blemish in this sea of blinding teeth, strong jaws, and perky breasts. Maybe if she really got to know them . . . but then, she'd known Brandon for several months now and he still seemed perfect. A legendary model whose face Debra Jo recognized not only from *Vogue* but from a number of rock videos draped herself over Brandon. She was spun-gold blonde and the walking embodiment of what Jackie called 'the three t's': tall, tanned, and toned. Her stomach was flat enough for women in *National Geographic* to wash clothes on. The rest of her was all limbs and hair.

'Hi, Bran, how ya doin'?' Bran? Brandon introduced Debra Jo. The model's eyes flicked over her, cutting her down to size, and dismissing her as competition, at least in the sexual sweepstakes. Under the bird's nest hairdo, Debra Jo could see the gears shifting into, 'I'll be medium nice to you. You're no threat but you can't do anything for me either.'

'Love your show. Not that I have time to watch. How do you like LA compared to Houston?'

'It's wonderful. I worry about the crime rate in our

neighborhood, though. I'm out here with my son, you know.' See, I'm a mother. No threat at all.

'Oh, no problem. You just have to surround your place with white light.'

'Really? Is that part of the Westech service?'

'No. I mean, the white light you carry with you. Most of us have it, although Bran's is one step higher. His light is gold.'

'Ah.' Debra Jo had no idea how else to respond.

'So give me a call,' she turned her attention back to Brandon. 'B.J. and I have split. I need you to console me.' With a kiss, and a wave of octopus tentacles, she was gone.

Brandon laughed. 'Don't mind her, she skips the stratosphere, that one. More wine?'

'Please.'

'Is your pasta all right?'

'I think so. I've never had black spaghetti before. What makes it black?'

'Squid ink.'

She put her fork down. She'd seen enough Jacques Cousteau specials. 'I better save room for dessert.'

A tall, reddish-haired man with bulging blue eyes stopped to say hi. 'Debra Jo, how are you?'

'Fine,' she tried to place him.

'How's Danny doing?'

'Great.' She must know him if he was asking about Danny.

'What school's he at again?'

'Oh, he's doing real well at . . .'

Brandon put a hand on her arm and interrupted. 'Excuse me, if you want dessert, you better be thinking about it now.'

'Catch you later,' the man said and melted away.

'Do you know that guy?' Brandon asked.

'I'm not sure. Why, do you?'

'No. He's probably OK, but you need to be careful, Debra Jo. You shouldn't give out information about Danny's school. You don't want someone tracking him down for an interview.'

'Oh, no.' She shivered then, spotting someone across the room, 'Is that Goldie Hawn and Kurt Russell?'

'Looks like them. You want to be introduced?'

'Please, please,' she was half-way out of her chair, when Brandon stopped her.

'Hang on, sit tight. I'll give them a wave and they'll come over.'

In between celebrity drop-ins, Brandon regaled her with tales. He had the true actor's gift for storytelling, a few names dropped here and there, embellishment just barely to the point where it strained belief. He kept her either enthralled or laughing all the way through dinner.

They went on to Stellini's for dessert (the owner was a business partner to an agent at CAA), on to the Monkey Bar, dropped into the VIP area at Roxbory to dance for a bit, then they were in the car and speeding toward Topanga Canyon. It was three o'clock in the morning but Debra Jo couldn't resist seeing where he lived and Brandon promised to drive her home afterwards. Just at the crest of one of the tallest mountains, set into the hillside, looking as though it had been carved out of the mountain itself, was a palatial Spanish ranch-style adobe hacienda. It had a spectacular view looking down toward the San Fernando Valley. Brandon threw open the doors to the terrace and she went straight out to look over the edge.

The drop-off took her breath away. The night sky was studded with stars, the mountains jutting sharply up into the sky surrounded by a hazy glow, the lights of the city far off in the distance. Brandon handed her another brandy and stood behind her, the two of them looking out over the panorama.

She was very aware of his presence behind her. He smelled wonderful, a sharp, tangy male smell, a mixture of leather from his jacket and the sweet spice of his natural body so close to hers. She felt the warmth of his breath on the back of her neck. Her heart was pounding so loud she could actually hear it reverberating in her ears. He lifted her hair and let his lips brush against the soft exposed skin of her neck. One little touch and her entire body ignited. She was afraid to move. His arms went around her, his hands just below her breasts. Trembling, she leaned back against him. He whispered in her ear, 'I want to kiss you, Debra Jo. Is that all right? I want to turn you around, take you in my arms, and kiss you.' She nodded mutely. Slowly he turned her to face him. She couldn't look at him, it was too intense, but he lifted her chin up and brought her lips to meet his.

His tongue sought hers and she moved her body in to him, melting, melting.

He picked her up in his arms and carried her into the bedroom, just like Ted Danson did with Shelley Long on Cheers. She was in heaven. They were in his bedroom, their arms wrapped around each other, kissing again, deeply. His mouth went to her ear, tracing its outline, and she sighed with pleasure. 'I'll be back in a minute, darlin',' he whispered, 'and then I'm going to undress you slowly, piece by piece.' She was left there, quivering with desire, aching for him to do just that, undress her, slowly, piece by piece. But what if he saw her body and no longer wanted her? What if the fantasy was over before it had started? Quickly she got out of her clothes and climbed into the enormous bed. When he came back, he was wearing a green silk robe, exactly the color of his eyes. He stopped when he saw her and in one swift movement, took off the robe. She peeked around the edge of the sheet. He was just as she had imagined him to be, so handsome and so huge. He sat on the edge of the bed.

'Are you going to be shy with me?'

'I don't know what to do,' she stammered. 'I don't know how to please someone as . . . experienced as you. I don't know any tricks. I'm afraid you'll be disappointed.'

He leant over and kissed the tip of her nose. 'You could never disappoint me. Nothing could please me more than to pleasure you tonight. Let me make you happy, that's all I need.' Delicately, he rolled the sheet away from her, leaving her nude body completely exposed. Instinctively her hands went to her breasts and crotch but he took her wrists and gently held them above her head. 'You are so lovely,' he said, his eyes sweeping up and down her body. 'You're so real.'

Real. There was that word again.

'Real breasts,' holding her wrists with one hand, he let the other move down to stroke her breasts, cupping them, caressing them. 'Soft and round, not hard.' His hand followed the indentation of her waist down to the curve of her hip. 'Nice cushiony hips.'

'I'm trying to lose a couple of pounds,' her voice caught in her throat as his hand slid between her legs and then moved back up to her nipples.

'What for? They're so welcoming. Makes me want to dive

right in and lose myself in you.'

'I'm sorry about the scar.' She wished she could hide the evidence of her Caesarean.

'I'm not. You've given birth, you've created life, it's magic, it's miraculous.' He bent down and let his lips slide up the scar and down, up and down. She was in ecstasy. It reminded her of one of her favorite movies, *Shirley Valentine*. When Shirley's sexy Greek lover kissed her stretch marks, the women in the movie theater sighed *en masse*. Of course, maybe Brandon had seen the same movie. So what, he was kissing her down there and it felt heavenly. His mouth was moving in circles, his tongue painting a personal design on her belly, moving lower and lower, looking for her center, his fingers joining the search, finding her, opening, fingers then mouth, mouth then fingers, until she couldn't tell the difference. His tongue flicking inside her, his hand entering her. For one brief moment, a crazy thought flooded her. Brandon Tate, *the* Brandon Tate, is going down on me. If only Jackie could see this. Then all possibility of thought vanished as she gave herself over to the unbelievable sensation. Her hands went to his head, clutching his hair, that thick, sexy, famous head of hair, twisting her fingers in it, pulling on it, shoving herself closer to his mouth, up and down, back and forth, the series of melting circles getting smaller and smaller and deeper and deeper until she exploded like the Fourth of July at Six Flags under Texas.

Finally he came up for air, his mouth glistening with her. 'Baby, you're a little fire cracker. You don't have any trouble getting off, do you?'

'Nope.' That was one of the things she was proud of. That part of her body worked like a charm. Then instantly she was insecure again. 'I feel kind of inadequate. Shouldn't I be doing something here?'

'Oh, honey, you don't know what a gift you are. You're so responsive. I touch you here,' her nipple sprang immediately to attention. 'Or here,' she was positively flowing. 'Or here,' he kissed her and she found herself moaning. 'Now I am going to come inside you and make love to you until we can't do it any more.'

He was the one who was forced to give up first. They made love four times, each more explosive than the last. 'I adore making love with you,' he whispered, kissing her gently on each eyelid before his own closed. Too excited to sleep, she lay next to him and let her mind float free. They had done all the things she'd ever seen on any X-rated video. All that and more. He was really good at this, so expert, so skilled. He must have had hundreds, even thousands of women, but still, he wanted her.

How was she ever going to tell Eddie? She spun a few variations. 'I can't help it, I've changed. I'm not the stupid little girl you married, Ed. I belong in Hollywood and I'm going to marry Brandon Tate.' 'I realize this will come as a shock, but I want a divorce. I'm about to become Mrs Brandon Tate.' 'Jackie, you are never going to believe this. Brandon has asked me to marry him. Will you help me find the right way to break the news to Eddie?'

PAUL GREEN KEEPS WIFE LOCKED UP!
PART OF ANCIENT CULT RITE

Makeover star Paul Green has a shocking secret lurking in his private life. He and his wife are members of a bizarre male-dominated religious cult. The sexy comedian's wife must bow to pressure from both her husband and her religion and adhere to strict rules and regulations which govern every minute of her waking life. Like thousands of other followers of this strange sect, she has been forced to:

(1) Take a new foreign name. Her real name is Carol, now she must be called Chaya.

(2) Adhere to a rigid dress code. She is not allowed to wear pants or to show any cleavage. She must wear long sleeves and the length of her skirts is dictated by rules of the cult. Her head must be covered. Like many others belonging to this sect, Paul does not want his wife inspiring lustful thoughts in other men who should have their minds on more lofty business.

(3) Eat only special, proscribed foods. Paul and his family follow a strange diet based on ancient rules and regulations which forbid the eating of certain foods. Their kitchen had to be completely renovated in order to accommodate their weird tastes.

And that's not all. For a full twenty-four hours each week, they are not allowed to answer the phone, turn on a light, drive a car or listen to music.

Even their sex life is dictated by the tenets of this bizarre sect. For certain days every month they are not allowed to sleep in the same bed. Women must be kept apart and men may not even shake hands with them. Can this be a called a normal family lifestyle? Friends and members of the Make-over company are wondering if Paul's marriage can survive the strain.

A source close to the *Insider* says, 'Very few people have met Paul's wife. Paul insists a woman's place is in the home with the kids. Those who have seen her say she could be a beautiful woman but the way she dresses makes her look like a matron of fifty. We've never seen her real hair. For all we know, she might be bald. We're talking about a young woman here, barely thirty years old.'

Chaya is rarely seen at Hollywood parties. She never travels on the road with Paul when he does his stand-up concerts. She never even comes to the Friday night taping of the wildly successful sit-com her husband is starring in. Is Paul so ashamed of his wife he has to keep her hidden away?

Paul defends his unusual relationship with: 'My wife has more important things to do than accompany me on the road or watch my show on television. Our life together is separate from my work and that is how it should be. We do our best to keep the media out of our private lives. We don't want our kids' heads turned by dollar signs and the moral quagmire of Hollywood.'

But others view the marriage with suspicion. 'Privacy is one thing, obsession is another. Paul is a control freak. We're not living in the Middle Ages. This is the nineties. Women are supposed to be independent. What's next for Chaya, a chastity belt?'

Paul skyrocketed to stardom with Makeover. His first feature film, *Shooting Blanks*, did well at the box office. His professional future seems assured. But his personal life may be in trouble.

A spokesperson for Paul Green issued this statement: 'Paul is a practicing Jew. Judaism is a recognized religion that has been around for centuries. In fact, much of Christianity, the religion followed by the majority of Americans, is based on Judaism. There is nothing weird or bizarre about it.'

Chapter Thirty-seven

'You happy now?' Paul waved the *Insider* front-page article in Brandon's face. 'They finally got me.'

'Guess you're not as boring as I thought, New York.' Brandon let out a whistle. 'Your story got better placement than my paternity suit, right between "Granny Gives Birth to Two-Headed Baby" and "Elvis Is Alive in Bill Clinton".'

'It's not funny,' Paul raged. 'OK, so I'm a Jew. I'm also a citizen of the United States. I feel like I'm in a time-warp pogrom in Czarist Russia: people spying on me, tapping my phone, taking aerial photographs of my house. I'm a comedian, an actor. Why don't they go after some slimy politician? There have to be a lot more dangerous people out there worthy of their attention.'

'The real danger is when you get a politician who's also an actor,' Brandon quipped. 'Ronald Reagan. Never knew if he was really the President or just playing one.'

'This is all just one big joke to you, isn't it? You don't have a reputation to uphold, but I do. Now everybody in middle America thinks I'm a sexist Svengali who keeps my wife in sack-cloth and ashes, pregnant and chained to the stove.'

'Well, she is about to bear your fourth child, isn't she?' Brandon started to laugh, but stopped at the look on Paul's face. 'Take it easy, New York. Believe me, this is big news today, but everybody will have forgotten about it by tomorrow. OK, maybe not tomorrow, but give it a couple of weeks.'

'What do you care? You've been waiting for me to look like an asshole along with the rest of you.'

'Hey, enough of this, all right, buddy?' He held out his hand to Paul. 'You and I have been feuding for too long. I'd like to be the one to extend the olive branch. We've got a much more serious problem here. The shit is flying all over the place now and there's practically no one on the show who hasn't been hit by it. I figured Theresa was just being paranoid at first, but now I think she may be right. Someone close to us has to be leaking information to the *Hollywood Insider*.'

'Well, now we know it's not me,' Paul said sharply.

'Can I buy you a drink and we'll talk?'

'I don't think so,' Paul regarded him with suspicion. 'I'm not into male bonding. Hanging out at bars is not my style.'

'No? Well, maybe it should be. You want to know what Mr and Mrs America think, there's only two places to find out: Oprah Winfrey or a sports bar.'

'I don't know.' Paul was reluctant. Could this be a set-up? Brandon was looking at him expectantly, his hand still outstretched.

'Look, you and I are the only two men on the show. The women are going snaky about the *Insider* onslaught. Even Julia, who's usually a rock, is starting to show the signs of strain. I think we need to be together on this.'

'All right. I agree with you as far as that.' He tentatively shook Brandon's hand.

'Great, then let's go hoist a few. Come on, you can stick to ginger ale if you want. I've got an idea for the show I want to talk to you about.'

'I really should get home. I hate leaving Chaya on her own unless I have to. She's been kind of on edge waiting for this baby to get born.'

'She's not due for another two weeks, isn't that what you said?' Everybody on the set had been primed for the birth, ready to halt production so that Paul could rush to his wife's side. He insisted on being close to a telephone every minute of the day.

'Yeah, but I'm worried. She looks like she's ready to pop. Right now she's as big as the Imax. Sorry, I shouldn't have said that, but the *Insider* has made the atmosphere at home pretty tense. You know what? An extra hour won't hurt. Sure, you can buy me a drink. Where do you want to go, Fracas? It's right nearby.'

Brandon snorted. 'No way, José. That place is a meat market. The *Insider* will think we're having an affair. Now that could really destroy your reputation. And mine. No, I'm going to force you to do the macho thing. Take you to a real bar, the Silver Saddle. Lots of smoke, hard liquor, it's a real billiard hall, not one of these LA-hip pool pubs.'

'You didn't let me win, did you?' Paul asked anxiously as they made their way through the noisy, smoke-filled room, back to the table, after shooting a couple of rounds of pool.

Brandon laughed. 'You know, for a fast-talking big city boy, you are one insecure guy. No, I did not let you win. I admit, pool's not my game, but I'm usually pretty good at it. You beat me fair and square.'

They had a table off in a corner, away from the big TV screen and the curious eyes of other patrons. Brandon was a regular at the Silver Saddle and most people knew to leave him alone, but no point in putting himself on view. He signaled for the waitress who strutted over wearing a suede halter, cut-off jeans and cowboy boots. She had dark roots and a long, bleached ponytail. Brandon sized her up in one quick look while she tried hard to stay cool and not ask him to autograph a cocktail napkin.

'I'll have a couple of shots of Tequila Gold, darlin',' he flashed her his killer smile, then turned to Paul. 'You want to try it? Strong stuff. J.C.'s got me hooked on it. Has to be the gold though. The silver tastes thin in comparison.'

'Sure,' Paul nodded, his eyes sliding after the waitress as she walked away, her butt cheeks fighting to remain inside the frayed edges of her shorts. Brandon didn't watch her go. Apparently he'd appraised her and dismissed her with that one initial glance and she'd been found wanting. Paul wondered why. Maybe, given the paternity suit, he'd sworn off waitresses for good.

'Where'd you learn to play pool like that?' Brandon asked.

'Jackson Heights. Queens.' They were still not completely comfortable with each other, but the game had relieved some of the tension. 'The pool hall was on my way home from school. Used to stop in and shoot a few. Had to find some way to be accepted. I was the only Jew in a neighborhood of Irish and Italians. Don't ask me why my folks decided to move there. Made me doubly ostracized in high school. Jewish and a brain.'

The waitress bounced back with their drinks and a basket of peanuts in the shell. The Silver Saddle was the kind of place where you were supposed to open the peanuts with your teeth and spit the shells on the floor. 'Thank you,

392

darlin',' Brandon said. The waitress giggled. He shoved one of the shotglasses toward Paul and lifted the other to his lips. The waitress hovered. 'Anything we can help you with, darlin'?'

She brought the tip of her ponytail forward and chewed on it. 'Um . . . well, is everything all right?'

'Give us a few minutes to find out and you'll be the first to know.'

'Sure thing . . . darlin'. You, too, Troy, I mean Paul,' she giggled at her own bravado and boldly bounced away.

Brandon raised his glass again. 'To the buddy system.'

'*L'chaim,*' Paul said. Brandon downed the tequila in one gulp and Paul did the same. It had an odd taste, smoky but not unpleasant. Reminded him of every bad novel he'd read about Mexico.

'So you made it through high-school angst,' Brandon smiled, 'and now you're living Revenge of the Nerds.'

'I've always known how to survive. I've been a bullshitter all my life. Now it's actually working for me. They like that out here.'

'You can say that again.' Brandon tossed back his next shot and Paul did the same.

'I've always been a funny guy, only now I get paid for it instead of being sent to detention. You start out making your friends laugh. Then all of sudden you're being paid big bucks to make strangers laugh. It's been so easy that I feel a little guilty, you know?'

'Why?' Brandon regarded him with lazy amusement. He signaled for the waitress to bring them another round.

'I used to be a doorman at the Improv.'

'A doorman?'

'Well, I ended up playing there, of course. But I started as a doorman. So did Keenan Ivory Wayans. Now we're doing TV and movies and making an obscene amount of money while most other poor schmucks are chained to a desk, nine to five, working their asses off just to meet the next car payment. I can afford to lease two luxury cars . . .'

'Wait a minute,' Brandon put the shotglass down with a bang. 'You don't own that car?'

'I like leasing,' Paul shrugged. 'In New York, I never bothered with a car. When I'd fly out to LA for a spot on Carson and later, Leno, I always rented. The habit just stuck. You don't have to pay insurance. If it breaks down, they give you a new one. I've got enough responsibilities in real life without owning a car. Besides, this is a great car. It's got a CD player, a sunroof, a cellular phone. Although I have to tell you it's hard to drive and deal at the same time. Like patting your head and rubbing your stomach, you know?'

'This is LA,' Brandon said. 'You live here now, you're putting down roots. Are you and Chaya still renting?' Paul nodded. 'Oh, man, give your kids a break. Buy a house with a view and pool.'

'I can't deal with open space and I'm allergic to chlorine.'

'Then at least get your own car. You must need it for deductions. It's Porsche time, pal.'

'You sound like my accountant. Anyway, the point I'm making is that what I do is easy. I can't claim to be an abused child, I don't come from despair, I didn't have to work very hard to get here.' Paul crunched a peanut shell into a fine powder and pushed it into a pile in the center of the table. 'I feel guilty.'

Brandon laughed. 'Do you remember that fight we had on the set last season? When you told me that stand-up is more honest than doing a series? I was pissed off when you said that. I thought you were just farting around and wasting everybody's time, but the results are worth it. When it comes to comedy, you're a genius.'

Paul ducked his head. 'Yeah, well, I wasn't always sure where it was going. Making the crew laugh strokes the ego and J.C.'s right, I have a big ego that demands extra stroke time.'

'I think what you do is hard, much harder than what I do,' Brandon said seriously. 'I trained to be an actor and I happen to think I'm pretty good on film. But the fact of the matter is, you can take somebody with an interesting face right off the street, put them in a film with a good script and a clever director and, if you shoot them right and edit carefully, you can create a film actor, maybe even a movie star. As a stand-up comic, you're out there, all on your own, isolated in a spot. The audience is restless and rowdy and knocking back the booze and you're right, most of them are thinking about making the next car payment or whether they're going to get laid tonight.'

Paul leant forward. He was surprised how accurately Brandon had pegged his former life. The waitress set their drinks in front of them and they each downed another shot.

'You're teetering on the high wire,' Brandon continued. 'No script, no character to hide behind. The audience either laugh or they don't. If they don't, you fail. Right then and there. No "we'll fix it later in the editing" or, "sweeten it with a laugh track." That's life or death, man.'

'Maybe, but what real contribution am I making?' Paul tried to focus his thoughts. The first shot of tequila had appeared to have no effect on him, but the minute he drank the next, he seemed to have gone from sober to pissed in about thirty seconds.

'You mean, what are you doing about world hunger?'

Paul nodded. 'Something like that.'

'So call up Whoopi and Robin and do a benefit. Hell, I think you're already performing a social service. A good laugh is better than a good shit. Or even a night of great sex. Don't let the *Insider* know I said that. It's a release. It brings people together and at the same time takes us out of ourselves. Alone, in a hotel room, on location somewhere, after a bout of marathon sex with some faceless face and matchless body. She gets up, goes home; I'm left on my own. I flip on the TV and watch old reruns of Saturday Night Live or SCTV. That's when the real release comes.'

Paul was trying to follow Brandon's line of reasoning and at the same time formulate his own. 'I guess what I'm trying to say here is the fact that it's been so easy is now hard to handle. Overnight, I've gone from being eccentric and quirky, an acquired comic taste, to mainstream, a household name. I've got a Winnebago for a dressing-room this year, complete with TV, VCR, another CD player, and a minibar. I don't even feel comfortable in it, but my agent says I have to take it because the perks are part of the image. In addition to my agent, I've got a business manager, an accountant, a lawyer. I'm incorporated now and I'm saving like crazy because I don't know how long this will last. I've got a press agent and a personal assistant. Not to mention fifty million women who want me to go to bed with them. Women who wouldn't have given me a second look in high school are now sending me their underwear.'

'Used or new?' Brandon raised an amused eyebrow. 'You poor guy. The seduction of Hollywood is the ultimate fuck.' He studied Paul for a moment and then said, 'What do you do when you want to be wild?'

'Wild?' Paul said blankly.

'Yeah, have a little fun. Not be so neurotic.'

'What do you want, I'm a Jew, I was born with a double set of neuroses.'

'And guilt in triplicate,' Brandon laughed. 'The way I see it, you've finally got all these perks and you're not even allowing yourself to enjoy them because you feel guilty about having them.'

'True.'

'Or maybe you're afraid to enjoy it because you worry you'll wake up tomorrow and it'll all be gone. That's a legitimate fear. You've got to be strong enough within yourself to know you can live with that possibility. But not to take advantage of it while you've got it is a useless form of self-flagellation. It doesn't help the people who don't have it and it's not doing you any good either.'

'Maybe you're right,' Paul said slowly. He felt relaxed for the first time in weeks and he had to admit what Brandon was saying made a lot of sense.

'I'm willing to bet that's why you've been so antagonistic toward me right from the beginning. You see me as lazy, you think I take my cock more seriously than my work, am I right?'

'Not exactly.'

'I didn't become a star because I like to fuck. Now I'm not trying to play devil's advocate here to your Dr Faustus, but this is your time on earth and if you can't enjoy it, even a little, then what's the point?'

Paul didn't know how to respond to that so he changed the subject. 'So what's your idea for the show? You said you had something you wanted to talk to me about.'

'Yeah, I want to do a weekly segment called Jock Talk. Just you and me. A couple of minutes where Travis and Troy get together and shoot the shit about sports. I've already run the idea past Julia and she loves it, but she doesn't want to write it. She wants us to improvise it. Now that scares the hell out of me, but I'm willing to give it a try if you are. You're the master of improv, Paul. We'd choose a different sport each week and just go wild with it.'

'But I don't know anything about sports.'

'You play a mean game of pool. Anyway, that's the point. Neither does Troy. That's what makes it funny. Although I think it would be great if every once in a while Troy surprised Travis. The way you did by beating me at pool. Maybe Troy has certain bits of nickel knowledge about the history of sports so that he can sharpshoot Travis.'

'Yeah,' Paul's eyes lit up, 'like, for instance, why is it called the World Series when until 1992 it had never been played outside the US?'

'I don't know. Why is it called the World Series?'

'Because the very first series was sponsored by a now defunct newspaper called the *New York World*.'

'Exactly.'

'This is a good idea,' Paul said. 'I like this idea. It could make a great routine.' He leaned forward, took off his baseball cap, scrunched his hair and began, 'What if . . .?'

'Troy, hey Troy, over here,' a patron of the bar came lurching toward their table.

'*Oy vay*,' Paul mumbled under his breath, 'I really hate this. I wish they wouldn't call me Troy, my name is Paul. This is my worst nightmare. I don't want to get known as a TV actor, be stuck on Makeover for the next ten years, until people can only see me as Troy.'

'I know what you mean,' Brandon concurred. 'Next stop, dinner theater in Florida.' The man was hanging over them.

With his three-day growth of beard, earring in one ear, and loose shirt hanging out over his jeans, he looked like he'd seen *Die Hard* once too often. 'My wife loves you, Troy,' his breath was in danger of setting the table on fire.

'That's nice,' Paul said politely. His head felt fuzzy. He wished this guy would go away.

'She wants to fuck you.'

'I see. That's interesting.'

Now he leaned in toward Brandon. 'She used to want to fuck you, but now it's Troy.'

'Well, that's life,' Brandon said. 'Now why don't you head back where you came from.'

'No,' the drunk blurted, shifting back to Paul. 'I gotta get your autograph. Take it home to the wife.'

'Forget it Paul,' Brandon muttered.

'No, no, it's all right.' Anything to get this asshole to leave them alone. He scrawled his name on a cocktail napkin and held it out.

'No, this, Troy, how about this?' The man shoved the *Insider* article under Paul's nose.

Paul recoiled. 'Get out of my face.'

'Is this shit in here true?' The man was weaving.

'You heard my friend,' Brandon said. 'You better leave.'

The man ignored him. 'You think my wife will still want you now she knows you're a kike?'

Paul sat frozen in silence. The room was spinning, there was a whirring sound in his ears, and he couldn't marshal any of his usual forces. Go away, he pleaded silently, just fuck off.

Brandon stood up. 'On your way, pal.'

'I ain't talking to you.'

'No, but I'm talking to you. You've over-stayed your welcome. Now move it.'

'Whatsamatter? The Hebe can't stand up for himself?'

'That's enough. You got what you came for, now fuck off.'

The man leaned over and poked Paul in the chest. 'If I touch him, you gonna do something about it, is that it, Jew lover?'

'You're damned right, you anti-Semitic bastard.' With one easy punch, Brandon laid him out cold on the sawdust-and shell-covered floor. He took out his wallet, threw some bills on the table, and gestured to Paul. 'Let's go.' Paul couldn't move. He was stuck to the chair. Gently but firmly, Brandon lifted him up by his shoulder, gripped his arm and headed for the door. 'Come on, buddy, time to travel.'

Numbly, Paul followed him out to the parking lot. He was having trouble maneuvering over the gravel. Brandon strode on, cursing under his breath, 'Godamn *Insider*, this has gone far enough.' As they approached Paul's car, they heard the cellular phone ringing.

'Damn.' Stumbling, Paul rushed ahead, unlocked the car door and grabbed the receiver. 'Hello, Paul Green here.' He listened for a moment, slammed it down and then turned to Brandon. 'I'm in deep shit,' he said.

'No, it's OK, we handled it all right back there. The question is what do we do next?'

'Forget all that. You don't understand,' Paul looked stricken. 'That was my next-door neighbor. Chaya's at Mt Sinai. She just gave birth to twins.'

'Twins? *Mazel Tov*.' Brandon raised a fist in the air.

'I missed it,' he was stone-cold sober now. A hammer had invaded his head and a hacksaw was attacking his gut. 'I missed the whole thing. Chaya's never going to forgive me.'

'Well, they must have slid out pretty quick,' Brandon looked at his watch. 'We've only been in there for two hours max.'

'I've got to get to the hospital right away.'

'Give me your keys. I'll drive you.'

Chapter Thirty-eight

'What the hell is this?' J.C. burst into the new offices of Hudlow/Turgov at Pac Vic and slammed a copy of *McCall's* magazine down on Julia's desk. Marty was sick at home and Julia was doing her best to cover for him at a studio/network meeting with Tim and Kathryn. 'Would one of you like to tell me what this is all about?' J.C. pointed to a glossy, customized insert in the middle of the popular woman's magazine. 'Kelly's Kids' Kurls Are Hot' and 'Kelly's Kids' Kosmetics Are Kicky' read the copy for a new set of hot rollers and an accompanying line of hair-care products and natural cosmetics bearing the endorsement of Kelly Carmichael. The Kelly's Kids line was aimed at pre-teen and young teens. There were shampoos, mousse and sprays specially formulated for 'young, natural hair', and make-up with 'the purest ingredients, safe for the youngest skin'. Kelly's name and face were splashed all over them.

'It's a joint promotion for Makeover and Kelly's Kids,' said Tim. 'I think, once you understand the concept, you'll see it's quite exciting.' He was using his business voice. 'We're going after the youth market, so Melissa will be working closely with Kelly, but all of you will be involved. There's a six-page spread in there, one page for each woman on the show.'

'Whose idea was this?' J.C. demanded, looking straight at Julia.

'Kelly's, of course,' Tim said. Julia didn't know what to say. She had known this was going to cause trouble, but Tim and Kathryn were so insistent on the promotional campaign, there was little she could do about it.

'I guess that's why her face is on the first page of the spread and mine is on the second!' J.C. was madder than an angry hornet.

'The insert is to advertise the hair-care products first and, incidentally, Makeover,' Kathryn tried to explain. 'I think it's going to do well for us. The make-up is light and none of it is tested on animals. The hair-care products all smell wonderful: apples, coconut, vanilla, bubblegum.'

'Spare me the commercial.'

'Kathryn's right, it's going to have national impact and all of us will benefit,' Tim said enthusiastically. 'We've got in-store displays in all the Wal-marts across the country.'

'Who's the star of this show anyway? Every time I turn around I see Kelly Carmichael's face staring at me. Just take a gander at this.' Bam! A video-cassette went down on the desk. '"For Adults Only. Kelly's Kosmetic Magic, How You Can Highlight and Shadow Your Cleavage Just Like Makeover's Samantha." Who does she think she is, an X-rated Donna Mills?'

'These promotional deals help sell the show in a way that's unique to what the show is about: make-up and hair,' Kathryn went on, a little uneasily.

'Fine. Except that it's exactly what Mac and I were planning to do with the hiatus, produce our own line of beauty products,' J.C. turned to Julia. 'Are you involved with this?'

Julia opened her mouth to speak, but Tim stepped in. 'It's a four-way deal: CBN, Wal-mart, Pac Vic and Hudlow/Turgov. Having the production company involved allows the stars of the series to appear throughout Wal-mart, in ads and TV commercials. That gives all of you extra exposure, which is great for the show, and it's added incentive to get people into Wal-mart. Creates consumer excitement.'

'I don't need extra exposure, thank you very much,' J.C. was spitting nails. 'I've never played a Wal-mart and I don't want to start now. You've got a picture of me doing Melissa's hair and Kelly doing her make-up. You can't use my picture without my permission.'

'I'm sorry, but we can,' Tim said determinedly. 'It's our show, it's our product. We aren't using any publicity photos connected with J.C. Austin, singer. But any publicity that is generated by the studio or CBN of you as Janine is perfectly acceptable. The contract you signed states that we may use your persona as Janine in any way we deem fit in order to sell the program.'

J.C. turned her eyes to Julia. They were full of anger and hurt. It was clear she felt betrayed. 'Julia, you knew Mac and I were talking about a hair-care sideline. When you first came to see me in Nashville to try to talk me into doing your show, you heard me tell Mac we could do a spin-off business. You were standing right there. That was one of the reasons Mac finally agreed to let me do the show.'

'That was two years ago, J.C.,' Julia said quietly. 'I honestly forgot. When Kelly came up with the idea and pitched it to us, it seemed like it was for a good cause.'

'What cause? Kelly's making money off my name and fame.'

'Kelly isn't getting a penny of this, I promise you,' Julia said firmly. 'Her part of the revenue goes straight into Kelly's Kids, her foundation for pediatric AIDS. That's why it's called Kelly's Kids. None of us are making a profit here, it's just good publicity.'

'Oh,' J.C. looked taken aback, but she didn't apologize. Julia had never seen her so angry. She swallowed and then said, 'I been doing my best to get behind this ensemble thing of yours, Julia, but Janine is the main character. I'm starting to get ticked off. I feel unappreciated here and I'm not the only one. You're using Debra Jo's voice now to say, "Ya'll don't go away. Makeover will be right back." Linda Earl always used to do that and she's not too happy to have it taken away, let me tell you.'

'Yes, we know,' Tim said.

'So what's going on around here? Are you trying to pressure Linda off the show?'

The question hung in the air for a moment before Kathryn jumped in and said, 'No, of course not.'

J.C. looked at Julia hard. 'Y'all are messin' with a good thing here and I'd hate to see it fall apart. I have another life to go back to. I'm not so sure about the rest of you.'

'Whew,' Tim let out a long whistle after J.C. had left. 'I bet we haven't heard the end of that. That husband of hers has been filling her head with all kinds of crap. Encouraging her to throw her weight around.'

'What's he doing back here in LA?' Kathryn asked. 'For a while there, he seemed to be spending most of his time in Nashville.'

'The minute she starts feeling insecure, she summons Mac to her side to protect her. He's got her seeing everyone around her as an enemy.'

'She's right and you both know it,' Julia said suddenly.

'I'm doing my best to keep the show balanced. I've even got staffers counting the number of lines attributed to each actress, but there's only one pie to go around. I'm worried that we're upsetting a delicate mix here. Linda Earl is just about ready to blow.'

'Wait till she finds out about the personal appearance tour we have lined up for Debra Jo,' Tim wrinkled his brow. Thanks to the success of the show, mall makeovers were the latest craze sweeping the nation as women flocked to their local shopping centers to get a bargain-basement beauty transformation and photo metamorphosis. Make-up, hair-style, and a sexy outfit were provided for a glamour photo shoot, all for the cut-rate price of under twenty dollars. According to *Star Weekly*, the photo-makeover industry had become a seventy-five million dollars-a-year business with clients from six to eighty. As a publicity gimmick, Debra Jo had been approached to tour the US, 'dropping in' on various mall makeover shops to sign autographs and plug the show. Debra Jo was thrilled by the idea because she would get to travel free to some of America's hot spots and meet with other women just like her.

'Linda's been missing rehearsal days from the set,' Julia went on. 'Stomach problems, her agent keeps telling us.'

'She's lost a lot of weight,' Kathryn observed, 'do you think something's physically wrong? An ulcer, maybe? She looks like a walking skeleton.'

'I don't know. If she has to work with Brandon, she is sullen and difficult. She accuses Debra Jo of not feeding her the lines properly. Then she comes to me and bitches that I'm beefing up Debra Jo's role at her expense. What can I tell her? It has been cut down, that's the truth.'

'She's no fool,' Kathryn sounded almost sympathetic, 'she knows there's not enough room for the two of them.'

'Linda has never really caught on with the viewers,' Tim said. 'Research and development has been telling us that for the past year.'

'Well, she thinks that's because I don't give her anything funny to say. She's complaining about her dialogue and demanding script changes. I don't know, maybe she's right, maybe I have been neglecting her.'

'She can't get laughs even with your best lines,' Kathryn said. 'Face it, the woman is just not funny.'

'And Debra Jo is,' Tim said. 'Stan feels Linda's days are

numbered. He'd like to see her gone by the end of January. He's convinced Debra Jo can take over.'

'Well, that remains to be seen,' Julia said stiffly. What would she do if they demanded Linda Earl be axed? Threaten to quit? She had to keep her focus on the main objective, the good of the show. She couldn't let anything like empathy take her off track. She felt sorry for Linda Earl, but she'd had reservations about her right from the beginning. Was she really worth fighting for? Her main concern had to be keeping J.C. on board. If J.C. got ticked off enough to jump ship, there could be no Makeover. They were supposed to be friends and now J.C. was looking at her like she was the enemy. She remembered Marty's warning, 'The bigger we get, the tougher the decisions. The more successful you become, the fewer people will like you.' She could feel it happening already. Oh God, where was Marty when she needed him? Lying at home on the sofa coping with self-induced anxiety while she was in very real danger right here at the studio with a dilemma that could send her off into true panic. How had they gone from a tight, happy company to a bunch of insecure, backbiting enemies? Enemies was the right word. She felt like she was in a war and she was no longer sure which side she was supposed to be fighting for.

The intercom on her desk buzzed. 'Your two o'clock is here.'

Julia sighed. Theresa Ruiz and Shirley Bunting had requested a meeting and she had a feeling they weren't coming in to tell her how happy they were with the way things were going. The door opened and Theresa and Shirley marched in followed by, surprise, surprise, Alex. What next?

'Shirley and I have been talking and we feel it's time for you to make a "color adjustment" to the show,' Theresa wasted no time in getting to the point. 'We feel like a couple of dark faces in a sea of white.'

'Don't ask me to add another character to the show,' Julia begged.

'No, but we want you to think about saving a guest spot for an actor who represents an ethnic minority. We've come up with a couple of story ideas we want to run past you. Can't Janine and Kelly do a makeover on someone who's African-American?'

'Or Asian or Hispanic,' Shirley said quickly. She was clearly nervous but determined to back up Theresa.

'I don't mean some jive-talking hip-hop character or somebody's maid, but an average minority woman who happens to want a makeover.'

'Don't they usually go to their own shops?' Kathryn asked timidly.

'Just my point,' said Theresa. 'The beauty techniques are different for people of color. African-American hair or Asian make-up, different skin tones, different textures. I'd like to see Concha and Shirley teach Janine and Kelly a thing or two. It could be interesting for our viewers who aren't white to see their own problems dealt with, no?'

Julia agreed. 'I like the idea, Theresa, I mean it.'

'Most of our guest shots are already reserved for the rest of the season,' Tim said hastily. 'We're going after some big name country stars and none of them are black.'

'That's because there aren't any,' Theresa said. 'The country music business is one of the most racist around. Look, you let Kelly make over men into women for that episode and we got one of our highest shares for that show. There's an audience out there that isn't totally white bread. What about a storyline where a black man comes to the Changing Room to be made over into white, to see what it's like to be white for a day in a city like Houston? Eddie Murphy did it in *Coming to America*.'

'These are good ideas,' Julia could feel a story formulating. 'I wish I'd thought of them.'

'With all due respect, Julia,' Shirley said softly, 'you wouldn't think of them. There's no black voice behind this show. Your staff writers are white. Your co-producers are white. The black presence may be making itself known on the other networks, but you don't have one black executive at CBN, Mr Talbot.'

'It's tough for anyone to break into television,' Tim said defensively, 'even me. There's a system. You have to come up through that system, create and write your own shows.'

'Then how do you get into the system?' Theresa was itching for a fight. 'There sure are some wonderful black playwrights out there. OK, so they don't have a track record in TV, but they can learn, if you're willing to take the time to train them.'

'Theresa's written a play that's a big hit in Miami,'

Shirley recognized her cue. 'It's been running for eight months. Do you even know about it?'

'We're in a primetime ratings race,' Tim began.

'We've got stats from your own research department,' Shirley flipped open a file folder. 'A study shows that blacks watch more network than any other racial group. Forty-eight per cent more, nearly seventy hours a week.'

Theresa cut to the chase. 'Julia, I've got an Emmy to prop open my front door. That proves somebody thinks I'm worth watching, but I don't know why. It's the middle of the second season and all I do on the show is answer the phone, adjust my stockings and come on to any guy who walks through the door of the Changing Room. You promised me change; when is it going to happen?'

Tim broke in, 'Do you think you have to deliver some heartfelt message or social commentary with every episode?'

'*Si, claro. Por que no*? J.C. says the set's not right, you tear it down and redesign the whole pinata. Kelly has a commitment to pediatric AIDS, that goes in the show. Shirley and I have opinions, too, and we want a chance to be heard. That's why I wanted to be an entertainer in the first place.'

'The operative word is "entertainer".'

Theresa ignored Tim and focused her blazing eyes on Julia. 'You promised me I'd have a say in the development of Concha. You said you'd listen to me. Where's the growth that was supposed to happen? This part is a dead end.'

'I didn't promise you anything.' God, she was tired of this wrangling among the actors. Look at me, Mom. Play with me. 'I had to fight to get you on the show in the first place. Tim and Kathryn can attest to that fact. You're lucky to have this job at all.'

'I fought for Shirley,' Alex spoke for the first time. Shirley looked surprised. 'She's been kept in the background long enough. I'd like to see her get a chance to show what she can do.'

'I want to do good work, that's all,' Shirley said. 'There's not much out there for women. For black women, it's even tougher.'

Julia looked at Alex. Thanks a lot, she thought. Nice of you to warn me about all this beforehand. Alex dropped his eyes, embarrassed. He had let it slip to Julia that he was falling in love with Shirley. At this point, he'd probably do anything to back her up. Oh, that wasn't fair. He believed in all this, too, of course he did. The trouble was so did Julia. It was just that she was beginning to feel inundated, attacked from all sides.

'I've got twenty-two minutes per show,' Julia said sharply. 'What do you want from me?'

'We want you to do for us what you did for Kelly.'

Something inside her snapped. 'I can't do it for all of you!'

It was a stand-off. Wordlessly, Shirley and Theresa gathered up their charts and papers and followed Alex out the door.

'I guess this isn't the time to tell you that Stan wants you to write another episode featuring Debra Jo,' Tim said wryly.

'Why won't you all leave me alone?' Julia lost it. 'I'm giving you a show that's on time and on budget. It's profitable. The numbers are great. What more do you want?'

'Stan wants CBN to make it to number one this year,' Tim said. 'He believes Makeover is the key.'

Julia stared at herself in the long row of mirrors over the banks of sinks. She was standing in the main washroom on the first floor at Pac Vic. She should be on her way home, the traffic would be heavy at this time of the afternoon, but she was exhausted by the day. She remembered what a friend of Marty's had said, 'It's a lousy business. It brings out the worst in everybody. You get beaten up so badly that by the time you get the power it's hard not to turn into a monster.' Had that monster been chained up inside her all along and only now released? Get a grip, Julia. You've had a bad day, that's all.

Someone had guessed her right age today. That had never happened to her before. She had always looked younger. Well, so what? She no longer had that 'deer caught in the headlights' look. I look older now than I did just a year ago, she thought, appreciably older. Like Gorbachev just before the break-up of the Soviet Union. The strain of this job is beginning to show on my face. What about the rest of the body? She began to unbutton her blouse and take a look when there was a light tap on her shoulder. She whirled around to see a thin, neuresthenic looking young woman wearing a blazer two sizes too big for her. The shoulder pads hung off the edges of her shoulders making her sloping frame sink into the jacket.

'Aren't you Julia Hudlow Turgov?'

'Last time I looked.' What was the matter with her? Taking her clothes off in a public washroom at the studio to see if her breasts were starting to sag? Jesus!

'I just sold a script to Murphy Brown and I wanted to thank you.'

'Why?'

The woman swallowed. 'Oh, of course, you don't even know me, but you're my role model. You're the reason I got into this business.'

'I hope you don't grow up to be me,' Julia said dryly. 'I'm not terribly happy just at the moment.' God, why had she said that. It sounded so bitter and mean-spirited. But 'you're my role model'? It made her feel a hundred and two years old.

'Gee, I'm sorry.' Her shoulders hunched further down in the blazer and she looked as though she might cry.

'Forget it, bad day,' Julia said. 'You sold a script? What's your name?'

'Carla Hanson.'

'That's great, Carla Hanson. I'll watch for you.' She flashed her what she hoped was a warm, earth-mother smile, and got out of there as fast as she could.

I'm not going home, I can't handle it, I deserve something else. Into the car, over to Liam's. He opened the door and wrapped his arms around her. She never knew the meaning of 'his eyes lit up' until she saw Liam see her. He wasn't wearing a shirt and the hair on his chest sent sparks through the thin silk of her blouse as he embraced her. 'I willed you to be here,' he said.

'I can't stay long, but I just couldn't stay away.' She told him about her day.

'You're way too hard on yourself, Julia,' he hugged her close. 'I admire your perfectionism. It's one of the reasons I love you.' Her heart stopped. He said it casually, slipping it in, when there was an unspoken agreement they would not say those words to each other, but she knew he meant it. He kissed her gently. 'I know what you need, a hot tub.'

'No, no, no,' she protested. 'I'm not a hot tub kind of person. Really.'

'Are you telling me this is something I can actually introduce to you? You've lived in southern California all this time and you've never experienced the joy of jacuzzi?'

'I thought I'd escaped it.'

'You'll love it, I promise you. Besides I've got it all fired up; you have to try it.' He looked at her shyly, suddenly awkward. 'May I undress you?'

'Please.'

'Thank you.' They both laughed at their own politesse. He stood in front of her and, carefully, one button at a time, undid her blouse, slipping it off her, leaving a pool of silk on the floor. He knelt in front of her to unfasten her suede skirt, sliding it down over her hips. He brought his mouth to her half-slip, his face so close she could feel his warm breath on the silk; he was about to kiss her, then his fingers pulled the slip off. Reaching up, he unhooked her bra, the satin straps falling off her shoulders. His hands brushed against her skin, setting it on fire. She wanted him to make love to her right then and there. Slowly, gently, he inched her panties off, until she was standing in a circle of her clothes. He took her hand to help her step out, then reached for a thick, soft beach towel, which he wrapped lovingly around her, and took her out on to the deck.

The patio doors were flung wide, she could see the steam rising from the hot tub which was built into the deck, all she smelled the clean, fresh scent of the natural wood. All the lights were turned off in the house, it was already dark out, moonlight streaming down and a few stars twinkling in the black sky. There was a high fence around the deck so no one could see in, but Julia felt nervous. 'Should we be wearing bathing suits?'

'What for? It's completely private. No one can see in. We may get a visiting cat or two. The woman next door must own at least fifteen. Sometimes they climb the trees, walk along the fence, and drop down on to the deck. But the point of having your own hot tub is to be naked.'

He had brought a ghetto-blaster out on to the deck and a low, sultry jazz piece filled the night air. There was an ice bucket with champagne chilling next to a large china vase filled with blood-red roses.

Gingerly, she stepped down into the steaming water, letting the towel go at just the last moment.

'How does it feel?' he asked.

'Heavenly,' she said.

He poured champagne into a crystal goblet and handed it down to her.

'Are you sure this is OK? Haven't I read that alcohol and hot tubs don't mix? If you get overheated, you die?'

'I love seeing you overheated,' he said, 'but if it'll make you feel better, you drink and I'll stay sober so I can save you.'

She took a sip of champagne. The icy cold liquid was a sharp contrast to the hot, steamy water. 'Are you going to stand there and watch me enjoy myself or are you coming in?'

He unbuckled the belt to his jeans and slipped them off, his body gleaming in the moonlight. It never ceased to amaze her how at ease he was with his own body. Most men, when they were naked, hunched over a little, one hand protecting their balls, but Liam moved as if man was meant to be naked, graceful, proud, like a lion. She looked at him. She hadn't touched him and already he was hard.

'Wait a minute,' he said. He took the roses from the vase and, one by one, tossed them into the swirling water.

'This is exquisite,' she said, as he came down into the water. His eyes were such a pale blue in the moonlight they appeared almost silver. They lay back and looked at each other. Her body, which was small and delicate, in the water felt lush and full, the refracted light of the moon on the water magnifying the curve of her breasts and hips, the length of her legs. She was completely open and wet.

'Watch,' he pushed a button and the water began to churn wildly as colored lights turned it red, the roses wet and black against the colored water, dancing dramatically.

She laughed and kicked her legs with the man-made waves. 'This reminds me of your artificial moonlight,' she said.

'I haven't got it quite right yet. But that's OK, you haven't used it yet.' He flicked the switch and the water slowed down as the lights changed to blue and green.

She closed her eyes and let the water and the music wash over her, remembering the way they had sat on the set, drinking wine and talking.

'I was already in love with you by then,' he said. He had said it again. 'I wanted so much to touch your beautiful breasts but I didn't dare go any further than this,' lightly, he traced her collarbone. 'Now I can.' He dipped his fingers in the champagne, anointed her nipples with the wine, then leaned over and sucked it off. She ran her fingers over his chest, the dark blond hair wet, even darker, defining the muscles of his body, swirling downward to where his cock lifted out of the water, straining toward her. She felt the pull between her legs and, as if reading her mind, his hand slid down, pressing against her as she arched forward to meet him. The moon was round and full, eerily erotic above them. She looked up and gasped.

'What? What is it?'

'Look.' She pointed up toward the trees. 'We've got an audience.' She counted twenty cats, of all different breeds and sizes, sitting in the branches of the trees, staring down at them, Cheshire-like, little cat faces glowing fuzzily above. They both began to laugh and then Liam stopped abruptly.

'Did you hear what I said a moment ago?' he asked.

'Which part?'

He reached out and took her face in his hands. Her mouth opened to receive his kiss, but instead, he ran his fingers over her wet, glistening skin, again and again, as if committing the bones of her face to his memory. 'Julia, please let me say this. I know it's not what you want to hear, but I have to, I must. I'm in love with you and I don't want to give you up.'

MAKEOVER SISTERS THROW REAL-LIFE TANTRUMS

The women on Makeover are feuding and fighting, causing major problems on the sit-com set. Although producers are trying to keep a lid on the trouble, things are about to blow, according to an *Insider* source.

'This used to be the happiest bunch of people on TV. But now you walk on to soundstage six and the air of tension is so thick you could cut it with a knife, especially between beauty queen Linda Earl and newcomer, Debra Jo Fawcett.'

'Show execs are sick and tired of the beauty queen's tears and tantrums. She's not a favorite with the viewers either.'

Debra Jo Fawcett, housewife turned TV star in just a few months, is already more popular with audiences than Linda Earl is after two years. 'The female viewers love Debra Jo because she's a real woman who understands their problems. She watches her weight, shops at K-Mart, juggles her finances and has to balance her checkbook at the end of the month.'

Fans appreciate the fact that Debra Jo, who recently moved to LA with her son, Danny, is raising him on her own while her husband looks after their other child back in Houston, Texas. Despite her sudden success, Debra Jo still makes all of Danny's meals and does his laundry herself.

'It's not fair,' Linda Earl complained to a friend. 'Debra Jo's getting paid to play herself. I have to play the character that's written for me. It's not my fault that people think that character is stuck-up and boring.'

There's no love lost between the male stars, Brandon Tate and Paul Green, either. Known to call each other by derogatory nicknames, last season the two men, arguing over script changes, came to blows right on the set.

The stress of dealing with all of this is also taking its toll on show's principal star, J.C. Austin. J.C.'s hoping an upcoming episode where personal friend, country singer George Jones, is set to guest star as Janine's dad, will help get the focus of the show back on track.

The presence on the set of a number of 'significant others' doesn't help matters either. The cast hates it when Mac Austin comes to town. 'He likes to throw his weight around,' says an insider. 'He may be his wife's manager, but he's got nothing to do with Makeover. He should butt out.'

Power-tripping Bonnie McKimmie, mother to teen star Melissa McKimmie, is causing problems, too. 'She failed as an actress up in Canada, but she thinks she knows it all. When she tries to coach her daughter, the results are embarrassing. It's obvious Melissa prefers to take direction from her real director, Alex Jordan, and that makes Mom mad.'

Meanwhile, show execs are running scared, and the actors are all walking around looking over their shoulders to see who's going to get axed from the hit sit-com. 'It's a case of too many people now. Something's got to give. Somebody's got to go.'

Chapter Thirty-nine

The telephone was off the hook. The door to the bedroom was shut tight. The shades were drawn and the skylight blocked off to keep out the afternoon sun. Wearing a T-shirt and a pair of bikini panties, Linda Earl lay in bed, the covers of which were strewn with candy wrappers, broken potato chips, magazines and newspapers. The *Hollywood Insider* was having a field day trashing Makeover. What did she care? None of those people were her true friends anyway. Brandon had pretended to like her and then turned on her in Houston, playing her for a fool. He deserved to be publicly raked over the coals. They all did.

In bed, she felt cozy, safe. Steve was in San Francisco on business. Two-and-a-half-year-old Maggie was downstairs taking a nap with the housekeeper, Concepcion. Good. Naptime for everybody. Linda had instructed Concepcion to phone into the studio and say she was sick. They didn't need her anyway. Or at least that's what they thought. Let them see what they could do if she didn't turn up at all. The episode would have to be rewritten to exclude her. Could cost them money. So what? Not her problem. She deserved some time off. Everybody kept telling her to relax. The pill had allowed her to sleep till noon. She felt pleasantly drowsy even now at – she craned her neck – two-thirty, which was a lot better than feeling her heart was about to implode in her chest. Her two Burmese cats, Cleo and Fateetata, curled on either side of her feet. She had redecorated the bedroom herself. Tones of beige and off-white before, now it was all dusky pink. The heavy, rose-coloured, brocade drapes were backed with blackout cloth and, when drawn, closed off the outside world, creating a pink, womb-like atmosphere. Steve complained that it was too feminine and wanted to know where he fit into the color scheme. Like sleeping in a sea of Pepto Bismol, he said. Damn. The curtains weren't

414

completely closed. A crack of light shone right into her blurred eyes. Should get up, pull them together. Too lazy.

Bed was so warm, sheets laundered several days ago, soft, lightly wrinkled. She was vaguely hungry. Could buzz down for Concepcion to bring her tea and toast. No, she didn't want to be discovered this way. Concepcion would only look at her disapprovingly. Layabout. Not fair. She worked hard, damned hard. She deserved some time to herself.

Now she felt ravenous. Was there anything left up here? From the food she'd ordered last night? Was it last night? She shifted her legs, careful not to disturb the cats, and leaned over the edge of the bed. The floor was littered with an array of takeout delights. She must have gone nuts dialing Waiter-on-the-Way again. Let's see. A pint of chocolate, chocolate-chip ice-cream had melted and overflowed the top of the container on to the carpet. Fifteen per cent butterfat. Not a good idea. Pork satay, coconut shrimp, and meekrob noodles from Thai Seed Pearl. Barbecue wings and rib combo from El Pollo Loco. Feta cheese and sundried tomato calzone from California Pizza still looked inviting. Pizza was good cold. In addition to all this, there was the breakfast Concepcion had cooked for her and left on a silver tray beside her bed. Huevos rancheros, grits, biscuits with sausage cream gravy.

The shrimp smelled a little off (how long had they been sitting there?), but the ribs and chicken looked OK. She wolfed them down, greedily licking the grease from her fingertips. Roll the biscuit around in the gravy, creamy, soft, hot spicy pepper, the hole in the stomach is starting to go away. Eggs, scrambled, full of chili, onions and cheese, just the way she liked them. Cold, but who cares? Shove it in, no need to taste it, feels good in the mouth, wash it down with white wine, it's warm, but what the hell? Hot peppery bits of sausage a perfect contrast to the creamy blandness. More wine. Her head was a little fuzzy. Cleo and Fateetata came sniffing around. She offered them each a shrimp, but they eschewed it. Definitely off. Lucky she hadn't eaten them. But, oh, dear God, what had she eaten? The containers were empty, the plates licked clean. All gone. No, please, oh no. She felt stuffed, her stomach was stretched, bulging out, her skin exploding. No, wrong, all wrong, bad feeling.

Into the bathroom, make sure to lock the door. The white walls, glistening porcelain fixtures, too bright, blinding. Open the medicine chest. Bottle of ipecac. Empty. Shit! Maybe more, somewhere, there in the back, no. Bottles out on to the floor, broken glass on the tiles, doesn't matter now sweep it up later. Plastic cup, fill it with water, add lots of salt, hold your breath, drink it down, straight down, lean against the sink, drop down on the floor, lift the edge of the toilet seat and wait. Yes, there it is, here it comes, get it out, all out. Talking on the big white telephone to Ralph, as her model friends used to say. Oh God, there's more, it's pouring out. Clinging to the edge, gripping it with her hands, letting go, all of it. Oh, the release, the blessed release. Better than orgasm.

She felt calm, relaxed, peaceful. No point looking in the mirror, she knew what she would see. Drawn face, circles under the eyes, stringy hair. So what? No need to be perfect. It was her day off. She smelled bad, a sour, stale smell. She reached for the perfume atomizer. Why bother?

Nobody else around. It was her own smell, it didn't bother her. In fact, it was comfortingly familiar. The walls of the bathroom shifted. Whoa. A little shaky on the pins there. Time to go back to bed. Take another pill. Get some rest. Step by step, hold on to the furniture, got to make it back to the bed.

She was crawling up on to it when the door flew open and the production assistant for Makeover stalked in, followed by Concepcion.

'So sorry, señora,' the housekeeper's broad face was lined with worry, 'she no wait downstairs.'

Cindi was a nervous, twitchy, plain girl whose stop-watch seemed to be soldered to her left hand. 'I've been sent to see just how ill you are,' she said officiously, and then stopped, her mouth dropping open, at the sight of the glamorous Nadine, clinging, half-naked to the side of the bed. 'Jesus, Linda,' she whispered, 'what's wrong with you?'

'Flu, twenty-four hour, running at both ends,' Linda managed shakily. 'I'll be okay. Concepcion's looking after me.'

Cindi's frightened eyes swept the room, taking in the whole scene, the empty cartons of food, the wine bottle tipped over on the floor, the sticky mass of ice-cream on the carpet. The smell was gagging. 'I'll let them know at the studio,' she said, then turned and bolted.

Linda felt too feeble, too tired, to stop her. She let Concepcion help her back into bed. Tuck the covers around her, turn the air conditioning up, let the white noise block everything out.

'Mommy?' a little voice said, 'Nap over. Time to get up.' Two-and-a-half-year-old Maggie, wearing a ruffled halter top and shorts, was standing at the foot of the bed, rubbing her eyes. 'You said swimming today.'

'Mommy's tired,' Linda mumbled, barely able to look at her.

'But you promised. You said.'

The perfection of her daughter's angel face, the blonde curly hair, the amethyst eyes, stared at her. She was going to grow up to be beautiful. Linda burst into tears.

'Mamacita is sick today,' Concepcion explained, taking Maggie by the hand and leading her out of the room. 'You and me, we go down to the kitchen and get some ice-cream, no?'

As if ice-cream could make it all better. Crying weakly, Linda pulled the covers up over her head. Darkness, sleep. Please, oh God, let this be over.

MAKEOVER BEAUTY QUEEN IS BULIMIC

The secret is out! Linda Earl suffers from the deadly, body-destroying disease, bulimia nervosa. This binge and purge syndrome affects many women in the US and now it has apparently afflicted the beauty queen turned actress who plays J.C. Austin's sister on the red-hot sit-com, Makeover.

An inside source tells us that the beleaguered beauty is so depressed that she can't kick the destructive habit of stuffing herself with junk food and then vomiting it all up. In recent weeks, friends and fans have been shocked by Linda's continuing weight loss. 'Remember the camera adds at least ten pounds,' says the source. 'If Linda looks that thin and ravaged on the show, imagine what she looks like in real life?'

'On the set she either eats nothing or everything, no in-between. She's either splurging or starving. I've seen her polish off a whole chicken, plates of nachos, and an entire pecan pie with ice-cream. That's as much as 7,000 calories in one sitting.' Others say they've seen her eat nothing but iceberg lettuce and mustard for days at a time.

'I've been out for dinner with Linda,' says one friend. 'She will eat a full meal, just like a normal person, then excuse herself to go to the restroom. I know she's in there sticking her finger down her throat to make herself vomit. The woman is really sick. She needs help.'

Linda has always been obsessed with her appearance. Remember you read it first in *HI* that the former beauty queen has had enough plastic surgery to make an entirely new human being.

Many famous stars have come out and admitted they're bulimic, including rock singer Elton John, actress Jane Fonda, and tennis player, Carling Bassett. But Linda refuses to admit she has a problem. 'She's playing Russian roulette with her life. It's only a matter of time before the gun goes off.'

Worried friends don't understand it. 'She has a beautiful little girl who needs her. Her handsome husband is madly in love with her and rich enough so she never has to work another day in her life, but all she cares about is how she looks.'

Ironically, Makeover is all about body image. Apparently nobody is more obsessed with that than Linda Earl.

Chapter Forty

Someone was shaking her. Leave me alone, let me sleep. She awoke to see Steve's face floating before her eyes. 'Hi, honey, you're home,' she reached out to draw him down into an embrace, but he roughly pulled her up to a sitting position.

'How could you hide this from me?' he demanded. Her picture was on the front page of the *Hollywood Insider* with the lurid headline, 'Makeover Star Flushing Her Career Down the Toilet, story and photos inside.' 'How could you let my colleagues read in the newspapers that my wife is constantly running to the bathroom to stick her finger down her throat. And I don't know anything about it? You've made me look ridiculous. You don't give a damn for our marriage or for Maggie's happiness. You're ruining your health. I'm putting you in the hospital right now.'

In the offices of the *Hollywood Insider*, the phone rang three times before staff reporter Leonard Pollack picked it up.

'Hi,' said the voice on the other end of the line. 'It's me.'

'I was hoping you'd call. It's been a while. I was thinking of getting a hold of you.'

'No, I don't think that would be a good idea.'

'So, what have you got for me this time?'

'Linda Earl's about to get the ax from Makeover.'

'That rumor's been circulating for months. Tell me something new.'

'This time it's definite. They're waiting to make a formal announcement, but she's off the show as of now. Her husband's been told. She's in the hospital. I'm offering you a genuine scoop.'

'Good stuff.'

'How are things at your end? Dug up anything on Kelly Carmichael?'

420

'We've got her mailbox staked out. A couple of our guys are busy playing mailman, but so far they've found zip.'

'OK. Keep digging. The Linda Earl story is hot. Once her firing is official, there'll be gang-bang coverage on this. Better move on it right away.'

'Thanks for the tip. I'll wire payment to your account as usual. Should clear in a couple of weeks, OK?'

'No problem. Whenever.'

There was a click and the voice was gone. With a smile, Len Pollack hung up and turned to his computer.

Linda was lying in bed at St John's Hospital. Bright sunlight streamed in through her corner room window. For the first two weeks she'd been on intravenous feeding. Now that she was managing liquids – soup, yogurt, milkshakes – she was in confinement with round-the-clock nurses to make sure her food stayed down. She was in therapy, about to start a twelve-step program for bulimics. Linda recognized her body had become a battlefield for the war raging within her.

She'd bribed the day nurse to bring her a copy of the latest *Hollywood Insider*. It was about as bad as it could be. 'Troubled TV Star Dumped from Show. Luscious Linda Leaves Makeover.' In the article, Julia graciously explained why she had to be written out of the show with only a few episodes in the season left to go. Linda wondered where the *Hollywood Insider* had got these quotes. She couldn't imagine Julia ever giving an exclusive to the tabloid. 'Hudlow/ Turgov, the show's creator, said with regret, "Linda Earl is a highly talented actress with a lot to offer. She tried her utmost and so did we, but it was simply not meant to be. The character wasn't going anywhere. Linda was the wrong person in the wrong part. Even though we will miss her, it's best for all of us that she move on. We wish her well and hope for her speedy recovery." When asked if Houston housewife, Debra Jo Fawcett, would now play a larger role on the show, Ms Hudlow Turgov hedged with, "No decision has been made on that as yet. We will just have to wait and see." '

Linda folded the newspaper neatly and dropped it into the metal wastebasket beside her bed. The worst had happened. She was no longer on Makeover, but at least she was still alive. The door to her room opened slowly and a pair of legs walked in, obscured by an enormous bouquet of orchids and tiger lilies. 'Hi, lovely lady,' Steve peeked around the flowers. 'How's my honey doing today?'

'I lost my job,' Linda said.

'I know.' He put the bouquet on the bedside table. 'They came to me last week but I didn't want to tell you until I was sure you were up to hearing it. How did you find out?'

'The good old *Hollywood Insider*.'

'Damn it, I'm going to kill that night-nurse.'

'It's OK. I made her bring me a copy. I needed to know for sure. I'm off the show for good.'

'Yeah,' Steve sat on the edge of the bed and took her hand. 'How do you feel about that?'

'I guess I should be depressed or upset but, funnily enough, I'm kind of relieved. I feel a little bit like Maggie's hamster, B.S.' Maggie had named him after Bart Simpson. 'It's like the wheel in the cage has finally stopped and I get to jump off and rest in the wood shavings. Do you think we can survive if I'm unemployed?'

Steve's eyes filled with tears. 'I'd be happy living in a trailer as long as I have you. All I want is my wife back. Maggie misses her mom. Who cares if you're on TV? God, I love you so much. I can't believe I almost lost you.' He hugged her, hard. 'Listen, I fired Concepcion.'

'Oh, no, why?'

'I suspect she told the story to the *Insider*. Besides I want it to be just us at home for a while. I've taken a leave of absence from the firm. I swear to you, Linda, I'll do everything I can to help you take control: control of your house, your child, your life.'

Chapter Forty-one

It was slipping away from her. Everything had happened so fast. Since coming to LA six months ago, Debra Jo had been on a roller-coaster of emotional highs and lows. Let's take you way up and then we'll hurtle you way down with a force guaranteed to shove your gut right into your throat.

People kept saying they loved her on the show. She was 'great, just great'. But she didn't know why she was great. Or how she could repeat it. What if she stopped being great? How would she find her way back? 'Just be yourself,' they said, but she had come to realize that even J.C., who was the other person on the show supposedly playing someone close to herself, wasn't really. J.C. Austin, the public persona, was a lot different from J.C. Austin, the real person.

Seeing herself on television was not such a happy surprise either. Is that me? I really look like that? Gotta lose some weight. No more donuts on the set. And my voice. I don't sound like that, do I? 'A delightfully daffy persona with a nutty-crunch voice,' was how one critic described it. Debra Jo didn't think that was necessarily a compliment.

And now Alex was starting to bug her about her Texas accent. Telling her she was hitting her r's too hard. 'That's what a real Texas accent sounds like,' she informed the director. 'It's not soft southern like Bill Clinton's Arkansas or Jimmy Carter's Georgia.' The show was set in Houston, for God's sake, she was from Houston. How could her accent be wrong? 'It has to blend with the other voices on the show,' he told her. 'If you're going to be an actress, you'll have to be able to adapt.' Playing herself was a a lot harder than she'd expected.

Next week she was going to be on Jay Leno's show. She'd even been offered a movie of the week, playing a Texas waitress who gets lured into a prostitution ring and ends up killing her pimp in order to keep her daughter from being drawn into the ring as well. It was one of those reality-based dramas. 'Out of the pages of today's headlines' read the first line of the 'cover', the brief description of the 'coverage', the story, attached to the screenplay. Not based in any reality she knew of. She would have no idea how to go about playing a part like that.

Debra Jo was having trouble enough staying based in her own reality. Here she was, a wife and mom, playing a wife and mom, having to be a wife and mom a) without her husband and b) in a city far away from the rest of her family. During the summer hiatus, she was scheduled to start her publicity tour of malls all across America. She'd been hoping Eddie and the boys would tour with her, but Eddie's business was on the upswing and he wanted to stay in Houston to get behind it. Beau had baseball camp. Danny didn't want to leave LA. He was going to bunk in with Tucker's family in Bel Air and, as much as she would miss him, she couldn't deny him the chance to see how the other half lived. According to Danny, Tucker had his own master bedroom with private bath, a music and TV room with the latest techno-gear and what sounded like an Olympic size swimming pool. Of course, maybe it would be a better life lesson if Tucker came and lived with them for a while!

The Christmas visit with the rest of the family had been a whirlwind. She and Danny showed Beau and Eddie all the fun LA places. Eddie complained about the smog, the food, the freeways, the pollution at the beach. He didn't have one good word to say about southern California.

The one bright spot was that Melissa and Beau seemed to hit it off. When Beau got off the plane at LAX, Debra Jo almost didn't recognize her own son. He'd shot up to over six feet. With his white-blond hair, athletic build, and shy, farmboy grin, he turned heads even in jaded LA. Melissa's own mother, who had to be Debra Jo's age at least, made no secret of the fact she thought Beau was 'a burning love hunk'. Bonnie was all over her son like a dirty shirt but, fortunately (she would have killed them both), he wasn't interested, he had eyes only for Melissa. The two kids had hung out together the whole time and, now that Beau was back in Houston, they were keeping the US Postal Service in business with letters going back and forth.

All during the visit, Debra Jo kept trying to find the courage to confess she had slept with Brandon. Eddie had a right to know, especially if any kind of trial separation was imminent. Except she herself didn't know what was going on with Brandon. Their one night of ecstasy had not been repeated. He smiled at her in the same way he always had, and touched her casually, but it was almost as if that night had never happened. How could he treat her this way after what they had shared? She kept looking for ways to be alone with him again, but it was almost like he couldn't be bothered with her any more. No, that couldn't be it. He was being discreet, that was all. How could he forget so quickly?

She remembered every single moment of their night together as if it had been written down and handed to her to memorize. Every bite of food they ate. The fizzy, sharp-sweet taste of the Kir Royale, a drink to which she was now addicted. The way he gallantly took off his suede blazer and put it around her bare shoulders. His hands brushing across her skin. The wild drive through the winding roads, up the mountain path, to his place in Topanga Canyon. How he swept her up in his arms and carried her off to the bedroom. His sensitive hands making their slow, expert discovery of her body. The way he had kissed her scar. Maybe he was worried about getting involved with a married woman? If only they could be alone together once again so she could let him know that she was willing to take a risk or two to see how their relationship might develop. She kept trying to send him signals, but so far he wasn't picking up on any of them. What was the guy, deaf, dumb and blind?

Finally, in desperation, she broke down in tears and confessed the whole thing to J.C. She was tight with Brandon, maybe she'd have some insight.

'I'm so confused. Brandon's the best lover I ever had. I'm only thirty-four, my kids are almost grown, it's not too late to have another life, but if he loves me, I need to know for sure.'

'Did he say he did?' J.C.'s lips tightened.

'He told me he absolutely adored me. He said he adored making love with me. We made love all night long and in the morning he . . .' Debra Jo was anxious to give her all the details but J.C. stopped her.

'Brandon loves to fuck, that's what he loves. I wouldn't start buying a new trousseau just yet if I were you.'

'But what should I tell Eddie?'

'I wouldn't tell him anything. I realize this kind of thing is probably front page news where you come from, but out here, one night doesn't even make the paper.'

'I've never lied to Eddie about anything, J.C. When we got married we agreed we'd always be honest with each other.'

'Men say they want honesty but they don't mean it. The entire world of most men is something that could be called Fantasyland. I wouldn't give Eddie a reality check just yet.'

'Well, do you think I should let Brandon know I'm looking into a trial separation?'

'Brandon's like a ornery bull. You got to give him a lot of rope. He'll either come on back when he's good and ready or he'll hang you. What's important for you is that you got to protect your softer parts.'

J.C. let her cry it all out. Afterwards, she felt better, but she was still confused.

Brandon was confused, too, and, without understanding why, feeling something close to guilt. He must be losing his edge. His sex life had always been guilt free. Two consenting adults, in the privacy of the home, anything goes, no questions asked, that kind of thing. Maybe he should never have slept with Debra Jo. Not that it hadn't been great on the night. It was comforting to sleep with someone so normal, without neuroses or sexual dysfunction or bizarre orgasmic demands that were so much a part of the LA fuck scene. She was warm and eager and that had been more than enough to arouse him. Now she aroused nothing in him except guilt. There it was again. She was soft, willing, and pliable, which couldn't hold his attention for very long. He had tried gently to make her understand. A more sophisticated woman would have gotten the message. Kathryn Grady was back in town. Time to give her a call.

Kathryn looked different since her marriage: softer, less contained, but at the same time less approachable. Her wild dark hair was loose around her shoulders instead of in her trademark knot, and the lines of her dove-gray suit were less severely tailored. They met for lunch on neutral ground. A restaurant. Kathryn's choice. No matter. He'd soon be able to redirect the meeting so they ended up at his place. The restaurant was the Topanga Fish Company. His choice.

'You look glowing,' he said, kissing her fingertips. 'You're not pregnant, are you?'

'No, not yet. But Jonathan and I are having fun trying.'

They talked business over lunch. Kathryn admitted that Pac Vic was worried about the strife surrounding Make-over.

'I know they intend to give you an episode to direct next season.'

'Yeah, well that's what they've been saying for two years now. My agent is ready to break my contract if they don't come through this time.'

Kathryn confessed her own concerns about Julia. 'The strain of trying to keep it all together is really starting to show. There's not much I can do to help her. Stan King's determined to ram CBN into first place and he's got Pac Vic by the balls.'

'I love it when you use that aggressive language,' he murmured. 'The iron fist in the silken glove.'

Kathryn ignored him. 'He's trying to keep the lid on Julia as well, but she's tougher than she looks. And this is the age of the female creator-producer giving the good old network boys a run for their money. I just hope she can hang in there. I don't know if she's willing to play Hollywood hardball. It's not that easy if you're a nice person, which Julia actually is.'

'Unlike you. How are things with you? All this flying back and forth between New York and LA tough on the marriage?'

'On the contrary. It keeps us from getting bored with each other. We both like our freedom.'

'I couldn't agree more.' His hand went under the table and on to her knee. He loved the fact that she wore stockings even in this heat. Most women in LA went bare-legged, not realizing how a smooth, shapely, visible but covered leg could stimulate the senses.

'What are you doing?' Kathryn put down her cup of decaf cappucino.

'Letting you know how much I've missed you. Don't make any noise, we don't want to attract attention.' He allowed his hand to move to the inside of her thigh and caress it. They both used to love this, putting the moves on each other in a public place until they were both so hot they had to rush off and do it in the washroom or the car.

Quickly she crossed her legs, trapping his hand between her thighs. Now this was more like it. Except that she was gripping him almost too hard. His hand was caught in a vice. She beckoned him towards her. He leaned across the table. 'Now listen, my friend, and listen good. You think we can just pick up where we left off?'

'Why not?' He was suddenly uneasy, not sure where this was leading. 'I've been patient, I've given your marriage a year, but now I would like us to start seeing each other again.'

'No.'

'Just "no"? That's all I get?'

She sighed. 'I like being married, Brandon. You really ought to try it. It's a tough old world out there and it's nice facing it with someone as part of a team. Get it together, sweetheart. Anyone can see you're in love with J.C. Austin.'

Brandon frowned. 'That's a lost cause.'

'Nothing's a lost cause.'

'Except you.'

'Except me.' Kathryn's tone hardened again. 'You don't really want me, Brandon. You want J.C., but you won't fight for it. You're afraid to commit. You're addicted to the chase. Where will that leave you in the end? Old and bald and fat.' With one swift move, she freed his hand and stood up from the table. 'I wish you well, love. Nothing would please me more than to be able to dance at your wedding.'

J.C. summoned Brandon to her trailer. She looked madder than a wet hen. 'You keep your dick out of Debra Jo Fawcett, you understand?' She was chewing furiously on her lower lip.

'What have you heard?' He prided himself on being discreet and considerate.

'Debra Jo told me what happened. But I didn't have to be told. She's been slinking around after you like a kicked puppy.'

He looked away, embarrassed. 'It was nothing serious.'

'Not to you. In her mind, she's already divorced her husband, married you, and is fighting to get custody of her kids. Didn't your mother ever tell you charm can be a curse as well as a blessing?'

He smiled weakly, but she wasn't finished with him.

'You ought to be ashamed of yourself. That was like

giving candy to a baby. Your dick is not a toy. Where you're concerned, it should come with a manufacturer's warning on it. Now take this fish off the hook and let her down gently. I don't want to see her flopping all over the deck for the next six weeks. Debra Jo deserves better.'

'What am I supposed to tell her? If she's dreaming marriage she's not going to be very happy with a kiss off.'

'Tough shit. I'm telling you to fix the situation and fix it good, before the hiatus, so she can make up with her husband.'

She was disappointed in him, that was obvious. He had violated a secret code of hers that he was somehow supposed to know about. On the other hand, she was also blazing with an anger that was out of proportion to the sin he had committed. She'd chewed her lower lip to a furious pulp. He wondered if way down deep a part of J.C. wasn't a little bit jealous. Could that be why he had gone after Debra Jo in the first place?

Chapter Forty-two

'Where have you been, Bon?' Melissa opened her dressing-room door to let her mother in. 'I haven't been able to find you for three whole days.'

'Miss me?' Bonnie was looking even more deeply tanned but much the worse for wear. 'You told me you were spending the weekend with Debra Jo and Danny. I'm surprised you even noticed I was gone.'

'I was really worried. I kept calling our apartment to check in with you, but the answerphone was always on. Usually you call me back when I leave a message for you.'

'Yeah? Well, I was kind of busy.' Bonnie lit up a cigarette.

'Please don't smoke in here, OK? I can't breathe.'

'Well, excuse me.' Bon dropped her cigarette into an open juice can.

Melissa snatched it up and threw it into the trash can. 'Where did you go? Did you leave town without telling me?'

'Good guess. I spent the weekend in Mexico with Christopher Max. I wanted to stay in Tijuana but that was a little too scummy even for Chris, so we wound up in Encinada.'

'Isn't he supposed to be getting married next week? To that girl on his show?'

'Yep. That was the point of our little trip. A private bachelor party, just me and him, one final blast.' She sighed. 'I wish I could marry him myself. Boy, the *Insider* would have a field day with that one.'

'Real funny, Bon. You scared me half to death. I thought something bad might have happened to you. And what about me? Weren't you at all worried about me?'

Bonnie shrugged. 'Why should I be? I knew you were safe at Debra Jo's living The Waltons with Dan-Boy.'

'You make it so hard for me, don't you realize that? I

can't tell you any of my problems because I'm always listening to yours.'

'I think I know why. Guess what I found out about you and me?'

'What?' Now that her fears had been alleviated, Melissa wanted to get back to the latest draft of the script. Any minute now, they would be calling her to the set, and she was still unsure of the new lines. Usually she was a quick study, but she'd been so worried about Bonnie that it had been hard to keep her mind on her scenes in this week's episode.

'Psychically, you're the mother and I'm the daughter.'

'Yeah? Tell me something I don't already know.'

'I mean in a past life. Chris took me to this incredible channeler who told me you and I have shared many lives together but in the past our roles were always reversed.'

'Oh Mom, don't be such a flake. I can't believe you really believe this.'

'No, wait, don't you see, it makes a lot of sense? That's why we're having problems. I'm used to you being my mother in the past so it's hard for me to tell you what to do now. Weird, huh?'

'Yeah,' Melissa's face softened. 'I'm just glad you're back in town and everything's OK. You want to hear my lines for me?'

'Not really. You'll be fine. You always are.'

'But I want to be word-perfect for this one. George Jones is the guest star. He's playing J.C.'s father. He's really cool.'

'"No Show Jones?"'

'Don't call him that! It's not true any more. Wait till you hear him sing. I think he's just amazing.'

'Isn't he amazing?' Debra Jo whispered to Melissa. They were standing to one side on the floor watching the white-haired, still handsome George Jones rehearse a scene with J.C. 'The Ol' Possum's fought booze, drugs, bankruptcy, and he just keeps coming back for more of life. I really admire him. Everything he's lived through is right there on his face and in that voice. He's one of a kind.'

Julia had come up with another power-packed ending to the episode entitled, 'Daddy, You Hardly Knew Me'. The log line read: 'Janine's dad, Clay Lamar, a has-been country singer (played by veteran country star, George Jones), on the comeback trail, lands in Houston and drops in on the Changing Room.'

FADE UP:
INT. THE CHANGING ROOM BEAUTY SALON – EARLY EVENING
THE LAST CUSTOMER HAS GONE. JANINE AND CLAY SIT ALONE TOGETHER IN THE SHOP.
CLAY: I'm sorry I ran out on you and your sister that way. I missed out on so much. But I couldn't stop myself from goin'. I belong on the road. (Looks around the salon.) Looks like you done all right for yourself, kid.
JANINE: Can't complain. Except with Carl gone, it's pretty lonely.
CLAY: It's pretty lonely out on the road, too. (Looks up and sees the guitar hanging on the wall.) That's my old Gibson! You kept it for all these years?
JANINE (Nodding): Some things are hard to let go.
CLAY: (He takes the the guitar down from the wall. He begins to play an old George Jones favorite, 'He Stopped Loving Her Today'. After a moment, J.C. joins in. They sing harmony.)
CLAY (Looking at her with surprise): You've got a soulful voice there, girl. How come I never knew that?
JANINE: You never really knew me, Dad.
CLAY: (He kisses her on the cheek.) Maybe. But I never stopped loving you.

There was a hushed silence as J.C. and George looked lovingly into each other's eyes. He put his arms around her and gave her a big hug.

'Isn't he something?' Debra Jo whispered. 'Now that is real country. His voice sends shivers up and down my spine. Don't you just love him?' She looked over at Melissa. The girl was standing stock still, staring straight ahead, tears streaming down her face.

Debra Jo walked through the commissary, balancing a plate of fresh fruit and cottage cheese in one hand and a bottle of lemon-lime Perrier in the other. She needed to lose three pounds this week if she was going to fit into her costume. It had taken her several months to get over the presence of the familiar faces of big stars eating their lunch in the Pacific Victory commissary. She knew enough now not to rush up to them and ask for their autograph while they were in the middle of their pasta primavera. She didn't want anyone bothering her while she scarfed down what few calories were allotted to her before rushing back to the set for the afternoon's rehearsal with cameras. Quickly she scanned the room until she found Bonnie McKimmie, sitting by herself at a table at the back, reading a copy of *Première* magazine. Melissa was still on set, rehearsing a scene with J.C.

In Debra Jo's purse was a letter from Eddie with some vital information concerning the whereabouts of Melissa's father. Her instinct told her to go straight to Melissa with what Eddie had found out, but maybe she owed it to the girl's mother, the woman who'd actually been married to Gordon McKimmie, to tell her first.

'OK if I join you?' she asked.

'It's a free country.' For the life of her, Bonnie couldn't understand what Melissa saw in this woman. OK, so she was friendly enough, but she never shut up. Overweight, nothing hair, she dressed like an ad for toilet-bowl cleaner, yet the whole country seemed to have fallen in love with her. What was the big deal? Bonnie kept her nose in her magazine.

Debra Jo got Eddie's letter out and set it beside her plate. 'Listen, Bonnie, when Melissa was staying with me in Houston that time, she asked my husband to see if he could track down her dad.'

'She did?' Bonnie closed the magazine with a snap.

'Yes. She told Eddie, that's my husband, that her father had been in the service. Eddie was drafted in '75 just before the end of Vietnam. He took his basic training and he thought for sure he'd be sent to 'Nam but by the end of the eight weeks the war was over so he ended up as a jeep driver for an intelligence officer in order to finish out his service. He was driving this officer, Colonel Beaudry, all over the place, and they got to be good friends, and even after Eddie got out of the service, they stayed in touch, you know exchanging Christmas cards, that kind of thing . . .'

'Yeah, yeah,' Bonnie nodded impatiently, 'where is this leading?'

'Well, Eddie contacted Colonel Beaudry. Now this is a man who's got access to top government files and, to make a long story short, I know where your husband is.'

'You do?' Bonnie's jaw dropped in amazement.

'Yes. It's all in here.' Debra Jo shoved the envelope over to her and ate her lunch in silence while Bonnie read the letter.

Hoping President Carter's amnesty applied to him, Gordon McKimmie had snuck across the Canada/US border. He had got a job as a shipping clerk with an electronics firm in southern California and worked there for six months until the firm got a government contract which meant that all employees were subject to a security check. Gordon's social security number linked him to his service record, which revealed he'd deserted during basic training and fled to Canada. Desertion while in training, especially during the Vietnam war, did not automatically warrant incarceration in a military prison, but he had been sentenced to a couple of years in a civilian prison. Serving time had not rehabilitated Gordon McKimmie to re-enter American society. According to his record, since 1985, he had been in and out of prison on numerous charges, the latest being a series of breaking and enterings which had landed him once again in the state penitentiary.

Bonnie read the letter twice before handing it back to Debra Jo. 'Well, that's that, I guess,' she said.

'Melissa's going to want to know. She may even want to see him. The Chino Correctional Institute is not far, maybe a hundred miles from LA. You'll have to tell her.'

'I'm not going to tell her anything. Look, Gord can't do either of us any good now. He can't help me get a green card and he can't exactly build a relationship with his daughter while he's behind bars. Nothing for me to do but divorce the son of a bitch and forget about it.'

'That's not fair to Melissa. We both know she's stuck on this idea of finding her dad,' Debra Jo felt her frustration rising. Bonnie was always so thorny. 'She needs things settled one way or the other.'

'That's for me to decide,' Bonnie said loudly. 'It's got nothing to do with you.'

'I'm her friend. She asked for my help.'

'Yeah? Well, in case you've forgotten, I'm her mother.'

'Then why don't you grow up and act like it.' Debra Jo

tried to keep her voice down, aware that everyone in the room had stopped chewing, forks in mid-air, to listen. 'It's a crime the way you treat that child. You can't blame her for looking somewhere else for what she doesn't get at home.'

'You're trying to steal my daughter away from me.' Bonnie reared back and slapped Debra Jo so hard she lost her balance and fell on the floor. 'Keep your fucking nose out of our business.'

'Mom, what are you doing?'

Bonnie whirled around to see Melissa and J.C. standing in the doorway of the commissary.

MAKEOVER MOMS BATTLE IT OUT IN STUDIO COMMISSARY

J.C. Austin and Melissa McKimmie, the mother-daughter team on Makeover, looked on in horror as Melissa's real-life mom, Bonnie, and newcomer to the series, Debra Jo Fawcett, engaged in a slanging match involving more than harsh words.

The thirty-four-year-old mother of the teen star landed a punch that toppled the housewife-turned-actress and left her bleeding on the floor, then jumped on top of her and proceeded to pummel her, despite her cries for help.

'They were rolling around, kicking and screaming, pulling each other's hair,' says a source close to the *Insider*. 'It was a real cat fight.'

A burly security guard, apparently stunned by the scene, watched in amazement as MO's star, J.C. Austin, had to wade into the fray to separate the two women.

'Get your hands off my kid, you scheming b——' Bonnie was heard to scream. Rumored to be a heavy drinker, you may remember, earlier this year, it was *HI* that brought you reports of Bonnie's all-night partying at some of the city's top spots.

'You're an unfit mother. You don't deserve a child as wonderful as Melissa,' retaliated Debra Jo, who is known to have a close personal relationship with the young actress. Since joining the show this season . . .

Chapter Forty-three

Without finishing the rest of the article, Debra Jo wadded it up and threw it away. Look what she got for trying to help? A black eye and her good name trashed in the tabloids. The *Hollywood Insider* made it sound so much worse than the truth, and the truth was bad enough. The article described a prize heavyweight match that went on for many rounds instead of a quick skirmish that was over as fast as it had begun. Debra Jo had never been involved in a physical fight with anybody, and she was caught off-guard when Bonnie attacked her. The woman reeked of alcohol, even in the middle of the day. She was damn lucky that J.C. had pulled her off, literally saving her face. Bonnie's nails were razor sharp and, as it was, one of her rings had left a big gash under her right ear.

Of course the *Insider* made it sound like she lay there for hours bleeding to death on the floor. It was so embarrassing to read this in a national publication. Despite the sensivity of the rest of the Makeover company, Debra Jo had secretly wanted to get her name in the *Hollywood Insider*, so that all her friends back home would know she'd made it for real. But so far their coverage of her new career had been less than flattering. First she was accused of being out to get rid of Linda Earl, now she was being portrayed as a yowling street fighter, ready to beat up on another woman. Her friends would read this and think that Hollywood had really changed her.

As bad as it was for her, it must be devastating for Melissa. Her own mother exposed as an alcoholic and a street fighter. Poor kid. She'd had to cope with a lot in her fourteen years. No wonder she acted like a miniature adult sometimes. That was why Debra Jo agreed to take Melissa to the Chino Correction Institute to meet with her father after all. She had warned Melissa that she might not like what she saw, but Melissa insisted that she needed to know, once and for all. Gordon McKimmie was behind bars but he hadn't murdered anyone. Right now, she didn't believe her father could be worse than her mother.

'Hey, guys, this is my daughter, my little star,' Gordon McKimmie introduced her around and Melissa waved a shy hello. The Chino Correctional Institute didn't look all that much like a prison. When Debra Jo offered to take her to meet her father, she had somehow envisioned him being in a real cell. Maybe that was where he slept but, at the moment, they were sitting stiffly in a sun-filled dayroom, one group of men gathered around a TV set which was blaring 'One Life To Live', while another group played cards in the corner.

'You're the spitting image of me,' Gord sounded pleased.

'Same hair,' Melissa nodded. Actually his red hair, now mixed with gray, a sort of sandy, gold-beige color, didn't look anything like hers, but she wanted to find a connection too. This man, sitting across from her, was nothing like she had imagined. He had hair to his shoulders, but it was thin and straggly; his skin was pale, his body soft, flabby. Well, where would he get a tan, dummy? Still, didn't they work out in prison? Somehow she'd expected him to be more lean and hard-bodied, like Bruce Willis or one of those criminals on Top Cops. Not sad and tired, slump-shouldered, nervously rolling one hand-made cigarette after the other. Every once in a while he would crack his knuckles.

'So, let's have a picture,' her father said. 'That's why you brought the camera, isn't it?' He gestured to the Polaroid tucked under Melissa's arm. 'Maybe your friend will take it for us?'

'OK, sure.' Melissa handed the camera to Debra Jo and went over to stand next to Gordon. When he put his arm around her, she felt awkward, but that was silly. He was her father. This was the moment she'd been longing for. Debra Jo aimed and pushed the button, father and daughter smiled, and the camera whirred. Nobody said anything as they all stood around waiting for the photo to process and slide out.

'Thanks, that's great,' Melissa took the photo and showed it to him. They both looked weird. Well, what could you expect? She put it in her shoulder bag.

'Hey, how about me?' said her dad. 'I want one, too.'

They had to do it all over. Again, they were all silent watching for the photo to be ready. 'Great,' her dad took the snapshot and tucked it in his shirt pocket.

Nobody knew what to say next. Melissa looked at Debra Jo. 'Well, I guess I'll pop down to the cafeteria for some coffee.' Debra Jo moved reluctantly toward the door.

'I'll take good care of her,' Gord said. 'I'm not going anywhere.' He laughed, a rattling, choked sound.

'You'll be OK?' Debra Jo looked at her nervously.

'Oh yeah, fine,' Melissa reassured her. 'I'd kind of like to talk to Dad on my own anyway.'

'Gord,' Gordon corrected her. 'You're old enough to call me by my first name, don't you think?'

'Sure. Gord.' Melissa gave a little jerk of her head to Debra Jo. 'See you later.'

'I'll be back in half an hour.' Glancing over her shoulder a couple of times, Debra Jo left the room.

Melissa swallowed. 'So, I guess it's been a while.' Boy, what a stupid thing to say. Everybody in the dayroom was staring at them. It was hard to tell the difference between the inmates and the guards, they were all dressed the same.

'You're a star now,' Gord gave her a lopsided smile. 'You're on TV.' She nodded. 'You know, I can't believe I never made the connection. I watch the show, but I didn't think it could be you. I guess that was pretty stupid, huh? But, I mean, Canada's a long way from California. I should have known your mom would have pushed you to do what she couldn't do. How is Bonnie?'

'Fine,' Melissa said politely. She couldn't believe he'd actually watched the show and didn't realize it was her. For so long she'd been clinging to the idea that the moment he saw her he would instantly recognize her and come for her. Of course she was barely a year old when he left, she was bound to look a lot different now. But still, same name, same age, red hair. Was his brain completely fried?

'Looks like she hasn't changed much.'

'What do you mean?'

'Same hellcat as ever. That picture made me laugh. Old Bonnie and your friend there – what was her name, Debra Jo – rolling around on the floor, scratching each other's eyes out? Man, that was something else.'

Her stomach turned over. 'Oh, no, you mean you saw

that? You get the *Hollywood Insider* in here?'

He laughed. 'Newspaper of choice for those in the know. *HI*'s got the best personal section of any of the tabs. I've found a couple of great penpals through it.'

She was mortified. 'Those papers, they make up a bunch of stuff, doesn't really happen.'

'I bet this did. I can believe it of Bonnie. She never took any shit off anybody. Neither did I. I bet you're the same way, right?'

'Right.' She felt the tears sting against her eyelids.

'You know, I was glad when they told me you wanted to come and see me.'

'You were?' Please, please, don't let me cry.

'Yeah. You know me and Bonnie never got a real divorce.'

'I know.'

'I mean, there wasn't anything I could do. I got back to the good old US of A and I had to lay low. You understand, right?'

'Sure.'

'But I was thinking of trying to track her down myself.' His hand shook as he painstakingly piled the loose tobacco on to the paper, rolling it up neatly and lighting the end. She waited for him to continue. He seemed to have lost his train of thought. He put the cigarette in his mouth and cracked his knuckles.

'You were saying about Mom?' she prompted. So he wasn't ideal casting for your average dad. He'd had more than his share of rough breaks, it wasn't really his fault. Vietnam screwed up a lot of guys. You could see that every time they showed footage of visitors to the Memorial in Washington DC. Rubbing names off the stone, crying, even after all these years, leaving presents for men who had been lost long ago. 'You were looking for her?'

'Yeah. I want to get married again. A chick I met through the personals. See, I told you they work,' he chuckled. 'I'm due to get out in fourteen months, but she don't want to wait, she wants to go ahead and tie the knot. Now that I've found you, you think Bonnie will give me a divorce?'

Her heart plummeted. 'Probably. She's actually mentioned the idea once or twice.' She'd only just found him and already he was leaving again. Suddenly she wanted to

440

reach out and hold him there, make him really see her. She started babbling. Telling him everything all at once. About their life back in Vancouver, their house that they were subletting to friends while they were here in LA, the teachers she'd had, her favorite color, her favorite foods, the cat they'd had to leave behind. As if she could give her father a crash course in the daughter he was meeting for the first time, not as a baby, but on her way to being a young adult. She tried to be funny. Maybe if she could make him laugh, he would like her; if he really got to know her, maybe even love her. She was lovable, after all, wasn't she? Millions of people she didn't even know loved her. Why couldn't he?

He sat there nodding and smoking. When she finally ran out of steam, he said. 'Hey, that's great, baby. I'm glad you're happy. That's what we all deserve. So what do you think? Is Bonnie ready to set me free?'

Fuck him. She had never used that word before in her life. Never even thought it. But now she said it out loud, over and over again. 'Fuck you, fuck you, just fuck you, you fucker.' He stared at her in utter amazement. The guys in the room didn't say a word as she called her father all the worst things she could think of. She wouldn't give him the satisfaction of seeing her cry. She had already cried it all out that day at the beach when Bonnie told her about Gordon abandoning them so long ago. That was when she had really lost her father. She just hadn't realized it until now.

'OK, everybody, let's settle. Not bad for a first read, but I think Julia would like to hear that all again.' Alex clapped his hands to get their attention. They had just done the Monday table-reading of the season finale, 'Like Mother, Like Daughter'. The Judds were guest-starring as mother/daughter makeovers. It was a very funny episode in which Wynona ended up looking like Naomi and vice-versa.

'That was a nice spin you ladies put on the last scene. Melissa, you appear to be sleepwalking through this. Get with the tour. Give it some energy, OK?'

'Why should I? Monday doesn't really count.'

'Excuse me?' Heads around the table snapped to attention.

'I said, Mondays don't count,' she yawned, barely disguising it with her hand. 'I mean, lots of other shows, they just do a half-day on Monday.'

In an instant, Julia was at her side. 'Mondays count, Mel. The Monday read-through is where I make my decision about the script and that impacts on the rest of the week.'

'So?' For an instant she felt guilty embarrassing Julia, who had always been particularly nice to her. The faces around the table looked concerned. Let them. This was the new, tougher Melissa. Get used to it. 'That's your job.'

'And this is yours. Do you get paid for Mondays?' Melissa nodded. 'All right then. Mondays count. Every day counts.'

'This is not the Melissa McKimmie show, you know.' Alex reminded her.

'Looks like this week it belongs to the Judds.'

'OK, everybody on break for ten minutes. Mel, into my office.'

He didn't have to go ballistic on her. Everybody else got a chance to throw their weight around but the minute she made one little peep, he was hauling her on to the carpet. She slouched after him into the office.

'Now, what's with the prima donna act?' He shut the door. 'Talking back in front of our guest stars, behaving like a spoiled brat, this isn't like you.' He put his arm around her, but she shrugged it off and moved over to the Mr Coffee that Alex continually kept going in his office. She helped herself to a cup of coffee. He raised an eyebrow. She stared back at him, slumping down into a chair. Alex sat on the edge of his desk and looked at her quizzically. 'Where's Bonnie? She wasn't here on Friday and she's not here today. You two have a fight?'

'I don't know where she is. I'm not her mother.' When she had told Bon that Debra Jo was taking her to see her dad, Bon had flown into a rage and stomped out of the house. That night, when Mel had got home from the 'pen' – that's what she was already calling it – her mother hadn't been there. She'd ordered a pizza, eaten it all herself, and gone to bed. In the morning, no Bon. So she'd telephoned Pac Vic and asked them to send a studio car and driver to pick her up for the set. She hadn't seen Bonnie for four days. So what? She could handle things fine on her own, she didn't need anybody to look after her. She was fourteen and she felt she'd already lived as much as someone twice her age.

'Has she called in?'

'Nope.' Melissa lit up a cigarette.

'And just what do you think you're doing?' Alex grabbed the cigarette out of her hand and dropped it right into her mug of coffee.

'Oh, gross,' Melissa peered down at the cigarette fizzling and then floating in the thick, dark liquid. 'You had no right to do that.'

'Yes. I do. You know there's no smoking in my office. When did you start smoking anyway? This isn't like you.'

'You're riding me too hard,' she accused Alex. 'On Friday, you made me do that one scene over and over again. Today, it's the same thing.'

'You're usually much harder on yourself than I am.'

'You're harassing me. Get off my case.'

Alex studied her intently. 'I happen to believe in you. You're a gifted actress, Mel, with a major future in this business, small screen and big screen, if you want it. Your instincts are spot-on. You've got brains as well as talent. I don't like to see you wasting either. Nor holding up the rest of the company while you work through your private demons. I suggest you take Jodie Foster as your role model instead of Drew Barrymore.'

Melissa stared at him defiantly.

'Look, I know this is hard work. You're not having a normal childhood, but them's the breaks, kid. Is there something going on at home that I should know about? I mean more than the usual tension between you and your mom? Anything I can help you with?'

She was about to speak when there was a feverish knock at the office door. Cindi, the production assistant, came running in, glancing over her shoulder. 'Sorry to interrupt, but Melissa, this concerns you. A representative from the LAPD is out here for you.'

'The police? For me? Why?' Surely she hadn't been that bad. Then the real fear struck. 'Oh no. Is it Bon?'

'Oh, honey, don't panic. She's not hurt. She's just, well, the charge is drunk and disorderly. They picked her up on the street in Venice and they're holding her at the precinct.'

Immediately Alex began issuing orders. 'Cindi, we'll skip the second read-through. The actors can go to wardrobe. This afternoon we'll start with blocking on the set. Explain the situation to Julia. Smooth things over with the Judds. If we have to, we'll go into overtime tomorrow. Come on, Melissa, I'm going to the station with you.'

MAKEOVER'S SECOND SEASON DRAWS TO SHATTERING CLOSE

MELISSA'S MOM LANDS IN DETOX CENTRE

What is the future for Makeover? That's the question on everyone's lips now that the company has lensed its season finale and dispersed for the summer hiatus.

Last month, Bonnie McKimmie, mother to Melissa McKimmie who plays smart-talking Carlene, was ordered to enter a detox center outside LA. This happened only days after Melissa discovered her father is a convicted criminal kept behind bars in the California Pen. The *Insider* was able to obtain this photo of father and daughter at their heartbreaking first meeting in thirteen years.

But Melissa's troubles are only part of the problems that continue to plague one of the most successful sit-coms in TV history.

This season, Makeover garnered its highest ever Neilsen ratings, the program often placing number one in the top ten. Its network, CBN, is now moving into first place ahead of all the others. But the show itself has become a battlefield littered with the corpses of axed actors, family feuds, and broken marriages.

'The hair-raising stories connected with the salon sit-com are hot enough to curl your hair,' says a source close to the *Insider*. In just one year:

Linda Earl, resident beauty queen, was revealed to be bulimic and dropped from the show.

Paul Green, popular comedian turned actor, has lost his wife and kids as, after giving birth to twins, Chaya Green returns to NYC with all five children.

Brandon Tate threatens to walk unless his contract is honored, allowing him to direct an episode in the third season.

Hot tamale Theresa Ruiz threatens to quit unless more attention is given to her and Shirley Bunting as 'representatives of ethnic minorities'.

Houston housewife Debra Jo Fawcett, brought in to replace Linda Earl, ends up in fistfight with Bonnie McKimmie.

Makeover's number one star, J.C. Austin, is reportedly jealous over rising star Kelly Carmichael's popularity.

'J.C. is furious because Kelly's getting more and more lines when the show is supposed to be about Janine. Kelly started off with a cameo role, but viewers demanded to see more of the sexy Samantha. Both stars can't be number one. Makeover should be renamed Whose Show Is it Anyway?

Network bigwigs hope that time away from each other will resolve the actors' differences. But an insider says, 'The wounds are deep, the show is in danger of self-destructing.'

Writer-producer, Julia Hudlow Turgov, along with some of the show's stars, blames the tabloids for creating the controversy. All we can say to that is, 'Hey, we calls 'em as we sees 'em.'

Could this be the last year for Makeover?

Lance J. Sutton

HIATUS

Chapter Forty-four

Paul was staying in LA for the summer. Chaya and the kids were going back to New York. Visit all the relatives. Show off the twins to Max and Ruth Gottlieb. Ostensibly that was the purpose of spending the summer away from each other. Neither of them wanted to acknowledge this as an actual separation, but each knew the possibility existed. There had been too much tension between them lately.

'What are you going to do here all by yourself all summer?' Chaya asked. 'Won't you be awfully lonely?'

Paul didn't want to tell her that being by himself sounded like absolute heaven. Excited to be sprung for the summer, the kids were chasing each other around the house, slamming doors and shrieking with laughter; the twins, Shulamit and Shoshana, had kept them up all night with colic. His nerves were now continually on edge, and he could no longer count on Chaya to soothe them. Maybe he should make himself a cup of herbal tea?

'I want to stay in town, keep my ear to the ground. TV ends careers. I can't afford to get stuck in it. I need another film.'

'You've turned down everything offered to you.'

'That's because they're all cheap rip-offs of *Shooting Blanks*,' he grabbed a glass mug and filled it with steaming water from the special filtered hot water tap they'd had installed at great expense. He could have tea at any time without waiting for the kettle to boil, although he had to admit it didn't taste quite as good. 'I've got to be selective about my next project. Did I tell you I'm in development for a film with Brandon Tate?' They'd started out competing, now they were playing off each other, trading jokes and choice lines. Jock Talk was now his favorite part of the show and was fast becoming a cult.

'Don't you see enough of him during the regular season?'

Chaya turned her back to rummage in the cupboard for the Sleepytime tea. He knew she resented his friendship with Brandon. She still blamed him for Paul's being absent at the birth of the twins. 'You'd co-star with Brandon?'

'He'll direct and I'll star. I promised him I'd stick around and help him raise some money for the project. He wants to shoot it next summer. I've got some stand-up gigs scheduled, too. That will keep me out of trouble.'

'Stand-up?' A gentle frown creased her smooth brow. 'Why? I thought you wanted to leave all that behind.'

'I actually miss it. A studio audience of two hundred people doesn't do it for me. I miss the hit of a crowd that's there just to see me.'

Chaya looked at him quizzically. 'You were just voted the Funniest Man on TV by the readers' poll. How many more people do you need to tell you you're wonderful?'

'You think this is all about ego, don't you?' The water in his mug was already cold. He dumped it into the sink and refilled the mug.

'You're great with a crowd, Paul. Not so hot one-on-one.'

'What's that supposed to mean?'

'I think you're using this as a way of avoiding dealing with us.'

'Us?'

'The family. Me and the children. Our lifestyle.'

'I'm in a profession that is a religion in and of itself. They don't take kindly to my having another religion.'

'You can either be trapped by our tradition or empowered by it.'

'Are you planning to give me the tea?' he said irritably, 'or just hold on to it for the rest of the day?'

'Oh,' she looked down at the box in her hand, 'sorry. Here,' she tossed it to him.

'Look, I'm feeling a little weighed down, OK? I mean, in our day and age, maybe we don't need to express our feelings through praying and fasting?' His hand shook, he dunked the teabag into the mug of water which was rapidly losing its steam.

Chaya's frown deepened. 'Kosher laws are designed to let man be put on earth in order to carry the message: man must not be an animal or a robot. Man must improve, man must civilize. I bet it was easier being a Jew in Poland than it is in Hollywood. Seduction is its own kind of persecution.

The cost of prosperity has been a loss of spiritualism.'

'I'm trying to tell you how I feel,' Paul said with increasing irritation, 'and you're trying to trap me in a philosophical debate.'

'Well, believe it or not, Paul, how you feel is not the most important thing in this world.'

'I'm going to tell you anyway. I feel schizophrenic, torn apart.' There, it was out. 'I'm trying to live in both worlds and I'm not doing justice to either one.'

Chaya shook her head. 'I can't help you with this, Paul. You see me as your problem; the problem is within yourself.'

'You read the *Hollywood Insider*. They see us as freaks. For shock value and titillation, there's very little difference between the two-headed babies and us.'

Chaya shuddered. 'I don't want to even think about that horrible trashy paper. I hate having that kind of attention focused on me. It makes me sick the way they took all the wonderful things about the way we live and twisted them into something weird and ugly.' Paul put down his tea and went to hold her, but she shook him off. 'I can't stand living in a fish bowl, Paul. I can't cope with all this. I need to get away.'

'I'm going to miss you,' Paul said, but even as he said it, he felt guilty. Part of him was panicked at the thought of being on his own, the other part was already experiencing a heady, exhilarating sense of freedom.

'You need time for yourself, too. I can see you're feeling crowded and cramped. We're just not listening to each other the way we used to.'

'You know I love you,' he said quietly.

'If you love me, you'll understand that I've got to get out of here.'

The stand-up concerts were exciting, they made him feel alive again. Although it was weird in the beginning. It was hard for him to tell whether he was genuinely funny any more. He had become a famous funny man. They laughed right away at everything he said. Plus, they expected to see him do stuff from Makeover. They didn't understand or remember that his stand-up act was different, that he was Paul Green not Troy Morrison. When he walked on to the stage, the audience would yell out, 'Where's Janine?

451

Where's Travis?' They wanted to know what Kelly was really like and if that was Theresa's natural accent. He wanted to say, 'Hey, I'm not Entertainment Tonight, I'm a comic.'

But for his sold-out gig at Carnegie Hall, he got Brandon to go onstage first and try and sell the audience some sports equipment. When they realized who he was, they went wild, clapping and cheering. Then Paul joined Brandon for a little impromptu Jock Talk just like they were now doing on the show.

'I never thought I'd end up being the warm-up act for Paul Green,' Brandon grumbled good-naturedly as they stood in line at the fish market on the Santa Monica Pier, where they were meeting for brunch to discuss strategy for their film project.

'You were great,' Paul clapped him on the back. 'I feel guilty,' he stared at the array of shrimp, mussels, clams and oysters laid out on a vast bed of ice, 'I really shouldn't be eating here.'

'You keep kosher outside the home?' Brandon selected a variety of oysters on the half-shell and ordered the Mexican cook to steam up a couple of pounds of clams.

'Well, there are some great kosher restaurants in LA. Chaya always packed me lunches for the studio. If I've got a power lunch, I suggest Le Dôme and the Palm, because they let me brown-bag it. I just hand my food to the maitre d' and ask him to put it on a plate with some lettuce.'

'You're kidding!'

'Nope.'

'Then, it's definitely time for you to live dangerously. Want to try some fresh crab? They've got them live here and they'll boil them up right in front of our eyes.'

Paul gulped. 'Sure, why not?' But as the fishmonger reached into the tank, the crabs went crazy. Right. They were not fools. They recognized the hand of death. Paul wasn't sure he could accept responsibility for the death of a living creature. He felt like a Roman emperor at a gladiator fight. The unlucky crustacean was kicking and undoubtedly, in a high-pitched frequency unrecognizable to the human ear, was screaming as the fishmonger held it triumphantly aloft. Paul was tempted to give the thumbs up and let Spartacus live but he didn't want to appear a wuss in front of Brandon. Ouch. The crab was instantly plunged into a huge caldron of boiling water over a gas flame. He beat a hasty retreat to the dock out back of the market café. It was a gloriously sunny day and he and Brandon sat at a picnic table and drank Corona beer from tall, clear glass bottles until the steaming red crab was brought to them wrapped in newspaper along with a large, heavy, wooden mallet.

'You want to do the honors?' Brandon held it out to him.

'No, no. You go ahead. I'll watch.' Paul winced as he slammed the mallet down on the back of the broad carapace. He half expected the crab to come back to life and go scuttling off the edge of the pier and into the ocean. Brandon removed the back and cracked open a claw, neatly extracting, intact, the prized pink and white meat. He plopped it into Paul's paper plate where it lay there quivering. Amazing. Even without the shell, the meat retained its claw shape. It glistened in the sun, shiny and moist, purple veined. Paul nibbled at it tentatively.

'You pop the whole thing in your mouth,' Brandon urged.

'I know, I know.' He dunked it in the melted butter, swallowed it whole, followed by a slug of ice-cold beer. Any minute now he was going to throw up right over the edge of the dock. Chaya would probably prefer that he screwed one of the blonde beach bunnies playing volleyball on the sand than eat this traif.

'Delicious,' he hoped he sounded convincing. 'So how's our screenplay coming along?'

'We've got a great working title,' Brandon sucked on one of the crab's legs. '*Fish Out of Water*.'

'What are we talking here? Jews on Horseback, Duelling Jews, Blazing Jews?'

'It's a comedy-thriller with a romantic twist. I see you as a comedian who can play leading man. Funny but smart, outrageous and sharp. Billy Crystal type of thing.' Brandon went on to explain the plot of the film. A professor of Hebrew at NYU, former Peace Corps worker in Africa, is asked to help a group of Ethiopian Jews who have settled in New York. They speak little English, but they do understand Hebrew. Jewish professor has to team up with a black woman, a social worker, who is also supposed to help the newcomers integrate themselves into American society. They're instantly hostile to each other. 'She knows nothing from Jews, he knows little from American blacks, the Ethiopian Jews know nothing about the US. All of them are . . .'

'Fish out of water,' Paul finished. 'Sounds good.'

'Urban life is not without its dangers. We get some gang warfare, we've got a murder . . .'

'Romance?'

'Of course. Our Jewish hero's got a princess of a girl-friend. Thinks he should play it safe and suck up to her daddy, who happens to be the NYU department head. But of course he ends up falling in love with the African-American woman. Could be controversial, but inter-racial themes are hot right now and I think, if it's handled right, it could be funny and thought-provoking. We should have a first draft next week.'

'Jewish writer?' Paul wanted to know.

'And black. One of each. The dialogue has to ring true. How's our other project coming along?' Brandon and Paul had made a deal to do a little digging on their own to find out all they could about the *Hollywood Insider*. It was hard to counter attack without knowing the enemy.

'A little progress, not a lot. I've found out the headquarters for HI Publications is located in a place called Mentira. It's on the south-east coast of Florida. So far, I've come up with zip on either Susan Carroll or Lance J. Sutton, but I'm still poking around.'

'Good. The *Insider* seems to be cooling it during the hiatus anyway.'

'Probably just lying in wait for Makeover to start up again.'

'Yeah,' Brandon nodded. 'Listen, if you're free Friday night, I've got an invite to Stan and Demeter's party. It's guaranteed to be an A list affair, good opportunity to do some dealing.'

'Friday night. I don't know. Chaya—'

'Has left you,' Brandon said.

'That's right.' Paul took a bite of crab and chewed it determinedly. 'You're on.'

'Holy shit, she looks like she's seen *Batman Returns* one too many times,' Paul nudged Brandon toward Demeter King who stood alone on the deck looking down on the roaring ocean. The party was supposed to be black tie, but Demeter was wearing a black, reptile-patterned, wet-look bodysuit, silver-studded belt and four-inch spike heels. Every inch of her tall, rapier-thin figure was outlined by the clinging material and her waist-length blonde hair was blowing dramatically in the wind. Her small, sharply pointed breasts were outlined in glittering sequins making them look, as Paul observed, like two silver bullets. 'You could kill a vampire with those things,' he whispered.

Paul pegged the Stanfield Kings' rectangle of glass in Pacific Palisades as 'a public incentive to throw stones'. The starkly modern building housed one of the biggest art collections in the civilized world.

'Stan may not know a thing about art,' Brandon said to Paul, 'but he knows what he likes – a good investment. Tim's taste runs more to Classic Comic Book kitsch.'

Paul and Brandon had schmoozed and hustled and networked their way through two hours of the Hollywood cocktail party which mixed television primetime players with studio heads, entertainment power brokers, producers and high-profile agents. 'If a bomb blew up in here right now, there wouldn't be a Hollywood,' Paul joked.

'Would that be considered a national disaster or an act of God?' Brandon quipped. They had been quick to admire Stan's newest art acquisitions and careful not to avail themselves of too much of the first-class liquor for which Stan was famous.

'Better go say our goodbyes to the hostess,' Brandon said, pulling Paul out toward Demeter.

'Do we have to? There must be a reason nobody else is out there with her. Could be the fact she's standing pretty close to the edge.'

'That's Demeter. Life on the edge.'

Demeter turned to greet them with a glittering smile. 'Ever have the urge to throw yourself over?' she asked, indicating the crashing waves below.

'No,' Paul said hastily, stepping three feet back. He could easily picture himself falling to his death over and and over again.

'I think everyone has that feeling from time to time,' Brandon said smoothly. 'You can't move forward, you can't get back. The lure of the water. That old attraction-repulsion thing, you know.'

'Yes, I do,' Demeter stared into his eyes. She had a low,

smooth voice with one of those posh eastern school accents instead of the usual California quack. Radcliffe? Bryn Mawr? It was hard to place. She put a cool, elegant hand on Brandon's face and let her fingers trace the scar over his left eye. 'Self-mutilation?'

'The accident,' he said shortly.

'Oh yes,' she said. 'I remember. Well, it suits you. You're looking much more rugged these days.' Her hand moved down the side of his face, her fingers lightly touching his lips, before she drew it away.

Brandon recognized a worthy sparring partner when he saw one. They'd already gone a few rounds together at several studio parties. There was a sense of unfinished business between them. He felt that familiar surge of the blood. She was on his list and he was on hers.

'Would you like to join me for a private drink at the pool house?' Surely she wasn't suggesting tonight, here on home territory, right under her husband's nose? 'Stan's about to screen *Nosferatu* from his classic film collection, but I've already seen it.' Yes, she was. He felt another thrill of excitement. Her eyes swept over Paul, trembling like Baby Roo in the background. 'You, too. I've got a lovely single malt scotch.'

'No, thanks,' Paul stammered. 'I happen to love film classics. Wouldn't want to miss Stan's show.'

'Suit yourself,' she gave a shrug of her elegant shoulders, then flashed a smile at Brandon, teeth whiter than the foam on the waves below. 'The pool house is just down there. You can take the elevator or there's a rock path if you care to be adventurous. See you in about ten minutes?'

Brandon nodded and the two men watched as she slipped back into the crowd.

'Are you out of your mind?' Paul clutched at his sleeve. 'She's Stanfield King's wife.'

'She offered us a drink, that's all.'

'I don't think so. She's like the mechanical shark in *Jaws*; open wide, she'd snap it right off.'

'You're overreacting, Pauly boy. I think I can handle myself in the situation. Sure you don't want to come along for a little more adventure?'

'No thanks,' Paul shivered. 'Eating crab was enough excitement for one day. Give me a call when you get home and tell me all about it. If I don't hear from you in twenty-four hours, I'll send out a posse.'

The pool house was also built out over the ocean, and even more stark than the main house, all black and white, with a circular area in the middle with low-slung leather seats and a chrome bar. Surrounding that were a series of cubicles. For changing, Brandon supposed. There were full-length mirrors on the outside of each cubicle. As they sipped their scotch and chatted, Brandon could see himself reflected many times over. It was kind of like a bizarre locker-room. The dark side of desire. Already he felt excited. And more than a little curious.

Demeter drained her glass, stood up, and turned down the already low lighting to a murky glow. He could hear the sound of the waves pounding the beach outside. She unzipped her catsuit to her waist, revealing a black velvet demi-bra which lifted her breasts, but left the nipples completely exposed. Jesus. His gut contracted. The message was clear.

Just in case he missed it, she said, 'I'm not into vanilla sex. Can you handle it?'

'Vanilla sex?'

'You know straight sex, the old in and out. I prefer to be adventurous. I'd like you to surprise me.'

'Sure,' his heart was beating like a sledgehammer, 'I'm game.'

'Good,' her voice was calm, almost serene. 'Let's play.' Her long, elegant fingers began circling her own nipples, the slice and dice nails flicking them into erection. Christ! He was starting to sweat. 'I pride myself on being intuitive. Just think about what you want. I can read your mind. Let your imagination run wild.'

As if in a dream, he moved toward her. He kissed her lightly at first, then more searchingly, her mouth opening under his, their tongues doing a clicking, castanet flamenco.

She tore her mouth away from his, licking down the side of his neck, then she sank her teeth into the flesh. Ahh. It made him jump. He grabbed her black top, pulled the sleeves down to her wrists. Leaving her hands trapped in the clinging black cloth, with one hand he pulled them behind her back. He let the tips of his fingers brush, ever so delicately, across her nipples. 'Harder,' she whispered. 'What?' 'Don't be gentle. Harder.' If that was what the lady wanted. He applied pressure, pinching them into hard points of pleasure. She writhed under his touch, hissing like a snake. Roughly he moved his hand between her legs and, discovering the body suit was in two pieces, he unsnapped the crotch, revealing the thick, dark triangle of hair. He pushed her back on to the black leather chaise-longue and straddled her wide, bending down to bite her nipples as she arched up under him. Still holding her hands away from him, he moved down her body and brought his mouth close to her pulsating mound. This was something he knew how to do. This, he was good at.

'No,' she said sharply. 'I don't like that.' In one swift move, she jack-knifed him off her and on to the floor.

He lay there for a moment, panting, confused. She might be able to read his mind, but he was having a hell of a time following hers. 'What do you want?' he was forced to ask.

'I want to see you strip.' Her voice was low and authoritative. 'Take off your clothes. Do it slowly.' She stretched on one of the black leather lounge chairs and lit a Sobrani. Nice. Color coordinated cigarettes. She lay back, smoking silently, as he took off his teal-blue Armani tux and laid it over a chair. Two seconds later he stood in front of her, naked. Her eyes swept him up and down. 'Turn around,' she said. 'Nice ass.' She was treating him like a piece of meat, but he felt compelled to obey. 'Bend over.'

Gripping the edge of a chair, he did as she asked. In a moment, he felt her there, right there, behind him. She gripped his ass, her nails digging into the flesh, hard. Her tongue was wet, moving all over him. His cock was rock hard, straining for her, he wanted to be inside her, but she was still behind him. She was biting the inside of his legs, sharp little nips, his muscles jerking involuntarily each time her mouth came close to him. His legs were shaking, he was afraid he was going to fall. 'Please,' he whispered hoarsely.

'Get up,' she commanded. He turned to face her. There was no emotion in her eyes, no connection between them, other than sensation. With her stiletto heels, she was almost as tall as he was. He reached out for her, but she struck his arms away, surprisingly strong. She grabbed his hair, pulled his face to hers, and kissed him. Open-mouthed, tongues thrashing wildly, then suddenly she was pushing him, back, back; he could feel the cold mirrored glass of the cubicle door against his bare skin. The door gave way and they were inside the cubicle as she shoved him up against the wall. She was raising his arms above his head, pinning them. He could see what she was doing. There was the sound of metal against metal, he felt something cold around his wrists. 'Jesus Christ.' She had handcuffed him to the wall. He tried to move, but she shoved his legs apart and bound his ankles. He was immobilized, completely help-less. 'What the hell are you doing?'

'Surprising you.' She reached into a drawer.

'Yeah, well, be careful you don't do any permanent damage.'

'It would be silly of me to break something,' she said, taking out two long, knotted, silk scarves, 'when I might want to use it again.' She tied the first scarf around his eyes; he couldn't see a thing. He felt the other scarf come between his legs, winding around, in and out, as she proceeded to tease him and tantalize him with the silk, bringing him right to the edge and then retreating until he thought he would go crazy with the need for release. She rubbed her breasts against him, nipple against nipple, raking across his chest, down to his belly. She pressed her crotch against his and slid her cool, dry body over his wet, slippery one, sliding up and down his spread-eagled body. His cock was throbbing, he was gasping for breath, she was rubbing herself off against him, faster, harder, her breathing quickening. He was panting and crying out, strange, harsh sounds, torn from his throat, but, aside from a slight quickening of breath, she didn't make a sound. It was eerie. He became frantic, his arms and legs were trapped, he tried to use his hips to guide himself into her, but she eluded him at every twist and turn, never allowing him to enter her.

Everything became a blur; he didn't know where he was or who she was or what was happening to him. Finally the muscles of her thighs tightened against his and, without making a sound, he felt her convulse against him. The relief was so great that he came seconds later.

She pulled away from him and disappeared. He heard the sound of a door closing. He had a moment of sheer panic. Was she going to leave him here like this? Bound and blindfolded, with half of Hollywood's élite getting pissed to the gills right overhead? After a moment, he heard her heels clicking across the floor and he felt her presence near him again. Without any sense of urgency, she removed the scarf from his eyes, freed him from his bonds, stepped away and looked at him. There was no acknowledgement of what had just occurred. 'You can get dressed now,' she said crisply, doctor to patient. 'See you back at the party.' She gave him a cool little wave and went out the door.

He stood there staring after her.

Chapter Forty-five

'You've got to admit your mother loved me.' Alex and Shirley had just returned from a trip to Charleston where he had been allowed to meet her mother for the first time. For almost a year now, Alex and Shirley had been involved in their affair, but they were keeping it secret. 'Olivia thought I was splendid.'

'She was just impressed with your accent. Mama's a sucker for Masterpiece Theater.'

'Not true. When you were on the phone chatting up your girlhood friends, she took me aside and gave me her blessing.'

'Mama did?' Shirley walked to his fridge, opened it up, and poured herself a glass of white wine.

'I asked her for your hand in marriage.'

'You did what?' The glass crashed to the floor.

'She said yes.'

'Fine. Then marry her. I'm not saying yes.' Shirley grabbed a broom and began sweeping the shards of glass on to a piece of paper. 'Damn. You really need to get yourself a dustpan, Alex.'

'Leave that.' Gently, he took the broom away from her and pulled her over to a stool by the bar. 'Look, I know you don't love me the way you loved – probably still love – Roy; but I'll take what I can get.'

'Don't go acting all noble on me. It's not you.'

'I'm not being noble, I'm being extremely selfish. I want to spend the rest of my life with you. You can't have Roy Williams, but you can easily have me.'

'So I've heard.'

'Things could be worse.'

'Next you'll be getting down on one knee and saying, "You could learn to love me, Shirley, couldn't you?" Damn. This isn't some Jane Austen novel, this is real life in

461

the good old US of A. There's no shit harder.'

'Oh yes,' Alex sat down next to her, 'there definitely is. We're lucky. You and I are making pots of money. I have been for some time, you're starting to get there. We can afford to pick and choose where we want to live. It's much easier here.'

'It wasn't so easy in Charleston, was it? The stares, the glares, the whispers, the open hostility?' They were both quiet for a minute, remembering walking down the street together as an inter-racial couple, white people looking daggers at them, mumbling under their breath. Black men calling out to Shirley, 'Yo, mama, what you doin' with him, baby?' Black women saying, 'Hey, sister, you got your nerve.' The fear, the jealousy, the implied threat to their own choices. 'You think you're too good? Or not good enough?'

'You can't let other people live your life, Shirl. Stop listening to all those old tapes. White women are weak, black women are strong, black men are lazy, white men are boring. We've got to blow those myths out of the water.'

'How?' Shirley looked at him fiercely. 'It's not getting any better in this country; if anything it's getting worse. I don't want to live my life as some kind of political statement. I don't have that kind of strength. You sleep with me but you don't really know me.'

'Yes, I do.' He took her hand and kissed it.

'No. We're so different.'

'I love those differences. I thrive on them.'

'So what I am to you? A novelty act?'

'Hardly.'

'There's a privacy to the black world, an insulation; we speak a language among ourselves which you could never understand.'

'The English have their own secret club, too. More than one, depending on the class. You could never fully understand that and, trust me, you don't want to.'

She shook her head. 'No, I'm telling you, it's different.'

'Then you and I will just have to create our own world, population of two. Hey, we already have our own language.' He kissed her fingers and then her mouth, with a surprising strength and passion. 'Look, I realize you have another love with which to compare me. I know that's part of the problem for you. It's all wrapped up in history and pride

462

and loss. I don't have that. I've never come close to loving anyone the way I love you. It's not because you're black, it's because you're you. OK, OK, I realize that sounds like a line from a very bad film, but I can't help it. I want to say all those corny things to you, because I am literally desperately in love for the first time in my life and it's how I feel.'

'I'm not ready yet.'

'You can't just leave your life on hold, Shirl. I'm the most reserved person I know. I like to plan my life the way I plan my camera shots, right down to the last angle. But if I'm willing to take a chance, why can't you?' He kissed her again. 'I don't even care if I make a fool of myself, because when I'm with you, I just feel . . . right.'

She pulled away, her eyes searching his face. 'I can't say the same, you know,' she said hesitantly. 'I don't feel right, but I have to admit, I feel better. Being with you I feel better than I have in a long time.'

'Then go with that feeling. At least move in with me so we can see what we're like when we're really together, please, please.' He took her face and planted little kisses all over it. 'God, listen to me; all my natural reserve has flown right out the window. You see what you do to me?'

'All right, all right,' she was half-way between laughing and crying.

'What did you say?'

'You can stop wearing me down with words. I said all right. I'll go next door and get some things.'

'Wait a minute.' He wrapped his arms around her and pulled her on to his lap, 'I'm afraid if I let you go you won't come back.'

'I will, I will, I promise.' Now she was really laughing. 'I just don't want to have to sleep in your T-shirts for the next six weeks.'

'Oh my love,' he kissed her and stroked her hair, holding on to her tight.

Shirley had been gone maybe twenty minutes when the doorbell rang. He raced to open it and was surprised to find Melissa McKimmie standing outside.

'Hello there,' she said briskly. 'I'm glad I caught you in.' She didn't sound like Melissa. Her speech was cool and clipped. She didn't look like Melissa either. Dressed in a sophisticated summer suit with white pumps and a matching purse, she looked twenty-five. Her hair was up and she was wearing pearl earrings. 'May I come in?'

'Sure.' He opened the door for her. 'Are you on your own? How did you get here?'

'The Miata,' she sat down gracefully on the very edge of a chair. 'I parked it out front. It's not a towaway zone, is it?'

'You have a license?'

'Beginner's.' She smoothed a wayward red curl off her forehead. 'I'm licenced to drive with somebody else in the car.'

'And where is that somebody else?' Alex pretended to look around.

'I needed to talk to you on my own.' She crossed her bare legs and let one hand rest on her newly acquired bosom. 'My, it's warm out there.'

Alex blinked. 'Would you like a cool drink?'

'Thanks. I'll take a beer.'

'I don't think so,' Alex laughed. 'I had in mind juice or a soft drink.'

'You let me have a glass of champagne sometimes after the taping.'

'Hmm-mmm. I'll have the beer, you'll have a Koala Springs, how's that? Mango and passion fruit.' He popped the cap, poured it into a wine glass, and handed it to her.

She took it and looked around the room. 'Nice photographs. You take them?'

'Yes.' He opened a beer for himself.

'Excellent.' She sipped her drink.

He wondered what she wanted. 'So, how's it going at D.J.'s?' Since her mother had landed in Cri-Help, a strict live-in facility in North Hollywood for multiple addiction, Melissa had been staying with Debra Jo and Danny out in Sherman Oaks.

'All right, I suppose. The house is charming. It's convenient being close to the studio; I don't have to get up so early. I love Debra Jo. She has to win the prize for best mother in the whole world, but I have the feeling, you know, that maybe I'm kind of cramping Danny's style? Not that he's around all that much. We hardly see him.'

'He might be a little jealous. You and D.J. are pretty close.'

'I know, and that's important to me, but I don't want to crowd their relationship. I feel I'm somewhat in the way.

That's what I wanted to talk to you about. I'd like to move in with you.'

'I beg your pardon?' Alex choked on his beer.

'My father's in jail, my mother is "recovering" in rehab. Accommodation has become a problem for me.'

'You want to move in here?'

'Why not? We could share expenses. It would be a business arrangement.'

'I have a feeling that might cramp my style,' Alex said dryly.

'You mean sex?' She brushed the hair back from her forehead again. 'That's OK, I'm willing to sleep with you.'

'Excuse me?'

She put her glass down and came over to sit next to him on the sofa. 'I've been thinking about this a lot, Alex,' she said earnestly. 'I want you to make love to me. It would be my first time. I'm a virgin, you know.'

'I rather suspected that.'

'Why? None of the girls in my class are still virgins. They're all having sex.'

'I doubt if that's true and, even if it is, that doesn't make it right for you.'

'Oh, I know. When Debra Jo's son Beau was here, we went out quite a bit. He wanted to, of course, but I didn't feel ready.'

'Good for you.'

'And now I know why. I love you, Alex.' Her hand went on to his knee. 'I want my first experience to be with a man who knows what he's doing. I want it to be perfect, with someone I love.'

Gently he took it off. 'Honey, you're fifteen years old. You want to get me arrested for statutory rape? This isn't you, Melissa. Now go into the bathroom, take down your hair, and wash that muck off your face.'

'I love you, Alex, and I know you love me.' Back went the hand on to his knee.

This time he took it off and held it. 'I'm very fond of you, Melissa, you're right about that, but I don't love you.'

'Yes you do, you must,' her eyes were brimming with tears. 'I can see it in your eyes. The way you look at me when we're on the set, in rehearsal, it's different from the way you look at everyone else. It's like we have this special secret. You love me, I know you do.'

'Sweetie, I love what you do. You're such a wonderful actress. You're always able to surprise me and I love that. I delight in the choices you make. That's the secret you think I'm telling you.'

'Oh, please,' she was crying now, hard, 'you just have to. I don't have anywhere to go. Nobody wants me.'

'Honey, I can't. Not the way you're asking me to.'

'Why not? I think I've gotten pretty gorgeous this year, don't you?'

'Absolutely.' He wanted to put his arm around her to comfort her but, at this point, he didn't dare make physical contact. 'You've become quite stunning.'

'Then why can't you love me?'

'Because I'm in love with someone else.'

'Who?'

The words were out of his mouth before he had time to think. 'Shirley Bunting.'

Her little freckled face twisted with pain and betrayal. She tore herself away from him and ran out the front door. He sat there for a minute, in frozen disbelief, then jumped up and ran after her calling, 'Melissa, wait a minute. Let me explain.' But by the time he got to the edge of the balcony, she was in the pink Miata, speeding away.

'Shit, shit, oh shit.' He rushed to the phone, looked at the contact sheet posted over the desk, found Debra Jo's number in Sherman Oaks and frantically dialed it. It rang five times and then the machine clicked over. 'Hi. You've reached 213–458–7765. We really want to talk to you so leave a message when you hear the tone.' He left a message, slammed down the phone, and paced around the room. He thought about going next door to talk to Shirley, but no, he had only just managed to convince her, he didn't want this to screw things up between them. Come on, D.J., call me back, this is an emergency. Half an hour later, his hand was on the phone to try her again when it rang, making him jump. He snatched it up. 'Hello?'

'Hi, Alex, it's D.J. Listen, she's fine, she's here, she told me what happened. She's feeling really embarrassed about the whole thing.'

'No, no, that's perfectly OK.'

'I think with her dad and all, she's a little confused right now.'

'Understandably so.'

'She was looking on him as her last hope. That bastard really broke her heart.'

'I know. Are you able to talk freely?'

'Yes. She's gone into her bedroom and shut the door. Poor little thing.'

'You know, we should have seen this coming. We should have seen the signs. Has she been talking with you at all?'

'Well, sure, all the time, but not about this.'

'I guess with kids you have to listen, even when they're not saying anything. How is the living arrangement working out for you?'

'Not great like I'd hoped. I love Melissa like she was my own daughter, but she's not. I'm worried about Danny, if you want to know. He used to adore Melissa, but now that she's under the same roof, his attitude has changed. He's got a real sharp mouth on him now. Yesterday I heard him telling her to F off – well, you know the word. I don't allow that kind of talk in my house and he knows it, but I think he wanted me to hear him saying it so I would do something. Bonnie's going to be in Cri-Help for who knows how long? I don't want to put Mel out on the street, but we've got to find another solution.'

'I'm already thinking of one,' Alex said. 'Let the dust settle over the next few days. I'll check things out with a lawyer friend of mine and let's plan a family conference at your house for the end of next week.'

The three of them sat in lawn chairs out on the back porch.

'Those wild plums look wonderful,' Alex said, 'are they edible?'

'Sure.' Melissa bounded off the porch to pick a few.

'How's she doing?' Alex asked when she was out of earshot.

'OK.' Debra Jo sighed. 'She's a tough little nut, you know. I don't think it helped that the picture I took of her with her dad at the correctional institute wound up in the *Hollywood Insider*. She figured out that Gord must have sold it to the tabs himself. That hurt her pretty badly.'

Melissa came running back to hand them each a couple of plums.

Alex brushed the fuzz off the purplish-blue fruit and took a bite. 'Oh God, this is heaven,' he let the juice run down over his chin. 'When I was a little boy growing up in

London, I never thought I would live in the Garden of Eden. This place is so beautiful. OK, down to business. How's your mother progressing?'

'OK, I guess.' Melissa sat at his feet. 'They've got her in a twelve-step program. Bon's lucky to be alive at all, you know? When she went into detox, she had to have a complete physical and the doctors discovered her liver is twice as big as it's supposed to be. That's from all the booze. She was killing herself and I didn't even know it.'

'It's not your fault, sugar pie,' Debra Jo said quickly.

'Anyway, Cri-Help seems to be an OK place. I hate going to visit her there though. Bunch of losers who can't control themselves.'

'That's one way of looking at it,' Alex said. 'Another would be that it took a great deal of courage for your mother to ask for help.'

'Maybe you're afraid that you've inherited your mother's weaknesses,' Debra Jo said gently.

'Don't even think that,' Alex said. 'You're not self-destructive, no matter how hard you try.'

Melissa drew her knees together and rested her chin on them. 'You know, I used to love the fact that my mom was so young. She was like something out of a storybook. The princess not the queen. The queen is old and ugly, the princess is young and beautiful. She kept telling me if you're a woman, youth and beauty is where it's at, but you know what? I think she's wrong. Power is where it's at, and that's what I want to get for myself. Not power, exactly, but control somehow.'

'You had to grow up the hard way,' Debra Jo reached out to stroke her hair, 'you've brought yourself up.'

'It's only going to get better,' Alex said, 'I promise. But you can't live with me.'

'I know that,' Melissa sighed. 'That was so stupid.'

'Hey, most of the time you're super bright. You're allowed one fall from grace. But never offer sex in exchange for something you really want.'

'I can't believe I came on to you like that. I'm really sorry.'

'You can't live with me,' Alex repeated, 'but you could live near me.'

'How?' her face lit up.

'Shirley Bunting's moving in with me' – he waited for

some reaction from Melissa but she appeared to take the news calmly – 'so her condo will be free. It's in the same building. We could both keep an eye on you. You need to feel that even though you're living on your own, you're not alone. We're here for you, both of us, if you want us to be.'

Melissa blushed. 'I know I acted jealous, but really I think it's wild about you and Shirley.' She popped a plum in her mouth. 'You're pretty cool keeping it a secret from all the rest of us, but when I think about it, you two are perfect for each other.' Debra Jo nodded in agreement.

'I've talked all this over with Shirley and, if you're really serious about wanting some control over your own life, we will help you investigate the possibility of becoming an emancipated minor.'

'You mean like Drew Barrymore and Corey Haim?' Obviously she had already been thinking about the possibility herself.

'That way, you could be considered a legal adult before you are eighteen. The court would declare you independent, free from both your parents. You'd be able to move into your own place, handle your own money, the restrictions are quite clear. You're young, but if, as you think, some of the money you've earned has disappeared, that could influence a judge. Shirley and I would be willing to give testimony that you are a responsible person, committed to your education and your career. We would also agree to keep an eye on you to make sure you stay that way.'

'You think I'm mature enough to handle this?'

'Despite what happened last week, yes I do.'

Melissa turned beet-red. 'Every time I think about what I did, I'm so embarrassed I just want to die. It was like I was possessed or something.'

Alex smiled comfortably. 'Desperate people do desperate things. Listen, you show up for work every day. That's more than a lot of kids your age would do. More than a couple of the adults could manage last season.' All three of them were quiet for a moment, thinking of Linda Earl. 'Look at it this way, kid. You survived your childhood. You've already been through the worst.'

'It's weird being a star,' Melissa said. 'Who are all these people who are watching me? I don't know them. They don't really know me, but they think they do. I get letters from other kids asking for advice. Like I know how to help them.'

'You're in a very special position, Melissa,' Debra Jo said, 'especially for your age. You can influence other kids because they'll listen to you. Lots of kids have something to say. They care about the world and they want to change it, but they don't get the chance. You have the chance and that gives you power. Use it wisely.'

Melissa nodded, then said, 'You know, these have been the best and worst times of my whole life. I've never been so happy, or so miserable.'

Debra Jo sighed, 'I know exactly what you mean.'

Chapter Forty-six

Writing Linda Earl out of Makeover had not been easy for Julia. Visiting her in St John's Hospital to make it official was even harder. But she felt she owed it to the actress to tell her in person how her disappearance would be dealt with on the show.

'I've decided that Nadine, after years of failing with men, finds a guy, gets married, and moves to Denver. We're giving you a happy marriage, which it looks like you already have.' She smiled at Steve who sat on the other side of his wife's hospital bed, holding Linda's hand. Linda looked shockingly thin, her face white against the pillow. Who is this woman, Julia thought. I never really got to know her. She hesitated and then plunged ahead, 'With your permission, Linda, I'd like to do a Makeover episode on bulimia and I'd like to dedicate it to you.'

'You don't need my permission,' Linda said. 'You can write what you want.'

'I know, but I don't want to take advantage of your illness. It's just that the whole body-image thing is what Makeover should be about, and to address it on the show will bring the problem out into the open for a lot of people.'

'Haven't you used her enough?' Steve said bitterly. 'The talk has finally died down, the papers are on to another fresh scandal, and you want to dredge it all up again?'

'I'm so sorry,' Julia said. Looking at the thin face, gaunt against the pillows, she felt ashamed. She remembered asking herself whether Linda was worth fighting for? Was any television show worth risking a human life? What was happening to her?

Linda touched her husband's arm gently. 'Steve, honey, it's OK. Bulimia is a scary disease. The more people who know about it, the better. I've spent too much of my life trying to hide what I was I going through.'

'Thanks,' Julia pressed her hand gratefully. 'I really am sorry about all this, Linda. I feel we could have helped you more than we did. And who knows? Denver, it's not that far away, Nadine could pop in for a visit.' But as she looked at Linda, hooked up to an IV and lying there exhausted, she doubted it.

These days Julia felt surrounded by illness on all sides. In addition to Linda and Marty, her mother called from Houston to inform her that Leigh was back in the hospital. Marty was pleading with her to go away with him. She didn't want to leave the city. Her work. Pre-production for the show's third season. Let's be honest here, she didn't want to leave Liam. But she owed it to Marty. Maybe if they'd been able to grab a few weeks' vacation last summer, he would never have gotten sick. She wouldn't have fallen in love with Liam, which she could not deny she now was. Guilt was like a familiar sweater she wore every day.

'Where do you want to go?' she asked. 'Carmel? Catalina?'

'No, I've got to get away completely, out of California altogether. No professional demands, no responsibilities, no stress. Isolated. Preferably on a beach. Didn't you say you had a cousin with a place on Padre Island?'

'Mustang Island. Between Padre and Port Arransas.' Normally Julia would have resisted going back to Texas, especially in the summer, but she wanted to accede to Marty and she also had the uneasy feeling she should be close to her parents. She called Liam and told him she was leaving town for a month to go to Mustang Island.

The minute they were there, she knew it was a mistake. The beach house was right on the ocean, self-contained, a couple of miles from the nearest town. Gulf breezes, temperate waters, sandy beaches – except for the occasional black spots from an oil spill – fresh seafood. And cut off from everything that defined them. Nothing to do except lie in the sun and look out at the sea, counting the days until the vacation was over and she could go back to real life. The worst of it was, Marty didn't seem any better. With nothing to focus on except his illness, he grew more anxious every day, calling his doctors back in LA, seeing new ones in Corpus Christi and Port Arransas, looking for someone, anyone to give him the answer.

He went through a phase of agoraphobia. Getting him to

leave the house during the day to go to the grocery store was almost impossible. He would creep along, make it to the bus stop a block away, collapse on the bench, afraid either to go on or go back. One of the new doctors told him to try self-hypnosis through relaxation.

One day though, when she came home from a swim, the house smelled of garlic and onions, a Gulf breeze was blowing through the open windows, and the sound of Vivaldi came fluting through the living-room. Marty was in the kitchen, stuffing a red snapper with olives and herbs. He looked up, beaming, and gave her a kiss. 'I went to Spain today,' he said. He'd washed his hair and he smelled of shampoo and a spicy, sweet new aftershave. Flushed with the heat from the grill, his face was the one she knew and loved. It was Marty. Here in the kitchen. Back in the land of the living.

She tiptoed to the fridge and poured herself a glass of white wine, as if any loud noise might scare him away again. 'Tell me more.'

Marty began to explain his meditation process. 'I started with the usual relaxation techniques, but this time I managed to get past simple muscle relaxation and into what Lorna calls my "private pleasant place". I was thinking of Cabo de Gata on the south coast of Spain and I started to drift into this incredible meditative state. I mean, I wasn't really in Spain and I wasn't asleep either, but I certainly wasn't here. I was aware of my body and the room but they were of no importance. I was aware of light coming through my eyelids in brilliant orange and gold. There was a central pulsating circle all around me, like a giant eye. I began to understand the inspirational origins of the religious art style of India or the primitive Mayan civilization. Are you following this at all?'

'Yes.' Despite her misgivings, Julia was being drawn into his description. Marty had never been interested in the spiritual or metaphysical before.

'I didn't see Krishna or Rama, but I did see the kind of setting in which they are often painted. Finally I drifted even deeper, toward sleep or unconsciousness, I don't know which.'

'And then?'

'I got scared. I had gone further than I wished to go and I caught my breath to pull back and started the count up to ten to open my eyes. But I'm going to try it again tomorrow. I feel like I'm getting close to something.'

'I'm so glad.' She hugged him, hard. It felt like such a long time she had been missing him. 'I'm going to take a shower and wash my hair. I'll be quick.'

'That's fine,' he said cheerily. 'Take your time. Dinner will be ready in about a half-hour.'

She stood in the shower, the scalding water streaming down on her, mingling with the tears that ran down her face. Please, God, let him be all right, make this last. She came out of the bathroom, wearing the peach-colored silk kimono he'd bought her for Christmas. He was waiting for her in the bedroom, naked. He pulled her down on top of him and whispered, 'I've missed you so much, Jules. I've missed holding you and kissing you and making love.' She wrapped her arms around him and kissed him, her wet hair dripping all over his face. He smelled so good, his body felt wonderful under hers. In a tangle of arms and legs and silk, they began to make love. So familiar, but feeling new. Such a long time. Magic still. The strength of his body against hers, so hard, the softness of his mouth on hers. Oh God, I love you, how could I ever have thought that was gone. My first love, my only love. It's come back, you've come back. So good, so right, being together. Building up, up, into the peaks. Breaking through the clouds with a burst of fiery sun. Then floating, drifting, high above the earth together. Magritte floating over Paris. In the kitchen, the fish on the grill hissed away until it burned itself to a crisp. Neither of them cared.

Two days later he had her paged at the grocery store. He was hysterical, begging her to come home at once. She left her cart, piled high with groceries, in the middle of the store, ran out to the car, and drove like a bat out of hell. Marty was curled in the fetal position on the sofa. She rushed over to him. 'What happened, what's wrong?'

'I got lost,' he started to cry. His face was drawn again, he was sweating, and there was a strange smell in the air. 'I did my meditation, I got way down, almost immediately, and then this black thing, this force began pulling me under, sucking me straight into its vortex and I was petrified I'd never get back up again. Oh, God, Julia, what is the matter with me? I feel like I'm losing my mind. They say this never

474

lasts more than two years, but I can't stand two whole years of this, I can't.'

I can't either, Julia thought. She put her arms around him and held him tight.

There was a clinic she'd been reading about, one that specialized in panic and anxiety disorders. It was attached to the Feighner Research Institute in San Diego. She told Marty about it and, within twenty-four hours, they were packed and on their way back to California.

It felt strange, J.C. thought, to be back in Nashville, like wearing a summer dress out of the back of her cupboard. Still a nice color, but too short, a little tight across the bust, some buttons missing, it just didn't fit any more. Nashville had been her home for almost twenty years but now the Lone Star Estate, which was once her dream palace, had the feel of a museum. The air was better here than it was in LA, but she knew enough now to recognize the people were pretty much the same. Hustlers out to make a buck. Country was big-city business now.

The fifties had been boom years for Nashville. During the sixties times were tough for country music because its themes were out of step with social protest and the sexual revolution. The seventies saw the crossover to pop and the outlaw movement, the early eighties the urban cowboy craze. The nineties brought a meteoric rise in the popularity of country music. As sales of rock continued to drop, country sales were way up. It gave her a chuckle to see rock and pop singing stars trying to 'cross over' into country, because that's where the money was to be made. So many falling pop singers were turning up in Nashville that the city had earned a new moniker: 'the Mayo Clinic of the music business'.

In the fifties, nothing was cut in the Nashville studios except country-and-western music. Then the Atlanta rock and soul players moved into Nashville and opened their own recording studios. Big-league production standards had taken over the town and now there was nothing in music Nashville couldn't do. It even had a world-class symphony orchestra and the facilities with which to record it.

All that was well and good, but the face of the place had changed. Now Nashville had enough all-night joints lit up like Christmas trees to rival Vegas. Expensive-looking but with the smell of something cheap. Like a high-priced hooker: lady on the outside, dirt trash on the inside. Why hadn't she noticed this before?

Telephone Road, her 'confessional' album, had been hailed as a ground-breaking work and had sold better than any of her previous albums. She'd been afraid of revealing her true self, but if anything, the controversy had only served to boost sales. Trouble was, you had to keep topping past successes. Now that she'd broken silence about her past, gone back to her emotional roots, she wanted to dig deeper and explore some of the musical influences that had been part of her childhood. Blues, of course, some rock and roll, and Tex-Mex, a sound that was part authentic Mexico, part pure Texas. She was willing to spend more money on this new album, *Heart of Texas*, to get a new and different sound.

Mac had always been in charge of setting up her studio sessions, calling in the musicians, calling the shots. He'd balked at the new directions of *Telephone Road*, although he was happy enough now with the dollars and awards it continued to pull in. But this time around, J.C. wanted to lay down some working tapes on her own with the guys, so she could give Mac a better idea of where this new album was headed.

She no longer used the 'Nashville cats', the studio musicians who used to play for everybody's sessions, preferring her own band to record as well as tour with her. They were her boys, her brothers, they loved and trusted her. The 'pickers' had all made a bundle on the last album; she knew she could count on them to give her her head on this one. She was paying them each a flat fee of twenty-five thousand for the album, which meant she could call them in to rehearse whenever she liked.

For the new Tex-Mex sound she was after for *Heart of Texas*, she had to add accordion plus a bunch of Mexican fretted instruments. Some of them were highly traditional such as the guitarron, the acoustic bass guitar which mariachi bands played in the streets, and the charanga, a little baby mandolin the size of a ukulele, its back made from the shell of an armadillo. The musicians who played these instruments were as authentic as the instruments themselves, capable of handling the range of emotions and intricate rhythms she was after. She was excited at the prospect of bringing them together with her brothers for one big jam session.

She'd managed to score a recording engineer she'd been after for a long time. Bob Jacks had one of the best ears in the business. As a mixer, he was a magician and a technical genius. She'd been aching to get him into her studio.

She'd booked the pickers for the regular three-hour call. Because this session was simply to lay down a work tape, they'd set things up casually, miking the instruments, but not worrying too much about isolation. It was just something to show to Mac as a demo. As she looked around at all the musicians she had pulled together, she got a thrill of excitement. There was enough hot talent in this group to generate the steam to blow the lid off anything she had recorded up to this point. Her job now was to lay the tune out for the band and see what each of them could bring to it. Mac's unspoken direction to the band was always understood as 'play your parts, shut up, and take your check', but J.C. wanted to keep the atmosphere relaxed and easy-going, allowing the pickers more creative input. She had always been good at handling macho musicians; her language could get as rough as theirs, her jokes as raw. It felt good to be wearing plain old jeans and a T-shirt and hanging out with the guys.

She had already explained to them what she was after. 'We'll stay away from the synth on this album. Want the sound to be real and true, nothing hokey, or predictable. It'll be traditional but it's my own personal tradition, what I was raised with.' Her basic instrument was guitar but she knew enough piano to block out the basic tune for the title song.

'OK, guys,' she ran through the basic tune on the piano and then said, 'you can work on your parts, I'll play past you, and when you feel comfortable, just jump in. I know I want to lead off with the twin fiddles. That's real stone country and that's what they're going to expect, but then we do a shift on them, here, see? We bring in the accordion, that'll take them by surprise. Then add a touch of guitar-ron. That'll tell them, you think you know J.C. Austin? Well, here's something new.'

They played through once and everybody was beaming. They caught on quickly and were soon flying together. 'OK, let's do a test track. Then we'll get Bob to play it back.' J.C. was gaining confidence. Her instincts were good, she was right to trust them. She knew that, to get the sound she wanted, the one she could hear in her head, would require the patience and precision of a chamber orchestra and the creative freedom of progressive jazz. They played through again. Bob Jacks punched the talk-back button inside the control booth, and asked, 'You want to hear a playback?' J.C. nodded and they all listened. It sounded even better than she'd expected and this was just a rehearsal tape. Mac was going to be so impressed.

'We're getting close to magic, guys,' she praised them all. 'So what do you think? I can hear horn coming in somewhere in here and maybe beef up the guitarron, Manuel?' The guitarron player nodded, his dark eyes alive with excitement.

They were half-way through again when the door of the studio was flung open and Mac stormed in.

'What the hell is going on here? You're doing a session without me?' The musicians stopped playing, fingers and bows frozen in the air.

'We're just doing some work tapes for you,' J.C. said, trying to hold on to her calm.

'Bob, whatever you were paid to do this gig, I'll pay you double not to do it. You're out, as of now.' His face was a tornado cloud ready to whip across the prairies. 'The rest of you, sit there till we sort this shit out. J.C., I want to see you outside. Now.'

'Y'all take a break,' J.C. said. 'We'll get back to you in five.' The guys shuffled off.

Mac grabbed her by the arm, hard, his face right in hers, his voice low and angry. He held her up against the studio door. 'I don't want Bob Jacks in the booth. Why do you think I've never used him before? Because he's shit, that's why. I don't like what he does, I don't like the way he does it. I don't recognize half those faces in there. Who are these folks? What are all the taco benders and beaners doing here?'

'These are traditional musicians,' J.C. started to explain, but he rode right over her.

'You know I don't want greasers and niggers playing for me. I don't know what tradition you're talking about. I got nothing personal against these people, but they're not part of country music, never have been, never will be.'

'Now, Mac, don't get all pushed out of shape,' J.C. tried to get around him. 'When I called you from LA, I told you I was going after something different for this album. I wanted to get the jump on things and surprise you with a new sound, that's all.'

'Surprise me, hell. Let's get one thing straight here. I don't mess with what you're doing in LA, you don't screw up what I do here. You got your show, I got mine. Now maybe what you have in mind is just perfect for the album, but we got to talk about it before you go doing it, you understand?'

'Yes, Mac,' she said quietly. She was embarrassed, but she knew the pickers would take it in stride. They'd seen it all before. Once they walked out of the studio, they'd forget about the blow-up, it was like erasing a tape. But she wouldn't forget.

Okay, maybe these were extreme circumstances, she'd pushed him too far. Mac was feeling threatened, Julia would probably say. Except that she didn't have to push Mac for him to be yelling and ordering everybody about. She'd learned you can't scare musicians into getting the sound right. Musicians were like kids, they wanted to please you, but as teacher, Mac still ruled by the rod. He hadn't changed in twenty years. How many times had she seen him throw his weight around, blow his stack, and she'd just accepted it? The way he talked, taco benders, beaners. It wasn't like she hadn't heard all that before. That was the way Mac talked, it was part of him. But why should that kind of attitude, right out in the open, with no regard for those people's feelings, be allowed to be a part of anyone? Mac had always been a dictator. You couldn't even call him benevolent. It was his way or no way. But now J.C. was far from sure it was the right way.

J.C. flew back to LA early, leaving Mac, as usual, to finish the mix. He directed the session just like he'd always done. They'd managed to lay something down: it wasn't totally as she'd wanted it to be, but it should be different enough to attract the right attention. He'd fired Bob Jacks, but he'd gone with her choice for the musicians. Compromise, that's what a real marriage was all about, right? Yeah, but then why did she feel she was compromising herself?

She called up Brandon to tell him she was back in town

early. He wasn't home. Probably out partying somewhere. She called Julia, who told her Marty was away in San Diego, her other friends, meaning Liam, were out of town, so why didn't she come over and spend the weekend?

'Are you talking a pajama party?' J.C. teased. 'In high school, I could never manage to get an invite to one of those. I was the pajama party type, but not where girls were concerned. Are we going to make fudge and do each other's hair and dish the dirt?'

'Forget the fudge,' Julia said. 'Just bring your Tequila Gold, I'll provide the lime. We'll sit out back by the pool and trash everybody we know.'

They didn't. They ended up talking about their men. Julia broke down and told J.C. Marty was sick and in the hospital in San Diego. 'I'm real sorry about Marty,' J.C. said. 'How's your daddy doing?'

'Still hanging in there. He's a tough old bird. There's so much unfinished business for me back in Houston,' Julia sighed, 'but I really don't feel like opening up that box and taking a longer look. Not with Marty sick.'

'How are you surviving? Got anyone else in your life to make you feel better?' Julia didn't know J.C. knew about her involvement with Liam, but this was LA, half the town knew. 'A little dessert, maybe?'

'Yes,' she said hesitantly, 'but I'm not sure how it's going to work out. Dessert's just not enough to keep either of us satisfied.' She didn't feel comfortable discussing it any further, not even with a close friend like J.C., and the concept of sex as dessert was completely alien to the agonizing situation she found herself in at the moment.

J.C. confessed to Julia what had gone on back in Nashville. 'I'm sure Mac don't have any idea how ticked I am with him. He's so used to throwing his weight around and everybody going along with it, including me. It's getting better, but country music is a man's business. Used to be if you were a female vocalist, the only time you were allowed to open your mouth was to sing. I think it's about time for girls' night out.'

'I've never asked you this, J.C., but do you still love Mac?'

J.C. sighed. 'I can't imagine my life without him.'

'Really? Whenever Marty and I used to fight, I'd decide that was it, we weren't meant to be together, I would have to leave him. I'd lie in bed at night planning where and when I'd go.'

'So how come you didn't leave?'

'I only had to picture him injured in a car accident or sick and lying in a hospital bed somewhere. Immediately I'd start to cry and then I'd feel all the love coming back.'

J.C. chuckled. 'I've done that, too. The old death-bed scene. I wonder if men ever think about that?'

'I doubt it.' She poured herself another tequila, sloshing a little of the amber liquid on to the ground. 'Now he is sick and I'm really frightened for him, but it doesn't make that feeling come flooding back. Most of the time, I feel numb. I don't want the next ten years of my life to be like this last one.'

'I say amen to that.' They both sat quietly for a while, sipping tequila, and looking at the moonlight reflecting off the pool. 'You and Marty, though, I just can't imagine y'all really fighting bad. You seem too civilized to get ticked off with each other.'

'It used to tick me off,' with the tequila working its liquid gold magic, Julia was starting to sound more and like J.C., 'that Marty's so sure of himself. He knows everything about anything.'

'I like that in a man.' J.C. bit down on the lime and took another shot, savoring the sharp, cold tang of the citrus as it cut through the fire of the booze.

'Well, fine, but there was nothing left for me to discover on my own. He'd already been there and done it first and couldn't wait to tell me about it, all about it.'

'That's exactly what I loved about Mac. Course I was only fifteen when I met him, but man, all I wanted was a guy to take care of me. Now I can take care of myself only he just can't seem to see that.'

'He sees it all right,' Julia said. 'That's why it's giving him grief. You going to call him tonight?'

'I got to, I always do. Since the day we were married, if we're apart, we talk on the phone every night. We used to talk so long, I'd get a cramp in my hand and my ear would be all sweaty when I finally hung up. Now I don't have anything to say to him. He doesn't understand half of what I tell him anyway. It's like he's stayed the same and I've moved on to another place, you know what I mean?'

'Yeah,' Julia sighed. 'You know it's funny,' she put her

481

glass down and leaned forward. 'On the surface, you and I couldn't be more different, but we're coming up against a lot of the same problems.'

'All women are. For a long time somebody else was calling the shots. Now we're wearing the boots and nobody knows who's supposed to carry the gun. But you and I are more alike than you might think. Sisters under the skin. I've known that ever since you turned up in Nashville.'

'Really? I thought you were so tough, so sure of yourself.'

'Why? I may cuss more than you do, I'm more up front, but you knew what you wanted and you hung on to it like a dog with an old felt slipper. You stood up to Mac pretty good as I remember.'

Julia gazed down into her drink.

'I never thought I would stop caring what other people thought about me. First my parents,' Julia had told J.C. about Claire and Leigh's opposition to her marrying Marty, 'then the network, the studio, even the media. Secretly I've always been a rebel. I guess I was hoping for a peaceful revolution but now . . .'

'But now you just don't give a shit,' J.C. finished for her.

'That's right, I just don't give a shit.'

Chapter Forty-seven

Kelly watched Carlito as he raced up and down the brick walkways of the Century Plaza shopping center, chasing after Brandon, shrieking with laughter. Any other adult would have been tempted to put the kibosh on such natural exuberance and tell the kid to pipe down, but to Kelly, it was music to her ears. Let him scream, let him cry, let him rage. Let him live. In the beginning, he had been such a silent kid. He never laughed. Even when he cried, it was soundlessly, as if his pain was not worthy of anyone else's attention. Now his innate mischievous, hell-raising spirit had resurfaced. He was rambunctious, talkative, and loud. He would chatter away, switching effortlessly from Spanish to English, and when he cried, it was a lusty wail. Capable of throwing a tantrum, he had a strong temper. He would need it for the fight ahead.

Getting better didn't mean getting well. That was so hard for Kelly to accept when he looked so vibrant. Almost six now, he was still small for his age, but he had a lusty appetite that matched hers, reaching out for any part of life she was able to give him. He resented being undersized, but he still wanted her to call him Carlito. She was still Sam to him, although often, when they were hugging each other, he would call her Mamacita, which made them both laugh a lot because there was nothing little about Kelly. Maybe it was baby machismo, a small male's attempt to put her in her place, although she was doing her best to direct him away from sexist attitudes which, even at six, were already surfacing. Where did he learn this? At the hospital?

'You throw like a girl,' he said scornfully one day when they were tossing a softball around in her backyard.

'Well, so?' Kelly laughed. 'I am a girl.'

'Girls can't play good ball,' he stated emphatically.

'Plenty of girls play great ball,' she assured him, 'and

483

plenty of boys bake great cookies, as you are about to find out.' And she marched him into the kitchen to teach him how to make his favorite oatmeal chocolate chip cookies.

When he came to her place for an extended visit, she had to make sure her apartment was AIDS ready. The array of medicines, syringes, surgical gloves – even oxygen, should he suddenly need it – were enough to sink the heart of an adult, let alone a child, but Carlito took it all in stride. A beeper was strapped to his hip, butt-purse style, and when it went off, he knew it was time to swallow whatever was required.

'Yuck,' he would say, his little face grimacing at the bitter taste.

'You know why you have to take this?'

'*Si*. I want to live for a long time.'

He said it so matter-of-factly, she thought her heart would break. He was just a little boy, goddamn it; something had to be done.

The Marathon Makeover at Century City Plaza was forty-eight hours of makeover magic to raise funds for Kelly's Kids. The indoor-outdoor mall, big department stores and luxury boutiques had all opened their doors and their hearts to her. The best make-up artists in Hollywood, together with top hair stylists from all over the world, had gathered to do hair and make-up for the general public who, normally, would never even get an appointment with some of these people. 'Hairdressers to the stars' gave haircuts for ten dollars, and special effects make-up consultants were willing to do face-painting for kids. The stars themselves, from all the comedy shows on all the networks, along with some of the top TV executives, were very much in evidence. 'Network cross-pollination', Kelly called it. 'We may never get these people together in the same room again.' The atmosphere was carnival-like, relaxed and casual, a welcome change from the black tie, thousand dollar-a-plate fund-raisers.

Makeover Marathon gave the fans an opportunity to see their favorite stars face to face. There was a Liz Taylor lookalike contest with Liz herself judging. There was an Elvis lookalike booth where men and women lined up to get greased pompadours and sideburns. J.C.'s country music cohorts had set up an outdoor karaoke for amateur country singers and Brandon was overseeing pony rides in the parking lot. Kelly and J.C. were doing hair, Debra Jo, Shirley and Theresa were helping out with make-up, and Paul, Troy's camera in tow, was hawking, 'Get your picture taken with the stars.' The Market, the famous Century Plaza food court, was going strong, donating all their soft drinks' proceeds for the entire weekend to Kelly's Kids. Most important of all, parking was completely free.

Kelly had become a crackerjack fund-raiser. She wouldn't take no for an answer from anybody. She would also take a yes from absolutely anybody. A couple of the members of her board of directors for the foundation wanted her to disassociate herself from the gay community, but she'd refused.

'We'd be even further behind in the fight if the gay community hadn't given us complete support. They're the ones on the front lines of this disease. They got out there and lobbied and pushed to raise funds for research, education, AIDS awareness, and just plain acted up. We all have to act up.'

Now she was addressing the crowds in the mall with equal fervour. 'For a long time no one realized what was happening with children and AIDS. The people who watch Makeover are just your average Americans. These are the people who need to know more. We are all afraid of what we don't know. It's time we all knew about a virus that doesn't discriminate. HIV takes no prisoners. AIDS belongs to all of us.'

She finished her impassioned plea and moved away from the podium. A tall, odd-looking man came up to her, holding out a microphone and a tape recorder. 'I'd like to ask you a few questions, Kelly, about why you chose to get involved with this particular cause? Is someone in your own family afflicted with the disease?'

'No,' Kelly looked at him strangely. 'I work with the Pediatric AIDS foundation because it needs all the help it can get.'

'Of course, but what is your personal connection?' He shoved the microphone up to her mouth.

'Which paper are you with?' she asked sharply. 'Where's your press pass?'

'Like an idiot, I left it at home,' the man said.

'Then get out of my face,' she said sharply. There was no

485

way she was going to talk about Carlito to a creep like this.

'Oh, got to go,' he said instantly. 'I want to grab Liz before she leaves. Catch you later.' He disappeared into the crowd.

'Who was that?' Julia came up beside her.

'Some creepoid rat trying to crash the event and get a hot quote, I guess.'

'Well, you can't blame him. This is turning out to be the fund-raising event of the year. Everybody's here.'

'Of course. Because it's fun. You don't have to wear black tie and eat rubber chicken. You can have a great time and still feel virtuous. Have I figured this town out or what?'

Julia laughed. 'You enjoy life more than anyone I know.'

'That's because I know how much it's worth,' Kelly said, a shadow coming across her face. 'But hey, I owe this life to you, Ms Julia.' She brightened again. 'I'm having a ball. You can't possibly know what you've done for me by giving me the chance to be Samantha.'

'I would never have dreamed the character would become so popular. I can't even take credit for creating Sam. You've really done that on your own. So what do you think?' Julia asked. 'Maybe a spin-off series, something that focuses on horoscopes? Samantha's Stars? Makeover can barely contain you. I'd love to develop something that would really showcase your talent.'

'You mean you'd write something just for me?'

'It's still in the crazy idea stage, but I am thinking about it, yes. I've got to come up with a new project for CBN.'

'You know, I'm really happy where I am on Makeover. It's just the right size for me. Gives me time to do stuff like this. I used to be driven to act, I think most actors are, otherwise they wouldn't stick it out in this nutsy biz. But now Kelly's Kids is just as important a part of my life, maybe even more so. It's like I'm finally making a difference.' She stopped and pretended to stick her finger down her throat. 'Oh, puleeze, will you listen to me? Gag me with a spoon.'

'No, I think you're on to something,' Julia said wistfully. 'I wish I could stop being a workaholic. You're racking up all these good deeds. In the end, what's going to count? Writing about life or actually living it?'

J.C. Austin was blow-drying a young man's hair. It was

brown and thinning; he had the gaunt, hollow-eyed look that marked him as a PWA, his slender neck supporting his proud head like the fragile stem of a flower. So young. They were all too young. She gave him a quick spritz of hairspray, whipped off the plastic cape, and showed him the results in a mirror.

'That's amazing,' he marveled. 'I didn't think I had that much hair left.'

'You just got to comb it right,' she patted him on the shoulder, 'blow-dry it opposite your natural part to get extra lift, and if you want to save what hair you've got, don't shampoo too often.'

The young man looked surprised. 'Did you research all this for Makeover?'

'Gosh, no. I used to earn my living as a hairdresser back in Nashville. José Eber ain't got nothing on me. If I lose my job tomorrow, I'd just go back to stylin' hair.'

'I don't think there's much possibility of that.' He held out the throwaway plastic cape for J.C. to autograph. 'My name's Scott. Glen and I never miss your show. We both love you.'

'Well, Scott, you tell Glen I just gave you the best blow job you ever had.' He laughed and handed her a check for three hundred dollars. 'No, no, it's only ten bucks.'

'I can afford it,' Scott said, with a rueful little smile. 'Maybe it'll buy me some extra time. Besides, you're worth it.' He took her hand, made a funny, gallant little bow, and then wandered away.

Kelly came up just in time to hear the end of the conversation. 'Your booth is a big hit.'

'I know. Nobody's paying the ten-dollar fee, they're all giving more.'

'It's really good of you to do this,' Kelly said gratefully.

'I can't say I've always had it easy, but people have been awfully good to me. I've got so much now. I need to give something back. Listen –' she glanced at the line-up of people waiting to get a haircut – 'I need to say something to you.' She flipped a 'Back in Five Minutes' sign over the edge of her stand and drew Kelly to one side. 'This is a wonderful event. You've done a great job of organizing everything.'

'Thanks.'

'I want to apologize for the way I iced you out last season.

487

I hate to admit it, but I got bit by the envy bug.'

'That's OK.' Kelly was surprised, almost embarrassed by J.C.'s honesty. It was true, things had been tense between them. She thought she knew why, but she never expected the star to acknowledge it herself.

'No, it's not. I'm the most insecure person around, but I appreciate that you never called me on that. Just went on being your usual self, while I worked things out. I guess what I'm trying to say is "I've missed you." '

'Me, too.' Kelly felt tremendous relief. She knew unless the star liked you, you could be hung out to dry, but more than that, she'd started out on especially good terms with J.C., which had made it all the more confusing and hurtful when their friendly, teasing relationship had suddenly cooled.

'The Kelly's Kosmetics, the camp, the promotional stuff, I admire all of that. You're funny, you're talented, and you deserve every bit of the attention you're getting.'

'The only point to the attention is this,' Kelly did one of her swooping hand gestures to indicate the crowd. Everyone in Hollywood was turning out for the Makeover Marathon. If it did as well as she hoped, it would be worth making it an annual fund-raising event. Her goal was one million in proceeds and an extra mil in donations. But as young Scott had said, was that enough to buy a little boy some extra time?

Pneumocystis pneumonia. Pneumonia was to be the most feared and at last it had struck Carlito. Pneumonia was fatal for twenty per cent of HIV adults the first time around. For infants and children, it was sixty per cent fatal. He was back on the AZT, but this time it was not helping. The pains in his stomach and arms and legs had come back, the high fevers. His immune system was shot to hell. By now Kelly knew all the signs.

She was practically living at the hospital. First thing, early in the morning, on her way to the studio, she stopped in to try to get him to eat even a little breakfast. God, he was losing weight so fast. After work, she returned to stay with him until he finally fell asleep. By now she knew most of the hospital staff by their first names, no matter how often their shifts changed. She held him so they could do the painful medical procedures – drawing blood, putting him on IV, taking him for a CAT scan – and when the hurt was blessedly over, she rocked him and soothed him. His features, always large and well-defined, now seemed enormous in his sunken little face; his eyes, rimmed with red, looked huge. They remained curious, sometimes fearful, but never empty, the way they had first appeared to her two years ago. At least she had given him that.

Like many kids his age, he was obsessed with dinosaurs, loved reading dinosaur comic books and watching Dinosaurs on TV. She bought him an enormous rubber stegosaurus for his room and papered all four walls so that Liam Carey could come in and paint a mural of the prehistoric reptiles. When her child was sick, Kelly had no qualms about calling in all her favors. Carlito loved Paul and Brandon's Jock Talk routine on Makeover. Even though he didn't understand all the references, he responded to the attitude. Paul and Brandon put a couple of their best routines on a home cassette so he could listen in the hospital, and J.C. did the same thing with his favorite songs. He liked Christmas carols the best. Whether it was November or July, he always wanted to hear a Christmas carol.

Did he comprehend what was happening to him? Did he really know how quickly he was losing ground? Sometimes she thought he did.

'If I die, Mamacita, would you miss me?'

'Of course,' Kelly was sitting in the chair, rocking him back and forth, the way she had done what seemed like lifetimes ago. 'You're my best buddy, my favorite pal. I'd miss you, but I'd also be just a little jealous.'

'Why?'

'Because you'd be up there in Heaven baking cookies without me.'

She didn't know if she believed in Heaven. All she knew was that if there were a God who could do this to a child, He – she no longer imagined a She – bloody well better provide some sort of Heaven to make up for all this pain. Other times she knew there was no cosmic system of trial and punishment, no ultimate reward. It was just a virus. The tragedy it wreaked was epic but there was no spirituality attached to it whatsoever. Other than the triumph of each individual human spirit who fought against it.

'*El mejor nino del mundo,*' she said as she rocked him and

rocked him, whispering softly, 'the best little boy in the world.'

He seemed to relax, for a moment, in her arms, and then 'It's dark,' he cried suddenly, 'I can't see. *Yo soy miedoso.* I'm scared.' His little hands were reaching out, clutching the front of her blouse, her sleeve, trying to grasp the material and hold on.

She looked outside the hospital window. It was getting toward evening, the sky was gray, but she had a frightening, gut-wrenching feeling that this was not what he meant.

'*Yo soy miedoso,*' he repeated over and over again, '*yo soy miedoso.*' He was lapsing competely into Spanish and she found it hard to follow what he was saying.

Oh God, please don't let him go blind. For a little child, how would life be worth living if he couldn't see the world around him for the brief time allotted him. It was not as though he had already stored up a wealth of images to remember. 'Close your eyes, Carlito,' she said as calmly as she could, 'then you won't see the dark. Close your eyes and go to sleep. *El mejor nino del mundo, el mejor nino del mundo,*' she said over and over again, trying not to let him know how frightened she was.

She was trying to maneuver herself toward the call button to ring for the nurse when suddenly, with no warning, his arms and legs began to twich, his body jerking in her arms.

A seizure. Oh sweet Jesus. She had no idea what to do. Strange, unintelligible, guttural cries were coming from him.

She was trying to hold on to him, his limbs flailing, reaching with her foot for the buzzer. Hurry, please. Get in here. She didn't know what to do. His movements were so violent he was in danger of jerking out of her arms. Footsteps moved quickly down the hall, outside the door, and the door was flung open. The nurse took one look. Code blue. Dr Marker. Room 325. Stat. She heard the urgent call over the PA system. More footsteps, running this time, plunging through the door. Team of medical personnel, snatching her baby away from her, slamming him down on to the hospital bed, pulling the slats up into place, locking him in. Still thrashing wildly. Superhuman strength in such a tiny, frail body. They held him down as they worked over him. Oxygen. IV. Pumping in a sedative.

She stood there, frozen with fear, unable to move or

speak. Then suddenly everything stopped, just as suddenly as it began. He slammed on to the bed one final time, then went limp, perfectly still. Oh no. Please. Not so quickly. No time to say goodbye. No time to whisper I love you.

The medical workers moved in again, hovered, circled like a pack of green birds over the stark white bed. A look passed among them, a murmur ran through them. Then up, back and away. All the eyes turned to her. Like the parting of the sea, they made way for her to come to the side of the bed. She didn't want to go, felt if she stayed there, fixed to the spot, nothing would have happened; she didn't see, she doesn't know, she could go back in time. Like walking through water, slow motion, the force holding her back yet moving her forward, she came to the side of his bed.

She sat on the edge and looked down at his face. His eyes were closed, the thick lashes dark against his smooth skin. His hands relaxed, no longer reaching for anything. She put her arms around him and lifted him up, cradling him to her breast. He was light as a feather. Gently she rocked him back and forth, whispering in his ear, '*Adios me Carlito, el mejor nino del mundo. Te amo.*'

He had always been leaving and now he was finally gone.

THE THIRD SEASON

Chapter Forty-eight

'I want to play around with form a bit this season,' Julia told Stan. Once again they were gathered in her office at Pac Vic, gearing up for a new fall season.

'What do you mean?' Stan looked worried. He didn't like the sound of anything new.

'Wait till you hear this, Stan, you're absolutely going to love it,' Tim said. He was wearing his baseball cap further back on his head these days, now that he was half-way through a hairplug replacement process.

'I've got a storyline,' Julia explained, 'that will start with the first episode in September and go through five episodes. Janine will decide her period of mourning for Carl is finally over and she's got to get out there and find a man. We'll follow her search from week to week.'

'Are you talking about serializing a sit-com?' Now Stan was looking really worried.

'Well, each episode will work on its own, but they'll all be connected. It's a five-story arc culminating in Janine's realization that Mr Right may just be the boy next door.'

'You mean Travis?' Stan perked up.

'Yes. You'll be happy to hear I'm finally getting Janine and Travis together.'

'Well, it's about time. The chemistry between Brandon and J.C. is hot enough to implode. Both on and offscreen.'

'What's with those two?' Tim asked.

'I don't know,' Julia answered. 'I don't think they know, but if we don't let Janine and Travis get it on pretty soon all of America's going to have blue balls.'

'Julia!' Tim pretended to be shocked. Stan looked disgusted.

'We're going to give Brandon a chance to direct that episode himself. He was prepared to walk if we didn't give in to his demands to direct and he certainly deserves it by now. Alex has done a great job of setting the style of the show over the first two seasons. We can stand a fresh approach and, anyway, Alex has asked for some time off to do an MOW starring Shirley Bunting.'

'Really?' Tim raised a quizzical eyebrow. 'Something personal going on there?' He was always up for hot gossip.

'I think so. I'll leave it to Alex to tell you himself. Anyway, after our five-story arc with Janine and Travis, I'm going to concentrate on further development of Samantha. Kelly and I are talking about . . .'

'You're really pushing the envelope with Kelly,' Stan grumbled. 'Samantha's character is written larger-than-life and she doesn't do anything to play against that. Too controversial. I can't tell you how closely Standards and Practices has to monitor her and how many complaints we get.'

'We've had this argument before, Stan,' Julia retorted. 'Who wants to see smaller-than-life? It's boring.'

'The favorable letters outnumber the complaints three to one,' Tim remarked.

'But they're all from gay men.'

'So, 'mos aren't allowed to watch TV, too, is that what you're saying?' Tim snapped. 'Julia's right about this one, in my humble opinion. Kelly's Halloween episode with the drag queens got a bunch of new viewers to "sample" the program and they liked what they saw enough to stick with us. Controversy may cause an initial drop, but eventually we pick up new viewers who are more discerning.'

'That's right,' Julia said defensively. 'A lot of people who initially dismissed the show as being too "blue collar" have caught up with us now. We used to be chasing Roseanne, now we're rivaling Murphy Brown. The show is attracting a more sophisticated, upper socio-economic audience.'

'Don't give me that R and D doubletalk,' Stan said sharply. 'Who cares about a handful of intellectual snobs? The cultural élite aren't regular viewers anyway. They only watch TV sporadically.'

'Surely you're not bitching about the numbers, Stan?' Tim chided.

'No, I'm not. They're terrific. Though, Julie, I have to tell you I have increasing reservations about the tone of the show. It's too . . . political.'

Julia took a deep breath. 'I think it's time, Stan, for you

to call me Julia like everyone else does. And Makeover doesn't deal with political issues. We examine social issues, the things that are dividing our country right now. I'm trying to find a level of reality that most sit-coms don't have and even you must admit it appears to be working when you look at the numbers.'

Stan was growing red-faced with the exertion of trying to keep up with her. 'Reality? Bulimia, drag queens, black people who want to see what it's like to be white? That doesn't represent reality for the majority.'

'Look around you, Stan. It's out there. This is what pop culture is all about.'

'I don't approve of your hiring Theresa Ruiz to write for the show.'

'I haven't hired her to write for the show, I've hired her to write *a* show. She wrote an episode on spec, we all liked it, we're going to do it. Pac Vic agrees with my decision to take advantage of Theresa's many talents.'

'You mean Kathryn Grady agrees. Haven't you heard, Julia, that Kathryn's days are rumored to be numbered?' Stan had an almost malevolent look in his eye.

'She's thinking about relocating to New York. To be closer to her husband. That's what she told me.'

Stan shrugged. Tim sat silent. 'You're a very clever woman, Julia,' he was careful to say it properly this time, 'but I think you're listening too much to minority factions. You're giving in to too many other people's demands.'

'You mean instead of yours?'

Stan got up angrily. 'You going to push me now, is that it? That would be a mistake, Julia. By the way, give my regards to Marty. Perhaps, if you stay away from him, he'll be able to make a speedy recovery.' He stormed out of her office, slamming the door.

'What's he talking about?' Julia turned to Tim. 'Stan just seems to get weirder and weirder.'

Tim flushed a shade of heliotrope matching the flowers in his Hawaiian print shirt. 'I'm afraid he means this.' He reached into his pocket and brought out a crumpled copy of the *Hollywood Insider*.

Julia's heart sank. 'Oh no. They've been so quiet for most of the summer I thought they were finally off our case. Who are they after this time?'

'You.'

MAKEOVER CREATOR SIGNS HUSBAND
INTO MENTAL INSTITUTION

High-profile producer, Marty Turgov, the power behind the scenes for CBN's monster hit, Makeover, has landed in a psychiatric clinic. Apparently Turgov collapsed while vacationing on the Gulf Coast of Texas and was rushed back to California to undergo treatment at San Diego's famed Feighner Institute where he will remain indefinitely for observation and counseling.

Those close to Turgov, once known as 'The King of Pitch', say that he is normally a strong and positive person, but the well-respected veteran of the TV industry may be suffering from more than a usual mid-life crisis.

Friends blame the business brain's hard-driving wife, Julia Hudlow, for pushing her husband so hard he crumbled under the pressure.

'Julia is a workaholic and she expects everyone around her to be the same way,' says an inside source. 'She'd work the cast and crews right around the clock if the unions would allow it. She can't understand that some of us would like to have a personal life, even if she doesn't.'

Others say Turgov had become despondent watching his hitherto unknown wife's star rise in a business that was supposed to be his domain.

'The irony of the situation is that it was Marty who pushed Julia into TV in the first place. Now her success is literally making him sick with envy.'

Neither half of the wealthy Hudlow/Turgov producing team could be reached for comment.

Julia knocked gently on Marty's door and then pushed it open. Sitting at his computer, hacking away, he looked up when he heard her come into the room.

'Hello, darling,' she said, putting her arms around him and kissing the top of his head. 'I brought you a printer. How's my laptop working out?' Marty was trying to keep on working out of the clinic. She had brought him her personal computer with a built-in modum, a numbers pad on the side, his disks, and a fax so that he could send work to the office.

'Great. I must be getting better. I'm beginning to find all this peace and quiet boring instead of relaxing. Do you think you could supply me with a different view next time you drive up?'

'What's wrong with this one?' She looked out the window at the broad expanse of green lawn and tall trees.

'Nothing. Except that I've already seen it.'

She laughed. He was beginning to sound like the old Marty. Or, hopefully, a new Marty with a different spin on things.

'Looks like the *Insider* is finally zeroing in on you and me,' he said. 'The tabs rarely go after people behind the scenes. It must mean we've really made it.'

'I was hoping you hadn't seen it.'

'How I could miss it? They sell the *Insider* at the news-stand. I'm walking by, I see a picture of me in what looks like a strait-jacket, it caught my attention; what can I tell you? Of course, I know and you know that the photo is of me in catcher's gear at the studio-network baseball game, but I look pretty crazy even to me.'

'Oh, honey, I'm so sorry.'

'Don't be. If we can't find the humor in this, then we've both lost our minds.' He sounded surprisingly sanguine about the whole thing.

'Yeah, well, they make it sound like I strapped you down and had you committed. I feel like something out of *Gaslight*. "Bella, Bella, this brooch was here yesterday, Bella? Where have you hidden it?" '

'Naw, you're much prettier than Charles Boyer. I particularly like the end where they refer to the "wealthy producing team". Who do they mean, not you and me surely?'

'Well, we are getting closer to syndication. If we can just get through this third season. How are you feeling? You're sure you're not working too hard?'

'No, that's the point. I'm not here to veg out, I'm here so they can monitor my therapy and medication. Dr Richardson says that was part of the problem with the vacation on an isolated island idea. If you lose what defines you, it's easy to feel lost; if you stop work completely, you may fall apart. On the other hand, if all you do is work, then you're only pleasing other people, you're not doing anything for yourself. Want to hear Dr Richardson's first step to dealing with anxiety?'

'Yes. After what I'm going through with Stanfield King,

I need it.' Julia pulled up a chair and sat next to him.

'He says to find three things to do every day: for yourself, by yourself, to please yourself. Want to know how I responded to that?'

'How?'

'But doctor, three times a day? My hand would get tired.'

Julia laughed. 'You'd be in danger of going blind three times faster.'

Marty laughed, too. He was looking better, more relaxed. Then his face turned serious. 'The *Insider* is wrong about one thing.'

'The *Insider* is wrong about a lot of things.'

'No, but this is really important. You're not the reason I got sick, Julia. Your success did not cause this stress and anxiety. It's something in me and I have to find a way, on my own, to get through it. I'm proud of what you've accomplished. I'm thrilled with the changes you've made. I want to see you go as far as you can. I want to see you fly.'

Julia lay in bed next to Liam. They had just finished making love. 'What are you thinking?' she asked.

'Nothing,' he said.

'Really nothing?'

'I don't think, I visualize. I'm playing a series of images in my head and then I'll replay them again and again when you're gone. Conversation's not my strong point. I'm not good with words like you are. I'm not really from the hearing world, you know.'

'I know.' It had taken her some time to adjust to that after coming out of a relationship where talking was a high art. Every moment of the day had to be analyzed and reviewed and put into perspective. Otherwise it didn't exist. With Marty, there was debate and there was sex, both equally volatile and passionate. The only problem was that when one went wrong, it was almost impossible to get to the other. If they weren't talking to each other, they couldn't make love, they just couldn't. With Liam, there was all the in-between. There was a peacefulness about him, a contained quality, almost a femininity. Yet when they made love, it was plenty explosive, as if all the energy had been stored for that release. No, Liam was not good at talking. He was good at being. He asked very little of her at a time when she felt the world was gobbling her up.

The phone rang.

It was the props master from the studio, wanting to know some design details about the ashtray Theresa would throw against the wall in one of the new season's episodes. The storyline centered around Concha's atempts to give up smoking. Julia had written this into the storyline because Theresa herself had decided to quit smoking and she liked to incorporate bits of the actors' real lives into the show.

Liam on the phone was amusing to watch. His eyes were always wandering over the surfaces of whatever room he was in, looking at shape, taking in size and color. Often his voice would drift away as he got caught up in the visual and forgot the aural. Even Julia, who usually had his undivided attention, would hear his voice drift away at the other end of the phone, and she would have to say, 'Stop looking at whatever it is you're looking at and come back to me.' Mind you, she loved it when he looked at her with that same attention to detail, studying every inch of her, finding the beauty and grace in even her simplest actions. It was very seductive. He hung up the phone and rolled over.

'Now, where were we?'

'Visualizing. Swimming in the senses.'

'Oh yes.' His hand went between her legs, his artful, sensitive fingers stroking gently, almost idly at first, then with increasing intensity until she thought she would faint with pleasure. The second orgasm was sometimes better than the first. Or the third. Or the fourth. He never disappointed her. He never failed to surprise her.

She came back to earth and looked up into his eyes. Those beautiful, compelling blue eyes, that seemed to draw her right into him. 'I love watching you come,' he whispered. *La tendresse, la tendresse, c'est la source.*'

'What are you saying?'

'Where the excitement really lies is in the tenderness, the personal. You've taught me that.'

'I did?'

He nodded, struggling with the words and the emotion. 'I don't know how to say this, Julia, but you chose me. You took me by surprise. You reached out for me. That never happened to me before. I wasn't planning this. I wouldn't allow myself to even conceive of it. I'd been through enough bad experiences to know what I didn't want. I saw myself as a loner. Just short of being a hermit, at least in my heart. The possibility of sharing my life with somebody had always seemed an impossibility until you. Now I've discovered the secret.'

'What's that?'. Her breath was coming in short little gasps. His hands were moving over her again.

'You just say "yes". Don't close yourself off. Say yes, say yes, say yes.'

SHOCKING SECRET REVEALED: J.C. AUSTIN HAD ABORTION

Nashville songbird turned TV star J.C. Austin claims the biggest tragedy of her life is not being able to have children.

'I'd give up all my gold records, all the money I've earned, every spec of my success in exchange for one little baby of my own,' the Makeover lead actress says, 'but I can't seem to get pregnant.'

Now a Mexican nurse has come forward to reveal the shocking secret that the country queen was, in fact, pregnant, seventeen years ago, but did not have a miscarriage.

According to Nurse Doe (the *Insider* will not divulge the woman's real name in order to protect her privacy), the pregnancy was terminated in a back-alley abortion across the border in Mexico when the singer was only a teenager.

'Conditions were *muy malo*,' confesses the nurse, now in her fifties. 'It was not a real operating room. Sheets were put on a table and the doctor's instruments were *cochino, sucio*, dirty, not always properly cleaned. She was so young, so small. We could not even give her the anesthetic because after the operation she must be awake enough to get up and leave. *Pobrecita, mucho dolor*, the pain was so bad, she screamed and cried.

'When she came into the doctor's office, she said she was sure she wanted to get rid of the baby and the man who was with her agreed. He held her hand. Half-way through the operation, she tried to change her mind, but it was too late. You made your bed, now you lie in it.'

According to private medical records, the abortion, though technically successful, scarred her Fallopian tubes which may be the reason why she has not been able to become pregnant since. Although she soon skyrocketed to fame and fortune, thanks to her manager husband, Mac Austin, the couple have spent thousands of dollars going from doctor to doctor in search of a medical miracle. But all the money in the world has not been able to buy them what they really want, a child of their own.

J.C. has been married to Mac for twenty years and has often been heard to say, 'For a woman, family comes first. Mac is my family. I wish God had seen fit to give me more.'

A practising Christian and the granddaughter of a gospel

singer, she says, 'The Bible is my favorite book and I try to live my life by it.'

But a disillusioned friend thinks otherwise. 'Abortion is a sin. J.C. was not raped. In fact, the father of her lost child was none other the man she is married to right now. It was pure ambition that blinded her. She had her eyes on the prize of a recording career. Nothing and nobody was going to get in her way. There is no excuse for what she did.

'Given J.C.'s amazing talents, her baby could have been a musical genius or a movie star. Now we'll never know. She can never let go of the shame of her tragic act.'

Nurse Doe shares in that shame and wants to clear her conscience. 'I feel so bad this beautiful lady cannot have another baby. I cry myself to sleep at night because I am afraid this is partly my fault. I pray that God will forgive me – and J.C. Austin.'

Chapter Forty-nine

J.C. was devastated. She called Mac right away, begging him to come down to LA. Now that he was managing other artists, he was spending more time than ever in Nashville. He had just signed a new mother-daughter team that he hoped would have some of the original appeal of the Judds. They were due to go into the studio tomorrow.

J.C. started to cry over the phone, but Mac was in no mood for her tears. 'How could you do this?' he shouted at her. 'It's all over Nashville. We agreed we would never talk about this again.'

'I didn't, I swear.'

'You must have let it slip to someone. I paid Maria Hidalgo enough money to keep her mouth shut for a lifetime. She was the only person left alive who knew. That quack of a doctor is long gone.'

'Somebody must have tracked her down and offered her more, I don't know.' J.C. was crying so hard she could hardly hold on to the phone.

'I'm sorry, baby,' Mac's tone softened, 'but this could lose you a lot of your hardcore country fans. Damn, we work our butts off to create a squeaky clean family image and now one little article blows it all away.'

'I feel like I should say something, defend myself, us, somehow.'

'I wouldn't do that. Didn't Stanfield King tell you the best thing to do about trash like this is to ignore it?'

'Yeah, but this hurts so bad. This is the worst they've ever done me.'

'I know, baby. I wish I could be there with you, but I'm set to go into the studio tomorrow. We're just going to have to hope your fans stick by you. They could handle the rumors of the drinking and carousing, that was all in the past anyway, but I don't know how they'll stomach this.'

Mac was right. Within a few days, the vitriolic letters started to pour in, calling her everything from selfish and ambitious to murderess and baby killer.

'I've thrown out all your records and tapes. I will never listen to you again or watch Makeover. I'm getting rid of you just like you got rid of your baby.'

'You don't deserve to call yourself a woman. I've raised four children, all by myself, on welfare. With all your millions, you didn't even have the guts to raise one. And you have a husband. I am disgusted and heartbroken.'

'How dare you? You are such a hypocrite . . . no different from those Nazis who killed the Jews in World War II.'

J.C. answered every one of the letters by hand. Meanwhile, Pro-Choice was hailing the revelation as a breakthrough, a blow against the sexism and moralism of country music. Sally, Phil and Oprah wanted her to come on the show to talk about her painful decision, past and present, but she refused. It was nobody's business but her own.

At Pac Vic, the switchboard was continually lit up with callers phoning in to voice their opinions. Yes, you did the only thing you could. No, you deserve to burn in hell. Outside the entrance to the studio, Operation Rescue, Lambs of Choice, and the Right to Life, picketed, carrying banners and placards reading, 'Pro-Choice? What Choice Did Your Baby Have?' 'Terminate Abortion, Not Babies'. The protestors were either singing hymns or screaming invectives at J.C. when the limo delivered her to work each morning. As she got out of the car, a man in a tan raincoat managed to push his way through the crowd and get next to her. 'This is for you, J.C.,' he said softly as he placed a small, beautifully wrapped present, the size of a jewelry box in her hand. In the sea of angry, spitting faces, his thoughtfulness touched her deeply. Safely inside her dressing-room, with trembling hands, she opened the little box. Nestled against the plush red velvet was a miniature, plastic fetus.

She couldn't stand it any longer. She had to make a statement to the press. Mac was still stuck in Nashville so she asked Julia to join her in a hastily called press conference. 'I know Stan doesn't want us doing this, but we can't go on taking this shit lying down. Will you back me up?'

'You bet I will,' said Julia. 'I know now these people will stop at nothing. I have no idea how they found out about

Marty. Maybe there's a spy at the clinic or somebody in the doctor's office was paid to talk.'

'Like Nurse Doe must have been,' J.C. said bitterly.

'They're probably bluffing about the hospital records. It would be illegal of them to have them, much less to have paid for them, which the tabloids are always denying they do. I'd really like to get these guys and get them good. The least we can do is declare war.'

Julia and J.C. stood together on the podium to issue their statements to the mass of reporters and photographers. Head held high, the tremor in her voice only barely discernible, J.C. gripped the microphone and, without any notes, simply began to speak. 'Y'all know just about everything there is to know about me; I know very little about you. All I ask is that you try to put yourself in my shoes. I'm going to try to speak from the heart.' She took a deep breath, 'How would you feel if your most private business was written in the sky for the whole world to read? Because that's what's happening to me, and it really hurts. Yes, I wanted to be a public entertainer. I know the price of success is some loss of privacy and I've done my best to be honest with you. But I didn't reckon on anything like this. What I did when I was seventeen is something I will never get over and neither will my husband, Mac. Now you are making us relive that pain, over and over again. Why? I'm not royalty. I am not a politician that y'all have elected. I am not answerable to anyone except God. I made a mistake a long time ago and I will pay for it the rest of my life. None of you could hate me any more than I already hate myself, and you can't punish me any more than I've already been punished. I'm not trying to forget about what I did, but I am trying to go on living and make the best of my life. That's all any of us can do.' Half-way through her statement, the tears began to slip down her cheeks, but she brushed them away and forced herself to make it to the end. The room was completely silent when she finished; after a long moment, the reporters and photographers burst into applause.

Then it was Julia's turn. She was visibly nervous as she stepped up to the mike to read a written statement. She didn't trust herself to wing something as important as this. 'The *Hollywood Insider* appears to have a personal vendetta against my show, Makeover. I admit I'm a woman with strong opinions. Most people find what I have to say interesting enough to make Makeover one of the most watched shows on television today. We have a lot of power and I don't take that power lightly. Obviously some of you out there don't like us and are doing your best to make us look crazy and un-American. The private lives of some very good people are being held hostage by the media. It's a new form of celebrity terrorism and I can tell you it feels like being held at gunpoint. Rumor is not fact. But when rumor gets reported, it becomes quasi-fact. By the time a denial may be printed, it's too late, because in the minds of the readers, what they read first has now become truth. For those of us in the Makeover family, it's frightening to be the object of all this intense scrutiny just because we write and perform a little show. Just because we are famous.'

She faltered and then J.C. came to the rescue, 'We may be famous, but we work for a living like you do. We pay taxes and we're supposed to be guaranteed certain rights. The tabloids are sick. It's time to shut them down.'

The entire room stood up and gave them an ovation. War had been declared; their battlecry had been heard.

Chapter Fifty

THERE AIN'T ONE WITHOUT THE OTHER

> There's a big ol' country world
> That's sittin' right outside the door
> And sometimes it makes me wonder
> What it is we're livin' for
> We are tested with decision
> At our moments of growth
> If we're blessed with the vision
> We can see the truth in both
>
> There ain't one without the other
> There ain't black without white
> There ain't sister without brother
> There ain't day without night
> There ain't six without seven
> There ain't land without sea
> There ain't hell without heaven
> There ain't you without me

This was it. The episode that all America had been waiting for. Finally, after two-and-a-half years of Makeover, Travis Kyle would get up the courage to kiss the woman he now knew he loved, Janine Barnett. Which also meant that Brandon Tate would finally kiss J.C. Austin.

Janine has come to accept Carl's death and to realize she must get on with her life, so she begins to date other men. Travis, convinced that his wife Marcia will never return, is busy making up for a long period of celibacy by going after everything in skirts. At the start of the episode, 'A Kiss Is Just a Kiss', Janine and Travis have been comparing notes on their dating marathon. They still regard each other as

509

friends, ignoring the obvious attraction and jealousy thing which has been building between them.

J.C. had written a special song for this episode, 'There Ain't One Without the Other'. The audience would have to wait till the very end of the episode for the kiss. It looked like J.C. would have to wait until the end of the week to even rehearse the kiss. Brandon was directing this episode which meant that a stand-in had been rehearsing with J.C. while he blocked the actors, set up the shots, and worked with the camera crew. Travis had a small scene at the beginning and then, of course, the climactic scene at the end culminating in 'the kiss'.

In the meantime, there was a poignant flashback of Carl Barnett saying goodbye to Janine before leaving for the Gulf War, telling her that if, God forbid, he didn't return, he would want her to find someone new to love.

INT. THE LIVING-ROOM OF THE BARNETT HOME. A COZY BUNGALOW. MORNING. SUNLIGHT STREAMS IN THROUGH THE FRONT WINDOW.

CARL: At least keep those feet of yours warm. For a hot-blooded woman you sure got cold feet.

JANINE: What are you saying? I couldn't get married again.

CARL: If you don't, it looks like what you and I had was so bad you're afraid to try again.

JANINE: Nobody could ever match up to you.

CARL (Looks at himself in the mirror. Smooths his hair): That's true. I admit it, I'm a ten. But you might find somebody who was maybe an eight. No wait, make that a six. Just promise me one thing, darlin'?

JANINE: I hate even talkin' about this, but what?

CARL: No English accents. I don't trust those guys. And he's got to have all his own teeth and hair.

The way Brandon directed the scene, it was a tear-jerker that ended with a laugh. Especially since over the five-arc story Julia had created, the viewers had seen Janine embark on a frenzy of dating culminating in tonight's episode with a guy who appeared to fit all the qualifications until he lost both his teeth and his hair (toupee and dentures) on a hair-raising ride on the roller-coaster at Six Flags over

Texas. They had already shot that sequence on location at Magic Mountain. For the Friday night filming, the audience would see a copy of the roller-coaster scene on video with the real thing edited in later.

As a director, Brandon had the magic touch for J.C. Her small role in *Vengeance* had brought her good reviews and further scripts to read, thanks to Brandon's coaching, and she trusted him completely. All he had to do was press the right emotional buttons and the tears flowed copiously as Janine hugged Carl, unwilling to let him go. He was able to get a sharp, comic delivery out of her in the beginning of the episode where Travis tells Janine the reason she hasn't hit the sack with guys she's been dating is because she's too picky. Janine snaps back at him, 'Too picky? I realize that for you, Travis, if it's warm and barely moving, it's a romantic possibility, but I need a little bit more.' In a later scene with Kelly and Paul, Samantha and Troy give their advice to Janine on how to score a guy.

SAMANTHA: You can't tell anything about a guy unless you've kissed him. One kiss says it all. Oh, and if you do get lucky, make sure that the first time you make love you do it standing up. That way everything stays in the right place.

TROY (Sarcastically): Good advice, Sam. No wonder she's nervous. You got to learn to cut loose and go with the flow, Janine. You got to say to yourself, 'The next guy that walks in here, no matter who he is, I'm going to haul off and kiss him.'

CUT TO THE FINAL SCENE. ENTER TRAVIS. JANINE SITS ALONE IN THE SHOP, ON HER STOOL, PLAYING HER GUITAR AND SINGING 'There Ain't One Without The Other'. TRAVIS WANTS TO APOLOGIZE FOR THE SPAT THEY HAD EARLIER. WHEN HE HEARS JANINE SINGING, HE STOPS IN AMAZEMENT. HE HAS NEVER HEARD HER SING BEFORE. WE SEE BY THE LOOK ON HIS FACE THAT HE IS IN LOVE.
SHYLY, HE JOINS IN THE SONG. THEY SING TOGETHER AND GO INTO A NATURAL HARMONY.

511

THE SONG ENDS.
SLOWLY, AWKWARDLY, THEIR LIPS COME
TOGETHER FOR A BRIEF, FUMBLING KISS.
JUST A PECK REALLY. THEY LOOK INTO
EACH OTHER'S EYES.
THEN A LONG, SLOW, DEEP KISS. FINALLY
THEY PULL APART.
THE MOOD SHIFTS INTO BEDROOM FARCE.
THEY BEGIN TO TEAR OFF EACH OTHER'S
CLOTHES, TOSSING THEM INTO THE AIR. IT
IS OBVIOUS THEY ARE THROWING CAUTION
TO THE WINDS AND INTEND TO MAKE LOVE
RIGHT THERE IN THE SHOP.

It was Friday afternoon. Dress rehearsal. For some reason
J.C. was on tenterhooks about this kiss. Silly. Brandon was
her best friend. They knew each other's secrets. It was well
over a year since he had put the make on her in Banff.
They'd never mentioned it again. They continued to have
loads of fun and he'd always been a true gentleman. But all
this week, every time he got close to her, J.C. felt the need
to step back and give herself some air. She was getting all
twitchy and jumpy. Something was definitely going on.

Maybe she was nervous because of Mac. He'd been
worrying about this moment ever since she first signed to do
the series. He just didn't want her kissing Brandon and he
sure wouldn't be happy when he saw the show aired. She
had the perfect excuse ready for him. 'Baby, I have to kiss
him. It's in the script. I'm getting paid for it. It'll be like
kissing my brother.' Never mind that the episode was so hot
that everyone connected with the show, from publicity on
down to set dressing, had been sworn to secrecy.

The stand-in was gone and Brandon was in. The first part
of the scene went fine as they sang 'There Ain't One
Without the Other'. Brandon had a surprisingly good
singing voice. Hadn't he told her he'd once sung in *The
Mikado* at the Sydney Opera House? The longing, the pain,
the loneliness, the hope, their emotions were perfectly in
sync. They got the harmonies just right, individual sounds
blending perfectly and then floating as one out into the air.
Coming up on the kiss now. Don't panic. This is just a dress
rehearsal.

★ ★ ★

The Kiss. Take One. OK. Deep breath. Move in for the kiss. Little peck first. Shy, tentative, awkward. Perfect. Now look into his eyes. Oh, Jesus God, talk about connecting. The electricity was palpable. She could feel the heat radiating off his body. His arms went around her. Her heart was pounding. Suddenly she couldn't breathe. She tried to swallow. Mouth on hers, open, soft, now stronger, urgent, searching. Oh Lord, this man knows how to kiss. A connoisseur of the lips and tongue. Every inch of his well-defined body, hard against hers. Heat flooded her, her bones were dissolving, she was melting into a little puddle. His mouth came off hers, no, no, put those lips right back where they were, I haven't finished with them yet, leaving her breathless. Whoa, what was going on here? She didn't think she was going to be able to get up off the stool, she was stuck right to it. She couldn't remember what she was supposed to do next. Did she have a line here? Was it her move? What? Helpless, she looked up at Brandon. He was studying her with just a hint of a smile, the crinkly lines around his eyes deepening with secret amusement.

'Cut,' he said finally. 'Not bad. We can do the rest of the business tonight. We'll have to wing it.'

'Business?' she said faintly.

'This is the point where Janine and Travis tear each other's clothes off and go at it, right?'

'Oh, right.'

'Don't worry. That was just fine,' he patted her on the top of her head, 'for a dress rehearsal.'

That smug, self-satisfied son of a bitch. Talk about unprofessional. Giving her a tongue sandwich. Getting her all worked up, making her lose her place, and then standing there with a big, shit-eatin', I-told-you-so grin on his face. OK, buddy, you asked for it. Tonight, at the taping, you better get those lips ready. Audience or no audience, it's gonna be payback time.

Take Two. The studio audience held their breath. Two years of flirting and feinting and circling and teasing, a caress here, a bite there, two-and-a-half seasons of agonizing foreplay. Now, finally, Travis and Janine, together at last, alone in the shop, sparks flying back and forth between them, hot enough to light a Christmas tree. On the first kiss, the peck, there was a collective sigh. Nice, sweet, romantic, a promising start. Now turn up the heat so we can feel the sizzle.

On the second kiss, J.C. opened her mouth, slipped him her tongue and kissed him right back. She felt him react with a jolt, and then his arms were around her, their bodies pressed together, imprinting each other, lost in a slow-motion dance, while the studio audience erupted wildly. If the First AD hadn't yelled 'Cut' they would have done it right there on the floor.

They both knew where this was headed. They weren't sure how long it would take them to get there. Smiling, nodding, shaking hands with all the network execs, 'excellent directing, Brandon', 'good job, J.C.', 'hot stuff, kids'. 'Terrific episode, should get us the numbers, a thirty share for sure, maybe another Emmy, who knows? Is it hot in here?'

Acknowledging all the compliments in record time, without saying goodbye, they slipped away from the wrap party. J.C. left her car in the studio parking lot and got into Brandon's forest green Cadillac and drove.

'Wait a minute,' J.C. said. 'Aren't you taking me to your place?'

'I am.' Brandon assured her.

'But you live in Topanga Canyon.'

'I'm taking you to my real home, my secret hideaway in Laurel Canyon. I figure you're not a woman I can impress with display, so I might as well show you what I really love. Laurel Canyon has a certain kind of funky cachet but it's not trendy, although it was when Joni Mitchell first moved here. Remember Queen of the Canyon?' He turned at the Canyon Country Store on to a winding mountain road which brought them to a little house tucked away, almost obscured by the foliage, thick vines, bushes and flowers. They parked at the top of the road and walked down, hand in hand. 'I thought this was pretty romantic, especially in the early seventies. I bought it with the money from the first film I ever made. Paid for it outright. I figure if I lose everything, I'll always still have this.'

'This is real sweet,' J.C. said in surprise. The house was of a nice size, but very simple, a combination of wood and stone. Surrounded by tree-covered hills, with the crickets chirping and a full, round moon rising, it felt like they were far from the city.

'Nobody will find us here. Very few people know I've still got this place.' Brandon opened the screen door, unlocked the front door, and let her in. It smelt musty, but not unpleasant. He opened the windows to let in the night air and turned on a couple of lights. They knew each other so well, they didn't need illumination to see with clarity.

'Wow, just look at this,' J.C. exclaimed. The place was filled with cowboy memorabilia. Trophies and saddles, a six-gun and holster, a whip, it looked like a museum of early western movies. 'Where did you get all this?'

'Some of it comes from my dad. Remember I told you he was a rodeo rider? The trophies are the prizes he won for steer wrestling and roping. A couple are mine for bronc riding. The rest of the collection is from some of the early westerns. I'm a sucker for the cowboy mystique. That's Lash Larue's original whip and Hopalong Cassidy's Long Horn neckerchief holder. The white ten-gallon cowboy hat actually belonged to William S. Hart.'

'The collection's probably worth a fortune,' J.C. said, fingering a hand-tooled leather belt.

'I don't see it as an investment. I keep it to remind me of where I came from.'

He put on some music, low, funky, bluesy guitar, the sort of thing they both liked. She looked so beautiful, standing in the small living-room, the soft light framing the cascade of red hair. She smiled at him. He was aching to touch her, but he didn't want to rush it. Rush it? Hell, he'd been waiting two-and-a-half years for this. It was all he could do to keep from grabbing her and kissing her all over. She was here. In his private home. They were about to make love. It was going to happen.

He was nervous. He wanted it to be perfect. 'Are you hungry? I don't keep a lot of food here, but I have someone stock the place once a month. I could easily whip something up. Believe it or not, I'm quite a good cook.'

'No thanks,' she said softly, standing there, not moving, just smiling at him. 'I'm not hungry.'

'Would you like a drink?'

'No, really, I'm fine.' Her blue eyes never left his face.

'What would you like then?' His heart was in his mouth.

'I'd like you to hold me. Just hold me.'

He opened his arms and she moved into them, easily, naturally. Even in her red cowboy boots, she was so tiny, her head just barely reaching his chest. God, the feel of her, the smell of her, the shape, the touch, the taste of her. He kissed her hair, inhaling its scent. His lips went down to her neck and he could feel her shiver next to him, then he kissed her mouth, and it opened so naturally under his. The kiss seemed to go on for ever, longer even than Janine and Travis's. They could freeze-frame right here and he would die a fulfilled man. When they finally broke apart, they were both breathless.

'I think we want this pretty bad,' J.C. said, breaking into a laugh.

'I know I do,' he could hardly speak.

She lifted her chin and looked up at him. 'All our parts fit real good together, don't you think?'

'Want to see if it's the same fit in the bedroom?' All his artful words of seduction seemed to escape him.

'Unless you're aiming for the floor.'

'You mean like this afternoon?'

She blushed and they both laughed. He took her by the hand and led her up the stairs to the loft bedroom.

His hands were trembling as he undressed her. Look at him. He hadn't been like this since he was sixteen. No, fourteen. He didn't know what to say to her that he hadn't said before to someone else, what he could do that she hadn't already tried. Her body was so beautiful, at least it was beautiful to him, because he wanted it so much. He flashed back to Banff and the hot springs. The little black bathing suit that he wanted to tear off her right then and there, to make love in the water, with the steam rising from the surface, and the mountains and the dark all around.

She sized him up approvingly. 'I never thought I would see you buck naked,' she said.

'Butt naked.'

'That, too.' She reached out and let her fingers lightly trace the contours of his chest and down toward his belly. She was good at this; she knew what she was doing. Her eyes widened as she looked at his body. She touched his nipples, already swollen with wanting her. He felt a shiver of deep-rooted pleasure run all the way through him.

516

'I love you, J.C.,' he whispered. 'Will you let me say it now? Do you believe me now?'

'Oh yeah,' she said, 'I believe you now.'

She was looking at him so lovingly, with such genuine emotion, that he knew it was true. They kissed and licked and sighed and touched and it was all wonderful, and, shit, what was wrong with him? She kissed him and their tongues did a dance and his body was straining. Her eyes glazed, she reached for him, and then drew back, surprised. She stroked him, lovingly. He willed himself to get hard. She knelt down and took him in her mouth, sucking, gently at first, then harder, down, down, way down. He was moving back and forth with the rhythm of her mouth. She was good at this. In fact, she was better at it than any woman he knew including the ones who were paid for it. But it wasn't working. Why? Why? He wanted to die. Why was this happening to him now, goddamnit, why?

'I don't understand,' he was forced to say, his voice betraying all the frustration, anger, and desperation that he had never expected to feel. 'This has not happened to me before. I know men are supposed to say that and you know that they are lying, but for me, it's true. You must believe me, this has never happened before.'

'I do, darlin', I do.' She sounded completely unconcerned about it.

'I love you so much. I want everything to be perfect for you. I don't know what's wrong. Maybe I can't make love if I'm in love. That's ridiculous, that's crazy . . .'

She put her hand over his mouth. 'I didn't ask you to make love to me,' she said gently. 'You've been doing that all year long, Brandon. With your eyes, with your voice, with the way you've cared for me and helped me get through some of the darkest moments of my life. And I love you for it. I just asked you to hold me. It doesn't have to be perfect. It just has to be us.'

So he did. And it was.

> We can have our cake and eat it
> In the best days of our lives
> And the one who joins with others
> Is the one who now survives
> We are facing many choices
> We are challenged to decide

So just listen to your voices
When you reach the great divide

There ain't this without that
There ain't rain without sun
There ain't dog without cat
There ain't work without fun
There ain't head without heart
There ain't think without do
There ain't done without start
There ain't me without you
There ain't one without the other
There ain't dark without light
There ain't father without mother
There ain't wrong without right
There ain't take without give
There ain't her without he
There ain't die without live
There ain't you without me

Chapter Fifty-one

Debra Jo Fawcett was not having a good day. That's why she was shopping at Gelsen's, the grocery paradise in Century City, a far cry from the Piggly Wiggly. When she was down, the only thing that would bring her back up was treats. So what if the prices at Gelsen were out of this world? So was the food. Fifty varieties of fresh baked breads, at least that many different mustards, exotic fruits and vegetables to provide a taste of far-off lands. Gigantic, live lobsters and crabs swimming, well, at least wiggling, in a miniature in-store swimming pool. Gelsen's had everything under the sun, and that was what she needed right now.

Two weeks ago she had put Danny on the plane and sent him back to Houston. He and Tucker had been caught stealing electronics equipment and selling it on the street. Danny'd been in danger of going to a juvenile detention center but, thanks to the efforts of Julia and some pull at the studio, the authorities settled for him leaving LA altogether. The company had been very supportive when she told them of her trouble. She'd been so upset she'd offered to quit the show, but they talked her out of it.

Eddie was absolutely furious; he blamed her, of course, and she accepted that blame. She had neglected Danny. Not that she'd meant to, but Melissa's problems seemed so much more pressing and dramatic. You get one child sorted out and then the other one starts acting up. She should have known something was wrong. What was it Alex had said to her? 'You have to listen to your kids even when they're not saying anything.' It was dumb of her to think Tucker was a good kid just because he lived in Bel Air and his folks had money to burn. Back in Houston, it was the kids from ritzy River Oaks that were always getting into trouble. Shoplifting, auto theft, unwanted pregnancy, drugs. Drugs. She shivered, thanking her lucky stars Danny had missed getting into that. Of course drugs were probably next on Tucker's list. Not that she would have known. She'd been completely obsessed with Brandon. Crazy. Like living in a dream world. To think that one night meant the promise for a lifetime. He'd been very sweet when he told her it was over. Said she was too good for him, he couldn't intrude on her marriage. She wasn't stupid. She knew he was letting her down easy and she was grateful, but it hurt. God, it really hurt. And then Danny's pain overtook everything else. She felt so guilty. She hadn't been home enough, it was all her fault.

She didn't want to go home now either, the house was so empty. Melissa had moved into a condo next to Alex and Shirley in Marina del Rey. Maybe if she'd moved out sooner, that would have helped Debra Jo to open her eyes and see what was going on with Danny. But there was no point now in crying over spilled chocolate milk. That's what Danny insisted on saying when he was five years old and spilled his milk. Even as a baby, he had been precise, and precision was important to him even now. He'd only been gone two weeks and she missed him like crazy. She missed Eddie and Beau, too. Funny how the mind and heart could shift so quickly. Last year, she'd spent a lot of time fantasizing about leaving Eddie and marrying Brandon Tate. It embarrassed her even to think about it now. Brandon was sweet, but marriage? That man didn't know the meaning of the word, or at least understood a very different definition of it from her and Eddie.

To Eddie, marriage meant: You've got a hankering for some Cherry Garcia ice-cream? I'll jump in the truck, speed over to the mall, be back in time to feed it to you myself. It meant rubbing your feet when you were tired. Or scrubbing your back in the tub and not assuming that would necessarily lead to making love although, with Eddie and her, it usually did. She smiled, remembering what an animal he was in bed. There was only one Eddie. They'd be seeing each other at Christmas and, this year, it couldn't come fast enough for her.

She looked up to see a woman staring at her from across the frozen food section. Probably wondering why she was standing there grinning like an idiot over the Lean Cuisine. Or maybe she recognized her from Makeover, although Debra Jo, as popular as she had become, was rarely recognized – as long as she didn't open her mouth and reveal her trademark squeaky voice. She looked like everybody else; that was her selling point on the show, and that made it possible for her to move among the people without being recognized. She nodded and smiled. The woman tentatively smiled back – was that sympathy in her eyes? Then she went all red, turned on her heel, and began vigorously pushing her shopping cart in the opposite direction. Not an easy task. The Gelsen shopping carts were the size of a VW beetle. She didn't have to split so fast. Debra Jo would have happily given her an autograph if that's what she wanted.

Reaching into the chilly treasure chest, she selected a rum cake with whipped cream. To think she used to find Sara Lee chocolate brownies a big treat. She scooped up frozen Chinese dumplings, duck and coriander enchiladas, smoked salmon canapés, and caviar blinis. On to the meat and poultry counter. Hormone-free chicken? If it was free of hormones, how could it reproduce? Double cream brie, tangy goat cheese, crumbly feta, she'd come a long way from velveeta cheese dreams. Pita chips, chorizo, shitake mushrooms, marinated lotus root, her shopping cart was piled high with gourmet goodies. She was attracting unusual attention today. Shoppers turned to stare and when their eyes connected with hers, they immediately looked away. Her TVQ must be increasing she thought, as she wheeled the cart to the checkout.

Then she saw it. Her face, a huge head shot, plastered all over the front cover of the *Hollywood Insider*. 'MAKE-OVER MOM FAILURE AS WIFE AND MOTHER', blared the headline. Her head was down, Princess Diana style, looking as though she were about to burst into tears. There was a picture of Danny, looking startled and very hostile, in front of his school, with the sub-heading: 'Favorite Son Arrested for Theft'. And in the corner, a photograph of a couple in bathing suits, standing close together, looking very cosy – oh Lordy, it was her husband, Eddie, and her best friend, Jackie. That's exactly what the caption said, too: 'Debra Jo's Husband Eddie with Best Friend Jackie. For the Story on Debra Jo's Two-Timing Hubby, Turn to Page 17.'

Her hands were shaking so hard she let the magazine fall to the floor; she had to reach down and pick it up and find the right page all over again. The story seemed to go on for pages. It wasn't really that long, but there were photos of Debra Jo all over the article. In her yellow chicken dress being crowned Mrs Houston. With Mac and J.C. at the baseball game in the Astro-dome. 'In happier times for the estranged couple', said the caption under that one. Of course, they had to re-run that humiliating picture of her and Bonnie rolling around on the commissary floor. And the photo of Eddie and Jackie. Her eyes kept returning to that one, over and over again like Ripley's Believe It or Not. They were both wearing practically nothing. All that bare skin, sliding over each other, touching, kissing. Jackie was thin, much thinner than Debra Jo, even after the weight she'd lost for the show. Eddie had always said Jackie had a boney ass. Did he like that now? Was that what he wanted?

There was a roaring sound in her ears. Her stomach heaved. The rich, buttery croissant smell coming from the in-store bakery was enough to make her lose her lunch right then and there. She didn't know which one she wanted to kill first. Eddie was weak, he was lonely. The man loved to screw, he had a big appetite for sex, she'd been away a long time. Stop making excuses. He was a pig, a butthole. Hadn't Jackie warned her about this when she put her on the plane for LA? Or was Jackie planning even then to go after Eddie the minute Debra Jo's back was turned? How could she have been so dumb? Her face was hot, throbbing. Her eyes were stinging with tears jammed up against the back of her eyeballs.

Everybody was staring at her now. Of course, why wouldn't they be? Nothing had turned out the way she'd expected it to. It had all gone to ratshit. She felt like bawling her eyes out, right here in the middle of the store, sinking down on the cool tiled floor and crying, 'I want to go home.'

MAKEOVER MOM FAILURE AS WIFE AND MOTHER

Debra Jo Fawcett, who plays the spunky housewife of the same name on America's favorite sit-com, Makeover, is paying a high price for her overnight success.

'Debra Jo's close-knit family is being torn apart by Mom's unexpected fame,' said one source close to the *Insider*.

Recently her twelve-year-old son, caught stealing high-priced electronics equipment, had to be shipped back to his dad because Debra Jo couldn't handle him.

'The kid was out of control. He went from a normal suburban homelife in Texas to a Hollywood headtrip that turned his basically good morals upside down. Danny was a sweet boy when he came to town, now he's obnoxious. What can you expect? He's only a kid.'

According to a source, Danny begged her to 'stop playing a mom and be a real one again'. But Debra Jo didn't listen to her son's cry for help. Nor did she heed the advice of friends who warned her she might be putting her marriage in jeopardy by leaving her husband behind in Houston while coming to LA to make it big in a business not known for long-term wedded bliss.

'Eddie is a proud man. It must burn him up that his wife is the breadwinner in the family now. Debra Jo had counted on her husband accepting her surprise stardom, but it looks as though he's not prepared to sit around and wait for her to come back home and heat up his TV dinner.'

Rumors that the fifteen-year Fawcett marriage was rocky have surfaced from time to time. Now there is evidence with this photo. While Debra Jo is working round the clock to earn enough money to send her boys to college, sexy Eddie is seen in this sizzling photo cavorting in the sun with his wife's skimpily-clad best gal pal, Jackie Berry.

We did not reach Mr Fawcett or Ms Berry for their comments. The *Insider* has learned, however, that Jackie Berry has started divorce proceedings to extricate herself from her third marriage.

Debra Jo has always claimed, 'My husband and my two boys are the most important things in my life.' Now she may have to put her money where her mouth is and give up her new-found fame and fortune in order to salvage the true treasure of her family's happiness.

Susan Carroll

Chapter Fifty-two

The disclosure of J.C.'s abortion did cause her popularity to dip, but it soon bounced up again. The wind of public opinion on a woman's right to choose was shifting and, anyway, hadn't she made this particular choice a long time ago? Where was Mac in all this? There was a general perception that, given a seventeen-year-old from the boon-docks with a golden throat and on the threshold of a big career, her much older husband manager might have a hand in this choice.

Along with the hate mail came letters of support and admiration for her courage in speaking out. She might have lost a few hardcore country fans, but now, due to the success of Makeover, she was reaching a much wider audience to replace them. The Emmy nominations were announced. Thirteen nominations for the show and, for the first time, J.C. Austin was nominated for Outstanding Actress in a Comedy Series. She phoned Mac in Nashville to tell him the good news.

'I know awards don't mean a damn thing, but it makes me feel great. Like maybe finally they're accepting me out here. I figured all the fallout from the abortion would do me in this time for sure, but I guess people respect my honesty. I feel better bringing it all out in the open anyway. I been carrying that weight around my heart for too long. The *Insider*'s going to have to find somebody else to pick. I don't have any more skeletons to come out of my closet.'

'I'm glad for you, baby,' Mac's voice on the other end of the line sounded low-key, subdued.

She wanted to cheer him up, make him laugh. 'We're taping our Christmas episode this week. Guess what it's called? "A Mall and the Night Visitors". Get it?' That elicited a chuckle. 'I think it's one of Julia's funniest. Janine and Travis are supposed to be doing a nativity pageant in

524

the mall. I'm playing Mary. That's a stretch. Brandon and Paul are the Wise Men. Wise asses is more like it. I can't believe Julia talked Paul into doing a Christmas show. Of course it ends up with Melissa making this speech about how it doesn't matter what you are, Christian or Jew, what matters is the human spirit.'

Mac snorted derisively. 'That sounds like Julia. That guy she's married to is a Jew, isn't he?'

J.C. winced. He was always talking like that. At this point in his life, he wasn't likely to change. She'd just have to learn to tune it out. 'Anyway, at the end of the show, where I usually sing my song, Julia wants us all to sing together. This is the episode where the rest of the Changing Room staff find out what only Travis and Janine's dad know, along with millions of viewers, of course, that Janine is a great singer. So Julia asked me to do a voice check on everybody. Paul couldn't carry a tune in a bucket. The rest of them sound real good. But the big surprise was Kelly.'

'Why?'

'I put her through the scales and her range is D below middle C up to C above middle C. That makes her a true tenor. So I'm having her sing Third Wise Man, isn't that a hoot?' Mac laughed, but he still sounded down. She knew he was hurting from all the negative publicity. He loved her to be in the spotlight, but he shied away from having any of the glare focused on himself. 'Mac, I know these last few weeks have been real hard on you. The sorry part about the whole mess is how it's affected you. I can take anything they say about me, but when they start bringing you into it, I just see red. You didn't ask for any of this. It's so unfair.'

His tone softened. 'Don't fret yourself, baby. I'm glad things are going better for you. I can take care of myself. We have to concentrate on what we've got together. You feel so far away right now. I really miss you.'

'I miss you, too. Love you. Bye.'

She was drowning in guilt, not just because the mud slung at her had landed on Mac, but because every minute she wasn't on set, she was in bed with Brandon. After his initial false start, things had got going so hot and heavy, they had barely come up for air. Because very few people knew about Brandon's other home in Laurel Canyon, that became their secret hideaway. After the heavy security, monitored luxury of their day to day lives, the simplicity of the little house was more romantic than the most sumptuous hotel. It was a relief to get a break from the star treatment and live almost normal lives. The backyard was a garden enclosed by a huge wall, which guaranteed them privacy so they could sunbathe and hold hands and kiss until kissing wasn't enough.

'Talk to me in Shakespeare,' J.C. would say. 'Even if you never touched me, I could get off just listening to your voice.' So Brandon would read to her from the sonnets. Usually he only made it through one or two before he had to put the book down because she was all over him. Sometimes they would light a fire in the fireplace, spread out a blanket in front of it, and picnic on pizza and beer. J.C. would play the guitar and they would sing together. For her, singing harmony with the man she loved was like making love.

'You can make my nipples hard just from hearing you sing,' Brandon whispered. 'The way you hit the note and then hold it for ever. Your total surrender to the lyric, when you go four or five syllables past where I'd expect you to break for a breath. Man, I love that. The first time I heard you sing, there was this amazing, intimate intensity. I hoped, oh God, I hoped that the way you sang was the way you would make love, that somewhere else in you that intensity had to exist.'

They were in that glorious state of discovery where everything seemed fresh and new. Even though they had been friends before they were lovers, the comfort of familiarity was suddenly shot through with the excitement of the unknown.

They grabbed every night of passion they could get. A weekend was a luxury. Both of them sailed through the regular week of readings, rehearsals, wardrobe calls, everything connected to Makeover, with silly grins on their faces, because they were looking forward to ten o'clock Friday night when they could go into hiding. The minute the taping was done, they got into their separate cars, so as not to arouse suspicion, and drove straight to his place. They couldn't get enough of each other.

As good as they were together on set, they were even better in bed. Sometimes they spent forty-eight hours without leaving the house, making sure they were surrounded by what Brandon called 'necessary provisions': wine, bread, cold salad, flowers, music and candles. He was trying to woo her away from her beloved Tequila Gold. 'This stuff rots your gut and I want you to be around for a long time,' he said. Funny, when Mac told her what to do, it just ticked her off, but Brandon's protectiveness warmed her heart. And she had to admit that when she was with him she didn't need hard liquor to heighten her senses. He kept her flying.

They would lie in each other's arms and talk and talk until desire stopped the words and took them somewhere else and back again. 'You really love making love, don't you?' J.C. lay back with a contented sigh. 'Some men make love only because they're compelled to, you know what I mean? It's a drive and they can't stop themselves but they don't really enjoy it. You get the feeling there are parts of a woman's body they don't really like so they give them a lick and polish and then move on to what they consider the good stuff.'

'With you, it's all good stuff,' Brandon rolled over and kissed the inside of her elbow. 'I love every inch of you. If you give me a chance to catch my breath, I'll prove it.'

J.C. snuggled closer. 'I guess what I'm saying is, maybe a lot of men don't really like women. They have this idea of what a woman is and they like that OK, but they're not partial to the real thing.'

'That's because basically they're afraid of women and want to control them.' Brandon let his tongue trace a pattern along the inside of her upper arm. 'Otherwise they risk being controlled.'

'You are so right. All the other men I've been with, we may be equals outside of bed, but once we're in bed, they have to take charge or they're not happy. You and me, we both like to fuck, we're both good at it, and neither one of us is in charge. All the other men I've been with . . .'

'Will you please stop saying that?'

'What?'

'All the other men. It makes me think of row upon row of foot soldiers marching over your pillows and committing unspeakable acts upon your all too willing person. Do you have to sound like such an expert?'

'Hey, you should talk. With your reputation? I guess we've both looked around enough to know what we really want.'

'Oh, darlin', I do.' He pulled her to him and kissed her

for a long time. 'I used to wake up with some woman and think, "What am I doing? I don't want to be here." You know, that awkwardness of "why are we here?" '

'Oh yeah. That sounds familiar. All those years of touring with a bunch of road dogs. Of course that's the easy answer to the question, what are we doing in bed together? We're on the road and what you do on the road doesn't count. You try and block it out of your mind by getting faced and the minute you're drunk enough to forget the last guy, you're drunk enough to pick up the next. I'm surprised I'm still alive.'

'I know. It seemed like one long free ride. If I'd known then what was going to happen now, I would have done more.'

'More? More?' J.C. smacked him in mock amazement. 'From what I've heard, you didn't have room for more.'

'You have been misled by rumor. I told you I've always practiced serial monogamy. I'd get into a relationship and think, this is it, this is for ever; then after a year it would become routine: not boring exactly, but just routine.'

'Maybe that will happen with us,' J.C. said.

'No. We've already passed the two-year mark. I've been in love with you for over two years. Sleeping together is just the icing on the cake.'

'Umm. Gimme some more of that cake.' She reached out for him.

'I love your greediness.' He stroked the curve of her thigh.

'Well, all the other men I've been with . . . Excuse me, you are the only man who's been able to keep up with me.'

'Not an easy task,' Brandon said, 'even for me.' His hand moved to her breast and he caressed it, then stopped, suddenly very serious. 'With you, J.C., there's staying power. There's strength. Usually for me, the attraction wears off, it doesn't stay. With you, it's stayed. For a long time, I wanted nothing more than to wake up and say "hi" and be glad to be there. With you,' he held her close, 'I am. I can't imagine the rest of my life without you.'

'Please don't say that,' J.C. whispered miserably. 'I can't imagine not being married to Mac.'

Julia drove up to San Diego to the Feighner Institute. Marty was being discharged today and she had promised to pick him up and bring him back to LA.

'You look great,' she said as he tossed his bags into the trunk of the car. He did, too, tanned and relaxed, the tension around his eyes and mouth gone, his face recognizable as the one she knew and loved. 'You want to drive?'

'No, you drive, I'll talk. I want to tell you what I've been doing the past six weeks.' As they headed down the coast, he began to explain what he had discovered about himself during the time they'd been apart. 'In the beginning I was still agoraphobic. I was afraid to leave my room, much less go outside the hospital. You figure, the tighter the boundaries, the safer you are.'

'I know what you mean.' So much was going through Julia's head that she couldn't express to him. She was glad she was driving because it gave her an excuse to focus on the road without having to give him her full attention. Marty knew her like a book; she was afraid of what he would read in her eyes.

'So here I am, stuck in this room, with only two things, a television and a computer. I'm using the computer to try and keep my hand in at work and to keep notes for Dr Richardson. But all this focusing in on myself is making me feel worse. I need an escape. I leave the computer, I turn on the TV. That's why it's there, but for me, TV can never be an escape. Watching is work.'

'Oh, boy, do I understand that now,' Julia murmured.

'Right, but you've only had a few years of it. I've got a history with it that dates back twenty-five years. I know everybody, on the shows, behind the shows, at the networks. I realize this is my whole life, always has been.'

'Your whole life?' For an instant their eyes connected in the rearview mirror.

'If I'm honest with myself, yes. Now I'm really depressed. I'm even more depressed as I watch the fast-food junk that constitutes today's primetime entertainment on TV. I go back to the computer, type a few notes, my thoughts on the current state of television, where it came from, where it's headed, because I've been part of it, you know, and I can see that everything's changing. The days of the networks ruling the roost are gone, something else is coming, it remains to be seen exactly what. There used to be just a few channels. Now there are one hundred, and they're talking five hundred. With all the advances in cable, there's a vast smorgasbord out there. How do you convince people not to eat the smoked salmon in favor of the butterfly shrimp? What Stan and Tim and the other network guys don't realize is that they're programming themselves right out of existence. The big networks will go the way of the big car manufacturers.'

'Bite your tongue,' Julia murmured.

'It's not just television, Julia, it's everything. We're in the middle of a revolution. The whole world is. We don't know it. We don't even know who the revolutionaries are. It may well be you and me. Anyway, I'm typing away and I'm still thinking of this as notes for the doctor, to explain how I've come to how I feel this way.'

'Right.'

'Only it doesn't come out in notes, but complete thoughts, full sentences. Pretty soon the document is full and I'm starting another. I'd written volumes before I realized what I have here is the makings of a book, one that will blow the lid off the television industry.'

'It sounds like an exciting idea.'

'More than an idea,' Marty said eagerly, 'it looks like it's going to be a reality. I faxed the first three chapters to a publisher in New York and they've already accepted it for publication. Well, they've made me a tentative offer. I've handed the negotiations over to Michael Taylor. If we agree to the deal, once the contract's signed, I'll get an advance. The money in publishing is nothing like what I'm used to getting, but the point is, Julia, it's all mine. Television is a collaborative business, this is something I've done all on my own. I feel good when I'm writing and when I'm finished, I've got something I can hold in my hand. I guess it's what Dr Richardson calls, "getting with your passion". All I know is, I've come back to life.'

'Why didn't you tell me about this before?' She was really surprised. As far as she knew, Marty had never written anything other than a postcard.

'I felt sort of weird about the whole thing. I mean, you've always been the creative one in the family, I'm the business-man. Of course, this isn't fiction, it's an overview of the industry and how television impacts on pop culture, but still, it requires analysis and structure and interpretation, not just a budget. Julia, the words are coming out of me so easily. I have a lot to say and I can't wait to say it. I'm really looking forward to getting home, back to my office, so I can finish the damn thing. The lead time for books can be years and the TV business is changing daily, but I'll just keep updating until the book actually comes out.' He stopped, breathless, his eyes shining with excitement. 'So, what do you think?'

'I think it sounds . . . marvelous.'

They stopped for lunch in Carmel at a place that was famous for its crab salad and sourdough bread and its view of the sea. Julia was so quiet over lunch that eventually Marty called her on it.

'You're letting me do all the talking. Usually you fight for equal time. What's going on here?' His warm brown eyes were anxious. 'Are you worried about what such a book will do in terms of your career? Makeover has remained in the top ten. The people who watch it aren't going to read this book and, even if they do, believe me, it won't make them stop watching television.'

'I'm not worried, I mean it,' Julia picked at her salad.

'You think it's going to cause problems for you within the industry? Is that it?'

'I've already got problems. The technicians are threatening an industry strike and we've only got a few episodes in the can. If they strike, we'll be able to air what we've got, but we'll have to stop production on any more. They're already talking about postponing this year's Emmy Awards. The tabloids are hounding the cast. Every time I turn around there's another hatchet job on one of us. There's tension between the CBN execs and me — and it has been just me, because you were out of the picture — and I'm really up against it. I don't get it, Marty. They wanted me because I was new to the business, they said they were looking for a fresh approach, but every time I try to do something different, they're on my back. I believe in this show, I love doing it, but it's become a daily battle to do it my way.'

'You mean Stan?'

'Stan's just one guy, but Stan and his sensibility is reflected over and over again in all the other guys. There are a bunch of Stans out there. They just wear different suits. I'm not getting the support I need from Kathryn. There's some kind of shakeup going on at Pac Vic: maybe she's being pressured out, she keeps talking about moving to New York. All I know is, millions of viewers think what I'm doing with Makeover is right, but I can't seem to convince Stan.'

'You've got a hit show, Julia. What's he going to do, fire you?'

'I'm making so much money, my life has changed so much. I look in the mirror, I don't even recognize myself. I'm beginning to question my own integrity. Maybe I am taking the show in the wrong direction, who knows? I'm juggling so many balls in the air, if one of them drops, they'll all fall.'

'And you're afraid that my book might bring it all crashing down? That's part of my whole point, Jules. Stan and Tim and the rest of the boys don't know it, they're still clinging on for dear life, but the game is already over, at least the way they've been playing it.'

'I'm not worried about the book,' Julia repeated. 'I'd be happy to see them all strung up by their balls.'

'Because if you are, I won't go any further with it. I mean that. It's not worth it to me.'

'Don't say that. It just makes me feel worse.' Her eyes were starting to well.

'OK,' he reached out for her hand, 'you better level with me, Jules. This isn't about the book or the show is it? When you start questioning your integrity, that has to mean something else. I know you feel abandoned because we've been apart for a long time. I mean, I was already apart from you in spirit before I even went into the hospital so that makes it seem even longer, but—'

'I need to be apart,' she blurted out. 'I've been doing fine on my own.'

'You've just been telling me you haven't . . .'

'And now that you're feeling better you think you can just pick up where we left off only you're not really back to work for Hudlow/Turgov and Makeover, you're writing a book instead, so where does that leave me?' She was surprised at the fury she felt.

'What you're telling me is you don't want me to come home right now,' Marty said quietly.

'Yes . . . no . . . I don't know.'

'I can't say I blame you. Watching someone go through panic and anxiety is probably worse than having to experience it yourself. You must have felt helpless. And cheated. Maybe even angry.'

'Yes,' she said, grateful he understood at least part of it.

He looked at her and then looked away before he said, 'Are you involved with someone else? No, wait, don't tell me if you are. I don't want to know. I'm feeling better, but that I couldn't handle right now.' He let go of her hand and reached for the check. 'There's an apartment hotel close to the studio in Burbank. I used to stay there before I met you. When we get back to LA, you can drop me there.'

'Are you sure?'

'Yes. You know, it's funny. Somehow I thought that when we made love on Mustang Island, we'd found each other again. I guess I was wrong.'

'No, no, you weren't. I felt that, too,' Julia said sadly, 'but then we had to come back to California and I—'

'It's OK. Don't tell me any more. I have a feeling that fighting for you, at least right now, is not the thing to do.' He forced himself to look at her. 'I love you, Julia. Maybe you think everything's changed, but that hasn't.'

The pain in his eyes was almost more than she could bear.

Chapter Fifty-three

The doorbell rang at two o'clock in the morning. He had phoned to say he had something to show her, some pictures he thought she might like to see. Kelly had been expecting this for a long time. She took a deep breath and opened the door.

He was well-dressed, in a blazer and casual slacks, and he carried a briefcase. Tall and thin, he had reddish, sandy hair and blue eyes. I've seen you somewhere before, Kelly thought, but she couldn't place him.

'Hello, Kelly, I'm Len,' he said politely. 'May I come in?' He was soft-spoken, with a slight British accent and an air of urbane charm.

'Do I have a choice?' Kelly asked, allowing him to enter the apartment.

He laughed. 'You are even more magnificent in person than you are on the show. A real work of art.' He spoke with what appeared to be genuine admiration. 'I love the show, by the way. One of the few interesting things on the tube these days. Your success is well-deserved.'

How could he stand there and say that? When the sleazy, muck-raking rag he worked for had been hounding Make-over almost to the exclusion of all the other shows. How could he even look her in the eye knowing his paper's methods of researching and reporting were so dirty and underhand, cloaked in darkness and secrecy, ignoring any right to privacy and human dignity? How could he smile so warmly at her when he was about to destroy her life?

'Show me what you have,' she said sharply.

Len unlocked his briefcase and brought out a file folder. 'We don't usually do this,' he said, handing it to her, 'but I thought it only fair that you should have a look at these.'

She sat on the sofa to read it, knowing the only way she could handle what she suspected were the contents of this file was sitting down. She took her time and went over everything. It was as damaging as she thought it would be. Records, files, even photographs, a meticulously researched, thoroughly documented exposé of her past.

'What do you intend to do with all this?' Kelly asked.

Len looked very serious. 'Firstly, the *Insider* believes you deserve a chance to tell your own story.'

'I have nothing to say on this subject.'

'I understand how you feel,' he said sympathetically, 'but you must have realized it would have come out sooner or later.'

'Maybe not. Without your help.'

'You chose a high-profile profession. What did you expect?'

'My past is my own business.'

'Guess again, sweetheart.'

For one brief moment, she tried pleading with him, 'If this gets out, do you realize what it will do, not just to my career, but to everything in my life? How can I continue to represent Kelly's Kosmetics? Do you think the President will allow me to stay on as Chairperson of the Federal Pediatric Aids Committee? Is it really worth it just to sell a couple of thousand extra copies?'

'I'm afraid that's part of our job. Once we know, we have to let our readers know. Perhaps you would like to give us an exclusive? Tell the story from your own point of view? We're prepared to make you an excellent offer, say, in three figures?'

'I don't think so.'

'With the right approach, you can make this another one of your causes. Like Kelly's Kids. I admire you greatly for your work in that area, by the way.'

'No.'

'We want to put you in a unique position. We'd like you to become a "friend to the *Insider*".'

'What does that involve?'

Len leaned forward. His tone was conspiratorial. 'Nothing major. Simply making yourself available to give us the odd interview. Keeping your eyes peeled, your ear to the ground for anything you think we might want to know. Granting us the favor of allowing us to contact you directly rather than having to go through your publicist.'

'You mean you want me to spy for you?'

'I wouldn't put it quite like that,' he said smoothly. 'Certainly the return would be worth it.'

'How can you do this?' Kelly whispered. 'How can you use my personal private pain to flog newspapers?'

'There are certain things we believe the public has a right to know. It's a matter of journalistic integrity.'

'Integrity?' She felt sick to her stomach. 'You wouldn't know what that was if it bit you on the ass. Once you pay for it, integrity goes out the window.'

Len's face hardened. 'I'm sorry. We're going to go with the story anyway, with or without your cooperation. We'll pay you a million bucks for the exclusive rights. You might as well go for it.'

'No way.' Kelly handed him back the file. She moved to the door, opened it, and held it open. 'I'm giving you exactly ten seconds to drag your ass out of my house and into the gutter where it belongs. If you're not out of here by the time I count to ten, I'm calling the police and having you arrested for trespassing.'

It was Sunday night. The *Hollywood Insider* would be on the stands tomorrow morning. Her story would undoubtedly make the cover. Kelly had just completed her Sunday night ritual of cleaning the house from top to bottom followed by a long, hot bath. She enjoyed puttering around the house, cooking, doing laundry, a little respite of domesticity before jumping back into the fray of the series bright and early Monday morning.

The apartment smelled comfortingly fresh and clean. The appliances in the kitchen were gleaming and there were streaks and swirls on the pile of the carpet from having just been vacuumed. She'd put fresh flowers in every room, even the bathroom. The large bathroom with its oversize tub had been one of the main selling points of the condo. Kelly walked through every room in the apartment, making sure each of her most treasured objects was neatly in its proper place. There was a picture of Carlito on the antique sideboard in the living-room. She flicked away a particle of dust she'd missed the first time around, automatically kissed her fingertips and placed them on the likeness of Carlito, the way she always did. The sideboard was intricately carved; it came all the way from Tours in France, home of some of the most exceptional cabinet-makers. It had cost a fortune and she was very proud of it. After struggling so long and so hard, it felt good to be able to own even a few beautiful things.

She slipped a CD into her player and turned up the volume. Handel's *Largo*, nice and soothing. She took out one of her prize Baccarat crystal glasses, poured some icy cold Chablis into the glass, and drank it straight down. She poured herself another, slipped off her heels, and padded into the bathroom.

Bath salts into the tub. Ombre Rose, her favorite. Turn the hot water on, nice and easy, to let the heavy, sweet, sensual smell escape slowly into the room. She inhaled deeply, letting the spicy sweetness tingle.

For a special treat, she lit a couple of candles and placed them high on a shelf.

As she disrobed to get into the steamy, luxuriant bubbles, she caught sight of her naked body in the full-length mirror and stopped to admire herself. She knew that most women found fault with some aspect of their bodies, but not Kelly. She loved every womanly contour and curve, was proud of her femininity.

For a brief moment, she held her magnificent, full breasts in her hands, cupping them lovingly. You've got great tits, lady, she said to herself.

As the gentle, lyrical sounds of *Largo* filled the apartment, Kelly climbed into the bathtub, took a razor and cut a neat, six-inch gash in each of her wrists.

SAMANTHA IS SAM!

Oh Boy Bombshell! Kelly Carmichael Is Transsexual!

Producers and execs of Hollywood's bright light sit-com, Makeover, are completely in the dark about one of their top stars.

The sexy, salty-talking star, who created the catchphrase, 'don't tease my hair', has a shocking secret buried in her beehive. Kelly Carmichael has had the ultimate makeover, changing from a man to a woman.

Kinky Kelly walks, talks, looks and sounds like a girl, but was born a boy, Carl Michael Kelly. Apparently little Carl grew up in Chicago, wearing Mommy's clothes and playing with dolls.

A tip to the *Insider* from a source close to Makeover led to an investigation of the star's personal and professional background. Kelly Carmichael started her career as an actor, then went to England to become an actress. David, the man Kelly refers to as her husband, was really her lover when she was still a man. Kelly claims she never 'remarried' because she was so blissfully happy with David, but obviously not happy enough.

Carl Michael Kelly always wanted to be a woman. Psychiatrists who examined the young man recommended gender reassignment surgery quite early on when a physician discovered that Carl had the classic XXY chromosome make-up symptomatic of the condition known as 'gender dysphoria'. But first Carl had to undergo a rigorous two-year, 'true-life' test, where he was forced to live and work as a woman for two whole years before being allowed to go ahead with the sex change.

While performing with the Paper Doll Players, an avant-garde theater in London, England, 'Kelly' was taking female hormones and having 'her' breasts enlarged with implants. After sex-change surgery, Carl changed his name to Kelly Carmichael and returned to the US as a full-fledged woman.

The description of this gruelling, five-hour operation would be enough to scare off all but the most determined and desperate. Surgeons remove the penis and testicles, at the same time constructing a 'vagina' and external female parts that supposedly look to all intents and purposes like a real woman's. Ouch!

Kelly had the agonizing surgery so that she would look on the outside the way she had always felt on the inside. Even her closest friends don't suspect the truth.

A member of the crew of Makeover says, 'This rumor is utterly ridiculous. The cast is full of talented, sexy women, but Kelly is by far the sexiest.' He admits to having a brief, but satisfying relationship with the actress. 'Believe me, if she were a man, I would have been able to tell the difference. I can't believe there's a word of truth to this garbage.'

Well, sorry to disappoint you, but photos and records prove beyond a shadow of a doubt that Carl Michael Kelly and Kelly Carmichael are one and the same.

The star used to work for peanuts and is now raking in the big bucks far beyond her wildest dreams. But she must know only too well that this revelation could put her sizzling career on permanent hold. Not to mention her sideline job as spokeswoman, er, man, for Pediatric Aids.

How are Makeover fans going to feel when they discover their favorite gal is really a guy?

The saddest part of all of this is that, legally, Kelly Carmichael must remain a man. She can never truly be the woman she longs to be.

Lance J. Sutton

Chapter Fifty-four

Kelly's death rocked all of North America, but Julia was completely devastated. When a letter with no return address arrived through the mail marked 'personal', she had an instant gut realization that it was from Kelly and had been mailed just before she took her life. No suicide note had been found with the body, but the lurid *Insider* exposé left no doubt as to why the star had killed herself. With trembling hands, Julia opened the letter.

Dear Julia,

This is meant for your eyes only. Analyzing gender and personality from now till Kingdom come will never get to the heart of this. For all of us, sex is illusive. Like magic. A wonderful, beautiful mystery. I've spent too much time on psychiatrists' couches trying to be normal to attempt to explain too much of myself here and now.

When David died, I realized that life can be cut off at any point. I'd already wasted a lot of time trying to be something I wasn't. I wanted to live the rest of my life, however long it might be, as a woman. In my heart I'd always felt female since the time I was old enough to know there was a difference.

One in thirty thousand men in the world is a transsexual. In North American native society and in India, crossdressers are respected, shamans and healers. But in the world you and I live in, I'm a freak.

I want you to know, Julia, that I have never been happier than when I was working with you on Makeover. I loved being Samantha and I loved the freedom you gave me to create her. You've been a good friend, Julia, and I know you would have supported me through all the brouhaha that will occur once the news comes out. What has gotten me through this so far has been my sense of humor, but now, I'm afraid, the laughs have run out for me.

My life would never be the same again. I don't want to go through the rest of my life labelled transsexual when all I ever really wanted to be was just 'the woman next door'.

As far as Makeover is concerned, I know I'm leaving you in a tough position, but hey, kid, you can handle it. I give you carte-blanche to find a way to kill off Sam that is crazy and wild, a real kick in the head. Let's put it this way, I'd like to go out with a bang. Give those viewers a shock, something they'll never forget.

I make no apology for my life or my death. Death is the last adventure I will go through. As always, I make my exit with style. All my love,

Kelly

Julia was facing a real dilemma. The strike was now over so they could resume shooting. All they had in the can was the five arc episodes with Travis and Janine, the Christmas special, which now they would have to reshoot without Kelly, and an episode featuring Kelly which was supposed to air next week! The circumstances surrounding Kelly's death were sensational. The thought of airing the episode in full without acknowledging Kelly was gone seemed wrong. She had a crazy idea which could not only save some of the Kelly episode, but serve as a tribute to the character and the person, both of whom were greatly loved. They would keep the first half of the show. It had lots of laughs and featured absolutely the best of Kelly; funny, mouthy and big-hearted. Sam would actually die right in the middle of the show. Not at her own hand, that was too close to real life. Something that was wild and off the wall, in keeping with Sam's (and Kelly's) own sense of humor. Sitting under the hairdryer, doing her nails, an electrical accident, the dryer blows up and Sam is killed instantly.

They would rewrite and quickly reshoot the second half to deal with the death of Samantha and her subsequent funeral. At the funeral, in the same shocking way everyone in America had learned Kelly was transsexual, the staff of the Changing Room would find out that Samantha was also transsexual as all of her friends in drag (they could use the same actors who had appeared in 'There Is Nothing Like a Dame') came to pay tribute to her.

It was a pretty zany, bizarre idea but Julia felt it would give the right send-off to a zany, bizarre actress. She had to run it past Tim because Stan was away on vacation on an island in the Caribbean and couldn't be reached. Which was just as well because she knew he would never approve of this.

'We've got to write Kelly out of the show by the next time it's aired,' she told Tim. 'Her death has to be acknowledged and dealt with. Otherwise, it's just, I don't know, ghoulish. Everybody knows she's dead and how she died. We can't pretend it hasn't happened, not even for one show.'

'I'm with you on that,' Tim agreed, 'but I don't know about bringing the whole transsexual thing out into the open. Some people find it creepy.'

'That's why I think it's so important to validate what Kelly was, not try and hide it. Make people understand that they loved her before they knew and finding out that she was once a man shouldn't make a difference.'

'OK,' Tim said. 'We'll have to get this moving quickly. Bring the cast back together early, reshoot, edit and get it on the air. Standards and Practices may balk, though.'

Julia took the plunge. 'They've already approved the episode as it was originally written. There isn't time to run it past them again.' She knew Tim understood the hidden message. 'Ultimately, it's the Entertainment Division that determines whether I can do this or not.'

'All right,' Tim came to a sudden decision, 'let's try.'

Julia gathered the entire cast together on soundstage six. She gave them the new scenes and as they read the dialogue aloud, everyone alternated between laughter and tears. They loved the twist that all of Sam's 'friends' turn up at the funeral dressed as Sam as a special tribute, and are surprised to learn the Changing Room staff are unaware of her secret, 'Didn't you know she was one of us? That's why we always came to the Changing Room.'

> CARLENE: Wow, I can't believe Sam was really a transvestite.
> JANINE: She wasn't a transvestite, honey, she was a transsexual.

CARLENE: What's the difference?

JANINE: A transvestite gets kicks from wearing women's clothes. A transsexual wants to be a woman.

CARLENE: Sam had it all backwards. Who would choose to be a girl? I'd rather be a boy any day.

JANINE: Give yourself another year, you'll change your mind.

CARLENE: Sam worked here every day for two years and it's like I never really knew her.

JANINE: Yes you did. In the only way it matters, we all knew the real Sam.

'We'll do the wake scene right in the salon,' Julia said. 'Using a closed coffin, of course. I'd like to find an extra kicker for the end, but so far, I haven't come up with one. This is black comedy, folks. We want to go all the way and do Kelly proud.'

Brandon and Paul were getting pissed at the Silver Saddle. Rehearsal was long over, but neither of them felt like going home.

Paul knocked back a double scotch and ordered another. 'Man, I had no idea about Kelly, did you?'

'Not a clue,' Brandon shook his head in disbelief. 'And we were good friends, pretty close. Just between you and me, I always found her, him, quite hot.'

'Me too. A little heavy on the paint job, but what a body. Even if it was man-made.'

'Want to know a secret?' Brandon leaned heavily on the table.

'Sure.'

'I made a pass at her once.'

'Did you . . .? Was she . . .?'

'She turned me down. Although it might have been an interesting experience, who knows? I miss her a lot.'

'Yeah,' Paul sighed. 'She loved doing the show, being on the set. For the rest of us it was just a job, but she was like a kid allowed to stay up late for the big party.'

'Too bad she's going to miss her own funeral,' Brandon said. 'I wish she was here right now.'

'Did you ever hear the story of W.C. Fields?' Paul asked. He was feeling more than a little drunk. 'How after he died, John Barrymore and a bunch of his pals stole the body from the funeral home and trotted the corpse around from bar to bar so they could toast him before he was laid to his final rest?'

Brandon looked his friend straight in the eye. 'Are you thinking what I'm thinking?'

'Well, it would be a fitting send-off,' Paul said slyly, 'and Julia said she was looking for a kicker.'

'Let's go for it, buddy.'

Together they tossed back their drinks and slammed the empty glasses down on the table.

It was the evening of the taping. The afternoon's rehearsal had gone fine, although they hadn't had time to scrounge an audience because it wasn't a regularly scheduled taping and they were only doing fifteen minutes worth of show. Julia sent Cindi, the production assistant, next door to soundstage number five where another Pac Vic sit-com, Dads in Bondage, was taping, to try and get some bodies into the bleachers. Cindi told a very rowdy Dads crowd, 'We need your help. We have to reshoot a couple of scenes from Makeover and we need a surrogate studio audience. You get to see J.C. Austin and Brandon Tate and there's a party afterwards. Food and booze on the house.' She came charging back, happy to be able to deliver the required number of bums on seats.

Although the cast had been on the verge of tears at having to say goodbye to Sam and Kelly with this episode, the studio audience got them back on track as they roared with laughter at all the jokes and whooped and hollered as a long parade of men, all dressed and wigged to look like Samantha trooped past the big, ornate wooden coffin to pay their last respects.

At an agreed-upon cue between them, Paul and Brandon suddenly began to change lines and improvise business over the coffin. Alex and Julia were down on the floor, watching the taping.

'What's going on with those two?' Alex asked. 'Did you give them a later rewrite without telling me?'

'Of course not,' Julia said. 'I have no idea what they're doing.'

PAUL (Troy) (He holds up his camera): I just wish I

could have got one last shot of Sam before that hairdryer electrocuted her. She always looked stunning in black.

BRANDON (Travis) (He urges him closer to the coffin): It's not too late. (He throws open the lid of the casket.) Be my guest.

PAUL (Leaning in): As always her make-up is perfect. (He smiles down at her, then snaps a picture.) So long, Samantha. *Syonara*, Sam.

'Oh my God,' Alex and Julia whispered together. At that instant, they, and everyone else in the studio audience saw that there was a real dead body lying in state in the casket. Kelly Carmichael looked as glamorous in death as she had in life, her make-up a work of art, every hair in place, a quirky, sly smile curving her lips as if to say, 'Hey, fellas, ain't this a gas? I couldn't have planned a better exit myself.'

Paul kissed his fingertips and brought them down to Kelly's lips. And the body of Kelly Carmichael was committed to film for all of posterity.

At the wrap party, in a corner of the room, apart from the rest of the crowd, Brandon and Paul were huddled together, talking.

'We pulled it off, good buddy,' Brandon chortled.

'Fucking A. And the best part is, Kelly would have enjoyed the hell out of a stunt like this.'

'Did you get the feeling she was smiling at us?'

'Yep. Giving us a wink, too,' Paul laughed, then said, 'Do you think they'll have the guts to air it?'

'Who knows? They have this afternoon's rehearsal on film as a back-up anyway.'

'Right. I forgot. They could edit in that ending if they're too chicken-shit to go with what we did tonight.'

'Personally, I put my faith in Julia,' Brandon said. 'If anyone's got the balls to push it through, that lady does.'

'I'm still angry, though,' Paul said.

'About what?'

'The *Hollywood Insider*. That slimy rag is responsible for what happened to Kelly. This thing has gone far enough. I want to put a stop to it once and for all.'

'How?'

'I want to go to Mentira, find out who the source is, and shut them the fuck up.'

'We can't get all the way to Florida and back in forty-eight hours. We have to be on the set, ready to go, bright and early Monday morning. We're starting a new episode.'

'We could easily get there and back,' Paul said eagerly, 'if we charter a plane.'

Brandon turned ashen. 'You know I don't fly. I haven't been on a plane since the crash six years ago.'

Paul gripped him by the shoulders. 'Brandon, we have to do this and we've only got this weekend to do it. If we're not back Monday for the table reading, we'll both be in deep shit. I can't take care of it all by myself. I'm telling you, we have to charter a plane right now.'

Brandon took a deep breath. 'OK,' he said, 'OK.'

Chapter Fifty-five

Brandon chartered a Lear jet with a private pilot to fly him and Paul to Mentira, Florida, headquarters of the *Hollywood Insider*. Even first-class on a commercial airline would subject them both to being hassled, and requesting the use of the Pac Vic jet was out of the question. They were on reconnaissance and they did not want to alert anybody, including the studio, to the nature of their mission.

As the plane took off from Burbank, Brandon's gut turned over. He felt like the top of his head was about to explode. His hands gripped the armrest on either side of the seat.

'You OK?' Paul asked.

'It's OK. Really, I'll be fine as soon as the Jack Daniels clicks in.'

'How do you think I feel? I'm flying on Shabbat. The last place I'm supposed to be is up in the air. But this is something we have to do, and do it fast!'

'You're right,' Brandon agreed. 'If we have to storm the place, butt heads, and shove their entire news team up against the wall, we're going to find Susan Carroll and Lance J. Sutton and demand an answer.'

'I figure whoever's leaking this stuff has to be doing it for the bucks, no?' Paul asked.

'Not necessarily. It could be for any one of a whole lot of reasons,' Brandon said. 'I mean, the stories have all been such privileged information, too personal to come from some lowly production assistant or lighting grip. The mole's got to be someone who's much more on the inside of Makeover.'

'Who do you suspect?'

'Shit, man, I don't know. Every week, it's somebody different. At first, I was positive it was Linda Earl. I mean there was one fucked-up babe. Insecure, jealous, always on

547

the attack because she couldn't really defend herself. Once she was off the show, I thought OK, that's it, the stories are going to stop, but the shit just kept on coming. At one point, I thought it might be you.'

'Yeah, well, I hate to admit it,' Paul said sheepishly, 'but I definitely thought it was you. I was so smug about being left unscathed and you said it was because I was too boring to make good copy and then, boom, they latch on to the religion angle. Coincidence? I didn't think so.'

'What would I have to gain? You have to look for a motive, buddy. After Linda, I had Kelly pegged.'

'Why? Kelly was such a private person. She wasn't the type to inform on anybody. She kept to herself because she had plenty to hide.'

'That might be the point,' Brandon said eagerly. 'The mole who's their source may not be a willing spy.'

'What are you talking?'

'The *Insider* could have something to hold over one of us. They could be blackmailing that person into becoming an informant, so their own secrets don't see the light of day.'

'That would have fit Kelly's situation all right.'

'I miss her a lot,' Brandon said thoughtfully.

'Me too. Some of the life's gone out of the show, no joke intended.'

'That's OK,' Brandon smiled. 'Kelly would have loved that kind of a joke.'

Paul nodded. 'So whoever got the goods on her has to be more of an "insider" than either you or me. Boy, I'd like to make the son of a bitch pay for Kelly's death. We've got to get to the bottom of this.'

'I have a feeling we're not going to like what we find,' Brandon said grimly, as the plane flew over Lake Okeechobee, then south from West Palm, heading for Mentira, a tiny place half-way between Boynton Beach and Delray Beach. To avoid the recognizition factor, they would land at a small industrial airport where they'd arranged to have a rental car waiting.

'The building doesn't look all that imposing,' Brandon said, as the rented Geo Prism pulled up to the headquarters of HI Publications, home of the *Hollywood Insider*, circulation five million plus. 'Are you sure this is the right place?'

'You were expecting maybe the *New York Times* or *El*

Herald?' Paul snapped. 'I've got relatives all over south Florida and I've worked every club in Palm Beach County. Believe me, I know the area, and this is the place.' He took a couple of deep breaths to calm himself. Since starting their own two-man undercover investigation of the *Insider*, they hadn't been able to discover much, but what they had learned made him uneasy. Very little was written about the tabloids.

'I don't know, I just thought it would be bigger,' Brandon said. 'The *Insider* isn't the only thing they publish.'

'Small building, big money-maker.' He wiped the sweat that was pouring off his forehead. Florida had it all over California for heat. 'These guys don't want to make a splash. Their aim is to keep a low profile. Look how long it took us to track down their headquarters. You're right, though, it does kind of look like your average small-town community centre.'

The *Hollywood Insider* was housed in a gray building, low to the ground, surrounded by dense south Florida foliage: sea-grape trees, casaurinas, and the ubiquitous palm. Across the street was a water treatment plant. There was no identifying plaque at the entrance. Those connected with the *Insider* knew where to look, that was all that mattered.

'OK, all systems go,' Brandon leaned over and opened the door to let Paul out. 'You know what to do?'

'I think so,' Paul said. 'Why do I feel like I'm in a rerun of Miami Vice?'

'You'll be fine. You're much smoother at this kind of thing than I am. Think of it as a high-risk improv. As soon as you've made contact, meet me back at the motel. If everything's on track, I can take it from there.' He gave Paul a thumbs up and drove off quickly into the blazing Florida sunshine.

Paul opened the door and walked into an air-conditioned chill. It was not at all what he expected. There were no dirty old men in raincoats with smoke-stained teeth and beer bellies. In fact, there were quite a few female reporters along with the men, clean-cut, well-dressed, looking more like the staff of a college newspaper than purveyors of sleaze. There was a bustling air of pressure and deadlines common to any newsroom, or at least what he knew of them from his favorite TV show in high school, Lou Grant. The walls of the office were banked with state-of-the-art computers, telephones and fax machines. Trash goes high-tech. In the middle of the room, a group of staff reporters huddled around a large table, on top of which were stacks of folders. Paul, slipping into his New York City 'I'm in a hurry, of course I have a right to be here and if you question me you're going to be in big trouble' mode, strode past the receptionist up to the big table. As he got closer, he could see that the file folders were labeled with the name of a tab celebrity fave or a popular TV show and were full of background info, quotes, and articles from conventional newspapers. 'Ted Danson', 'Whitney Houston', 'Murphy Brown', 'Designing Women' (that one took several folders, all stuffed to the limit). Next to the folders were lead sheets on which the headline for this week's stories had already been written along with pertinent quotes.

He spotted the pile for Makeover – it took up the biggest corner of the table – and moved in next to the young woman who was poring over the file. There was a photo, blurred and grainy, it might be a hill-top shot, looking down on Brandon and J.C. sunbathing together. The picture was fuzzy, he couldn't make out where they were, but it was definitely the two of them, in very close proximity. He was just able to make out the headline, 'J.C. AND BRANDON CAUGHT IN SECRET HIDEAWAY . . .' when she closed the file with a bang and whirled around to face him. She recognized him at once and her hand flew to her mouth.

Paul gave her a wink and smiled his off-kilter Troy smile. 'Hey there,' he said, 'are you Susie Carroll?'

'Um,' she looked around nervously, 'well, no.' She was blonde and cute, with a Chynna Phillips haircut and round blue eyes. Probably a snap for her to worm her way into the confidence of a celeb's unsuspecting friends and relatives and get them to spill their guts.

'I'm Paul Green.'

'I know.' She didn't volunteer her name.

Firmly, he took her by the arm and maneuvered her away from the other reporters. 'You want to stay anonymous, that's fine. I'm not here to make trouble for you, but I have some questions and I'm not leaving until I get the answers.' He kept his voice soft and his grip hard. He had never played a part like this and it wasn't easy. 'You follow me?'

She nodded, wide-eyed. 'Are you responsible for the Make-over file?'

'Oh, there's no one person in charge of that,' she assured him. 'We all write about everything.'

'But most of the articles have the same couple of bylines.'

'Um, well, yeah,' he could almost see her mind rapidly running through a series of false responses before she decided to admit to what was probably the truth. 'But those are just pen names. We just pick a name depending on the type of story it is.'

'So you're not Susan Carroll?'

'Oh no.'

'Or Lance J. Sutton.'

'No.'

'Uh-huh,' Paul nodded noncommittally. 'So, who's your editor then?'

'We've got lots of those, too,' she gulped.

Paul leaned over her shoulder and tapped the stack of folders she was still clutching in her hand. 'Enough with the chat. Take me to whoever's in charge of this *tsouris* and do it now.'

Without a word, she led him to a glassed-in office at the far end of the newsroom. 'His name is Len Pollack,' she said, 'and that's his real name.' She disappeared.

Paul knocked briskly on the door and went straight on in. In his polo shirt, blazer, casual pants, and Nike hightops, Len Pollack would have been right at home in LA. The Rolodex on his desk rivaled the fabled one in Stanfield King's office. Paul stared at it. There must be three or four thousand names in there, contacts, sources, he guessed.

The fax was spitting out reams of paper. The phones were constantly ringing. On Len's desk, there were three more phones. Two of them were ringing. Len was on the third. Hunched over a computer, inputting like mad, he was talking a mile a minute while his fingers flew over the keys. It looked like the receiver was permanently welded to his ear. But no. As soon as he saw Paul, he slammed down the phone.

'Paul Green,' Len stood up to shake his hand.

'I'm your man.' Good. At least he wasn't going to pretend not to recognize him.

'What can I do for you?'

'I shouldn't really be here, but—' Paul shifted uneasily,

from one foot to another. Now that he was face to face with one of the senior editors of the *Insider*, it was important for him to look like a nervous actor. Which wasn't that hard. So far, everything was going according to plan, but it was all moving so fast. Like one of those tightly edited episodes of Law and Order. 'I just had to see you. Mind if I close the door?'

'Sure, go ahead.' Len continued to eye him warily.

Paul closed the door, shutting out the cacophony of sound. 'The article your paper wrote about me and my wife, it caused me a lot of trouble . . .' He stopped for a moment as if it were almost too painful for him to go on, and then continued, 'My wife ended up leaving me.'

'Yeah, I heard that,' Len said flatly.

The schmuck wasn't even going to apologize. For a moment Paul forgot his role. He was so angry he wanted to punch the guy out. He put his hand to his forehead as if searching for the right words. 'I got a good career going here, Len. Mind if I call you Len? I have to make sure that something like that doesn't happen to me again.'

'That's hard to guarantee,' Len said.

'Look,' Paul let his eyes meet Len's, 'you've got lots bigger fish to fry. If you can guarantee to take the heat off me personally, I could make it worth your while.'

'Oh?' Wariness gave way to interest.

'There's a lot I could tell you about Makeover.'

'Really.' Len sat on the edge of his desk.

'I . . . I don't feel comfortable talking about it with so many people around.' He glanced out through the glass to the hectic newsroom. 'If you could, I don't know, meet me for a drink? Tonight? I'm staying at the Motel 6 right off the I95.'

Len picked up a pink piece of paper intended for phone messages and held it out to Paul, who wrote down the address of the motel on the back. 'Eight o'clock?'

'Eight o'clock.'

At eight-thirty Len Pollack had not shown up. In the cheap, fake-wood-panelled room, decorated with prints of a team of Husky dogs pulling a sled across the snow – a bizarre design choice for a motel in south Florida – Brandon stretched out on the tufted orange bedspread, watching CNN. 'The weasel's late.'

'He'll be here, I'm sure of it,' Paul was sitting in the one chair, also covered in neon bright orange. 'You should have seen his eyes light up when I offered to be an informant.'

'What does Len Pollack look like?'

'Like his name. A fish. That stuff they use for fake crab. Expensively dressed, but at heart, a cheap imitation. Kind of lanky, reddish hair, pink skin, nasty eyes.'

'So if this were Len Pollack's life story, who would you cast?'

'Good question. Ed Begley Jr maybe? with a Michael Caine accent? Or he could be Australian. I don't know.'

They were interrupted by a light knock at the door. Brandon stayed where he was. Paul went to answer it.

'I had a hell of a time finding the place,' Len said as he stepped inside. 'Must be a dozen of these motels out this way.' For a clandestine meeting, he sounded relaxed and confident. He was carrying an expensive leather attaché case. Paul wondered if there was pay-off money inside, just like he'd read about.

At the sight of Brandon Tate, Len froze. He was sharp enough to know that he wasn't likely to be getting two celebrity spies for the price of one. He had walked into a trap. He tried to bolt for the door, but Paul instantly blocked his way, giving him a push that sent him stumbling backwards into the room.

In a flash, Brandon was off the bed, grabbing the reporter and slamming him down into the chair. 'Not so fast, pal. Time for a chat.'

'Fuck you,' Len said aggressively, but he looked scared.

'You low-life scum,' Brandon leaned into him, 'don't you have any morals at all?'

'Look, mate, things are tough all around. There's some kind of wheeling and dealing at the top that we're not party to. All I know is I'm being pressured to get as much dirt on you lot as possible. There's a lot of competition out there. Grab headlines, push sales, increase circulation. Everybody wants to read about Makeover. You've got to admit you give us plenty of ammunition. It's not like we make this stuff up. We check all our facts.'

'Oh sure,' Paul broke in. 'You may start with the truth but by the time you've finished blowing it up and twisting it into a pretzel, it's completely unrecognizable.'

'We're in the entertainment business, just like you,' Len

553

said defensively. 'You celebs seem to forget that you're human. Your shit stinks, too. All we do is let our readers smell it.' He made an attempt to rise.

Brandon put his hands around his throat and lowered him back down into the chair. 'How can you live with yourself? How does it make you feel knowing you're responsible for the death of Kelly Carmichael?'

'That was not my fault,' Len's eyes were darting around the room, looking for a way out.

'The hell it wasn't. She got pushed too far. Trying to kill off the show is one thing, murdering a human being is another.'

'I was only doing my job, mate,' Len said. Paul was actually close enough to smell the sweat of fear on him.

'Whose orders were you carrying out?'

'I don't know, really I don't. We've got over a hundred staff members and reporters. Our job is to take little bits of information and blow them up into big stories. But if you're asking where our orders are coming from, none of us can answer that, because we don't know.'

'All right then,' Brandon said, 'if you can't tell us who's above you, then who's below you? Who's your source for Makeover?'

'We never reveal our sources.'

'We're prepared to sue the ass off you,' Paul said. 'Every actor on the show has banded together in a joint litigation.'

'You want to sue, you've got to prove malicious intent,' Len said belligerently. 'Lawyers go over every word we write with a magnifying glass.'

Brandon lifted the chair, with Len in it, up into the air and slammed it down, hard. The reporter went green around the gills. 'Don't fuck with me, Len. You're risking jail time. We've got enough to have you arrested.'

'For what?' The wind was knocked out of him.

'How about tampering with mail, that's a federal offense all by itself. Theft of private hospital records. Kelly Carmichael's surgery. J.C. Austin's abortion. It's illegal to have those documents in your possession.'

'I didn't steal them,' Len was gasping for air. 'They were given to me by the source.'

Brandon grabbed him out of the chair and slammed him up against the wall. 'All right, you slimy son of a bitch, who's the fucking source?'

In the plane, flying back to LA, Paul and Brandon sat silently, not even looking at each other. They were still reeling from the shock of what Len Pollack had told them.

'We're going to have to confront J.C. with this,' Paul finally broke the silence.

'I'll talk to her,' Brandon said.

'Are you sure?'

'It's not something I'm looking forward to. But at this point, I think it has to be me.'

Paul stared out the window at the Florida coastline. 'So long Mentira. What does Mentira mean anyway? You know Spanish.'

'Falsehood.'

J.C. AUSTIN FILES FOR DIVORCE

(AP) Los Angeles

Actress/singer J.C. Austin has begun divorce proceedings against her husband of twenty-two years, producer/manager Mac Austin.

The surprise announcement comes hot on the heels of yesterday's announcement that the cast of Makeover has filed a joint suit against the tabloid newspaper, the *Hollywood Insider*.

In a short statement issued directly to the press by Ms Austin herself, she said, regarding her marriage, 'It's over. That's for sure and final. I'm not one to look back. I'm keeping my eyes fixed on the future.'

When asked what that future might hold for the country singer turned television star, Ms Austin stated that she would continue to pursue film and television opportunities along with her recording obligations and that she would be taking full control of the multi-million-dollar business that is her career.

'The popularity of Makeover and the phenomenal success of *Telephone Road* has made me realize I work best when I can be my real self. I will be rerecording and producing myself the album I have currently in the works which is called *Heart of Texas*. All personal and professional ties with Mr Austin are in the process of being severed.'

Ms Austin cited, as grounds for the divorce, the often invoked 'mental cruelty'. When pressed by reporters to expand on this, she would say only, 'The bond of trust between my husband and myself was stretched so thin it finally broke.'

Ms Austin declined to respond to questions about whether the divorce proceedings were linked to the suit against the *Insider*. Neither would she confirm or deny the rumor that she is romantically involved with co-star Brandon Tate.

'I could not have handled any of this without the love and support of all my friends. I have walked through fire and come out the other side.'

Chapter Fifty-six

'How could you do this to me?' Mac was livid. He had flown in from Nashville to confront her. 'I get to find out you're divorcing me by reading it in the newspaper? How am I supposed to defend myself?'

'Now you know how I feel,' J.C. said. 'For the past three years, I've seen my private business splashed all over the tabloids. That was bad enough. But to find out that it was all coming from you is something I can't forgive.' She still wasn't over the initial shock and anger. When Brandon had told her it was Mac, she had refused to believe him at first. Whatever problems she and Mac had, he would never do something like that, it just wasn't in him. She couldn't accept that the man she had loved so loyally and so long could have that depth of ruthless, mean-spirited, manipulative vengeance. Once she was forced to acknowledge the truth, her disbelief was replaced by a white-hot rage.

'I know everything, Mac. You're the "source close to the *Insider*".'

His face went ashen. 'How did you find out?'

'Brandon went to the *Insider* headquarters in Mentira and had a little talk with a Mr Len Pollack. How could you, Mac? You gave Len the hospital records, and then you lied to me about it, crying crocodile tears over the phone about how I was ruining your reputation in Nashville. You tracked down the nurse and paid her triple the amount to reveal the abortion that you paid her twenty years ago not to reveal. You've been lying to me all along.'

'I had to do it,' Mac said without flinching. 'I had to destroy the show in order to save your career.'

'My career's doing just fine, it's my love and respect for you that's been destroyed. You abused the trust that we had, the honesty that was supposed to be the basis of our marriage. I told you everything that was going on with the show and every single person on it. You encouraged me to confide in you and then you used it all against us. Even after you went back to Nashville, you kept pumping me for information and, like a fool, I never caught on why. I thought you just wanted to stay a part of my life even though you were no longer in it.'

'That's exactly how I felt,' Mac was desperate to defend himself, but J.C. cut him off.

'How did you find out about Kelly? You didn't get that from me because I didn't know.'

'Well, now I kind of did. You told me she was a tenor and that just confirmed my suspicions. I always felt real uncomfortable around her. There was something not right with her, made my skin crawl. And right from the beginning she was trying to steal your thunder. I figured you wanted her off the show.'

J.C.'s anger with Mac was so deep-seated and powerful, she wasn't sure she could contain it, but she had to get the truth out in the open. 'So you had her followed to see if your hunch was right?'

'Yeah. We didn't have much to go on, trying to trace a paper trail of phone numbers and addresses. For a long time it didn't lead anywhere, but then we got lucky.'

'You hired a detective?'

'No. The *Insider* did that. I just gave them the tip. And a copy of her résumé.'

'How did you get it?'

'Easy,' Mac sounded almost excited. 'At one of the wrap parties, after a taping, I got into her dressing-room and went through her files. I didn't know then what I was looking for. I just knew there was something weird about Kelly. I held on to her résumé and then handed it over to the detective. She had listed a whole bunch of shows with this theater in England. We tracked down the theater, took a look at their programs and there it was. C. Michael Kelly. We traced C. Michael Kelly back to Chicago. In Chicago C. Michael Kelly was a male actor, but in England, C. Michael Kelly was playing women's parts. Then there was a big gap on the résumé, two years with no credits at all. Then Kelly Carmichael turns up in LA.'

'I don't get it. What does that prove?'

'Before she could be approved for the surgery, she had to dress and live as a woman for a year. That's when she was acting with the theater, playing female roles, but still technically a man. She had the surgery in England, dropped out of sight, legally changed her name, and resurfaced in LA as Kelly Carmichael. She covered her tracks pretty good, but once you tipped me off, I just put two and two together.'

J.C. listened with a mixture of fear and pity. He was so eager to lay it all out for her as if this explanation could somehow make her understand his actions. 'Why, Mac? Why would you do this?'

'For us,' he said. 'The minute you joined that show, you started slipping away from me. I was so afraid I'd lose you.'

'You weren't scared of losing me as a wife, you were scared of losing me as a meal ticket.'

'That's not true,' Mac was crying now. 'You don't understand, I love you. You've got to believe me. Please, you've got to forgive me.'

The strange thing was, on one level, she did believe him; but he was talking about something that was crazy and twisted and possessive, not love. 'I can't forgive you for Kelly's death. We're going to court, Mac. We've filed an injunction against the *Hollywood Insider* to stop them from printing any stories on Makeover for the next twelve months until this whole mess is settled. According to Brandon, the First Amendment protects the paper as long as the articles were without malice, but that won't do a thing for you because malice was guiding you every inch of the way.'

'Well, I guess I was right about one thing,' the side of Mac's mouth curled up in distaste.

'What's that?'

'Brandon Tate. He was poaching on my territory all along.'

'No,' J.C. said firmly. 'You dumb son of a bitch, you still don't get it, do you? You lost me all on your own. You held me down, you held me back, and you wouldn't listen to anybody else, including me. Blind, deaf and dumb, you just keep plowing ahead.'

'You knew what I was like when you married me,' he said defensively. 'I can't change.'

'That's what living means, Mac. Change.' She looked him straight in the eye, pleading with him, willing him to understand. 'I could have stood any of that, so long as you were on my side, but all this time you were working against me. You didn't get tricked into it, you weren't even doing it for the money. You deliberately set out to hurt me and my friends and you wound up killing one of them.'

'You can't lay the blame for that all on me. She was fucked up, anyone could see that. You and I, we both made mistakes, but I don't think it's fair to throw away twenty-two years of good together, for one that was bad.'

J.C. looked at him sadly. 'You've known me since I was sixteen, Mac. I'm basically a trusting person. I have to be hit over the head with proof before I'll stop believing someone is good. This time I think I finally got the message. I'm loyal to the last, but once I move on, I don't look back.' Her anger was gone now. She felt completely dead inside. All she wanted was for him to leave, get out of her sight, but he just stood there staring at her.

'I deserve a second chance,' he said stubbornly.

'Do you have a clear idea at all about what you've done? You hurt a human being so bad, she couldn't stand to go on living. She doesn't exist on this earth any more. Doesn't that mean anything to you?'

For a moment, she thought something flickered behind his eyes. Then he shrugged. 'What's one faggot more or less?'

At last everyone on Makeover could breathe a little easier. The tabloid attacks had ceased. The enemy had been confronted and defeated.

Brandon and Paul were back at the fish market on the Santa Monica Pier, sitting on the deck, watching the orange sun slip smoothly into the sea.

'You want some of this crab?' Brandon asked.

'No thanks,' Paul took a slug of his Corona. 'I hate to disappoint you, but I don't think I'm ever going to like it. You go ahead. Enjoy.'

'You're missing something great.'

'I know,' Paul said. '*Naches.*'

'What?'

'*Naches.*'

'Sounds dirty.'

Paul laughed. 'No. It means the joys of family life. Comfort. Emotional security.' He let out a small sigh. 'I want Chaya back. LA is just too hard without her.'

'Then go and get her,' Brandon ripped the back of the crab, allowing a mound of golden-green glop to slide out.

Paul winced. 'She hasn't forgiven me for missing Shoshana and Shulamit's birth.'

'I give you full permission to blame me for that.'

They both remembered that afternoon in the Silver Saddle which was the beginning of their friendship.

'I don't blame you, I blame myself. I've missed half a year of the twins' lives. I'll never get that back.'

'So call Chaya and tell her you want to get back together,' Brandon prompted him again.

Paul sighed again. 'To get her back, I'll probably have to give up the show. What really drove us apart were all those Friday night tapings. I wanted her to be there. Not only did she not want to be there, she didn't want me there. And she was right. I miss being together with my family on Shabbat.'

'Then talk to Julia,' Brandon suggested. 'Not every show out here works Monday to Friday. Roseanne only goes Monday to Thursday, some others switch the schedule around completely. Tell Julia you have to be finished by sundown on Friday. You're a hot property, man. Given the attrition rate on this show, Julia won't want to risk losing you.'

'You think so?'

'Well, it's worth a try.'

'You know, I really used to envy your freedom, Brandon.'

'What for? "Freedom's just another word for nothing left to lose." '

'Uh oh. We're into quoting Kris Kristofferson. That's a bad sign.'

'I think I feel the need of a little *naches* myself,' Brandon said.

'What about you and J.C.?' Paul felt OK mentioning the big affair because it was out in the open now.

'I love her, there's no doubt about that.' He reddened slightly. 'I've asked her to marry me.'

'Hey, way to go.'

'So far she's said no.'

'Why? You losing your touch in the sack, buddy?'

'I haven't heard any complaints. No, J.C. just came out of a dysfunctional partnership and . . .'

561

'Dysfunctional partnership, what is that? Some kind of men's movement psycho-babble?'

'Well, mainly she feels it would be unfair to get married because she can't give me a child. That's the way she keeps putting it, "give me a child", like it was some sort of Christmas present. I've told her I don't care, but . . .'

'What are you talking? The woman's never heard of adoption? If you love her, go for it. It's not like you to roll over and play fuckin' dead.'

'You're right,' Brandon grinned. 'We kicked butt pretty good in Mentira, didn't we?'

'Damn straight we did.' Paul raised his beer bottle. 'To the buddy system.'

'To the buddy system.'

'I've come to take you home, Debra Jo.'

Her heart did a flip-flop. There he was, her husband, Eddie, large as life, standing in her kitchen. She was awfully glad to see him but damned if she was going to give him the pleasure of knowing it. 'Oh, I see. You think you can come waltzing in here, unannounced, and just scoop me up in your arms and carry me back to Houston. After you've been fucking my best friend Jackie? Forget it.' Debra Jo never used the F word. She wouldn't even allow it to be used in her presence.

'I wasn't fucking Jackie,' Eddie said hotly, 'and I don't think it says very much for our marriage if you won't even give me the chance to tell you that.'

'Pictures don't lie.' Debra Jo pointed to the page she'd ripped out of the *Hollywood Insider* and pinned up on the bulletin board in the kitchen to remind her why she wasn't going to take any of Eddie's frantic phone calls or respond to Jackie's urgent messages. Jackie had even written her a letter. Without reading it, Debra Jo had torn it into little pieces, stuffed all the little pieces back in the same envelope, and marked, 'Return to sender', on the front.

'This one does,' Eddie ripped it off the bulletin board, tore it into strips, marched over to the sink, and stuffed it down the garburator. That would be hell to clean out in the morning. 'Now, you are going to sit down and listen to what I have to say,' he ordered. 'You owe me that much.'

'I don't owe you jack shit,' Debra Jo said but she sat down.

Eddie swore he hadn't slept with Jackie. He said the photo of the two of them was one of the ones taken when he and Debra Jo went on their two couples vacation with Jackie and her third husband to Nashville. It was him and Jackie by the pool at the Shoney's motel where they'd stayed on the outskirts of town. It was true Jackie was divorcing this husband, too, but he, Eddie, had nothing to do with it. 'I don't know how you think either one of us would do that to you. Not that I haven't had my chances, mind, while you were out here getting to be a big star in Hollywood, but you're the one with lots more opportunity. How do I know you haven't been playin' around on me?'

Debra Jo didn't have an answer for that one so she just sat tight.

'I mean it, Debra Jo. I want you to come home with me right now.'

'You can't order me what to do. I make lots more money than you do now.'

'All right, I'm beggin' you then.' Eddie got down on his hands and knees and put his hands together as if he was about to do 'here is the church, here is the steeple.' 'Please, Debra Jo, please, please, pretty please?'

The corners of Debra Jo's mouth started to twitch. He looked pretty funny. She stood up and went over to the fridge to get herself a cold Pepsi. He scooted after her, on his knees, and wrapped his arms around her hips. 'I miss you, I love you, please give this up and come back to Houston.'

Debra Jo took a long time to finish her Pepsi. Then she looked down at Eddie and said, 'I'm intending to quit the show anyway.'

'You are?'

'Yeah. I'm not happy out here any more. It's too dirty, too dangerous, and this acting thing is too hard. I proved I can do it, but now all I want is to go home.'

'Oh, baby,' Eddie started to kiss his way up her.

'But not until the end of the shooting season,' Debra Jo held him away from her. 'I can't leave the company in the lurch. It's been a real tough year for all of us. I'll finish out the season and then I'll come back to Houston, OK?'

'OK, fair enough. But in the meantime, I'll stay out here with you until you're done.'

'You mean it?'

'Absolutely. You're a star now. You deserve your own houseboy to cook and clean and service all your needs.' His hands were already tugging at her, pulling her down to the floor with him.

'Ed Fawcett, we can't do it on the kitchen floor,' Debra Jo squealed.

'You bet your sweet little ass we can. By the time we've finished making love, there won't be any doubt left in your mind that I've been savin' it all for you.'

Chapter Fifty-seven

The letter came by courier. It was on CBN letterhead and it was brief and to the point. 'It is with the utmost regret that we inform you of the Currie Broadcasting Network's decision to terminate its agreement with Hudlow/Turgov Productions. Said termination to take place two weeks from the date of receipt of this letter. As of 1 November, the services of Julia Hudlow as writer-producer of Makeover and of Hudlow/Turgov as producers of same will no longer be required. Neither will said producing entity be allowed to retain consultancy privileges. Effective 1 November. Signed, Stanfield King on behalf of Charles Currie for CBN. cc Frank Weiser, VP Pac Vic.'

Julia stared at the letter in disbelief. She had expected Stan to be upset that she had changed the ending of the episode and that the episode had been aired without his approval, but she never would have predicted this. After all, they had been up against it with the strike, short of time, a decision had to be made and she had made it. Along with the entire company. And what about Tim? He had allowed the episode to go to air. Was his head going to roll?

The phone rang. It was Marty. 'Have you received a letter from Stan?'

'Yes,' Julia said. 'I'm standing here, holding it in my hand. It's so brief. No explanation, no nothing. What do we do now?'

'I don't know. I'm completely in shock.'

'Does this mean they're cancelling Makeover?'

'Are you kidding? They're not going to dump the only show they've got that's consistently in the top ten.'

'Well, can they do it without us?'

'Of course. Legally we don't own the show. They've got the cast, they've got the sets, they've got your writing staff. They'll have to hire a new producer but, other than that, what's to stop them from going ahead with business as usual?'

'Where's Pac Vic in all of this? Who's Frank Weiser?'

'Kathryn's replacement, obviously. CBN's got the studio by the balls. The network is their best customer. Pac Vic will do anything they say, including doing the show without us.'

'But they can't. Makeover has got my stamp all over it.' The fact that she no longer had a job had yet to sink in. All she could think about was the future of the show.

'They'll attempt to duplicate it, of course,' Marty said.

'What about Tim? Where's Tim?'

'I don't know,' Marty said. 'I just called him but he refused to take my call. It's what I've always hated about this business. You can't trust anybody.'

'They can't do this to us. Cut us off just like that after two-and-a-half years of partnership. We're owed an explanation at least. I'm going over to CBN to talk to Stan.'

'Julia, I wouldn't do that,' Marty warned. 'The Emmys are barely two weeks away. This could be some kind of power play or even a bluff. We need to talk to our lawyers, get hold of Kathryn, arm ourselves with the facts before . . .' The phone went dead. He knew Julia was already out the door.

'You can't be serious about this,' Julia faced off with Stan who was safely behind his desk.

'Absolutely,' Stan said. 'You completely ignored firmly entrenched network rules not running the episode past Standards and Practices, and airing it without my approval. It doesn't get much more serious than that.'

'S and P had already approved the script for the episode. The first half of the show was exactly the same. We didn't have time to resubmit the changes. Because of the strike, the only other episode we had in the can was the Christmas special. We couldn't air that.'

'You didn't submit the rewrite because you knew it would be turned down. Ultimately, the decision was yours.'

'There was a death in the cast, not just any death, but one that occurred under extraordinary conditions. The entire US knew what happened to Kelly, there was no way we could ignore it. I had to deal with it in an extraordinary way.'

'No, you chose to deal with it in a way that was in highly questionable taste, sensational and shocking,' he said firmly. 'I'm convinced now that you knew about Kelly all along.'

'I didn't, I swear I didn't. And I'm not responsible for her body being in the casket, surely you don't believe that.'

'I don't know what to believe.'

'But Tim viewed the tape of the finished show. He made the decision to let the episode go to air.'

'I am aware of that, but Charles and I feel that you're expendable and Tim is not. At this time.'

'You and I both know this isn't the real reason you're firing me,' Julia went on the offensive.

'Being a writer-producer isn't just turning out scripts, Julia. It's managing the star acting talent as well. Linda Earl off the show, Kelly's suicide, Debra Jo quitting at the end of the season. You can't seem to hold on to your actors and the ones that are left are out of control. I don't like it when actors take matters into their own hands. Statements to the press, lawsuits against the *Hollywood Insider*, assault and battery on a reporter. I warned you if you tried to do battle with the tabloids you'd get into trouble, and you have.'

'But the source has been tracked down and stopped. Everything is back to normal. We won.'

'Not without a hell of a lot of negative publicity for all of us.'

'You told us yourself that doesn't matter as long as attention stays focused on the show. "What a Way to Go" brought in the best numbers the network has ever seen.'

'That's true. But the advertisers are threatening to pull out due to questionable content. You just went too far, Julia.' Stan's tone shifted. 'I thought you were a bright, creative new talent with a big future. On behalf of CBN, I did everything I could to support you. But you just weren't willing to softpedal your convictions. If you don't want to cooperate, if you're not willing to compromise, write a novel, not a network TV show.'

'Stan, please, think about this. I created Makeover. The show is me,' Julia said desperately. She never thought she'd be begging to be allowed to stay in a business she hadn't wanted to get into in the first place.

Stan allowed himself a small, mirthless smile. 'You have an inflated sense of your own worth, Julia. As far as the viewers are concerned, Makeover is J.C. Austin and Brandon Tate. It survived the loss of Linda Earl, it will even survive the loss of Kelly. You, I can assure you, will not be missed.'

When Julia came out of Stan's office, she found Marty waiting for her. He looked at her expectantly and she shook her head wordlessly. They both wanted to get out of the CBN building as fast as they could, but neither wanted to go home alone. In a nearby fast-food restaurant, over cups of weak but bitter coffee, they sat in silence.

'They got me,' Julia finally said. 'I don't know why, Marty, but somehow I thought I was inviolable.'

'Maybe it's a blessing in disguise,' he tried to comfort her. 'A sign that it's time to get on to other projects.'

'Easy for you to say. You have another project, the book. You didn't want to work in television any more anyway. I hate to admit this, but I'm still hooked.'

'Jules, you can go to another network, create a new series. You're not exactly yesterday's fish, you know. They'd probably be thrilled to get you away from CBN. Undoubtedly you'd get a better upfront deal now than we did three years ago when you were an unknown quantity. If you think you really want to go through all this again. In the meantime, you're not going to starve. We've still got the pay-or-play clause in the contract. That's worth three million to us right now. Even if CBN intends to sever all connection with us, drop everything we're in development for with them, they have to pay us. Within two weeks, as I recall.'

'I can't stand the thought of Makeover belonging to other people now.'

'For the sake of the cast, I hope it survives without us, but if it doesn't survive, well, it's not the end of the world, just the demise of yet another TV show.' He stirred his coffee for a moment and then said, 'Hey, did you hear the one about the two brain surgeons? Their patient dies on the operating table and one of the doctors bursts into tears. The other doctor says, "Take it easy. We're not producing a sit-com!"'

Only Marty could make her laugh at a time like this. She was surprised he could be so sanguine about everything that had happened. Maybe he really had changed. Funny, it was almost as though they'd switched places. Marty was the one who was able to put things in perspective while she was freaking out. She sighed and picked up her purse. 'Well, I better get home.'

'Yeah,' he pushed his coffee away, 'get some rest.' Their eyes met. She read such love still there, such concern for her. 'I miss you, Jules. The door's always open for you to come back any time, no questions asked.' He grinned wryly. 'Of course, right now, you're the one with the house, so I guess it has to be your door. Anyway, for what it's worth, I miss you.'

Her eyes filled with tears. 'I know. I miss you, too. There's something I may need to talk to you about . . .' She stopped herself and stood up briskly.

'What?' She could feel the hope radiating from him.

'Nothing. It can wait.' She was all business again. 'We better keep in touch. If I don't see you before then, I'll catch you at the Emmys.'

'See you there.'

She had come close to telling him there was a very good chance she might be pregnant. She'd been so caught up in recent events she'd missed one, maybe two periods. Two home pregnancy tests had turned out positive, the little blue ring glowing as plain as day. But those kits were never reliable, so now she was on her way to the doctor's for a battery of tests. If she did turn out to be pregnant, whose baby was it? Half of her was sure it had to be Liam's, the other half was convinced it was Marty's, from their time together on Mustang Island. Neither half of her wanted to have a baby at all. She'd shoved the dilemma to the back of her mind while she dealt with what she thought of as more pressing problems. That was a laugh. Everything was now rolled up into one giant problem. She might be facing the future as a single, unemployed mother.

Julia kept waiting for the miracle to happen, for CBN to reverse their decision, for Stan to call and say she could come back to work. It didn't happen. When she managed to get a meeting with Tim, he was sympathetic but didn't hold out any hope.

'I don't know what's going down, Julia,' he said. 'I went out on a limb for you the last time and nearly got fired. I'm afraid to do that again.'

The cast of Makeover were up in arms.

'What are we going to do?' J.C. cried.

'The show won't be the same without you,' Brandon said.

'Well, hopefully you won't notice that much of a difference,' Julia tried to reassure them. 'They're bringing in another producer, but luckily the writing staff is staying on intact. They know my sensibility, they understand my style. You know your characters inside out by now, so everything should stay on track.'

'But you'll be retained as a consultant, right?' Paul asked.

'I have no official on-going relationship with the show. But we're all friends here. If you or the writers have any questions or problems, of course you can call me at any time. If Marty and I have done our jobs right, the show should go on indefinitely. It has a life of its own now. You'll all be just fine, believe me.' The company looked as betrayed and panicked as Julia herself felt. It was like trying to explain to your children that Mummy and Daddy still loved each other but they couldn't live together any more so they were going to get a divorce but nothing was really going to change. Kids rarely bought that explanation and neither did the cast.

'What about the episode I've written, is it still going ahead?' Theresa blurted out, then caught herself with, 'Sorry, I know that's not what's most important here.'

'That's OK,' Julia gave her a hug. It was a natural reaction. In a business where practicing your craft was reliant on decision by committee, the minute a shake-up was announced, any artist's first thought was 'What about me?'

'I've still got two years to go on my contract,' J.C. said. She looked stricken. Julia couldn't blame her. The bond the two of them shared was at the center of what made Makeover such a success. 'You can't leave the series.'

It was not until Julia said, 'This is not my choice,' that the full implication she had been fired set in.

'I don't want to stay without you. Nobody can replace you,' J.C. declared.

Several of the other actors threatened to quit, but Julia convinced them that it would be in nobody's best interest. The cast determined to band together and lobby for Julia to be reinstated as writer-producer but, given Stan's feelings about 'actors taking things into their own hands', she didn't hold out much hope.

Kathryn didn't either. She herself had been pressured out of Pac Vic and was heading back to New York. Tomorrow Jonathan was flying in to help her clear out the house.

'It happens to women in this town,' she said bitterly. 'It's been happening for years. I don't know who or what's going to stop it. And the worst thing is, we can't even cry about it because we're not allowed to show our emotions.'

'I feel so powerless,' Julia agreed. 'It's ignominious to be fired by someone I've never even met.'

'Now you know it's not Charles Currie's decision,' Kathryn said. 'This had to have come from Stan. But these guys stick together. What do you expect?'

'Well, that's what's so confusing about this whole thing. Usually with those guys the bottom line is money. Makeover isn't losing money, it's making a fortune.'

'I thought Stan told you some of the advertisers were pulling out. That could mean a huge drop in revenue for CBN.'

'He did say that, but then Marty phoned Sackville-Peters, the firm CBN uses to handle all the advertisers, and they told him the advertisers are thrilled with the ratings and have no thought of withdrawing sponsorship.'

'So either Stan was afraid they were pulling out. Or he lied to you in order to have another reason to terminate the contract.'

'Exactly,' Julia said. 'I can't shake the feeling that there's something more to Stan's agenda, something personal.'

'Wouldn't be the first time. How are you holding up?' Kathryn asked, her voice full of concern. 'You don't look so good.'

'Then I guess that means I must really look like hell,' Julia joked. 'In Hollywood the first thing people say to each other is "you look wonderful", no matter how far from the truth it may be.'

'Your face is kind of pale and puffy, that's all. Could be stress. Could be PMS.'

'Could be I'm pregant.' It had slipped out before she knew it. At Kathryn's surprised expression, Julia tried to backpedal. 'I mean, it's possible. Late in the game, totally unexpected, inconvenient, but anything's possible.'

'That's wonderful. I'd trade places with you in a minute. Jonathan and I have been trying for two years and, so far, nothing. Of course you and Marty have been married for what, fifteen?'

'Actually, Marty and I are separated,' Julia admitted. 'I mean, legally, we're still married, but I'm with someone else now.'

'Oh, I see.' Kathryn said delicately. 'Bad timing?'

'I don't know. I haven't figured it out myself.'

The doctor said she was almost three months pregnant. That placed the time of conception mid-July. On Mustang Island. With Marty. She didn't know what she was going to do, but she owed it to Liam to at least make him aware of the situation. When Julia told Liam she was pregnant, he was so excited he didn't wait for her to finish before his eyes filled with tears. He swept her up in his arms and whirled her around, a gesture of spontaneity uncharacteristic of him. For one brief moment, as he held her close, she had a wild thought that she could just go on letting Liam think it was his child. Divorce Marty, marry Liam, raise the baby together. No one need ever know. A crazy impulse. That might work on a soap opera but not in real life. Besides it would be totally unfair to Marty who so desperately wanted to be a father. She could have the baby and give it to Marty to bring up. Equally crazy. She was missing entirely from that equation. Liam would have other chances. Gently she told him the baby couldn't possibly be his.

'Are you sure?' he looked shaken, tears of joy still hanging, unshed, in his eyes.

'Very. The timing puts it firmly in Marty's camp. It was when you and I were separated last summer.'

'Does Marty know?'

'No. I wanted to talk to you first.'

'I don't care whose baby it is. I want to marry you anyway,' he said fiercely, instantly hooking into her own fantasy. It was the first time he had come out and said what she'd suspected all along. He was counting on them spending the rest of their lives together. 'Please, Julia. I know this is all coming at you at once. You've lost your job, you found out you're pregnant, I want you to marry me. You're not sure of anything, but you can be sure of me. The baby could be mine. As far as I'm concerned, it will be. Please, marry me.'

'Don't tempt me. Right now I would give anything, Liam, if the baby were yours. It would make it all so much easier. But as it is, I'm not ready to open up my secret garden to public view.'

'What are you talking about?' He looked bewildered. 'What garden?'

She explained how in the beginning she had thought of him as her place to escape to, be taken out of herself, her secret garden, how she fantasized about him, fantasized about him every night before she went to sleep. When she thought she was going mad with work and pain, how she would tune out and drop in to the secret garden. 'A place where there's no arguing, just continual love-making, private, magical, beautiful, perfect.'

'Is that all you think we have together?' Liam demanded. 'I've tried to be that for you, but I hope I'm more than that.'

'You are. We have. But opening it up to public scrutiny would destroy it. Look what's happened to me the last couple of months. My private and personal business laid wide open, dragged through the mud, things that no one else has a right to know becoming common knowledge. I wouldn't want that to happen to us.'

He looked as if she had slapped him. 'Wait a minute, I don't understand. I'll be right there with you. I'm in love with you and you're worried about what people think? I'm talking about a life together, and you're saying let's not spoil what we have? What are you telling me, Julia? That I'm just some personal X-rated video to get you through a bad patch in your life?'

'No, no, of course not . . . I didn't mean . . . I'm not explaining this very well . . . I'm sorry.'

His eyes were full of shock and betrayal. 'This was part of Julia Hudlow's own personal makeover? Produce a hit, make money, screw a younger man? You're a bored wife who wanted a fling because her husband was too tired, too old to get it up, is that it? Was it just sex for you? Because it wasn't for me.'

'Marty was sick,' Julia began, 'and I needed—'

'No! How can you defend him?' he shouted at her. 'He doesn't love you, he doesn't even know who you are except in relation to him. He dropped out of your life just at the time you needed him the most. How can you excuse that? Your fucking husband wasn't there for you. I was, I am, and I want to stay there.'

'I wish it were that simple . . .'

'To me, it is. If you love me. Jesus, Julia, I was in love with you long before we ever made love. From the moment we started working together. Because of Marty, I rationalized that it would have to be a different kind of relationship. I wanted to be near you and I was willing to take what I could get – friendship, a special understanding, artistic partnership, anything – because I didn't think more was possible. You're the one who changed everything. You reached out and chose me and made me believe it was possible.'

'Liam, that's not fair—'

'You chose me, don't you understand what that did for me?' His voice was choked with anger. Tears were rolling down his face, but his eyes were blazing with fury. 'I come from an emotionless family, Julia. We don't invite danger into our lives, we won't even allow it. But you wouldn't let me be. You opened me up, you made me feel so much it frightened me, but I trusted you, I let go, I went with it, and now you're saying it was just a sexual illusion, thanks for the heat? Fuck you. I hate you for doing this to me. I won't feel this way again.'

'You will, Liam, I know you will. After all, I did,' Julia felt helpless in the face of his rage and grief. 'I loved Marty and then I fell in love with you.'

'No, you didn't. You fucked me. I serviced your fantasy. Hasn't any of this been real to you? It was to me. I'm real. Don't you care at all about what you're doing to me?'

'Of course I do.' She reached out to touch him, but he pulled away.

'No. Don't put your hands on me if it doesn't mean anything to you. A farewell fuck? I won't do that for you any more.'

'Don't, please,' she said gently. She didn't know what to do. She wanted to put her arms around him and comfort him, ease his pain, but she couldn't because she was the one who had caused it. It wasn't true that you could only love one person, that only one man could make you happy. There could be more than one, each offering a different choice that involved an entirely different life. She couldn't say, 'I don't love you,

Liam' or, 'It would never work', the way it was said on television or in the movies, because she did love him and it could work. It would just work differently, that's all, and ultimately that was the choice. 'I know you think I'm not hurting, but I am. I don't know what to do.'

'Why won't you even consider the possibility of marrying me?'

'It wouldn't be right for you,' she said finally, knowing it wasn't a very convincing response. 'I think, eventually, you would find it hard. You've got so much to give, Liam. You don't want to have it compromised before you even start.'

'Let me make that judgment for myself.' He was in such a fury she was almost afraid he was going to lash out and strike her, too caught up in his own pain to understand hers. 'I think you're secretly grateful you're pregnant with Marty's baby. It resolves everything for you.'

'No, not everything,' she was starting to cry, 'but maybe you're right. I guess, ultimately, a decision has been made.' She reached out for him, but again he pulled away. 'Liam, please . . . I'm so sorry. I won't stop loving you, but I must stop seeing you.'

He picked up the little bird sculpture and threw it across the room. It shattered on the floor. For a moment the two of them just stood there staring at it. Then Liam looked up at her. 'Of course you can't see me any more,' he pinned her to the wall with his accusatory eyes. 'That way you get to keep your secret garden intact.'

The Pasadena Civic Auditorium was packed for the Annual Emmy Awards. Due to the delay, because of the strike, the excitement was higher than usual and there was not a seat to be had. This year, Paul Green was one of a triumvirate of comics hosting the Awards.

'Boy, this is a switch,' he joked. 'Just two years ago I was sitting at home watching this on television and throwing cold pizza crusts at the screen. Do you think I should really be up here?' The crowd roared an approval and Paul went on to rattle off a stream of topical jokes about TV, current events and politics.

The glittering, glamorous event was already running forty minutes late by the time Paul took over. Julia sat in the audience, wearing a defiantly red dress, a Giorgio di Saint Angelo. It was just the right shade of rusty orange to set off

575

rather than clash with her red hair. As she said to Alex and Shirley, who were sitting on either side of her, 'If I have to go down, I might as well go down in flame.'

Predicting Emmy winners was always a risky business, but by now the buzz in the hall was that Makeover could sweep the Awards. They had dominated the nominations, and so far the show was picking up the prized trophies for virtually every category in which it was nominated. It looked to be Makeover's night. The irony of the situation was not lost on Julia. A little over a year ago she'd sat right here, happy and triumphant. A year ago she'd boosted the network into the lead, made an actress out of a singing star, and found a new career for herself. A year ago, she'd fallen in love with Liam. A turbulent, crazy, fucked-up twelve months that had brought her right back to this very spot, sitting in her plush seat waiting to see if this time she would catch the big brass ring. She watched as the members of the Makeover 'family' made numerous trips up to the podium to pick up their awards.

Earlier in the evening, Paul had won Best Supporting Actor in a Comedy, his second year in a row. A posthumous Emmy was given to Kelly Carmichael as Best Supporting Actress and the entire audience stood to give her an emotional ovation. The show picked up awards for art direction, editing and costume design. Brandon snagged a Best Actor. The last acting award of the evening was Outstanding Comedy Actress, and Julia was thrilled when it was won by J.C. for her work with George Jones in 'Daddy, You Hardly Knew Me'. Julia herself had received another writing award for the same episode, but she wouldn't be satisfied, wouldn't feel vindicated, unless the show she had created won for Outstanding Comedy Series. Then, and only then, could she let it go.

Paul ripped open the envelope and a wide grin split his face. 'In the category of "biting the hand you feed", nobody qualifies for the Outstanding Comedy Series Award more than Hudlow/Turgov Productions for Makeover!' She'd won it! As Julia made her way to the podium, the crowd in the Civic Auditorium rose to their feet for the second time that night to give her a standing ovation. Shouts, cheers, whistles, it went on and on until finally she had to raise her hand to get them to stop. It had only been two weeks ago, but everybody in town knew she had been fired, and they were all silently praying that in her acceptance speech she would flip a finger to the network.

Julia had no idea where Marty was. It seemed so strange to be standing there all alone. 'Thank you, friends – and I do know that most of you out there are my friends,' she began falteringly. 'I'm glad the Academy has chosen to honor me in the same month that CBN saw fit to fire me.' The crowd booed and there was a long, low hiss. 'We are the artists who create what the networks market and sell. We must take back what we created in the first place, our own work. I realize the network sees me as a little woman with a big mouth, but I accept full responsibility for everything I've done in connection with Makeover. I'm picking up this award because I made this show happen.' The hall went nuts again, cheering and applauding. 'Thank you so much for giving me a terrific send-off. Although this award means everything in the world to me, I may have to hock it because, as of tonight, I am out of a job. Thank you all very much.' She turned to leave the stage but was stopped by a procession, led by Marty, of cast and crew members from Makeover: J.C., Brandon, Paul, Shirley, Theresa, Debra Jo, Alex, the technicians, make-up and wardrobe, her writing staff, everyone, even Liam, they all streamed on to the stage to hug her. Marty kissed her and she kissed him back, hoping she could let him know, with that one kiss, how sorry and glad she was about everything that had happened over the past twelve months. Hand in hand, they walked offstage together, as the band played a triumphal march version of the theme from Makeover.

Lying in bed, Marty let his hand rove over her stomach, back and forth, round and round, stroking his unborn child.

'You're not going to feel anything yet,' Julia teased. 'I'm barely three months pregnant.'

'A lot you know,' he scoffed. 'There's definitely a little person in there.'

'I don't know how good I'm going to be at this,' Julia sighed. 'I never thought I was cut out to be a mother. You're going to have to do more than your share. I'll have the baby, then it's over to you, OK?'

'Listen, I'd love to be a sea-horse and carry the baby for you. I promise to do my share, more than my share, if that's what it takes. You can go off and create another series. Baby and I will stay home and write my book.'

'Right, sure.' Julia could just picture Marty hunched over his computer with a toddler clutching at his knees. 'What do you want, a boy or a girl?'

'I don't care. It really doesn't matter. The name I have picked out would work just fine for either.'

'You already have a name? Wait a minute, don't I get a say in this at all?

'Nope,' Marty said seriously.

'All right, what is it?'

'Mustang. In honor of where she/he was conceived.'

'Mustang Hudlow Turgov? Forget it, no way, no, no.' They both collapsed in laughter, laughing until, at the same moment, they each rolled over to reach out and hold each other tight.

Chapter Fifty-eight

The ringing of the phone woke Julia from a sound sleep. She glanced over at the clock on the bedside table. Seven a.m. What the . . .? She groped for the receiver. 'Hello?'

'Hello, darling,' said the chirping southern accent on the other end.

'Claire? Mother?' Julia nudged Marty and he came to life.

'I know it's early out there, dear, but we just couldn't wait any longer to call. Leigh and I watched the entire Emmy Awards ceremony last night on TV. Congratulations!'

'Thanks.' For a minute, Julia wondered if she was still dreaming.

'Your father's here, he wants to say something.'

'Julia Catherine?' His voice sounded weak, but clearer than when she had last seen him.

'How are are you doing, Dad?'

'I'm hangin' in there. They thought they'd be rid of me long ago, but I'm a tough bird.'

'Good for you, Dad.'

'And so are you. You've got my spunk, Julia Catherine. You really gave those assholes what-for last night. Tore a strip off them, up one side and down the other. Too bad they cut you off right in the middle of your speech and went to a commercial. Sorry we missed the last part,' his voice was fading out. 'You done good, kid. Gotta go now. Your mother says to tell you we're really proud of you.'

Julia swallowed hard. There was a lump in her throat, she knew she was dangerously close to tears. 'I love you, Dad. I'm really glad you called. We'll talk again soon.' She hung up the phone and turned to Marty.

'I've never heard you say I love you to either one of your parents,' Marty said.

'Yeah, well, better late than never.' Quickly she got out of bed.

'Why didn't you tell them about the baby?'

'Those bastards cut me off.' She began to get dressed.

'What?'

'Last night, at the Awards ceremony, they only aired the first half of my speech, then cut to a commercial.'

'Well, the print journalists were all there. It should get into the papers. Where are you going this early in the morning?'

'To the studio to clean out the offices and pick up our things. I want this to be really over.'

But at the entrance to the Pac Vic lot, Julia was stopped by security. 'I'm sorry, miss, but I can't let you on to the lot.'

'I'm Julia Hudlow Turgov. Makeover. You know perfectly well who I am.' Julia was fuming. She wanted to get this over and done with as quickly as possible.

'Oh, I recognize you all right ma'am,' said the stocky female security guard. 'And even if I didn't, I got your picture right here with instructions not to allow you into the area.' She pointed to a photo of Julia which was posted just inside the guard booth.

'You've got to be kidding? Who at Pac Vic ordered this? Surely not Kathryn Grady?'

'No ma'am. Ms Grady no longer works here.'

'I know that, but . . . look,' Julia tried to control her frustration, 'I'm simply here to collect my things. There are files in there that belong to Hudlow/Turgov Productions and not to Pacific Victory.' The guard shook her head. Julia wanted to reach into the booth and throttle her. 'What the hell is this anyway? They can't do this to me. It's my office.'

'Sorry, it's no longer your office. The space is leased by CBN for shows that are being produced for the network. The new producer is moving in tomorrow. Your offices have already been cleared. Your things are scheduled to be delivered to your home address.'

'When?'

'Who knows?' The guard shrugged.

'Thanks for nothing.' Julia backed the car up, whipped it around and sped away.

All the way back to Brentwood, she replayed the events of the past two weeks in her head and, every time she rewound the tape, she got more angry. How dare they lock her out of her own offices? Just because she made a few disparaging remarks about the network that had fired her? Talk about paranoia. What were they expecting her to do, run wild and trash the place? If they thought strong-arm, fascist tactics would keep her mouth shut, they had another think coming.

As she whipped along the 401 through the Sepulveda Pass over the mountains, she saw a large white van up ahead, bearing the letters CBN. She sped up to pass it and, as she went by, she opened the sunroof and flipped the driver of the van a bird. Hopefully he would recognize her vanity license plates, MAKEOVR, and know where the gesture of contempt was coming from. Those fuckers! If she ever saw the CBN logo again it would be too soon.

She parked the car in the garage and ran into the house to tell Marty what happened.

'We've got another problem,' he said grimly. 'I called CBN accounting to see why our buy-out hasn't clicked in yet. We should have received our first check by now. Nobody in accounting knows anything about it. They haven't received an order to issue any checks for Hudlow/Turgov except for your royalty payments.'

'You think they might try and get out of paying us what they owe us?' Julia said in dismay.

'I don't know. Maybe they just forgot to check the contracts. Or maybe they're doing us a dirty, who knows? We've got to get our hands on our copies of the contracts.'

'How? I can't even get on to the lot and into our office to get to the files. If I set even one toe on to Pac Vic property, security will be all over me.'

'Maybe I can,' Marty said. 'I doubt if my picture's been posted at security; I've been away from the studio for so long they've probably forgotten all about me. Come on, we'll take my car and go back to Pac Vic.'

'It's a long drive to Burbank. I don't even want to see Pac Vic, I don't want to face that guard again. The whole thing was so humiliating.'

'I know, but we've got to get our buy-out activated right away. I'll leave you at the deli across the street while I grab the contracts out of the files.'

They walked out the front door just in time to see the white delivery van with the CBN logo pull up and begin unloading their effects from the office on to the front lawn.

'Oh no,' Julia moaned. 'That's the guy I just gave the finger to.'

'Who knew? Try and get him to unload the right file cabinet first. I'll go get my keys.'

The driver and another burly man got out. 'You Julia Hudlow?' he asked.

'Yes.'

'Sign right here.' He shoved the clipboard in front of her so that she could sign the receipt. As she sprawled her signature all over the bottom of the form, he said in a surly tone, 'I'd recognize that little hand anywhere.'

'Just get the stuff unloaded,' Julia snapped.

Of course that meant they took their time, unloading each piece of furniture with a desultory air. Julia stood there, unable to move. It was monumentally depressing to see the working symbols of the last few years of their lives unceremoniously dumped all over the front lawn.

Marty bounded out of the house with the keys. 'Any sign of the filing cabinet?'

'No.'

'It's probably buried inside the truck. Come on,' he said impatiently, 'let's shift some of this ourselves. These guys are incredibly slow. The sooner we locate that contract, the sooner we can swing into action on the money side.' He jumped on to the back of the van and began hauling furniture out himself in order to get to the files. 'Found it,' he shouted. He grabbed hold of the filing cabinet and, as he handed it down to her, the drawers slid right open.

'Whoa.' Instantly he stood up in surprise. 'It's not locked. I always keep it locked. Looks like someone broke the lock to get into it.'

'Are the contracts in there?' Julia asked, her heart pounding so loud she could hear it in her ears. 'What do you want to bet they've been stolen?'

She held her breath while Marty rifled through the papers. 'No, the contracts are right here.' They both let out a sigh of relief. 'OK, now I know that clause was right on the first page.' He scanned it quickly. 'Shit, it's not here.'

'Maybe it wasn't on the first page.' Julia grabbed the document out of his hands and began flipping through it. 'No, nothing, damn. Is this the right contract? Could they have substituted another one?'

'No. This is it. At least the rest of the pages are the original. Look, here are our original ink signatures on the last pages: Stanfield King. Marty Turgov. But you're right, they could have replaced the first page.'

Julia rounded on the driver of the van. 'The lock is broken on this cabinet. Have you been into these files?'

The delivery man backed off, holding up his hands. 'Hey, lady, all I do is drive the truck. You got problems with the contents, take it up with someone else.' He disappeared back into the van.

'We can sue the ass off CBN for this, can't we?' Julia said angrily. 'Intent to breach the contract. I mean, just breaking into the files is an illegal act, right? Malicious mischief? Theft? Something.'

'The network's got armies of lawyers. It could take years of legal fighting, we don't have those kinds of funds. We have no proof. Right now, it's our word against theirs that that clause ever existed.'

'Are you sure,' Julia persisted, 'are you absolutely, positively sure that clause was there? I remember you negotiating for it, but did you actually get it?'

'Of course I did. I wouldn't have signed this otherwise. I can see it, in my mind, clear as day, right on the front page. It was three million dollars, Julia. I wouldn't forget that. I mean, the whole event was so extraordinary. You remember, that vicious tennis match where I thought I was going to lose the top of my head? Tim's triple-strength margaritas? Stan kept being interrupted by all those phone calls. It seemed to take for ever to get to what we were there for in the first place, the actual signing.'

'The tennis match,' Julia said slowly, 'we signed the contract after the tennis match.' She grabbed her car keys. 'Call Tim. Maybe he'll be decent enough to fax us the network's copy of the contract so we can compare them. And check with the Writer's Guild. They should have a copy on file, too.' She headed for the garage and her car.

'Where are you going?' Marty called after her.

'I just remembered something. If it pans out, I'll let you know. In the meantime, call Tim.' She jumped into the car and burned rubber as she sped away.

The USC School of Cinema and Television was at the corner of Hoover and Jefferson. She parked in the lot, and got her old Bolex camera out of the trunk of the car, where she always kept it. Her mind racing, she strode on to the campus, walking quickly toward the Spielberg building. In the basement was the processing lab and there, sitting at the Steenbeck – the flatbed editing machine – was the chief technician who had been lab manager when she was in film school, Mario Del Plano. He still looked like an Aztec god, with shoulder-length black hair, and a fiercely handsome face.

At the sound of her greeting, Mario stood up and gave her a hug. 'Hey, welcome back, Miss Success. How ya doing, kid?'

Julia didn't waste time answering. 'Mar, I need a major favor from you and I need it right away. I've got some exposed film here and I need you to process it ASAP.'

'For you, my prize student, anything.'

'I think it may have been sitting in here for quite a while. I haven't touched my Bolex in ages.'

'How old is this film?' Mario looked concerned.

'Two, maybe two-and-a-half years.'

'You left film in the camera for two years?' he shouted.

'Hey, at least it's black-and-white, not color. I didn't do anything with the film because it wasn't seriously shot.'

'That's a long time to be sitting there after exposure. There's bound to be a loss of quality over the years. You're going to get some contrast compression. Some parts of it may be grayish instead of sharp black-and-white, but I'll give you as much contrast as I can.'

'ETA?' Julia asked.

'An hour, hour-and-a-half tops. We just got some new high-speed technical equipment donated to us by Spielberg. I'll do my best.'

'Thanks, Mar, you're a lifesaver,' Julia gave him a kiss.

The film had to be developed, fixed, washed and dried. An hour and thirty minutes later, Mario set up the roll of film on the flatbed. Julia sat in a metal folding chair in front of the Steenbeck while Mario began rolling the film across the machine. With a pounding heart, Julia focused on the images that were appearing on the flatbed screen. Mar was right about some loss of clarity, but although the images were fuzzy, the event was clear.

'There, freeze frame,' Julia said suddenly. 'Hold on that, Mar.' And there it was, a zoom close-up of the contract.

The 'missing' clause was clearly evident. 'Bingo!' Julia shouted.

'Found what you were looking for?'

'Oh yes. You may have just saved our bacon. Now, can you do me one more favor and make me a video transfer of this? Record it at EP, Extended Play, so that if I need to, I can freeze frame on the video.'

'You got it.'

'Thanks, Mar. I owe you big.'

She checked in with Marty at home who told her that the contract had disappeared from the WGA files as well. In the meantime, he'd reached Tim who said he couldn't risk being directly in contact with either of them, but he had agreed to fax the network copy of the contract to Kathryn at her home. Julia drove straight to Beverly Hills where she found Kathryn and Jonathan packing up the house in order to move to New York.

'The movers are coming in three hours,' Kathryn said, 'and we're catching a plane tonight, so I don't know how much we can do at this point, but we'll do what we can to help.'

'Did the contract arrive?'

'Yes, but there's no buy-out clause on the first page of the network copy either. They're weasels,' declared Kathryn. 'If they took the trouble to break into your files and remove the clause from your copy, of course they eliminated it from their own. You've still got no proof.'

'Take a look at this.' Julia slipped the video-cassette into their VCR and fast-forwarded through the tennis game to the first close-up of the contract. 'This proves that the contract was changed.'

'But it doesn't prove how they did it,' Kathryn cautioned.

'And legally, this wouldn't hold up in court as evidence.' Jonathan was now standing behind them. 'The film could have been doctored. Have you got any footage of the actual signing? That would at least implicate Stanfield King.'

'I think so,' Julia said. The three of them watched as the tape rolled on. Stan answered a phone call and went to the other end of the court to talk, taking his copy of the contract with him. Then there was a zoom shot of Stan waving and punching up another number on his cellular phone. Then the film cut to another zoom close-up of the returned contracts about to be signed. 'Wait a minute,' Jonathan said. 'What's that number pencilled in the upper right-hand corner of Stan's copy?'

'I don't know,' Julia responded. The tape rolled ahead to where all the parties were signing and dating each of the contracts.

'Well, at least we've got a fixed date when it all happened,' Kathryn said. 'The film of the signing along with a blow-up still of a frame showing the original front page of the contract could be introduced into court.'

'But their lawyers will try to say that the film still could have been doctored,' Jonathan said firmly. 'There's something else that's bugging me, though. Wind back to that pencilled number again.' He wrote it down: 28274847. 'OK, now rewind to the first close-up.' Julia did and they all saw that the number was missing from the contract. 'That means that Stan must have written that number down on his copy of the contract while he was off taking the phone call.'

'So?' Kathryn said. 'That number could be anything.'

'Except that it's still bugging me.' Jonathan got out his laptop computer with built-in modem, which he plugged into Kathryn's phone line, explaining that as a director and officer of his financial company, he had access to even the most private files in all departments. He typed in a code and a command for a search, cross-referencing the number 28274847 with the date of the signing. As the numbers and letters began to flash up on the screen, Jonathan let out a long, low whistle. 'Well, this is interesting. On the very day of the signing, Charles Currie declined an offer for Curri-Com to acquire ownership of *HI* Publications.'

'*HI*?' Kathryn asked.

'The *Hollywood Insider* and all its sibling publications,' Jonathan informed her. '*HI* Publications was a client of ours and they were looking to sell out to the highest bidder. We were all disappointed when Currie turned it down but, surprisingly, on that very same day, an offer was made through another financial company, Richmond-Braunfield, to purchase shares in *HIP* amounting to a controlling interest. Richmond-Braunfield made their offer on behalf of a mystery client identified only as 'numbered company 28274847'. Two days later, *HIP* accepted the offer on receipt of a money transfer from the Cayman Islands branch of Buckley's Bank, drawn on account number 3498 542.

The holder of that account was unidentified, but the money was good, so the deal went ahead. And that was the end of my company's involvement because the next day we were told that *HIP* would henceforth be a client of Richmond-Braunfield.'

'If I'm following this correctly,' Kathryn said slowly, 'what you're suggesting is that Stanfield King is the mystery client. He was in a position to know Charles Currie had turned the deal down so he decided to buy *HIP* for himself, only he couldn't let anyone know because that would put him in competition with his own boss, not to mention conflict of interest. So he went the numbered company route which meant he could keep the ownership anonymous.'

'Wait a minute,' Julia said, 'are you telling me that Stan King owns the *Hollywood Insider?* The newspaper that waged war against Makeover right from the beginning? The tabloid we're suing?' At first the very idea seemed incomprehensible to her, but as she began to put the pieces together, it made sense. 'No wonder he fired me.'

'If you could prove all this, it would certainly help you get your buy-out, maybe even your job back,' Kathryn said.

'It would undoubtedly get Stan fired. From what I know of Charles Currie, he's a shark when it comes to a business deal, but the one thing he prides himself on is dealing honorably.'

'Then we've got him,' Julia said excitedly. 'We've nailed Stanfield King.'

'No, you haven't. This is almost impossible to prove,' Jonathan warned. 'You've got two numbers linked to each other, but neither is linked to Stanfield King.'

'What do you mean?' Julia demanded. 'One of them's right there on the top of his contract.'

'But it could be anything from a European phone number to a dog license in Rancho Cucamonga for all you can prove unless you can verify that it's Stan's company. It would take you for ever. That numbered company could be registered in any state and once you find which one, the state may not give out that information.'

'Can't we find it out from Richmond-Braunfield?'

'Hardly. They won't give the names to my company, let alone to you. Client privilege.'

'Then we have to link Stan to the bank account in the

Cayman Islands,' Kathryn said.

'Just as tricky. That's the point of having a bank account in the Caymans. You don't have to pay taxes and you're guaranteed privacy. I'm afraid the only person who can verify all this is Stanfield King, and he's never going to admit to it.'

Back in the car, Julia left Beverly Hills and headed straight for Century City. She felt guilty about not phoning Marty and filling him in on all the extraordinary developments, but she knew if she told him what she was planning to do next, he might try and talk her out of it. She had to confront Stan.

This time, facing him in his spectacular office, she felt no fear, only a murderous calm. Stan didn't seem surprised to see her. He probably thought she had come to bitch about the network's gestapo tactics on the Pac Vic lot.

'It's been over two weeks and you have not yet activated the pay-or-play clause in our contract,' she said. 'Why?'

'I don't believe there was one.' His expression was one of studied concern, as if he were trying to picture the contract but having great difficulty calling it to mind. He pushed the intercom button. 'Jenna, can you get me a copy of the contract for the Makeover deal?'

Julia had already pushed past him to shove the video-cassette into one of the office VCR's. 'I think this proves there was.'

Wordlessly, Stan watched as she showed him the entire tape from start to finish, then rewound back to the first close-up of the original contract and fixed on the image. His secretary came in with a copy of the network contract and placed it on Stan's desk. He didn't even bother to look at it.

Julia cut right to the chase. 'Unless I receive payment of the clause in full, I intend to bring criminal charges against you and CBN.' Julia saw the blood drain from his face, leaving his skin pale and waxlike.

'That would cause me a lot of unnecessary hassle,' he said quickly. I bet it would, Julia thought. If you've done what I think you've done, you don't want the police sniffing around. 'I will certainly facilitate activation of the buy-out as soon as possible, but we're talking about a couple of million dollars here. I can't authorize that large a payment without approval from head office in New York.' He glanced at his rolex. 'It's past eastern standard closing time.'

'The LAPD is on Pacific time and that's where I'm headed next –' it was fun watching him squirm – 'if I walk out of here empty-handed.'

'No, no, no.' He was edging backward as if she were a bank robber and he was looking for the secret button on the floor he could step on and call for help, 'No need for that. You and I should be able to come up with a viable alternative.'

Just what she was hoping he would say. 'How about an advance?' she said coolly. 'I think Marty and I would accept a personal check from you of no less than one hundred thousand dollars.' Stan swallowed nervously. 'Just to show your good faith.' Little beads of perspiration were breaking out on his forehead.

'That's quite a hefty sum, too.'

'Yes I know.' She was enjoying her own sense of power in the situation. Let him sweat, the prick. He had no idea what or how much she knew. Let him squirm, the bastard. Every time she thought back to the company meeting where he had advised them all to ignore the *Hollywood Insider*, that the vicious, personal publicity they were getting was better than no publicity at all, she wanted to kill him. Of course he didn't care how many people got hurt as long as it boosted sales of the tabloid, brought more dollars into the corporation, his corporation, money into his own pocket at their expense. When she thought of Kelly's death, the only thing that could make her feel better was to envision Stanfield King's face being smashed against the pavement, over and over again. 'It is a large amount of money, but right now we need it to tide us over. Certainly, once the buy-out comes through, we would be prepared to pay back every penny of this advance. Fair's fair, right?' She smiled innocently at him.

'All right, if that's what it takes,' Stan's legs appeared to collapse out from under him as he sank back down into his chair behind the relative safety of his massive desk.

'I have a lot of questions for you, Stan, but I doubt you're prepared to answer them at this time.' She allowed just the tiniest amount of the contempt she felt for him to creep into her voice.

'What sort of questions?'

'I hold you personally responsible for virtually everything

that went wrong with Makeover.'

'That's rather a blanket statement.'

'Well, if the foo shits,' she said with a minimal smile. 'Now, write me the check and I'll be out of your way.'

'Deal.' The sweat was pouring off him. He deserved to have a heart attack and drop dead in his office, right here and now, the slimy son of a bitch. But not before he'd written her a check.

Julia held her breath as he reached into his attaché case for his checkbook. Her heart jumped up to her throat when she saw him take out, yes, there it was, a Buckley's bank book. Gotcha!

His hand shook as he signed the check. She reached out to take it and gave him a chilly smile. 'Thanks, Stan. Don't worry about a thing. I'll be in touch.'

She was in the elevator on her way down when she looked at the account number on the check: 9003 219. Shit! It was the wrong number. She knew it wasn't right, she'd already memorized the Cayman Islands number, but maybe, just maybe. She hauled out the piece of paper and compared them: 3498 542; 9003 219. Not even close. Her hopes plunged to the ground floor along with the plummeting elevator. She had been so sure. She wished now that she had blurted out all her suspicions to Stan, nailed him to the wall with the evidence they had, circumstantial though it was. Maybe, in the face of her accusations, he would have come clean. But no, Jonathan was right. Despite his surface agitation, Stan was too smart for that. At least, with one hundred thousand dollars, she could retain one of the top litigators in town to take on the case. Despair flooded her. That could take for ever and, if and when she got her job back, by the time she did, Makeover would have changed irreparably. With a heavy heart, she got into her car and headed for home. Suddenly she slammed on the brakes. The address on the check Stan had given her was for a local branch of Buckley's Bank located near Rodeo Drive, right here in the good old US of A. California. Beverly Hills. Her own personal bank was in Beverly Hills. She checked the digital clock on her dash. Almost four o'clock. Still, it was worth a try. She whipped the car around and broke every speed limit going to get back to Beverly Hills. At her branch, she pulled into a drive-through automatic teller, endorsed Stan's check and deposited it into her own private account. Then she raced over to the address given for the Buckley's Bank, Beverly Hills branch. It was a tiny, pink-brick building tucked discreetly off the street, identified by a small gold plaque. As she came through the doors, a bank employee locked them behind her. She had made it in just before closing time.

Hastily she wrote a personal check for one hundred thousand on her own account and made out a deposit slip in the name of Stanfield King, account number 3498 542. Taking a deep breath, she strode purposefully up to a teller. There was no line-up, but the teller was not pleased to see her.

'Hi, sorry it's so late,' Julia did her best to sound contrite, 'but I need to get this into Mr King's account today.'

The teller looked as though she didn't want to wait a minute longer to get off her feet. She frowned and glanced up at the clock on the wall. 'This won't clear until the next business day, you know.'

'That's all right.'

'Does Mr King have an account with this branch?'

'Well, yes, I believe so,' Julia did her best to look just slightly puzzled. The teller tapped some computer keys, glanced at the screen and said tiredly, 'He has an account with this branch but not under the number listed on your deposit slip.' She looked at the screen again and her frown got tighter. 'You've left this awfully late in the day, you know. I can't take the time now to call Mr King regarding this transaction.'

'I know,' Julia said humbly, 'but it is, after all, a deposit. I'm really sorry, this is all my fault, but I did promise him I'd put it in today, and then I got really caught up with work, and the traffic was crazy and I don't know what to do, please, I could get fired for this, you've got help me,' she finished in a torrent of words.

The teller looked at her for a moment with a fraction of suspicion, then said, 'OK, OK, wait here a minute, I'll have to talk to my supervisor.' Reluctantly she moved off to a glassed-in cubicle on the other side of the bank.

Julia drummed her fingernails on the marble counter. Ten past four. She felt like she was trapped inside that clock up on the wall, that with every tick of the second hand, part of her brain was being chipped away. Over the top of the glassed-in cubicle across the way, she could see the teller talking in hushed tones to a severe-looking woman in navy blue, who kept shaking her head 'no' and then, looking again at the deposit slip in the teller's hand, gave just the barest perceptible nod. The teller came back with the message. 'The problem is that the number on the deposit slip is shown on the screen as another account of Mr King's.'

'Another account?'

'Yes. It's Mr King's account with the Georgetown branch of Buckley's Bank.'

'Georgetown? You mean Washington?'

'No. The Cayman Islands.'

Eureka! The pieces of the puzzle had at last come together. It was his account. Now she knew. Stanfield King was the mystery owner of *HI* Productions and the *Insider*. But she would need a receipt or her returned cancelled check with his account number on the back. 'So you can't make a deposit into that account?'

'Oh yes, we can, but I'm afraid it will cost you. There's an international deposit transfer fee of twenty dollars. Bureaucratic red tape, you understand. Sorry about that.'

'No problem. I'll give it to you in cash,' Julia pulled out a twenty and handed it to her. She smiled as she watched the check move through the electronic box and disappear from view on its way to Stanfield King's unidentified account in the Cayman Islands.

THE WRAP

Chapter Fifty-nine

There has been a major shakeup at CBN. Charles Currie fired Stanfield King. Stan was allowed to leave gracefully with the announcement that he is going into 'independent producing'. Tim Talbot is now president of CBN Entertainment, the youngest executive to hold such a position.

Julia has her job back as producer of Makeover. Marty's book is on the bestseller list. Julia has a first draft screenplay of the small, important film they first set out to do three years ago. They have a baby boy, Benjamin Mùstang Hudlow Turgov.

Melissa was awarded the status of Emancipated Minor. She lives in a condo in the same building as Alex and Shirley. She has just received notification that she has been accepted for early enrolment at Yale. Her dream is to become a film director like Jodie Foster, but first she must decide whether or not she will stay with the series.

Theresa is now a staff writer for Makeover. She and Shirley are working on a possible spin-off for Shirley's character, Lyla Kaye, which will explore contemporary black life in America.

Alex and Shirley got married and honeymooned in Saint Lucia. They are expecting their first child.

Paul and Chaya have reconciled. Makeover now tapes on Thursday nights which leaves the weekend free for family. Paul and Chaya have formed their own production company with a small studio housed in a long-defunct department store on Fairfax at Wilshire. They are producing short films for the Jewish community.

Debra Jo finished the third season and then quit. Eddie played house-husband and the experience made their marriage stronger than ever. Danny's doing well in school back in Houston. Beau wants to become an actor and Debra Jo is trying to talk him out of it. Sometimes she misses the glamor of the television world, but she wouldn't change the safe and happy life she has for any other.

Brandon and J.C.?

FADE IN:

EXTERIOR. BACKYARD HUGE HOUSE TOPANGA CANYON. AFTERNOON The view overlooking the ravine is breathtaking. The sun is just beginning to set, casting a golden-rose glow over the company assembled.

A bower of Texas bluebonnets and yellow roses is at one end of the vast acreage. Standing just inside it is MINISTER and the GROOM, a handsome man wearing a western tux and hand-tooled cowboy boots.

MUSIC: It is the wedding march played on banjo and steel, and blues guitar.

CAMERA pulls back: All turn as the BRIDE comes slowly and carefully across the field. We can see she's wearing a white cotton Mexican wedding dress with red boots. Her wild curly red hair flows all the way down her back.

She holds the hand of a small, dark-haired little girl with bright eyes. Two-year-old ANNA, her adopted daughter from El Salvador.

CAMERA ZOOMS IN as the BRIDE and GROOM and their DAUGHTER, all three, join hands for the ceremony which will unite them as a family.

MUSIC SWELLS

FADE OUT